EXTREME MEDICAL SERVICES BOX SET 7-9

Year of Doom

Extreme Medical Services Box Sets

JAMIE DAVIS

MedicCast Productions, LLC

Extreme Medical Services Box Set 7-9

By Jamie Davis

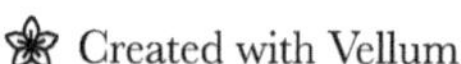 Created with Vellum

To all of the real paramedics out there, saving the world every day. This one's for you.

The Paramedic's Doom

Chapter 1

PARAMEDIC DEAN FLYNN flipped the switch on the ambulance dashboard and the red and white light bar on the roof started its dance of flashing strobes and LEDs. The emergency call came in just before noon for a behavioral emergency downtown in an office complex off of Hopewell Boulevard.

The dispatcher upgraded the 911 response protocol for this particular dispatch. The voice on the radio notified the crew to run in Delta Response which meant to run with full lights and sirens. Dean reached out to activate the siren as they approached the first intersection. It was strange for this type of full-on emergency response for an agitated subject and Dean wondered what could have triggered the dispatcher to raise the severity level of the call.

Dean's partner, Barry, who was driving, must have wondered the same thing.

"What's with the Delta Response? It's only a crazy person. They know ramping up our response this way puts us and the public in greater danger."

"I don't know. Pay attention to the road and don't run through any intersections without checking they're clear first. It's the middle of the day. The roads are going to be plenty congested."

The Station U ambulance squad was housed in an industrial park outside the city. It always took them a few minutes to get to the more congested city streets of the downtown business district. In the middle of the work week, it took even longer.

There were closer ambulance stations to the city's center but the Station U team was special. They treated the supernatural creatures, called Unusuals, who lived and worked in secret alongside their human neighbors in and around Elk City.

Dean picked up the mic and called in to dispatch.

"Ambulance U-891 to headquarters."

"Go ahead U-891."

"Do we have any additional information on the current situation?"

"All additional information we have is being sent to your data terminal now."

"Copy, dispatch."

Dean flipped open the newly installed laptop sitting on a swivel mount between the driver and passenger seat of the ambulance. He turned it in his direction and checked the screen after logging in.

Thirty-seven-year-old female. Co-workers report agitated behavior on return from a restaurant with carry-out lunch. She is now locked in an office conference room and threatening suicide. Police en route.

"It's a woman who's threatening suicide," Dean told his partner. "We'll need to be careful. People who want to harm themselves sometimes end up hurting others even if it's by mistake."

"You don't have to tell me twice. Any clues about the Unusual connection?"

"Don't know, but there must be something that triggered them to alert us at Station U rather than one of the closer ambulance units already downtown."

Dean shrugged. He didn't know any more than Barry did about the connection. The two paramedics would find out soon enough.

They pulled up on the street outside a four-story office building. A frantic man greeted Dean as soon as he opened the passenger door to get out.

"Thank God you're here. Stacey is acting crazy up there and we're all afraid she's going to hurt herself."

"Easy, sir," Dean soothed. "Which office is she in? Which floor?"

"She's up in the Global Traders offices on the third floor. Please hurry, this isn't like her at all."

"We need to grab some of our gear and then we'll have you lead us upstairs, alright?"

The man nodded and Dean pulled open one of the side cabinet doors on the outside of the ambulance. He grabbed the trauma and med bags. Barry would already be grabbing the oxygen bag and the heart monitor from the back, along with removing the stretcher from the rear compartment.

Stacking the bags next to the oxygen and the monitor on the ambulance cot, Dean closed and locked the vehicle, then he helped Barry lift the stretcher up over the curb and followed the impatient man inside.

"Sir, I'm paramedic Dean Flynn and this is my partner and fellow paramedic, Barry Winston. And you are?"

"Sorry, I'm Fred Tanner. I'm the office manager at Global."

"Can you tell us anything else about what happened? What set her off?"

"I don't know. It was her turn to go out and bring back lunch for the rest of us. She came back just like any other time and set the food down in the conference room. Then she grabbed her head and started screaming. When we tried to help her, she started hitting us and throwing things at us. Then she locked the conference room door."

"We received information that she threatened to harm herself."

"She said she 'needs to pay for what she's done' and she 'had to die for her sins.'"

Barry jumped in with a question.

"Has Stacey ever acted strangely like this before?"

"No, never. She's been with us since we opened the offices here in Elk City. Stacey would be the first to tell you she's painfully normal and boring. There's never been anything that would make me think she was dealing with any mental issues."

The three of them boarded the elevator up to the third floor. People gave them curious glances and started collecting in groups, trying to figure out what was going on. The doors slid closed as the bystanders congregated and the office rumor mill started just like it did every time the paramedics showed up on a location like this.

"Any sign of the police?" Dean asked.

"No, why? Do you think we need them?"

"They're dispatched along with us on situations like this. I was only checking to see if they'd gotten here ahead of us, that's all."

Dean and Barry shared a glance. Dean knew what his partner was thinking. They needed to decide if they should wait for police backup or go in and try to handle the situation as it was. A violent patient could be dangerous, especially if she were some sort of Unusual supernatural creature.

The elevator doors slid open on the third floor revealing a small vestibule with double glass doors opposite the elevators sporting a round logo topped with the words "Global Traders" in frosted white letters. There were other office workers clustered together on the other side of the glass. They all looked towards the paramedics as they exited the elevator. Worried but hopeful expressions showed on their faces.

Fred held one of the doors open while Dean and Barry wheeled their stretcher and all their gear into the reception area. They heard the shouting and occasional screams right away. The woman's voice was muffled so Dean couldn't make out what she was shouting about but the screaming and crying was easy enough to decipher. Someone was in pain of some sort. Whether emotional or physical, it didn't matter either way. It was up to him and his partner to deal with it.

"Dean, should we wait for police?"

"I think we need more information. Let's see if we can assess where she is and what her physical condition is before we decide for sure."

"Sounds like a plan."

Dean turned to Fred.

"Wait here and send someone else down to wait for the police officers. They should be arriving soon. My partner and I are going to head back and see if we can talk to Stacey and calm her down."

"Her best friend, Meg, is back there with her, now. She hasn't been able to get through to her."

"Well, we're gonna try anyway. Wait here."

Dean picked up the trauma and med bags while Barry grabbed the oxygen and the heart monitor. They could leave the wheeled cot where it was.

Neither of them needed a guide. It was easy to follow the sound of Stacey's anguished cries back through the office cubicles to the conference room. A distraught woman in her mid-forties stood outside the wooden door wringing her hands. A plaque on the wall read "conference room" next to the door.

"Meg?"

The woman turned and a look of relief crossed her face.

"Thank God you're here. I don't know what's come over her. She's gone completely insane. You've got to help her. This isn't like her and I'm worried she's hurting herself in there."

"We're going to see what we can do," Dean assured her. "Please go back out to the reception area and wait there. It'll be safer for all of us."

"Don't hurt her, please."

"We're here to help. We'll do our best to keep her safe, I promise."

After Meg left them alone, Barry looked from Dean to the door and back again.

"What do we do? She sounds like she's trashing the room in there. There's two of us and one of her but I don't wanna get banged up by a patient today."

Dean shook his head.

"We'll make sure we can get out without her getting to us first. Keep the door at our backs and don't let her get between us and the exit. That should be enough for now. No one has said she had any weapons on her. I want to see what her condition is. I'll open the door a crack and see what happens. Based on her response we'll reassess the situation. You ready?"

Barry nodded and Dean set his bags down and approached the

door. He placed a hand on the handle and listened to the woman's tirade on the other side, waiting for a lull in the shouting and screams. Much of what she said was unintelligible. He did keep hearing the words angel and wings. That got his Unusual radar going.

Pressing down on the handle, Dean pushed the door open a crack and leaned forward to peer into the room. A woman passed right by the door, her hands thrust into her hair as if she were trying to pull it out. She wore a floral print dress that was torn in several places so severely it barely remained on her body and didn't do a very good job of covering her up anymore.

Her arms were battered and covered in bruises, as was her torso, though the latter seemed older than the wounds on her arms. Dean pulled the door closed.

"It looks like she's pretty banged up from throwing furniture around and beating on the walls but there are signs she's taken a beating sometime recently. Her torso is all bruised up. I wonder if she might be a domestic violence victim."

"What's that got to do with her condition now?" Barry asked.

"I don't know for sure but maybe whoever is beating her is also the one responsible for her wigging out the way she is. There's no sign she's an Unusual herself which leads me to believe her condition is a side effect of contact with one. There are several types of supernatural creatures out there who have various powerful psychological effects on humans. We've both seen them."

Barry nodded.

"So what's the plan?"

"I'm going to go in. Stay behind me and keep the door open. If things get too hairy, I'll try to disengage and you can pull the door shut behind me to keep her contained in there."

"Alright, but you be careful."

"Don't worry. I have no plans on being any kind of hero. I have to try and talk her down, though."

"We could wait for police," Barry noted.

"Let's try this first. If it doesn't work, we'll pull back and regroup while we wait for more help."

Dean grabbed the door handle again, took a breath and then opened it, stepping inside the conference room.

The woman whipped around as soon as he stepped into the room. She snarled with rage and started to open her mouth to say something when her eyes softened and her face relaxed.

"You're just like him," Stacey said, pointing at Dean. "I can see it all around you. It's beautiful but not exactly the same. Can you help me get him to stay longer."

Dean didn't understand what the woman was talking about but he wasn't going to complain either. She'd settled down and whatever it was she saw, she wasn't attacking him or hurting herself.

"Stacey, I'm Dean Flynn. I'm a paramedic with the city fire department. Do you mind if I talk to you for a little bit and see what's got you so upset?"

"He was mine. I found him. I made him better. He should not have tried to leave me the way he did."

"Who, Stacey?" Dean asked.

"Reggie - uh - Reginald. He's been staying with me while he gets better. I thought he liked me enough to stay longer but he doesn't want to. He tried to get away this morning but I was able to keep him here. That's alright, isn't it? He's mine. I found him."

"I'm confused, Stacey. Is Reggie a dog or a cat?"

Stacey laughed. "No, silly. Reggie's an angel."

That took Dean by surprise, even given the words he'd overheard earlier. It made him reassess the origin of her wounds. Maybe she got them struggling with someone else and she was the aggressor. It was unusual, but then, in this line of work, that was the name of the game.

"I'll tell you what, Stacey. If you come with my partner, Barry, and me, we'll take you somewhere you can talk to people who will help you with Reggie. The only thing is, you have to tell me where Reggie is now?"

"I don't know if I should tell you. What if you try and go see him and he gets away. I found him. I nursed him back to life. I should get to keep him."

"I just want to make sure he's not hurt like you are. You don't want him injured and hurt without help, do you?"

Stacey shook her head. "I don't want him hurt. I nursed him back to health. You can check on him but promise you'll lock up after you seem him so he doesn't get away?"

"I'll make sure nothing bad happens to Reggie, I promise."

Dean was careful to never lie to patients, even in situations like this. He hadn't promised not to help Reggie escape, if escape was what Reggie wanted. Luckily, Stacey heard what she wanted to hear, just as Dean hoped.

He extended a hand towards Stacey and she started towards him, placing a battered and bloody hand in his. Together, they walked out of the conference room. The police officers from their law enforcement version of Station U had arrived and waited in the hallway for them.

"Hey, Jimmy," Dean said. Officer Jimmy Shorter was a cop who'd worked with Dean on cases before when violence was involved. He also knew about the existence of Unusuals in Elk City.

"Dean," the officer nodded. "I heard the tail end of that. It sounded like she —"

Jimmy stopped when Dean shook his head.

"Jimmy, this is Stacey. She is going to go with us while we go and check on a friend for her. Can you follow along behind us while Barry and I go and help her with her problem?"

Jimmy looked a little unsure of what was going on but he followed Dean's lead. They'd worked together enough that he knew Dean was trying to help the distraught woman. Treating people in these situations was seldom straightforward.

"Sure, Dean, but shouldn't she go to the hospital or something?"

"Maybe not. I'm going to check with the docs over the radio first then I'll explain when we get there. Just follow us, alright?"

The police officer nodded and they all walked with Stacey back to the lobby where the stretcher was located.

Chapter 2

STACEY'S APARTMENT was across town and before they left the scene, it took Dean several minutes on a conference call over his phone with headquarters and the ER doc on duty to explain the need to divert to a patient's apartment before transporting to the hospital. Dean stuck to his guns though and convinced the shift supervisor of the need to visit the woman's home first. The supervisor, a paramedic captain who understood the unique nature of the Station U calls, agreed with the assessment of his team on the street after listening to Dean. He approved the diversion once he had more information on the situation.

Barry climbed into the driver's seat while Dean, finished his call to the powers that be, and hopped in the back with Stacey. Officer Shorter got up from where he sat next to the distraught woman. He nodded at Dean and swapped places with him, stepping out to the street behind the ambulance.

"I'll follow behind in my police cruiser. Have Barry stop if you need me to help you back here."

"Got it. Thanks, Jimmy. I don't think there'll be any issues. Stacey is going to be just fine, isn't that right Stacey?"

The woman smiled and nodded. "You'll see. Reggie is at my place. You'll understand once you meet him."

"I can't wait to meet him," Dean replied.

Jimmy rolled his eyes and shut the back doors to the ambulance.

There was no need to run with the lights and sirens on the way to Stacey's apartment complex. Without the emergency lights engaged, it took them almost twenty minutes to drive across town. They pulled into the residential neighborhood where their patient lived.

Dean was playing this by ear at this point. He'd stepped outside any ordinary medical protocol he had, but that was not that strange for the paramedics of his unit. You had to be flexible when dealing with supernatural and mythical beings. He had confidence in his decision.

Their medical director, Doc Spirelli, had always told them to trust their instincts as paramedics in general and he doubled down on that statement when talking to the Station U medics. The doc knew the kinds of things they faced every day.

"Stacey, we're here. I'm going to walk up to your apartment with you. Then you can show me where you're keeping Reggie."

"You're not going to take him away from me, are you? I found him. He's my angel."

"Let me take a look at him first. He might need more medical treatment. You wouldn't want him to get sicker when I could help him out, would you?"

"No, I don't want that."

"Alright, then, let's go check on him."

Jimmy's police cruiser pulled in behind them as Barry slid the ambulance up to the curb and parked. Dean waited until both Jimmy and Barry stood behind the ambulance before he unbuckled Stacey from the cot and helped her get up.

Barry opened the back doors and helped her down. He looked up at Dean and quirked an eyebrow as if asking, "What now?"

"I'm playing this by ear, partner," Dean replied to the unspoken question.

"I'll follow your lead then."

Dean hopped down and closed the double doors at the rear of the ambulance. He turned to his patient.

"Stacey, do you want to take us to your apartment? Which one is it?"

"I'm in twenty-four J, over there on the third floor."

Dean followed her pointing finger and spotted building twenty-four in the complex of squat garden apartment style buildings. A central, open stairwell in each building led up to the second and third floors.

They crossed the courtyard and went up to the third-floor landing in Stacey's building. Four doors opened onto the third floor. The first started with apartment letter "I" marked on the door to their right. Apartment "J" was right next door. Dean had Stacey's keys and after getting her enthusiastic nod opened her door.

"Hello?" Dean called out. "My name is Dean Flynn. I'm a paramedic. I'm here to help you."

"Reggie's back in the bedroom, silly. He needs his rest."

"Alright, why don't you stay here with Barry and officer Shorter while I go back and check on him. I'll make sure he's okay and then we'll head out and get you some help."

Barry stepped up to stand on one side of their patient and Dean turned and stepped inside the apartment. The place was a mess. There were dirty dishes piled up and the smell of food rotting in the sink and garbage can wafted out at him from the kitchen.

He saw an overturned chair, books and knick-knacks knocked to the floor, and a broken lamp was lying on its side next to the end table. It all pointed to a recent struggle in the living room. Dean reached out and tried the light switch to put some light in the hallway. He tried a couple of the switches before he found the right one.

"Hello, my name is Dean. I'm a paramedic I'm here to help you."

He continued down the hallway to the bedroom door. It was closed and he listened pressing his ear to the door's cool wooden panel. He didn't hear anything in the next room. Reaching down, he turned the knob and pushed the door open, ready to jump back if there was trouble on the other side.

Dean spotted the ropes tied to the head and footboard. There was no one in the room, but someone had been tied up on that bed. He did a quick search of the closet and a looked under the bed just to be sure. There was a sliding door leading out to a small balcony.

The door was open and a slight breeze wafted the curtains into the room.

Whoever had been in this room, they were gone now. Dean called out to his friends still standing outside the apartment.

"Jimmy, you need to come see this."

The police officer entered the apartment and walked back to the bedroom.

"Hmmm, it seems like I need to have a talk with Miss Stacey. Unless she has some rather kinky habits in the bedroom, it looks like she may have been holding someone prisoner in here. I'd like to find out if she knows where that person is."

"Me, too," Dean said. "Especially since whoever she held here was likely some sort of Unusual and I'd like to figure out if they're okay."

"Dean, I'm going to stay here and call for a forensic team to come check out the whole apartment. Are you alright taking her to the hospital on your own?"

"Sure, she seems harmless enough. I'll call ahead and make sure security meets us at the ambulance entrance to the emergency department. Do me a favor. Let me know if you find out anything about who might've been held here."

"Will do, Dean."

Jimmy pulled out his portable radio and started talking to police dispatchers to request the crime scene investigators.

Dean returned to the third floor landing outside the apartment.

"Did you find him? Did you find Reggie?"

"There was no one there, Stacey. But, Officer Shorter is going to stay here and see if they can figure out where Reggie went. For now, though, why don't you come with Barry and me so we can get you checked out at the hospital."

The woman's shoulders slumped.

"He was my angel. He was mine. Now he's gone and I'll never see him again."

"Never is a long time, Stacey. Come on. Let's go back to the ambulance."

On the way back out to the parking lot, Dean kept his eyes open looking for some signs in the apartment complex courtyard of the missing angel, or whatever or whoever it was she'd kept prisoner in her apartment. He didn't see anything out of the ordinary, not that he was sure he knew what he was looking for.

They got Stacey situated and strapped into the ambulance cot, then Barry returned to the driver seat and they started on their way to the hospital. Dean picked up the tablet from its dock in the back of the ambulance and started filling out the patient report. It would electronically sync with the system both at the hospital and back at their station.

It didn't take them long to to get their patient situated with one of the nurses in the emergency room. Once Stacey was in an exam room and settled in, Dean and Barry put a fresh sheet on the stretcher and headed back out to load up their ambulance for the next call.

Soon Dean and Barry were on their way back to Station U on the outskirts of Elk City. They never made it all the way back to the station. Another call came over the dispatch and Dean and Barry found themselves tied up with one ambulance call after another. As Unusual ambulance calls went, they were all pretty routine with nothing too serious. Mostly it was people dealing with the flu this time of year. The back-to-back runs did take up a lot of time and it was well after dark when they were finally put off shift and started back to the station.

When they arrived at the industrial park that housed their ambulance building, Dean spotted a beat-up white van parked next to his pickup truck. Gibbie was here. He wondered what the frumpy, middle-aged vampire wanted with the Station U paramedics to bring him out to their neck of the woods.

After helping Barry back the ambulance safely into its bay, Dean walked over to the squad room door and poked his head inside. Brooke and Tammy where already there having started their shift while Dean and Barry were still out running calls. Gibbie was there, as well.

Tammy looked up from her work on the station's computer when he opened the door to look in.

"It's about time you two got back. I figured we were going to have to take that beat up old backup ambulance out if we got a call. You guys been running all day?"

"Pretty much," Dean said. "It's been one run after another. Hey,

Gibbie. What are you doing here? Do you need some more supplies for your first aid kit?"

"Yeah, that and I wanted to come hang out. It's been kind of boring and I was hoping you might be offering some additional training for myself and the other CERT responders soon. We miss meeting up together like we used to. Any chances you have something coming up soon?"

Dean remembered training Gibbie and several other members of the Unusual community to be CERT responders for community first aid in the case of local emergencies or disasters. For a while, Dean had even gone on runs with them while the fire department suspended him from the job. It had been a scary time for everyone. Despite that, he had fond memories of hanging out with Gibbie and the others while they prowled the streets looking for people in need of help.

"You know, I think it's about that time," Dean said. "I should probably talk to Brynne about coming up with some new training scenarios for you guys so you can practice your skills. I'll shoot her an email before I leave tonight. I think she's the shift supervisor on duty."

"That would be great, Dean. You know we miss you. You should come hang out with us sometime. We hold a regular get-together at Sabatani's. It would be just like old times."

"Are you kidding," Brooke laughed. "He doesn't have any spare time. Jaz has him wrapped around her little finger. Speaking of which, when are you going to put a ring on one of those fingers?"

"Haha, the joke's on you, Brooke. I've actually been thinking in that direction and have been saving up to make a purchase."

"So, the huntress becomes the hunted," Tammy said. "Are you sure that's what she wants, too?"

A knot started forming in the pit of Dean's stomach. He worried about whether Jaz would say no to him if he popped the question. She was the successful CEO of an international security firm as well as the last survivor of a prominent Hunter clan. It wasn't like he had all that much to offer her.

Tammy must have spotted the look of doubt on his face. She laughed.

"Dude, relax. You have absolutely nothing to worry about. I've seen the way she looks at you when she's come over to the station to meet you for dinner or breakfast or we've seen her out and about. She'll say yes for sure. I was just teasing."

"I hope you're right. I feel like the guy never knows for sure."

Brooke chuckled.

"That, my good friend, is all part of the mystery. We ladies like to keep you gentlemen guessing."

"Well, it's working, Brooke. I'm guessing alright." Dean looked around the squad room. "Is Freddy still here? I was hoping to catch a bite to eat before I headed home. I've got nothing in my kitchen."

A shuffling of feet from the hallway leading back to the station's bunk rooms drew Dean's attention. Freddy, their personal zombie chef, entered the squad room.

"I already cooked dinner, Dean. There are plenty of leftovers, however, so help yourself to one of the containers I put in the refrigerator."

"What did you make?"

"Pork chops with an apple glaze and green beans almondine."

"Wow, what's the special occasion?"

"A few of the families of fairies living out in the Barrens just butchered a hog. They dropped some of the meat off here as a thank you for all the times you guys have responded out there. There's plenty more in the freezer including freshly smoked bacon and a few roasts."

"Yum," Dean said, rubbing his belly. "That sounds delicious and it will cut down on what we have to spend to stock the kitchen for you."

"Every little bit helps," Tammy said. "It's not like we're making bundles of cash working as paramedics for the city."

"Amen to that, sister," Dean said. "Alright, let me help Barry finish restocking the ambulance for you guys and then I'll come in and grab some of those leftovers you've made for us, Freddy."

Dean ducked back into the ambulance bay. Barry was already in the back of the ambulance with the gear bags open, replacing the supplies they'd used on their various calls that afternoon and evening.

"Hand me the medication bag," Dean said. "I'll go draw the meds we need from the dispenser."

Barry handed Dean the blue med bag.

"What did Gibbie want? That was his van out there, right?"

"Yeah, I think he just wanted to hang out. He must be between girlfriends right now."

"Ah, the life of the five-hundred-year-old vampire. It must be tough."

Dean laughed. "Especially when you have his luck with women."

Barry laughed along with him. They'd both seen plenty of situations where Gibbie had gotten mixed up with the wrong woman.

Dean set to work refilling the medication bag, checking off the inventory list as he went. He returned the bag to its cabinet in the back of the ambulance. By the time Dean was done, Barry had finished restocking the other supplies as well. Their shift was finally over since Dean had finished up his reports while they were at the hospital following their last call. It was going to feel good to get home.

When Dean returned to the squad room, Freddy had already packed up two meals of leftovers in plastic containers for him and Barry to take with them when they left.

Dean grabbed his containers and headed for the door. Before he went outside, he remembered the earlier call with Stacey and turned back to Tammy and Brooke.

"Keep your eyes open tonight. There might be some sort of angel or another type of unusual I've never heard of out there running around." Dean recounted the earlier ambulance call with Stacey. "I'm not sure if this Reggie was even a real person or just a figment of her imagination. Whatever he was, if he's real, he's got some strange powers that affect people's sense of guilt and regret strong enough to make a person want to kill themselves."

"Sounds like a sin eater," Gibbie said from where he sat on the couch flipping through a book on demonology from the Station U reference library.

"A what?"

"A sin eater. They are pretty rare. Honestly, I haven't heard of one around these parts before, but that doesn't mean there isn't one here. The way you describe the effect on that woman makes it sound a lot like what I've seen before from one of them."

"What are they?" Brooke asked. "Are they some sort of angel or Eldara?"

"They are a lesser form of angel from what little I know about them. They're sort of a junior member of the Eldara clans. Usually, they only pop-up when big trouble is coming on the horizon. They seem to have a sense of dark times approaching. It's those times when people want to repent their sins. The sin eaters feed on the guilt that people feel for their past transgressions and draw off that energy leaving the individual feeling as if they'd been forgiven. If your woman was holding one prisoner, I suppose they could reverse that effect and intensify feelings of guilt to the point that someone might want to hurt themselves."

Tammy pursed her lips and whistled.

"Sounds like we all have some homework to do. I guess we should be looking up information on sin eaters tonight."

"You two can do that," Dean said. "I need to call Jaz. I told her I'd drop her a line when I was finished my shift tonight."

"Ooh, sounds like a booty call," Brooke said.

Everyone laughed, including Dean. You had to be able to take some teasing in this community. EMS crews grew very close to each other and there were few secrets between the close-knit ambulance teams in the city.

"You all are just jealous. I'll tell her you said hi, though. See you in a few days. I'm back on night shift this coming Wednesday."

Dean headed out to his pickup truck and pulled out his phone, tapping Jaz's name at the top of his contact favorite's list. He hadn't caught up with her for a few days and it would be good to see her again. He hoped she wasn't out on a stakeout or something for her security work.

"Hi, Dean," Jaz's voice answered on the first ring. "I was beginning to think you'd forgotten about me. Long day?"

"Yeah, I'm beat, but I wanted to come by and see you. I have some food. It looks like Freddy packed enough for both of us."

"Sounds good. What did he make tonight?"

"Pork chops, apple glaze, and green beans almondine."

"Sounds great. I've been bogged down with work stuff and haven't had time to get dinner. That will be perfect. Come on over. I'll buzz you up when you get here."

Dean smiled and headed out of the parking lot. He needed a quiet night at home relaxing with his girlfriend. The last week of six straight shifts had been brutal. He was ready for a break.

Chapter 3

DEAN PULLED up to the gate outside of the Errington Security building. He punched in a code on the keypad and waited as the gate rolled back allowing him entry into the parking lot.

The Errington Security building was brand-new, built on the lot where the former building stood before an explosion destroyed it along with Jaz's entire family. Not only did it hold Jaz's offices for herself and her security teams, it also had a full set of apartments including one large apartment on the upper floor reserved for her. Dean parked his pickup truck next to a line of black SUVs and got out, walking over to the double entrance doors on the side of the building.

Jaz was supposed to give him a personal code to get into the building, but her IT guy hadn't gotten around to creating a unique code just for Dean. Without the code, he stood and waited by the entrance knowing she should be able to see him on the security monitors mounted on the wall of her apartment's foyer.

He expected her just to buzz him up, opening the doors remotely from upstairs. He was surprised when the doors opened and Jaz stood there smiling back at him.

She had her blonde hair pulled back in its usual ponytail tucked through the back of the baseball cap she wore. She had a towel over one shoulder and wore a gray tank top and black leggings.

"I thought you were going to buzz me in from upstairs."

"I thought so too, but I've been spending too much time behind a desk lately. I decided to get a few more reps in on the weight bench and wait for you down here."

Jaz leaned in for a kiss which Dean returned, grateful as always for any contact with her.

"You don't mind that I'm all sweaty, do you?"

"Not at all. I kind of like my women sweaty."

"Eww, don't get gross," Jaz said, laughing. She gave him a playful punch on the shoulder.

"Hey, you started it," Dean complained, rubbing his arm as if in pain.

"Careful, or I'll show you what I can really do if I wanted to. Come on upstairs. You did remember the leftovers, right?"

"I did," Dean said, holding up the bag with the plastic container Freddy put together for him.

"Awesome, I am famished."

"You said you were working on something and forgot to get dinner. What's got you so tied up?"

"It's another project to provide corporate security for an executive traveling overseas. It's pretty standard bodyguard work but they want assurances that we're providing them the very best we have. Honestly, we are spread pretty thin right now and I'm having trouble recruiting the type of people I need."

"I wish there was something I could do to help," Dean said. "If you needed to hire a few tactical medics, I could put you in touch with some people, but for the kind of thing you're talking about you need a particular set of skills."

A thought occurred to him.

"Have you thought of talking to Rudy? He probably has some contacts among the Lycans, if you don't mind hiring people like that."

"If you're trolling to see if I've overcome some of my family's older prejudices against creatures of the night, I think you'll be disappointed. I actually already thought of that. A few of his people would be perfect for this job especially since the places this executive is traveling for his meetings has a large Unusual creature mob presence. It might be good to have a few werewolves around on the security team to discourage them from making a move on our client."

"Sounds like you've got it all figured out then."

Jaz laughed. It was a happy chuckle that warmed Dean's heart. He liked to hear her laugh like that again. She'd been through so much over the last year and it seemed like she was finally recovering. He was glad he'd been there to see her through it.

They rode up in the elevator to the top floor. The doors opened right into the apartment. She'd only been staying there for a few weeks and there were still unopened boxes left to unpack from her temporary apartment in the building across the street.

"It doesn't look like you've got much unpacking done," Dean observed. "I told you I would come by and help. You don't have to do all of this alone. That's one of the perks of having a boyfriend."

"I know. But you've been busy getting back into the swing of things at work since your injury and I didn't want to put anything else on your plate."

"Well, that's just stupid. If we're going to spend all our time tiptoeing around trying not to bother the other one, nothing is ever going to get done. Look, I'm off for the next couple of days. I was planning on staying here anyway so why don't I start unpacking all this stuff while you get your work done? I bet I can get most of it done in a day or so. With that done, this place will feel much more like home to you.

"I'm hoping it will feel much more like home for both of us," Jaz said. She looked at him waiting for an answer. She didn't have to wait long.

"I would like that a lot."

His confident statement, spoken without hesitation brought a beaming smile to her face. It lit up her whole expression and made him smile, too.

"Did you at least get the kitchen stuff unpacked? The last time I was here, all of your plates and utensils were still in boxes."

Jaz shrugged. "I did manage to unpack a few things but not much."

"I'll make do. You go shower and get changed while I heat up dinner. By the time I'm finished you should be out and feeling fresher."

"Sounds like a plan. Be back in five."

Jaz headed down the hallway towards the bedroom and master bath while Dean turned to go to the kitchen. She was right. She had barely unpacked anything in here.

He dug around until he found a couple of plates as well as the box with the eating utensils.

Freddy had arranged the food so that all he had to do was heat up the food from the container in the microwave. One side had the pork chops and the other had the green beans almondine.

While the food was heating up, Dean went ahead and set the small, round kitchenette table in the corner. He had to take a few boxes off the top and set them down in the dining room next door, but that only took a few minutes. By the time the food was done, he'd laid out the plates, napkins, and silverware for their meal.

He pulled open the fridge and grabbed a beer for each of them, setting a bottle down next to each plate. Jaz came in just as he was dishing up the food. She wore a T-shirt and shorts; her head tilted to one side as she dried her hair with a towel.

"Wow, that smells delicious. I am so hungry."

"Well, that's what it's here for. Dig in."

Dean sat down across from Jaz. His stomach growled loud enough that even she heard it. They both stared at each other for a second and then started laughing.

"Sounds like I'm not the only one who's starving."

"Not at all," Dean said. "We ran all day without a break. Things have been very busy lately."

"Anything strange I should be aware of?" Jaz always tried to keep abreast of anything going on within the Unusual community. She was the head of a Hunter clan, after all.

"There was one thing. Have you ever heard of a sin eater?"

Jaz shot him an alarmed glance. "Why, is there one in town?"

"Maybe," Dean said. "At least that's what Gibbie thinks."

Dean recounted the events surrounding Stacey and the missing angel she had stashed in her apartment.

"So this Reggie person, if he exists, is the sin eater?"

"That's the theory so far. I'm not sure there's much to it though. We only have a little bit of evidence he even exists."

"Maybe not on your end, but on my end, there are a few things that showed up on my radar recently that might point to a sin eater being in the area."

"Like what?" Dean asked. He hadn't expected to find corroboration from Jaz's side of things.

"Just rumblings from some of our contacts. I didn't think much of it until you said something about a sin eater being in town. Now that you say it, some of these other things are starting to make sense. You know how some Unusuals are more sensitive than others to supernatural phenomena, right?"

Dean nodded.

"I got word that one of our secretaries, a member of a banshee family, turned in her notice yesterday. When she was asked why she quit, she said she had the sudden urge to move far away from here. She told her supervisor to pack up his family and move away, too, if he knew what was good for him."

"That sounds ominous," Dean replied, concern in his voice.

"It does, especially in light of what you just told me."

"Gibbie said the sin eaters show up right before something bad happens."

"That's an understatement," Jaz said. "You've heard of the Black Plague? Well, there was a rash of sin eaters all over Europe right before the plague spread throughout the area. It was so bad; people started associating the plague with the sin-eaters. I know because the Hunter clans were tasked with tracking them down and dealing with them."

"But the plague is spread by fleas on rats, not people, and certainly not angels."

"We know that now but it was a different time and people didn't understand disease and germs the way we do now. They saw correlation as cause and effect." Jaz shook her head. "I agree. It wasn't our finest hour."

"It's stuff like that which causes all the bad blood between you and your Hunters and the rest of the Unusual community."

"I know it and I'm trying to be better, really I am."

Dean reached out and took her hand in his.

"I know you are. You've come a long way since we first met a year ago."

Jaz squeezed his fingers in hers.

"Who knew when we met back then we'd end up here? We didn't really hit it off all that well."

"That's an understatement. So much has happened over the last year between us, good and bad. No matter what has happened, I wouldn't want to change where we are now, not for anything."

"I'd like to have my family back."

Dean's heart sank. He was being selfish again. He saw Jaz as the best thing that ever happened to him, despite their rocky beginning. When she thought back to the first few times she met him, it only reminded her of the bomb that killed her parents and older siblings.

"I'm sorry, I just meant…"

"I know what you meant, Dean. It's alright. I'm grateful to have you in my life now, too."

She gave his fingers another squeeze then let go of his hand so she could go back to eating. She tried to change the subject.

"Freddy has done it again. I don't usually like pork chops but these are amazing, juicy, and tender. I'm used to pork that is dry and chews like shoe leather."

"Having a zombie chef who used to have two Michelin stars does have its perks." Freddy had taken to staying at the station after terrorist vandals burned down his house trailer. He paid for his room with his prodigious cooking skills, making meals for the paramedics on shift during the day.

"Make sure you tell him how much I appreciate him making enough for you to bring home to me. I can't help but think I'd be wasting away to nothing if it weren't for his leftovers."

"Don't worry. I will."

They finished dinner and Dean helped Jaz clean up. Afterward, the two of them spent an hour unpacking the remaining kitchen boxes until that room's stuff was put away in the custom cabinets lining the walls.

"See, I told you it wouldn't take too long. Imagine how much I'll get done tomorrow while you're downstairs in your office."

"I feel bad putting you to work like that," Jaz said. She threw her arms over his shoulders and pulled him close. He was always surprised by how strong she was.

"I suppose you could find a way to make it up to me."

She leaned forward and whispered in his ear.

"I'm sure I can think of something."

She tugged him by the hand back to the hallway and the bedroom beyond with a mischievous grin on her face.

Dean smiled and went along willingly.

Chapter 4

THE NEXT TWO days flew by for Dean. It surprised him when it took him most of both days to get everything put away and the boxes carted down to the recycling bin in the parking lot. He was proud of how much he'd accomplished, though. The apartment was much more homey now that everything was put away in its proper place. Jaz was happy with the results, too. Dean knew she hated everything to do with getting her apartment set up. She wasn't terribly domestic.

Dean stopped by Jaz's office on his last trip up from the recycling dumpster. She hunched over her desk, buried in paperwork with her reading glasses on. He knew she was self-conscious when wearing her glasses. Dean didn't understand what the big deal was. He kind of liked the bookish look on her.

"Hey, I just wanted to let you know I'm all finished upstairs. Maybe we can plan to go out tonight and celebrate?"

Jaz looked up from her work. She shook her head.

"I'm not sure I'm going to be able to get away early enough for dinner. Maybe we can schedule it for another time?"

Dean was a little disappointed, but he tried not to show it. He knew how busy she was with getting security operations ramped back up to the level they were at before her family died.

"We can do that. I do go back to work starting tomorrow night. But maybe after the next round of shifts we can plan to celebrate getting the move completed. Does that work for you?"

"Honestly, Dean, that would be perfect. I should have everything for this new project completed by then. Thank you for understanding."

"Hey, what kind of boyfriend would I be if I didn't cut you some slack for being the upwardly mobile career woman? Since you're working late though, I think I'll head back to my apartment for the night. I haven't been there for a few days. I need to check the mail and look in on the Baxters."

"That works. I'll call you tomorrow before you go to work."

Dean smiled and leaned over her desk, sharing a brief kiss before he turned and left.

He didn't like how the work stressed her out. She'd never planned to be the executive in charge of her family's security business. That had always been her brother. She was digging in with gusto, though, which he appreciated. Hard work had rewards of its own and he knew it would pay off for her in the end.

Dean headed out, driving across town to go back to his place. He wasn't sure his plan would work and he was glad he'd been able to keep the secret of why he really wanted to stay at home tomorrow.

He planned to meet with Gibbie to get together with a diamond merchant the vampire knew in the Unusual community. He knew almost nothing about jewelry but Gibbie's long experience with all of his girlfriends over the years had made many connections with various jewelers in the area. He'd offered to introduce Dean to one of them and promised to get him a nice discount, too.

The first thing he did when he got home was throw a load of his uniform shirts and pants into the laundry. His landlords, the Baxters, had recently put in a second clothes washer and dryer in the back of their garage right below his apartment. They told him it didn't make any sense for him to go and spend all his time off at the laundromat when he could do laundry at home.

The Baxters were a sweet old couple who rented him the apartment over their detached garage. They both treated Dean like he was the son they never had. At first, it made him uncomfortable, but over time, he grew to appreciate the way they looked in on him and took the time to get to know the young man who lived over their garage. He'd resolved to pay them back for their kindness with extra chores around their property and home just like he thought a dutiful son would do.

Dean was going to miss living here after he and Jaz got married. He thought they'd miss him, too, though Mrs. Baxter had told him on numerous occasions how much she liked that nice girl he was seeing.

While he was waiting for the laundry to get finished, Dean went ahead and logged in to his work email account from home. On the screen, there were the usual announcements and calendar item emails notifying him of updated training and protocol options for him to get his continuing education credits. He flagged them to look at later while he checked the other two emails that caught his attention. They were both from Tammy and the subject line read "Sin Eater."

Both emails contained links to patient care reports on calls she and Brooke had been on while he was off. He was logged in to the secure portal system allowing him full access so he clicked on the links and brought up the confidential medical reports on the two patients.

The first was a twenty-two-year-old woman who suddenly displayed cutting behaviors that alarmed her parents. When the paramedics arrived, the woman was carving designs that looked like runes of some kind in her forearm with a box cutter. Tammy had made a note in the report that she could not find any reference to the specific runes during her brief search. The woman had spoken about the need to atone for her past transgressions.

The second report linked dealt with an elderly man who had taken an overdose of pain medication in an attempt to kill himself. When Tammy and Brooke revived him, he told them he had to die to pay for all the people he'd cheated as a banker in the community over the years. There was a note in that report that local police had been informed and we're looking into the possibility of criminal activity in the man's past.

After looking through the reports, Dean agreed with Tammy's assessment that these both sounded like people who had run-ins with the sin eater loose in the community.

On a hunch, Dean pulled up a map of Elk City on the screen and looked up the locations of the two ambulance calls. He also cross-referenced the workplaces listed for each person in an effort to see if their paths might have crossed during the course of the day. While their homes were nowhere near each other, they both worked within a couple of blocks of each other which might indicate the sin eater was somewhere in and around the downtown business district.

It wasn't much to go on, but Dean figured he and Barry could head out on their shift and pick up a meal in that area while he scouted around to see if he could spot anyone matching the vague description they had for the sin eater.

Dean tapped a reply to one of the emails thanking Tammy for sending him the information. Anything they could do to cut down on the call volume they'd seen over the last several weeks would help. Even a couple of fewer ambulance calls translated to a break in their already busy days.

Dean spent the rest of the evening searching for information among the many myth and legend databases he'd discovered since he started working at Station U. While he waited for his laundry to be done, he typed in every version of sin eater he could think of using different keywords and phrases to learn everything he could about these particular rare creatures. He had to figure out a way to find this Reggie and figure out what dire situation or impending doom was about to occur in Elk City and its surrounding community.

By the time he was finished searching, it was late in the evening, well after midnight. Checking the last load of laundry and bringing the clean clothes upstairs, Dean turned in for the night. He had a busy day tomorrow. He was meeting Gibbie at noon to talk with the diamond merchant. When that was finished, he had to head back home and get ready for work at six o'clock. His first day of night shifts hit on the weekend which always led to a series of exciting 911 calls.

Chapter 5

IT WAS JUST after noon and Gibbie was running late. Gibbie being late didn't surprise him. The vampire was always a little disheveled and unorganized. What did surprise Dean was that he'd decided to go ahead with this significant purchase using Gibbie's jewelry guy.

The words "Gibbie knows a guy" were seldom considered an excellent review of services rendered in Elk City. Dean could hear the laughter and teasing he'd get if his coworkers heard him utter those words.

He checked his watch again for the third time and was just about to pull out his phone and call Gibbie when the familiar beat up white van with dark tinted windows pulled up across the street.

As it pulled to a stop, Dean's phone chirped with a text message.

Follow me into the underground parking garage after I enter the code.

Dean started his truck and, after checking to make sure there was no traffic, executed a U-turn pull in behind Gibbie's van. They drove a half a block down the street and then turned into a ramp leading down to an underground parking garage beneath one of the buildings.

He'd wondered how Gibbie was going to take him diamond shopping in the middle of the day. Vampires Gibbie's age were still very susceptible to the ravages of direct sunlight. The underground garage explained it. The Diamond merchant must have offices in the building above.

Dean followed Gibbie as he drove through the garage circling past many empty spaces all the way to the lowest level before parking. Dean pulled his pickup truck in next to the van and got out.

"Hey, Gibbie, why didn't we just park upstairs? There were plenty of parking places on the first and second level."

"We would've had to come down here anyway," Gibbie said. "The guy we are going to see is it located in the tunnels below this garage."

"Good grief, Gibbie. Why the heck would he have his offices underground? There're perfectly good offices upstairs. Who is this guy anyway?"

"He's underground because gnomes like to spend most of their time underground. It makes them a lot more comfortable, besides he's doing me a favor and meeting us here in his home so show a little respect, okay?"

"I'm always respectful. Next time, though, fill me in on the details beforehand."

Dean had never met a gnome in his work treating the emergency injuries and illnesses for the Unusual community in Elk City. It was always a bit of a thrill to meet a new kind of mythical creature, though he wished he'd known ahead of time. It would have been nice to look up some information on gnomes before they got here. Not knowing who or what an Unusual could do to him made Dean nervous.

Gibbie smiled. "There's nothing to worry about, Dean. I've known this guy for a long time, and he was happy to be able to do a favor for one of the paramedics who serve our whole community. From the way he talked when I called him, I think he's prepared to give you a very good deal on his merchandise."

"Lead on, then. I can use all the help I can get with this purchase. It's not like I can afford very much to begin with. Jaz already makes so much more money than I do it kind of makes me uncomfortable I can't afford a decent ring for her."

"You've got to lose some of those old-fashioned values, Dean. For goodness sake, it's a whole new millennium out there. Women are allowed to make more money than their male counterparts. Hasn't anybody filled you in on that fact? If I felt that way, I'd never have a girlfriend. Wow, and people say I have problems with women."

Dean couldn't believe he was having a serious discussion about relationship advice with Gibbie.

"I'm not having problems with my relationship with Jaz. The problems are all in my own head and have to do with getting her the diamond ring she deserves."

"You're putting too much pressure on yourself, Dean. I think she'd be happy if you gave her a ring out of the gum-ball machine. It's you she wants, not some random item of jewelry."

"I hope you're right. It doesn't mean I shouldn't do the best I can with what I have."

"Oh, you're absolutely right there. While she would accept a gum-ball machine ring, it doesn't mean she didn't expect you to put some effort into getting her a real one."

"That makes absolutely no sense, Gibbie. She either wants a nice ring, or she doesn't. Which is it?"

Gibbie laughed.

"It's both, stupid. Women get to contradict themselves all the time. That's what keeps us guessing and coming back for more."

Dean shook his head. He didn't think Jaz was like that, but he couldn't be a hundred percent sure. Better to be safe than sorry. Besides, he had some ideas to make the ring and the engagement a little more than your standard event.

"Lead the way, Gibbie. I'm right behind you."

The vampire led Dean to a dark corner at the back of the third level of the garage. Dean couldn't make out much and wished he'd grabbed his flashlight from the truck.

Dean was about to turn back to get it when a light flared ahead of him as Gibbie opened a secret panel set into the concrete wall. He entered a code on the hidden keypad there then stepped back.

A section of the wall slid backward and then to one side. On the other side of the opening, there was a long passageway lined with concrete heading off into the distance. A string of bare lightbulbs connected by a long electrical cable hung suspended from hooks in the ceiling above.

Gibbie motioned for Dean to follow him inside. Once Dean stepped into the passage, Gibbie turned back and closed the secret wall behind them.

"No sense letting anyone else know about this place. Alfonse is very particular about who visits him here."

"Given what he does for a living, I can understand that. Extra security would be preferred."

"Why would he need security? No one in their right mind steals from a gnome. The bad luck alone would chase you for the rest of your life. And that's if he didn't track you down and rip you apart, limb from limb."

"You make him sound like some sort of monster."

"He's no more a monster than any of us are, Dean. He is just capable of taking care of himself and his merchandise. You'll see."

Dean didn't know what that meant, but he was a little more apprehensive than he'd been before.

The passageway continued for about a hundred yards in a straight line before ending in an ornately carved stone door. There was a velvet rope hanging down from the ceiling next to the door. Gibbie tugged on it twice before taking a step back and waiting.

"He might have another customer or a house guest with him. This is the entrance. There's another passage that's the exit leading back to the garage. Alfonse takes great care to protect the anonymity of his clients."

"I'm just a simple paramedic. Why would I need to hide the fact I shopped here?"

"There are others, a more select clientele Alfonse sees. They like to have their identities kept secret. It's all part of the mystique, I guess."

"He's certainly got me wondering about all the mystery."

"See," Gibbie said. "That means it's working."

The door shifted a bit in front of them, then slid to one side with a slight grinding sound. It revealed a foyer covered with a plush red carpet leading to a large room filled with the most garish gold-painted furniture Dean had ever seen. Everything in the room was either painted gold or covered in red or gold velvet. He felt like he'd entered some sort of velvet Elvis painting. He also noticed what looked like moving boxes and open crates scattered around the room. It looked like this guy was packing up and going somewhere.

A short, squat man entered from a door opposite them and waddled over, a huge grin on his face. He had a broad, flat nose on his face set above a long waxed handlebar mustache stretching out on either side of his mouth.

"Gibson, my good man, how are you? It's been a long time since you graced me with your presence."

"I know, and I'm sorry. I've fallen on some unfortunate times and don't have the funds to shop from your exclusive collection of late. What's with the boxes, Alfonse? Are you going somewhere?"

"I am taking some precautions, that's all. There've been some rumblings of trouble on the horizon and I want to be ready in case things get too hot around these parts."

That caught Dean's attention. What did the gnome know? Did he have some information about some impending disaster or situation coming to Elk City? Dean wanted to ask outright but he hadn't even been properly introduced yet.

Most Unusuals put a lot of stock in protocol and manners. Dean would have to wait until it was a better time. He did clear his throat to remind Gibbie to introduce him.

Gibbie didn't pick up on the hint but the gnome did. He turned and gestured to Dean.

"Is this the young man you told me about? I've wanted to meet this paramedic who sent that vile bastard Artur packing with his tail between his legs. Your name is Dean Flynn, is it not?"

Dean shifted his feet. The whole situation with Artur had left a bad taste in his mouth and he didn't like to think about how close he'd come to losing Jaz that night.

He forced a smile on his face anyway and held out his hand. "Yes, sir. Dean is correct, and it was a team effort. I had a lot of help. In fact, I'd be dead without the aid of my friends."

"Nonsense, I heard it was you who tracked him down and cornered him in his lair. That was no easy task and a bold move to make. I salute you. Now, call me Alfonse. All my friends do."

The abandoned mansion Artur used as his hideout while he tried to overthrow the local Unusual overlord, James Lee, wasn't what he would call a lair. Dean didn't want to argue with their host, though. He worried it might drive up the cost of his diamond ring.

Dean opted to change the subject. "Thank you for agreeing to see me, Alfonse. I appreciate it. I have to admit, though, I don't know much about shopping for jewelry. Before Gibbie offered to introduce us, I was just planning on visiting one of the stores in the mall."

The gnome gasped, his hand coming up and covering his open mouth, but not before Dean spotted the rows of needle-sharp teeth inside.

"That hurts me just thinking about it. What kind of person buys the woman they love mall jewelry?"

"The kind who doesn't have a lot of money to spend, like me."

"Well, we'll see about that. Most people think money is the only currency in the world and therefore they discount the true worth they bring to a transaction. I believe you have more to offer than you know. The question for you, Dean Flynn, is what do you think? What is your real worth?"

Dean found his eyes drifting to the floor as he shifted his weight from foot to foot. The gnome's scrutiny made him uncomfortable for some reason. It felt like he was being x-rayed or something.

"I'm not sure I know what you mean, Alfonse. I'm just a city employee at the end of the day."

Alfonse stared at him, making Dean uncomfortable.

The silence dragged on for many long seconds until he finally raised his eyes from the floor and returned the gnome's gaze.

Alfonse shook his head in disbelief.

"You really believe that, don't you? Interesting. Well, never mind all that. I'm sure we can come to some sort of accommodation. Follow me and we'll take a look at some of the items I have to offer."

Alfonse took Dean and Gibbie through a series of winding passageways deeper into his underground apartment until they ended at a huge steel bank vault door set in the concrete wall. Considering the whole place was already sort of a vault in itself, Dean found it a little bit of overkill.

The gnome placed his open hand palm down on a glass panel. As soon as he did, the panel lit up with a red light from below. It pulsed a few times then flashed as it changed to green. A click sounded and the gears on the front of the vault door turned, pulling the huge steel bars back into the door from the sockets in the surrounding walls.

Alfonse gripped the door with both hands and pulled open the heavy steel panel. It opened smoothly on the massive hinges. Beyond, the gnome revealed a small room about ten feet on each side.

Straight ahead, opposite the entrance, was a metal wall with glass shelves. Each shelf contained a selection of various items of jewelry. There was everything there, from rings to necklaces, and bracelets and earrings. On the left and right were dozens of tiny metal doors set in the wall. It was very similar to what Dean had seen for bank safety deposit boxes. Each of the small metal doors had its own lock.

"Come inside, come inside," Alfonse said. "I like to think there is something in here for everyone no matter what you think you can afford to pay."

Dean followed the gnome inside with Gibbie close behind him. Dean wasn't sure he could afford anything among the items in view on the glass shelves. A knot started to form in the pit of his stomach. This stuff had to be worth a fortune. It was all far outside anything he could afford.

Alfonse must've seen the shocked look on his face.

"Don't get yourself all worked up, Dean. There are many items here of various levels of value. There is a ring and a stone here suitable for your fiancé. Now, why don't you tell me a little bit about this woman who's captured your heart?"

"Uh, I suppose she's a lot like many women. She has blonde hair, blue eyes, and she's very athletic."

Gibbie rolled his eyes.

"Oh for goodness sake. Dean honey we're never going to get anywhere if that's the best you can do."

Gibbie turned to Alfonse.

"Dean's fiancé is Jaswinder Errington."

Alfonse's eyes grew wide and he shot a glance at Dean.

"THE Jaswinder Errington?"

"That's the one. As you know, she's an accomplished hunter and currently the CEO of their whole international security firm. The girl seems rather down-to-earth on the few occasions I've met her but she comes from money and good things so she'd appreciate a value when she sees it."

"Good to know," Alfonse said. "That gives me somewhere to start."

"Look," Dean said. "I'm not sure this is such a good idea. Maybe I need to rethink what direction I go right now."

"Having second thoughts, are we?" Alfonse said. "Gibbie, fetch the boy a chair from outside while I get him a few things to look at."

Alfonse turned his full attention to Dean.

"Now that I know a little something about the lady involved, I have some good news for you. Given that she's, shall we say, an active sort of person, I'm sure she won't want a huge solitaire diamond and setting. That's good for you. They're gaudy and needlessly expensive. Plus, it would only get in the way of her more tactical pursuits."

"That makes sense," Dean said as he nodded.

Gibbie returned with a tall, mahogany, ladder back chair.

Dean sat down when the gnome paused and gestured to the seat.

"Now," Alfonse continued, "my gut tells me we should look at something more vintage, perhaps something with a little meaning beneath its selection. I have an excellent collection of antique rings with diamonds set in lower-profile settings more suited to your Jaswinder."

"It's Jaz," Dean corrected.

"Jaz. Isn't that sweet." Alfonse turned to the lefthand wall of cabinets and pulled out a large ring of keys from his pocket. Dean wasn't sure how he'd fit such a massive ring with so many keys in his small pants pocket but he'd obviously managed it somehow.

The gnome peered at the selection of keys dangling before his eyes then selected one and inserted it into one of the small locked doors at eye-level. Pulling the door open, Alfonse slid a long rectangular box out of the hole the small door revealed. He set the long box down on a small wooden table in the corner.

Selecting another key from the ring, Alfonse unlocked the small padlock holding the box closed. Opening the box, the gnome leaned over it, looking inside. Dean couldn't see the inside of the box from where he sat, so he waited while Alfonse scanned the contents inside it. After a few seconds perusing the selection, he reached inside and pulled out a small silver ring with a blue stone set in a low-profile, round setting.

Putting a jeweler's loop in one eye, Alfonse peered at the ring up close for a long time, turning it from side to side to look from many angles.

Tucking the viewing loop back into one of his many pockets with one hand, Alfonse held up the other, presenting the ring to Dean.

"This one is perfect, I think."

Dean took the ring and looked at it, turning it in his fingers to catch the overhead light from different angles.

"It is beautiful, but if it's an antique, it must be expensive."

"It's not just an antique; it's a powerful artifact. There is a powerful charm set on it."

"Magic? I'm not sure…"

"Not sure your hunter girlfriend will dabble with magic. Don't worry, the charm is harmless to its wearer and might come in useful in her line of work. This particular ring belonged to an heiress to a great Lycan family fortune. She came from a contentious family, though, and her father encouraged his offspring to fight it out for dominance among themselves. The werewolf mistress in question had this little beauty created to warn her when a surprise attack from behind her was imminent. Alas, she died from a silver bullet to the heart, fired from directly in front of her by an attacker in plain view. I'm told the person who shot her was her younger brother."

"That's an awful story," Dean said. "What woman would want a ring with such a sordid past?"

"A woman with an appreciation of magic. Your woman will see its value, not just because it's a beautiful piece of jewelry but also because of the powers the ring passes to its wearer. As long as she has this ring on, no one can attack her from behind and catch her unawares. I would think a hunter would find such a skill very useful in the course of her work."

Dean examined the ring again, trying to see if he could sense anything of the charm cast upon it. He didn't know what to look for, or how he would detect such things.

"It is beautiful. How much?"

Dean prepared to wince at the amount.

"Certainly more than a simple public servant could afford. But for a talented healer and person with other, hidden skills, quite affordable."

"That doesn't even make sense," Dean said. "I either have enough money saved or I don't."

"I do not have any need for your money, Dean Flynn. What I want is a favor from you."

"What kind of favor?" Dean's cautious wariness, born of his time on the street, raised a warning in the back of his mind. Unusuals took things like favors offered or given very seriously. It was not something to be taken lightly.

"Nothing you can't provide I assure you." Alfonse waved a hand in the air as if dismissing the concerns with a gesture.

Dean knew he had to tread carefully here.

"I cannot offer an open-ended favor. I am sorry if that offends you but I could never follow through on a favor that might harm another in any way."

Dean reached out to hand the ring back to Alfonse.

The gnome backed away from Dean.

"I don't want it back, I've already given it to you. It's yours now."

Dean shot Gibbie a glance and the vampire stepped forward.

"What are you playing at, Alfonse? I brought Dean here in good faith, not to have him trapped into some sort of unknown bargain."

"It is nothing to worry about I assure you, Dean. I would not be so foolish as to trap someone with your pedigree in an unfair arrangement. I only wish you to convey a message for me."

"You'll give me this ring and all I have to do is pass along a message? What's the catch?"

"No catch at all. Just tell your father I require a meeting the next time you see him."

"I can do that, but the joke's on you, Alfonse. I've never even met my father, at least not since I was an infant. I could pass him on the street right now and not know who he was. I doubt he'd recognize me either."

That shocked the little man.

"How could the sage be wrong?" Alfonse muttered to himself. He turned and paced back and forth in the small room, holding a running conversation aloud with himself. It was strange to hear one person discussing something voicing both sides of the conversation.

"Perhaps the boy lies."

"No, you fool, he doesn't lie. Maybe the sage knows something we don't and is trying to deceive us."

"What could the sage possibly want to hide from us that would put this at their advantage?"

"Could it be the father returns sooner than expected?"

"Yes, that must be it. You know what that means."

"I do, and it fits. The sage has always been correct but he would want to hide this from any prediction he pronounced. Imagine what would happen if word got out he was coming here, right now."

"It would change everything."

Dean watched the running discussion, trying to decide if this was for show or if the gnome was actually a split personality. Then the gnome stopped all of a sudden and spun around to face him. It startled Dean so much he jumped up out of the chair and stood behind it, placing the seat between himself and Alfonse.

"We accept the risk, Dean. Whether you know your father or not, will you keep the message safe until you either deliver it or leave this mortal life?"

"That's a strange way to put that," Dean said.

"Nonetheless, that is the offer. Take it or leave it."

Gibbie nodded at him. "Take the deal."

Dean considered what the gnome said, trying to detect any hidden meaning or holes in the bargain that might be used against him in the future.

He could find nothing.

"Fine, I accept your terms. What is the message for my absentee father?"

"Simply tell your father, the gnome king requires a meeting with him at his earliest convenience. That is all."

"You seem to know everything here, why don't you tell me who my father is. Maybe I can pass along the message sooner."

"If your father has hidden his identity from you, it is not my place to reveal such things. Simply hold the message until the time when you meet him again. That will satisfy the bargain and you may have the ring."

Dean nodded. If this guy wanted to part with a priceless antique magic ring on the outside chance he met his father again after all these years, Dean was happy to take him up on it.

There was still a nagging suspicion in the back of his mind there was more going on here than he could see, but he decided the value was worth the risk and pocketed the ring. He'd come here to procure a ring for Jaz and he'd done it for next to nothing in monetary terms. All he was out was the cost of the gas he spent driving here. He was pleased.

Dean was so distracted by his thoughts he didn't hear Gibbie calling his name at first.

"Uh, Dean, we'd better go."

Alfonse had taken to muttering and pacing again, as if no one else stood in the vault with him. The gnome seemed to become more and more agitated as the two guests stood watching. He was speaking in a guttural language Dean didn't recognize. Alfonse sounded angry and bared his teeth while making a growling noise deep in his throat.

"Dean, did you hear me? We should be going."

"Yeah, Gibbie, I think you're right. Let's leave him to his problems for now. I mean, the deal is sealed, right?"

"That's the way I understood it. Gnomes work on verbal contracts and it sounded settled to me. Come on let's go."

Dean followed Gibbie back through the winding passages to the entrance to the underground bunker. He was glad the vampire knew where he was going. Dean might have gotten lost before he found his way back on his own.

Gibbie pressed a panel on the wall and the concrete door slid back revealing the long passageway back to the parking garage.

A shout and a loud crash behind them made both Dean and Gibbie jump through the doorway. More shouting followed the crash and the two of them picked up their pace as the concrete door slid shut, silencing the increasing sounds of destruction and shouting behind them.

"I hope I don't regret you getting me into this, Gibbie."

"I'm sure nothing more will come of it. Plus, you've got the perfect ring for Jaz. I say celebrate the easy win."

Dean wasn't sure he agreed with Gibbie. Everything had a price and there was no such thing as an easy win where Unusuals were concerned.

Chapter 6

DEAN ARRIVED at work early later that day to be greeted by the delicious smell of whatever Freddy was cooking for dinner. The zombie chef stood working his magic in the station's kitchen over in the far corner of the squad room.

"Oh, my God, Freddy that smells good. What is it?"

"Pan Roasted Salmon served with mashed potatoes and sautéed spinach. You've also got a side dish of roasted red peppers sprinkled with feta cheese. Sit down and I'll bring you a plate before you start work."

"I'll be right there. I need to put some stuff away in my locker."

Dean headed back to the men's bunk room and his locker. He dialed in the combination on the padlock he used to keep his gear safe when he wasn't there and pulled open the locker door.

Reaching into his pocket, Dean pulled out a small jewelry box he'd bought for Jaz's engagement ring. He popped open the lid and ran his fingertips over the beautiful blue sapphire set into the ring's white gold band. It was a beautiful ring.

Closing the lid, Dean put it on the top shelf in his locker, closed the door and closed the hasp of the padlock. The ring would be safe here, especially since Jaz had the run of his apartment, on the rare occasions she stayed over at his place. He didn't want her to stumble upon it in some hiding place at home.

Returning to the squad room, Dean sat at the table just as Freddy arrived with a plate of steaming food. His mouth watered and he grabbed his fork and knife to dig in. The salmon's pink flesh was moist and flaky, almost melting in his mouth. Dean didn't usually like fish, but when Freddy made something, it was typically worth giving it a try. The zombie chef was the best-kept secret in the Elk City fire service and the paramedics of Station U planned on keeping it that way.

As Freddy shambled back to the kitchen to make another plate for Dean's partner, Barry, Dean raised his can of soda in the air.

"My compliments to the chef, Freddy! You have worked your kitchen mojo yet again."

"Thank you, Dean. It is my pleasure as always."

Barry slid into the seat next to Dean and grabbed a fork to stab a piece of salmon off of his partner's plate.

"Hey! Get your own," Dean protested as Barry popped the bite of fish into his mouth.

Barry's eyes closed while he savored the morsel.

"Man, that's good. Hurry up, Freddy. I want to finish before our shift starts."

"Don't rush him, Barry. You know things fall off him when he moves too fast."

As if to punctuate the point, Freddy's right ear fell to the floor while he hurried back with Barry's plate.

"That's on you, Barry. You get to re-attach it before we start work."

"Totally worth it," Barry said around a mouthful of his dinner.

Bill and Lynne had the shift before them tonight. Dean finished his dinner and watched as the two of them completed the final items on their shift checklist to wrap up their day. Bill came over and sat down to eat as soon as the clock struck six.

"Move over, Dean. I'm so hungry; I could eat an entire ocean of salmon."

"Long shift?" Dean asked.

"Yeah, we had a few more of those strange behavioral calls you told us to keep an eye out for. Every one of them was the same. They each were racked with guilt over their past sins and wanted to atone for them."

"I got an email Tammy sent while I was off," Dean said. "Are they all still centered around the same area downtown?"

"All but one. We picked up one woman down by the riverside near the water treatment plant. We figured she'd wandered away from home in a stupor and ended up there."

"That is strange," Dean said. "I'd hoped we might be able to localize the source of the problem and track down our sin eater to keep him from affecting anyone else."

Barry stopped eating long enough to add a thought.

"You know what is next to the water treatment plant?"

"What?" Dean asked, unsure where his partner was headed with this.

"The main sewer outlet for the city. I used to work for public works before I got into the academy and transferred to the fire department. That pipe leads directly back to the downtown sewer hub. It's big enough to walk upright inside, too. What if our sin eater is hiding out down there to keep out of sight. The lady in question could have fallen under his spell and ended up getting away to wander out by the river. It would have been easier for her to get out that way than return to the surface downtown. Climbing up a ladder in the sewers and lifting one of the heavy metal manhole covers from below is no easy task."

"That's worth checking out," Dean said. "I think the two of us should head that way if we get a break during the shift."

"We can try if things are slow enough."

Dean winced. Paramedics were superstitious and saying the shift would be slow was as bad as saying it had been quiet lately. It was just asking for trouble.

This time was no exception.

The first call came in two minutes later.

As the tones sounded on the overhead speaker and the dispatcher began giving them information for the call, Barry shoveled in two more bites of the salmon before grabbing his jacket and heading for the door.

The dispatcher's dispassionate voice read out the details while Barry dashed into the ambulance bay.

"Respond for a behavioral emergency in the alley behind 3247 State street."

Dean had already climbed into the cab and started the ambulance. He dialed in the location on the computer sitting between the front seats in the ambulance.

Barry climbed into the passenger seat and picked up the mic.

"U-891 responding."

"Received, U-891. Be advised, CERT responder called in the patient. He is still on scene."

Dean laughed.

"I'll bet you ten dollars that is Gibbie."

"I'm not even going to argue with you. Who else would it be? The others would have called us directly."

Five minutes later, they pulled up next to the alley. It was dark and there was no light in the narrow street between two high-rise buildings. Dean pressed the switch on the dashboard's control panel and activated the ambulance's floodlights on the driver's side. It helped but he still couldn't see very far down the alley.

"There's Gibbie's van," Barry said, pointing out the beat-up white van parked across the street.

"I told you. If dispatch's report is correct, he's probably down in the alley with the patient. I can't get the lights angled right from here to see very far. Grab the flashlights while you unload our gear. We'll take extra lights in with us."

"Gotcha."

Dean popped open the driver's door and walked to the back of the ambulance. Barry met him there after grabbing the lantern flashlights with their leather shoulder straps. They would help illuminate the alley as they got deeper inside.

After loading their bags and the heart monitor on the stretcher, the two paramedics wheeled their gurney to the mouth of the alley.

Dean walked in the lead and switched on his flashlight, letting it hang down at his hip on its strap. He pulled the stretcher into the alley while the light shined ahead down the narrow gap between the buildings.

The alley turned to the left ahead. Dean switched to guiding the stretcher with one hand while directing the beam of the flashlight with the other.

"Gibbie, it's Dean Flynn. You down there?"

"Dean," Gibbie's voice came from the darkness ahead and around the corner. "I'm so glad you're here. I saw someone who looked injured, so I parked and followed him into this alley. He's very upset and I can't calm him down."

Another voice sounded, a male's voice but high pitched with strain and tension.

"Who's out there? You can't have what I know. I can keep a secret. I promise I can."

Dean took a tentative step forward towards the bend in the alley, trying to angle his light so he could see. Despite getting closer, the light seemed to reach a point and then stop. It was as if something swallowed up the flashlight's beam.

"I can't see you, whoever you are. My name is Dean Flynn. I'm a paramedic. My partner and I are both here to help you."

"I can't trust you; I can't trust anyone."

A shuffling and then sounds of a struggle came from the strange area of darkness.

"Gibbie, I can't see what's happening."

"I'm trying to hold on to him. He tried to flee but I grabbed him."

Dean stepped up to the corner and shined his light around it. The light stopped as if hitting a black wall a yard away from him. No matter how he moved the light, he couldn't get it to penetrate into the darkness ahead.

A grunt and a crash of what sounded like trash cans knocked over came from ahead.

"Barry, I'm going in there. Gibbie needs help. If we're going to assist this guy, we need to detain him. Draw up some haloperidol and have it ready. We'll see if we can bring whoever it is out and use it to calm him down."

"Dean, you'll be blind in there."

"Hopefully, he'll be blind, too. I don't know what's causing this darkness but it seems to extend into the rest of the alley. If I need help, I'll call for you. Be ready with the med."

"Be careful, dude."

"Don't worry. I will."

Dean kept the flashlight on as he stepped forward into the wall of darkness. Part of him expected to bump up against an actual wall.

He didn't, though. The only thing that happened was a sudden and total lack of light around him. He couldn't see the glow of the city in the sky above him anymore and if his flashlight was still on, it's light was being swallowed as well.

Following the sounds of a scuffle from up ahead, Dean walked forward, both hands extended before him attempting to intercept any obstacles. He shuffled his feet rather than taking standard steps, trying to avoid tripping over anything on the ground.

"Gibbie, I'm coming, but I can't see anything at all. What's happening?"

"He's stronger than he looks, Dean, but I've got him."

Dean followed the sound of the vampire's voice until something bumped into his leg. He crouched and felt a shoe or boot.

"That's me, Dean," Gibbie said. "I've got my arms wrapped around him and I'm holding him on my lap. He's kicking something fierce, though."

"Can you hold his arm still long enough to let us inject him with something to calm him down."

"Just don't stick me by accident."

Dean tried not to think about what could go wrong with his current plan but he didn't know what else to do. Clearly, the darkness was magical in nature. Whoever or whatever this patient was, he somehow either controlled the light or created darkness.

"Barry, bring me the sedative. Just come around the corner and walk straight ahead into the darkness. Go slow and follow my voice."

"I can't see a thing, Dean," his partner called out. "Where are you?"

"Follow my voice. I'm waving my arm back and forth in your direction. Put a hand out in front of you until you feel it."

Dean slowly waved his arm back and forth sticking it out behind him. A few seconds later, he felt Barry's hand brush against his. They grasped each other's wrist and Barry moved up next to him.

"Hand me the syringe,"

Barry's other hand pressed something against his wrist where he held onto Barry's arm. Dean took the thin cylinder of the syringe from his partner.

"Got it. How much?"

"Ten milligrams. The cap is still on the needle, though I don't know how you're going to manage to do this in the dark."

"Carefully."

Barry let out a slight chuckle.

"Just don't stick yourself."

"Or me," Gibbie added.

"Gibbie," Dean asked. "What's he wearing?"

"Just a t-shirt. It's one of the things that drew my attention. It's cold out tonight. He should be freezing. He's not."

"Good, I can inject him right through the shirt. Hold him as still as you can."

"What are you doing?" the man's frantic voice called out. "Stay away from me."

Dean felt Gibbie's body move as the man's struggling increased.

"Easy, my friend, we just want to help you," Dean said. He tried to sound soothing even though he felt just a little stressed.

He reached around Gibbie and found the other man's shoulder. Gripping the shoulder with one hand, Dean brought the capped syringe over with the other. He knew he was only getting one shot at this.

He rested his wrists on the guy's upper arm to stabilize them. Then he tipped the needle forward and jabbed it into the shoulder between his two hands. He pressed the plunger down injecting the medicine.

Pulling the needle away, Dean pressed his hand holding the exposed syringe down on the ground at his side, while he waited for the medicine to work and calm the patient's agitation. He didn't want to move in the darkness with the sharp, bloody needle in his hand, so he kept it still at his side.

It took about thirty seconds for the medication to start working. The first indication something was working was when the thick, black darkness began to fade. It was slow, but a few seconds later Dean started to see shapes moving next to him.

As soon as the darkness had faded enough, Dean called back to Barry.

"Bring up the med bag so I can put this syringe away in the sharps box."

"Got it. Be right back."

Dean turned his attention back to the patient struggling feebly now in Gibbie's arms.

The man had shoulder-length coal-black hair, unkempt and with that greasy sheen from not being washed in a while. Like most homeless, he reeked of sweat and far too long between showers. His bearded face's expression had calmed some, but Dean could still see the panic in the man's eyes as they shifted around, like they were trying to see everywhere at once.

Barry arrived with the med bag. He'd unzipped the side pocket with the portable sharps box inside. Dean dropped the needle inside and slid the lid closed.

He shifted around to the other side of Gibby to make room for his partner. He positioned himself in front of the patient, trying to meet his shifting gaze.

"Sir, I'm Dean Flynn, I'm here to help you out. You were upset so I gave you some medicine to help you relax and talk with me. Can you tell me your name?"

"Peeps call me Will," the man answered, his words a little slurred now. His eyes had started to droop a little, too. The sedative effects of the med were working.

"Is it alright if my partner takes your blood pressure?"

"Uh-huh."

Barry took a set of vitals while Dean kept up a running banter with the patient, trying to discern what had upset him.

"Can you tell me why you were upset? We noticed you did something to the light."

"Did I? I'm sorry if I did. I don't like to do that kind of thing in public. Humans don't understand things like that."

Dean chuckled, "No they don't, Will. We don't mind, though, as long as we know you won't do it again. We want to help you."

Will held up his hand and a soft white light appeared over it. There was no heat coming from it, just the glow of the white light hovering there over his hand.

A thought popped into Dean's head. The light and the name triggered a memory of something he'd read.

"Are you a Will-O-the-Wisp, like in the legends? It's cool if you are, I just wondered because I've never met a person like you before."

Will nodded, and waved his hand in the air, making the light bob up and down like it was dancing.

"I like making the light do what I want. It's especially fun at night when people see my lights and follow them. It's not fun anymore. I saw him. I saw him and knew who he was. He's one of THEM. He didn't see me because I hid myself and cloaked in darkness first, but I saw him."

"Who? Who'd you see, Will?"

"The first horseman. He's here. He would have killed me for sure if he'd seen me watching." Will tapped the side of his head. "But I was too smart for that."

Gibbie shook his head and relaxed his grip on Will. He was no longer struggling at all. The medication and the conversation had settled him.

"That's not good," Gibbie muttered under his breath.

"You say something?" Dean asked.

"I'll tell you later," the frumpy vampire said.

Dean wanted an answer but Gibbie seemed distracted by something. He sat and stared off into space, his lips moving but saying nothing.

Dean shrugged. Gibbie had a whole level of strange all his own.

"Come on, Will," Dean said. "We have a nice warm ambulance around the corner. Let's go back there and get inside where it's cozy. What do you say?"

"You, you can do something about this, can't you?" Will said.

"I'd like to think so, Will. Let's get you up and walk to the ambulance. Can you do that if Gibbie and I walk next to you?"

"I think so. You made sure the horseman wasn't around, right?"

"I haven't seen a horseman all day," Dean said.

Will smiled at that and walked with Dean and Gibbie back down the alley to the street and the ambulance. Barry grabbed the bag and steered the stretcher after them.

High above, on the flat roof of the apartment building next to the alley, a cloaked figure watched the paramedics leave with their patient. With a flick of his pale wrist, the cloak closed around the man and then dissipated into the air like a tendril of smoke blown away by the breeze.

Chapter 7

DEAN WALKED BACK down the ramp at the ambulance entrance of Elk City Medical Center, returning to his unit. He tapped a few last words on the tablet in his hand before he closed the screen with a swipe of a finger.

Barry and Gibbie leaned up against the ambulance chatting.

"Everything ready to go?" Dean asked.

"Yep," Barry said. He patted the vampire on the shoulder. "Gibbie here was a big help."

"I try to be."

Dean smiled and tucked the tablet under his arm.

"Hey, what was all that cryptic talk back at the scene?" Dean asked. "You acted like what Will said made sense to you."

"Will-O-the-Wisps are hermits, vagrants. They usually keep to themselves, staying away from others. It's because they have visions all the time. Usually, the visions mean nothing, but something clearly scared this one away from his seclusion, making me think his vision was something more than just a random hallucination."

"Why, Gibbie?" Barry asked. "Couldn't it all just be the crazed ramblings of another homeless guy?"

"It's not just him," Gibbie said. "You guys are looking for a sin-eater, then there was the reaction of the diamond merchant earlier, and now this mention of the horseman. Don't you see?"

"See what? Come on, Gibbie. Stop being cryptic and spit it out."

Gibbie waved his hands in the air as if trying to wipe something away then lifted his eyes, meeting Dean's gaze.

"Will mentioned the horsemen, Dean. He meant the four horsemen of the apocalypse, the ones predicted in the Book of Revelations in the Bible. The ones who come and signal the end of the world."

"So we're looking for four bad guys on horseback?" Barry said. "That shouldn't be too hard to spot here in the middle of Elk City."

Gibbie shook his head. "They don't have to be riding horses. That is how they've been presented mythically in the past. The important part is their arrival signals the beginning of the end. The last battle is coming." Gibbie stopped and laughed, a hint of nervous hysteria leaking into his mirth.

"I'm probably just over-reacting, guys. Dean, you should go and talk to James about this. He's been around a lot longer than me. Tell him what's been going on. Tell him what Will told you and see what he says. I gotta go. There are things that need doing, just in case. I'll see you around."

Gibbie turned and started down the sidewalk next to the hospital.

"Don't you want a ride back to your van?" Dean asked, calling after his friend.

"I'll walk. I've got lots to think about."

Barry laughed watching Gibbie wander away down the street. "He's so strange. Come on, let's go. Maybe we'll have time to pick up a snack on the way back to the station."

Dean spared a last glance at Gibbie's back. The story of the four horsemen had spooked the vampire. While he was a creature of the night and an apex predator, Gibbie still had a lot of the personality from his human days a few hundred years before. That probably accounted for his skittishness about the myth of the end of the world coming.

Climbing back into the ambulance, Dean started the engine and decided he'd definitely head over to see James and Brynne after work.

He should probably heed Gibbie's advice and see the ancient vampire lord of Elk City. Plus it would be nice to see Brynne outside of work while she was at home with James.

Dean headed for the elevator doors in the underground garage below the Nightwing building. He rubbed his eyes. The shift had been long with little rest. He and Barry ran one call after another all night only returning to the station to restock in between each run.

Pressing the call button, he was surprised when the doors opened right away and Rudy stepped out, almost bumping into him.

"Hey, Dean. Sorry about that. I didn't see you."

"No worries. I'm in a bit of a daze. Long night."

"Me, too. Been putting out a lot of fires for the boss, lately."

Rudy referred to James, the vampire lord of Elk City, for whom he worked as the head of security as well as being the leader of the local werewolf pack.

"Anything we should know about at Station U?"

"Brynne's got a handle on that. She's back on as night supervisor in two days. She'll have a full update then. Hopefully, we have a better idea of what's making everyone so skittish by then."

"Yeah, hopefully. Have a good rest. I'll envy you getting to bed before me."

"Ha, that's what you think. My wife's visiting her mother and her original pack in Pittsburgh this week. I've got to get the kids ready for school and drop them off before I get near anything resembling a bed."

"Good luck with that, then. See ya," Dean said. He stepped into the elevator and stabbed the button marked "PH" for the penthouse. He swiped his access card enabling the elevator to travel to the upper, restricted floors. The doors closed and the elevator car started upwards.

Dean wondered what sort of problems James was handling right now. The Unusual community was pretty peaceful most of the time here in Elk City. James ran a tight ship and kept his subjects happy for the most part. It concerned Dean to hear that might have changed.

The door opened onto an entry hall with a table and two chairs. There were fresh flowers in a crystal vase on the table. Dean turned right and walked up to the double doors, ringing the bell.

"Come in, Dean, it's open," a familiar woman's voice called from inside the penthouse apartment.

He pushed the door open and went inside.

"Brynne? Is that you?"

"In the living room, Dean," Brynne Garvey answered.

She'd been his training officer and mentor when he first started working as a paramedic. He missed working alongside her. She'd almost died when a crazy co-worker had shot her in a fit of jealous rage.

Dean and James had decided changing her into a vampire was the only way to save her life. Now he only saw her when she came in to work as a shift supervisor on nights, and only when their schedules synced.

Heading around the corner into the large central room and living area of the apartment, Dean smiled. Brynne, dressed in torn, faded blue jeans and a black Ronnie James Dio concert t-shirt, sat on the carpeted floor in the middle of the room.

She had file folders spread all around her while she tapped away on her laptop. Dean could see the familiar screen of the patient care reporting software they used.

Brynne glanced his way as he walked in.

Dean pointed at the laptop and files spread around her. "You're supposed to be off, aren't you?"

"I couldn't rest, too much going on. So, I decided to get some work finished. This quality improvement stuff never ends. You guys are always messing up your reports."

Dean chuckled.

"That's why you get the big bucks, boss lady. Hey, is James here? I'd like to run something past both of you. It came up on a call earlier tonight."

"He and Celeste are tending to something downstairs. They should be back soon. Anything you want to talk about now?"

"I'll wait so I don't have to repeat myself."

"Suit yourself. How's Jaz? You two still resisting the urge to tie the knot and get it over with?"

"Well…"

Brynne looked up from her work and stared at Dean.

"Shut up! You proposed to her, didn't you."

"Well, not yet but it is in the plans."

Brynne shut the laptop and swung her legs around so she faced Dean.

"Out with it. What's the plan? How are you going to pop the question? I need details so I can make sure you don't screw this up."

Dean felt like a brand new probie paramedic all over again under her intense scrutiny.

"Well, I thought I'd take her out to dinner and then go for a walk in the park downtown. There's a place by the lake there with a bridge overlooking the water. I thought I'd pop the question there."

"You have someone to be there to record the moment, don't you?"

"Why, are you volunteering?"

"I could be persuaded to help out if you ask nicely."

"Ask what nicely?" James said. He came around the corner from the entry hall followed by his assistant Celeste Teal. James always looked impeccably dressed, even when he was wearing what most would call lay around the house clothes. His black jeans and his tight black t-shirt both looked like they'd been freshly pressed only moments before. It was one of a multitude of things that could annoy you about James if you let them.

"Dean just told me he is planning to propose to Jaz."

"Congratulations, Dean," Celeste said in her characteristic southern drawl. "She's a lucky girl."

Celeste was a vampire, too, like James and Brynne. She'd been with James since he'd turned her sometime back around the Civil War. Dean wondered if that made her and Brynne something like sisters. He didn't know much about that part of vampire subculture. He'd have to ask Gibbie when he got the chance. It wouldn't be appropriate to ask here and now.

"I feel like I'm the lucky one," Dean said.

"That is the key to a successful relationship, Dean," the red-headed assistant said. "Keep it that way, and you two'll last a long, long time."

"I don't see you out and about with anyone special, Celeste. Are you sure you're qualified to give me advice?"

"Oh, honey, I was fighting off the boys long before you were born. I've seen the relationships over the years that worked and the ones that didn't. Trust me. Treat her like you don't deserve her and the two of you'll last your whole lives."

"I'd listen to her, Dean," James said. "Lord knows her love life is the most successful one around here. How many girlfriends have you had now, Celeste?"

"Things are complicated for me, James. There aren't as many lesbian vampires as you'd think. Most of them are turned by you men because they're already dating you. It doesn't leave that many for me and my fellow sisters on the other side of the fence."

"Sounds like a perfect excuse to have one fling after another," James laughed. "But, hey, you do you."

Celeste grunted in exasperation and headed back to her offices in another part of the penthouse.

"What brings you by, Dean," James asked. "Was it to seek advice on your pending proposal?"

"No, there are some things happening out there that I wanted to run past you. It seems that we're both dealing with a little bit of upheaval lately and I wanted to compare notes, especially after talking with Rudy on my way in this morning."

Dean recounted the information about the sin eater being in town and also the incident with Will earlier that evening. He mentioned the vision of a horseman and what Will and Gibbie had said.

James had been paying attention all along but at the mention of the horseman, he tensed and clenched his fist.

"I knew it," James muttered under his breath.

"What?" Dean asked. "Am I missing something? You must know something. Tell me."

James stood and crossed the room to a metal carafe sitting on a hot plate on an ornate buffet table. He poured himself a mug full of fresh, warm blood from the carafe. He sipped while he stared across the apartment at nothing in particular.

"Come on, James. We've been through too much together at this point for you to keep anything from me. You trust Brynne; you can trust me, too."

"I'd hoped the sin-eater was just passing through and stirring up trouble," James said. He shook his head. "I guess that was just wishful thinking."

Brynne got up and walked over to James.

"What is it?" She asked, laying a hand on his shoulder. "Tell us."

"If I'm correct, and it all adds up now. Gibbie's right. The horseman your patient mentioned is likely to be one of THE Horsemen, though we call them the Agents of Chaos. They're the ones foretold by dozens of mythologies including the Judeo/Christian mythos."

"You sound like you've seen these Agents of Chaos before."

James nodded. "I've seen what happens when they've come to visit earth in the past. The chaos and death they bring makes the shorter-lived humans at the time talk about it like it's the end of the world. That is how they got the reputation they have. Usually they are only able to manifest one or two of them at a time. If all four come through, that signals the coming of the final battle between good and evil. If that happens, the whole earth is doomed to become a battleground."

"I guess I should be happy it's just hype then," Dean said. "I'd hate to have it end up being the real end of the world."

"It depends on your definition, Dean," James explained. "What if a plague struck us now with an effect like the black death that struck Europe in the middle ages. If one-third of the earth's population died in a matter of a few years' time, it would seem as if the world was ending, right?"

"But modern medical science can treat the plague," Brynne suggested. "It still crops up from time to time here in the U.S. But we take care of it and it's limited to just a few people a year, usually in the southwestern states.

"She's right, James," Dean continued. "The bubonic plague is easy to manage. It just requires a course of antibiotics. That type of disease wouldn't be nearly as effective now."

"I don't think you understand. Brynne, maybe you can help. Explain to Dean what would happen if a drug-resistant superbug version of the plague suddenly spread across the nation or the whole world."

Brynne's brow creased as if lost in thought; then she looked at Dean.

"He's right, Dean."

"Why?"

"Think about it. If an antibiotic-resistant variety of the plague or any of a number of nasty bacterial infections were to spread rapidly across the world, imagine what it would be like. The hospitals would overflow. Government services would be taxed beyond their limits until they failed as the public servants also succumbed to the disease. Public order wouldn't collapse everywhere but it would in many places here and around the world."

"And you think these horsemen are coming here, or might already be here?"

"Unless we can stop them," James said. "It will be like nothing we've ever seen in modern times."

"You said they came before," Dean said. "What stopped them before?"

"They were defeated in different ways in different ages. Sometimes it was enough to eliminate their agents on earth. In other times, it took whole armies to send them back to hell. It's different each time."

"That's not a lot of help," Dean said.

James shrugged.

"It's the end of the world, at least for that time. It doesn't have to be a plague either, at least not in the traditional sense. There are four horsemen, each with their own bag of tricks to bring to play. They'll each try their methods until one takes off."

Dean tried to remember what each horseman represented in the little he'd read about them.

"Okay, so there's war, and I guess plague or disease. What are the other two?"

"The four are Death, Famine, War, and Plague," James recited. "They have their own names and there are other interpretations of what they each represent, but that is a good way to remember them. The good news is, according to tradition, each one has an opponent, a human or Unusual champion, somewhere in the world. It is those four champions who must face off against each one of the Agents of Chaos, the four horsemen, in order to send all four of them back to the netherworld."

"So all we have to do is find these four champions and have them ready when the time comes to face them," Dean proposed. "It's like a vaccination. If we're ready for them before they get here, then we can send them back before they have a chance to do any real damage."

Brynne shook her head.

"They could be anywhere. We'd have to search the whole world for the right person or people to counter the horsemen. What if one of them is in the middle of China or something. It would be impossible to find them in time."

"I don't think so," Dean said after a thought came to him. "The higher powers don't intervene directly anymore but they also don't leave us totally undefended. We've seen that in the few demonic encounters we've had here. Help is always available; we just have to figure out how to use that help and who will provide it. I'd be willing to bet the four champions are closer than we think."

"You're putting a lot of faith in the gods above, Dean," James said. "In my experience, they leave us to sort out the mess on our own here on Earth.

"You forget. I've met angels. So have you. There are heavenly forces at work as well as demonic." Dean stopped and shook his head. He was tired from working all night. "I have to think on this more and I have to get some rest. Jaz is expecting me to be up in time to meet her for an early dinner before work, tonight.?"

Brynne nodded. "Get some sleep. James and I will do what we can to find out more from here. We should be able to find out what the rest of the Unusuals here in Elk City are saying about this. Others may have seen or heard something."

"Good, see what you can find out and we'll talk about it when you're back on shift in a few days."

"We'll all meet up again at the station in two days," James said. "I'll come, too. Let's just hope nothing blows up between now and then."

Chapter 8

DEAN WORRIED he'd have trouble sleeping with all the earlier talk of the end of the world with Brynne and James. Instead, he fell asleep almost immediately, as soon as he lay down in bed.

It wasn't a restful sleep, though. He had troubling dreams of his childhood. His mother cried and cried, and his younger self in the dream couldn't figure out why. She didn't listen to the young child standing next to her asking her what was wrong. She kept calling out a name over and over again. 'Gabe,' she repeated as if that was the answer to the question he asked.

Dean woke with a start when his alarm went off. He sat at the edge of his bed for a long time, staring at the floor, trying to make sense of what he'd seen in the dream about his mother. He struggled with what he remembered. He could only see bits and pieces as if the dream were a picture made with colored sand running away through a sieve even as he tried to grasp its meaning.

In the end, the only real image he remembered was his mother clutching her knees to her chest, rocking back and forth and calling out for someone named Gabe. It was such a vivid image; Dean wondered if it had really happened, memory lending definition to the dream somehow. If so, it had to be among the earliest of his memories. The child in his dream was only two or three years old.

Shaking his head, Dean went into the shower to help clear the cobwebs from his head. He had Bill covering the first six hours of his shift tonight so he could take Jaz out for a date. He needed his wits about him if he was going to pull this off. Tonight was the big night.

Jaz was naturally suspicious and he didn't want her to suspect the proposal was coming. Everything had to work out perfectly if he was going to fool her. He loved her but she could be infuriatingly clever sometimes.

The shower helped wake him up and relax him. Soon after, Dean stood looking at himself in the mirror. He wore his nicer bluejeans and a blue and white striped button-down shirt. His goal was to look nice but not so good that Jaz would think he'd done something special.

That was also why he let her offer to pick him up. On the occasions when he'd wanted to make their dates special in the past, he'd insisted on driving. He hoped by letting her do the driving it would put her off and make her think this was just a regular date for them.

Dean grabbed his keys off the table, along with the small box with the ring inside. He'd left a spare uniform at work the night before so he could change when he got there later without having to come back home first. As far as he could tell, everything should be ready.

He mentally ticked off the list of preparations in his head one more time before he left the apartment over the Baxters' garage and headed to the street. Jaz would be here any minute. Dean pulled the door shut behind him as Jaz pulled up out front and honked the horn twice.

Dean waved and hurried down the stairs to the driveway. Mrs. Baxter was out gardening in the front yard. He waved at her, and she waved back.

"Have fun on your date, Dean. Tell Jaz we said hello."

"Will do, Mrs. B. I'm working later tonight so I won't be home until the morning. I'll mow the lawn for you tomorrow when I wake up in the afternoon, is that alright?"

"That's fine, dear. If you don't get to it, Mr. Baxter can do it. He needs to get more exercise anyway."

"I'll take care of it. Don't worry."

Mrs. Baxter smiled and went back to her gardening.

Dean pulled open the door to the black SUV pulled up out front. Jaz sat behind the wheel, her blonde hair hanging down past her shoulders rather than pulled back in her usual ponytail. Maybe she did suspect something. She looked really nice.

She wore a satiny lavender blouse and black jeans. The top hung down past her waist, probably so she could hide the holstered Glock he knew she always carried at the small of her back.

"Hi honey," Dean said as he climbed in. He leaned over and kissed her as he got situated and then buckled his seatbelt.

"So, Dean, where are we going on this mystery date?"

"I told you, just dinner out. I have to go to work later. It's nothing special, I just hadn't seen you in a while and thought it would be nice to catch up."

"So, I can pick the restaurant?"

"Uh, no," Dean stammered. "I got us reservations at Sabatani's tonight."

"They've been booked up solid since they rebuild the place. How'd you get reservations there?"

"It helps if you taught the owner his CERT first aid training. Plus he called and said he had a last minute cancellation tonight. He wondered if I'd want to use it before he opened it up. I figured it was better than my original plan of taking you to Hanks Diner."

"Well, let's go then," Jaz said, a big smile on her face. "I could use one of Kristof's signature dinners."

Jaz pulled away and Dean hoped he'd managed to divert her attention from the special plans he had. She seemed to fall for it, at least for now.

So far everything was going according to plan.

Dean sat back from the table and patted his stomach.

"That's it; I can't eat another bite."

"Wimp," Jaz said. She stabbed at his plate with her fork nabbing two of the cheese tortellini and popping them into her mouth.

"I still don't know how you can eat so much. It's weird."

"Hunter genes. We have an increased metabolism. It gives us the ability to keep up with the supernatural creatures we hunted over the years, but it also comes with the need to fuel up more frequently and with more food than normal."

"I guess it comes in handy in keeping that girlish figure."

"I haven't heard you complaining," Jaz said hiding her smile behind her wine as she took a sip from the glass.

Dean held up his right hand as if taking an oath.

"No complaints here at all. I swear.

"Good, no woman likes complaints about how she looks."

Kristof, the owner of the restaurant, who happened to be a real live Djinn or genie, stopped by their table on his rounds checking on the patrons.

"How was your dinner? Everything was good, I hope."

"Everything was excellent, Kristof," Dean said. "Not that I'd expect any different. Thank you for thinking of us when you got that cancellation."

Kristof nodded.

"I have always tried to support our first responders, especially the men and women of Station U."

"We greatly appreciate it," Dean replied.

"I still want you to let me hire Freddy away from you. Since he started cooking for you all, you don't come in to see me as much as you used to."

"It's not because of the food, I assure you. We can't afford fine dining out all the time. Even with your discount, dinner here is still something your average public servant has to save up and use for a special occasion."

"That reminds me," Jaz said. "Can you put our dinner on my business account? There's no need for Dean to cover this, I'll let him pay for dessert later."

"Not a problem at all, Miss Errington. I'll make sure it is added to your regular bill."

Kristof left and Dean looked at Jaz. She had a satisfied grin on her face.

"You have a tab at Sabatani's now?"

"I also have a regular reservation three nights a week for my out of town clients to hold dinner meetings. That's the canceled opening you got, I suspect. It's sweet of you to think to bring me here, though. I don't usually get to partake of the dinners with clients. I let my account reps take care of that."

"Jaz, you've got to let me pay for some things. We talked about this."

"We did and I thought we left it with you understanding I make twenty times the money you make working for the city. You told me, again and again, you won't leave there and take a job with me. Training tactical medics for my security teams is not a slack job just to keep my boyfriend busy, by the way. Just be smart and let me pay for the expensive dinners."

"My work for the city is important; you know that. I like taking care of my patients and I like the challenge it offers for me."

"Which is why I usually don't say anything about it." Jaz paused and leaned across the table then took Dean's hand in hers. "Hey, I like the way you're committed to your patients and the community as a whole. It's one of the things I love most about you."

Dean gave her hands a gentle squeeze in return along with a smile acknowledging what she'd said. He leaned back and nodded to the door.

"Shall we head out? I thought we could go for a stroll in the park before it got too late. There's a concert of some sort planned for this evening. I saw a notification on it from the city in my email at work. It could be fun."

"You planned this date night, Dean," Jaz said as she took the folded napkin from her lap and slid out of the booth. "I'll follow your lead."

"Come on, then. I think the music is starting soon."

Dean and Jaz left the restaurant and, instead of retrieving their SUV, opted to walk the three blocks to the city's commons, the main park situated in the center of Elk City.

They soon reached the outskirts of the park and started on their way down one of the many paths there. In the distance, Dean heard the sound of a rock band's driving bass and drum beat drifting through the trees. He couldn't make out the song, though.

Reaching out to take her hand, Dean led Jaz towards the music. It was located in the park's central pavilion next to a small, man-made lake with several fountains in the center. He could hear the cover band well enough now to pick up the tunes from a few recent pop hits.

Taking a branch in the path, Dean led her to a footbridge across the narrowest portion of the lake, opposite the pavilion on the far shore. Dean's free hand patted the pocket of his jeans where he'd stuck the box with the ring. He'd caught himself checking for the ring so many times tonight; it was as if he was afraid it would somehow disappear if he didn't keep checking for it.

"You're quiet," Jaz said as they reached the center of the span.

"I'm listening to the music. The band's not that bad."

"I guess so," Jaz said, shrugging. "I've heard better, though."

"I think it's a local showcase and not a featured artist."

"In that case, I guess we should cut them some slack and hope they improve."

Dean laughed and Jaz joined him. She was right. The band was pretty terrible. They were butchering one of his favorite songs now.

In the midst of his laughter, he wondered if maybe the choice of a musical backdrop for the proposal wasn't such a good idea. He banished the thought as jitters and reached into his pocket to pull out the ring. Taking a deep breath, Dean prepared to kneel on the bridge's decking.

And then he stopped himself at the sound of Jaz's stern whisper.

She kept the smile on her face while she leaned in as if to kiss him and said, "Dean, don't react. There's someone else on the bridge behind you about ten yards away."

Dean almost turned and looked but managed to resist. He leaned in as well and kissed her.

"It's a public park, Jaz. There are bound to be people out and about."

"He didn't walk out here. He just suddenly appeared, Dean. He definitely wasn't there a few seconds ago."

Her hunter instincts were rarely wrong about things like this. She always kept an eye on her surroundings.

Keeping a smile on his face, too, Dean said, "What do we do?"

"Stay where you are so you're blocking their view of me."

Dean nodded and pretended to stare out over the water at the distant band in the lighted pavilion. He tried to get a look out of the corner of his eye at the threatening figure but he couldn't see anything but darkness.

Next to him, Jaz drew her Glock, holding it down at her side while she leaned in for another kiss.

"He's coming this way. When I say drop, hit the deck."

Dean's lips brushed against hers. The floral hints of her perfume wafted past his nose. Everything seemed to slow down.

"Drop!"

At Jaz's shouted command, Dean fell to the bridge's decking expecting an attack of some sort.

Jaz assumed a shooting stance above him, one hand bracing the other holding the pistol.

A soft white light filled the center of the bridge, coming from behind him in the direction of their assailant. Dean turned at the sound of a man's calm voice.

"You may relax, Jaswinder Errington. I mean you no harm. I am here to talk with your companion."

"You shouldn't sneak up on people in the dark like this if all you want to do is talk."

"Perhaps, however, I'm here now. May I approach?"

"You may, Eldara," Jaz said. The pistol dropped back to her side.

Dean twisted on the ground to look behind him.

A man in his early forties approached. He wore gray slacks and a black sweater. Well, not a normal human man, Dean admitted, not with the fading nimbus of white light still surrounding him. Jaz's assessment it was one of the Eldara seemed an accurate one. With a glow like that, it was a good bet he was one of those heavenly messengers from the gods, known as angels to some, and by many other names to others.

The fact he wanted to speak to Dean didn't bode well in his experience. Dean scrambled to his feet and stood next to Jaz.

The closer the man got, the more familiar he seemed to Dean as if he should know this Eldara. There was something about his face, something about the way he carried himself that triggered a distant memory in Dean's mind.

The nimbus of white light faded entirely by the time the Eldara reached the couple. Soon they were left with nothing but the soft glow of nearby lampposts spaced along the length of the bridge.

Dean resisted the urge to snap at the angel standing before him. All his plans for Jaz had been dashed by some sort of divine plan. Dean knew his anger would be wasted on the Eldara, especially if he was here delivering some message from above. Hopefully, he'd say whatever he had to say so Dean could get back to the business of proposing to Jaz.

Plastering a fake smile on his face, Dean met the man's eyes and said, "I'm Dean Flynn. You said you came to see me. I assume there's some sort of message from above?"

The Eldara shook his head and smiled.

"I'm surprised you don't recognize me. You should feel something, a distant memory of me, I would think."

"I'm sorry, I don't know who you are. You haven't introduced yourself yet."

The wrinkled brow and pursed lips showed confusion spreading across the Eldara's face. He didn't seem to know what to say at first. Then the man's smile returned, along with his confidence, it seemed.

"My name is Gabe, Dean. I'm your father."

Chapter 9

"I'M SORRY, WHAT?" Dean asked.

It was his turn to be confused.

"I'm your father, Dean. Your mother must've told you something about me."

Dean's mind raced with thoughts and memories swirling around all at once. After his dream earlier that afternoon, he remembered his mother calling for a man named Gabe. Now, that name attached itself to another hazy memory from his early childhood. It was so long ago, the man known as Gabe was little more than a shadowy figure to Dean. He couldn't have been more than two or three years old the last time he was around.

As some of those earlier memories were jogged, he remembered his mother had never referred to any one man as Dean's father. Other than the possible memory he'd dredged up in his dream, she'd never talked about anyone named Gabe at all.

Except now the man called Gabe stood here in front of Dean, claiming to be his father. He decided to try and get rid of the guy. Even if he was Dean's father, he didn't have any desire to get to know him now at this point in his life.

"I'm sorry, Gabe, my mom never talked about you. You must be thinking of someone else. You're not my father."

"You can't lie to me, Dean. You may not know much of who I am, but you remember something about me. I can tell."

Gabe moved closer while Dean tried to come up with an answer to the accusation. His emotions jumped around in his head from anger to betrayal to sadness about never having a father around.

Jaz stepped up next to him while he fought his internal struggle. Her voice was cold and hard like ice.

"I think you should take a step back, Eldara."

Gabe turned his gaze on Jaz. His eyes blazed with an inner light.

"I'm not accustomed to taking orders from humans, Huntress. You would do well to understand that."

Jaz didn't back down but neither did she threaten, Dean noticed. She kept her weapon down at her side. It would be of little use in this situation anyway unless she had some sort of Eldara-killer rounds in there.

"And I'm not one who responds well to threats from supernaturals. I'm not without my protections, Eldara, and I know the strictures as well as you do. If I offer you no harm, you may not attack Dean or me. Besides, I recognize you. I know who you are."

Jaz nudged Dean with her elbow, never taking her eyes off the angel standing opposite them on the bridge.

"This isn't just any random Eldara delivering a message, Dean. He's one of THE Eldara, one of the senior members of that clan of divine messengers. He's an Arch-angel. This the angel Gabriel himself and he's just as full of himself as all the stories say he is."

Gabe smiled and relaxed his stance, taking a step backward. He gave her a nod of respect.

"You remember your lessons well, Jaswinder. I applaud you for determining my identity so quickly."

"I've known others of your kind, and they're much more attuned to proper conduct in a situation like this. You aren't. That means you don't associate much with humans. There's only one Gabriel in the lore who fits that bill. It wasn't much of a leap."

Dean recovered his thoughts enough to jump in again. His anger took over as he shook a finger in Gabe's direction.

"How do you get to be my father and why should I care if you are? My father left my mother alone and destitute a long time ago. He never came back, not once. We learned to get along without you well enough and I don't need you in my life now either."

"That is all stuff your mother told you, Dean, but it is not true. I stayed as long as I was allowed to stay. Then I had other divine duties to attend to. I resisted at first but the higher powers finally tracked me down and I was called back to the upper realms to deal with those duties. I didn't want to leave. I never want to leave when I'm called to create a Nephilim, a child of my progeny."

Dean seized on that last point. His anger spilled over in his words.

"So I'm merely a creation of yours, a so-called Nephilim, something you just created with a random woman before you returned to the heavens above? You're just some sort of heavenly gigolo, taking advantage of women here on Earth."

"You're twisting my words against me, Dean. You're better than that. I may not have been part of your everyday life but I've watched you grow up. I watched you become the type of child any father would be proud of. When the time came to help you, help arrived, usually handled by one of my cousins here on earth while they tended to their other duties."

Dean searched his mind for what Gabe meant by his words.

"You mean help like Ashley? Like Ingrid? They were just placed here to help me out?"

"You know the answer to that already, Dean. Ashley said as much when she was here with you. She said she was searching for someone who needed her help. She told you that when you first got to know each other. There was no subterfuge involved. Perhaps she didn't tell you everything she knew, but there are rules about how much we can reveal to our charges on earth."

"But now, at this particular moment, you chose to come down to earth and reveal your true identity to me. I suppose that means I will soon need your help with something." Dean let out a wry, sarcastic chuckle. "It must be something pretty big if you decided to come yourself rather than send some lackey to deal with me. Let me guess; I'm in some sort of danger."

"You all are. You're in greater danger than you could possibly know."

Burning anger welled up like a volcano within Dean.

"Why, because the Agents of Chaos are on their way here to Elk City? Because I'm living in the midst of the apocalypse, the end of the world? I already know that, Daddy. I don't need you or your help."

Jaz's head whipped around and she faced Dean.

"The Agents of Chaos, they're coming here?" She asked, firing off questions in rapid succession. "How do you know that?"

"I didn't have a chance to tell you, Jaz. We weren't even sure it was real."

"We, Dean? Who? James and Brynne, I suppose."

"I stopped in after work this morning to check on something Barry and I heard while out on a call yesterday. The topic of the four horsemen came up with James and Brynne and James shared what he knew about the Agents of Chaos from the past. I was going to tell you but it never seemed to be a good time. I'm sorry."

"Dean you're telling me you forgot to let me know the end of the world was coming."

"It's just something we heard on the street. I wasn't even sure it was real."

Jaz pointed at Gabe.

"That's the Trumpet Bearer himself, Dean. He's the one who will call the heavenly hosts to the final battle. Now he's here, and he turns out to be your father to boot. I think it's a tad more important than you thought."

"I didn't know he was my father, Jaz. I've told you everything I know about my father, everything my mother told me about him. Besides, this could all be some sort of Eldara trick."

"Dean," Gabe said. "You know the Eldara do not lie. We might not reveal the truth at every opportunity, but when I say I am your father, I am not lying."

Dean tried to fight down the knots twisting his guts into pretzels at the moment. He felt like he was being pulled underwater and he couldn't find his way back to the surface. He needed to breathe.

This was all too much to process. Why had his mother lied? Gabe was correct. Dean did recall a vague memory of a man resembling Gabe from his childhood, but his mother never connected that memory to his father. According to her, his father was simply someone who drifted into her life and left her to raise a child alone.

"Does my mother know you are here?"

Gabe shook his head.

"I thought it would cause too many old memories to rise up to the surface for her. I cared very deeply for her during the brief time we were together. I still do."

"But you're alright turning my life upside down in the midst of one of the most important moments of my life?"

Jaz shot him a puzzled glance at his choice of words then looked back at Gabe again. She must have sussed out what Dean had planned. Her eyes blazed with fresh, hot anger that hadn't been there before. She seemed pissed at both of them now.

"I am sorry if I interrupted something important, Dean. I had to reach out to you and I thought it would be better here in this secluded space away from prying eyes and ears."

Dean clenched his fists. He wasn't going to let a simple apology make up for the ruined plans and the shocking revelation of his paternity.

"Fine, Daddy," Dean said, drawing out the name, letting sarcasm drip from his tone. "You're here now. Give me whatever cryptic message you came to leave me and go back to the heavenly plane you come from."

"Dean, I'm not here to deliver a message. The Agents of Chaos are coming. I've come to fight at your side in the final battle over who is to rule this earthly plane."

"What, fight in some armageddon of divine creation? I'm not interested. I'll take care of my own here in Elk City and the rest of you can fight amongst yourselves."

"You don't mean that, Dean," Gabe said. "I know what the humans and other people of this city mean to you. You'll fight to save them with every ounce of your energy, just as you have done in the past whenever they've been endangered by outside threats."

Dean ground his teeth together. Gabe obviously knew him. He knew Dean too well, it seemed.

"I said I've been watching over you," Gabe continued. "You've never truly been alone in the world. I or someone else has always been close to you, watching over you."

"Like Ashley?"

Gabe nodded. "And others, too."

Dean thought about that statement. Who else in his life was an agent for the gods, watching over him?

"So nothing in my life is mine. Every choice I've made has been made for me."

"Not true at all. There was guidance when you needed it but the choice was always yours to make, or not make. There were certainly times when you did not make the choice I thought you would or would have chosen for you. Still, it all worked out in the end. We are here and you are ready to assume your place at my side to help turn the tide in the final battle."

Dean searched for something to ground him and steady his resolve. He reached out and took Jaz's free hand in his. Her touch, the warmth of her hand pressed against his gave him renewed strength.

"I'm not playing the game by your rules, Gabe." Dean used the Eldara's proper name rather than name him as a father anymore. "You said I make my own choices. Fine. I choose to stop this fight from happening. There will be no final battle at all. If that battle happens here and now, in this city and around it, thousands, perhaps millions, will die. Many more will be injured. That is unacceptable."

"Once events start down a path, Dean, they may not be altered," Gabe said. "This is a prophecy told long before you or even I."

"James said the Agents of Chaos have come before and they've been stopped and send back to hell. If it can be done once, it can be done again, without the end of the world happening alongside it."

"Dean…" Gabe started to say.

"Don't tell me it can't be done. Go back to where you came from Gabe and tell the powers that be that I'm not playing their game or by their rules. They can have their war to end all wars somewhere else and at some other time."

A memory of something else came to him and he added one more thing before leaving.

"I almost forgot. A gnome by the name of Alfonse told me he needs to speak with you. I told him I'd deliver that message to my father if I ever met him. I never thought I'd have to pass it along."

Dean shrugged and tugged on Jaz's hand.

"Come on. I don't have anything else to say to this angel of bad tidings."

Jaz holstered her pistol and gave Dean a reassuring smile, nodding. He noted a hint of worry in her eyes when they met his but he also saw the support she sent him. He was more grateful for it than she knew.

Together they turned their backs on Gabe and walked towards the far shore, leaving the Eldara standing alone on the bridge behind them.

"Well, that went well," Ingrid chuckled as she landed on the bridge beside Gabe, tucking her white-feathered Valkyrie wings against her back as they faded from view. "If there was ever any doubt whose child he was, that stubborn streak proves it's you, cousin."

Gabe watched Dean and Jaz disappear into the darkness at the far end of the bridge.

"It's possible I miscalculated some in how I revealed myself to him."

"You think?"

"You would've chosen a different path?" Gabriel asked.

"This isn't ancient times or even the middle ages, Gabriel. You can't just show up and flash your aura and expect to get blind obedience. It might suffice to get you into some woman's bed but most of the people of this time want explanations. They need to understand the choices they face before they'll adhere to the will of the gods."

Gabriel felt his shoulders sag a little. He'd been so confident Dean would welcome him with open arms after never knowing his father. He'd not anticipated the vitriolic response from the boy.

"What would you recommend, Ingrid?"

"He needs to talk with someone he trusts, someone with whom he's confided before."

Gabe nodded. "Someone like your sister."

Ingrid's shock registered as she shot him a glance.

"I was thinking of myself, but Ashley — is that even possible? She's still regenerating her corporeal form after her body died during the kidnapping. It'll be years before she's able to return."

"There are ways to speed up that process. It's open only to the most powerful of us, and it is not without its own risks. Still, this situation warrants risk, does it not?"

The Valkyrie nodded.

"Then I have an important request to make up above. Let's see what I can do to expedite your sister's return to this plane."

Chapter 10

DEAN STARED out the SUV's passenger window. He and Jaz hadn't said a word to each other since they left the footbridge in the park.

His hand traced the lump of the jewelry box in the pocket of his jeans. He'd planned everything. He'd thought out every aspect of what he would say, imagining Jaz's response of surprise, joy, and eventually saying yes to his request to marry her.

Instead, some random guy, no, an arch-angel appears and ruins everything leaving Dean struggling with a wide range of conflicting emotions about his ruined proposal and the revelation of his father's identity.

His fingers tightened further in his already clenched fist. He pounded his hand down on his knee with a grunt.

Jaz broke the uneasy silence.

"Dean, talk to me. You can tell me what you're feeling. It's alright to be angry or confused or whatever you have going on in your head. But don't close up. Don't shut me out. We can get through this together."

Dean turned towards the driver's seat. Jaz stole a glance in his direction while she drove. She smiled a little when she saw him looking her way.

"That's better," she said. "I don't want to ruin our date night. I thought it was going well up to that point. Don't you?"

"Yeah, right up until the moment my supposed father came and crashed the party. I still don't know if I believe him, I don't care what he is."

"He was telling the truth, Dean. The Eldara cannot lie. You know that. Oh, I'm sure he was hiding something about his motives and what he really wants from you, but he is your father. That much has to be true."

Dean pounded his fist down on his knee again.

Jaz reached out and took his left hand in hers, wriggling her fingers until he relaxed his fist and grasped her warm, soft hand in his.

"Do you remember him at all from when you were younger?"

Dean nodded. "There was something — I don't know — something familiar about him. Something about his walk and his voice that I'd seen or heard before stuck way back in the deepest corners of my mind. It's kind of hard to pin it down. I think I was so little the last time I saw him I didn't understand who he was or what was going on."

"Maybe if you called your mother and asked her…"

"No," Dean said. "Telling her about this will only upset her. She'll either worry about how I'm taking it, or it will dredge up old memories she doesn't want to recall."

"But she could answer your questions, Dean."

"It'll also start a fight between us, Jaz. My mother and I haven't talked in a long time. She didn't want me to move away and come here. Calling her now with this news is only going to open old wounds between us. It's better to leave her out of it for now."

"You know best, Dean. You do need to talk to someone about it, though. Don't close me out of things regarding this. I'm here for you."

"I know you are, Jaz, but I don't know if I'm the talking type when it comes to stuff like this."

"If you expect me to stick around for the long haul, you'd better be, Dean Flynn. You'd better be."

The SUV stopped moving and Dean was startled to see they were parked in the lot at Station U.

Jaz slid the gear lever into park and leaned over the center console until she was very close to Dean. Once again, he caught a whiff of her perfume. She didn't wear it often and a twinge of anger roiled in his gut at the way the Eldara's unforeseen arrival ruined the night's planned activities.

"Dean, look at me."

She waited until he complied and his eyes met hers.

"We'll get through this. We'll do it together, alright?"

"I guess so."

"No, that's not good enough. We will do it. We have a lot to look forward to in this world, Dean. Don't forget; we already know we have a daughter together sometime in the future. Let's not let anything get in the way of us going down the path that lets us meet up with Joanna again. I'm looking forward to watching her grow up into the total badass she becomes."

Dean felt a hint of smile crease his lips. That time-traveling teen witch who was the daughter they were yet to have certainly had turned their lives upside down. Jaz was right. He wanted to see her again, too.

"Alright," Dean whispered.

"Alright, what?"

"Alright, I'll keep you in the loop on what's going on with me."

"Good, that's all I wanted to hear." She leaned closer and kissed him. "Now get in there before you're late. I'm sure Bill wants to go home to his family."

Dean climbed out of the SUV and waved as Jaz backed out of the parking spot and drove away. He turned and walked towards the building.

Stepping into the squad room via the parking lot door, Dean found himself amidst pandemonium. Barry and Bill were carrying the extra go bags from the closet to the ambulance.

Barry spotted him as he came in.

"Hurry up and grab your uniform. You can get dressed in the back on our way there. There's been an explosion of some sort and we have reports of multiple injuries inside a collapsed building over near the Witches coven's house on the other side of town. Fire units are already en route."

Dean nodded and ran back to the bunk room to get his uniform out of the locker where he'd left it.

The ambulance was already running and the garage bay door was rolling up as Dean jumped into the back, pulling the door shut behind him.

"Go. I'm in," he called to the front of the unit.

Bill sat in the driver's seat and he gunned the engine, slowing only long enough to verify the garage door closed behind them. Then he headed into the night, lights blazing and the siren's wail preceding them down the city's streets.

Dean was just tying the laces on his boots as the ambulance came to a halt along the curb in front of the address for their call. Dean looked out, recognizing the old Victorian house which was the central meeting place of the local Witches coven.

Or, Dean corrected himself as he looked on the chaotic emergency scene laid out before him, what used to be an old Victorian house.

The whole front half of the building had collapsed inward leaving the second and third floors of the home's rear half exposed to the responders pulling up out front. Dean climbed out and grabbed the rescue helmet from the side compartment on the passenger side of the ambulance. He grabbed the other two helmets in there and handed one to Barry as he stepped out, holding the other for Bill, who came around from the driver's side.

They were going to have to get in there if rescue operations were to begin and, with a collapsed building like this, helmets were a must. The kevlar woven into the fabric of their duty pants and jackets would help with exposed nails and splintered wood.

Deputy Chief Compton waved in their direction summoning the three of them over. Officer O'Malley from the police's Unusual unit was there, too.

Dean also recognized Asha, the coven leader. Dirt and debris from the house covered her, matted in her hair and all over her face. She'd either been inside when the building collapsed or had tried to go in and rescue her coven sisters on her own before help arrived.

The three station U paramedics headed over to the chief's command unit, an SUV with its rear liftgate open to reveal a slide-out workstation complete with a laptop computer and radio equipment so he could communicate and manage the various units on scene to deal with the situation.

"Good, I'm glad you three are here," the Chief said. "The High Priestess here says some sort of spell a group of junior witches were casting went wrong somehow."

Asha nodded. "It was a harmless practice spell. Then I felt the tenor of the spell change. Unfortunately, things progressed so fast I never had the chance to get there in time and stop them from continuing."

"What sort of spell was it?" Dean asked. "If it caused all of this, will there be residual effects inside the collapsed area?"

"I'm not sure," Asha said shaking her head. "All they were doing was attempting a basic scrying spell. They hoped to determine the source of some negative plane energy we'd detected recently. It was such a simple spell; I left it to the younger sisters. I figured I'd get a report from them when I woke in the morning."

Barry pointed at the collapsed building. "A simple scrying spell didn't cause that. What did they cast if it wasn't the spell you expected? I have to wonder if one of them sabotaged it on purpose."

Asha shook her head. "It started out correctly. I watched them start just to be sure before I went up to bed. What I felt later when I awakened was an intensification of the negative plane energy we'd detected earlier, only now it was centered here. That was just before the explosion and collapse. Something on the other side sensed their scrying and used it to break open a portal from the other side."

"A portal?" Dean said. "Your sisters opened a doorway to the netherworld? Did anything come through?"

Officer O'Malley spoke up.

"We were first on the scene. Neighbors who came to offer help reported seeing a tall, pale man, wearing an all-black business suit leaving the rubble. He was last seen walking towards the center of town. I have units watching for someone matching that description but so far we've heard nothing."

"Asha," Dean said. "How many of your coven aren't accounted for.

How many are injured and how many do you think are still trapped inside?"

"Most of us were upstairs in our rooms. That shielded us from the explosion. We got all of them out via the back kitchen stairs and those with minor injuries are being tended to in the neighbor's houses. I don't believe there are any serious injuries there. That leaves just the five junior sisters who engaged in the scrying spell. No one's seen them and we fear they are trapped inside the wreckage."

"The heavy rescue truck is on the way with the gear we'll need to stabilize the collapsed walls," Chief Compton said. "In the meantime, can you three see if you can localize any survivors without going too far inside?"

The three paramedics nodded.

"Chief, I'll take over medical control," Bill said, assuming the medical command function in the incident command system. "I recommend having the next two ambulances arriving check on the neighboring houses where those who were evacuated are located. They can double check the injuries there while Dean and Barry try and see who we've got inside the collapse."

"Sounds like a plan. Report back to me when you find out from them what we're dealing with. I'll assign channel two on the radio to EMS units so we don't talk over top each other. I'll also send a fire engine crew of four over with you in case you need help extricating anyone in a position you can get to safely."

Dean fished his tactical gloves from his pocket. They would protect his hands while he started searching through the safer portions of the collapsed building. The old, three-story home was large and this was going to take some time.

The frame of the front door and entryway was still partially intact. They decided to stage their med and trauma bags there in the foyer area and start spreading out towards the front of the home to either side. That way they stayed away from the places where the broken beams of the upper floors still hung dangling from the rear of the structure.

Dean moved right while Barry went left. He'd been here a few times before and this was the parlor area to the right of the entry hall.

It led to the room where the scribed casting circle had been built into the floor with a mosaic of tile and wood. Based on what Asha said, this would be the center of the blast.

Dean stepped carefully around parts of the roof and upper floors collapsed down. He stopped and listened for any sounds coming from the rubble around him.

"This is a job for an experienced urban search and rescue team, Dean," Barry called out across the wreckage.

"We can turn it over to the USAR team when they get here. Until then, let's keep searching, just take your time and be careful."

Dean picked his way around a portion of the roof propped at an angle against a fallen section of wall studs still jutting upward. He spotted the hand and forearm right away. It stuck out from under the rear of the collapsed roof section.

He reached out and touched the wrist with two fingers, feeling for a pulse. The hand twitched and grabbed his fingers.

"Oh my goddess, is someone there?" A panicked voice called out from below. "Please, help me. It's so dark and I'm trapped under these beams. I can't move my legs anymore."

"I'm Dean Flynn. I'm a paramedic with the city's Station U team. What's your name?"

"I'm Jessie, Jessie McMann. Hyacinth is somewhere close, too, but she stopped talking to me a while ago. Dean Flynn? Aren't you the one we helped with returning your daughter back to her future self?"

"That's me. Now listen for a second. Besides your legs, is anything else injured on you?"

"I don't think so," Jessie replied. "My legs don't even hurt so much anymore. The worst part is this infernal itching. It's like I have a terminal case of poison ivy all of a sudden."

Dean filed the itching away for later. He had no idea what was causing it and it wasn't likely to be life-threatening like the further collapse of the building could be.

"Alright, Jessie," Dean said, giving her hand a squeeze. "I'm here and we've got more help coming so hold tight. Can you tell me where you heard your friend earlier? Her name was Hyacinth, wasn't it?"

"Yes, she was closer to the center of the circle than I was. She tried to close the portal when it opened. The pale man who came through it struck her with his hand before he started pulling the house down around us. She flew away from him and bounced against the wall next to the fireplace. She was talking to me until a few minutes ago. Now she won't answer."

"I'm going to head over that way and see if I can find her. You hang tight and I'll be right back. My partner Barry will be here soon, too."

"Please hurry, Dean. I don't want to be alone. I'm scared."

"I understand. Just try and think of something to distract yourself until I get back. Do you have a favorite book or something like that? Focus on the story and try and recall the words from your favorite part."

Dean let go of her hand and hoped the distraction would help keep her from panicking until he came back from checking on her friend. Picking his way around the small portion of the interior wall still standing, he headed for the collapsed chimney where the fireplace was located.

Dean found Hyacinth, her vacant, lifeless eyes staring up from beneath a pile of bricks which had caved in from the chimney next to her. She was trapped underneath the pile, covered with broken and shattered bricks from her shoulders down.

Something looked strange about her and he shined his flashlight down on her face and gasped. Her skin was covered in what looked like some sort of large round burn blisters, or something like it. The blisters had turned black and some had burst, releasing a milky yellow fluid that ran down her skin to the debris under her head. It was unlike anything he'd ever seen before.

A thought occurred to him in the back of his mind and he crouched down to examine the woman closer. Burn blisters would have a clear discharge of cellular plasma. The thicker, whitish discharge from these blisters looked like — Dean froze, his hand an inch away from the woman's face. The fluid draining from the blisters looked like something from an infected wound.

Dean stood up and looked around then returned to where Jessie's hand stuck out from the rubble. Shining his flashlight on the exposed skin and examining it closely, Dean noticed something he hadn't before. There was a raised red rash spreading across her arm. Some of the tiny rash blisters had opened and a similar white liquid seeped from them.

He stood up and quickly picked his way back to their bags in the empty and intact foyer. He switched his radio to channel two and keyed his mic, clipped to his radio's leather shoulder strap.

"U-891 crew chief to medical command."

Bill's voice answered him back immediately.

"Go ahead, U-891."

"Medical command, requesting hazmat units to the scene for suspected unknown biological contamination at this location."

"Say again, Dean?" Bill asked, breaking radio protocol by using his name.

"There some sort of blister agent exposure on the survivor I found and a definite and widespread exposure on the one deceased individual I found. Looks like an infection of some sort but I'm not sure. I recommend we lock down the scene until we have more information. That includes the two neighboring homes holding the survivors who self-extricated."

"Received," Bill replied. "Notifying incident command now. Hold tight and take what precautions you can there."

"Already on it. U-891 clear."

Dean popped open the side pocket of the med bag and pulled out a pump bottle of hand sanitizer. He carefully peeled off his gloves and pumped out a sizable amount of the sanitizer in his hand. He spread the sanitizer all over his hands and exposed wrists under his coat's cuffs. It wasn't much but it was all he could do right now. If the infectious agent was airborne, he was already exposed.

"Dean, did I hear you right?" Barry asked, picking his way over debris back to the entryway.

"Yeah, there's some sort of advanced infection on both patients I saw. We hold out here until more help arrives. Did you find anyone over there?"

"No, it seems like that area was empty, just crushed furniture there."

Dean described in more detail what he'd found to his partner and handed him the sanitizer bottle.

"If you touched anything, get those gloves off and sanitize all exposed skin. I don't know if it will help but it's better than nothing."

"What do we do now?" Barry asked as he scrubbed with the sanitizer.

"We have three more people to account for so we'll keep searching where it's safe. Be careful. No physical contact until we have the hazmat team here. We have to wait."

Chapter 11

DEAN AND BARRY managed to locate the other three witch sisters in the collapsed room while they waited for the Hazmat team's arrival. They were each alive but all three were trapped under the rubble in some way and all three had signs of the strange rash.

"Barry, over here," Dean called, motioning to his partner to return to the entry area to talk.

Barry picked his way across the debris to Dean.

"What's up?"

"Hazmat will be here any minute. We need to be ready to decon when they get here which means we're done with patient care. We should give Bill a report now with anything else we know before we hand over care to the hazmat medics.."

"I was checking on the rashes on each patient again. It seems the closer they were to the center of the room, the more pronounced the rash and blistering are. Hyacinth is, by far, the worst case and she's dead, though I don't know what killed her. Then Jesse is next. The other three seem to have made it to the front of the house and were pretty far away from the central location, which I'd guess is where that portal opened. They all say they have a light rash and itching but it doesn't seem to be getting any worse. Without being able to see all of their bodies under the collapse, I have to take their word for it."

"It sounds like some sort of infectious disease or maybe a caustic gas release. Proximity to the portal and whoever came through is the key." Dean looked around, readying his thoughts for the report to Bill. "Can we get the other three free? I know Jessie is going to require some time to dig out."

"They all are reporting minor injuries but are trapped beneath a section of the collapsed porch roof. That's why we didn't see them right away. I think the heavy rescue can use airbags to lift it far enough off them to provide them an avenue to crawl out."

There was a commotion out front where the entire lawn was lit up with floodlights on stands from rescue truck. They were set up in an arc around the front of the home, filling the front of the collapsed structure with light. Dean couldn't see past the bright lights very well, but it appeared there was an arrival of another large vehicle. That would probably be the Hazmat team in their converted school bus.

His guess was confirmed when he spotted the first of the figures approach the house in the bright orange plastic suits. Dean waved and the figure headed his way. Dean sent one last message to Bill with the updated information they had and waited for the hazardous materials tech to reach them.

Dean was surprised to see Brynne's face inside the transparent plastic window on the front of the hood.

"What are you doing here?"

"We decided it was unlikely that any infectious disease would affect a vampire so I was allowed to suit up first. I'll take over patient care. You two head straight out into the yard and towards the command post. They have set up the portable showers there. You two will disrobe and scrub down per protocol then we'll take you two in to the hospital to get checked out."

"We don't need to go to the hospital. We're fine," Dean protested.

"No arguments," Brynne said. "Until we're sure you're clear, you two get checked out by a doc. Now tell me where your patients are and then go get cleaned up."

Dean pointed out the locations to Brynne then he and Barry

headed out to the yard, leaving the hot zone of the hazmat scene behind them. As they got closer to the perimeter lights, Dean spotted a trio of small tents erected just past the semicircle of lights. That would be the showers and transition area from the warm zone into the safe cold zone.

Two figures dressed in orange suits like Brynne's motioned them over to the first tent.

"Go inside here, guys. Strip down and put all your clothes in a plastic bag. Your radios, phones and other personal items can go in one of the small ziplocks you'll find inside. Put everything in the first bin by the door and go get showered. There are scrubs for you to wear in the third tent after you dry off."

"I don't suppose you guys have hot water in these showers?" Barry asked.

"Nope, the shower's being powered by the tank of water on the engine," the guy in the suit said, shaking his head inside the plastic hood. "Just tough it out and don't rush the process. Make sure you're clean before you come out. There are soap and scrub brushes inside."

"Oh, joy," Dean said. "Come on Barry. Let's get this over with."

The two of them headed inside and went through the steps of the decontamination procedure, shivering under the cold water but taking their time and doing the job right. Once finished, they moved at last into the third tent.

Shivering from the combination of the cold air and cold water, Dean toweled off as fast as he could and pulled on the blue scrubs and socks and slippers provided.

Bill waited for them outside.

"I've handed over medical command to the deputy EMS chief. I'm supposed to drive you two over to ECMC to get checked out in the emergency room. They have an isolation room set up to bring in patients and clean them up before entering the hospital."

Dean didn't want to leave the scene. He had a feeling something significant had happened here. There was no bucking the system, though. He had to get checked out. He reached for his phone to text Jaz and tell her what was going on, then realized it was bagged for decontamination back in the first tent.

The hospital had a few of the new ultraviolet light decontamination cabinets in the ER. Their phones would be taken there and placed inside after they were wiped down. Once the UV light did its job, he'd get his phone back.

Sure enough, someone handed them their bagged phones and personal items. The hospital staff would take care of decontamination after they determined what type of infection was involved.

At the hospital, Doc Spirelli, their medical director, did the exam on both of them. A tech drew a few tubes of blood samples from both medics. Dean waited in an exam room, watching the TV on the wall while he waited for the doc to come back and tell them what was up with them.

It was nearly five in the morning when the door opened and Dean expected the doc to come in the room. He was surprised when Gabe walked in, wearing scrubs and a stethoscope around his neck. He even had an ID badge on, though it wasn't Gabe in the picture.

"Oh, it's you. Did you use your Eldara mojo to get your disguise or did you knock some poor nurse over the head and take his badge and stethoscope?"

"You know better than that," Gabe replied. "I don't harm innocents. These were easy to come by in the staff locker room. By the time the owner discovers they're missing, I'll be long gone."

"Look, I don't want to talk with you. I thought I made that clear last night."

"The events of last night at the Witch temple have forced me to accelerate my plans. Tell me what you saw and learned at the temple. I need to know if one of the Agents of Chaos has arrived or not."

"If you mean a tall thin, very pale guy, then yeah, I think one of your demons has shown up. He seems to have brought some sort of disease with him from the netherworld."

"Malificar."

"What?"

"It's Malificar, known as Pestilence in some legends. He's one of the horsemen and it confirms what I'd feared."

"Let me guess; it's the end of the world as we know it." Dean shrugged and laughed. "I feel fine."

"You are correct, Dean," Gabe said, either not getting the reference or glossing over it. "The Agents of Chaos are coming. One of them is already here. Now they are going to try once again to force an end to this world and bring on the final battle."

"You've beaten them before and avoided the end of the world. I heard all about it from someone who's seen it and lived through it several times himself."

"Your vampire friend may have given you some insight into the past visits by the horsemen but that doesn't mean he understands what this occurrence means."

"Why not? I mean, the forces of good arrive and send the demons back to hell and everything goes back to normal again."

"It's not that simple. The Agents learn from their mistakes and try something different each time they return. We must be equally clever and use our foretelling to help us find champions on earth to push them back and counter their plans."

"Champions," Dean said. He didn't like the sound of that and leveled a stare at Gabe. "Now you're going to tell me how I'm some sort of 'chosen one' or something like that? Save your breath."

"Just because you don't like what someone tells you doesn't mean it isn't true. The first of the Agents is here. It won't be long before the others fight their way through to this world. When the last of them arrives, they will put their plans into effect. Will you let that happen?"

"No. I told you earlier. I'll do anything I can to stop them. But I won't play by your rules either. I refuse to accept their's no way out other than a full-on war signaling the end of the world. If they can be sent back to hell once, then they can be banished once again. Better yet, let's find a way to kill them once and for all and stop this cycle from repeating itself in a few hundred years."

"Dean, even if you could find a way to kill one of the Agents, it would be unlikely to unravel their whole plan."

"I don't play by the rules, none of us do. You'll learn, Gabe, that paramedics like me find a way to defeat death and impossible odds all the time. If I can fight off the grim reaper when death is all but certain, I can find a way to stop this, too."

They were interrupted by a phone buzzing in Gabe's pocket. Dean stopped and looked at the archangel.

"This thing has been vibrating like that off and on for an hour."

Gabe took a smartphone out of his pocket. Dean recognized it as his own right away. His custom Star of Life phone case was easy to pick out.

"Where did you get that?" Dean asked, holding out his hand.

Gabe handed it to Dean. "I overheard one of the staff say they'd cleaned it and had to return it to you. I picked it up when they weren't looking and brought it with me."

Dean looked at the screen. Jaz had left two voicemail messages for him over the last hour. She'd called a total of four times but had likely given up on leaving a message. He tapped the screen and put the phone to his ear to listen to the first message.

"Dean, I just got word of a Demon incursion from one of my informants. I'm assembling a team and meeting Rudy and some of his werewolves at an abandoned building downtown. I'll call when I know more."

Dean tapped to play the second message.

"We've got this demon trapped inside. I sent a remote drone on wheels into the building. It looks like there's just one of them. He's assumed the guise of a tall, pale man but it's got to be the one we're looking for. I suppose he's disguised as a human so he can mingle with the rest of us and not be noticed. Rudy is here now and we're going in after him. I'll call when the operation is over."

"Dean," Gabe said. "I overheard what she said. She cannot face one of the agents alone. She's no match for one of them, even with her enchanted sword and other hunter enhancements."

"We've got to get to her before they go in," Dean said. "I can't wait around here. I've got to get to her."

"I can get you out of the hospital. I'll cast a glamour on us so no one notices our passing. I have friends waiting with a car outside."

"Friends?"

"You seem surprised. You are not my only resource in the area." Gabe stopped in the doorway and looked back at Dean. "Are you coming or not?"

Dean didn't have to think twice. He knew he'd catch some flak over leaving without permission but he also knew he was clean. If he wasn't, Doc Spirelli wouldn't have let him just sit in one of the ER's exam rooms waiting for tests to come back.

"Let's go. Do what you have to do, Gabe. I'm right behind you."

Chapter 12

DEAN FOLLOWED Gabe through the ER. He avoided making eye contact with any of the nurses or doctors, afraid they'd stop him and ask where he was going. They were much too busy, though a few did nod a greeting in his direction as he passed.

Wending his way through the waiting room, Dean stepped outside, the skin on his arms suddenly covered in goosebumps from the cold pre-dawn air. He should have tried to find a coat or something to keep warm. Wearing nothing but scrubs was going to be uncomfortable.

Rubbing his hands on his exposed arms to warm up, Dean looked around.

"Where's your ride?"

"It'll be here in a few seconds. Follow me down to the corner. We'll meet them there."

Dean followed Gabe along the sidewalk in front of the ER entrance. An ancient, rusted-out white Bronco pulled up to the curb. Gabe pulled open the front passenger door and climbed in.

Dean chuckled as he climbed into the back. Gabe's friends apparently didn't have a lot of resources if this was the best they could come up with. A dark-skinned man of about thirty sat behind the wheel. Another, this one of Asian descent, sat in the back seat with Dean.

"Where to, my Lord?" The driver asked.

Gabe turned and looked back at Dean. He pulled out his phone from the pocket in the scrubs and opened up the find friends app. Selecting Jaz from the short list of people he shared locations with, Dean prayed her phone was on and she hadn't masked her position.

A blip popped up on a map and zoomed in until Dean could see the location precisely.

"Do you know where High Street and Beacon cross?"

The driver nodded.

"Head there and turn left down Beacon. I'll be able to give you better directions as we get closer."

The app would get him close to her location. Hopefully, he'd be able to spot her SUV when he got there.

Dean tried Jaz several more times on the way to the building on Beacon Street where the icon blinked on the screen. Each time, the phone went to voicemail. He hung up the last time to see them turning onto Beacon from High street.

"There," Dean said. He pointed to their left about a block ahead. There were three black SUVs pulled up in front of a five-story building with a brick facade. The doors were open on one of the vehicles but nobody was in sight.

This wasn't good. They wouldn't have left the vehicles completely unattended.

"They must've gone in after him. Hurry, there still might be time to stop her from confronting Malificar," Dean said.

The Bronco had barely slowed to park in front of the lead SUV when Dean jumped out.

Gabe called out something to him but he didn't hear or care what the archangel said. He ran to the building's entrance, pulling at the doors.

The one on the right popped open and Dean went inside. Very little light filtered in from the streetlights outside and he had to pause to let his eyes adjust to the darkness.

He knew the lack of light was of little concern to Jaz. The family amulet she always wore granted her the vision of a cat in low-light conditions as well as other protections she might need in her work as a demon hunter. Rudy and his werewolves would have no problem in the darkness either.

The door opened behind him and Gabe arrived with his two friends. Each of them carried assault rifles with flashlights mounted beneath the barrels.

The beams of light swung around illuminating the dark corners of the building's lobby. A central hallway stretched out to the left and right from his position by a counter that must've been an information desk at one time in the past.

"Your friends come well equipped, Gabe."

"The Knights Templar are always prepared to lend the Eldara aid in their work on earth."

Dean shook his head.

"You're not kidding, are you? These guys are real Knights Templar, like from the crusades."

"The order was officially disbanded by the Pope in the early four-teenth century at the urging of the King of France who owed them a lot of money. Since then they've operated from the shadows. They still prove useful at times like this."

"My Lord," the lead Templar who was their driver called out from down the left hallway. "I've found the stairs up. The dust is disturbed. I think our quarry went up here."

Dean and Gabe rushed down the hallway.

"You guys know there are friends of mine in here. Don't just shoot the first thing you see."

"We care not for your earthly associates," the driver said. "We are here to protect the Archangel."

"Thaddeus, you and Sebastian must show more respect to my son. He is important to my mission here at this time."

The two knights didn't hide their shock though they regained their composure soon enough. Thaddeus did offer Dean a nod of deference before turning his attention to the open stairwell door.

The gesture made Dean uncomfortable for some reason, perhaps because it acknowledged something he didn't want to believe, even though he knew it to be true in his heart.

The four of them started up the stairs, Thaddeus in the lead, followed by Gabe, Dean, and Sebastian bringing up the rear. A groan of pain from up above on the second-floor landing stopped them for a few seconds.

Dean darted past Gabe and Thaddeus. Someone was hurt up there, it didn't sound like Jaz but it could be Rudy or one of his team.

The werewolf security team he led was a pretty decent tactical team according to Jaz's professional estimation. It was probably why she called him for back up when she knew her own teams were tied up. You couldn't call the police for a Demon kill. They'd want to arrest the creature, especially if they looked human.

Reaching the landing, Dean found a man curled up in a fetal position. He flinched and looked up at the paramedic, the eyes so wide with fear, it seemed as if the pupils and irises had shrunk in the center.

Dean knew this man, he was a werewolf and definitely one of Rudy's team. He was the father of one of his CERT responder students, a teenaged werewolf named Marian.

"Mr. Gregory, it's me, Dean Flynn. I taught your daughter's disaster first aid training."

"Don't touch me. That demon did something to me, to all of us."

"Where's Jaz? Is she here?" Dean struggled with the fear rising up within him. It made him nauseous to think about Jaz being injured or dead upstairs.

"She's up on the third floor. I was supposed to watch the stairs in case the demon tried to escape. There was a lot of shooting and then he was coming down the stairs. He didn't even slow down when I shot him. He just put his hand on my chest and then the pain started. Then he was gone."

Dean didn't wait for more. He was already racing up the stairs to the third-floor landing. He yanked the door open and bolted through into a large open office space with concrete columns spaced along the floor to support the ceiling beams.

A cluster of bodies lay scattered around the center of the room. Dean spotted Jaz immediately laying prone on the floor in the middle of the other bodies. He rushed over to her, stepping over several moaning members of Rudy's werewolf security team dressed in black tactical gear.

She groaned when he rolled her onto her back but she didn't open her eyes. Dean stared at her, unable to process what he saw for a few seconds. Blackened pustules covered her face, similar to the ones he'd seen at the Witches' house earlier. From what he could see, they extended over her whole body. He couldn't believe she was still alive but he was glad she was. It must be her Hunter genes and protections helping her hold on.

Dean drew in a long breath and regained some of his composure. He reached out to take her pulse. He didn't care if she infected him or not. He had to assess her and see what he could do to help her.

There was a barely detectable pulse. It was weak, rapid, and thready. She struggled to breathe, gasping for air, and he detected wet sounding wheezes which could mean her lungs' air passages were constricting or filling with fluid.

Gabe and the two Templars caught up to him at this point. Dean turned to the archangel, his father, and pointed at Jaz, pleading for her with all his heart. His anger at his father forgotten in the terror he might lose her.

"Heal her. She needs healing and I know you Eldara can do that."

"Not all of us, Dean, at least not at this level. She needs a total body cleanse and healing." Gabe gestured to the security team around Jaz on the floor. "I may be able to help the others and their lesser injuries. Their Lycan blood has helped them withstand the infection Malificar spread before he left. Your friend, though, I'm sorry to say, is beyond my meager healing abilities."

"But, you have to. I'll do anything. Give anything." Dean looked back and forth between Gabe and Jaz trying to think of some way to convince the archangel to help her.

"She needs one of the Eldara Sisters, the healers of our clan, Dean."

Dean knew of them from his previous girlfriend who'd revealed herself to be not just a nurse at the ER but one of the healing Eldara. She was dead now, at least her earthly form had died. He'd been told she still lived on another plane but that meant nothing to him. He needed her or another of them now. There had to be others like Ashley somewhere on earth.

"Call one, Gabe. She needs it."

"It's not that simple, my son. None of the healing sisters are close enough to hear my call in time."

Dean's heart seemed to become lodged in his throat. He couldn't speak and he turned to stare at Jaz as she gasped with her last breaths of life there in front of him.

After several long seconds, Gabe spoke again, in a low whisper. It was quiet in the room and Dean had no trouble hearing him.

"There is one way but it requires great sacrifice and I would not risk losing you trying it."

Dean spun around, his voice returning as his fears were suppressed by hope. "It's worth any risk; I don't care what it costs me. She has to live."

Gabe hesitated and Dean felt white hot anger well up within him.

"Look if you want me to agree to join your stupid quest to kill this demon and his evil friends, fine, I'm in. I'll still try to do things my way but you and I can join forces if that's what you want. You have to save her if you want my help, though. As far as I'm concerned, this whole world can go to hell if she dies."

Gabe's eyes met his for several seconds before the archangel nodded.

"Very well, Dean. You've made your point. I will do what I can. You must understand, though, the sacrifice comes from you. This requires me to siphon some of your human life force directly from your soul. It will weaken you considerably for an extended time."

"I don't care," Dean snapped. He rechecked her pulse. "Just do it. Hurry, she's fading." He turned back to stare at Jaz.

"Very well." He leaned forward and the heavenly blade, summoned from another plane, plunged into Deans' back.

Dean didn't have time to turn around when the pain erupted from between his shoulder blades. He arched his back and tried to reach the source of the excruciating pain. His fingers came away bloody and torn from grasping at a razor-sharp sword blade extending up to Gabe's hand.

The pain went on forever. At least, that was how it seemed until it finally ended with his fading consciousness. He collapsed to the concrete floor, rolling to his side to stare up at Gabe. He thought he'd just been killed by his father and he couldn't understand why.

A blinding white circle of light extended out from the sword in Gabe's hand, it's end still red with Dean's blood. The circle of light expanded until Dean had to close his eyes against the searing brightness. He felt his life fading anyway and was sure he was slipping away into death.

The last thing he heard before blackness closed in around him was a familiar voice, a voice he hadn't expected to hear again until the afterlife.

"Dean, my love, what foolish thing have you gone and done now?"

"Ashley?" He heard his voice croak out the question just before what must be his death finally took him.

Chapter 13

DEAN COULDN'T MAKE sense of the afterlife. He'd tried time and again for what seemed like hours to sort it out, but it never worked. As far as he could tell he was blind here, wherever here was. Occasionally he heard snippets of voices, some of them familiar.

At one point Ashley was talking to Jaz. It was almost as if they stood right next to him, though he couldn't understand their words for some reason.

He tried to reach out with his hands to touch them, but when he did, it all faded away again. Of course, he had no body to reach with anymore. He was dead after all.

Another time he could hear Brynne, James, and even Celeste, though why the last two were there, in this afterlife dream world, was a mystery to him. While he and James had made peace with each other, he didn't consider the vampire lord to be a close friend, and Celeste was little more than an acquaintance.

Dean drifted in and out of awareness in the void wondering if he was a ghost, a bodiless spirit, caught between worlds. He decided if this was what being a ghost was like, no wonder they were pissed and scary all the time. The thought made him laugh, and for the first time since he'd died, he heard his own voice, laughing.

"He's starting to awaken."

"Ashley?" Dean asked. "Is that you? Are you hear to take me to the afterlife?"

"He thinks he's dead," Jaz said. "He's always so melodramatic."

"He was like that for me when we were together, too," Ashley said. "I found it endearing."

"It is one of his better qualities," Jaz agreed, laughing together with Ashley.

A warm hand slipped under his head and tucked a pillow under it.

His head. He could feel his head, and the rest of his body, too. Awareness returned. Like a sheet being drawn down to reveal his body, the feeling in his torso and limbs returned.

Dean tried again to open his eyes. He managed to open them but the light was brighter than expected or his eyes needed time to adjust. He squinted, trying to make sense of the visual cues around him.

"Wh-where am I?"

Two faces leaned over him, one on each side. One dark haired, one blonde haired, he knew both of them, though seeing them together at the same time confused him.

"You're in my apartment," Jaz said. "I had them bring you back here after I'd recovered enough to think."

Dean's eyes shifted back and forth from face to face. It made no sense.

"But, how?" He asked. "Ashley, you're gone, sent away forever, and Jaz you were dying of some disease I couldn't cure."

"I left, Dean, but I told you it wouldn't be forever. I needed time to regenerate my life force enough to manifest this body again. Usually, that takes years. This time, though, thanks to your gift, I was able to return sooner."

"My gift? I remember Gabe saying something about a sacrifice. Is that what you mean?"

Jaz nodded and spoke up before Ashley could respond. "You apparently shortened your human lifespan in order to bring her back. Ordinarily, I'd be pissed but you did it so she could heal me so I'll let you off the hook, this time."

"Here, Dean," Ashley said. "Let Jaz and I help you sit up. You need to eat something and get your strength back."

Both women, his ex-girlfriend and his current girlfriend, grabbed him under the armpits and lifted him up with surprising ease. Ashley stuck a few additional pillows behind him and they lowered him back to a reclining position.

Dean recognized his surroundings now. He was in Jaz's bedroom in her apartment.

Jaz held out a mug and spoon to him. "Try some soup. Ashley's right, you need to get your strength back. It seems like we're going to need you based on what she's told me about what is about to happen."

Dean took the warm mug of soup and sipped at it. Its rich, delicious stock warmed him to his core. He smiled after taking a few sips.

"This tastes wonderful."

"I'm glad you like it. Ashley and I went shopping for some things she thought would help rejuvenate you while Brynne and Celeste watched over you. It was fun and gave us a chance to get to know one another better."

Dean considered the oddness of this situation. While he was glad the two of them got along, it wasn't the kind of thing he'd ever thought would be a good idea.

No guy ever wanted his current love interest to meet an ex. It opened up too many opportunities for jealousy and competition. Except, on this occasion, the whole thing seemed to be working. The two of them acted like they'd known one another for years.

A thought occurred to him.

"You two haven't met before, have you?"

Ashley giggled.

"No, silly. I have known other members of her family over the years. We haven't always gotten along given their clan profession as hunters, but Jaz and I never met until yesterday."

"Yesterday! I need to get to work. I'm missing my shift."

Dean tried to hand them the mug while he simultaneously tried to get out of bed. Two pairs of firm hands pressed him back against the pillows.

"Don't be stupid, Dean," Jaz said. "Brynne took care of things for you at work. She applied for a short leave of absence for you so you could recover and help us deal with matters of greater importance than routine ambulance calls."

"We took care of everything, Dean," Ashley added. "I even went and told the Baxters you'd be staying over here for a while so they wouldn't expect you to handle the usual chores for them."

"It seems like you two have thought of everything. How long do I have to stay in bed? Can you tell me that?"

"Judging by your tone," Jaz said. "You are almost back to your usual self. It's up to Ashley, though. She's the nurse."

"I'd say you can get up once we get a decent meal into you," the Eldara Sister said after giving him an appraising look. "You finish the mug of soup and the two of us will go and make you something more substantial. If you manage to eat that without any trouble, you can get up."

Dean lifted the mug and took another sip. It was quite good. He smiled.

"You're the boss."

He glanced at Jaz realizing he'd left her out of the decision.

"I mean bosses. I'm sorry, but this is really confusing and weird."

That set both of them to laughing. Jaz reached out and smoothed his hair with one hand, leaned over and kissed him on the forehead.

"The only one who's confused is you, honey. We're fine. Eat your soup. Ash and I will be right back."

The two women left Dean and he shook his head again, trying to wrap his head around Ashley being back in his life. Then there was the friendship the two ladies had struck up while he was unconscious. Two days ago, he'd have staked a hundred dollars down against Jaz ever wanting anything to do with his exes, especially a literal angel like Ashley.

Chalking it all up to women being from another planet entirely, Dean sipped at his mug of soup and picked up the TV remote from the bedside table. It was noon and the news came up on the local channel. He was about to change the channel to something on one of the cable movie channels when something the newscaster said made him stop.

"…strange illness took another four lives overnight, bringing the total number of deaths to ten. Public health officials and Elk City Medical Center doctors all say they are baffled as to the cause but urge people not to panic."

The newscast cut away to a close up interview with Doc Spirelli from ECMC. "People should take ordinary infection precautions. That means frequent hand washing and the use of alcohol-based hand sanitizers. These are still the best way to keep from catching any illness."

"Doctor, are you and your colleagues any closer to identifying this illness?" The young blonde female reporter asked. "There are some unconfirmed reports it is Ebola or another tropical illness."

"I can confirm only that it is NOT Ebola. We have sent samples out to the Centers for Disease Control in Atlanta and are in contact with state and federal health officials about our efforts here. There is no reason to think we cannot contain this particular outbreak and identify a proper treatment plan for it."

The picture cut back to the male anchor at the television studio.

"Stay tuned here to Action News Central for updates throughout the day as they become available as well as full coverage again at six and eleven tonight."

Dean muted the TV as the anchors moved on to another news story.

"Jaz, Ashley," Dean called out. "I just saw a story on the news about a disease outbreak in the city. That wouldn't have anything to do with our missing demon, would it?"

Gabe walked into the bedroom and answered him. The archangel's presence caught Dean by surprise.

"Malificar is consistent, but he shows little imagination. All he knows how to do is cause illness and disease wherever he goes. He will likely try to stay hidden while he works to bring his brothers here to earth. These deaths you've seen on the news are related to limited exposures from his passage through an area. Once he goes to ground to wait, it should stop the spread of the illness temporarily."

"I didn't know you were here," Dean said, trying to sound disinterested in anything his father had to say.

"Of course I'm here. You are the lynchpin to our efforts to fight the Agents of Chaos in the final battle."

"I told you, I'm not buying the whole 'end of the world' thing you're peddling. There has to be a way to stop them without them opening the gates to hell and fighting a pitched battle with all the hordes of demons released by the four horsemen."

"There might be, but I'm not going to waste time looking for something that may or may not work. The stakes are too high for us to fail. It means the future of humanity, heaven, and earth if we fail."

"Humor me, Gabe. You want my help so answer a few questions. If you were to look for an answer to my earlier proposal on stopping this whole thing before it starts, where would you start looking?"

Gabe stared at him for a long time before answering.

"Very well, since you insist. Hopefully, you'll see how difficult the alternative is. We should be preparing for the inevitable final battle. The only way to stop the coming of the final battle is to prevent the four horsemen, the Agents of Chaos themselves, from combining forces and casting the spell to open the gateway to hell. That will signal the beginning of the end."

"So we just have to defeat each of them and we stop the whole process? That doesn't sound that hard."

"You don't understand, each of them can only be defeated and banished back to hell by one of four chosen champions, one for each of them. No one knows who they are or where in the world they will be found. Also, we can only challenge the four demons when they become vulnerable at the time they begin casting the spell to open the portal. As you can see, too many things have to happen for us to be able even to try and stop them that way. We'd have to find the champions, locate each of the Agents of Chaos and track them to the location where they plan to open the gateway. Fight our way through whatever minions they've assembled. And finally, fight each of them."

"It sounds a lot less impossible than the way you first described it to me. We find the champions, we find the demons, and we defeat them. That's it."

"I always marvel how you humans, who are so risk averse in most situations, are so bad at assessing the odds of success when there is a significant risk at stake. It's like you forget you're mortals."

Dean shrugged. "Blame the gods. Remember what was left when Pandora released all the troubles on the world?"

"I knew Pandora, Dean. She was a foolish girl who also didn't listen to reason. Don't break out that old parable to me."

"You didn't answer my question. What was left in the box?"

Gabe sighed. "Hope. It was hope."

"There's your answer. You didn't leave us humans much to hold on to in the midst of your battle for good and evil in this world, but you immortal types did leave us hope. As long as there's hope, I won't give up. If you knew as many paramedics as I do, you'd know how often we defy the odds and save our patients all the time. In fact, we laugh in the face of hopeless odds."

"But if you fail, Dean, all is lost."

"I think the alternative is worse. The devastation of the world in the midst of a battle where no one on earth wins no matter who comes out on top is something I don't accept. I refuse, so help me find these champions and defeat the Agents or get the hell out of my way."

Gabe turned away and started to walk out of the room. Ashley and Jaz were returning from the kitchen with some more food for him.

"Where are you going, Cousin?" Ashley asked Gabe.

"I need a break. I don't know how you manage to put up with these humans all the time. I couldn't stand living here among them for any length of time."

Gabe pushed past her and disappeared down the hallway.

Dean called out to him.

"I won't change my mind just because you leave. I know what I need to do and I'll do it with or without you."

Ashley laughed. "I recognize that stubborn streak, Jaz, and you're in trouble."

"What do you mean?" Jaz and Dean asked in tandem.

"Never mind. Now, settle down and eat something or I'm not letting you out of this bed. You may have some grand mission or plan in mind, but until I tell you you're well enough to get up, you are staying right where you are."

Dean grumbled under his breath but leaned back against the pillows and took the plate of food from Jaz. He started eating under the watchful eyes of both women.

He didn't care. His mind whirled while he chewed, trying to formulate a plan.

He had to stop the end of the world.

Chapter 14

WHEN HE'D FINISHED the plate of food, Ashley let Dean up to walk around the apartment a little bit.

"Take it slow, Dean," Ashley cautioned him as he started to get up.

"I'm fine. You and Jaz are worrying for nothing."

Dean swung his legs over the side of the bed and stood up. He knees buckled instantly, the sudden weakness in his legs catching him by surprise. A wave of fatigue swept over him and he barely caught himself in time, pushing backward with one hand on the nightstand to land seated on the side of the bed.

"She warned you, Dean," Jaz said.

"I don't understand. I felt fine laying in the bed just now but my legs felt like limp spaghetti noodles when I put my weight on them."

"Ash explained it to me as something like giving too much blood. You'll get your strength back but you have to give it time for you to replenish the life force you spent bringing her back."

Ashley nodded. "Gabriel shouldn't have risked you like that. Your Eldara half allows you some limited regeneration. You'll regain the life energy you spent, but it will take time. You remember what happened when I used too much of my power all at one time? I was bedridden for the better part of two days."

"I don't have two days," Dean complained, levering himself back up to the top of the bed where the pillows helped to prop him upright.

"I don't think you have a choice, honey," Jaz said.

"I always have a choice. Gabe tried to tell me there was no way to stop the impending doom about to descend on the world. After I questioned him, I found out there might be a chance of heading things off before Armageddon begins. We need to find four champions to stand up to the four Agents of Chaos. If we can do that, then we can defeat them before the battle is joined."

"Gabe knows what happens if we fail," Ashley said, "We potentially doom the final battle's outcome, too. That's a big risk to take. The final battle decides the fate of everyone who ever lived on this planet. Is that worth risking everything?"

"All the more reason to do it in my book, Ash. I'm hoping, now that you're back, you'll know of a way we can locate the four champions. Gabe said it's impossible. I don't believe him. We just have to find a way to do it. That's the key to this."

Ashley shook her head. "Ordinarily in a situation like this one, I'd tell you to wait and keep your eyes open and the champions will reveal themselves to you. That isn't going to work here. They are not the primary solution to the pending prophecy's fulfillment. The final battle is what the prophecy of Revelations predicts."

"That doesn't help us a whole lot, Ash," Jaz pointed out. "We need to find a way to circumvent the prophecy."

"She's right, Ashley," Dean said. "We need a way to locate the champions without me having to get out of bed."

The room fell silent. Everyone lost in thought as they worked through the possible solutions as that came to mind.

Jaz arrived at the answer first."

"It's a magical intervention we seek, one that will alter the events as they're supposed to happen. Right?"

Dean and Ashley nodded.

"Asha has to be wanting payback on Malificar, the first horseman, for destroying her home. We ask her if she can help us find our champions, then."

"Her temple is destroyed, at least for now. The casting circle and pentagram are covered in debris," Dean said. "Where will she find another location for a casting like that?"

"Here," Jaz said.

"What?" Dean and Ashley said at the same time.

"When I moved in, I put in a protection circle in the living room under the carpet. It took me a while but I painted the pentagram and runes myself. I took great care to make sure it was complete and intact."

She stopped and looked at Dean and Ashley. Both seemed a little shocked at what she said.

"It's a common practice in hunter families to have a safe room in the home where we cannot be touched by demonic powers. It should also be able to double as a casting circle, I would think. Asha can tell us for sure."

"Just when I think I know everything about you, Jaz, you surprise me yet again," Dean said reaching for his phone. It sat charging on the nightstand next to him. "I'll contact Asha and see if she'll agree to meet us here. I still have her on my phone from when she sent Jo back to the future."

"I'll call her, Dean," Jaz said. "You aren't doing anything but resting. You look pale enough to be death himself. If you lie down again, you'll be asleep in a matter of minutes. Ashley and I will take care of getting her here. Hopefully, you'll be stronger and can come participate, but only if you rest now."

Dean wanted to argue, but the wave of overwhelming fatigue swept in again. If he hadn't been laying down instead of standing, he'd have ended up on the floor.

"Just keep me in the loop," Dean said. "I want to know what's happening."

Both Ashley and Jaz smiled and agreed. He settled back into the pillows and fell asleep wondering if they were just telling him what he wanted to hear so he'd rest as they wanted.

"I can adapt my spell to work within this circle," the Witch High Priestess Asha said, looking over the circle of runes painted on the floor. "You're right. I'd like a chance to pay back that creature that destroyed my home and killed sisters from my coven."

"Thank you, Asha," Dean said. "I'd hoped you'd agree to do this."

"This spell is not without its risks. You're essentially forcing a fork in the timeline. If the world was supposed to end at this time and place and we alter that, there could be repercussions down the road we don't understand. Things might happen in the future none of us will live to see or understand."

"I can watch out for that," Ashley said. "If I see something in the future, I can try to work out a way to bring things back into line again."

"It's a chance I'm willing to take," Dean said. "Anything has to be better than the end of the world."

"Let's hope you're right, Dean," Jaz said. She pointed to the pentagram surrounded by a circle of runes on the floor. "Is there anything we need to change with the runes or circle itself?"

The carpet was rolled back and lay against the wall in the corner with the living room furniture. The gold leaf paint Jaz used to build the circle reflected the light in different patterns on the ceiling as the large candles flickering at the points of the pentagram cast their illumination on it.

"No, it is better if I alter the spell itself as I cast it to provide the best chance of success."

"Okay, Asha," Dean said. "We're yours to use as you need."

The High Priestess shook her head. "The three of you will only be in the way. Stand over there by the door and be ready to run if it looks like things are breaking down with the casting."

Jaz shot Asha a stern look. "I thought you said you could adapt the spell to my circle."

"I can and will. It's the spell itself that is problematic. The powers above and below will seek to counter it because we seek to alter fate's course."

"We understand the risks, Asha," Dean said. "Go ahead and attempt the spell."

Dean moved with Jaz and Ashley across the room to stand against the wall by the door. He moved with care, trying not to show the twinge of weakness and trembling he still felt in his legs. It had been two days since his collapse and he felt better, but he was in no way at a hundred percent.

He leaned up against the wall, using it for a little extra support as Asha closed her eyes and started chanting.

At first, there was no effect he could see. Asha kept chanting, repeating over and over a series of unintelligible phrases while walking around the inside perimeter of the rune circle. She paused each time she reached one of the five candles. When she did, she passed a hand over the flame, palm down. The fire rose a few inches higher with each pass around the circle until the tongues of flame from each candle extended a foot in the air and resembled the blue flames of five blow torches rather than the simple yellow fires of lit candles.

The chant continued in the midst of the flickering blue light from the tall candle flames. As it did, a soft white glow about the size of a baseball grew in the air, hovering above the center of the circle. As Dean and the others looked on, it grew and divided three times until four identical glowing balls of light hung there.

The lights circled around the center of the circle's pentagram, about five feet off the floor. Then one peeled off from the other three and sped across the apartment, passing through the glass of the double window in the far wall and disappearing into the night.

This happened two more times until there was a single ball remaining, hovering in the center of the room. Then it, too, began to move, this time away from the window. Dean was sure it was heading right for him but it swerved to his right at the last instant to hover above Ashley's head. It flashed brighter three times before fading from view.

When the glowing light above Ashley faded, the candles returned to normal with the flickering yellow flames they'd had when the spell began.

"Huh," Ashley said with a sigh. She had a strange look on her face. It seemed to be a mix of grim determination and apprehension.

"What just happened?" Dean asked.

"The spell located its first champion," Asha said. "Apparently, you already found her."

Dean pointed out the window.

"But, the other lights, we should have followed them somehow."

"No, they have not yet found their intended targets," Asha said. "I sensed uncertainty in their purpose as if the subjects of their search were not yet decided at this time."

"That doesn't help us at all," Dean said. "Gabe was clear when he told me what was needed. We have to have all four champions gathered together to have a chance of defeating the four Agents of Chaos."

"Perhaps," Ashley suggested, "it can't find the other champions yet because only one of the demons has come through the portal to this world."

She placed a hand on her forehead and nodded. "I have a feeling why I was selected. Malificar is also known as pestilence. He spreads disease. I'm a healer. It makes sense that one such as I must confront him. Perhaps, once the other demons arrive, we will identify similar connections to them as each champion is revealed to us. Then each champion can counter their demon's evil purpose."

"That makes sense," Asha agreed. She closed her eyes and tilted her head as if listening to something. After a few seconds, she smiled and opened her eyes. "The spell is still active and searching. When the other Agents arrive, your other champions will be revealed, too."

Ashley walked over to the window and looked out into the sky, across the expanse of the city outside the apartment. She pointed to something in the distance.

"It's strange," she said. "I have a sensation pulling me to the south. It's a sort of tugging on my consciousness. I don't know how to describe it."

"Are you alright?" Dean asked. He worried the spell might have had an adverse effect on her.

"I'm fine, I think." Ashley put a hand to her head. "There's something there to the south, not too far off. It's like I can point to it, whatever it is."

Dean had moved to stand next to the Eldara where she stood by the window. A familiar clicking of metal sliding on metal sounded from behind him. He turned around.

Jaz slipped on her shoulder holster and racked the slide on her second pistol after sliding a magazine into the grip.

"Isn't it obvious?" the hunter said. "The spell has given her the ability to track the demon. A hunter can spot a tracker from a mile away. Ashley can lead us to him, and this time, I don't intend to go in unprepared. I'm bringing extra firepower."

"But Gabe said we couldn't take them out before all four had assembled," Dean said.

"Why should we take his word for it?" Jaz said. "Gabe has an agenda of his own. He wants the last battle to come. He told you he didn't want you to do it this way. Maybe that was a distraction to keep you from tracking the Agents of Chaos down as they arrived."

"He's an Eldara, Jaz. He can't lie to me."

"No, she's right, Dean," Ashley said. "He can't lie but he can bend the truth pretty far. It's possible he misled you. I agree with Jaz. I have to see where this pull takes me."

"Asha?" Dean asked the High Priestess.

"I've finished everything I can do. If you want, I can pass a blessing from Gaia to you if you'd like. It will help fight against the demon's ability to infect you with its disease."

"That's perfect. Between you and Ashley's healing ability, we should be safer this time," Jaz said. She picked up her Katana and slid the scabbarded sword over her shoulder into the loops on the back of her harness built to hold it in place. She pulled open the apartment door. "Come on. We'll walk you down to your car on our way out. You can pass on your blessing there. It looks like we're going on a demon hunt."

Chapter 15

IN THE PARKING garage beneath Jaz's apartment building, the trio paused while Asha passed on her blessing spell. Dean felt a warmth wrap around him and through him as she completed the incantation.

When she lowered her hands, Dean realized he felt better than he'd felt in days. He caught himself smiling despite the seriousness of their mission.

"That should offer you all some protection for at least a few hours from the effects of most types of infectious disease. If nothing else, it will slow the progress of the illness long enough for Ashley or someone else to effect healing."

"Thank you, Asha," Dean said. "You've been a big help."

"I'll continue to do what I can. Contact me if you need anything else. In the meantime, I still have to prepare our coven for the possibility of a world-ending event."

Jaz pulled out the keys to her SUV. "Hopefully, Asha, before you get home we'll make sure that doesn't happen. Be safe on your way, though."

"You all be safe. I'm just driving across town."

Asha got in her small compact car while Dean, Ashley, and Jaz climbed into the black SUV parked in the reserved spaces next to the elevator. A line of similar vehicles sat next to it, all part of the fleet of Errington security vehicles.

A thought occurred to Dean that hadn't while he'd been upstairs.

"Jaz what makes you think we can take on Malificar now when you and a team of Rudy's werewolf security guys, including the pack leader, couldn't do it several days ago?"

"Two reasons. First, we have Ashley with us now. She has a heavenly blade, remember? I suspect any demon, even one as powerful as this one will be more than a little afraid of her. Second, I've upgraded my standard loadout since the last time."

"What did you add?" Dean wondered aloud.

"You'll see."

Jaz fired up the engine and followed Asha's car out of the underground garage. She reached the street and turned south on the avenue running next to her building.

"Ashley, I'm heading south in the direction you indicated, but you have to tell me when we're getting close and when to turn, alright?"

"I'm still trying to make sense of what it is I'm feeling. It seems like we're headed the right way, though. I'll try and tell when we need to alter our course."

Jaz continued driving south for about a mile then Ashley pointed to her left. Dean saw her point from the front passenger seat. Jaz didn't. She was driving and couldn't see Ashley seated directly behind her.

"Go left, Jaz. Ashley says go left."

"Uh, yeah, sorry, Jaz," Ashley said. "I forgot you couldn't see me. I'm trying to concentrate on the tugging I feel. The sensation is centered in that direction now."

Ashley shook her head as if trying to clear her mind. "I'm not usually this scattered. It's like there's another presence in my mind, talking over the input from my normal senses. I'm working on filtering it out. Give me some time."

"Do I need to pull over? We don't want to miss the location."

"No, but it would help to slow down a little."

"Gotcha. Does that mean we're close?" Jaz asked, glancing up in the mirror to try and see Ashley behind her.

Ashley shrugged. "We're closer than we were and headed in the right direction. That's all I know. I'm still trying to learn what the different sensations I'm feeling from Asha's spell mean."

Dean started checking the buildings as they passed down the street. They were in a more impoverished section of town with a lot of vacant storefronts and half-filled strip malls. This area had a large transient homeless community. If an infection started to spread among them, there'd be almost nothing they could do to stop it's spread among that group considering the squalid conditions in which they lived.

"Stop!" Ashley called out.

Jaz slowed the SUV to a halt, pulling over to the curb.

"Is this the place?" Jaz asked looking at Ashley in the rear-view mirror. "Can you tell which building it is?"

"The only directional sense is — down? But that doesn't make any sense."

"Not necessarily," Dean said. "In this older part of town, there are underground steam lines that used to run from a central boiler used to heat some of these buildings. The homeless use the tunnels for shelter now. I've been on a few ambulance calls when some of them called for help. There are more than a few transient Unusuals living in and among the human homeless population."

"Which way is the nearest access point?"

Dean twisted in his seat, trying to remember and get his bearings. He pointed behind them to an alley they'd just passed.

"There. I'm pretty sure there's a storm drain outlet that will give us access to the tunnels if we can open the grate covering the entrance."

Jaz spun the SUVs steering wheel and executed a U-turn that ended with them driving straight down the alley until they reached the end where it opened up on a storm culvert with a grassy bank.

"I thought you said people lived down there in the tunnels?" Ashley asked. "How do they get in if there's a grate?"

"The city tries to discourage them from inhabiting the tunnels so they install new gates each time the old ones are breached. Plus, there are dozens of other access points, including from the subway tunnels. It's a maze down there. This is just the closest entry point I can think of. Maybe the residents have opened this one for us."

"Don't worry about the grate," Jaz said, shutting off the engine and popping open the driver's door. She looked back over her shoulder as she slid out. "I can get us past anything the city may have installed. Trust me."

Dean wondered what Jaz meant by that. He wouldn't be surprised if she pulled out a block of C4 plastic explosive at this point. She had resources beyond anything he knew about.

He hopped out and met both women back by the rear of the SUV. Jaz had the liftgate up. She was loading up seemingly random bundles and small boxes into the rucksack she held. Zipping the bag closed she slipped the straps over her shoulder and picked up an assault rifle with a grenade launcher tube mounted underneath.

Jaz pulled a small grenade shell from the bandolier she'd buckled around her waist just above her gun belt. The hunter slid the shell home in the tube mounted beneath the gun barrel and closed the breech.

"You think grenades in an enclosed space is a good idea?"

"When I use this, it will be for the bad guys," Jaz said with a grin. "Don't worry. I won't blow us up. I'm a professional."

Dean rolled his eyes. Jaz's wild hunter genes showed up the most at times like this. She loved a good fight more than just about anything. The last thing she grabbed was her ancient Katana sword, enchanted by powerful hunter magic for use against supernatural enemies.

He reached into the back and pulled out the fully stocked tactical medic bag she had added there just for him. As he slipped the bag's shoulder strap over his head, Jaz reached into the gun safe mounted in the back of the SUV and pulled out a semi-automatic pistol from a rack, handing it to Dean.

He shook his head.

"No, thank you. We've talked about this before. I'll stick to the healing side of things. Besides, I'm half angel it turns out. I've got my own abilities when it comes to demons. Right, Ashley?"

"You've never been up against an archdemon before, Dean. They are a bit more to handle than a run of the mill possession in a psych patient."

Dean shrugged. "I'll stick to the med bag, just the same."

Jaz shook her head but put the pistol back in the metal safe and closed the lid, locking it in place and spinning the dial on the combination. She picked up her rifle and pointed down at the culvert.

"Which way to the access point?"

Dean looked both ways before pointing left. "This way. It shouldn't be too far down."

He led them down into the grassy culvert. It was about five feet deep and served to channel runoff from the streets when it rained. It eventually drained into the Elk River on the southern edge of town.

The trio headed along the culvert for about a hundred yards before Dean spotted the opening to the tunnels ahead. As they approached, he could see the galvanized steel of the newly installed grate over the opening.

He started to lose hope of gaining access that way, but when they got right up next to the grate, Dean saw the lock was cut and then replaced to make it look like it was intact. He reached out and pulled at the grate with both hands. It levered open against the metal hinges and he let it fall open to the grass beside the tunnel's concrete-lined opening.

Dean started to lead the way, pulling a flashlight from his bag. Jaz grabbed him by the shoulder and pulled him backward.

"Nope. I go first."

She slid a headlamp on an elastic strap over her head and switched it on before heading into the tunnel entrance at a crouch.

Dean followed her with Ashley right behind him. After he ducked through the entrance, the tunnel had steps down and it opened up enough so he could stand upright. He looked behind him and was surprised to see Ashley holding a shining silver sword, gleaming as if with its own inner light. He recognized it as her heavenly blade, the weapon every Eldara could manifest from thin air when needed.

Ashley saw him staring at her blade. She smiled. "I've never faced one of the archdemons before. Gabriel and some of the oldest among us have, but not me. I guess we'll find out if I've got the power needed to take one of them on."

Her doubt struck Dean and he worried for the first time if they weren't biting off more than they could chew by coming here. Ashley was one of the most self-confident beings he'd ever met. If she was concerned about the outcome here, it bothered him.

"Keep up, you two," Jaz hissed from a few yards farther down the tunnel.

Dean nodded and moved to catch up with her. When he got close, she looked back at him.

"Any idea how far we have to go until we run into people?"

"The last time I was here, they met us at the culvert by the entrance since they'd called us to come here. I don't know where in the tunnels they actually had their home."

"Well, we'll just have to be careful. Keep your eyes open and watch for any trouble from behind us or from any side passages."

She stared down the passage again, her rifle stock up tight on her shoulder as she scanned left and right for any dangers. Dean stayed close enough to see past her and try and shine his flashlight into the shadows her headlamp didn't illuminate.

They reached the first branch of the tunnel. There was a T-shaped intersection and Jaz stopped before entering it, playing her light across the dark openings to either side.

That was when they spotted the first body.

Dean moved up to the crumpled form and crouched down. He spotted the familiar black pustules on the face and neck right away. They were huge, spreading across every inch of exposed skin. A few had burst open to leak out pale, yellow fluid across the surface. Dean was careful not to touch the dead man with his bare hands.

"These are the same types of infections we saw at the Witches' home, and on you, Jaz. We must be close."

Jaz glanced back at Ashley.

The Eldara had her eyes closed, trying to locate their quarry. She turned at first to the left and then stopped. Lifting her arm, she pointed to the right.

"That way. I sense Malificar's presence more clearly now that we're on the same level as he is. He can't be far away."

Jaz approached the opening to the right and scanned the tunnel beyond.

"I can see a few more bodies scattered ahead but not the end of the tunnel. Let's be careful. Dean, Ashley and I can see in the dark. We might want to shut off our lights and approach with some stealth. Are you comfortable being led by Ash in the dark while we move forward?"

"Do I have a choice? We definitely don't want to alert him we're coming, do we?"

Ashley moved up behind Jaz and turned to face Dean. "Put your hand on my shoulder and stay close. I'll let you know if there's any uneven footing."

Dean did as she said, shutting off the flashlight in his other hand but holding on to it in case he needed light in a hurry.

Jaz reached up and shut off her headlamp. Blackness filled the tunnel and Dean had a moment of panic. Jaz's hunter amulet empowered her with the ability to see in the dark. She'd likened it once to what you could see with night vision goggles.

Ashley was fine, too. Most of the Unusual community had evolved the ability to see in varying levels of darkness. He took a step forward as he felt Ashley move forward into the tunnel. Dean scanned the blackness with his eyes, unable to see anything, totally blind and relying on the two women to help him move forward.

With his eyes no longer sending any images to his brain, Dean strained to concentrate on his other senses. He felt the smooth, sloped concrete of the circular tunnel beneath his feet, heard the soft shuffle of their feet along the ground, and breathed in through his nose, catching the unmistakable odor of dead and decaying flesh.

It was the latter that alerted him to their arrival at another body before Ashley stopped him.

"Pick up your foot and take a big step forward, Dean," she whispered. "There's a body in the tunnel in front of you."

Dean lifted his right leg and stepped forward. The bottom of his boot scraped against the body causing the escape of a burst of fetid gas from the bloated corpse. He retched and shuffled forward trying to escape the pocket of gas released by the body.

Taking short breaths through his mouth now, trying to limit the air passing through his nose, Dean pressed forward, his hand gripping Ashley's shoulder. After another two dozen steps, she halted again.

Dean was about to ask why they stopped again but stopped when he realized he could make out a greenish glow emanating from up ahead.

"What is that?" He asked.

"I'm not sure," Jaz whispered. "It looks like the passage opens into a chamber up ahead."

"Jaz, Dean, do you hear that?" Ashley asked.

"No," the two humans replied.

"I hear chanting. It's soft but it sounds like a spell of some sort."

"What kind of spell? Could he have detected us coming?" Jaz asked.

"I'm not sure. The spell's magic is what's causing the glow, though. I can sense that much."

Dean had a sudden sensation of doom. It washed over him with a chill that passed from his head to his feet, making him shiver.

"I think we need to stop that spell," he suggested. "Something bad is about to happen. Can't you both feel it?"

Both women shook their heads.

"Stay close," Jaz said. "Watch your step. It's still pretty dark in here. Let Ashley and me take the lead."

Dean nodded and the trio started forward again. He let his hand drop from Ashley's shoulder as they neared the opening at the end of the tunnel. The glow from the chamber had increased in brilliance and allowed him to see much better now.

As they stepped through the chamber's entrance, Dean was greeted with the sight of a round, green disk hovering vertically in the air. It was seven or eight feet across and covered one whole wall of the concrete chamber. There were at least ten bodies scattered across the floor. From his vantage point, Dean could see all had been infected just like the others they'd encountered in the tunnel.

Standing before the glowing circle on the wall was a tall man dressed in what looked like a black suit coat and matching pants. It struck Dean as odd that despite the grime in the underground room, the man's clothing was spotless and clean, shiny even.

The three of them stood still for a few seconds, transfixed by what they saw. The figure in black raised his arms and shouted the last few words of his chant. Dean didn't know the language but the harsh sound of the words made his skin crawl.

As the man's hands reached their height above his head, the green circle flashed with light and another figure emerged from within the glowing disk. He wore a leather kilt and a black metal breastplate. A flowing black cloak was attached to the breastplate at the shoulders.

The new arrival smiled. It wasn't the smile of friendship or happiness. It was the smile of a kid burning ants with a magnifying glass or setting kittens on fire with gasoline. The armored man scanned the room, his eyes stopping when they reached the trio by the tunnel.

He reached down and drew a Roman-style short sword, pointing at them.

He bellowed a single word.

"Interlopers!"

Chapter 16

THE MAN in the black suit, who must be Malificar, turned and focused his eyes on the trio by the tunnel entrance. The eyes glowed with red fire as if coming directly from the pits of hell. He lowered his raised hands and pointed one in their direction.

Malificar snarled a curse at them and started muttering a new chant. His hand wove an intricate pattern in the air.

"Back, get back!" Jaz shouted.

She lifted her rifle and sprayed a burst of bullets at the two figures while Dean and Ashley stumbled backward into the tunnel entrance.

A roar of pain and defiance sounded from the two demons.

"That's Bellum, the horseman of war," Ashley called out over the gunfire. "I'm not the one who must fight him. There's no way we'll prevail against them both."

"Get out of here," Jaz shouted as she ducked back into the tunnel and swapped in a fresh magazine from her tactical harness. "I'll hold them off long enough for the two of you to get back to the branch in the tunnel."

Dean reached out and pulled her back towards him as he started back down the tunnel.

"You can't stop them, Jaz. Come on. We all need to get out of here. If you stay behind, you'll die."

He switched on his flashlight. He noticed the raised blisters on his skin right away. Malificar's spell must be working on them despite the protection laid on them by Asha.

"Malificar's spell is breaking through Asha's shield. We need to go or we're dead for sure."

Jaz fired another full auto burst around the corner. A bolt of red-hot plasma struck the wall nearby, shot by one of the demons. It super-heated the air and concrete of the tunnel and started to burn their exposed skin.

"Dammit, we almost had him," Jaz said spinning around. She pushed at Dean with her free hand. "Go, go, go; I'm right behind you."

Dean turned and sprinted back down the tunnel, hurdling the body he'd tripped over before. He skidded to a stop to check and make sure Jaz was behind him. Ashley stopped beside him, her sword held out in front of her. Jaz ran a few more steps then turned back.

"Cover your ears. This is going to hurt."

Dean slapped his palms over his ears as Jaz lifted her rifle and shifted her hand to the trigger for the grenade launcher. She fired it down the passage at the two figures striding towards them.

The explosion was deafening and the blast wave threw Dean from his feet, even though it was fifty feet away down the passage. Howls of anger and pain sounded from the two demons.

Dean stood, checking to see if the grenade had been successful in stopping or maybe even killing the two demons. His heart sank like a stone in his chest as two black figures strode out of the dust and smoke from the explosion.

"Go! Run!" Jaz said.

He didn't need to be told twice. Terror propelled him scrabbling backward until he could twist himself around and run towards the tunnel intersection.

Dean skidded to a stop long enough to ensure Jaz and Ashley were right behind him.

Another bolt of that hellfire or whatever it was sizzled by to slam into the far wall of the intersection. Cinders of broken concrete struck him, burning his face and hands with little dots of red next to his infectious blisters.

Dean saw Jaz and Ashley stumble into the intersection and they all turned and ran for the chamber leading to the culvert and hopefully escape. They had to get out of these tunnels to have any chance of getting away from the demons.

They almost made it.

A shouted cry from Jaz made him turn around. Grabbing her from behind, the black armored figure Ashley'd called Bellum slammed Jaz against the wall so hard she dropped her rifle clattering to the ground.

Dean rushed forward to help but Ashley was faster. She drove forward with a wicked series of slashes and lunges with her heavenly blade.

Sparks flew as the demon parried the divine weapon with his own black sword, forged in the pits of hell. Fire played along his blade even as a white glow burned from Ashley's long sword.

Dean grabbed ahold of Jaz by the straps of her tactical harness and dragged her back towards the daylight streaming into the chamber from the culvert entrance.

Ashley shouted and cried out in pain as the demon sword wielded by Bellum cut a deep gash in her shoulder. She fell back as she struggled to bring her blade up to parry the next attack.

She barely got her sword up in time as the demon brought his sword down at her from above while she lay on her back.

Ashley managed to divert the blade away from her chest but the tip still scored a fresh gash across her shoulder.

Without thinking, Dean reached down and pulled Jaz's enchanted katana from its scabbard on her back. He ran forward, shouting at the top of his lungs to hide the terror he felt.

The fear of losing Ashley so soon after she'd come back drove him onward against the paralyzing fear. He hacked down in an awkward blow that sliced down across the demon's exposed arm where the shoulder armor of his breastplate ended.

The blade's razor edge left only a red streak against the demon's tanned, muscled arm. It didn't even break the skin.

It still managed to distract Bellum from his attack on Ashley.

The demon delivered a vicious backhand blow with his gauntleted hand that sent Dean flying through the air to land on the ground next to Jaz.

Ashley rose to her feet, holding her blade in front of her as Malificar emerged from the tunnel to stand next to Bellum. He already had another blast of hellfire ready to scour them from this existence.

Dean was sure they'd never make it out of this place alive.

A plump figure bounced past him down the stairs from the opening above and slammed into the armored demon, knocking him backward to the ground.

Gibbie stood up, straddling the startled archdemon and rained down hammer blows with all his vampiric strength on Bellum's exposed face.

Malificar snarled in anger and turned to face the new threat only to be knocked down himself by a growling, heavily muscled werewolf. Dean recognized the wolf form of Marian, the teen Lycan who'd joined Gibbie and a few others to form a Community Emergency Response Team.

Dean stood up and pulled Jaz to her feet. She was still dazed from the demon's attack. He pushed her up the stairs, knowing their two rescuers couldn't hope to hold the demons back for long.

The two of them stumbled up the steps towards the daylight. Another figure stood up there, and Dean recognized the Djinn, Kristof Algar, another CERT member. He beckoned at them to hurry. Ashley ran up the steps behind Dean.

Gibbie screeched in alarm as a punch from the now disarmed Bellum sent him flying past all of them out into the sunlight. Dean emerged to see the vampire's skin start to char under the ultraviolet onslaught. Then Wim and Dora, the final members of the CERT Team, ran up and covered him with a blanket. The twin Dryads must have been waiting to give it to him when he emerged again.

Marian ran out right behind Ashley, still in wolf form but with bloody, singed areas visible where her fur had been burned away. She spun around growling as soon as she emerged into the culvert, ready to dash back in and fight some more to hold the entrance.

Ashley pointed to him with her free hand.

"Dean, get them out of here. I'll hold them back long enough for you all to escape."

"No, I'm not losing you again."

She started to argue but was knocked backward by a blast of hell-fire coming up from the tunnel entrance.

Dean ran to help her but Kristof grabbed his arm.

"I can stop them but you have to help me do it, Dean."

Dean stared at the Djinn without understanding for a second before he realized what Kristof needed for him to do.

Dean stood and pointed at the entrance to the tunnels. He could see Bellum coming up the steps.

"I wish for that opening to be sealed forever."

A golden glow surrounded Kristof for a split second then the opening flashed with a similar golden light.

Suddenly, where there had been an opening into the underground steam tunnels beneath Elk City, there was now only a patch of the ordinary grassy slope just like the rest of the culvert extending in either direction.

It was like the concrete-lined opening had never been there at all.

"Come on," Dora called out as she and Wim helped the singed Gibbie remain covered and walk at the same time. "Gibbie's van is this way."

"How long will that hold them, Kristof?" Dean asked.

"The wild magic I possess did as you wished. That entrance never existed. No one who wasn't here today will even remember it was there. The demons will have to find another way out of the tunnels."

"That works for me." Dean turned and looked around. Jaz and Ashley were both back on their feet and following him and the battered CERT team up the slope.

They'd managed to escape, but only barely. It was apparent they were going to need a better plan than this if they hoped to defeat these demons, a much better idea.

Chapter 17

GIBBIE STEERED THE VAN. Its heavily tinted windows protected him from the daylight outside. The frumpy vampire's burns had already started to heal, though he looked like he had a nasty sunburn. It had to be painful but he was laughing like a maniac as he turned onto the main drag heading back to the center of town.

"Did you see that?" Gibbie shouted in triumph. "CERT team to the rescue. We rocked."

Dean looked up from where he was applying a sterile dressing to the blistered burn on Marian's back. The teen had shifted back to her human form and she winced as he pressed the gauze pad against the wound. Ashley sat in the seat behind his, tending to Jaz's injuries.

"You all were lucky you got out of there alive," Dean countered. "What did I teach you about scene safety?"

"Hey," Gibbie countered. "There's safe for humans and safe for badasses like us." He raised a hand to one side and one of the Dryad twins, Dean thought it was Wim, slapped a high five on the vampire's raised hand from the passenger seat next to him.

Dean knew he should be more grateful but he felt responsible for their safety, nonetheless. He'd trained them to be careful and let the trained professionals like police handle the violence in some situations.

Of course, in this case, the pros were getting their asses handed to them when the CERT team showed up.

"How did you know we were down there anyway?" Dean asked.

"We've been following you ever since you got hurt rescuing Jaz and Rudy's team a few days ago. Marian overheard her dad and Rudy talking about what was going on and how most of the Lycan security team was down for a while. We all decided we could take up the slack and cover your backs. Good thing we did."

"CERT team to the rescue!" Wim cheered from the passenger seat. The Dryad grinned from ear to ear. She looked like she was having the time of her life. Her sister did, too, for that matter.

The whole CERT team wore big smiles, even Marian though she winced as he applied another dressing to her burns.

Dean decided he couldn't take this victory away from them by yelling at them. They were all bruised and battered, but they'd made it out alive.

That was what counted.

"I'm glad you guys took the initiative. Thank you. Thank you all." Dean looked around and met the whole team's eyes to show his sincerity. Their grins were infectious and soon he was grinning right back at them.

"So, where are we headed, boss?" Gibbie asked.

Jaz chimed in with the answer.

"Head to Errington Security. I'll have somebody go and retrieve the SUV later. For now, we need to regroup. Plus we've got more first aid supplies there and we can rest in relative safety in my apartment while we figure out our next move."

"On it!" Gibbie said. He swerved the van to one side as he pulled an illegal U-turn in the middle of the boulevard and headed in the opposite direction.

As they drove along in the beat up old van, Dean wondered what would happen to the world if they all survived a demon attack only to die in a rather mundane car accident with Gibbie at the wheel.

Marian picked up a second meatball sub from the platter in the middle of the table and set it on her plate. Dean shook his head in amazement. The combination of teenage appetite and the needs of werewolf regeneration combined to give her the ability to put away a truly tremendous amount of food.

Dean leaned back, sliding his chair away from the table in Jaz's apartment. He smiled and patted his stomach.

"I'm stuffed. Good idea to order delivery while we got patched up, Jaz."

"It's the least I could do seeing as how these guys risked their lives bailing us out back there."

Gibbie lifted up his coffee mug. "Where'd you get the blood? I wouldn't think a hunter would keep blood around for visiting vamps."

"I had one of my assistants run over to the Nightwing building and pick up a few pints from James' private supply. I hear he keeps a selection of fresh, uh, vintages on hand."

"This is very good," Gibbie said, taking another sip from his mug. "The donor is young and it's very fresh. I usually have to take what I can get from bribing the night guard at the blood bank. He just grabs the first bag he comes to. Usually, it's blood from some junkie or vagrant selling it for money."

"There's another bag like that one in the fridge. If you don't finish while you're here, make sure you take it with you. I don't need it and prefer not to have it in my kitchen."

Gibbie nodded and raised his mug again in thanks and went back to savoring his meal.

Ashley came in the dining room from the back of the apartment. She leaned to one side while she wrapped a towel around her long brown hair and squeezed to remove the excess moisture. Jaz had set her up in the guest bedroom next to theirs and she'd gone back to shower and change. It made Dean more than a little uncomfortable to know Ashley was next door when he was sleeping beside Jaz.

Both of the women had laughed and shared a humorous glance between them when he'd brought it up. He decided the two of them were having way too much fun at his expense.

"Ooo, the food is here," Ashley said, pulling up a chair and sliding in next to Wim and Dora. "Now that I have washed the filth from that tunnel off, I can relax and eat something. Hand me the platter."

Dean knew Ashley was about to put Marian's appetite to shame. The Eldara had expended a lot of her energy in the fight and then healing his and Jaz's injuries afterward. She hadn't depleted herself to the point of exhaustion, as he'd seen her do in the past, but she still had to replace the energy she'd lost.

A chime from the intercom speaker in the wall sounded. Jaz finished what was in her mouth and said, "Go for Jaz."

"Boss," a man's voice said over the intercom. "There's a lady down here who insists her sister is upstairs with you. I know you have guests but you didn't say you were expecting anyone else. I scanned her when she came in. She's definitely not human. What do you want me to do with her?"

"Send me the feed from the lobby cameras."

Jaz pulled out her phone and opened a proprietary security app Dean had seen her use before to connect to her company's systems. Apparently, it also let her view remote video feeds as well as access internal data and documents.

She took one look at her phone and snorted a laugh.

"It was only a matter of time I suppose."

Jaz turned the phone around so Dean and the rest of the table could see. Dean recognized her immediately. Ashley giggled as the woman on the screen, dressed in torn jeans, a white tank top and a leather jacket looked up at the camera. She raised her middle finger gesturing up at them.

"Jaz," Ashley said. "You'd better tell him to let Ingrid come up. My twin's likely just to invite herself and come up without permission. We wouldn't want an incident."

Jaz raised her voice and looked towards the speaker on the wall. "Front desk, send her up and be nice. She's a friend."

Dean hadn't seen Ashley's twin sister, Ingrid in a while. The Valkyrie had duties that took her all over the world, collecting heroic souls from the battlefields of the earth in preparation for them to return and help in the fight at the end of the world.

It occurred to Dean that perhaps she was here because that fight was coming sooner than later and she'd sensed its impending arrival. This might not bode well for their quest to stop Armageddon from happening.

A few minutes later, the doorbell rang. Jaz and Dean went to answer it. Ingrid stood there, looking like a pissed off version of Ashley, except for the additional ear and nose piercings. Dean blushed as he remembered she had a tongue piercing, too. He'd discovered it during a somewhat embarrassing case of mistaken identity.

"I heard my sister's back in town and I thought she might be able to tell me why I've got this magic ball of light following me for the last three hours. I figure it's got to have something to do with the way you're all messing up Gabe's carefully laid plans."

Dean followed her pointing finger to see a familiar white glowing nimbus of light hovering over Ingrid's head. Given who'd they'd seen arrive that morning, it appeared the Valkyrie was the champion chosen to fight Bellum, the horseman of war.

"Come in, Ingrid," Jaz said, stepping back and leaving room for the new arrival to come into the apartment. "I'm sure you're hungry, come join us."

The scowl left Ingrid's face at the mention of dinner. "I never turn down food. It smells delicious in here. What do you have?"

Ingrid walked into the dining room followed by Dean and Jaz. As soon as the two sisters stood next to each other, the glowing ball of light over Ingrid's head flashed brighter three times and then faded from view.

"As soon as I saw him, I wondered if you were the one for Bellum," Ashley said. "It's a strange sort of universal karma and symmetry for two angelic sisters to fight two demonic brothers."

"Bellum, the second Agent of Chaos?" Ingrid asked. "He's here already?"

"I'm afraid so, sister. That's what the ball of light was. We had the Witch high priestess cast a locator spell for the four chosen champions who must assemble for the fight against them. You've been chosen to join me in this fight."

Ingrid smiled. "It won't be the first time. Besides, you know me. I never shy away from a good fight. Now, someone said something about food. I hope there's enough for me."

Marian had just grabbed the last of the foot-long meatball subs; it was her third. She had already taken a bite and looked a bit embarrassed. Timidly she returned the partially eaten sub to the platter.

Dean laughed. There had been a platter piled high with large meatball subs there when dinner first arrived.

"I thought ordering three times as much as I normally ordered would be enough," Dean said. "I guess I was wrong. Let me call over to Station U and have Freddy whip up some more food and send it over to us. Jaz can you have one of your guys swing by and pick up more food from the station?"

"Sure, let me see who's out and about."

Jaz tapped at her phone while she walked into the other room to make her call undisturbed.

Ingrid grabbed at the final sub, tore it in half and gave the half with the bite out of it back to Marian. She took a bite and looked around at the group.

"From the looks on everyone's faces and the scrapes and bruises I see, it looks like you guys just got your asses handed to you. I assume you ran into Bellum yourselves?"

Ashley nodded. "I was chosen to fight Malificar, according to the spell, just as it indicated you were chosen for Bellum. You'll find if you concentrate, you can localize which direction the demon is in. We used it to find Malificar in an attempt to stop him from summoning any others. When Bellum arrived, though, they were just too much for us."

"Who are the other champions?"

"We don't know," Ashley said with a shrug. "I suspect they will be revealed to us when the final two Agents of Chaos arrive."

"Why don't you just wait until the final battle and join my Valkyrie comrades and the heavenly host of heroes in defeating them."

Dean shook his head. "We're not going to do it that way, Ingrid. Too many people, the good, innocent people of this city, will die if we wait for the Agents to work their infernal plans before the final battle. We have to try and stop Armageddon from happening. That's why we had Asha cast the locator spell to find the chosen heroes."

"Gabe thinks the end of the world is near, Dean," Ingrid said. "He's the trumpet bearer, he would know."

"My father has his own agenda and I'm not sure it's the best option for the people of this city, human or Unusual. They're the ones I care about. If we can stop this place from being the center of the last battle and banish the four horsemen back to the pits of hell for another hundred years or more, I'm happy to upset Gabe's plans."

"You can't just stop the end of the world, Dean," Ingrid noted. "It's foreordained. That means —"

"I know what it means, Ingrid. I also know that I figure in this somehow. That has to be why Gabriel took time out of his precious heavenly schedule to come down to earth all those years ago and impregnate my mother. Apparently, the gods above decided they needed someone special for this moment. Well, they are all in for a rude awakening. I'm not going to play by their rules. I've learned enough to know that human free will counts for something in this fishbowl experiment of theirs called Earth. I'm not simply letting the divine forces of good and evil have their way with the people of this planet without trying to stop them from laying waste to everything in some sort of universal grudge match."

Ingrid shot a look at Ashley.

The other Eldara returned it with a quirky smile. "He's always been stubborn. You know that as well as I do. Who knows? Maybe he's right."

"Yeah, you think this is stubborn. Wait until Gabe finds out I'm on your side. He's gonna blow his top."

Dean looked at them both and smiled. "I'm counting on it."

Chapter 18

TWO DAYS later the blizzard hit.

Elk City wasn't a stranger to occasional snow storms, but the nor'easter that cruised up the coast slowed down and seemed to settle over the Elk City region. It dumped four feet of snow on the area in just four days.

It was more snow than the state had seen in anyone's memory. The state and local resources were unable to cope with the massive amount of snow and city services and businesses ground to a halt.

The only good thing about the blizzard was it kept people inside and from congregating in large numbers which was where Bellum seemed to like to wreak havoc. Several spontaneous riots had broken out at community gatherings for no apparent reason. It was so strange, they all decided the horseman of war was at the center of it.

Of course, the storm effects also meant those who were most ill from the disease spread by Malificar were unreachable by ambulance and who knew how many died in their homes because of it.

Dean paced in Jaz's apartment. The rest of the team sat around the living and dining rooms, trying to find something to keep them occupied. Gibbie and Marian played a first-person shooter on the game Jaz had bought Dean for his last birthday. Wim and Dora looked on, cheering for their friends and laughing with them at their mistakes.

Kristof had returned to his restaurant the day after the culvert attack and he hadn't been back since the snow hit.

The sound of the apartment door opening interrupted Dean's brooding. That must be Jaz returning from checking in with her security team downstairs.

Crossing to the entry hallway, Dean called out, "Hey, babe," as he turned the corner. He stopped when he saw Gabe standing there.

"Uh, it's Gabe, not Babe," his father said.

"I can see that."

"I let myself in. Jaz was busy downstairs and told me to come up on my own."

"Are you here to gloat over something or to complain about how I'm not living up to your expectations?"

"Neither. I'm here to tell you the next Agent is on his way. The storm is the precursor. Famis, the horseman of famine and hunger, is coming if he's not already here. This freak storm is his way of making a grand entrance."

The apartment door opened again and Jaz stood there, just behind Gabe.

"I think the next Agent of Chaos has arrived," Jaz said.

"How do you know?" Dean asked. "Did Gabe tell you on his way up?"

"Nope," Jaz replied. She pointed up to the ceiling and Dean noticed for the first time the white ball of light hovering there over her head. She was the next champion to be revealed. She came in the apartment and as soon as she did, the glowing white ball flashed three times and faded out.

"What was that?" Gabe asked. "I sensed the magic over her but not its purpose."

"That," Dean said, "is the spell we cast to help us locate the four champions destined to help us defeat the horsemen before they initiate the final battle."

"What? And it picked her?" Gabe asked. "Who else was chosen?"

"The Eldara twins, Ashley and Ingrid," Dean replied. "I suppose I should thank you for helping with that. If you hadn't had the idea of using me to bring Ashley back to earth, I couldn't have put my plan into motion."

"You're playing with things you don't know, boy. There are forces here that have been aligning for millennia, plans that were set in motion so long ago, even I don't remember them. You aren't going to change all that with your short-sighted plots and machinations."

"Is that what you came here to tell me, that I can't change the course of fate? If so, you can turn around and leave."

Gabe stood and stared at Dean for a few, long seconds. He looked as if he wanted to turn and leave but then he scanned all the people assembled in the room and something changed in his demeanor. He glanced upward at the ceiling and cocked his head to one side as if listening to something. His facial expression softened and he nodded while letting out a long sigh.

"I think it best that I remain here with you. It seems that a few among the higher powers like the mettle you and your friends show, standing up to the impossible odds of trying to stop this war from happening."

Dean felt a satisfied grin creep across his face. "So the gods are on my side, are they?"

"Some of them, yes," Gabe admitted. "Others are as committed as I am to ending this unending war once and for all. It seems as if we've been, um, overruled by divine consensus I guess you would say. That means I'm to put myself at your disposal."

Dean didn't know what to make of that last part. His mind also tried to figure out what Jaz's role in this was and how she was supposed to counter Famis. The Eldara had their heavenly blades. Jaz, even for all her Hunter instincts and genetics, was still only human. They'd have to figure out how she could stand up to and defeat the third horseman in a fight.

Gabe looked past Dean into the rest of the apartment. "Where're Ashley and Ingrid?"

"Ashley is at the hospital helping tend to the plague victims. She's trying to strengthen the ones with the most critical need so they can fight off the infection."

"And her sister?"

"She's with my teams," Jaz interjected. "Since Bellum is at the root of the disturbances around the city, they're working on settling some of the riots in coordination with the local police force. With our big SUV's and some Humvee's we had in storage at the port, we can get around better than most of the city vehicles in the storm."

Dean pointed to a portable radio system and walkie-talkies set up in chargers on the dining room table amidst the half-empty fast food containers scattered there from lunch.

"My supervisor, Brynne, has got us patched into the city's dispatch system so we can monitor things from here and try and nail down where the horsemen will strike next. Since Jaz received the latest glowing ball award, that means we only have to wait for one more of the Agents of Chaos to arrive; then we can plan our final assault to take them down."

"Yeah," Gibbie called out from the other room. "And this time, we'll do a lot better than the last fight. We're gonna be ready for a battle."

Gabe shot Dean a sharp look, his eyes seeming to drill into Dean's. "You went after them on your own after I told you not to, didn't you?"

Dean's anger rose to the surface all over again. "Hey, I don't know what you think is going on here, but I don't follow your orders."

"You could've been killed; then all would have been lost."

"What are you talking about? We survived."

"Barely," Gibbie called from in front of the TV.

Dean winced. Sometimes Gibbie could be a pain in the ass.

He needed to defuse this before he and Gabe started fighting again. They were going to need Gabe's help if they were to succeed in this. That must be why the higher powers had linked the two of them together.

"Look," Dean said, taking a deep breath. "We learned our lesson. If you want me to tell you that you were right, I will. We weren't prepared and we went in blind. That's not the case anymore. We are preparing to face them with all the champions together at our side at once. The next time, we'll be ready for anything."

"You may think that Dean, but you have no idea what these

demons are capable of. They've done things in the name of evil you could never fathom."

"That is why we have Ashley and Ingrid, and hopefully, you on our side. I don't pretend this will be easy or without risk. But the alternative is unacceptable. I don't believe the end of the world is the only possible outcome no matter who wins."

"Dean, this has been foretold before you were born. You cannot stop it from happening."

"I've figured that much out, but I only believe it to a certain point. I think there's a way to defuse this whole mess before it turns into the end of the world." Dean stopped and stared at Gabriel, the archangel, the man who was his father. "Why did you come here? You said you were told to come and help me. Are you only here because some divine entity made you come?"

"I know these demons. I've been fighting them, over and over again since time began. I can help you understand what they're capable of and how they think."

Dean recognized Gabe didn't answer the question but he let it drop. It wasn't important anymore. He could do without a true father. He was a grown man after all.

Jaz stepped beside Dean.

"That's a good place to start, right, Dean? We could use the intel. It could give us a leg up when we take the fight to them."

"Yeah, I guess so," Dean said.

"I know so. Gabe, come in and sit down. Meet the rest of our team. Learn what each of our capabilities are and how we can work together to counter the things we're likely to run into when we face the Agents of Chaos."

"Uh, guys," Wim called from the living room. "You might want to come in here. Another riot has started up."

Dean and Jaz, followed by Gabe, went into the living room. Gibbie and Marian weren't playing on the game console anymore. They'd switched to the local news channel and watched as the anchor in the studio played back footage of a female reporter and her camera crew accosted by rampaging people at what looked like a supermarket.

"Where is it?" Dean asked.

"It's all the way across town," Dora said. She shook her head. "With all the snow, we'd never make it before the crowd disperses or moves on to a new target. I heard one of Jaz's teams in two Hummers check in from nearby."

Jaz pulled a radio from the charging station on the table and switched it on.

"…moving west on High Street. There are only a few stragglers still at the supermarket. We're moving in now to check on any injured and render what aid we can."

Jaz keyed the mic on the radio.

"This is Errington-One, report in on the situation at the riot scene."

"Jaz, this is Rick, Team Two. We responded to reports of a disturbance, acting in support of local police. The size of the crowd caused us to reassess our ability to do anything other than observe. We have half the team shadowing the crowd as it moves west of our location. We hung back and are starting to assess and treat injured bystanders at the riot's original location."

"Good work, Team Two. Continue shadowing but be careful not to engage. Especially monitor for signs of supernatural intervention. That could be signs of one of our targets."

"Received. Team Two clear."

Jaz set the radio down and turned back to Gabe and Dean.

"The rioting is Bellum's work," Gabe said. "Open conflict is his work for sure, just like this freak blizzard has Famis' fingerprints all over it. He loves using weather to create situations where resources and food are in limited supply. He feeds on the hungry and weak in the face of famine and need."

"That's three of the Agents in town," Dean observed. "We're waiting for one more; then we can put together a plan to counter them before they initiate the final battle."

"Mortis is the worst of all of them," Gabe said. "He brings nothing but death and destruction with him. He pulls together all the things the others have done and multiplies their efforts. He's also the strongest of the four."

"They've all got to have weaknesses," Jaz said. "Everything does.

You've defeated them before, Gabe, in other meetings and battles. How did you manage to send them back to hell in the past?"

"I can tell you but I don't know how it will help you. They've always been quick to learn from their mistakes. I've never been able to use the same strategy twice. That's what makes them so dangerous. Each time we face them again, it becomes harder and harder to fight them."

"But this time we have adapted, too," Dean said. "In the past, it's always been Eldara warriors like yourself fighting them and their minions, archangel versus archdemon, right?"

Gabe nodded.

"This time we have a combined force of humans, Eldara, and Unusuals, all fighting side by side. Heck, Jaz is the head of a major Hunter clan. She shouldn't be anywhere near associating with all these Unusuals, and yet she has a vampire and a werewolf sitting here in her living room playing video games. We like to buck the system and are doing things they've never seen before."

"You think the cooperation between the humans and Unusual community is the key?" Gabe asked.

"I think it's the only thing we can do," Jaz said. "It's our biggest strength. The last time they were all here was what? During the black plague?"

Gabe smiled. "The last time they were all here, humans and Unusuals were at each others' throats, actively hunting and killing each other. You're right, it's different now. In this age, there is unprecedented cooperation between the two groups, even if the average human knows nothing about who or what some of their neighbors really are."

"Exactly!" Dean agreed. "This time, we will be the ones who've adapted and changed the most. When they put their plans together and try to implement them, we'll be ready to fight against them side by side in a way they won't expect. That surprise will enable us to catch them off guard and stop them before they open up the portal to hell and start the final battle."

"It might just work," Gabe said. "The timing would have to be perfect, but if we manage it, we could change the whole direction of history here on earth."

Dean offered a genuine smile to his father for the first time. "Let's sit down and plan this out. This could be the solution we're all looking for. Before we do, though, we have a few more friends to invite to the party."

Chapter 19

JAMES WALKED over to where Dean and Jaz stood watching the eclectic group mingling in Jaz's apartment.

"I like what you've done with the place, Jaz. Were you able to make use of the contractors I recommended?"

"Yes, they all worked out very well and finished ahead of schedule, which was a nice surprise. Thank you for sending them my way."

"I figured it was the least I could do in the spirit of our new understanding between your clan and my people here in Elk City."

"Yes," Jaz said. "It still takes a little getting used to. Don't forget, though, the other Hunter clans still aren't all on board with this new level of cooperation between us."

Dean slipped an arm around Jaz's waist. He felt the bulge of her pistol under the thin leather jacket she wore, nestled at the small of her back. She might be operating under a new paradigm when it came to cooperation with Unusuals but she still didn't trust vampires and other supernatural creatures very far, even in the relative safety of her own home. Maybe someday that would change.

"I'm sure the other clans will come around soon enough, especially when we defeat the demons here with the force of our new pact, right sweetie?" Dean said.

"That's why we're all here, isn't it, James?"

James cleared his throat, nodded, and took a sip from his mug of warmed blood. Dean remembered when the mere thought of James consuming fresh blood turned his stomach. He'd come a long way since that newbie paramedic, fresh out of the academy not that long ago.

"Let's get down to business, shall we," James suggested. "I want to get back. Celeste is back at the Nightwing building working to get food and aid to the outlying communities of Unusuals like the Barrens. They're cut off by the storm and with the city dealing with the riots, no one is focusing much attention on the outlying areas of the region."

"She's up to the task," Brynne told James. "It's more important we're all here and making sure we're on the same page about what to do about everything that's happening."

"Agreed." James turned to Dean. "You called us together. Why don't you and Jaz kick things off? What is it you want us to do?"

It felt strange to Dean to have James defer to him in this type of situation. Usually, the vampire lord was all about taking control of the situation.

"Thank you, James. I think most of you know each other or are at least familiar with who we have here."

Dean was pretty sure what he said was true as he scanned the faces turned his way to hear what he said. Rudy was there. So was Marian's father. The two them were some of the more prominent members of the werewolf and Lycan community in the city. All the CERT team members were there and they would be able to spread the word of what they needed out to their clans and connections. Ashley, Ingrid, and Gabe stood off to one side, a little apart. Everyone knew Ashley and most knew about her sister. Gabe was the only stranger to most of them. Time to remedy that.

"There is, however, one here who a few of you do not know," Dean said, gesturing to his father. "This is the Eldara archangel, Gabriel. He has come to help us in our quest to stave off the end of the world."

Gabe nodded in greeting but didn't say anything. He looked at Dean and offered a grim smile, so Dean kept going.

"Our plan, for right now, is simple. We wait until the final horseman is revealed. He is Mortis, the horseman of death. When he arrives, all four of the Agents of Chaos will have manifested on earth and they can begin the process wherein they start off Armageddon."

Dean paused to see if there were any questions. The silence caught him by surprise and he struggled for a few seconds to gather his thoughts enough to proceed.

"We think, based on past manifestations, it will take at least a day for the four demons to gather and start the ball rolling to opening a gate between our world and the netherworld. Our plan is simple. Once Death makes an appearance, we locate the final champion destined to face off against Mortis. Then we take the fight directly to them with the champions in the lead. Those of us who follow them will act in a supporting role, dealing with any backup the four demons call to their aid."

Gibbie raised his hand. "Uh, Dean, tell me one more time how we'll know who the final champion is?"

Dean wondered why Gibbie was bringing this up again. He was pretty sure everyone knew how it worked at this point. He went over it again anyway.

"As I'm sure most of you know, we had Asha cast a spell that will locate them. They'll have a small glowing ball of light hovering over their head when Mortis arrives."

There was silence from the people in the room. They all sat there and stared at him. The reaction confused Dean. He hadn't said anything that alarming. Most of them knew the answer already.

Gibbie pointed at Dean, interrupting his train of thought.

"You mean a glowing light like the one over your head right now?"

Dean glanced from side to side before he realized Gibbie meant him. Dean tilted his head back, looking up. Yep, there it was, the familiar ball of light. As the others had before, it flashed three times then faded from view. As soon as it did, a new presence took up residence in the corner of his mind.

Dean focused on it, trying to understand what he felt. It was as if someone else was standing next to him, off to one side, just out of view. He turned to see who it was, but there was no one there. He could still sense them but they were now somewhere that way, maybe in another room.

For a few seconds, he considered going to search the back bedrooms before he realized what it was. Mortis was now here on Earth and Dean could sense him and his general direction from their current location in Jaz's apartment. It also felt like he could reach out and touch the other's mind and presence with his own somehow. If only he could—"

A squeeze of his hand brought him back to the apartment and the gathering of friends and comrades.

"Weird, isn't it?" Jaz said.

"I'd say you have no idea but that's not right. You know exactly what I'm feeling. I guess this pushes our plans forward a little bit."

Several phones went off at once, interrupting them before Jaz could answer him.

James, Brynne, and Rudy all pulled out their phones and answered the calls.

It was hard to follow what they were saying, but Dean could tell something bad was happening.

"What is it?" Dean asked all of them at once.

Rudy finished first. The security chief's tone was grim.

"There's a riot forming outside of the Nightwing building. They've breached the lobby doors and my security team has locked off the elevators and stairwell doors. They're not sure how long it will be until they break through, though. It'll be bad if they start up into the upper floors."

Brynne nodded as she took her phone away from her ear.

"That was headquarters. They confirm the riot in that location. It caught police by surprise and they're advising all our ambulances stay out of the area until the police can regain control of the situation."

James was still on his phone talking to someone. "Are you sure…?"

He paused, listening then pointed to Wim sitting on the sofa. "Put on the TV, the news. Try channel 13."

The Dryad picked up the remote from the coffee table and switched on the TV. A newscaster sat behind the anchor desk. In the corner of the screen, there was a rectangle with a photo of Brynne seated at a table. Celeste stood next to her.

Dean couldn't figure out what Brynne did to earn the honor of making it onto the news.

"Turn it up," he called to Wim. "Let's hear what he's saying."

"…Dozens of disturbing videos like the one we're about to show you were turned over to every news organization in the area this evening. I remind you, what you're about to see is disturbing. Those with young children should make them leave the room now."

Brynne's usually pale skin had lost what little color it had. She turned away as the video next to the news anchorman started.

On the screen, the video, which had widened out to fill the TV, now expanded show a goat at the far end of the room. Celeste moved next to the goat, said something and then reached down with a knife and slit open the goat's throat. Blood sprayed across the room, some splashing on Brynne. On the video, there was a blur as Brynne reacted with all the blinding speed of her vampire reflexes. She threw the table to one side and pounced on the animal. Tearing into the throat with her fangs exposed for all to see, fangs that weren't there seconds before.

Celeste stood over Brynne and the goat, bared her own fangs, and shook her head. There was no sound but Dean knew what he saw. It was a recording from when they tried desensitizing the newly turned vampire Brynne to the presence of blood. He had not been aware it had all been recorded.

The next video in the feed played while the voice of the newscaster said they were still verifying the authenticity of the videos. He continued his explanation while a new video played of James and Celeste feeding on a pair of young women in the Penthouse apartment atop the Nightwing building.

"Based on all the accounts in these videos, along with the accompanying paper documentation that arrived with them, it appears there is some sort of monstrous cult of blood-drinking people living in the Nightwing building downtown. Our attempts at reaching management, including the owner, James Lee, pictured in that last video, have been unsuccessful."

James hung up the phone. "According to Celeste, these videos have been playing for the last hour on all the local stations. They're also available for download on several online video sites. People started gathering outside the building soon after. She wants to know if they should evacuate?"

"Can you get everyone out past all the people?" Dean asked.

James gave him a grim smile. "Of course I can. I've been around too long not to have built a secret way out of my castle, even a modern one like I have now. There's a hidden staircase on all the upper floors leading directly down to the lowest level of the parking garage. A passage from there leads to the basement of Sabatani's."

Kristof laughed. "I never thought you'd have to use it. Of course, that didn't keep me from charging you rent all those years to keep that part of the basement storage area clear."

Dora had pulled out her laptop and was tapping out something on the keyboard before turning it around.

"Look! It's not just James and the vampires in the videos. Here's one showing Rudy shifting to werewolf form and there are others like it, showing the powers and true forms of other Unusuals in the city. They've managed to out us to the whole city at one time."

Wim leaned over and stared at the screen. "There are hundreds of other videos just like these on there, Dean. Where did they get all this."

Dean shrugged. He didn't know. It didn't really matter now they had all been released.

Gabe had an answer.

"There are agents for Chaos here on earth just like there are heroes representing the divinities of good. They must have been surveilling the community for months, maybe years, to amass all this."

Brynn's phone rang again, the colorful ringtone not reflecting the mood in the room at all. She answered it.

"Are you certain?" Brynne said after a few seconds. "Call me back if anything else happens." She put her phone away. "That was Bill at the station. He just got a call from a frantic August Beche from the New Barrens Apartments. There's a mob there, too. His people were forced to flee the buildings when someone set a fire next to the complex. They've run into the woods, scattering in all directions. He needs help."

Gabe shook his head. "They're trying to divide you and your resources. You can't be everywhere at once. If you try, they'll take you down one at a time. The four of them know there's still an organized resistance to their coming here in the city. They're trying to flush us out so they can eliminate us piecemeal."

"It would have worked, too, if we hadn't decided to come here and hold this meeting tonight," Dean said. "I can't understand how they missed attacking here, too. They knew so much about us otherwise."

Ashley stepped forward, pointing at the TV. "They're attacking the usual places. They've targeted James in his stronghold and the closest thing to an Unusual enclave inside the city limits at the Barrens. My guess is, if they know who Jaz is, they're still under the assumption she's a traditional Hunter clan leader. They think if they expose the others and make them fight back, the Hunters will come in and help sow more chaos defending the humans against the rest of us."

"If it weren't for Dean, pulling us all together like this starting all those months ago, it might have succeeded," Jaz said. She pointed to him. "You're the common denominator that's messed up their plan. Everyone they're targeting is here and ready to fight back."

"Where do we go first?" Rudy asked. "We still can't be everywhere at once, even if we manage to mount a surprise attack and break the mob riots apart, it'll just spur the public to come out more strongly against us."

"Dean," Ingrid said. "Where's Mortis now? Can you sense him?"

"He's that way," Dean said after concentrating for a second. He pointed north.

"So's Bellum. Ashley, Jaz, where are your targets?"

The two women closed their eyes then opened them pointing north as well.

"It's a distraction," Ingrid said. "This is all started to distract and delay us while the four of them do what they need to open up the portal to hell."

"It makes sense," Gabe said. "They've got to act quickly to bring in more help or their whole plan to destroy the world is for naught."

"Then that's where we're going," Dean said. "If they're doing what you say, we're going to stop them. The city will have to fend for itself for a while. We've got to stop the end of the world. Everyone get anything you think you'll need. Jaz, give them access to your armory. We're going to have to be ready for anything they've already brought across to guard their backs."

"Already on it," Jaz said, pulling a key card from her pocket. "Follow me down to the basement. We'll get everyone equipped while I have my headquarters group fire up the transportation for us."

Everyone got up and filed out, following Jaz to the elevators. Soon only Dean and Gabe were left standing there.

"This is really happening, isn't it?" Dean asked.

Gabe nodded. "I've hitched my wagon to you and your plan, Dean. I hope the faith the higher powers have in you is well founded. I don't want to be wrong, but the odds are stacked against us."

Dean surprised himself when he laughed.

"That's the worst fatherly pep talk in history, you know that? Don't worry, Gabe. I'm a paramedic. The odds are always stacked against us. I hate to say this with you standing here, but I was born for this."

Chapter 20

ONE HOUR LATER, Dean and Jaz sat in the front of one of the Errington Security SUV's staring out at the County Medical Examiner's building from their vantage point across the street. He could feel the presence of something inside drawing him to this place. It had to be Mortem, the final horseman.

Dean glanced at Jaz and turned to the others behind him. Ingrid, Ashley, and Gabe sat in the back.

"Are we all in agreement? Each of our targets is somewhere in that building up ahead?"

Jaz, Ashley, and Ingrid all nodded. Dean keyed the mic on the radio handset. They were on a private channel licensed to Jaz and her security teams.

"They're somewhere in the Morgue, probably in the basement, at least that's my best guess."

"Should we contact the Elk City Authorities and call for back up?" Brynne asked over the radio from her vehicle with James and Rudy.

"No. There's no time," Dean replied after considering his plan for a few seconds. "Park where you are. We'll move forward on foot. Get everything you'll need from the trucks, though. We aren't coming back until this is finished, one way or the other."

Gibbie's cheerful voice came back over the radio from his van. "The cavalry is geared up and ready to go, boss. Marian wanted me to tell you this is going to be epic!"

Jaz rolled her eyes, but Dean found the levity from the melodramatic vampire a welcome break in the tension. They were only here to save the world, after all.

Dean hopped out and walked to the rear of their SUV with Jaz and the others. Jaz loaded up with a pair of hip-mounted semiautomatic pistols in addition to another in her shoulder holster rig. She picked up another rifle with the grenade launcher and stared at it for a few seconds. She reconsidered after glancing at the building. Setting the rifle down in its case, she closed the lid.

"It's going to be close quarters in there. I think I'll stick to the handguns for this one," she remarked. The last thing she picked up was the Errington sword, a katana in its scabbard which she settled into its harness straps over her shoulder where she could reach it in a hurry if needed.

Dean equipped himself again with the trauma bag. Jaz handed him a shoulder holster rig with a single pistol.

"Take it, Dean. You need to have some sort of protection."

He started to say no but reconsidered. They were going to need every advantage in this fight. Jaz had been training with him a little over the last few months and he'd become a fair shot with a pistol at close range. It couldn't hurt to have it on him just in case.

Dean nodded and slipped into the rig and then put his leather jacket back on over it. The holster hung down under his arm, the bulge feeling unusual and conspicuous to him since he wasn't used to it.

Jaz turned to the others and gestured to the arsenal displayed in the back of the SUV's armored compartment.

"Any takers? There's plenty here for you three as well."

Ashley and Gabe shook their heads. Ingrid laughed and held her hand out in front of her. A second later a gleaming silver sword appeared in it.

"This is all we'll need for the likes of any demon-kind we encounter. We've been training for this fight for an eternity, right Ash?"

"You have, sister mine. I always hoped there'd be other ways to resolve this conflict. I pray Dean can bring an end to this battle quickly."

Dean hoped so, too. He was used to having a lot riding on his decisions but this time the pressure weighed on him more than any life or death decision made in the back of an ambulance. He considered the alternative to winning here tonight and made himself shudder at the thought.

He started to say something to try and show the others how confident he was, even if he didn't really feel it. He stopped and burst out laughing as Gibbie came around from the back of the white van parked at the rear of the pair of SUVs.

The frumpy vampire looked like something out of a Rambo parody video. His black outfit and tactical harness bristled with weapons. He had two different rifles slung across his back in an x-pattern with a barrel poking up over each shoulder. He had a nickel-plated desert eagle revolver in one hand and a silver, basket-hilted cutlass in the other.

The grin on his face topped off the ensemble with the perfect expression of crazed optimism. The others from his group were more sensibly armed, but no less determined in their demeanor. Kristof, Wim, and Dora were each armed with an AK-47. Kristof had a bare broad-bladed scimitar shoved in his belt. Wim and Dora each had a scabbarded short sword hanging from their belts.

Marian, the young werewolf CERT team member, carried a single wicked-looking tactical tomahawk in each hand. The red glow in her eyes showing she was just on the cusp of shifting to at least partial werewolf form for the fight ahead.

Her father and Rudy stepped up on either side of her. Rudy was dressed in standard black tactical gear as James' security team. Marian's father was dressed in similar fashion. Each had a pistol on their hip and a tactical pistol-gripped shotgun in their hands.

James and Brynne were the last to arrive. James sported a medieval longsword on his hip, as did Brynne, though she didn't look comfortable with it. She also had a trauma pack slung on her back, though. That was good. It meant Dean wasn't their only medic ready to handle any injuries they took in the fight ahead of them.

Everyone stood in the street and looked at Dean, expecting him to take charge. He'd planned to come here and face off against the quartet of world-ending demons, after all.

Dean let his sense of Mortem's location rise to the top of his attention again. There was a sort of feeling the demon was located down from his current position as he stared at the imposing stone and concrete edifice in front of him.

"I think they must be in the basement of the building. I get the idea they're underground."

"I'm guessing they are down in the old emergency operations center located the basement of the building," Brynne offered. "It was closed down after the new EOC was built on the edge of town. If my memory serves me, it's a fairly secure location with only two exits."

"What's the fastest way down to that level?" Dean asked.

Brynne pointed to the side of the building where Dean spotted a ramp down on the left. A sign next to it marked it as the loading dock. It was hard to see much more because it was below street level.

"We can head down there," Brynne said. "That's where the coroner's teams drop off bodies for autopsy and storage in the morgue."

"Alright, then," Dean said. "Down the ramp it is. Everyone stay close and watch each other's backs."

He started across the street, Jaz trotting along by his side. Ingrid, Ashley, and Gabe jogged along just behind them. The others filed after.

The first sign of trouble came when Dean reached the base of the broad, concrete ramp. It opened up into a large parking area on the side of the building. There was ample room for vehicles like the coroner's black vans to turn around and back into the loading dock area. There were two people crouched over a body down next to the open door of one of the parked vans.

Dean saw the collapsed person and started to move forward. His instinct was to render aid to the injured man or woman. Then, the closest of the people turned to face him, exposing the ripped open chest cavity in the body on the ground, the body on which the two formerly dead people from the morgue, were feeding.

Ashley realized what had happened first. She called out a warning.

"Mortem can raise and command the dead. Watch out. They're under his control."

The two undead creatures stood and charged at the group with surprising speed. Dean was caught completely unawares and nearly fell over, backpedaling away from them. He was the closest because he'd started forward to lend aid.

Jaz was there to help him, though. She jumped in front of him and leveled her pistol in a two-handed grip, pumping off two head shots that dropped the charging undead to the ground.

She kept her pistol up and pointed at the loading dock and called back over her shoulder.

"Brynne, how full is the morgue? How many bodies can it hold? A rough guess is all I need."

"It's the central morgue for the whole county. It can hold at least fifty at a time in the coolers under normal circumstances."

Dean knew what Jaz was getting at.

"Hold up everyone," Dean said, as a new thought occurred to him. "This is going to be harder than I figured."

Jaz looked back at him, her glance asking him 'why.'

He shook his head. "The morgue has many more dead than normal right now. There's way more than fifty bodies in there. The staff has been doubling and tripling them in the freezer ever since the strange plague hit after Malificar arrived."

"How many then?" Jaz asked.

Brynne stepped up next to Dean. "Based on that assumption, I'd say at least a hundred fifty bodies are in there awaiting an autopsy. On the last report I read from headquarters, it detailed us to take all dead patients to the hospital or local funeral parlors for safe keeping. The county medical examiner has also asked for refrigerated trailers to be parked downtown for additional body storage."

"So we've got to face off against the archdemons while fighting an army of over a hundred ravenous zombies?" Jaz asked. "Great. I should have brought some grenades after all."

"You mean like these?" Gibbie asked.

The portly vampire pulled at one of the straps across his chest, bringing a canvas satchel into view. He flipped open the flap to show at least a dozen round fragmentation grenades inside.

"I didn't think I should leave anything behind in the truck so I carried as much as I could."

"Gibbie, my man," Dean said, clapping his hand on the vampire's shoulder. "Once again you prove yourself to be a man of rare worth and ability."

Jaz held out her hand. "Give me two and stay close in case I need more."

Gibbie nodded and handed her two of the grenades, one at a time as she attached them to the front of her tactical harness.

"Anyone else want one?" He asked, holding out a grenade in each hand.

Marian stepped forward with a gleam in her eyes at the thought of more firepower. Her father gripped her shoulder and shook his head. She growled low under her breath but stepped back to her place.

"It's probably a good idea we leave the explosives to Jaz," Dean suggested. "If we need them later, we know to get them from Gibbie."

Jaz raised her hand in the air, palm out towards them.

"Shhhh, do you hear that?"

Dean turned and tried to hear what she referred to; then he picked up on the dull roar slowly gaining in volume. It was coming from the double doors up on the loading dock.

"The shots," Jaz said as she raised her pistol and took a firing stance facing the doors. "They must have heard the rounds I fired to finish off these other two. Form a battle line folks; we're about to have company."

The team barely had time to gather on either side of Dean and Jaz. The double doors flung open and several dozen snarling, naked zombies ran out of the dark hallway beyond, heading straight for the group outside.

Jaz lobbed one of her grenades over the heads of the lead zombies into the hallway. More of the undead were coming but were caught by the explosion in the enclosed passage.

Dean had no time to see if the grenade stopped them or not because the leading wave of undead hit their line. He fired half of the rounds from his pistol into the chest of the one running at him before he remembered to switch to headshots. The impacting rounds slowed it down enough that he was able to shift his aim, though. He was a terrible shot and it took four more rounds from his fifteen round magazine to score a headshot.

Beside him, Jaz was having much more luck. Her pistol thumped with a series of twin shots, each double tap taking a different zombie out before they could reach the group. Rudy and Marian's father were nearly as effective with their pump-action shotguns firing again and again to Dean's left.

There were so many of them coming, though, all moving much faster than most zombie movies he'd ever seen. The group was going to be overwhelmed if they didn't do something.

To Dean's right, a flash of silver caught his eye. The three Eldara had formed three points of a whirling triangle of death, their heavenly blades slashing and stabbing as they advanced into the horde of undead. Ashley and Ingrid, in particular, worked in concert with a fierce complementary precision only twins could have achieved.

As they carved their way through the mass of bodies, Gibbie and the dryads fired their semi-automatic AK-47s into those who slipped past the angels' blades. That stopped the surge of undead on that side and Kristof finished off the few that made it through with his massive scimitar.

A ripping snarl sounded on the left and Marian, shifted into half woman, half wolf form, leaped over her father and Rudy and fell into the surge of undead facing them. Her tomahawks were soon coated in gore as she tore through the zombies on that side. She was able to hold her own for a few seconds but the weight of the pressing bodies started to blunt the force of her attacks.

James and Brynne surged forward to Marian's aid, their silver longswords out and carved a path forward with blurring speed.

Dean returned his attention to the battle in front of him, dropping another zombie with a headshot but emptying his magazine in the process. He fumbled at his pocket for another while he ejected the empty one from the grip.

"Dean, they're going to keep coming," Jaz shouted while she

reloaded. "We need to get in there and stop the demons with Ingrid and Ashley. Follow the Eldara. They're clearing the way for us."

She was right. The trio of angels cut a path through the surge of bodies and were almost at the double doors leading inside. He charged forward, pausing for just a second as he finally managed to slide a new magazine home and jack a fresh round into the chamber of his pistol.

Jaz was right beside him and she lobbed her other grenade over the heads of the angels, sending it deeper into the hallway before them. The explosion cleared a gap in the ranks of zombies in front of them.

"Push forward," Dean called out. "We've got to get inside."

He spared a glance back at the others still battling outside against the bulk of the zombie horde. Then they were gone from sight as he passed through the double doors and into the hallway beyond. Gabe slammed both doors closed and slid the bolts on the reinforced steel doors home to lock it against the zombies outside trying to get back in at them.

"What about the others? They won't be able to get in, at least not quickly," Dean said.

"They'll have to fend for themselves and hold the loading dock for us against our return," Gabe said. "What needs to be done in here falls to us."

The momentary lull in the fighting left Dean shaking as the adrenaline coursed through his body, seeking release in more fight or flight activity. He nodded and pointed down the hallway.

"Mortem and the others are that way. I can feel them. How about the rest of you?"

"Malificar is there as well," Ashley agreed.

"So is Bellum," Ingrid added.

Jaz's nod told him Famis, her target, was there, too.

"Let's go then," Dean said. "We have to stop them before they succeed in opening the portal. It can't be long before they're successful."

FORGING FORWARD DOWN THE HALLWAY, Dean, Jaz, and the three Eldara followed the signs pointing to the central morgue. They encountered a few isolated undead who hadn't followed the main mass out onto the loading dock.

Between Jaz and the Eldara, they dealt with the stragglers in relative silence using their swords. Dean approved of the quieter alternative to their pistols. They didn't need to alert the four horsemen of their approach any sooner than possible if they could avoid it.

As they got closer to the central storage area and the medical examiner's main autopsy room, a thrumming hum vibrated up through the concrete floor. The deep vibrations radiated up through his feet going all the way to his head. It increased in intensity as the five of them progressed forward.

By the time they stood outside the doors to the room, the vibrations were strong enough to rattle Dean's teeth. On the other side of the large, double doors, over the low-frequency resonating sound, deep guttural voices could be heard chanting in unison.

"They've started the ritual to open the rift between the worlds," Gabe said. "We've got to hurry."

"We don't know what we're rushing into," Ashley cautioned. "They've got to have more of the undead guarding them inside."

"We don't have a choice," Dean said, shaking his head. "If that rift opens the portal to the netherworld, it's all over anyway. Gabe will have to sound the trumpet and call forth the heavenly forces to fight the final battle right here in Elk City. No matter the outcome, it will destroy everything and everyone here. We have to stop them."

"Each of us has a connection to one of the archdemons," Jaz said. "We'll focus on taking the attack to our own demon. Gabe, you stay with Dean since he's only got the single pistol which isn't going to do much, I'm afraid."

"I'll watch his back," Gabe replied. "What if we can't take them out?"

"Then sound the horn and we'll take our chances," Ingrid said. "In the end, we can't let them have this whole earthly plane, no matter what that means to the people of this city."

Dean knew it was the truth but he still refused to accept it as the only option. He didn't know what he was going to do in there but he'd come up with something. He had to or everything he'd worked to achieve in the city, all the people he'd saved in his short career, would all be lost.

He placed the palm of his hand on the double swinging door leading into the autopsy chamber and pushed, walking into the current center of chaos on earth. Dean didn't know what lay on the other side; he only knew he couldn't turn back now.

Whatever the expectation, nothing prepared him for what greeted him as he stepped through the doors. Four robed figures, each in a different, muted color, stood around a throbbing nimbus of glowing blackness. The circle of darkness was the size of a basketball but it pulsed and throbbed as if it was struggling to expand and become larger.

Not knowing what else to do, Dean leveled his pistol at the black-robed figure he knew was Mortem and fired all fifteen shots into the flowing robes from behind. The slide on the pistol locked back as the final shot rang out. The chanting stopped and the black-robed figure turned to face the intruders, followed by the others, robed in red, green, and blue respectively.

Dean couldn't see a face in the depths of the black hood that faced him but he saw two burning red eyes glowing inside.

"Stop," Dean called out. "I'll not let you destroy this world. You and your brothers must be sent back to hell where you can't cause any more trouble."

"I've felt your presence drawing closer," the voice from the black hood hissed. "You are the one foretold in prophecy. The one who must be present so we may finish opening the portal."

"I'm not going to help you open that doorway to hell, I don't care what your prophecy says," Dean shouted back in defiance.

"It's not your help I need, boy," Mortem rasped. "It's your mixed blood, the combined blood of an Eldara and a human. The essence of a hybrid is needed to breach the wards and open the gates of hell finally."

The black gloved hand reached into the robes and emerged with a hand scythe, the curved black iron blade glinted in the faint, purple light emanating from the glowing black ball.

"Come and I will make your death quick."

Dean had no idea how he was supposed to fight back at this point. His pistol had no effect, and he was out of ammunition anyway. Mortem reached out with his free hand and beckoned to Dean. Without warning and totally out of his control, Dean felt his feet lurch forward, one after the other, towards the demon.

"No!" Gabe shouted and the archangel ran between Dean and Mortem, his heavenly blade flashing in a blinding arc downward at the demon's cowled head.

The iron scythe came up and parried the gleaming sword. A shower of red sparks flew when the blades met. As if that was the signal, each of the other three Agents of Chaos ran forward to meet their counterparts in the battle.

Malificar in blue robes squared off against Ashley, his black longsword blade sweeping out to be met by her heavenly sword. Bellum, dressed in red, now carried a giant two-handed battle axe. Ingrid summoned a gleaming silver shield from the same place she summoned her sword. She raised the round disk of silver metal just in time and caught the crushing downward axe blow. She lunged forward with her sword, causing the demon to dance backward, letting out a deep, booming laugh as if enjoying the challenge of a fight.

Jaz ran forward at Famis, the green-robed demon, her sword held high. The horseman of famine produced an iron-shod staff of black wood and parried her sword's downward sweep, knocking it aside with ease before sweeping the staff around in a return strike that sent her diving to one side.

The thrumming hum of the glowing black orb suspended in the center of the room drew Dean's attention away from the rest of the fight. Before he knew what he was doing, he found himself walking in slow shuffling steps towards it. He tried to stop himself, or at least part of him did. All he managed to do was lose his balance and nearly topple over backward as his feet kept moving forward while his arm reached back to a nearby autopsy table to hold himself back.

The closer he got to the sphere of black darkness hovering before him, the less strength there was in his resolve to stay back. Eventually, despite wanting to stay away, Dean found himself only a foot away from the magical object.

He assumed it was the beginning of the portal between the netherworld and earth's plane. It seemed to be waiting for something, or maybe someone to complete the spell that would open it fully.

What was it Mortem had said when he arrived? If he had some role to play in opening the portal, might he also be able to close it as well?

Dean raised his hand, his forefinger extended to touch the swirling black mass suspended in the air.

"No!" Gabe shouted behind him.

Dean turned in time to see his father parry a stroke by Mortem's scythe. He darted around the cloaked demon, running at Dean with one hand outstretched.

"Don't touch the portal. Mortem is correct. Your life force is what is needed to open it all the way."

Dean paused, his hand only a few inches away from the black surface. Confusion battled against resolve in his brain. Something, some voice in his mind, still foggy from whatever commanded him to move forward, shouted at him to stop. It echoed the words from his father but Dean's foggy mind didn't understand why his father was shouting at him or the words he shouted.

Mortem spun to follow the archangel as he ran towards Dean. The scythe's black blade swung down and caught Gabe behind one knee, cutting the hamstrings and buckling the leg.

Gabe stumbled and fell to the ground; his glittering heavenly blade flew from his hand as he went down. The sword slid across the floor out of reach. The demon behind him shouted in triumph and leaped atop the collapsed archangel.

Dean noticed then that his other friends were all fighting desperate, losing battles against their opponents, too. Jaz was bleeding and bruised from being battered by the enchanted evil staff Famis wielded. It didn't look like she'd done any damage to the demon at all, though it was hard to tell through the robes he wore.

Ashley cried out beyond Jaz's fight as Malificar's sword blade snaked past her guard and scored a piercing blow in her shoulder. The wound smoked around the black blade and Dean could tell it leeched away some of her life energy before the demon recovered from his lunging blow to assume a guard position.

Ingrid's enchanted shield finally collapsed and was torn from her arm by another vicious downward blow from Bellum's war axe. It looked like the strike broke her arm in the process from the way she carried it after shaking the broken shield free to clatter to the floor. She wasn't giving up, but he thought he saw a hint of desperation in her eyes as she tried an unsuccessful combination attack to try and disengage from the close combat.

Dean took all this in within a few seconds before turning back to the orb. It still called to him asking him to join with it with wordless whispers of urges in his mind. Unable to resist any longer, he extended his arm the final few inches and touched the surface with his forefinger.

Everything around him halted, frozen in time the instant he made contact with the black orb. He felt himself falling forward, his mind leaving his body behind as he flew through the darkness. As he fell or flew, or whatever it was he was doing, he passed scenes of battles, most of them ancient, though a few appeared to be more modern with guns firing and bombs exploding. In each of the scenes Dean could see at least one central robed figure, in a few of them there were two or even three of the familiar robed figures present, directing the battle, trying to win the day.

He noted there was never an instance when all four of the Agents of Chaos were present and in each of the depicted battles, while great carnage and evil persisted, the forces facing them, both human and Unusual, won the day. Even though the forces of good won the day, the harm wrought by the demons persisted in some way, living on in some vestige of persistent wrong or prejudice to carry on until the next battle could be joined.

Dean realized he was being shown the history of the battle between the forces of Good and Evil for dominion over the Earth. All of them changed the course of events in some way. All of them led to this day and the fight in the morgue.

In some way, his involvement in this place and time was preordained. That realization helped him understand why Gabe had come to earth to father a child with Dean's mother, and it pissed him off.

He was more than just a pawn in some celestial game played by powers beyond his ability to comprehend. Dean refused to believe everything he'd tried to do to make the world a better place meant nothing. There had to be more to the significant events and choices of his life than being a way to bring him here to settle this fight.

The more he thought about it, the more it twisted his anger into despair. Did he have free will at all?

"Son, don't!"

The distant voice distracted him and pulled his awareness back into his body. He'd seen what he needed to see.

Dean didn't know how long he'd been lost inside the orb but in the intervening time, each of his friends had lost their battles with the demons. Each of them now lay on the tiled floor of the autopsy room, held down by pairs of Mortem's zombie minions. The four demons stood over each of them with their weapons poised to deliver the death stroke.

Mortem's voice penetrated the haze over his mind.

"Your friends are all vanquished, boy, but I can still spare their lives. I'll spare yours, too. All you have to do is complete the task for which you were sent here. Command the portal to open. Open the rift between worlds so that the forces of heaven and hell may once again battle here on this earth, the place created to be our battleground. You humans were a mistake of creation. This place was built to provide a neutral plane for our conflict. It was never right for the Supreme Divine One to cast us out and banish us. The rise of your species came from a glitch in the system but the Divine One chose to favor you, the mistake, rather than the primary beings of creation."

"Don't do it, Dean. You can't listen to him. He lies," Gabe called out in desperation.

"I lie?" Mortem laughed. "I've done nothing but tell you the truth. The only ones who've lied to you here are the Eldara. They hide their true plans to keep the earth for themselves so they can manipulate your kind through their infernal machinations. Think about it boy. You know it to be true."

Dean hesitated. He kept one hand on the black orb. He could still feel it's pulsing presence and the potential to become something more. He knew he could open that gate with just a thought.

He considered what both the demon and angel told him. In some ways, Mortem was right about the Eldara.

Ashley had ultimately deceived him about his real purpose here on Earth. She must have known who he was. If she knew, that meant she wasn't the only one.

Ingrid had always been distant and attended to her own plans and needs when she'd dealt with Dean. She'd used Dean to rescue her sister and defeat an incursion from the netherworld. As soon as he'd completed his task, she moved on.

Gabe was the worst of all of them, creating the lie that followed him through his whole life. He'd even forced Dean's mother to lie about the identity of his father. Dean wasn't the only pawn caught up in this divine chess match.

The more he thought about it, the more the anger burned within him, growing hotter and hotter. It fueled intense feelings of despair and loss. Nothing in this world was real to Dean anymore. None of it mattered because everything about it was a lie.

Yet at the bottom of the well of darkness and despair, a thin sliver of light shined through. It was a single truth, perhaps the only truth he had left. It lay in the opportunity here to set it all right, to make it so the powers of heaven and hell could have their final battle and settle the fate of the earth once and for all. All he had to do was give in and let them have the battle they all wanted.

Dean turned his attention to the orb, preparing to open the portal and start the war. As he pressed his hand harder against the smooth, warm surface of the orb hovering before him, his awareness entered the void inside it and he found himself floating in darkness. Except it wasn't complete darkness. A silver, glowing, serpentine line separated the interior of the orb into two halves.

He hadn't seen that before.

He traced the line with his eyes. Dean recognized the familiar shape of yin and yang. The two shapes separated by the thin line represented opposite sides of many things in Eastern philosophies. Here, in the center of the black orb, there were the two halves of good and evil.

Dean was surprised the two sides weren't represented as different in some way. One should be light and the other dark, he thought.

Except, they weren't different. That realization struck him and he saw Good and Evil for what they were. The two sides were completely alike; each were two sides of the same supernatural coin, each had their own agendas.

All he had to do to bring them together at last in a final battle, the fight deciding the fate of the world, was press his awareness into the gap between them and open up the portal. His existence would end at that moment but that meant all his pain and despair would also disappear.

Dean considered the two options before him. He could open the portal and end the lies once and for all, or refuse to open it, allowing the battle to continue behind the scenes for countless centuries until another champion, in another age, faced the same choice once again. Two options and his decision would either doom the world to its eventual end or prolong the lies and pain and suffering of everyday life.

Dean reached a decision. He sent out his mind, ready to open the portal and end the world as he knew it.

It made him sad that he had only those two choices. He wished for another option.

And then it came to him.

Amidst the darkness and despair, Dean recalled a conversation he'd had with Ashley once about humans, Unusuals, and the gift and responsibility of free will. Gabe had come here expecting the end of the world. The Agents of Chaos, the four horsemen, had arrived with a similar agenda. They each wanted the same thing.

They wanted their final battle.

While Gabe had joined Dean's side and agreed to his plans to confront the four horsemen, perhaps that was just a ruse to get him here. As long as Dean came here, he could open the portal and begin the final battle for them.

Dean pulled his hand back from the silvery gap between the two sides. They wanted him to believe there were only two choices. It was yet another lie told to force him to make up his mind.

He couldn't give them what they wanted and end the world. He also couldn't let the responsibility pass to the next generation's champion. There had to be a third choice, a way for free will to triumph.

Dean examined the silvery thread that was the gap in the darkness. As he studied it, he realized how fragile it was. It was nothing more than a seal over containers holding the two sides. It kept Good and Evil apart, holding the world in between and acting as a bridge from each side to the center that was the earth.

At that moment, the third option came to him in an instant of inspiration.

Dean had the solution and knew what he must do.

Letting his awareness return to the outside of the orb, Dean turned to where Gabe and Mortem watched him.

"What are you doing, boy? Open the portal." Mortem ordered. "End the circle of lies you've been told."

"What would happen if that thin barrier between your two sides were to be broken?" Dean mused. "Not opened into a portal, but broken completely?"

"Dean," Gabe said from where he lay on the floor held down by Mortem's booted foot. "What are you doing?"

"A thought occurred to me while I was inside the darkness of the orb. You both arranged for me to be here. You both hoped I would despair and lose faith in myself long enough to give up in the face of impossible odds."

Dean smiled at the puzzled look on Gabe's face. He imagined a similar look on the face hidden inside the black hood shrouding Mortem's face.

"Except, I'm a paramedic. Impossible odds are what I face each and every day. I find hope in the most hopeless of situations. I bring back life to the lifeless. I refuse to accept either of the options you've set before me. Instead, I choose freedom."

Dean held out his hand, palm open towards Gabe's heavenly blade on the floor nearby. The hilt twitched and then it lifted from the floor and flipped end over end through the air until the hilt settled in his hand.

The warmth of the grip under his fingers tingled and revealed the power within the divine weapon in a way he hadn't felt on the occasion when he'd held Ashley's blade in a previous adventure. This was the point of real truth. This was the moment when he saw the actual power given to the men and women here on earth.

"I choose free will."

Dean swung the blade in a broad arc, spinning in place until the shimmering, silver metal cut in a horizontal plane through the orb. The sword cut through the dark sphere from one side to the other, severing the thin, silver thread at its center, severing the bridge between the planes.

Chapter 22

MORTEM AND GABE BOTH SHOUTED "NO" at the same time. Their pleas for him to stop came too late.

The archangel Gabriel and the four archdemons all collapsed with a unified anguished shout, each falling gasping and weakened to the floor. The demons writhed as they landed, their robes smoldering with wisps of smoke, their bodies shriveling within until their cries faded and nothing was left but a pile of colored cloth robes on the ground. The undead bodies holding his friends down collapsed lifeless again to the floor.

Gabriel struggled to rise to his hands and knees but then his eyes rolled up in his head and he fell over unconscious. At first, Dean thought he, too, had perished like the demons.

The archangel still breathed, though. He was only unconscious. Dean had severed his primary connection to divine power.

For the demons, who'd spent their energy spreading their evil plan as fast as they drew it in, the loss of their power source had ended them. They had nothing left to sustain them the way Gabe did.

Ashley and Ingrid, lesser Eldara, were affected, too, but in a minor way. He'd weakened them, as well. The pale, shocked looks on their faces confirmed it.

Jaz stood and recovered her family's sword from the ground. She held it before her, ready to defend herself as she backed away from the shriveled heaps that were all that was left of the demons. She stepped to the right and moved closer to Dean.

"What did you just do? One minute I was sure we were dead and now? Now I'm not sure what I'm seeing."

"I dealt with the problem, taking away the threat of Armageddon once and for all. No longer will this threat hang over the minds of mortals here on Earth."

Dean pointed to where the orb had hung in the air. It was gone now. "Mortem and the other arch-demons, along with Gabe, all wanted me to open the portal and initiate the final battle between them. They presented a binary choice to me. I almost did what they wanted, Jaz. I almost brought on the end of the world. But then I realized what I saw as a barrier between the two sides, between good and evil, was really a bridge connecting them both to us here on earth. At that moment, I knew what to do. I cut the bridge and removed the connection to both sides of the equation."

"But they're all still here?" Jaz turned and surveyed the archangel and the weakened Eldara. "Why didn't they go back to where they came from, as the demons did?"

"I think it has to do with a side effect of their living among humans for so long. It held them on this plane without destroying them. They're now trapped here, at least for the time being."

Ashley raised her head. She wore a smile. "You are correct in a way, Dean. The Eldara had always played by the rules set by our masters, manifesting true human bodies with many human limitations alongside our divine powers. The demons refused to do that. They have always come to Earth in their true forms, refusing to give up their power and control. Your actions doomed the four archdemons to permanent banishment when you severed the connection between our worlds."

Ingrid crawled over to her sister and rolled over onto her back, staring at the ceiling.

"I can't feel Vahalla anymore. I don't hear the call of fallen heroes."

"I lost my connection to the higher planes as well, sister," Ashley said. "Be patient. It may return in some fashion given time."

"You've always been the patient one, Ash, not me."

"There's always time to turn over a new leaf."

A groan sounded from Gabe and he raised his hand up to his head as he struggled to a sitting position. Dean crossed to him, holding out the silvery blade of the archangel's heavenly sword.

"Here, this is yours."

Gabe shook his head. "No, it is yours now. It will not respond to my call anymore. You have used it for a greater purpose than I thought possible."

"What do I need with a sword? I'm a paramedic, a healer."

"You're so much more than that, son. The sooner you realize that, the sooner you'll discover the next purpose you're called to serve."

"Ashley and Ingrid mentioned they feel cut off from the higher planes. I guess you're stuck here forever."

"Our connection is weakened but still holds. I can sense the barest thread of it. It is the advantage of taking these human forms. I think, given time, we will find a way back when the time is right. Perhaps this is an opportunity to learn about this time and place. You have proven to me there is more worth here than I originally thought."

Dean struggled with an answer to that statement. He was going to have to get used to having his father around. He wasn't sure how he felt about that, given how Gabe had manipulated him. At this point in his life, he wasn't sure he needed a father, anyway.

A booming sound came from the outer hallway. Someone was bashing at the doors leading out from the central autopsy room. The demons had sealed them to keep Dean and his friends from retreating when the fighting started. That magic seemed to still hold, though it must have been weakened with the demise of the horsemen. The pounding on the outer doors continued until the double steel doors burst inward to crash to the floor.

Gibbie, Brynne, James, and the rest rushed in, weapons at the ready. They each sported various injuries and were covered in blood and gore, but they lived and seemed none the worse for the battle they fought all the way from the loading dock to here.

Gibbie slowed his charge, looking around for signs of an enemy to fight. He had the chrome-plated Desert Eagle revolver in one hand and his pirate cutlass in the other. He looked quite the modern-day urban warrior, despite the slight paunch spilling over his gun belt.

"Aw, crap. Did you finish them all off before we got here? I wanted to help you kill one of those demons."

"I'm afraid so, Gibbie. Sorry I didn't leave one of them alive for you to fight."

Gibbie holstered the huge pistol at his waist and slid the cutlass into its scabbard on the opposite hip. He looked like he was pouting.

Dean changed the subject and pointed to the doors leading to the hallway. "Is it all clear out there?"

"Yep, we had to cut more than a few into little tiny bits to get it done, though. It's going to be a major pain for the medical examiner and his crew to make sure all the bodies are put back in the same bins with the original pieces."

"Not my problem," Dean said. "Right, Brynne?"

She nodded. "As long as it's done, we can leave that mess for someone else to clean up. It is done, right?" She glanced around the room, looking for a foe to engage.

"Yes. They're gone, for good, I hope," Dean replied. "I think once the city settles back to normal, we should all be back to our regular routines within a few days."

James held up his phone. "Celeste says the riots outside the building broke up a few minutes ago. The people seemed to lose their rage and the will to press forward. They're all wandering away in a confused daze."

"Bellum controlled them," Ashley said. "He used their rage to push them into violence. Their desire to harm those different from themselves disappeared when Dean destroyed him and the others."

A crashing sound in the distance, as if someone had dropped a platter of silverware in another room, caught their attention. Rudy pointed out the door.

"We should check and make sure the whole building is clear of any more undead before we leave. It wouldn't do to leave any of these mindless zombies wandering the city. They aren't under their own conscious control like Freddie and others like him."

With murmurs of agreement, the rest of the group, joined by the three Eldara, dispersed to search the building. In a few seconds, all was quiet and Dean found himself standing alone with Jaz. It felt like the first time they'd been alone since Gabe had shown up on the bridge at the city park.

Dean's hand fell to his pocket, feeling the lump of the jewelry gift box. He'd been carrying it with him in the faint hope another opportunity would present itself to him.

In a moment of spontaneity, Dean thrust his hand into his pocket and snatched out the box. Dropping to one knee, he reached out and took Jaz's hand in his.

"Dean, what are you doing?"

"Don't you know?"

"I do but I don't think this is the best time or place to do this. Why don't we wait until things are back to normal?"

"If I've learned one thing in the course of our time together, Jaz, it's that, for us, there is no such thing as normal. As soon as I wait for something better to come along, we're likely to find ourselves caught up in another fight or mystery that needs solving."

"But—"

"Jaz, don't. I've got to get this out before anyone comes back and ruins it again."

Jaz closed her mouth and stared down at Dean. After a second's pause, she nodded, a grin spreading across her face.

"Jaswinder Errington, would you do me the honor of accepting my proposal to be my wife and grant me the privilege of being your husband. We know from Jo it was fated to be, but that's not the same as having the feelings we've come to share over the last year. I love you, Jaz. Please be mine."

Jaz's grin broadened into a full smile and she nodded an enthusiastic yes while holding out her hand, fingers extended.

Dean fumbled with the box for a moment until he managed to free the antique ring from its confines and slipped it over the ring finger of the extended hand. It slid on with ease.

Jaz lifted her hand up and he watched as she admired the ring before she crouched down before him and leaned in for a long kiss to seal the commitment.

"If you two are finished making wedding plans," Gibbie said from the doorway. "The rest of us are headed back out to the loading dock. James says the building is clear. Should I stand guard out here to give you both some privacy, or are you coming with us?"

Dean and Jaz laughed and stood, their hands clasped together.

"Tell the others we're on our way," Dean said. "It's time to put this city, and our lives, back together again."

———————————————

Chapter 23

———————————————

SIX WEEKS LATER, Dean stood in the middle of Sabatani's restaurant downtown, staring at Jaz as she recited her vows of marriage to him. The words washed over him and past him without really hearing them. He should probably pay better attention, but he felt the sentiment behind them. At the moment, the way she looked in the plain white dress, holding the small bouquet of flowers before her, captured all of his attention.

So much had happened since the fight at the morgue. The city had returned to normal.

Almost.

The presence of Unusuals in Elk City had been made public by the arrival of the four horsemen and many neighbors had received photos and descriptions of one or more of their friends, neighbors, or colleagues, outing them as creatures of the supernatural. At first, there was a wave of denial that such things were real. More than a few people called the videos posted online as some sort of Hollywood special effects.

Then, something incredible happened. Unusuals started sharing who they were with their human neighbors. It was as if they were tired of the long centuries of their families hiding their real identities. They overcame the fear of rejection and judgment and came out of the shadows, into the light.

There had been a few incidents and problems as one would expect. For the most part, though, the whole city experienced a period of uncharacteristic peace and goodwill as everyone got to know each other again.

The paramedics from Station U still had a job to do. They settled back into the usual routine of calls for their special patients almost as if nothing had changed. It was different for Dean, though. He'd discovered enough about his origins that he identified more with his patients than ever before. It also separated him from his human colleagues, at least in his mind. Maybe it was time for him to move on to something new.

Returning his attention to the matter at hand, Jaz completed her vows and met his eyes with hers. Dean held her hands in his and smiled at his bride. This was a time of new beginnings.

Beside them, Gibbie reached out a hand and placed it over theirs.

"By the power vested in me by the internet and the state of Maryland, I hereby pronounce you both husband and wife. Dude, kiss the bride already."

Dean smiled. For the first time in a long while, he felt comfortable in his own skin and knew he was on the right track with his life. He leaned forward and pulled Jaz in tight as he complied with Gibbie's command.

This paramedic had a new life, a new family, and a new path ahead of him. The whole world was a better place now, all because one paramedic did his job.

The End

The Paramedic's Amazon

Prologue

HANGBE SURVEYED the empty village from the ridge before heading down. She cursed under her breath. She was too late again.

She pulled the Land Rover to the side of the single gravel road passing between the cottages. The police constable's van sat across from her. As she climbed out of the SUV, the Scottish constable got out as well.

"You the inspector I was told to wait for?"

Hangbe nodded, her black braids rattling a little as the beaded ends touched. She pulled back the side of her leather jacket to show her ID badge clipped to the inside pocket. The maneuver exposed the black, contoured body armor she wore underneath.

The constable leaned forward and nodded after a brief look.

She ignored him. The mystery of these disappearances deepened with each site she visited. Hangbe stood in the middle of the small seaside community trying to get a sense of what it would take to clean out a place this size. She counted ten homes that she could see. There could be a few others nestled out of sight down along the water, but probably not many. She guessed less than fifty people had called this community home.

The constable, a heavy-set fellow with a bright red nose and rosy cheeks, took off his cap and scratched at his thinning brown hair. "I have to say you're not what I expected an Interpol special agent to look like."

"Met many of us, have you?"

"Um, no." He scratched his head again and changed the subject away from his surprise at meeting the West African woman in blue jeans, custom-fitted tactical body armor, and a long leather jacket.

He shifted his attention away from her after staring for too long. "Any idea where they all went?"

"I was going to ask you the same thing, Constable. Has there been any trouble among the villagers, perhaps with others living in the towns nearby?"

"No, in fact, I hardly ever come up here at all. The people here have always been clannish and keep to themselves. If they have trouble with one of their own, they keep it within the community and don't call for help."

Hangbe only half listened as she walked down the road. The gravel crunched under her knee-high boots and she cast outward with her otherworldly senses. The Constable had to jog a little to keep up with her long strides.

Common smells and sounds of the seaside met her as she strolled along past the empty homes. A glance to the left and right at the open doors told her whatever had happened had been hurried. Who leaves their homes open to the elements if they're planning to return? Other than that and the missing people, everything seemed the same as the others she'd seen. These small Unusual shifter clans all had similarities, no matter where she encountered them around the world. They'd avoid interacting with nearby humans, keeping up the pretense they were as normal as every other small fishing community.

"When did you first realize something was wrong?"

The constable stopped walking, snaking his forefinger up under his cap to scratch at his head again. Hangbe rolled her eyes, keeping her back to him so he wouldn't see her reaction. It was as if he couldn't walk and think at the same time.

"The first curious thing happened when old Joseph didn't bring in the village's catch yesterday morning. He usually sells it to one of the wholesaler trucks that passes through on their way into the city."

"So you sent out someone to investigate?" Hangbe asked after she realized he wasn't going to continue on his own.

"Oh, no. We figured they hadn't caught anything and left it at that."

She resisted the urge to turn and glare at him. It was almost night-fall the following day. He'd let the trail go cold because he didn't like coming all the way out here to look in on the strange little village and its people.

"So when did you finally realize they were gone?"

The edge of her voice cut like a knife, and the constable bristled a little as he caught the tone of what she said. "Now, look here, missy. I'm a busy man. There were other things to attend to yesterday, and I had no way of knowing there might be trouble."

"When?"

"This morning. When Joseph missed the second day's fish market drop off, I drove out. I thought maybe his truck had mechanical prob-lems. That's when I found it empty. The whole place was just empty. There were thirty-seven people living here."

Hangbe turned and looked back up the street towards her vehicle. "Just like the others."

"What's that?" the constable asked. "There are others?"

Hangbe nodded. "You must have suspected it when you filled out your report and my BOLO popped up in your system."

She'd had her team back in London submit the *Be On the Look Out* notice to all the UK police units for any mysterious disappearances of more than two people at a time.

"I wondered, but we get those kinds of things all the time from headquarters. They rarely apply to the outlying areas in the country-side. We don't pay much attention to them."

Hangbe surveyed the empty village. The open doors glared back at her. Two whole days had gone by. It was unlikely she'd be able to find any evidence of what had happened, even with her special skills. Still, she had to try.

"Alright, Constable. I'll take it from here. I'll loop you in on anything I discover."

"Um, my Superintendent probably wants me to stick around and assist you with your investigation."

Hangbe fixed him with a level stare. "Is that what you want to do?" She reached up and rubbed her middle fingertip across one of the ridged beads on the ornate necklace she wore. The magic worked instantly.

His eyes glazed over and the constable said, "No, I want to go back to the station so I can hit the pub with my mates."

Hangbe nodded, holding his gaze. "Then you should do that. I'll work things out with the Superintendent."

She dropped her hand from the necklace and the policeman's eye's cleared.

He opened his mouth to say something but stopped as if trying to remember a comment that had slipped his mind. He shrugged, nodded once, and walked back to his van.

She waited until the police van was out of sight before she started her search for clues. With her right thumb and forefinger, Hangbe rolled a different bead, this one orange and green with a pebbled exterior, back and forth as she walked back up the street. She took her time, waiting for the images of what had happened here to manifest. Two days was a long time, but if the emotions were strong enough, there should still be at least a shadow of an imprint left.

A few fleeting images of women running from dark figures crossed her path. They never lasted more than a few seconds. She pressed with her will to make them linger. All she got was a stabbing headache behind her eyes. It had been too long. Cursing aloud this time, Hangbe let go of the pebbled bead and stopped beside her car. She shifted her fingers to a different bead, this one black as the moonless night sky. This time the magic worked instantly, and she frowned knowing what she would find.

The tug on her mind pulled her between two nearby cottages and down to the water lapping at the stony shore. Fishing boats sat beached along the strand of shoreline nearby. The pull from the magic took her away from the boats and around a small headland to a small isolated cove. The magic wasn't needed anymore. The gulls and crows battling for scraps from the dead caused enough noise to tell her right where to go to find the bodies.

A dozen men and older boys lay in a heap, huddled together to shield each other from the hail of bullets that had rained down on them from the top of the cove. She knelt down and plucked a shell casing from the stones at her feet. The bastards had stood right here when they did it.

She glanced at the 9mm brass casing in her hand, then slipped it into a small plastic bag from her pocket. She'd submit it for evidence to her superiors. She'd catch the bastards. She always did, eventually. That was why she was given the latitude she had from her bosses, the humans overseeing international crimes against Unusuals. The evidence she gathered now was important. They'd want proof linking the trail of bodies she left behind once she caught up to the ones who'd done this.

Hangbe snapped a few photos with her phone of the bodies and of the surroundings in relation to the boats. That constable wasn't too bright, and she didn't want to have to come back to lead him to what he should have found before she'd arrived. She hoped the sight made him lose whatever he'd had for dinner tonight. She knew her appetite had left for the evening.

Returning to her Land Rover, Hangbe sat behind the wheel giving the village with no name one last look. This trafficking ring was slippery and careful. It was why she'd had little to go on so far. There'd been no concrete leads at all over the months she'd been tracking them down. She just needed one break in the case. One little slip by whoever had done this. Then she'd descend on them like an angel of death. Then she'd show them how an Amazon dealt with those who threatened the innocent.

———————————————

Chapter 1

———————————————

THE AMBULANCE VEERED around a car which slowed for no apparent reason. Paramedic Dean Flynn gripped the grab handle beside the passenger door even though his seatbelt was buckled.

"Easy does it, Barry. We need to get there in one piece, or we don't get to help anyone."

Barry, Dean's partner and fellow paramedic grimaced. "Sorry, Dean, I expected them to pull over like everyone else. What's the use of running with my emergency lights and the siren blaring if no one is going to pay attention to it or do the wrong thing when they do hear it?"

"You're preaching to the choir here, bud. If people did what was smart all the time, we'd be out of jobs."

Barry's eyes stayed on the road, though he did smile in response to Dean's comment. He peered through the nighttime street lit by the isolated pools of the streetlights ahead. "Did the printout from HQ have anything else on the patient?"

Dean glanced down at the paper in his other hand and then shook his head. "It just says injured subject from a fall. It could be anything. I'll call in and see if I can get them to give us a clue what we're walking into."

Reaching forward, the senior paramedic grabbed the mic from its clip on the dash and called the dispatch center. "U-191, we are almost on location. Do you have any additional for us?"

"Negative, U-191. Twenty-two-year-old female, injured in a fall is all we've been able to get from the caller. They disconnected and haven't picked up when we called back."

Barry frowned. "That doesn't sound good."

"No, it doesn't," Dean replied. Something about this particular dispatch didn't feel right. Learning long ago to trust his instincts, he keyed the mic again. "U-191 to Dispatch. Requesting a police unit to the scene for a check."

"Received, U-191. Police unit en route."

Dean replaced the mic on the dash and leaned forward to look out into the night as Barry turned off the main road and down a residential street. This was a run-down working-class neighborhood. Four and five-story buildings lined the street. They had broken most up into small apartments with various shops and businesses occupying the first floors.

Barry spotted the correct street number first. "There it is. I don't see anyone out on the sidewalk waiting for us. What's the unit number?"

Dean checked his sheet again. "Apt 3. I'm guessing that's on the third floor. It's usually two per floor in these places and that dry-cleaners takes up the first floor."

Barry pulled to the curb in front of the building and slid the gear lever into park. "Should we go in or wait for the police backup?"

Dean shrugged. "It could be nothing. Maybe I'm still jumpy, even after all these months since the—" Dean trailed off.

Barry finished for him. "Since you stopped the four horsemen of the apocalypse from ending the world as we know it?"

Dean grimaced. He hated it when people said things like that. Not that they were wrong. But to Dean, he'd done what anyone would have in that situation. He wasn't anything special. Besides, there were other people just as valuable there beside him. He couldn't have done it alone. That was for sure.

"Let's stay focused on the job at hand," Dean said. "We'll go in.

Just keep your eyes open for trouble. The cops will be here soon enough."

He hopped out and moved back to the compartment doors down the side of the ambulance. He grabbed the med and trauma bags and walked around to the back. Since Barry was driving today, it was Dean's turn to take the lead with the patients. They traded off and took turns every other day, even though Dean was senior to Barry, at least in Station U terms. He'd been working there longer and had more experience handling their supernatural patients.

Barry had already opened up the back and climbed inside to retrieve their heart monitor and oxygen and airway bags. He climbed back out to stand next to Dean on the street. Dean nodded and together they started across the sidewalk with their gear.

The entrance to the apartments above the storefront was up several steps. Dean glanced back at the ambulance. They were going to need the stair chair to save them from hauling the stretcher up to the third floor. He turned to Barry to say something, but his partner had already opened the side compartment housing the folding chair with wheels. It was invaluable to assist them in getting patients up and down stairs safely.

Dean walked up the steps and reached for the buzzer to contact apartment 3. He didn't push the button. One glance at the door told him the door's latch was broken.

Barry stepped up behind Dean carrying the stair chair along with the heart monitor and oxygen and airway bags. With the straps from the monitor and bags across his chest and the stair chair held in front of him, Dean knew his partner was loaded down. He pulled the door open and waited for Barry to enter first before following him inside.

The interior lights did little to illuminate the entry hall. Everything seemed grimy and more than a little run-down.

Dean headed forward to the bottom of the stairs and climbed to the second floor. Apartments one and two were to the right and left. That meant, three was one more floor up, as he'd suspected. He started up the next set of stairs and heard the sobbing right away. It sounded like a woman, but he couldn't be sure.

Heeding his own earlier warning to Barry, Dean proceeded with caution, ready to defend himself or run if need be. As he neared the landing, the door to his left stood ajar. The one to his right was closed. A tarnished brass number four was tacked to the wooden frame above it.

A glance to the left to check the frame above the open doorway revealed no number, though there were holes where the screws had once held a number in place. Still, this was likely the location they sought.

Dean glanced inside, past the partially open door.

A woman sat on a ratty, brown plaid couch in the center of the room. A tall, heavily muscled man in a grimy white tank top paced the floor next to her. She flinched a little every time he walked past her.

"Hi, I'm Dean Flynn," he said as he rapped on the door. "Did someone here call paramedics?"

The man spun around, his motions fluid, almost catlike. Dean, given the type of patients they treated, wondered right away if the guy was a shifter of some sort. There had to be a connection to an Unusual creature of some sort with this call.

"It's about damn time you got here. I've had to listen to her whining for too long as it is."

The woman looked up at Dean, her sunken eyes making the dark circles around them look even worse. Her whole emaciated body looked as if she had had little to eat or drink for days. She clutched her left arm tightly to her stomach and hunched over it.

The guy pacing next to her looked like he hadn't missed a meal in a long while. He wasn't overweight, but you didn't get muscles like that if you missed a lot of meals. Something wasn't right here.

Barry arrived in the doorway.

Dean moved inside to kneel on the floor next to the woman. "Hi, I'm Dean. What's your name?"

"You don't need her name. Just fix up her arm. She had another stupid accident."

"I need to know her name for my report. I'll need yours, too, since you're the one who called us."

"I'm Manton. Her name's Verity. You don't need our last names."

Dean turned back to the woman and smiled. "Hi, Verity. Can you tell me what's wrong? Is it your arm?"

"Of course it's her arm. She was clumsy as usual and fell down. Again."

"I'd like to hear it from her directly, if you don't mind."

Manton stopped, glaring down at Dean. His fists clenched and he loomed over the kneeling paramedic.

Barry must've decided the situation was getting a bit too tense. He came up to stand behind Dean, ready to back up his partner if needed. Dean was glad he was close by. Everything about this call seemed odd. A chill of danger ran down his spine.

"Alright, Verity, why don't you tell me what happened while I get your blood pressure and pulse."

"She don't need none of that. She just needs you to fix her arm."

Manton leaned over Dean again.

Barry slid into place between them, causing Manton to take a step back. "Sir, I'm going to need you to give my partner some room to work. Why don't you show me where she fell?"

Manton muttered something unintelligible in a way that almost resembled a deep, rumbling growl. Dean ignored it and focused his attention on Verity.

While Barry distracted the man, Dean leaned in to take her blood pressure. He pushed up the long sleeve covering her unhurt arm and concealed his gasp with a disguised cough as he spotted the bruises all along her arm.

While he wrapped the blood pressure cuff around her arm, he studied the bruises. They varied in color from deep purple and blue to paler yellow and green, showing various stages of healing. This woman had taken a beating, and more than once judging from her injuries. This didn't happen falling down the stairs, and if she was a shifter, too, she probably healed faster than a human did. That meant these past injuries had been even more severe than he'd normally expect from such bruising. It all had him questioning how today's injury had happened.

Dean glanced at the open doorway to the stairs outside, wondering how far out the police unit was. He couldn't call to check on them over the radio. Manton would overhear him, which might escalate his already edgy temper.

Dean pushed the button on the heart monitor to pump up the automated blood pressure cuff and smiled at Verity. "While that's working, why don't you tell me what happened in your own words."

She glanced past Dean at Manton and then said, in a thick Scottish accent, "It's like he said. I'm clumsy and had a bit of a fall."

"Okay, why don't you show me your other arm. I need to see what I can do about to help you."

She was afraid of Manton. Given everything he'd seen so far, Dean was pretty sure the hulking brute had injured her. There could be any number of reasons she lied about it. It didn't change the paramedic's obligation to help treat her injury at the moment. The circumstances did affect his need to report his suspicions to the proper authorities. He glanced at the door again, wishing the special station U police units arrived soon.

Turning his attention back to Verity, Dean examined her left arm. It was pretty obvious it was broken. The deformity stood out as soon as she shifted her body far enough for him to see it clearly. Her injured arm had as many bruises on it as the other one did.

Dean's anger welled up inside him as his imagination fueled his suspicions. He wished Jaz was here. While he was a healer and not much of a fighter, his wife was a different matter. If Jaz was here, she'd take Manton outside and teach him a thing to two about roughing up women.

Jaz, as the leader of a Hunter Clan, was a formidable martial artist and fighter. Some would say she was also a killer, at least if you were a demon or rogue supernatural of some sort. Dean didn't like to think of her that way, though. She wasn't the same bloodthirsty hunter he'd thought she was when they'd met over a year before.

Dean moved his hands with care as he palpated the injured arm around the deformed area. He could feel the crepitus, the slight vibration from the movement of the broken bones rubbing against each other under her skin. The swelling around the injury was already pretty substantial. It looked like it had happened as much as a few hours ago. Under the bruises, he spotted a unique sort of tattoo on the inside of the forearm. It looked like a panther's head, or maybe a mountain lion of some sort. Did it denote her shifter type?

"Verity, when did you injure your arm?" Dean studied her face, trying to see past her pain and determine what sort of Unusual she was.

"Um," she checked to see where Manton was before continuing. "It happened just before we sat down to eat. Manton likes me to make sure his food is ready as soon as he gets back from work. I was a little late tonight. I guess he startled me when he came home. I just sort of tripped and fell, that's all."

The kitchen table sat a few feet away. Dean scanned the single place setting with a few scraps remaining on the plate. It was clear at least one occupant had finished their meal before calling 911 for the ambulance. He could guess who that was. His anger flared again.

Wrestling his temper under control, Dean smiled at Verity, "I'm guessing from your accent you're not from around here? Where are you from originally?"

Verity shot another look in Manton's direction, then back at Dean.

"Don't worry about him, Verity. My partner will keep him busy talking while we chat. I'll fix it so your arm doesn't hurt as much while you tell me. I hear a bit of a brogue in your voice. Scottish, right?"

Verity nodded. "I came here about a year ago. It's hard to say exactly when. I used to live near the coast on one of the Orkney Islands."

That surprised him. He didn't think there were any big cats native to the U.K. "So you're not a werepanther or some other cat shifter?"

She frowned and flashed a little anger of her own. "No, I'm a Selkie. Why would you think I'm one of them?"

"It's just the tattoo on your arm. I figured…"

Verity immediately swiped at the tattoo with her free hand, as if trying to wipe it away. The anger flared in her eyes again, then faded as quickly as it came.

Dean changed the subject while he worked on stabilizing her arm. "What brought you here to Elk City?"

"Um, I came when I was, uh, brought here. I don't know how long ago it was. I came here to, uh, work. That's why Manton got me; to keep his apartment nice."

Dean doubted she was an ordinary maid. Not in this neighborhood. Plus, no actual maid would put up with the abuse, would they?

He pulled two short, padded splints from the trauma bag and began stabilizing Verity's arm. He started by attempting to align the bones as much as he could, then carefully wrapped gauze around the splints to hold the arm in place on either side of the break.

While he worked, Dean thought back to the previous year. Her words triggered a memory from a refresher class he took at Headquarters. The continuing education program taught the paramedics how to recognize human trafficking victims in the field. This had all the hallmarks of that sort of relationship: The controlling over-watch of the trafficker, the fear and deference of the trafficked, the evidence of abuse.

If he was right, he needed to get her separated from Manton and try to take her to the hospital where he could get her the help she needed. If her trafficker was a werepanther or other were-cat type and she was a Selkie, a seal shifter, it was definitely odd. Shifter varieties like that rarely mixed.

Dean looked back over his shoulder. Barry was doing a good job keeping Manton away, continuing asking questions and jotting the answers in an open note taking app on the tablet. The male shifter kept craning his neck past Dean's partner to see what Dean was doing.

Finishing up splinting the arm, Dean got Verity ready to go to the hospital. She needed an X-ray and a follow-up with an orthopedic surgeon to see if she needed surgery or just a cast.

"Verity, let me pack up my stuff, then I'll help you up and we can head out to the ambulance."

The instant he said she was coming with him to the ambulance, her eyes darted to Manton and then back to Dean. She looked down at the floor. "I may not leave."

"Verity, you need an X-ray for your arm. A doctor needs to look at that break and make sure it'll heal straight. You understand that, right?"

Verity shook her head and behind Dean, Manton pushed past Barry and came over to stand beside the frightened woman.

"She doesn't need to go anywhere. You wrapped her arm. She will heal on her own. You two must go. Now."

The order to leave was as clear as the threatening stance the male shifter had taken. Dean didn't care and opened his mouth to argue. He stopped as a familiar voice sounded from the apartment's doorway.

"Dean, Barry, I was in the neighborhood and spotted your ambulance. You two need any help?"

Officer O'Malley, one of the Elk City police department's special officers dealing with Unusual cases and crimes, stood in the doorway. He placed one hand to rest almost casually on the butt of his holstered pistol as he waited for an answer.

Dean smiled, glad to have O'Malley there at last to give them some support. "Hello officer, I was just telling Verity here that she needed to go to the hospital so we can get her arm checked out. I'm pretty sure it's broken. Her companion is hindering us from caring for our patient."

The officer set his lips in a firm line and nodded.

Dean was pretty sure the policeman understood at least part of the situation. He was as good at his job as the paramedics were at theirs.

O'Malley crossed the apartment to stand next to Manton. He stared into the looming were-cat's eyes for a few seconds, then glanced down at Verity. "You go with these nice paramedics while I chat with your friend here for a few minutes. He can come meet you at the hospital once I'm finished."

Manton started to say something.

O'Malley glared at him and the werepanther backed down.

Dean stood and gathered the gear.

Barry came over and stopped him. "You help her down the stairs. She can walk herself out with you along to steady her. I'll make a couple trips and get the gear loaded up."

"Sounds good. Thanks." Dean turned to the woman and said, "Let me help you up." He offered a hand to her and waited.

This was a critical moment. He knew she needed help, in more ways than one. But, if she didn't want to go to the hospital, he couldn't force her. He forced himself to relax with a deep breath while he waited patiently for her response.

Verity looked at Manton, who stood glaring at Officer O'Malley, then shifted her gaze to Dean. With a small nod, she reached up and took his hand, letting him help her up to her feet. Without looking back, the woman followed Dean out of the apartment and down the stairs to the waiting ambulance.

Chapter 2

IT DIDN'T TAKE Dean long to get Verity settled in the ambulance once he got her downstairs. By the time Barry had everything packed away from their call, Dean had taken another set of vitals and started an IV to deliver an initial dose of four milligrams of morphine for her pain.

"Let's see if that takes the edge off for you. I can give you some more if you need it."

"Thank you, it doesn't hurt so bad."

The way she winced when she shifted in her seat on the stretcher told Dean otherwise. He made a mental note to reassess her pain level in another five minutes. They were about fifteen minutes from the hospital, and he could give her up to ten milligrams without having to call in for a doctor's order.

Given how she was handling the pain so far, he figured it would be enough. They could always give her more once she got to the emergency department at Elk City Medical Center.

The door opened in the cab up front and Barry shouted back through the narrow passageway leading back to the patient compartment. "You all set?"

"We're good to go. ECMC, nice and easy. Mind the potholes, too."

"Already on it, partner. I'll make it a nice smooth ride for you both."

The big ambulance could bounce a bit on its suspension, especially on the local streets with all the potholes after this year's heavy winter. The city was still way behind on filling in all the gaps. Barry would have his work cut out for him trying to avoid them on the way to the hospital. Luckily, they didn't need to rush using their lights and sirens, so they could take their time.

The ambulance started forward. Behind them, Manton ran out into the street, calling for them to stop. Dean turned to the front and called out, "Keep going. He can get his own ride to the hospital."

"I agree," the other paramedic replied from the driver's seat.

Dean nodded at how they'd separated Verity from Manton. It was essential to get her to the hospital alone. Dean would report his suspicions to the nurses at ECMC. The staff had an excellent relationship with local social workers and local shelters. If anyone could get her to safety and in a place where she would open up and tell her story, it was those specialized resources. Dean and Barry had done their jobs by recognizing it in the field. Now they had to follow up and send the report up the chain of care.

It took almost twenty minutes to arrive at the hospital. Barry had taken a round-about route, driving them over some of the better maintained roads rather than going the quickest way. As he backed into an open slot in the ambulance bay outside the ER, Dean gathered his supplies and prepped Verity to go inside.

He'd given her two more doses of morphine, maxing out the ten-milligram dose he could give. It seemed to be enough for now. Verity no longer winced at every movement of the surrounding ambulance.

"Verity, once we get inside, you'll be safe. You can talk to the nurses and doctors in there and they'll help you, with everything you might need. Do you understand? They can help with everything."

"I do. Thank you. Will—" She stopped and looked out through the back windows of the ambulance. "Will Manton be here?"

Dean shook his head. "If you don't want him to come back to your room and see you, they can keep him away. Just tell them what you want. No one can hurt you here."

Verity nodded and fell silent, continuing to search the street outside the back windows.

Dean and Barry unloaded her on the stretcher and rolled her inside the ER. Dean looked to see who the charge nurse on duty was. They posted nursing assignments on the big dry-erase board by the nurses' station. Next to the word "Charge" was the name "Moore."

A smile spread across Dean's face. Ashley was working tonight. He hadn't seen her in a while, but he knew she was taking some shifts at the hospital now that she was back in town.

An Eldara Sister, Ashley was an angelic messenger of the gods or whoever the beings were that lived in the higher planes. In her case, she was one of the Sisters, a healing angel and a more than competent nurse. She had a history throughout time of helping others advance medical and nursing care. She had been one of his companions in the fight against the four horsemen months before.

He smiled as Ashely's tall form walked from behind the counter, a broad smile on her face. "Hey, Dean. I heard Barry on the scanner announcing you were on the way. What do you have for us?"

The first thing Dean noticed was her hair. She'd cut it short, very short, in a sort of pixie cut. It surprised him. He'd never seen her without her long brunette hair, usually pulled back in a ponytail. He had to admit, though; the look didn't detract from her angelic features. He shook himself. He was married now.

He and Ashley had a history, once, long ago. But that was in the past, and Dean had moved on. Now, she and Jaz were close friends, which was more than a little awkward for him at times.

Dean shifted his mind back to his patient. He nodded to the woman on the stretcher beside him. "This is Verity. I'm pretty sure she fractured her arm. She also might benefit from a room with some privacy because of some special concerns."

Ashley's eyes narrowed a little at the request for a room isolated from the others. He hoped she trusted him enough to follow his lead until he could explain the situation.

Ashley smiled at Verity and said, "Take her back to room sixteen. It's near our break room in the rear of the ER, which should be off the beaten track enough to keep her from any prying eyes."

Dean nodded. With Barry's help, he rolled the woman to the room at the back corner of the emergency department.

Another nurse, Barbara, came in as they moved their patient over to the hospital bed. She took Dean's verbal report on Verity's injury. He didn't expound on his suspicions here. He'd fill in Ashley out front and let her handle the relevant referrals. That was her job as the charge nurse.

"Verity, Barb here will take good care of you from here. Don't be afraid to share anything you want with her, or any other people on the staff. You can trust the folks here to take care of you."

Barb was one of the nurses who knew of the existence of Unusuals living among the human inhabitants of Elk City. She'd protect Verity's Selkie identity from the normal human patients in the ER. She'd also work with Ashley to get the girl the help she needed.

Dean and Barry took the stretcher back around front. On the way, Dean heard a familiar voice shouting in the waiting room through a pair of double doors. It was Manton, and he didn't sound too happy and being told to wait there.

"Barry, you got the stretcher and the supply restock? I want to fill Ashley in on the situation with the noise out front. We don't want Manton barging back here without someone to stop him."

"I got it. I'll see you back out at the ambulance."

Dean nodded and crossed over to the nurses' station. Ashley and the others had heard the commotion. As Dean approached, Ashley hung up the phone on the desk in front of her.

"Hey, Ash, that guy shouting out in the waiting room was at the scene earlier. He says he's Verity's boyfriend. Something weird is going on with them and we had a hard time separating him from her."

"I just called security down. Do you think he's got some kind of charm going on or other magic?"

"Not sure. My gut reaction is she's a victim of human trafficking or whatever you call the Unusual version of it."

"They're all humans, Dean," Ashley chided him. "You know that."

"Yeah, I do. Sorry." Dean of all people, having recently found out he was half-Eldara himself, should be more careful with his words.

"Anyway, if you can, I'd keep them apart until you can get her to open up about what's going on."

Ashley nodded. "I'll get back to see her myself once we get the guy out front calmed down. I don't want him upsetting anyone else."

"Officer O'Malley came to the scene and dealt with him there. You know him?"

"I do," Ashley turned to one of the clerks seated next where she stood. "Jack, see if you can call in to ECPD's station U team and get O'Malley to stop by if he's in the area. Tell them we have a situation and individual here he just handled at an ambulance call."

Jack nodded and picked up the phone to dial in.

"Uh, I haven't seen you since just after—" Dean said, trailing off.

"What? The end of the world?"

Dean couldn't hide his wide-eyed expression. He looked around at the nurses nearby to see if they overheard.

Ashley laughed, "Don't worry, the whole shift today is clued in. Most of the ER staff is at this point. There was no way to contain everything the four horsemen caused without explaining about the supernatural world all around them."

That surprised Dean. He hadn't heard that before. "Okay, somebody should've passed that down to us."

"I'm sure it's much the same for your colleagues in the Fire Department."

Dean thought about it and nodded. When he'd first started on the job just over two years before, he'd been part of a very small collection of responders and health professionals who knew about the secret world all around them. Since the near apocalypse, it was less of a secret. Having the living dead walk the streets opened more than a few eyes.

Still, the vast majority of the Elk City population had bought the health department line about a viral encephalitis outbreak that caused violent behaviors in those infected.

Deciding to change the subject, Dean pointed to Ashley's head. "I like your hair. When did you cut it?"

"Not that long after things settled down. It has been so long since

I've had short hair. It's been at least a thousand years. I'd forgotten how light it makes my head feel. I'm surprised Jaz didn't tell you about it."

"Why would she?" Dean hadn't known Ashley and his wife had been in contact recently.

"Jaz and I have lunch every week or so when she's not traveling. She likes to keep up on what's going on in town from a supernatural perspective."

His wife had not told him about it, and Dean wondered why she hadn't mentioned it.

Ashley must have spotted the perplexed look on his face. "Don't get annoyed with her. No woman likes to remind her husband of an ex-girlfriend, no matter how safe she knows it to be. Don't worry. We didn't talk about you, at least not too much."

She said the last with a little giggle and picked up a tablet computer from behind the nurses' station as two security guards entered through the doors leading to the rest of the hospital. "I have to go help these two deal with the disturbance out front. I'll see you again. I'm on shift all week while a few of the regular charge nurses are at a conference."

"That's nice to know. It's always a relief knowing you're here when we bring in critical patients."

As Ashley left, Dean checked his watch as he headed out to the ambulance. The shift was almost over and that meant he could get home and see Jaz. She'd returned that afternoon from a week-long trip to check on her company's European operations. It would be good to have her home again. She was supposed to be in town for a few weeks this time around. The apartment would be much less lonely with her there.

Chapter 3

BACK AT STATION U, tucked away back in a nondescript industrial park on the edge of town, Dean and Barry got the ambulance parked and restocked just in time for Bill and Lynne to arrive and take over for the next shift.

As Dean entered the crew quarters, a wonderful smell struck him and saliva flowed into his mouth from whatever Freddy had going in the kitchen.

"Freddy, you culinary genius, what glorious thing have you come up with for dinner?"

A shuffling gray form walked out of the small duty kitchen at the far side of the room. "I got some fresh mussels in from Kristof over at Sabatani's. He had some extras in the shipment he just got in, so he called over to see if I wanted them. I said sure. It's a good excuse to make you all a seafood chowder."

Dean gave Freddy a gentle high five. He had to be careful, so he didn't knock anything loose. Freddy was the station's resident cook. He also was a homeless zombie who traded his pre-death skills as a top international chef for a place to live.

"That sounds awesome, my man. Can you put some in a container for me to take home? Jaz just got back from her trip and I'd like to take some dinner home to enjoy with her."

Bill laughed from where he sat at the computer terminal, checking in with the daily reports. "What's wrong with the rest of us? You too good to eat with us heathens?"

"Leave him alone, Bill," Lynne said. "The two of them are still technically honeymooners."

"It doesn't count if the two of them haven't actually gone on a honeymoon," Bill countered. "Dean can't seem to get his act in gear to plan one."

"Hey, I'm working on it. I've just got to find a time when Jaz is in town for longer than a few days and when I can get off work." Dean wasn't lying, nor was he trying to evade Bill's point. He'd been working through a few ideas on where to take Jaz for a real, honest to God honeymoon. He didn't need his coworkers to remind him they hadn't been able to go away together yet.

Barry came in from the ambulance bay and let out a sigh. "I'm hungry enough to eat an entire hog. I hope you made a lot of whatever it is I smell, Freddy."

"I did, don't worry. I'll have it on the table in a few minutes."

"Don't forget to check for missing bits before you serve it," Barry cautioned. "I found your pinky finger in my salad last week."

Dean laughed. That had been hilarious, even if he'd almost had to Heimlich his partner to clear the choking zombie finger from his throat.

"It's not funny when it's in your food, believe me," Barry chided all of them. "I could have died and then what would you have done?"

Dean waved off Barry's comment. "We'd have saved you just like we do for everyone else. Stop complaining. You can't expect food this good for free and not have some trade-offs." Dean turned to check himself out of the shift on the computer.

Bill finished what he was doing on the other terminal and turned to Dean. "Anything interesting on your shift today?"

"There was our most recent call. It seemed like we'd stumbled on a woman who'd been a victim of human trafficking or something like it."

Dean related the events of the last call of the day and what he'd done at the hospital to report it. "I hope she takes the help she's offered."

Lynne shook her head. "I was in that same class as you were, Dean. You heard what the instructor said about the percentages who were rescued and those who opted to remain under the control of their captors. It has conditioned a lot of them to think no one will help them."

Bill said, "Didn't Brynne say something about a few similar calls being reported recently by some of the other shifts? I seem to remember seeing it here in one of her daily updates."

"If she did, I must have glossed over it," Dean said. He'd have to go back and check his email for that notice. "Where is Brynne? Isn't she on as supervisor tonight?"

Lynne nodded. "She'll be here later. She texted me she had a meeting to attend with the Chief before he went home for the night. The paramedic class just graduated, and I think she has her eye on at least one of them for Station U."

Brynne had been Dean's training officer until she'd nearly died from a gunshot wound. Only a last-minute save by her vampire boyfriend had saved her, sort of. Now she was back at work, but she could only work night shifts after sundown, and that limited her contact with the rest of the human fire department leadership who worked during the day.

"What did her email about trafficking say, Bill?" Dean asked.

He couldn't put his finger on it, but the fact that the other station U staff might have had similar ambulance calls told Dean that Verity's plight wasn't an isolated one.

"What are you thinking, partner?" Barry asked. "You think there's some sort of ring operating here?

"I don't know, but if there were, why bring them here where more people know about Unusuals," Dean said. "I could see a regular human trafficking ring setting up shop here. Putting one in place dealing in Unusuals here seems like they're asking for a run in with us or our police counterparts."

"Maybe you should ask Jaz that question," Lynne suggested. "With her connections both here and abroad, she might be able to find out something."

"I'll mention it to her. I know she'd want to help out. That's not something she has much patience with at all." Dean scanned down through his old emails but didn't see the one to which his colleague was referring. "Bill, I can't find the message."

"I remember it was a Merrow girl they found. She was in pretty bad shape when the crew got to her. I'm not sure if she survived or not. She had numerous health issues when they brought her in." Bill had turned back to the computer. He scrolled down the screen and pointed at one entry. He must have found the email because he clicked on the reference link to open the actual patient report.

"Merrow?" Dean asked. "That's an Irish sea fae, right?"

Lynne nodded. "They're the classic mermaids and mermen you hear about in most sailor's stories. They have tails and gills when in the water, but they can shift to human form to walk around on land if they want, at least for a limited time. There aren't many of them ashore, though. They usually prefer their home waters and communities."

"How did she get all the way over here, then?" Dean asked. "It's strange. I can't help but think there's a connection of some sort between the two calls. Mine was a rare variety of water Unusual, too. This one was a Selkie, a seal-shifter."

Bill shook his head. "They're even rarer than the Merrow are. They come from the islands off the northern coast of Scotland if I remember my legends and lore correctly."

Dean tried to pull the pieces together in his head. It felt like it was all connected, but he didn't have enough pieces yet. "Let's all keep our eyes open and check with the community when we get out and about. Maybe someone has heard something. I'll get with Gibbie and the rest of the disaster CERT response team to follow up for us, too. They've been champing at the bit for a chance to get some action again. Maybe if between us we turn over enough rocks, we'll kick something loose to see the connection."

The others nodded. Dean knew their informal paramedic community in the station would keep an eye out for similar patients and situations. Hopefully, they'd see something else that would lead to a clue.

Freddy came from the kitchen again, carrying a large Dutch oven to the break room table where he set it down next to a bowl of salad and a basket of rolls. He smiled at the assembled paramedics with a snaggle-toothed grin. "Dinner's ready. Get it while it's hot."

"Hand check," Barry called.

Everyone laughed as Freddy held up his hands, displaying all ten fingers, mostly intact. Dean had reattached the detached pinky finger the previous week using some super glue.

Freddy pointed back to the kitchen. "Dean, I have a plastic container back in the kitchen so you can take some home to have with Jaz. I added some dinner rolls and the salad, too. They're in a reusable nylon bag next to the container. Don't forget to bring back the bag and the containers, please."

"Thanks, Freddy. I'll remember. I know Jaz'll appreciate it." Dean stood up and said, "I think I'll get going. I'll follow up later with you all if I find out anything from my wife."

"I'll start an email chain with the different shifts so we can bring Brook and Tammy, along with the backup shift, into the conversation."

Dean nodded and walked over to the kitchen to grab the food Freddie had packed up for him.

Barry, Lynne, and Bill had changed subjects and were grilling Barry about a recent date. Dean chuckled to himself as he headed out to the parking lot. The crews of Station U were a close-knit group. There were very few secrets between them.

As he walked towards his pickup truck, he realized how oddly dark it was. A glance back at the Station told him why. The light on the pole by the building was out. It usually lit up the parking area bright as day. Dean shook his head. He'd have to tell Brynne about it. She'd report it to the industrial park's owners and get it fixed.

Dean turned back towards his truck and set the food containers on the hood so he could reach his keys. He grunted in surprise and pain as something slammed into him. The force knocked him down so hard he skidded on his chest across the asphalt for several feet. It took the wind out of him and he struggled to catch his breath.

Trying to gather his wits while getting up onto his hands and knees, Dean turned his head to see what had hit him. Expecting to see a vehicle, it surprised him to see a dark form stalking his way, red eyes glowing in the blackness of the parking area.

A ripping snarl followed by a guttural voice came from the figure. "You shouldn't have interfered with Verity, human. She was mine to do with as I pleased."

The dark form had gotten close enough now that Dean made out the humanoid form of a werepanther, the cat-like features blending with Manton's human face.

Dean pushed upward, trying to rise to his feet.

Manton took two steps towards the struggling paramedic, kicking Dean in the gut as he rose.

The air whooshed from Dean's lungs as the powerful blow lifted him from the ground and rolled him over and over until he came to rest against the curb beside Barry's SUV.

He put out a hand to use the vehicle to help get to his feet so he could defend himself. Dean didn't have too much hope to hold off an attack by an enraged shifter of any type for long. Still, if he were on his feet, he could make a dash for the station door. Help was there if he could reach it.

Gasping to catch his breath, Dean tried to call out for help. The building was pretty well insulated. He wasn't sure they'd hear him inside or not, but he had to try.

Manton stalked forward; his clawed hands extended towards Dean.

"H-help." He still hadn't caught his breath. The croaking rasp of Dean's voice had little volume, certainly not enough for the other medics inside to hear him. He worked to draw in a deeper breath to call out again.

Dean got to his feet, swaying as he stood. He propped his back against the SUV's rear door to steady himself and let out another pitifully weak call for help.

The shifter came closer and Dean lifted his fists, ready to defend himself as best he could, even if it seemed like a futile gesture.

Manton had almost reached him when a shadow streaked by, coming out of nowhere. It knocked Manton from his feet and sent the shifter rolling across the parking area.

Dean stared into the night, trying to see who or what had rescued him. The shadow moved to his right and he tried to pierce the darkness to see who it was.

"You alright, Dean?" Brynne asked.

He let out a sigh of relief at hearing his former partner's voice. "Yeah, I am now that you're here."

The vampire turned towards the werepanther who had regained his feet. A low snarl came from Manton's throat as he readied himself for a fight.

Brynne rushed forward, moving so fast, she was little more than a blur. She charged the shifter, colliding with Manton at full speed.

This time he was ready for her and took the hit without getting knocked down. For a while, the two of them were an indistinguishable swirling mass of battling darkness in the middle of the parking lot.

Dean considered running for the station door to get more help, but the fight ended before he took a step.

Brynne knocked Manton to the ground. Before he could rise, she kicked him so hard he flew over twenty feet across the parking lot to slam into the wooden telephone pole beside the building.

The werepanther rolled away from the pole and climbed back to his feet. From the way he carried himself, Brynne had injured him, perhaps seriously.

Before she could move in to follow up on her attack, Manton completed his shift to full panther form. The big cat, black as night, ran off into the darkness behind the Station U building.

Brynne stared after the cat, peering into the murky darkness around them. She glanced at Dean. "He's gone. Are you okay?"

"I am now. Thank you for saving me."

"You'll always be my probie, Dean. I'm not going to let anyone hurt you on my watch. Who was that guy? Did you know him?"

"He was the companion of a patient we had earlier. We thought she might be caught up in a human trafficking thing and separated them long enough to get her some help. Ashley was the charge nurse tonight and said she'd take care of it. It looks like she was successful separating them based on what that guy said when he attacked me."

Dean took a step towards his truck and groaned, clutching his ribs.

He didn't think they were broken, but he'd be sore for the next few days.

"You're hurt. Come on inside so we can check you over."

Dean shook his head. "No, I'm okay. I'll get Jaz to help me manage the scrapes and bruises when I get home."

Brynne looked like she was about to order him to come inside, but she changed her mind. "Call in when you get home and if it gets worse, get yourself to the ER. Don't be a hero. Got me?"

"Me, a hero? You know me better than that. I'll be fine. I promise."

"I'm serious. Either tell me you'll do as I say, or I'll pick you up and carry you inside right now."

Dean held up his hands in surrender. "I'll call, I promise."

Brynne nodded. Dean picked up his keys from the ground by the pickup truck. He unlocked the doors and put the food inside on the seat, pushing it over to the passenger side as he climbed in.

A glance out the window as he backed out showed Brynn standing there with her arms crossed, lit by the taillights from his truck. He waved before he pulled onto the street and headed home.

Chapter 4

DEAN WINCED as his wife tended to his injuries.

"You should have listened to Brynne. Your ribs could be broken." Jaz wiped at the scrapes on his arms with a damp washcloth, cleaning the remaining dirt and grit from the parking lot out of his wounds.

Dean twisted around where he sat on the closed lid of the toilet and probing with his fingertips at his side. "They're not broken. Just bruised, I think."

Jaz snorted in response as she turned to soak the cloth in the sink full of warm water.

Dean knew she didn't approve of his decision to avoid getting checked out any more than Brynne did. He didn't care. He just wanted to eat and get some sleep. There was nothing wrong with him he couldn't deal with in the morning. He'd head in to the ER if it seemed more serious then.

"Tell me who it was who did this to you again? You said it was a werepanther?"

"That's how I'd describe the guy. I knew he was some kind of cat shifter based on what I picked up from him during the ambulance call. Seeing him in the parking lot confirmed it. He was a big black cat. That's a panther, right?"

Jaz nodded; her lips pressed together in a thin line. She dabbed at his scrapes, saying nothing.

Dean knew his wife well enough to know she was plotting revenge of her own against the creature who'd made the mistake of attacking her husband. He didn't want her to go off on some sort of vengeance hunt.

"Hon, look at me. I'm going to be fine. Brynne scared him off and I don't think he'll be back. Besides, he has to know I'm aware of who he was. He's probably a hundred miles away by now, figuring the police are after him. I'm sure Brynne reported it."

"The police are the least of his worries. They won't put a silver bullet in his skull."

"Jaz, seriously, let it go. It's more important that we focus on the good news from the attack."

"Good news? Like what?"

"His attack means we freed Verity of his control," Dean replied. "I call that a win. She can get the help she needs, and the authorities can find out where she came from."

Jaz nodded. "If there's a trafficking ring set up here in Elk City, it's got to be rooted out. There has been no werecat activity from the Cartels around here for quite a while. My father made sure of that. Maybe they think they can come back now that he's dead."

"I didn't know there was a cartel of werepanthers."

"Most of the werecats in North and South America answer to one or two criminal cartels run by old-school families of werejaguars. They're very rare and supposedly super powerful among their own kind. They have an agreement with Errington regarding this kind of thing. I have to look into this."

"O'Malley was there, Jaz. Let the ECPD handle it. If there's a ring like that operating here, they'll take care of it."

He could tell from her expression Jaz wasn't convinced. She threw the supplies they didn't use back into the first aid kit and dropped it on top of the toilet tank lid. "You know as well as I do how the Unusual community is with getting help from human law enforcement agencies. They're afraid to reach out for help for even the simplest of reasons. Something like this would go unreported by almost everyone."

Dean shrugged. "I had to report it and help Verity deal with it. It's required. Besides, it's just the right thing to do. Brynne's looking into it, too, so that means James and Rudy will get involved. You've got enough on your plate working to get Errington Security's international operations back online. Let someone else handle it."

The Hunter clan leader shook her head, her blond ponytail swaying behind her. "Nope, keeping this city clean of scum like that is as much my job as it is the local authorities. I want this place to be a place of safety and refuge when I come home. It should be somewhere my family and I can relax without worrying about getting jumped in a parking lot."

Jaz turned back to the sink, wringing out the washcloth. She stared in the mirror for a few seconds than sighed. "Look, I'll stand down. Let me have my intel guy check into some things, though. These types move in certain circles. We might be able to get a handle on them where local police investigators can't."

Dean knew better than to argue with her about stuff like this. It was her company, and it was her decision to make if she wanted. He could've had a say, but he'd turned down the executive vice president position she'd offered him. He wasn't ready to give up working on the streets just yet. Of course, that meant he didn't have the right to say no to things like this, other than to express concern as a spouse. The dynamic between them might change someday, but for now it was the way they'd drawn the lines between their two jobs.

He changed the subject. He checked his injured arms. "This is good enough. I feel better already. Let me get a shirt on and we can go reheat the dinner Freddy made for us."

Jaz smiled and nodded. "It smelled good." Anger spread across her face. "I'm glad that shifter waited until you put the food down. If he'd ruined dinner, nothing would keep me from hunting him down."

"Great, at least I know where your priorities lie," Dean said, laughing.

"What can I say? Freddy's food is just that good."

The two of them went into the kitchen and started working side by side on getting the meal together.

Fifteen minutes later, as they sat eating, Dean asked, "Have you thought anymore about getting some time away from work so we can finally take that honeymoon trip we've been talking about?"

Her hesitation to respond was all the answer he needed. "Jaz, you promised. You said after you got back from Europe you'd have some time to do this."

"I know what I said, but I have more on my plate now than when I left. I deal with one issue, and three more crop up. I don't know how my father did it all."

Dean leaned over the table and put his hand atop hers. "He delegated the small stuff to his management team."

"There isn't any small stuff. And there isn't any management team." Jaz shook her head. "There's a rogue pack of werewolves roaming around Eastern Europe. I've had two teams in Budapest go missing while tracking them. I'm going to have to go myself if the head of European ops doesn't get it under control."

"I haven't met him yet, have I?"

"Her, and no, you haven't. I just put Elsa in place two months ago when I found out the last guy, a former German special forces operator, was taking payoffs to look the other way on some of our security accounts."

"How did you find her?"

"Rudy recommended her to me. She's the oldest daughter of the senior pack leader in Belgium."

Dean's eyebrows shot up. "You hired an Unusual for the job? That's pretty progressive of you considering where you were on the subject when we first met."

Jaz smiled. "I've had a change of heart. After all, I'm married to a half-Eldara."

"I might as well be plain old human if I'm going to keep getting my butt kicked by every evil bad guy to come along."

"I've offered to teach you some weapons and self-defense techniques. I could get you a concealed carry permit once you're trained."

Dean shook his head. "No, you know how I feel about this. I'm a healer, not a fighter. Let's just call it a division of labor in our marriage. One total badass is enough."

"Flattery will get you nowhere, dear. I'm serious. You need to be able to protect yourself. You'd think after everything that's happened to you over the last year and a half, you'd understand that."

"Nope, we both have our roles in this family. I'm happy with the way things stand." Uncomfortable with the talk about weapons and fighting, Dean shifted the conversation. "So this Elsa you hired is a Lycan, just like the ones you're trying to hunt down? It seems like she'd be a good fit if she's willing to do the dirty work. Most werewolves I know don't like packs breaking the rules. It only draws unwanted human attention."

"The biggest problem is getting the strike teams to listen to her. That she's both a woman, and a shifter is causing a problem among the older, more established members."

"They listen to you, right?"

"Mostly," Jaz replied and held up her hand. "Before you say anything, I'm dealing with the ones who are the worst. It's not just my gender. It's my age, too. They don't think I have the experience to lead the organization. I've got some ideas on how to show them I'm the boss in more than title only."

"How?"

"That's one reason I've had to keep going back over there. I've fired three of them so far, and two of those poached their friends from the team to go into security operations for themselves. I can't afford to lose experienced hunter team members. This whole last week, I've had to run damage control to keep the bulk of the remaining strike groups from running and hiring out for someone else."

"What does this Elsa say you should do?"

"She suggests hiring more Unusuals to fill the gaps, but I'm worried it will cause more problems than it solves."

Dean shrugged. "It seems to me that the people you're losing are dead weight, not the cream of the crop. If these losers are quitting because of their prejudice, they aren't going to be open-minded when on an operation either. I say good riddance. Let Elsa put together hybrid teams so everyone learns to trust each other."

Jaz paused, considering Dean's suggestion. "You're just voting for Elsa to take over the hiring so you can keep me home here with you."

"Of course I am, but that doesn't mean I'm not right. Let her do her job. Have her send regular reports for you to review but, let her have full control for a while and see how she does. It works for us in the fire and emergency medical services. The Chief has to let the line medics have the option to be unconventional sometimes. A good leader trusts her crews to use their own skills and intuition. They know best when to be creative and when to follow the letter of the rules."

Jaz stirred her spoon through the remains of the stew at the bottom of her bowl. "That might work. I have to go to Ireland next week and handle the opening of a new branch office there," Jaz said. "Elsa will be there, too. I can have a chat with her about what you've said. I'll see what she thinks about giving her more latitude in operational decisions and hiring."

"Perfect! I could go with you."

"Go with me? Why?"

"We can kill two birds with one stone. You can go do your grand opening thing and meet with Elsa. Then we can take a few days and tour the Emerald Isle. I'll bet if we ask Dougie down at the Irish Shop, he'll even let us use that magical doorway in his place to travel to Dublin."

Jaz smiled. "It would be nice to take a little time. A few days wouldn't kill us. When's the last time you talked to the leprechaun?"

"It's been a few months, but he's always said I could use the portal again if I needed to. It worked out well the last time with the CERT team. We went to debrief in a pub on the other side after the Barrens fire."

Jaz smiled. "Well, I guess it's a date, then. You set everything up with Dougie and I'll make arrangements for a hotel and transportation while we're in Dublin."

"Perfect," Dean said. He forgot how sore he was from the fight earlier. He stood and leaned over the table to kiss Jaz. "I'll get to show off my hot hunter wife to everyone we see."

"Who's saying I'm not going to show off my new boy toy, too."

They both fell into a round of chuckles and cleaned up their dinner. Dean tried to hide his pain when he moved and hoped he'd heal up before the trip came around. He didn't want to go on his honeymoon all gimpy from this injury.

They finished the dishes and got ready for bed. Dean pulled out his phone and sent off a text message to Dougie to check about taking the secret portal doorway in his shop to Ireland.

It pleased him he'd been able to get his wife to slow down a little and spend some time vacationing. They both could use a break and she was the type to work all the time if someone didn't make her slow down. It would be the perfect opportunity for both of them.

Chapter 5

THE NEXT FEW days flew by as Dean and Barry continued running the routine calls that made up the bulk of their days. Most were a lot like the current call on which the pair found themselves.

"We're almost there, Barry. You grab the med bag and monitor and get inside. I'll bring in the rest of the gear. This chest pain patient sounds like she's in the middle of a major cardiac event."

Barry nodded. "The additional dispatch information was pretty detailed. It's weird, don't you think? Who notifies the 911 operator they have chest pain, radiating pain down the left arm, and diaphoresis?"

Dean shrugged as he turned off the highway and down into a residential neighborhood. "Beats me. Maybe they have some medical training of some sort and knew what to tell our dispatch team. Either way, if it's accurate, we'll need to make sure they don't code on us before the hospital."

Barry pointed out to a house on the left. "There. That one is number 874."

Every one of the Victorian homes sat on large, grassy lots with trees lining the street on either side. Because the homes sat back off the street, it was hard to spot the house numbers from the road. Dean squinted in the darkness and tried to make out the numbers by the door.

"How can you even see that? Those numbers are tiny."

"I didn't look up at the house. Look down at the curb. The house numbers are stenciled there beside each driveway."

Dean grinned. "Good catch, partner."

He pulled into the driveway and Barry hopped out of the passenger seat to grab his gear and go. Dean worked quickly but didn't rush. He pulled out the stretcher and lowered the wheels until it stood by the rear of the unit, ready to go.

Loading it down with the airway bag and trauma bag just in case, Dean unhooked the stretcher from the rear of the ambulance. He wheeled it towards the house across the grassy yard when he spotted a familiar white van parked on the street in front of the home.

As if on cue, a middle-aged, slightly balding man came down the house's front stairs and jogged towards Dean, waving and offering a broad smile to the paramedic.

"Gibbie, what are you doing here?"

"Oh, I was just here for my weekly reading. When I got inside, she wasn't looking so good."

"And this woman's our patient?" Dean asked.

"Yeah, the Yakshini who lives here."

"The what?" Dean wracked his mind to remember where he'd heard that word before. He did regular research on the Unusual community, but there were a lot of creatures to learn about, especially when you added in all the international variations on the theme out there.

"The Yakshini, the woman inside. The Yaksha are a variety of Asian shape shifter. Tahira works as a Buddhist spirit finder. She helps work on people whose souls are out of alignment with their karma."

"But you're not a Buddhist, Gibbie. You once told me you didn't follow any religion since you became a vampire."

"Oh, it's not a religious thing. I'm just coming here so she can help me find my soul mate."

"You mean like a sort of dating service?"

"Yeah, but much more reliable than any of those online things. I tried the swipe left and right thing for a while, but none of them ever swiped me the right way."

"I wonder why," Dean muttered under his breath.

"Hey, I heard that." Gibbie pointed to his head. "Enhanced vampire ears, remember?"

"Sorry, Gibbie. Here, help me get this gear inside and then you can help us get her ready to go to the hospital."

"I don't think she's going to want to go. She didn't want me to call you in the first place, but I could tell her heart wasn't doing well. I could hear it sort of skipping beats and running real fast."

It sounded to Dean like she might have atrial fibrillation going on, but he'd need Barry to confirm it with the heart monitor. His partner knew what he was doing and probably already had the monitor hooked up and running a check on the woman's heart. No matter how good it was, Gibbie's enhanced hearing wasn't a reliable clinical benchmark.

Once he and Gibbie got the stretcher inside, Dean left it in the entry hall and entered a room filled with velvet upholstered furniture and stained-glass appointments to the windows and lampshades. Barry had already hooked up an old gray-haired woman to the heart monitor, as expected. The tiny, white-haired woman leaned back on an ornate, red divan.

Barry pushed a button on the screen to run a twelve-lead EKG. It looked at multiple areas of the heart at one time rather than just one tracing at a time. It would give them a better picture of what they had here.

Barry glanced at the printout as it came out the front of the machine and looked up at Dean. "A-fib. Draw me up some Cardizem while I get the IV started."

"Got it. Gibbie, help Barry get the IV line and bag ready to go."

"Will do, Dean."

The vampire started assembling the intravenous line tubing and inserted the spiked end into the opening on the plastic one-liter bag of saline fluid.

Dean smiled as he opened the med bag to draw up the syringe of medication Barry would use to treat the woman's rapid and irregular heartbeat. Training Gibbie and the others as Community Emergency Response Team or CERT members had been one of the best ideas he and Brynne had come up with during their time together as partners. The team had come in handy around town on more than a few occasions.

Once the IV was ready and Barry had taken another set of vitals, Dean handed over the medication and Barry began administering it via the IV tubing running into the woman's arm.

Dean reached out and held her other hand to comfort her. A spark flew between them as he touched her fingertips. Instead of jumping and pulling away from the surprise shock, her fingers clutched at his with surprising strength. He stared down at his hand and then up at her face.

The Yakshini's eyes bored into his. "Eldara-spawn, you must save her. It has fallen to you to rescue her amidst the sandy caves. Many things hinge upon your success."

Her eye still wide and wild, she turned to Gibbie. "The one you seek will soon be here, child of the night. Watch for the sign of the golden eagle."

As soon as the final words left her mouth, her eyes rolled back in her head and she slumped to the side. Dean searched her wrist for a pulse, staring at the heart monitor. A more-normal rhythm had replaced the irregular heart rhythm.

He waited to see if there was a pulse to match what the monitor showed. Dean followed the mantra taught him long ago. Treat the patient, not the monitor. He breathed a sigh of relief when his searching fingertips found a sudden, strong pulse in her wrist, matching what he saw on the screen. Nice and regular.

"What was her pulse like when you first came in, Barry?"

"Rapid, thready, and weak as hell. I almost couldn't find it."

"Well, it's nice and steady now. The med converted the rhythm."

"But I didn't give it yet." Barry held up the full syringe Dean had handed to him moments before. "I started to but stopped when she started talking to you. Her voice went all weird and I forgot what I was doing."

"Well, whatever happened, it converted. It doesn't explain why she's unconscious. She might have thrown a clot and had a stroke. Let's get her loaded up and out of here."

"What was that she called you?" Barry asked.

Gibbie beat Dean to an answer. "She called him Eldara spawn. That means Dean's dad is the Archangel Gabriel."

Barry shook his head. "I still don't know if I can get used to having a partner be able to do super stuff like that."

"Trust me, Barry. I didn't get anything fun from my sperm-donor of a father. I'm a normal guy, just like you."

"I don't know, Dean," Gibbie said. "You did use your powers to stop the end of the world."

"That wasn't what happened, believe me. Besides, you weren't even in the room when it all went down."

"No, but I know what Ingrid said about it once you all came back outside."

"She exaggerated everything," Dean snapped. Gibbie's eyes widened at the sharp retort. Dean realized he'd spoken louder than intended and drew in a deep breath. "Look, let's focus on the patient. Help us get all this stuff packed and loaded up. Barry and I will get her on the stretcher and into the ambulance."

Gibbie nodded. Despite his attempt to make it right, Dean saw the hurt reflected in the vampire's eyes. He hadn't meant to lose his temper like that. Something about thinking about Gabe and how he'd tried to end the world stirred up angry emotions inside him.

Gabe had wanted to stick around a little while to help Dean after they defeated the horsemen. He'd nipped that idea in the bud right away. His father had tried to trick him into starting the last battle between good and evil. The archangel wanted to bring on the end of the world to further some heavenly destiny or something. When Dean had figured a way to stop either side from having their way, he had made it clear he wanted nothing to do with powers from heaven or hell.

And now this woman had pronounced a prophecy of some sort over him. All the supernatural stuff lately sickened him. He wanted nothing to do with any of it, at least where it intersected his personal life. Pushing thoughts of his father from his mind, he focused on helping Barry roll the woman out to the ambulance. He'd ponder what the woman had said later. Right now, he had a patient to care for. It was more important to stay on target and get her to the hospital alive.

By the time Dean pulled the ambulance into the bay at ECMC ten minutes later, the woman had awakened in the back of the unit. She chattered away at Barry about her grandchildren and other random things during the last half of the drive.

In the ambulance bay at the hospital, Dean opened the back doors to unload the stretcher. The Yakshini smiled at him, as if she'd never seen him before. She nodded a greeting, but there was no mention that she'd said anything to Dean. He didn't want to bring it up.

Had he imagined all of it?

They rolled her into the hospital and Barry took charge as the lead paramedic on the case, giving his report to the nurse once they had moved the woman to a bed.

Dean took the stretcher out to make up the sheets.

Ashley spotted him from behind the nurses' station and came out to say hi. He stood by the stretcher in the corner tucking the edge of a white hospital sheet in under the mattress.

"Dean, what happened to you?"

"What do you mean?" Her concerned tone startled him.

"There's Dweomer around you. It looks recent."

Dean checked behind him. Was there something there? "What are you talking about? What's a Dwoomer?"

"A Dweomer. It's the magic residue of a spell. Did someone cast something on you during this call?"

Dean thought back to the spark he'd felt between him and the Yakshini. "I didn't think so, but there was something that happened. Can you tell what it is? It's not a curse, is it?"

"I don't think so. I don't sense any ill intent." Ashley leaned forward with her head tilted up slightly as if she were trying to smell him. Maybe she was. He didn't know all the abilities the Eldara Sister had.

"Well, what is it? I can't be running around with some spell ready to go off at the wrong time."

"Did she say anything when she put the spell on you?"

"She made some sort of prophecy about me being Eldara spawn or something like that. She said I have to rescue someone in a cave filled with sand. It was all nonsense. She was in the middle of a major cardiac event. As soon as she said it, she fainted. By the time she got here, she'd forgotten all about it."

Ashley nodded. "I think the Yakshini cast a Geas on you."

She'd used another word he didn't know. It sounded like "gesh." "Okay, are you going to explain that to me, too?"

Ashley looked around and pointed to the EMS break room by the ambulance door. "Come in here. I'll try to explain it to you where no one is listening. This is serious."

Dean didn't like the sound of that. He didn't have the time to lift some sort of curse. The local witch's coven had become a little gun-shy when it came to casting spells when he was around. Bad things had a way of happening when they did.

He followed Ashley into the break room with its computer terminal and half-size fridge stocked with soda and water for EMS crews between ambulance calls. "Okay, I'm here. Tell me what it is."

"A Geas is a special kind of magic that isn't used much anymore. It imposes an obligation on the recipient that can cause conflicts until they complete some sort of quest that resolves the obligation."

"Wait, so I'm bound to complete some sort of quest whether I want to or not?" Dean started pacing back and forth beside Ashley.

"Hold still while I try to figure it out. It usually won't work if it's something totally against your moral code, so you can stop worrying about that." Ashley reached out with both hands to grip Dean's head while she leaned close with her eyes closed.

At that moment, Barry walked into the EMS break room, took one look at the two of them and pivoted around 180 degrees back out the door. "Uh, sorry, I didn't see anything."

"Dammit," Dean said, pulling away from Ashley's hands. "Now Barry's gonna think I'm cheating on Jaz."

Ashely laughed, "Nonsense, Dean. He knows you better than that. He should know me better than that, too."

"I've got to go. If you figure out what's going on with this Geas thing, let me know. I'll try to see if Jaz can do anything about it. She's got to have a hunter charm or something I can use to block it."

"Don't be so sure. This is an ancient magic spell. It's better to figure out exactly what the old Yakshini meant when she cast it."

Dean nodded. "Maybe I'll come back here after work and visit her in her room upstairs after she's admitted." He broke out in a sweat as anxiety rolled over him.

"Dean, take a breath. This isn't the first time you've stumbled into something like this. You know when the time comes, you'll know what to do. It's part of who you are."

Dean shot Ashley as sideways glance and paused at the door. "You know, Ash. It would've been nice of you to tell me you knew who my father was all along. It's the one thing that sours my memory of our relationship a little when I think about it."

"It wasn't my place, Dean. I didn't know at first. By the time I figured out who you were, I'd gotten close enough to realize you weren't ready to know."

"Maybe, maybe not. That wasn't yours to decide. You still should have told me."

Dean left before Ashley could say anything else. He still had to deal with what Barry thought he saw. Once he put that fire out, he had to figure out what the Geas magic had done to him. Things had been normal for the last few months since they'd defeated the four horsemen. He'd thought maybe he was beyond this sort of thing for a while.

He should have known better.

Chapter 6

OUT ON THE hospital ambulance ramp, Barry stood beside the unit chatting with one of the hospital security guards. He smiled as Dean approached. "You get finished with everything you wanted in there?"

"Ha, ha, Barry. I know what you think you saw in there, but it was nothing. She was trying to figure out what kind of spell Tahira cast on me back at her house."

"Oh, is that all it was." Barry laughed and rolled his eyes.

Anger bubbled beneath the surface as Dean struggled with what to say. Then saw Barry smiling and realized his partner was teasing him. He forced a laugh. "Yeah, that's all it was. You're lucky, Barry. You try to run into one of your exes on a regular basis and see if you don't get caught in a potentially awkward situation sometime."

"Dean, if I had exes as hot as yours, I'd be getting caught in awkward situations all the time. You're a better man than I am."

"You've got that right. Ready to go?"

Barry pointed to the security guard. "In a second. You remember Verity from a few nights back?"

Dean nodded.

Barry continued. "Dirk here told me that her boyfriend came into the hospital late last night, threw some people out of his way and dragged her out here to the street. A few bystanders saw him force her into a black SUV before it drove away. The staff called the police, but they didn't get here in time to do anything but take a statement."

"Really? Why didn't Ashley tell me?"

Dirk said, "She wasn't working yesterday. She might not know."

Dean shook his head. "I'd hoped getting Verity here would finally get her to a safe place."

The hefty security guard shook his head. "That guy she was with was super strong. He tossed my partner aside like he was a rag doll. He's still upstairs with some pins in his leg because of it."

"Damn, Manton came back even after Brynne ran him off. I thought he'd be long gone by now."

"Too bad Ashley wasn't here."

Dirk shrugged, "Good thing, she wasn't. He'd have hurt her just like everyone else who tried to stop him."

Dean resisted laughing. Dirk wouldn't understand why he thought what he'd said was funny. Dean knew the Eldara would have been more than a match for the werepanther if it had come to a confrontation. It was likely the shifter had waited until she'd left on purpose just to avoid running into her.

As Dean thought about Verity, a vision of a different girl, younger, with red hair popped into his head. A strange, warm tingling sensation ran up the back of his neck. It raised the hairs there and despite the warmth of it; he shivered. Tahira's voice came back to him as if played back on a recording in his head. "Eldara-spawn, you must save her. It has fallen to you to rescue her amidst the sandy caves. Many things will hinge upon your success."

The voice trailed off in his mind and the sensation faded.

Barry stared at Dean. "You alright, partner? You just turned white as a sheet."

"Uh, yeah, just trying to shake of the weird stuff that woman said to me back at her house."

"Oh, about you being the chosen one and all?"

"She didn't say that, and you know it."

Barry raised his voice into a loud falsetto. "Help us, Obi-Dean. You're our only hope."

"Hilarious. Get in the unit. We need to get back on the street. You're the medic on call tonight. Maybe it'll be nice and quiet for you."

Barry groaned at the use of the "Q" word. "I'll get you for that, Dean. Now you've doomed us to the shift from hell."

As if to punctuate his words, their radios chirped with alert tones and the dispatcher called out their unit number. "U-191, are you back in service?"

Dean smiled and reached to key the mic clipped to his uniform shirt by his collar. "Affirmative headquarters."

"U-191, respond to the scene of a house fire at 8713 Cree Terrace for burns."

"U-191 responding."

Barry grunted, "I hate burns."

"Me, too," Dean replied. He walked to the driver's side of the ambulance and climbed in. Once Barry was in and settled, Dean started up the unit and pulled away from the hospital on the way to their next call. Even as he drove across town to another set of patients and more injuries, a nagging notion floated in the back of his mind, wondering where Verity was and if she was alright.

Chapter 7

DEAN REGRETTED USING THE "Q" word on Barry by the end of the shift. Every EMS provider knew that word brought on a very real jinx everyone feared. Even though they were supposed to get off work at six the next morning, Dean and his partner didn't get finished with their paperwork until nearly nine.

A glance at the clock as he clicked send on the last report made Dean wince. It was late, and he had a lot to do. He leaned back in the seat with his arms raised over his head and stretched.

Barry glanced his way from his seat behind the computer workstation beside him. "Dean, I hope my eyes aren't as bleary and bloodshot as yours are."

"They're worse, I'm betting. You had most of the patient care tonight. I was just the driver."

"Yeah, well, I'm gonna go home and climb in my bed and not come out again until this time tomorrow."

"It will be good to have the day off. I've got to get Jaz and I squared away for our trip."

Barry smiled. "Yeah, that's right. You two are finally going on that honeymoon thing. You'll have to tell me how it is. I might want to check out using that magic doorway with my girlfriend, too."

"Which one is it this week?" Dean quipped.

"Aw, you're just jealous that I can still play the field while you're tied down to the same old woman for life."

"I'd be careful who you call 'the same old woman,' Barry. If Jaz finds out you called her old, you might have to move out of town for a little while."

"You wouldn't tell her, would you?"

Dean laughed. "What happens at the station, stays at the station. I wouldn't throw you under that bus. My wife can be a stone-cold killer if she wants to be."

Barry laughed, too, but there was a hint of desperation behind it. He knew Dean wasn't kidding. Jaz was, after all, a trained Hunter.

Dean stood up and went over to grab his coat. "I'm out. You're all finished, too, right?"

Barry nodded. "Yeah, I just need to email the training officer about an upcoming slot in a class he's teaching. I'm behind on my continuing education. As soon as I'm done that, I'm out of here."

"Good, get home and get that sleep. You look like hell."

Barry chuckled and waved as Dean headed out to his pickup truck. He needed to pick up a few things on the way home and then he was going to hit the sack, too.

At least that was the plan.

As Dean drove home, he found his mind drifting back to Verity, wondering where she was and if there was some way to help her. He became so lost in his thoughts, he soon discovered he'd driven off track instead of going straight home. He found himself in an old, working class neighborhood on the northern edge of Elk City, down by the river front.

"Damn, I'm more tired than I thought," Dean muttered to himself. He needed to get some sack time.

His phone chirped and he clicked the hands-free button to pick up. It was Jaz.

"Dean, what are you doing up there on that end of town. Did you get called out on another run?"

He'd forgotten she had an app that could track his phone's GPS. "No, I just got distracted by something and sort of got turned around.

I'm getting back on the expressway now. I'll be home in fifteen minutes. I'm sorry."

"I blocked out time this morning to plan that trip to Ireland. I've got a call coming up I can't miss, so we're going to have to reschedule if you don't hustle home."

"I hear and obey, Ms. Errington."

"That's enough of that. Just get home. I'll make you some breakfast. I'll bet you're as hungry as you are tired."

"Take that bet and you'll be correct. Oh, and thank you in advance for breakfast. I'll be home soon."

Jaz hung up and Dean twisted his head around to find the fastest way back onto a main road. He passed several streets before he found what he was looking for. Turning the corner next to a run-down warehouse, Dean saw the intersection for Philadelphia Road three streets away.

He smiled as he thought about eating one of Jaz's omelets soon. It would fill the empty pit in his stomach. The hunger distracted him from the tugging in the back of his mind, telling him to turn around and go back to the building on the corner.

Chapter 8

DEAN DROVE up and entered his code into the keypad by the entrance to the Errington Security parking lot. After the gate opened, he pulled his beat-up pickup truck into a spot amidst a row of immaculate black SUVs.

Jaz had offered him the opportunity to get a new car or to just take one of the company vehicles on multiple occasions. She kept telling him he was in the family now and since it was a family-owned company, that gave him the right to drive anything on the lot. Dean still resisted, and he didn't know why. Deep inside, he'd like to drive something new.

Maybe stupid pride kept him from driving a vehicle he hadn't paid for. It might be a minor distinction to some, but to Dean, it was his last holdout against the massive monetary difference between what he made working for the Elk City Fire Department and Jaz's income as the head of a Hunter clan. Most of that income came from her international security and executive protection enterprises.

Dean grabbed his coat and duffle bag from behind the seat and headed into the building. He needed to swap out the clothes so they could go in the laundry.

Inside the employee entrance, the guard at the desk smiled and greeted him. "Good morning, sir. You're running a little later than usual for this shift. Rough night?"

Dean chuckled. "Yeah, you might say that. And Jed, you don't have to call me 'sir'. I've told you I'm fine with you and the others calling me Dean."

"I appreciate you saying that, but I can't. The boss says you're to be treated the same as her. That's all the reason I need. It's not like I want to get on her bad side. She signs the checks."

Dean sighed and returned the guard's smile. "I get that, Jed. I don't like it when I'm on her bad side either. Have a good day. I hope your shift goes by quickly."

"Thank you, sir. Get some sleep."

"Thanks," Dean replied as he punched the button to head up on the elevator. The doors opened right away, and he stepped inside, hitting the key for the fourth floor.

All the apartments were on the top floor. His and Jaz's place was the largest, but there were smaller ones used to house visiting company personnel from other regions. He stepped out into a hallway and walked all the way down past a series of doors on either side until he reached the door at the end. He reached down to pull his keys out. The door opened before he could get them.

"Hey, babe," Jaz said as she stepped aside to let him come in. "I have breakfast on the table. Come on in and eat something. You'll feel better."

"I hope so. I've been out of sorts all night."

"Why?"

Dean hesitated. He'd talked to her earlier to tell her he was running late, but he didn't tell her about the spell Tahira put on him. She saw through his evasion right away.

"Dean, what aren't you telling me? We talked about this."

"It's no big deal. Ashley said a patient put a Geas on me. I'm sure it'll work itself out."

"A Geas? What for?"

Dean shrugged. "She pronounced some sort of prophecy on me and then fainted. When she woke up, she didn't remember any of it."

"That's obviously bull. Where is this woman? I think I need to have a little talk with her." Jaz's hand rested on the Glock holstered on her hip. She wore it always, even in the apartment. Dean thought it was overkill, especially with all the muscle working downstairs around the clock.

"Jaz, calm down. We've talked about this before. There have to be boundaries between us at home and from our work. I can't have you flying off the handle every time I get roughed up by a patient or something happens to me on the job. I can take care of myself."

"Apparently not. This is why I wanted to get you a protection charm of your own. Its spells would have probably stopped this magic from affecting you."

"I told you why I can't have that. If one of the patients spots it and recognizes it as a Hunter charm, it'll ruin my credibility with them as a healer. It's bad enough I'm married to a Hunter."

Dean winced as soon as he heard the words leave his mouth.

Jaz glared at him, staring down from where she stood across the table from where he sat with his breakfast. "I'm sorry if my family's calling bothers your precious patients. Maybe you should have thought about that before you married me."

"Jaz…"

"I've got some work to do down in my office. Get some sleep. When you wake up, we're doing whatever it takes to get this spell removed. Be ready."

Before Dean could say anything else, Jaz stormed out. She slammed the apartment door hard enough that a picture in the hallway crashed to the floor. The sound of the frame's glass breaking punctuated the sudden silence after her exit.

For a few seconds, Dean considered running after her and apologizing before she got on the elevator, but his stubbornness wouldn't let him. He shoveled another bite of the omelet into his mouth.

He frowned as he chewed. It felt like chewing cold rubber now, and it wasn't any tastier.

He shoved the plate towards the center of the table. Maybe she'd settle down about this and realize he could handle it himself while he slept. They were supposed to pack up that afternoon so they could head over to the Irish Shop first thing in the morning. That was contingent on whether they were still talking to each other, of course. He got up and went to clean up the broken glass before heading to get some sleep.

He stripped off his shirt as he walked down the hallway to their bedroom. He finished getting undressed and climbed into bed. Tapping the small remote on the nightstand, he keyed the button that activated the automated blackout curtains and turned off the lights. Dean pulled the covers up around him and closed his eyes.

His sleepy thoughts drifted back to images of Verity, except it didn't look exactly like her. Her face kept shifting into someone else, someone younger. The girl wasn't alone, but danger seemed to stalk around her. The shifting face steadied into Verity's again as the viewpoint widened. There were others who looked enough like her they could be her sisters. They all sat on a concrete floor with their backs against a cinderblock wall. For an instant, before he drifted off to sleep, she looked up and stared back into his eyes. It was almost as if she was trying to say something to him, but he fell asleep before she started.

The dream stuck with Dean after he got up that afternoon and through most of dinner. It set off a sour mood and his surly, one-word responses to Jaz's attempts to make conversation set her off, too. The thoughts distracted him, and he didn't even notice her mounting anger.

Jaz stood, clearing the dishes. She stopped and stared at him. "Dean, what is going on with you tonight? Are you still annoyed with me from this morning? You're the one who should apologize to me."

"It's not that." Another image of the girl who wasn't Verity popped into his head. He shook it off. "I am sorry about this morning. What I said came out wrong. You know I appreciate all you're doing to change the way Unusuals perceive hunters. I should support that better."

Jaz didn't say anything. She nodded and took the plates she held into the kitchen. Dean grabbed a handful and followed her, setting them down on the counter beside the sink.

"So?" Jaz asked.

"So what?"

"So, what is bothering you, then? You aren't usually like this. What else happened at work?"

Dean struggled with how to explain what he'd dreamt. It was just a dream, after all.

"I didn't sleep well today, that's all. I guess I was anxious about our trip to Ireland tomorrow."

Jaz put down the plates. "Dean, I told you. I have two meetings in Dublin, that's all. After that, I'm all yours for three whole days. Promise." She crossed her heart with a finger.

"Well, as long as you promise. We've had so little time alone together like that. It's okay for a guy to get a little nervous about things like this."

Jaz let out a laugh. "Like what? It's not like it's a real honeymoon. We've been married for months now, and we lived together before the wedding. What's there to be nervous about."

Dean shrugged. "Expectations? We've built this up to be a huge thing, and now that it's almost here, I want to make sure it's absolutely perfect. No patients for me. No outlaws, terrorists, or rogue Unusuals for you. Just you and me as normal people."

"Like you and I will ever be normal."

Dean started to protest, and Jaz held up her hands in surrender. "I told you. I promise. I'll be just normal old Jaz, an ordinary girl from Elk City, Maryland. We'll be like every other tourist on vacation."

Dean laughed at the way she switched on her innocent, dumb blonde voice in the middle of what she said. He reached out and pulled her close, kissing her for what felt like the first time in days.

She melted into it and they stood there by the sink with the water running for a long time, enjoying each other's company.

When they finally parted, he felt a little flushed from the encounter. He was pleased to see it had the same effect on Jaz, too.

He decided to change the subject so they could both focus on cleaning up and packing for the trip in the morning. There'd be plenty of time on the trip for that kind of closeness.

"What are your meetings about in Dublin? Anything interesting?

"Not really. An old friend reached out to me recently and asked when I'd be over in Europe next. I told her I'd let her know. She's traveling down from somewhere to the north to meet me there tomorrow. The other meeting is just a quick check on my Irish operations team. I haven't stopped there to see them on site, they've always come and met me in some other European city. I thought it would be a good idea to check in with them and look over their offices and set up."

"A surprise inspection?"

"Not really. I told them this morning I was going to be dropping in tomorrow or the next day."

Dean laughed. "So they only have twenty-four hours to hide the bodies before you get there."

"They better have hidden any bodies long before that. They have had no active ops of their own for months. That's one of the reasons for the drop in. I want to make sure they're keeping their eyes open and covering our local clients appropriately."

"I love it when you go all boss-lady. You sound all tough."

"And I'm not tough other times?"

"Oh, no. I'm not falling for that one. You, my dear, are the epitome of a tough bad-ass Hunter every single day of the week."

Jaz flicked a wet tea-towel at him as he turned away. She snapped it with a pop so it stung him on the backside as he jumped out of the way.

"Hey! I'm unarmed here."

She dropped the towel and chased him down the hallway to their bedroom. Dean ran, laughing all the way and wondering if the honeymoon might start a little early. He decided, as Jaz tackled him onto their bed, he was a hundred percent okay with that.

Chapter 9

"YOU GOT EVERYTHING, DEAN?"

Dean checked the back of the SUV one last time and nodded at Jaz. "I have the suitcases, as well as my laptop bag. I loaded some new games to keep me busy while you're at your meetings tonight and tomorrow."

Jaz nodded and closed the driver's door, thumbing the key fob to lock the doors. She shouldered her own leather briefcase and followed him down the alley to the front entrance to the small Irish gift shop on a busy downtown street. Dougie O'Nolder, the leprechaun owner of the store, had told Dean in an email to park in the small lot behind the store and then come around front.

She checked her watch after Dean knocked on the front door for the second time. "What time did you tell him we'd be here? It doesn't look like anyone's inside to let us in."

"I said we drop by around nine-thirty. He opens at ten, but he said he'd be in early."

Jaz check her watch. "It's only a little after nine. We're early."

Dean gave his wife an awkward smile as they stood on the street with their two suitcases and shoulder bags. "I'm sure he just forgot we were coming. His car was there in the lot. It sat a few spaces from ours. Let me knock again."

He rapped on the glass door and leaned in close to the glass. He cupped his hands around his face to peer into the dark interior. The shelves of random Irish gifts packed the place and blocked most of his view to the back of the shop. He was about to pull out his phone and call the owner when he spotted some movement in the shadows.

"He's in there, I think. He must've been busy with something. Like you said, we are early."

Dougie moved out of the shadows inside and waved at Dean, holding up a finger to wait. Other figures moved about in the shadows, and Dean tried to see what was going on. Maybe he was doing inventory with his employees before they opened for the day.

A muscular form in a black T-shirt slid into view just inside the glass door. The guy was taller than Dean, and he had to tilt his head back a bit to see the face scowling down at him.

"What do you want? Shop's closed." The guy's thick Irish brogue was almost unintelligible.

"Dougie knows we're coming. I just saw him. He said to wait a minute. We're good unless you want to let us in so we don't have to stand outside with our luggage."

The man inside glanced around Dean and took in Jaz and the bags on the sidewalk. "Going somewhere?"

"Uh, yeah. Just a brief trip." Dean wasn't sure how much the guy inside knew about the owner's secret door to a pub in Dublin.

The guy inside made no move to open the door, and Dean's temper started rising. This guy was rude, especially since Dean had told the brute he knew the shop's owner.

Before he could say anything, Dougie showed up. The six-foot-tall leprechaun bustled over, nudging the bigger fellow out of the way. "Uh, Dean, I told you nine-thirty. You're early."

"Force of habit, I guess. Is it still okay we come in and use your little, uh—" Dean glanced at the big guy.

Dougie smiled. "Sure, sure. You're welcome to use the door. I just wasn't expecting you so early and I had some other business to attend to." He looked over his shoulder and seemed distracted by something going on in the back of the store.

Dean tried to move so he could see past Dougie, but the big, muscular guy slid over to stand in Dean's way. It irked Dean, but he didn't want to make a scene. He didn't need Jaz jumping in and putting this refugee from bouncer school in the hospital.

"Doug, if this is a bad time—"

"No, not at all. I think they're finished up with what we were packing away. Cyril, go back and make sure the storeroom door is closed."

Cyril scowled at the shop-owner, but he left and disappeared into the back of the store.

"Come with me and we'll get you two ready to go. You must both be excited to take this little excursion."

"We are. I really appreciate you letting us use the portal."

"Think nothing of it. It's the least I can do after all you did to save us all with that Armageddon mess."

Jaz smiled. "We're all very proud of him." The smile disappeared as quickly as it showed up. She nodded at the back of the store. "What was that all about? That Cyril guy seemed a little nervous to have us around."

"Jaz," Dean said. "Don't start interrogating Dougie. We are here on vacation. His business is his to deal with. We don't need to get involved."

His wife started to object, but he glared at her. To his surprise, she backed down.

Not wanting to give her any time to ask any more uncomfortable questions, Dean said, "Can we get going? We're kind of in a hurry to get on with our trip."

"Certainly, let's get the portal fired up and you can be on your way."

He led them back to the storeroom door Cyril had just closed. Dougie opened it and gestured for them to walk past him. Dean expected to see others in there, but whoever they were, they'd left with Cyril. The storeroom was empty.

Dougie pointed to a large steel door at the back of the storage area. "That's the back door. You're parked in the lot out back, right?"

Dean nodded.

"Good, then when you return after your trip, if the shop's closed, just go out that door and let it close behind you. It'll lock itself once you make sure it's latched."

Dean gave a thumbs-up. "Got it."

Dougie led them to the large green door set in the wall between tall floor-to-ceiling shelves. He unlocked it with a black iron key from his pocket. He tugged at the stout wooden door and the strange magic portal opened in the wall.

Dean grabbed his suitcases and nodded reassurance to Jaz as he stepped into the small room on the other side. The worn hardwood floor had the dark stained look of something ancient compared to anything he'd see in Elk City. Jaz followed him.

"Have fun," Dougie said. He winked, then shut the green door behind them.

"So what now?" Jaz asked.

"We go through that door and we're in Ireland."

"It's that simple?"

Dean nodded. "Come on. I'll show you."

He opened the door and led his wife into the common room of the Mulligan's Pub in downtown Dublin.

He noticed the difference from his last visit right away. It was nothing like the bustling, busy Irish pub he'd visited a few years before. For a moment, Dean thought they'd somehow ended up somewhere else. The dark hallway leading to the equally dark common room confused him.

Once he got his bearings, he realized they were in the right place. But it was empty. No people. Not a sound. As he walked around the common room and looked behind the bar, he corrected himself. This was the pub formerly known as Mulligan's. It appeared to have been closed for some time. Someone had stacked the chairs on the tables, and the shelves along the wall behind the bar were empty of the liquor bottles that had lined them the last time he was here.

"This isn't what I expected, Jaz. I didn't know the place was closed."

She tapped away on her phone for a few seconds. "It says here the owner, Jason Mulligan, died suddenly about six months ago. The pub closed down and an unknown investor bought it from the estate."

"That's a shame. The food and atmosphere here were great. I wonder why Dougie didn't tell us?"

Jaz glanced back at the door leading back to Elk City. "There was something strange going on back there in the Irish Shop. I couldn't put my finger on it, but now it makes sense."

"What? You think those other people must've come through ahead of us?" Dean looked around. "If they came back, they left already."

"Dean, I think your leprechaun friend is involved with some sort of smuggling operation." Jaz walked around, looking into the kitchen and returning to her husband. "It could be drugs or any other sort of contraband."

Dean didn't like her assumption but stopped. Dougie had acted distracted and a little annoyed they'd come early. Could he have been in the middle of a secret he didn't want Dean and Jaz to see?

"Jaz, is this something we need to get involved with? I mean, there's no actual evidence of a crime. We're just speculating. I think we should continue on with our plans."

From her hesitation to answer him right away, Dean could tell she wanted to push forward with an investigation. She gave a brief shake of her head. "You're right. I'll hold off, but I am going to put someone from the office on it and see what they uncover while we're here."

"Fair enough, as long as you keep your hands off. So, what now? We're not staying here for a bite as planned, so my itinerary is already out the window."

Jaz tapped on something on her phone and held it up to her ear. "I'll have someone from the Dublin office stop by and pick us up. They can take us to the hotel. We'll check in and I'll catch up with my first meeting a little early."

She opened her mouth to say more, but someone must have picked up on the other end of the line. Jaz held up a finger for Dean to hold on. "This is Jaz Errington. I need a car to come pick me up. I've pinged your system with my phone so you can get my location."

After a brief pause for the reply, she continued. "Good. See you in twenty minutes." She put the phone back in her pocket. "So, husband of mine, we have a few minutes to do some local sightseeing. What else is around here?"

Dean laughed. "I have no idea. We never left the pub. Let's go outside and find out."

With a nod, the two of them grabbed their bags went to the front door. It was locked but opened from the inside. A quick check showed the door would lock behind them. "Good thing you can pick locks, hon. Otherwise, we'd have to find another way home."

Jaz rolled her eyes. "Given how many things on this trip have already proven a little sketchy, I'm thinking I need a contingency plan. Maybe we should book a flight home."

"No, no, that's not necessary," Dean said with a groan. "I've got this all figured out. I promise. Everything else will go fine."

"If you say so, I'll hold you to it." Jaz pointed to a small independent bookseller across the street. "Come on, let's browse for a bit in that shop. I'd like to get a local guide to the city just in case you get us lost."

"Very funny." He lifted the suitcases off the curb and rolled them across the street. "It looks kind of cramped in there, especially if we take in our bags. I'll hang out here and wait for the car. You go and get your guidebook."

"I was just kidding. You're my guide for the trip." She glanced in the window for a few seconds. "I would like to go in and browse, though, if that's alright?"

"I'll be here. Go have fun."

Jaz entered the bookstore. Dean watched through the display window as she looked through a few books. The shopkeeper, a woman in a grey cardigan came over to help her and soon the two were deep in conversation. Now and then, one would look his way with a smile on her face. When both glanced at him and laughed at one point, he smiled back and waved. That only got them laughing even more.

A few minutes later, Jaz emerged, stuffing a *Guide to the Emerald Isle* in her shoulder bag. She glanced at her phone. "The car's almost here."

"Did you have fun making a new friend?"

"Oh, yes, Saoirse's very nice. She thought you and I make a cute couple. She also told me some more about the pub's sudden closing. The owner had complained to her that someone tried on many occasions to get him to sell the place. They'd put a lot of pressure on him, but he still said no. About a week after he told her this, he died."

"You see a mystery everywhere you look, don't you?"

"And you don't see potential illnesses with every person you meet."

Dean smiled. "Not all of them. I've never diagnosed you, though I do like to play doctor."

Jaz gave him a playful shove. "Save if for later, big boy. There's the car."

A black SUV pulled up and the passenger window, on the wrong side of the car, wound down. The woman behind the wheel leaned over and asked, "Ms. Errington?"

"Yes. You must be Niamh." Jaz said.

"Yes, Mum." The young blonde got out and walked around back. "If you and your husband will climb into the Range Rover, I'll get your things loaded into the back."

"Nonsense. Stay put. We can load our own bags."

Dean nodded, following Jaz to the rear of the vehicle. Niamh popped open the lift gate and they both slid their suitcases inside. Dean noticed a familiar black lockbox bolted in the back. He suspected it carried an array of weapons, just like the Errington Security vehicles back home.

Jaz got in the front passenger seat and Dean got in the seat behind hers. Having the boss sit up front flustered the driver a little, but she regained her composure and pulled out into traffic.

"You're new with the Dublin office, aren't you?" Jaz asked.

"Yes, Mum. My father recommended me for the position. He's a retired member of the Garda."

Jaz smiled. "You wanted police work, and he knew enough to find you a job that paid a lot better."

"Something like that. He also knew I loved reading all kinds of fantasy and mythology books growing up. I guess I've studied for this job all my life. He couldn't wait until my first day home from orientation to see my face."

Dean laughed. "I take it he was part of the Irish National Police version of our Unusual stations?"

Niamh nodded. "Yes, sir."

"No need calling me sir. I answer to Dean. You work for her, not me."

She glanced to her left, waiting for a slight nod from Jaz. "Yes, s—, I mean, Dean."

It was a minor victory, but he took it. He knew why Jaz had to maintain some distance and authority with her subordinates. That didn't extend to him, at least, not in his mind. Jaz might not agree, but on this Dean didn't care. He enjoyed being on a first name basis with folks.

Niamh talked about ongoing projects with Jaz for the rest of their brief trip, so Dean took in the sights as they drove through the city. In some ways it looked much like any other modern city, but now and then he got a sense of how old this country was compared to his home.

As they unloaded their luggage, Niamh pulled a folded black duffel back from a pocket in the rear compartment. She opened the locked security box with her thumbprint and a six-digit code. As expected, the armored box contained a variety of weapons, including handguns and a few blades.

"Do you have any particular preference, Mum?"

"The Glock and four spare magazines. I can't use a Katana. Too hard to hide here. I'll take the silver dagger, though."

Niamh glanced at Dean.

"Nothing for me, thanks. I'm a healer, not a fighter. Besides, we're on our honeymoon."

The woman shrugged and closed the box after transferring the pistol, a clip-on holster, magazines, and the dagger to the duffel bag. She zipped it closed and handed it to her boss.

Jaz slipped her arm through the duffel bag's handles and moved it up to carry over her shoulder. "I'll see you at the meeting tomorrow at our offices. It's a pleasure to meet you."

"You, too, Ms. Errington." She nodded at Dean and got in the Range Rover.

Dean extended the handles on both their suitcases and rolled them behind him as he followed Jaz into the hotel. It was very nice, as he expected. His wife didn't skimp when she traveled. She'd told him once that she spent far too much time sleeping on the ground in creepy old ruins not to take advantage of a good bed when she could. He didn't disagree with the practice. He liked staying somewhere posh, and she was paying for it, after all.

Ten minutes later, they were in their suite getting settled. Dean started unpacking his suitcase in the bedroom, putting his clothes away. Jaz turned her attention to the duffle bag. She fetched a towel from the bathroom and sat on the bed as she field-stripped the pistol, laying the pieces on the towel as she went. After she reassembled it and checked the magazines, Jaz pulled the dagger from its sheath and checked the edge before putting it away.

"Jaz, is there something you're not telling me? We don't need all the firepower for the trip I have planned."

"I've learned the hard way that it pays to be prepared for the worst. You know I feel naked when I'm unarmed."

"How's carrying that pistol even work over here. I know you can carry just about anywhere in the U.S., but things are different outside those borders, aren't they?"

"I've got a diplomatic waiver on my passport. As long as I don't flaunt that I'm armed, we shouldn't have problems. If we do, that waiver should cover us."

"If you say so. What's next on your agenda. You wanted to meet up with that friend of yours, didn't you?"

Jaz nodded and pulled out her phone. "Let me reach out and tell her we're here." She tapped at the screen as she walked into the bathroom.

She hadn't told Dean much about this friend of hers, and the mystery intrigued him. He wanted to know who this person was. His wife's secretive nature about it had his imagination working overtime.

It turned out, Dean didn't need to be worried, at least not that first night. Jaz's friend had been delayed getting to town and that left the night open for just the two of them. As soon as he had the opening, Dean jumped into action and reached out to the front desk for a special dinner he had originally planned for a few nights from now. The manager was glad to bump up the reservation to that evening.

They spent the rest of the afternoon relaxing in the room together. As it got dark, they got dressed and went down to the lobby to meet the concierge. Soon Dean and Jaz sat in a private dining room while a personal chef prepared a fine dining experience for them in the small kitchen next door. Their dedicated server opened a bottle of champagne and served them their food as each course arrived.

Jaz lifted her glass to her husband in a toast. "This is nice. You pulled out all the stops. I like it."

"I stayed within the budget we discussed; I swear."

"I already told you that wasn't necessary."

"It's important that I cover half this trip with my city salary. I have to pull my weight in this relationship."

Jaz shook her head but said nothing. They'd hashed out this topic frequently, and both of them knew the other's position well enough.

She smiled and sipped at her bubbly. "Thank you for planning this. I appreciate how hard you work and how long you've saved for this trip."

"I want us to enjoy the night since we suddenly have nothing else planned. This way, when your friend shows up, we won't have to miss out on something else."

"I hope it works that way. She's seemed distracted in her messages and mentioned being in the middle of something."

"You still haven't told me much about her. Come on, who is she, some sort of 007 character?"

Jaz smiled. "She'd wipe the floor with Bond if they met in real life. No, she's someone I met on a demon hunt a few years ago and we hit it off. Since then, we've traded intel and helped each other when we could on various missions."

"That still doesn't tell me much."

Jaz shook her head. "Sorry. Anything else, she'll have to tell you herself if you get the chance to meet her."

Dean shrugged. Jaz's reluctance to share more irked him, but he figured the mystery would solve itself once this friend showed up.

The server came in carrying their next course, and soon their meal distracted them from talk of Jaz's friend. Dean settled into having a good night on vacation with his wife. So far, the trip was going pretty well.

Chapter 10

DEAN SPENT the next day hanging out in and around the hotel while Jaz attended to things with her Dublin office team. It was all an opportunity for Errington Security's Dublin crew to show the boss what they had going on. Jaz asked Dean if he wanted to come along to the office and join in the briefings and threat analysis.

He declined.

Jaz ended up having to add a second day of meetings when Elsa Behringer, the leader of European operations, came to Ireland to meet with her. The move to put her in a job previously only held by humans made Dean proud of how far his wife had come from the Hunter assassin he'd first met over a year before.

At the end of the second day, he gave in to another invitation and met up with Jaz and her employees at a restaurant. She was taking the whole Dublin team, along with Elsa, out to dinner to wrap up her official visit. They'd each be bringing along their significant other, and he figured he should be there, too. He could play the part of the dutiful husband. It turned out to be a lot of fun, and it gave him insights into why her teams respected her so much. Her two days here had been well spent, creating a synergy that would open lanes of communication from now on. The easy-going conversations around their dinner table showed how well everyone got along, not just with Jaz, but also each other.

Afterwards, they all said their goodbyes. It was raining as they left the restaurant. Niamh and her girlfriend, Sasha, offered them a ride back to the hotel, which they accepted.

As they rode alone in the elevator up to the twelfth floor, Dean reached out and held Jaz's hand. He took in his wife as she stood beside him in dark gray slacks and a matching blazer. She looked every bit the successful corporate CEO.

"I'm proud of you."

She glanced up at him, a smile curling the corners of her mouth. "What brought that on?"

"I don't always get to see you as the big boss lady like that. They all look up to you. It's good to see you in that light. It suits you. Back home, I've gotten to know the gang at the office, and it feels much more relaxed. I see now that is something you take with you when you visit these places."

"You could see it more often if you wanted to."

Dean shook his head. "No, not right now. After everything that happened a few months ago, I need a return to normal."

Jaz tried to hide her disappointment, but he spotted it in her expression.

"A no right now isn't a no forever, Hon. I will get to the point someday where a desk job will appeal to me more than being on the street. Every paramedic hits that point where the hard work is better left to the younger crews. When that time comes, I'd much rather ride a desk as part of Errington than for the city."

She gave his hand a squeeze. "I guess that's a bit of a win."

"It is."

They'd reached their floor and Jaz fished their room keycard from her blazer jacket. She passed it over the reader on the door and pushed open the door to their suite.

Dean headed for their bedroom. "I'm going to see if I can dial up one of our streaming TV services on the flatscreen in the bedroom. We can settle in for some binge-watching in bed."

"I like the sound of that," she replied, veering off for the bath-room. "I'm going to wash up. It's been a long day."

Dean picked up the remote from the bed as he kicked off his shoes. He stopped as his socks soaked up water from the carpet and he stepped back away from where he'd been standing, trying to under-stand where the water had come from.

Their bedroom had a small balcony with a sliding door. It was open about a foot. The sheer curtain waved slightly as the rain blew in. Thinking the maid must've left it open, Dean walked over and closed it. That was when he noticed a puddle in the carpet by the door and over by the bed, but not in between. It was like something wet had dripped the water on that part of the carpet.

A chill ran down his spine. He stared around the room, searching each shadow for something or someone. There weren't many places to hide in here. He ducked and checked under the bed and then over in the closet.

Moving to the living room to check there, his sock squelched in another wet spot on the carpet. Whoever or whatever it was, they had passed this way.

Across the living room, Jaz came from the bathroom. Dean froze and caught her eyes with his. She took one look at his face and stiff-ened beside the floor to ceiling windows overlooking the street below.

"Dean, what?"

"Someone's here."

As soon as he said it, a shadow detached from drapes behind her.

"Jaz, watch out!"

Before he could get his warning all the way out, Jaz reacted. She dropped to the ground, swinging her left leg wide as she spun to face to the rear.

The spinning kick caught the attacker by surprise. The shadowed figure stumbled backward into the wall, barely blocking the heel of Jaz's foot as it swept past their head.

That was all the opening Jaz needed. She jumped up from her crouch, leading with a double punching combination to the attacker's body.

The dark shadows in the living room kept Dean from seeing everything. Neither of them had turned on the lights beyond the foyer and he couldn't see in the dark the way Jaz could with her Hunter charm. He ran to the panel by the door and clicked on the overhead lights.

The recessed lighting in the ceiling revealed his wife and a dark-skinned woman in blue jeans and a black leather trench coat trading blows in a flurry of punches and kicks almost too fast to follow.

He thought Jaz had the advantage until the woman dodged a punch at her face, grabbing the extended wrist and twisting to the side.

The maneuver yanked Jaz off-balance, and she cried out in pain. The other woman pulled harder and threw her hip outward, catching Jaz's falling body and flipping her to the floor.

"Jaz!" Dean yelled as the intruder lifted her foot to stomp down at her prone target.

Jaz rolled out of the way at the last moment, but moved towards the other woman, not away. The evasive maneuver rolled her up against the other woman's planted ankle.

Reaching up, she hooked her fingers over the thick leather gun belt beneath the swirling trench coat. Jaz kicked upward with one foot at the same time she yanked down on the woman's waist.

Dean's alarm turned to a cheer as the kick launched the woman up and over the sofa to crash into the coffee table. The wooden table collapsed under the woman's weight.

Jaz had already regained her feet. She leaped over the table to land atop the attacker as she struggled to get up. Jaz delivered a rapid series of powerful punches to the woman's chest.

Ordinarily the attack would have been devastating to an opponent. Dean wasn't sure what effect it had, though. The other woman wore tight-fitting black body armor of some sort beneath her coat.

Jaz brushed aside the attempts to block her attacks until the woman let her hands relax to the floor beside her head.

The flurry of punches stopped. Jaz snarled, "Give up?"

The other woman stared up at Jaz with her stunning brown eyes. The two glared at each other for a few seconds, then the intruder nodded.

To Dean's surprise, both their faces broke into broad grins. Jaz leaned down to offer the other woman a hand up. The attacker took the offered help with another nod.

Once she stood, the newcomer leaned in and the two women exchanged an embrace that seemed almost—friendly?

"Jaz, what the heck is going on? Who is this woman?"

"Dean, I'd like you to meet Chief Inspector Hangbe Dahomey, though I'm pretty sure that's not her actual name. She's the friend I told you I had to meet up with while we were here."

Dean spluttered as he searched for an answer. He'd just witnessed one of the fiercest fights he'd ever seen. Neither of them had pulled any punches. "But, I mean, why all the—?"

Hangbe smiled. "Jaswinder and I like to test each other. We've always been sort of competitive." She had a slight British accent with a hint of something else in the background, maybe West African?

"You started it," Jaz responded. "You began that string of practical jokes while we investigated that demonic incursion in Nigeria."

"You can't really blame me. You were so shiny and new, you practically squeaked. Someone had to take the polish off you once you were out from under Daddy's watchful eye."

"Yeah, well, I'm not under anyone's eye, not anymore."

The inspector's eyes turned sad. "I'm sorry about that, Jaz. I was half-way around the world and the news was weeks old when I found out what happened to your family. If I was closer, I would have come to help you right away."

"I know. It turned out I did alright with the help I had. That's where I met Dean." She held up her hand, flashing her wedding ring. "I guess it was worth it."

Hangbe cast a doubtful glance at the bling. "I can't believe you've finally settled down."

Jaz shook her head. "No settling down here at all. If anything, I'm busier than ever. We had to squeeze in our honeymoon on a business trip."

Hangbe looked from Jaz to Dean and back again. "Oh, so this is him? I thought I'd crashed another one of your infamous one-night-stands."

Dean looked from Jaz to Hangbe and back again. "What does she mean by that, exactly?"

Jaz laughed, but her expression wasn't all that joyful. She glared at her friend. "She's just stirring up crap. It's her favorite past-time." She kicked a piece of the table from in front of the couch. "Come and sit down. I had them make sure the mini-bar was fully stocked for you. Can I offer a drink?"

The taller woman sat down and shook her head. "Better just a sparkling water tonight. I've got some more leads to run down after this."

Dean waved off Jaz. He tried to forget the earlier comment as he said, "I'll get the drinks. You go sit and chat. Bubbly water for her and single malt scotch on the rocks for you, dear?"

"That would be perfect. I suppose you can have a beer if you want."

"Gee, thanks, honey."

Jaz laughed, sitting beside her friend.

Dean pulled open the cabinet hiding the minibar. He fetched the drinks and studied his wife and the other woman. It was clear they knew each other, probably pretty well from the way they riffed off each other. He listened to their conversation. He knew little about Jaz's early days before they met. This could be his way in to get some interesting stories about his wife's earlier exploits.

He grabbed a bottle of French soda water and two miniature bottles of scotch from the minibar. He dropped a few ice cubes from the tiny ice tray in the freezer into two glasses and carried them over to the sofa. Jaz and Hangbe took them, each offering a nod of thanks without breaking their conversation. They seemed to be catching up on the locations of a few mutual friends.

Dean went back and got himself a bottle of German lager from the fridge and sat down on the chair across from the broken coffee table. They didn't even glance at him as he sat back, watching them and sipping on his beer.

When a lull in the conversation finally presented itself, Dean asked, "Hangbe, what kind of investigation are you working on that has you out after you leave here. It's already late. It must be important."

Hangbe glanced at Jaz.

She nodded. "He's okay. I wouldn't have married him if he wasn't. Also, he's a half-Eldara, though he's all human in the ways that matter the most."

Hangbe cast a glance at him. He got the impression she had reappraised him instantly based on Jaz's comment. "Hopefully not *all* the ways."

Jaz blushed and Hangbe let out a loud burst of laughter.

Dean wasn't sure what she meant by that, but he let it slide. He could ask Jaz later.

"In response to your question, Dean, I'm heading out to interview some sex workers downtown. They were busy working earlier in the night and I don't want to interrupt their trade. Later on, after the traffic slows down, I'm hoping I can convince a few of them to talk with me."

"Are they in some sort of trouble?" Dean asked. "Shouldn't you involve the local authorities if they need help?"

"I will help them, if that's what they want. Right now, I'm trying to figure out how they all got here and who brought them. There's a huge trafficking ring based around here somewhere and following the money has proven difficult. The trail goes cold here in Dublin."

Jaz asked, "Is it just sex trafficking or are they smuggling all sorts of folks?"

"Lately, they've been dealing in various sorts of shifters, but the non-violent varieties."

Something tweaked Dean's memory. "You mean like Selkies?"

Hangbe shot him a look. "Exactly like Selkies. I've just come from a small village on the coast of Scotland. They cleaned the entire place out. One day the people were there and the next, someone drove into the village and everyone was gone."

"That's not good," Jaz said. "Any signs of killing or violence?"

"Sadly, yes." Hangbe fiddled with the beads on an ornate and colorful necklace she wore tight around her throat. "I used a bit of necromancy, though, and raised a recently dead Selkie gramfer. He couldn't tell me much. Dark figures burst into his home, rounded up his children and grandchildren. Then they dragged he and wife into a nearby cave with about a dozen other elderly villagers, able-bodied men and boys, and killed them."

"That's awful," Dean said. "If you could communicate with him, he must have been able to give you a description of who did it."

Hangbe shook her head. "They wore all black and were masked. They spoke in a language he didn't know. He thought it might be Spanish, but he wasn't sure."

"What about the others who went missing?" Jaz asked. "Do you have any idea where they were taken?"

"Traffic cameras picked up a rental truck that came over on a ferry from England. I tracked that down and it led me to here. Since then, I've been trying to track them down. I figure they've been put to work somewhere in the Republic, but I can't figure out where."

Dean had been listening, drawing lines and connections in his mind. More questions came before he could stop himself. "Was this the first such empty village full of Selkies who went missing?"

"No," Hangbe said. "There are four that I know of. The local police investigated but couldn't find evidence of who killed the ones they didn't take. They have swept it under the rug. They're telling the locals the small clans just moved on or left to go back to sea. They have closed the cases." Her voice turned hard as she said the last bit.

"You don't believe that." Jaz said.

"Of course not, but it's all the same. There's a lot of distrust for Selkies along the northern coastal areas and islands. They've been given a bad rap for things since the days of the Black Plague. People aren't sad to see them go, so the authorities won't dig into what might have happened. It's the perfect place to kidnap people."

Dean nodded. "What if they're not in Ireland at all?"

"Where else would they be? I've checked the sea and airports. There's no evidence they've left for anywhere else. If that was what they wanted, they could've smuggled them into container ships leaving from Liverpool. No need to shuttle them over here."

Dean glanced at Jaz. From the tilt of her head, he could tell she was thinking what he was.

"Hangbe, you and Dean are both right. They wouldn't have come here unless there was an easier way to transport people elsewhere here in Dublin."

"Jaz, if you know something, tell me. I've been on this case for months."

"Give Dean and I a few days to wrap up our honeymoon time. You keep tracking down the leads you have. Talk to your ladies on the street and see what you find out. We can meet back here at the hotel for breakfast when we return. While we're gone, I'll have my local team do some digging, too. We'll all share everything we've got and see if anything clicks."

"That should work." Hangbe downed the rest of her sparkling water and set the bottle down on the floor beside the broken table. She stood and stretched her arms over her head. "I should get going. Nice to meet you, Dean. It's good to see someone tamed that girl. I wouldn't have believed it had I not seen it myself."

"Careful how you put that, my friend," Jaz said. "Someone might tame you, too, someday."

"Not a chance. There isn't a man alive who can satisfy me long enough to make me want to stay."

"If you say so."

"I do." Hangbe headed for the door.

Dean pointed to the bedroom. "Don't you want to go out the way you came in?"

"Why? I don't need a key to get out."

She winked and left Dean and Jaz sitting alone in their suite.

As soon as the door shut, Jaz asked, "You think her case has something to do with what you uncovered in Elk City?"

"And you don't?"

Jaz paused, thinking for a few seconds. "There's something bigger at play here. I need to have my people do some checking on who closed that pub down. Once we get that and Hangbe tracks down her leads, we can compare notes. Maybe we'll see the bigger connection once we have more pieces."

"And until then?" Dean asked.

Jaz pulled him close and whispered in his ear. "Until then, I'm on my honeymoon."

Chapter 11

DEAN AND JAZ slept in the next morning, enjoying the first official day of their delayed honeymoon. As they got up and packed for the next phase of the trip, Jaz found a text from Hangbe sent in the very early morning hours. A call had come in from police in Northern Ireland. There'd been more disappearances there, and she was already on the road to check them out. She'd reach out if she found anything useful.

Dean and Jaz filed the message away, determined to continue on with their much needed alone time together. Dean swallowed hard, trying to clear the anxiety that roiled his stomach. He'd selected a quaint bed-and-breakfast place on the coast. The two of them would have a personal cottage all to themselves. The owners had stocked the kitchen with a few requested items for them to have for lunch and dinner, and they would deliver breakfast each morning. It had looked perfect, but now he wondered if it was right or not. He put on a smile and pressed forward. Too late to change anything now.

Jaz had requisitioned one of the company Land Rovers and she got in to drive to their little retreat while Dean navigated while he took in the passing countryside. The rolling hills stretched to the horizon on either side. To Dean, it seemed a lot like some rural regions of Maryland back home. Using his phone's GPS, he guided them to the turn toward the cottage. Jaz steered the SUV down a long gravel lane.

The location was just like the pictures on the app Dean had used to book the place. It sat on a bluff looking out over the Atlantic Ocean. He'd called ahead when they were a half hour out and the caretaker named Clive waited for them with a key. He told them his wife, Bess, had left something special in the kitchen. He also said she would be back in the morning to cook them an authentic Irish country breakfast. He mentioned they would especially like her Irish soda bread. The thought of fresh-baked bread alone had Dean already looking forward to breakfast the next day.

After the old man left, they entered and unpacked their suitcases. They had left a vase with fresh flowers on the kitchen table with a bottle of Irish whiskey. The note wished them a happy honeymoon. Besides the kitchen, there was a bathroom, a small bedroom, and a living room. It was just the right size for the two of them.

After settling in and checking out the cottage itself, Dean and Jaz went for a walk outside to get the lay of the land. At the edge of the bluff overlooking the ocean, a path led down to the rocky shore below. Dean's eyes scanned the beach, enjoying the foamy surf crashing on the thin section of beach he could see from where he stood. As he turned away to follow Jaz back to the house, he had a nagging feeling he was missing something he should've seen there. He shrugged, chalking it up to just being tired. He decided it might be nice to head down there for a run along the beach before breakfast the next day.

He and Jaz headed back to the cottage hand in hand. Dean's usually taut EMS senses had settled to a gentle murmur in the back of his mind, leaving him to focus on his wife. It was something he hoped she felt as well. They both had jobs that kept them on some version of alert most of the time. This was a much-needed opportunity for some downtime.

Back in the cottage, they made themselves sandwiches with the sliced lamb roast left in the fridge. There was a nice wedge of a sharp farm cheese, too, along with bottles of local beer. Taking a bottle each along with their plates, Dean and Jaz headed out to sit outside on a blanket they spread on the grass in back of the home.

Dean finished his sandwich and leaned back on one elbow while he sipped at his beer. "This is exactly what I needed. How about you, hon?"

Jaz smiled. "Me, too. You were right. We both needed to get away from home for a few days. Even with the work stuff when I got here, I could feel the relief of not having to deal with every little detail back home."

"See, I have a good idea every once in a while."

"Okay, but that's your one for this year."

"Hey, that's not fair." Dean laughed and then leaned in to kiss Jaz. The scents from the wildflowers and the sea breeze coupled with his wife's favorite perfume made it the perfect moment.

When they parted a few seconds later, Dean said, "Maybe we should clean up and head inside."

"What, afraid the locals might see us naked?" She glanced over her shoulder at the distant ribbon of country lane. "We're far enough off the road."

"I don't think there's anything wrong with a little privacy. Besides, I have a few surprises for you."

Jaz's grin turned wicked. "Me, too." She grabbed her plate and utensils and headed for the cottage. "Don't take too long cleaning up the rest. I might just start without you."

Dean didn't need to be told twice. He scooped up the rest of their dinner remnants, grabbed the woolen blanket, and ran in after her. He wouldn't keep her waiting.

The afternoon turned to night and both Dean and Jaz slept well with the help of a few shots of the whiskey, another quick sandwich, and more time alone together. It was early the next morning, when the sunlight beamed in the bedroom window, that Dean finally awakened. He shielded his sleepy eyes with his hand as he sat up and walked over to pull the heavy curtains closed. The room darkened and Dean checked to make sure Jaz still slept. He decided not to wake her. He'd dreamt overnight of running on the beach like he'd planned. He decided to take some time for himself and get some exercise at the same time.

Dean glanced at the clock over the stove in the kitchen. The caretaker's wife wouldn't be here to make breakfast for at least a half hour. It gave him just enough time to hit the beach below and still make it back in time for breakfast with Jaz.

He sent his wife a quick text message telling her where he was and headed outside. Making his way to the bluff overlooking the beach, he started down the narrow track. The trail down the bluff was steeper than it looked from the top, but it wasn't too treacherous. He took his time and soon he reached the bottom.

Dean looked both ways up and down the coast. A gentle tug at his subconscious he barely noticed drew him to the north, and Dean shrugged. It was as good a choice as any. He jogged along the shore, enjoying the way the early morning mist still clung to the rocky beach in many places.

He'd gone about a mile north and was about to turn back when that strange tugging sensation made him stop. Earlier it had been barely a hint. Now it physically pulled him away from going back the way he came. When he tried to turn back, something wrenched his shoulders back around to face northward again.

Realizing he couldn't fight whatever supernatural event had ahold of him, Dean scanned the beach and the cliffs above. Something held him here. Maybe he could find it and whoever was behind it. Up on the cliffs above he spotted a large box truck parked halfway down a gravel lane that wound down towards the beach and stopped at the edge of the high tide line a quarter mile farther to the north. No one was around it, and he wondered why it was there.

He started towards it, but before he'd taken two steps, it started up and drove away up the lane and disappeared. He stared at the empty lane for a few long seconds, then started walking up to where it had parked. Reaching the tire imprints in the wet gravel, Dean stopped. He had the driving urge to do something, but he couldn't figure out what. The truck was gone. Was he supposed to follow it?

Not having a better idea, Dean started up the gravel lane. He hadn't gone fifty yards farther before he picked up the faint sound of someone crying. He stopped and looked around. With the crashing waves, it was hard to pick up exactly where the sound came from.

Dean spotted some rock outcroppings jutting up at the base of the bluff below where he stood halfway up the lane. Turning around, he returned to the beach and walked around to the rocks.

They were each taller than he was and in a way that forced him to walk through several knee-deep tidal pools before he rounded the last one. As he did, the sobbing grew louder.

There at the base of the rocks was the broad opening of a cave with a sandy floor. A girl of about thirteen with long red hair crouched behind the outcropping. She wore a blue-green dress and had no shoes on, despite the rocky shoreline. Two long green streaks colored her hair on either side. The strips ran from just in front of her ears and down the hair over her shoulder.

As soon as the girl spotted him, she stood and craned her neck back and forth in a frantic search for a way out past him.

"Hey, hold on. I'm not here to hurt you. I heard you crying and came to see what was up."

She stopped looking past him and shifted her surprised gaze to his face. "You're an American. Does that mean you're not with them?"

"With who? I'm on vacation with my wife at a cottage to the south. I'm alone otherwise."

The girl craned her neck, trying to see past Dean.

He twisted his head to see what she was looking at. There was no one there.

"We're alone. It's okay. Tell me what's wrong and maybe I can help you. I have a phone. We can call for the police."

As soon as he pulled out his phone, she got more agitated. She stepped forward, pulling at his hand to keep him from dialing it. "No, the local constable is with them. If you call, it'll tell them where I am. You can't let them take me, too."

The girl turned her head and he spotted thin lines down the side of her neck. The parallel lines rippled and opened, revealing pink membranes underneath. He nodded, realizing what he saw. She had gills. That meant she was some sort of Unusual.

She caught him staring at her and clapped a hand to her neck. When she took her hand away, the lines had disappeared, leaving smooth skin behind. Like most Unusuals, she could hide who she was from humans.

Taking a chance that she might trust him better if she knew he was aware of people like her, he held out his hand where he had the invisible tattoo only members of the supernatural community could see. It was a paramedic's star of life with a snake and staff cadeusus emblazoned on top of it.

Her eyes widened. "What is that?"

"It's a sign of who I am and what I do. I'm a special paramedic, a helper who has sworn to take care of people like you. You can trust me."

She hesitated, her eyes shifting every few seconds to scan all around for trouble.

He kept talking, keeping his voice calm and soft. "My name is Dean Flynn. What's yours?"

"Kaylee."

"Hi, Kaylee. Do you mind if I ask you a question? I noticed your neck. Were those gills?"

Kaylee's hand drifted back up to her neck for a second, then she nodded. "I guess I was nervous, and I started to shift."

"What kind of Unusual are you? I can tell a little about folks I meet, but not everything."

"I'm a Kelpie. We have a small community that comes ashore from time to time when we want to trade with the villagers."

"Where are the rest of your family? If you're lost, I can help you find them."

She shook her head. "The cat-men took them. I swam back out into the surf when they jumped out of the truck and started attacking the others. I don't think they saw me. I swam around here to hide in this cave. I watched them load my family and the other villagers into the back of their truck. They'd tied up everyone. That's when I saw the constable. The leader of the cat men gave him an envelope and he drove away in his police van. I thought maybe I could set them free. But then the truck drove away."

"I saw the truck leave. It just drove inland."

Kaylee's shoulders dropped. "Then they're gone. I'll never find them."

"We don't know that. My wife is here with me and she's great at finding things, especially bad people like those cat-men."

Dean was pretty sure he knew who those men were, and why they were here. He wondered if there was time to track down the girl's family before the traffickers took them through the door to Elk City.

"Come with me back to the cottage. My wife is there, and she can help. We can get you some breakfast, too, and maybe some dry clothes, too."

Kaylee thought for a long while before she answered. She kept looking back out to the ocean waves crashing nearby.

Dean turned to look at the water. "Is there someone back there that can help you? I'll find a way to take you to them if that's what you need."

"No. There's no one there for me now. The entire village came ashore to trade."

"Then let's get started back to my wife. She's your best chance at finding your family again."

Dean backed up to give the girl room. He smiled as he moved to work his way back around the rocks. Kaylee followed along, hesitating a little at first, but then keeping up as Dean started back down the beach. The strange tugging sensation he'd felt before had disappeared. A feeling of accomplishment and satisfaction replaced it.

As they walked, he texted ahead to warn Jaz. She didn't like surprises like this, and he didn't want the caretaker's wife to see Kaylee. If some locals were in on this, there was no way to know who was safe and who wasn't. Luckily, Jaz was awake. She texted back that she'd come outside at the top of the bluff for him once the woman prepared breakfast and left them alone again.

When they reached the trail, Jaz stood along the path at the top. He'd been afraid she'd dress in her Hunter gear, but she didn't. She wore a skirt and blouse and smiled as Dean and Kaylee approached.

"You must be Kaylee. I'm Jaz. My husband says you're having some sort of trouble."

"Yes, ma'am. They took my family from the beach and drove away in a truck."

Dean nodded. "It's okay. You can tell her everything you told me.

She knows about the cat-men and about Kelpies." He pointed up at the cottage. "Maybe we can go inside and talk?" He glanced at Jaz. "Is it clear?"

"Bess is finishing breakfast. I told her I was meeting you out here and wanted some privacy. She said she'd leave everything on the table for us and leave out the front. I thought it best not to involve her with this until we knew what was going on."

Dean let out a long sigh. "Good thinking, hon. Let's remain out here for a bit until she leaves."

Jaz smiled and nodded. "Kaylee, tell me what happened and maybe we can help you."

Kaylee related the story she'd told Dean. When she mentioned the cat-men, Jaz shot Dean a look. She pulled out her phone and tapped in a message while the girl talked. As Kaylee talked, a small compact car drove away down the lane. That had to be Bess leaving. They could go inside.

Dean pointed up the hill. "Kaylee, come inside with us and we'll get you some food. Then you can tell us more of what you know. Any detail might be important."

Once inside, Kaylee spotted the breakfast laid out on the table and sat down, filling a plate with eggs and sausages. Dean sliced a thick piece of the steaming soda bread for her, too. Then he and Jaz watched as she ate for a few seconds. Seeing she was taken care of, the two of them sat and filled their own plates to join her. A few minutes later, Jaz's phone rang. She showed Dean the screen. It was Hangbe.

Jaz excused herself to step into the other room.

"Where did she go?"

"It's okay, Kaylee. My wife has a friend who is investigating people disappearing like your family. I think that's who she is talking with."

Jaz came back a few minutes later and sat down. Dean and Kaylee had continued, filling their plates with another helping of the warm Irish soda bread, smeared with chilled sweet cream butter, along with more of the sausages and eggs.

Dean waited until Jaz sat down then asked, "How'd the call go?"

Jaz finished her bite before responding. "She is heading back this way. She'll be here this afternoon. I also reached out to Niamh to look into any underworld werecat clans operating in the area."

Kaylee fixed Jaz with a hopeful gaze. "Does that mean you can find my family?"

Jaz reached out and laid her hand on the girl's arm. "I'm going to do whatever I can to help find them and bring them home. You're lucky you ran into my husband. We kind of specialize in this kind of thing."

"You do?"

Jaz nodded. "Finish your breakfast and then I want to have you talk to one of my friends back in Dublin. She has some questions for you. Tell her everything you know. The more she can find out, the better chance we have of catching the people who took your family."

Kaylee nodded and went back to eating. Dean and Jaz shared a glance and finished their meal in silence. He wondered if his wife felt the same way he did. Once again, events out of their control dashed their plans for a relaxing honeymoon.

Chapter 12

AFTER EATING, Jaz took Kaylee into the sitting room and set up a video call with Niamh to get more details about the people who took her family. The Dublin team had some facial recognition software that could approximate a sketch of the perpetrators, and Niamh wanted to try it with Kaylee. Any small bit of information could make a difference, and Jaz's Dublin team would make sure they got everything they could from the young Kelpie to help find her family.

After Jaz got the girl set up on the call, she came over to where Dean stood in the doorway. She stared at him for a long time, holding the silver Hunter charm around her neck between her thumb and forefinger. After a few long, uncomfortable seconds, she nodded and smiled.

"What?" Dean asked.

"The Geas seems to be gone. I think finding the girl was the event the Rakshini foretold in her viewing on you."

Dean glanced down at his body and ran his left hand down the front of his shirt. A chill passed down his spine as he thought about the spell's magic effects on him. Had it helped him find the Kelpie girl this morning? "Are you sure?"

Jaz nodded. "I can't sense it anymore. I think you fulfilled the quest or whatever it was."

"It's not done until we make sure she's safe. How long until Hangbe gets here?"

"It shouldn't be long. She said she'd hurry." Jaz glanced back over her shoulder to where Kaylee chatted with Niamh on the video call. "I should get back over there and supervise. This could be important."

Dean pulled out his phone while Jaz returned to sit beside the Kelpie girl. He leaned against the door and checked his Station U email account before sending in a series of emails to his colleagues to see if they had any more information about Verity or the trafficking ring. Barry replied right away, telling him to stop worrying about it and to relax and enjoy the honeymoon.

He appreciated his partner's concern. Barry knew how much this trip meant to him. However, now that he had a patient to take care of, all his thoughts for himself went out the window. There had to be a connection between this and Verity's situation in Elk City. He intended to find it and track it down to find the missing girl and maybe Kaylee's family, too.

After the video call ended, Kaylee settled on the small couch and watched some game show on the TV. Dean and Jaz left her alone while they stepped outside the front door to talk. It was time to go over their next steps.

They'd barely started going over their options when a speeding sports car turned down the long, gravel lane in their direction. It swerved so hard to make the turn, Dean feared it would overturn as it slid to the side. It regained traction at the last possible instant, straightening out and racing down the lane in their direction. The speed and apparent recklessness alarmed Dean.

As it got closer, he tried to make out the driver through the tinted windows. He couldn't see more than a shadowed figure behind the wheel. The silver coupe slid to a stop near the cottage's front door in a spray of gravel. The door popped open and Hangbe climbed out.

The inspector pointed to the cottage. "Is the girl in there?" The tension and hint of alarm in her voice made her urgency clear to both of them.

Jaz nodded. "Why, what's up?"

"The local police are on the way. I overheard a radio transmission about picking up some runaway. Somehow, they know she's here. We have to get her out of here."

Based on the yelp of fear from inside, the girl must've heard Hangbe. Kaylee ran from the house, trying to get by Jaz, who blocked her way. Her head jerked from side to side, her body poised to bolt in either direction. "They've found me. I have to go."

"Stop, Kaylee," Dean said. He kept his voice level and his tone friendly. "You're not in immediate danger. This is our friend, Hangbe. She's here to protect you, just like we are. No one will take you anywhere you don't want to go."

Jaz caught his eye and shook her head. He realized he'd broken a cardinal rule of earning a patient's trust. Don't promise something you can't deliver. If the proper authorities showed up to pick up a minor child, they'd have to turn her over.

He shrugged, glancing from Jaz to Hangbe. "What do we do?"

The Interpol agent pointed to the car. "Girl, if you want to avoid the people coming for you, you need to come with me, now."

"I don't know." Kaylee glanced from the car to the ocean beyond the bluffs. Dean knew she wanted to run; she just didn't know which way.

Hangbe turned to Jaz. "There's no time. Tell her. Once the local police get here, it'll be out of our hands. I can't overrule a local officer on something like this."

"She's right, Kaylee," Jaz said. "Go with our friend. She can take you to Dublin where Niamh is. We'll pack up our stuff and follow as soon as we can. We'll wait just long enough to point the police in the wrong direction. We can meet up with you both and continue the search for your family once we know you're safe."

The girl didn't seem sure what to do. She needed someone to decide. Dean took charge. He walked over and gently ushered her to the passenger side of the sports car. "Get in. Hangbe won't let anything happen to you. We'll see you later tonight."

"Promise?"

"If we're not there, it's because it's not safe for us to come to you.

We'll catch up eventually, though. Trust Hangbe. Jaz and I will see you as soon as we can."

Kaylee sat down and buckled her seatbelt. Hangbe nodded and climbed back in the driver's seat. "I'll head to Dublin. I'll leave a message for you at the front desk of your hotel. Check there if you don't hear from me."

Jaz nodded. "Contact Niamh at my offices there. She'll have additional resources for you and maybe some information. She's already started on tracking the people who took Kaylee's family."

Hangbe answered with a grim smile and closed her door. The sports car drove away, kicking up a fresh a shower of gravel as it took off back down the lane.

The car got out and disappeared down the road just in time. She hadn't been gone for more than five minutes before a police van drove down the lane. A rotund police constable got out. A tall, powerfully built man in a black leather jacket climbed out of the passenger side.

The pair walked up to the house where Dean and Jaz stood. The constable said, "I'm Police Constable Kelly. I understand from Bess Byrne that you two found a missing girl down on the beach?"

"We did," Jaz said. "Why, is there something wrong?"

"She's a runaway. This gentleman here is her uncle. He and the rest of the family have been looking for her. She's a troubled girl and likes to get folks all worked up with wild stories."

"I see," Jaz replied. She shrugged. "That's a shame. We fed her breakfast. As soon as she finished, the girl told us she had to leave. We tried to stop her, but she got away from us and ran off down the beach. I do hope she's alright. She's not dangerous to us, is she?"

The tall man growled under his breath, saying, "Why didn't you go after her? You two appear more than capable of taking care of a young girl."

Dean held up his hands. "Hey, we're not the bad guys here. We didn't know who she was. We just tried to be nice. Once she ran off, she's someone else's problem. We're just visitors here. We didn't know."

The constable and the one pretending to be Kaylee's uncle exchanged glances. Constable Kelly stepped forward. "Can I see some identification? I'm going to need to write this up and I must know where you'll be staying."

"Oh, I hope this will not cause an issue for us," Jaz said. "We were thinking of heading back to Dublin tonight."

"As long as I know where you'll be staying and you don't leave the country, that will be fine. My superiors may want to question you further."

"About what?" Dean asked. "We told you what happened."

"You told us what you said happened," the tall man replied. "we must verify your statements to see if you're lying. There will be severe consequences if we find out you did. Where will you be staying?"

Jaz stepped forward, her hands on her hips. She stopped a few feet away and stared at the man. "I'm sorry, are you a distraught uncle or a police investigator? Which is it?"

Dean tensed. Jaz didn't back down from anyone. He prepared for trouble.

The constable let out a nervous laugh. "He's just concerned for his niece, miss. He meant nothing by it. Just let me jot down some information from your passports and you can go back to the city. I'm sure this will all work itself out. No need to make an international incident over it."

Dean went inside and fetched their passports, handing them to the constable.

He snapped a photo of their documents with his phone and handed them back. "Where did you say you'd be in the city?"

Jaz answered the Constable but kept her eyes leveled on the taller man. "You can reach me at my offices. Just contact Errington Security. They can tell you where we are."

At the mention of the company name, the tall man's body stiffened. He stared long and hard at Jaz, studying her while considering this new information. He'd fallen for the innocent tourist act until now. Dean wondered why Jaz had let out the information that way.

A second later, the uncle nodded. "I think we should leave these two alone and get back to searching for my niece, Constable. You have everything you need, correct?"

The constable nodded, confused by the sudden change in direction. He smiled and said goodbye.

The van drove off and Dean realized he'd been holding his breath. He was sure Jaz was going to end up fighting the uncle right there in the driveway.

"That was close. I was worried."

Jaz cocked her head to the side. "Why were you worried? I had everything under control."

"How? What if he had attacked you? Were you just going to shoot the guy?"

Jaz laughed. "You have no idea how much I wanted him to make a move. I'm almost positive he's the head of the werecat clan that took those people. I could smell the musty shifter odor coming from him."

"But you're unarmed. Your sword and guns are in the SUV."

Jaz leaned down and pulled up one side of her long skirt to reveal a small holster strapped to her leg, mid-thigh. She pulled out the pistol and checked the chamber before returning it to the holster.

"I'm never unarmed. You know that. Especially not when we have things like this going on around us. If he'd so much as twitched in our direction, I'd have filled him full of silver slugs before he'd taken two steps."

Dean knew she wasn't kidding. When he'd first met her, she was a shoot first, ask questions later kind of person. He thought she'd mellowed a little since they'd gotten together. Every now and then, though, she reminded him just how deadly she was.

"What should we do now? He's got to know we've hidden her somehow."

"We pack up and head back to the city. If he has taken those people and they're part of the same werepanther clan that you ran into back in the Maryland, then there's only one way for them to get those people to Elk City. If we hurry, we can stop them there."

"You think they're using the Irish Shop portal to transport their victims?"

"And you don't?" Jaz asked.

"I'm not sure. I guess I don't want to think that Dougie is mixed up in something like this."

"He might not be a willing participant. Remember how the local pub owner died mysteriously? They probably threatened the leprechaun, too."

Dean hoped that was the case. He went into the house and started packing up. So much for their spending a couple of relaxing days here with all the peace and quiet. The honeymoon was definitely over.

Chapter 13

ON THE DRIVE back to Dublin, Dean's mind kept going over how their nice belated honeymoon trip had gone off the rails. He wondered if there was any way to salvage something from the trip. In the end, he gave up on the idea. There were more important things going on and he felt selfish for focusing on his meager problems while others were dealing with kidnappings and family disappearances.

As he caught glimpses of the city in the distance, Dean broke the silence. "What are we going to do with Kaylee if the were-cats have already taken her family through the portal?"

"I've been trying to work through that problem. We can't take her through with us. She'd be just another illegal if she got into any trouble. I need to ask around and see if there's anywhere safe to put her here until we find her family."

"You know there's a chance we won't find her family, Jaz? It's hard to track down traffickers and their victims. If we don't intercept them here in Ireland and they get to the U.S., they could go almost anywhere."

She shrugged. "We'll find someone here who can take in a long-term guest until we either locate her family or find her next of kin. Let me call in to the office. They might be able to help."

Jaz tapped the phone icon on the dashboard screen and selected the number for the local Errington office.

Niamh answered. "Errington Security, Limited. Niamh speaking. How may I help you?"

"Niamh, it's Jaz. I'm on my way back into the city. I need you to arrange a room at the same hotel we stay at before. We should be there to check in within the hour. Meet us there."

"You cut your trip short, ma'am?"

"With everything that happened with the girl, we followed up ourselves. I'll get you more info once we get in. Tell the others in the office you're on detached special duty as of now under my direct orders."

"Yes, ma'am. I'll have everything set up when you arrive at the hotel. Should I prepare for anything special while on this duty with you, ma'am?"

"No, just requisition one of the SUVs with a standard load out. I'll explain more when you meet us at the hotel." Jaz hung up. She glanced at Dean. "That's one thing down. We can work out the rest of the details about this issue once we make sure Kaylee's safe."

Jaz had Dean send Hangbe a text to meet them at the hotel once she checked it out. The other woman replied with a simple thumbs up. Dean showed it to Jaz and settled back in his seat, wondering what Jaz had planned.

Niamh waited for them on the curb as they pulled into the hotel's driveway. Jaz and Dean climbed out as the porters removed their bags and the valet took the SUV to park it.

Niamh handed Jaz and Dean two keycards. "I got the same suite you had before, Ms. Errington. I hope that is acceptable."

"Perfect. Let's go up now. They've got our luggage loaded on the cart."

Once they arrived upstairs and the porter finished unloading their luggage, Jaz took charge and filled them in on what she had planned. She pointed to the chairs in the suite's living room. Niamh sat down on the couch while Dean took one of the matching chairs. Jaz remained on her feet.

"Niamh, I'm about to ask you some unusual questions. There's no wrong answer, and if you decide what I need you to do is too much, there will be no repercussions. Okay?"

"Yes, ma'am. I'm sure there won't be any problem with your request. What is it you need?"

Dean hid a smile. The whole clandestine nature of things had the girl leaning forward in her seat with anticipation. He feared she might topple to the floor.

"You live with your parents, right?"

"Yes, ma'am. It's me, and my ma and da. My two older sisters have their own families. They have homes not too far away."

"Is there room in your parent's home for a special houseguest? This is a person who needs protection from certain underworld groups. I need a place where they're unlikely to look for her."

"I suppose so, ma'am. I'd have to ask my parents to be sure, but I think they'd say yes. It's the girl, right?"

"I cannot tell you until your parents give you an answer. That is all I can say right now."

Niamh nodded and pulled out her phone. "Let me call them right now and I'll get an answer for you." She crossed to the far side of the living room to make her call. She kept her voice low as she talked to her parents, but Dean could still pick up on most of what she said. Whatever their response was, it didn't seem to upset the girl.

It didn't take long to get an answer. Niamh's father had been in the Garda and it seemed his background protecting Unusuals carried into his retirement. Both parents agreed to help without reservation.

Jaz nodded and Dean got the sense she'd known what the answer would be before she'd made the request. His wife had a good sense for the type of people she worked with. That included their family backgrounds. She liked to know she could count on the team members to have her back.

Once Niamh returned to her seat on the couch, Jaz filled her in on what was going on with Kaylee, especially the fact that they had reported her as a runaway and the authorities might be looking for her in addition to the traffickers. The instructions were simple. Keep the young Kelpie safe while Dean and Jaz searched for the family, probably somewhere in the U.S. It might be an extended stay, so Niamh would need to create new identification papers for the girl as a visiting cousin or something.

"How about an exchange student?" Dean suggested.

"That's a good idea. What do you think, Niamh?"

The girl nodded. "That would help with the questions my sisters will have. I can say they arranged it through my work with the company. They should accept that."

"Good. That's settled then." Jaz started to say something else but stopped when there was a rap on the door.

Dean checked the peephole. It was Hangbe and Kaylee.

He opened the door and let them in. Jaz filled the pair in on what they'd already planned. After making sure Kaylee seemed confident enough to go along with the plan, Niamh got the SUV keys from Jaz and left with her charge. The Errington employee was closer to Kaylee's age and knew how to chat about things to keep her mind off all that had changed in her life. The distraction helped calm her down, and she went along with no further delay.

With that taken care of, Jaz, Dean, and Hangbe sat down to work through the next steps dealing with the larger problem.

The Interpol agent jumped in with what she'd uncovered, or rather, failed to uncover. "I've found nothing. This group is very good at covering their tracks. I followed them to the city. I know they came here, but then they disappear. Either no one knows where they go, or they have enough clout to keep people from talking."

"Dean and I think we know something that might help explain their disappearance." Jaz explained about the portal back to the U.S. She described the strange encounter on their way here and her suspicions related to Dean's encounter with his patient the previous week.

Hangbe smiled. "That's good news. Plus, I haven't been to the States in a long time. It'll be fun to visit and follow this investigation over there." She paused and looked up at the ceiling as a potential problem came up. "I don't know my way around Elk City at all, though. I'll need someone there to help show me around, someone who knows the Unusual side of the city. Any ideas?"

Jaz scratched her head. "None of my local team are available right now." She looked at Dean.

He shrugged. "I can make a few calls. James might be able to free up someone from his organization. It's in his best interest to keep this sort of thing out of Elk City."

"Who's James?"

Jaz jumped in with an answer. "Vampire. He's the local lord. He's decent enough, but he has his own agenda."

"They all do. Maybe I should look into his business dealings while I'm there."

"No," Dean said. "If you're involving James to get his help, then do that, but don't double cross him. He's done a lot to help us both out. I don't know all of his business dealings, but I'm sure he's mostly legitimate."

Hangbe shrugged. "As long as he gives me someone competent, I'm sure it'll be fine. I am a sworn law officer, though. If I discover something untoward, I have to investigate."

"Fair enough. Let me see what I can do." Dean pulled out his phone and started tapping in a message to Brynne. She'd be able to get the help he needed.

It turned out James was traveling, along with Rudy and his primary security team for a few days. That meant James' assistant, Celeste Teal, was also unavailable, which was a shame. She would have been a perfect choice. Brynne said she'd try to come up with someone else, but she wasn't guaranteeing anything.

Dean slipped his phone back into his pocket and returned to sit next to Jaz.

"Well?" Jaz asked.

"We're working on getting someone. The people who would've been on the top of my list are not available, though. Brynne's trying to dig up someone else on short notice from James' organization, but I don't think she's too hopeful."

Dean went down the list of potential guides in his head. The paramedics he worked with would make excellent choices, but they couldn't afford to take off work for more than a day or two and there was no telling how long this might take.

After going through the list again, though, a sort of crazy idea popped into his thoughts. Jaz noticed the smile on his face.

"What? From the look on your face, you've thought of something. What's that crazy brain of yours come up with?"

"It's too early to tell. I don't know if it will work yet. Let me reach out and check on a few things first. When would we be heading back?"

Hangbe said, "Now. The trail has gone cold here. That means they're already gone. If they did what you think and took the portal to Elk City, we'll find evidence of their passage on the far side."

"Okay," Dean glanced at the time. It would be getting into the evening hours back home. The shop would be closed soon. That might be a good thing, though. He didn't want a confrontation with Dougie about the trafficking ring until he had time to dig up more information. He still couldn't believe the leprechaun was part of this mess.

Dean sent out two different messages and waited for replies. While he did that, Jaz and Hangbe completed their plans for when they got to the other side. He listened to their conversation as he checked his phone. There were still a few days left on his vacation. He might help out should the opportunity arise. Finding these missing people was on the top of his list.

Chapter 14

A FEW HOURS LATER, the three of them stood in the shadows across the street from the pub. The lights were out except for a single light Dean could make out through the front window. It shined over the bar, probably left on for security purposes.

"It looks empty," Dean said. "What are we waiting for?"

"It's possible they left a trap," Jaz replied. She had changed out of her pretty skirt and blouse. She wore her standard tactical outfit, black cargo pants, black T-shirt and a leather jacket. She'd included a single pistol rigged in a shoulder holster hidden by the coat.

Hangbe wore black jeans with molded black body armor with a pistol at her side hanging midway down her right thigh. In response to Jaz's warning, she said, "Let me check."

She reached up to her ornate multi-colored bead necklace and pinched a large red bead between her thumb and forefinger. She moved her fingers, rolling the bead back and forth while she stared at the pub.

After several seconds, she said, "There are no magical wards, though something must mask the portal. I can't sense it at all. Is it open all the time or is there something you need to do to operate it?"

Dean shrugged. "You open a door in one place and walk through a room to another door that leads to the next place. I don't think there's anything else, at least not that I saw."

Hangbe's eyes narrowed as she concentrated on what she saw. Her finger and thumb moved faster, rolling the red bead back and forth with increased speed. "Curious. I sense nothing to indicate something with that much power resided within."

"It's there, I promise," Dean said.

A grin creased her serious face for a moment as she glanced sideways at Dean. "I believe you, but I dislike mysteries I cannot explain."

"That must be hard in your line of work."

"A little."

Jaz said, "Let's get this over with. I'll go first, then Hangbe once I open the door. Dean, you come over once we're inside."

He nodded. He knew he came last in case there was trouble inside. Had he gone first, and they ran into trouble, he'd just be in the way. He wasn't a fighter. Dean felt no shame in admitting that. He was fine with his wife being the badass in the family. He kind of liked her that way.

Jaz checked the street one last time and stepped from the shadows. She darted across the street, crouching down by the pub's front door. She pulled lock picks from the pouch at her belt and worked at the door for ten long seconds.

For a moment, Dean thought she wouldn't get it, then she stood, flashing them a grin before she pushed open the door and went inside.

Hangbe ran across the street, following Jaz in before the door closed. Dean waited a few seconds, checking for any traffic, then followed them, hauling the luggage.

Inside, Jaz and Hangbe finished checking the side rooms and behind the bar.

"It's clear," Jaz said.

"Here, too," Hangbe added, coming from the kitchen.

"Good," Dean said. "Let's get home. All this sneaking around makes me nervous."

The two women exchanged grins. They followed him down the hallway to the plain wooden door at the end. Dean opened it and stepped into the small room. Jaz closed the door behind the three of them and Dean leaned forward, pulling the key from his pocket and opening the door leading back to Elk City.

It opened with ease and a few seconds later, they stood in the darkened Irish Shop, back in Elk City again. Dean closed the wooden door guarding the portal and returned the key to its hiding spot, as Dougie had told him.

Hangbe looked around, picking up a few random items from the shelves. "Who would buy this junk?"

Jaz chuckled, "You'd be surprised. A lot of people here have a thing for the Irish."

Dean gathered their suitcases and started towards the back door leading to the parking lot behind the building. "I'm taking these out to the SUV."

"Go ahead, we'll be right out," Jaz said.

Dean hauled the suitcases outside and smiled when he saw the beat up white van pulled in beside Jaz's company SUV. Gibbie climbed out of the van and walked over to help Dean with the bags.

"Hey, I got your message. What's the big secret you couldn't tell me in the text?"

"Jaz and I have a special guest who needs some help getting around the city for the next few days. I thought you might want some extra work, and it's for a good cause."

"And you thought of me? Dean, I'm honored. I won't let you down. What's it pay?"

"It's coming from Errington. It's a few hundred a day and if you keep track of your mileage, she'll reimburse you for that, too."

Gibbie rubbed his hands together, a huge grin on his face. "Just show me who this VIP is and I'll give him the full Gibbie tour."

"She's inside with Jaz. They'll be out in a sec."

"It's a girl?" Gibbie's eyes got wide. "Um, you know I'm not really all that comfortable around women, Dean. I don't think they like me all that much. Are you sure I'm the right person for this job?"

"You have to be. There's not anyone else I'd trust with this." Dean didn't add that James couldn't spare Rudy or any of his shifter security team right now. Gibbie was literally all that was left from Dean's initial list.

Gibbie's chest puffed out with pride. "I guess I have to do it then. I mean, how hard can it be to show someone around town. Who is she, anyway?"

Jaz and Hangbe came out of the store's back door right on cue. Dean said, "Gibbie, meet Hangbe, special agent for Interpol. Hangbe, meet Gibson Proctor. He's—"

"A vampire." Hangbe shot Jaz a hard glare. "You got me a vampire to tour the city with?"

Dean stepped in before Jaz could answer, anger rising in him. "Gibbie is the perfect person to show you around. He's connected with all the Unusual groups in the city. He knows the town like the back of his hand, and I'd trust him with my life. He's the best man for this job, hands down."

He gestured for Gibbie to step forward and stand next to him, but he held back. Dean turned to face a dumbstruck expression on the frumpy vampire's face. He didn't move. He just stared at Hangbe.

"Does he have a voice, or does he just stand around with a stupid expression on his face?"

"Of course he does," Dean said. "Gibbie, come forward and greet the inspector."

Gibbie shook himself, swiped his palms down the front of the grey hoodie he was wearing. "It's a pleasure to meet you, Inspector. I'm honored to be the one to show a person of such stature and grace around town."

Dean couldn't get over the goofy grin on Gibbie's face. Jaz had noticed it, too. She shot Dean a stern stare. He shrugged. They were committed now.

"Don't call me Inspector. I'm undercover. Hangbe will do just fine."

"Hangbe it is. Undercover is great. I'm all about low key. They call me low key Gibbie. Well, not really. But they could if there were a reason to. Like now." Gibbie cringed and tried to reset, the words pouring out in a rapid jumble of excited syllables. "Here, let me take your pack. I'll put it in the back of my van."

"I'll need a place to stay. Can you take care of that?"

Jaz said, "You can stay with me at the Errington headquarters."

Hangbe shook her head. "No, too much chance someone could see me come and go."

Gibbie cleared his throat. "I could get you a temporarily vacant apartment above a restaurant downtown."

Dean nodded. "Above Sabatani's?"

"Yeah, Kristof has a place between tenants. I'm sure he would let us use it for a while." Gibbie turned back to Hangbe. "It's already furnished, so it should be perfect and low key, since you're undercover and all. It can be your hide-out on the down low, you know, until you're ready to go all inspector lady on people."

"I suppose that will be acceptable," Hangbe said, her lips curling up in a slight smile. She looked Gibbie over from head to toe while he fidgeted with his car keys. "I guess you'll do. You certainly are amusing enough. Let's go take a look at this hide-out you've found me. If it doesn't work out, I'm sure we can find other accommodations."

"Of course," Gibbie replied. "I'm yours to command. Just say the word."

The smile broadened on the woman's face. Dean swore she did a quick check of Gibbie's butt as he walked by. She handed him the backpack. He took it from her, pausing to admire the ornate leather and wood scabbard strapped to the side. It was just over a yard long and had leather-wrapped hilt jutting up from it.

"That's marvelous work. Western Africa, if I recognize the design."

Hangbe nodded. "Very good. Few people recognize the origin of my blade."

"It's a hobby of mine. I've always been interested in the history of that region. Your necklace caught my eye as soon as I saw you. It's very old, but I don't recognize the specific country from which it comes."

"It's my homeland. It belonged to my grandmother."

The two of them kept talking all the way over to Gibbie's van. He pulled open he passenger door and quickly shoved some random papers off the seat to make room for his guest. Hangbe climbed in and waved back at Dean and Jaz. A few seconds later, the van pulled away into the night.

"I'm not going to lie," Dean said. "That went way better than I expected."

"I hope he doesn't screw this up. She'll probably kill him if he does."

"What?"

"Relax, I'm just kidding. Probably. Let's just get home. We're both tired, and I have to follow up with Niamh on how Kaylee's doing first thing tomorrow."

Dean climbed in the SUV's passenger side as Jaz got in and started the engine. She pulled out of the parking lot and drove off towards the Errington building. They were back home again, with another mystery on their hands.

Chapter 15

DEAN PAWED AT THE NIGHTSTAND, trying to silence the persistent buzzing of his phone. His searching fingers closed around the annoying device and he brought it over towards his pillow. Cracking open one eye, he spotted the number. It was Brynne.

Groaning, he swiped at the screen to pick up as he sat up on the edge of the bed. Jaz rolled over to check on him. He waved a hand to tell her he was fine.

"Brynne, what's up?"

"I heard you were back in town. I know you're supposed to be on vacation til tomorrow, but no one else is available."

Dean got up and hurried from the room, pulling the bedroom door shut as he entered the hallway.

"I was hoping for a few more days of a break."

"Bill was supposed to come in today to cover for Tammy. She's out with a sick kid. Somehow, Bill broke his ankle playing basketball last night. I just saw him in the ER. Lynne and Brook are out of town for training, and Barry's already maxed his overtime this week. I need someone to come in from the squad or I'll have to defer Station U calls to regular paramedic units from the city."

Dean looked back at the closed bedroom door. Jaz had already told him she was planning on working today. He could pick up an extra shift or two. "I guess I can come in. I reserve the vacation day to use later, though."

"No problem. See you in an hour."

Dean ran his fingers through his unruly hair. He needed a shower. That would wake him up. He stumbled towards the bathroom as he worked to wake up.

He made it into the station with twenty minutes to spare. The smell of Freddy's latest fresh breakfast cooking brought a smile to his face. He still had time to eat.

Brynne looked up from where she sat at the double workstation across the room. "You don't look too bad for coming in on short notice. Thanks for doing that."

"No problem. How's Bill?"

"He'll survive, but he's gonna be on desk duty for four to six weeks with that ankle fracture."

Dean winced. They didn't have that many medics trained to work on the Station U team. It would force the rest of them to pick up even more hours when they were already stretched thin. "Maybe it's time to bring on some new blood."

"Funny you should say that."

Dean frowned. "Uh-oh, I don't like the sound of that. What do you have planned for me today?"

"The academy just graduated a new class—"

"A probie? Brynne, you remember how green I was? You said you'd never bring a squeaky new medic in like that again."

"Let me finish. The new class includes a special candidate. She's an Unusual herself who wanted into the program. She's excelled at her classes, and she already has a degree from Elk U, in psychology. She's smart, talented, and motivated to do the job. All you have to do is keep her straight and show her the medical ropes. She's already got the Unusual stuff down."

Dean grumbled, "I should've stayed in bed."

"I heard that," Brynne said, tapping her ears. "Vampire hearing, remember?"

"I don't care. This is a hell of a thing to spring on me first thing like this."

"It wasn't something I planned. Tammy was supposed to be her training officer. Now it'll be you."

"Okay, Brynne. You win. Just remember, paybacks are hell."

A voice from the doorway behind Dean said, "I'm sorry, am I interrupting something?"

A woman in her early twenties, probably about Dean's age, stood in the doorway with a backpack over one shoulder. She wore the crisply pressed uniform of a brand-new paramedic.

"Not interrupting at all, Leah," Brynne said. "Come on in. This is Dean Flynn. He'll be taking you on during your probationary period with Station U."

The woman crossed to Dean, extending her hand. She shook his hand with a firm grip and smiled. "I'm Leah, Leah Casado. It's a pleasure to meet you. I've heard quite a bit about you, Dean."

Her confidence and easy-going manner brought a smile to his face despite his annoyance at having a new probie. "I'm sure only half of it is true. I'm just a medic like you, trying to save some lives and do right by people."

"I'm excited to get on the unit with you. I'm sure you've got a lot you can teach me. There's only so much I could do while in the academy sessions in the field."

Dean studied her face. He had no idea what kind of Unusual she was, and he couldn't pick up any clues from this initial encounter. He'd figure it out soon enough, or she'd volunteer it. Until then, she was just another squeaky new medic who needed some polish rubbed off so she could do her job.

"Rely on your training and listen carefully when I tell you something. If you do that, I'm sure you'll do fine."

Leah smiled and glanced around. "Is there somewhere I can put this?" She lifted her backpack off her shoulder.

Dean nodded. "Come with me and I'll give you the full tour." He led the way back to the men's and women's bunk rooms. There were lockers in there for each medic in the station. Once she stowed her gear, he showed her around the station, including the ambulance bay, empty now with the ambulance still out on a call. He finished up back in the squad room.

"What is that wonderful smell?" Leah asked.

"That is the best kept secret in the Elk City Fire Department."

On cue, Freddy stepped out from the small kitchen carrying in a tray filled with individual eggs Benedict servings, a plate of bacon and sausage, and freshly squeezed orange juice.

"Leah, meet Freddy, the famous zombie chef of Station U."

"He cooks breakfast for you?"

"And lunch and dinner, too," Freddy said. "If there's something special you like, you let me know and I'll see what I can whip up for you."

"That's great. I'll let you know."

"Sit down and grab a bite. I'll check the GPS tracker on the computer to see where the ambulance is. They should be back soon. Then we need to be ready to roll if a call comes in."

Leah nodded and sat down to breakfast. Dean logged in to one of the two desktop terminals connected to the city's dispatch and reporting system. According to the tracking system, the station's ambulance was on the way back now. Dean figured they'd have about five minutes to get breakfast down. He'd make it work. Eating fast and on the fly was in the paramedic's job description.

Barry and part-timer, Kisha, walked in a few minutes later after parking the ambulance in the garage.

"Hey, Dean. I thought you were off for a few more days?"

"Me, too. I got back early and Brynne found out, so here I am."

"Sucks to be you."

Dean shrugged. "I'll survive. Can't let you grab all the OT. I could use some, too."

"How was the honeymoon?"

"Cut short, but mostly pleasant."

Barry shook his head. "Trouble with the newlyweds already?"

"No, work stuff with Jaz. We had to come back sooner than expected. That's all."

Barry turned to Leah. "You must be the noob. I'm Barry. Keep an eye on Dean. He's a magnet for trouble. All the crazy calls come his way."

"At least my life isn't boring," Dean said. "Come on, Leah. Let's go over the checklist for the start of shift. Then we can talk about how we'll handle the patient care on calls to start."

Leah got up and followed Dean out to the ambulance bay where he took her through the ambulance from front to back, and top to bottom. He brought up the checklist on the tablet in the rear of the ambulance and watched as she went through it, checking the bags and cabinets to make sure they were fully stocked before the first emergency call came in.

About halfway through the process, Brynne poked her head into the back of the ambulance. "Hey, my ride is here, so I'm going to head out before the sun's all the way up. You two good?"

"All set here, boss," Dean said.

Leah nodded as she looked up from her work.

"Good, I'll be back this evening. Call if you need anything."

Brynne opened the bay's garage door so the driver James gave her could drive inside out of the sunlight. Brynne hopped in, disappearing behind the dark tinted windows as she closed the car door. It drove off and Dean walked over to close the garage door.

"What's it like having a vampire as your boss?" Leah asked.

"Not as weird as you'd think. I knew her before she was turned, so I'm actually glad to see her back on the job."

"Really, so she hasn't been undead that long?"

"Almost a year and a half now. Maybe if you work out for a few weeks, I'll even tell you the full story. Until then, just know she's about the best medic I've ever met."

"I'll keep that in mind. Sorry about prying."

"Don't worry about it. Everyone in the station has a story of one sort or another. You'll hear them all, eventually. Give it some time. For now, keep you mind focused on learning the ropes and taking care of patients.

As if the EMS gods had read his mind, the radio speakers in the bay squawked with the alert tones followed by the dispatcher's voice.

"Ambulance U-191, respond for a fire at 1516 Eastern Boulevard. Still awaiting confirmation about injuries."

"Jump in the passenger seat, Leah. Time to earn our keep."

Dean headed for the driver's side. As the new probie, Leah would take on primary patient care while Dean acted as an observer. He'd only step in if she had trouble or there was a second patient.

He clicked the button to raise the bay doors again and started up the ambulance. Thirty seconds later, Dean and Leah were speeding down the road, lights flashing and sirens blaring as they headed towards Leah's first official call.

Chapter 16

IT WASN'T hard to find the location of the fire. The column of black smoke led Dean right to it. Located in an older section of Elk City, the two- and three-story brick buildings on either side of the street were from a time when this was the bustling industrial district of the city. Now, at least half the buildings were empty or used simply as warehouse space by businesses with more modern buildings elsewhere.

The fire crews had put out the blaze by the time Dean pulled the ambulance in behind the last fire engine in the long line of vehicles. Fire crews milled around down the street on the sidewalk in front of the gutted brick building. The structure took up most of the block.

Despite the grim situation with the fire, Dean smiled. Time to break in the new kid and see what kind of grit she had inside. Burn victims were particularly challenging. "Call in to command on the side channel and see where they want us. This fire has been going on for a while so we can't be the first ambulance on the scene."

Leah hesitated a second before reaching out for the mic clipped to the dashboard. Her hand trembled a little as she brought it up to her mouth and keyed the button on the side. "Um, incident command, this is ambulance U-191. We're on location about a block away. Where would you like us to stage?"

The gruff male voice on the radio replied, "Don't stage anywhere. Get up here. We've got another patient for you."

"Uh, okay, U-191 received. Proceeding into the scene."

Dean nodded. "Good job. It'll get easier as you practice."

"He seemed a little annoyed over the radio. Did I mess up?"

"No, that's just Assistant Chief Jonas. He always sounds like he just finished chewing on broken glass while smoking two packs of cigarettes." Dean slipped the ambulance into gear and pulled back into the street. "Keep your eyes open on your side. Firefighters like to dart out into the street between the engines when they're fetching equipment. Let's try not to run over any of them."

He caught the hint of a smile from Leah out of the corner of his eye. It disappeared as she stared ahead at the street and the line of fire engines and trucks.

Dean concentrated on avoiding any of the fire hoses arching out from the engines before curving around towards the building. Ahead, one of the ladder trucks on the scene had extended its long ladder, so the nozzle mounted at the top could shoot down into the remnants of the building.

As he neared the spot where Chief Jonas had parked his command vehicle, the incident commander turned and pointed to a spot on the pavement just behind his vehicle. Dean nodded and pulled over, slowly pulling up over the curb until he had two wheels up on the sidewalk and had cleared the way for other vehicles to pass if needed.

"What should we grab?" Leah asked.

Dean looked around the command vehicle in front of them. He shrugged. "Not sure. I don't see a patient anywhere. Let's go ask the chief, then we'll know what we need."

The two paramedics got out of their ambulance and approached a short, squat figure that was Assistant Chief Jonas. His round figure barely fit into his turnout coat, but his white helmet fit atop his bald head just fine.

He spotted the two medics approaching. "Ah, Dean, I'm glad it's you. We had no idea this one involved any of your Unusual patients until we started overhauling the building after we knocked down most of the fire."

Dean's eyebrows raised in surprise, and he glanced at the building again. "Someone survived that?"

"We pulled two survivors from the basement. They'd broken their way through barred windows from the inside. They didn't speak English, and we couldn't figure out if they were the only ones in there. The fire was fully involved and there was no way to send any of us in safely, anyway. We had the medics on the scene load them up and take them in. We didn't know they were special patients until we saw the rest of the basement."

"What did you see?" Dean asked. He still didn't know what the patient mentioned earlier needed or where they were.

"It's better if I show you. Grab your gear. Your patient's on the far side of the building."

"What injuries are we talking about?" Dean asked.

The chief shook his head. "I know he's not too bad off, just some minor burns, and a possible broken leg. One of the engine crews on that side of the building has been treating him while the police monitor him."

"Police," Leah asked. "What for?"

"Like I said, come with me and I'll show you."

"Give us a second to grab what we need. We'll be right back."

The two paramedics returned to the ambulance. Dean glanced at his partner. "What do we need? This'll be your patient."

Leah ticked off on her fingers as she named the equipment to load on the stretcher. "Trauma bag, oxygen and airway kit, patient monitor, med bag for pain management. Anything else?"

"No, that sounds about right." He pulled the stretcher out from the back and extended the undercarriage while Leah grabbed all the gear.

Once they'd loaded up the stretcher, Dean nodded at the head for her to take the lead. From this point on, he was there to observe her handling of the situation.

They joined the chief at the command vehicle, and he led them down the street to the front of the building. "Park the stretcher here. I need to show you something before we go any farther."

Dean stepped on the pedals to lock the wheels on the stretcher and followed the chief and Leah over to the open doorway closest to them.

This corner of the building wasn't burned as badly as the rest. The metal stairwell leading down was still in pretty good shape.

As soon as they reached the bottom, Dean caught the unmistakable whiff of burned flesh. That gave him a little warning of what he was about to see, though nothing prepared him for what greeted them inside.

The smell didn't alert his probie to anything special, though her wrinkled nose told Dean she thought the acrid odor was unpleasant.

Chief Jonas pointed at the double steel doors at the bottom. "These were chained closed when we finally got in here. If we had known what was down here, we would have come in this way first."

"Why?" Leah asked. "You said the building was a total loss by the time you got here."

The chief's grim expression turned sad as he said, "Because we might have been able to save a few of them."

As he said it, he yanked open one of the doors, warped by heat. Through the open doorway, he switched on the bright LED flashlight mounted on the side of his helmet. The light played across the floor near the doors. Charred bodies lined the floor, dozens of them, piled up by what had been a locked doorway. Dean picked up on the animal features of a few of them. At least some were shifters, though it would take a full autopsy to find out the particular variety.

"My God, Chief, how many?"

"We're up to thirty between here and near the barred windows where we rescued the two survivors. Some of them had shackles around their ankles, Dean. They were prisoners down here."

A low snarl put Dean on alert for trouble until he realized it came from Leah. She shifted her gaze from the floor to him, and he caught the flash of yellow in her eyes before her irises returned to those of a normal human. He could have sworn they had a feline cast to them before switching back.

Dean had seen enough. "Where's our other patient? Is it another survivor from down here?"

"Not exactly," the chief said. He had a slight growl to his voice now, too. "Come on. I'll take you to him."

The commander led them back up to the sidewalk and around to the far side of the building. Two firefighters crouched beside a man propped up against the rear of the fire engine, in the shade. They'd spread a tarp on the ground for the patient and they were splinting the leg using the basic trauma kit they carried on the fire engines.

Officer O'Malley stood a few feet away with a stern expression. He watched as the two firefighters treated the injured guy.

"Okay, Leah, this one's all yours. I'll be over by the police officer if you need anything. Don't worry, I'll be watching what you do."

Leah nodded and grabbed the monitor and oxygen bag from the stretcher. She moved to crouch with the firefighters beside the injured man. Dean had a better look at his injuries. Besides the broken leg, he had burns on his hands and forearms.

Chief Jonas joined Dean and the police officer as they watched the new paramedic get to work. The fire officer asked, "Has he given you any trouble?"

O'Malley shook his head. He took off his hat and ran his fingers through his greying brown hair. "No, he knows better than to mess with me. Besides, that break's pretty bad. Even if he can regenerate, it'll be a while before he's running anywhere."

Dean asked, "You know him, then?"

O'Malley eyebrows raised in surprise at Dean's question. "You don't recognize him? I heard from Brynne you and he had a run-in back at your station."

Dean's head spun towards the man on the ground, looking more carefully this time. He hadn't seen through the soot and grime from the fire at first, but now he did and recognized Manton, the werepanther.

"What's he doing here? I figured he left town after he attacked me, especially after taking Verity from the hospital."

O'Malley crossed his arms, saying, "He's in a lot worse trouble now. They found him just inside one entrance, trapped by a smoldering beam. He had a pair of heavy chains and two padlocks with him. They were just like the ones on the doors to the basement. Once the arson investigation is complete, I suspect he's going down for setting this fire and killing all the people trapped below. Two detectives are already waiting at the hospital to interview the two survivors."

Dean had heard enough. He crossed to kneel beside Manton and leaned in as Leah finished taking his blood pressure. "Where's Verity? You snatched her at the hospital. We know that. Where is she now?"

Manton's sneer and quick glance towards the burned out building was all he needed to see. Clenching his fists, Dean wrestled his anger under control. It sounded like O'Malley had him dead to rights on the fire and deaths here. He had to remember his place and job right now. It was hard to swallow his boiling rage, though.

Taking a few deep breaths, Dean asked, "Is he stable, Leah?"

"His vitals are a little high, but consistent with someone in considerable pain. No arrhythmias on the monitor. I was going to get an IV and start some morphine if that's okay?"

Dean wanted to tell her to hold off on the pain management, but he didn't. This was her patient, and she was right to treat him strictly according to protocol, despite what she had undoubtedly overheard.

"Good treatment plan. I'll get the stretcher ready. Once you've given the morphine, we'll load him up."

Manton sneered at Dean as he turned away. His burned hand clutched at the paramedic's arm. "You got no balls, Flynn. Here I am helpless as can be and you don't have the guts to do anything. Don't worry, though. I won't forget you. I'll heal fast enough. Once I'm out on bail, I'll come find you and we can finish our little tussle."

Dean wanted to threaten the man back, but he knew Manton would see anything like that as bluster.

To his surprise, Leah leaned in close. Her eyes had gone all cat-like and yellow again. She whispered something to Manton that made his eyes go wide for a second. After staring into her shifter gaze, he nodded and looked away, focusing on the ground beside him. His bluster and confidence drained completely.

Leah nodded with a grim smile on her face. Her eyes returned to normal and she went back to her work starting an IV and preparing the morphine dose.

Dean went to prep the stretcher, wondering what she'd told the werepanther that made him back down. What kind of Unusual was she that could have that effect on the outlaw cat shifter?

Chapter 17

MANTON DIDN'T SAY another word to anyone all the way to the hospital. He just lay there, casting a wary glance towards Leah occasionally, but otherwise staring straight ahead. O'Malley followed them to the hospital in his police SUV and escorted them into the ER. Dean checked the board by the nurses' station, hoping to see Ashley's name. He knew she could handle the werepanther if he made trouble.

The Eldara wasn't working, but O'Malley must have called ahead. Two uniformed security guards awaited them at the ER's entrance and stayed with Manton after they moved him to the hospital's cot. Leah gave her report to the nurse while Dean took the stretcher and put on a fresh set of sheets.

O'Malley came over as Dean worked. "What's with the new medic? She got that shifter to back down mighty quick."

"Yeah, I'm not really sure. She's a recent graduate from the academy. She seems to know her stuff well enough from a medical standpoint. I know little else about her."

"She's gotta be a shifter herself to get that kind of response. Only other shifters and maybe a vampire get that kind of response from people like him. It was broad daylight, so she isn't a bloodsucker."

"Hey, you know I don't like those kinds of terms. We need to treat them with some respect if we want them to trust us."

O'Malley held up his hands in apology. "Didn't mean to offend anyone. She did a good job from what I could see. I just wonder who or what she is."

He shut up and pretended to check his phone as she came over with the tablet computer after checking in the patient. From the glance she shot the police officer, she'd heard at least part of the conversation. She said nothing, though. She set the tablet on the stretcher and took her spot at the head.

"Ready to go, Boss?"

"Uh, yeah, sure. Did you want a water bottle or snack from the EMS ready room before we go? We get to grab stuff since they know we miss a lot of meals while running calls."

"No, I'm good. Still full from breakfast." Leah grabbed the bar at the head of the cot and tugged it towards the exit.

Dean shrugged and followed along, guiding the cot's back end out to the ambulance ramp. They loaded the stretcher and took a few minutes, throwing out some trash from their call and making sure everything was ready for the next call. Dean didn't have to tell Leah what to do, she seemed to know what he expected of her and jumped to it until the work was completed. He kind of wished he had her initiative and confidence when he got started.

Climbing back into the cab, Dean started the ambulance and started back towards Station U. "Put us back on the street, Leah."

She nodded, grabbing the microphone with more confidence the second time around. "Dispatch, this is U-191 clear and returning."

The radio reply from dispatch came right away. "Copy 191. Clear and returning to station."

They drove in silence for a few minutes while Dean tried to come up with a non-threatening way to ask her what she'd said to Manton. Finally, he decided she was his probie, and he didn't really need a reason when it concerned one of their patients.

"Leah, I have to ask you about what happened back at the scene. That guy and I have a history, as I guess you figured out. I was perfectly alright dealing with it. Then you said something to him, and he changed his demeanor completely. What did you do?"

Leah sighed and her shoulders sagged a little against the bucket seat. "No matter what I do, I'm never going to get away from him."

"Who, Manton? He's no danger to us. I didn't think you were afraid of him."

"Not him." She lowered her eyes, staring at the floorboard by her feet. "My father."

"What's your father got to do with all this? Are you in some kind of trouble? Believe me. I understand when your dad causes issues in your life."

"He has a certain amount of pull with the shifter cat community, that's all. I didn't like how that guy was throwing around threats at you so I told him my father wouldn't like it if something happened to you."

"Sounds like something out of *The Godfather*." Dean thrust out his jaw and tried a horrible Marlon Brando impersonation as he said, "I have an offer you can't refuse."

Leah shook her head and snapped, "I don't like to talk about it. I'm nothing like him and want nothing to do with him. I'm not part of that world anymore. Can we drop it?"

Dean realized he'd crossed some line with the reference to Don Corleone. "Hey, everyone has family they don't want to own up to. I completely understand that. Consider it dropped, okay?"

She gave him a curt nod but said nothing. Dean let the silence settle for a while as he headed back to the station. He'd let his curiosity get the better of him, and he needed to make up for that. Leah deserved his professionalism on the job, not his prying questions.

Back at the station, as he backed into the ambulance bay and parked the unit, Dean hooked a thumb at the rear of the ambulance. "I'll do the restock if you want to get started on your report in the squad room."

Leah shook her head and frowned a little. "No, I need to know how to do all this stuff. Show me what needs to be done. I can do it."

"Leah, I might be your training officer for the next little while, but that doesn't mean we aren't partners, too. You can help me. That'll get it done faster and I can show you where to get the fresh supplies from the cabinets in the garage bay."

Dean walked towards the row of storage cabinets along the wall, but Leah stopped him. "Dean, I'm not angry with you for asking about my dad. I guess I still have to get over my hang-ups. You did nothing wrong."

"Fair enough, but I could have kept my curiosity in check."

Leah laughed.

Dean cocked his head to one side in question. "What's so funny?"

"One of my academy instructors had a saying. She said, 'a paramedic who isn't curious, isn't much of a medic.' I guess that makes you pretty good at your job."

Dean laughed along with her this time. "I guess it does at that. Come on, we could get called out at any minute. Let's get this done and see what Freddy's making us for lunch later."

The rest of the day turned into a pretty routine day, at least where you could say such a thing where Station U was concerned. Dean observed Leah handle a patient with chest pain and some ventricular heart arrhythmias that needed some attention at the hospital. She took on a few respiratory distress calls, including a pediatric asthma patient in the Fairy community at the New Barrens. Overall, she proved to be both knowledgeable and compassionate, the two traits Dean most appreciated in other health care professionals.

As they backed in after the last call of the day, Dean was pretty confident Leah had the makings of a top-notch paramedic. He told her as much while they completed the end of shift checklist together and returned to the squad room. Brynne was there, as was Barry, Dean's former partner.

Barry pointed at Leah and shouted, "I knew it. I've joined the first wives' club. You've traded me in for a newer model."

Dean laughed. He was happy to see Leah smiled as well. "Leah, may I present my previous probie and partner, Barry Winston. He's the reason I learned to be such a hard-ass the first day."

Brynne asked Leah, "How did you do?"

The new medic shrugged. "Okay, I guess. I don't think Dean has too many complaints, right?"

Dean nodded as he took off his jacket and sat down to send off his last report of the day. "She's every bit as good as you said she was, Brynne. Whoever spotted her at the academy and pointed her this way, they should get a big high-five."

"It was me," Brynne said. "I ran into her about six months ago and she asked about the paramedic job. She jumped into the new accelerated program almost right away."

Dean clicked send on the last report and spun around in the chair. "Wow, Leah, she must've said something pretty impressive to get you to join up just like that. What was it?"

Leah blushed a little and shook her head. "I think I'll save that story for another time. My mother always raised me to keep a little mystery going with folks."

Brynne laughed and winked at Leah. "Well played. Your mother raised you right. Now Dean'll be wondering what got you into this field for weeks."

Dean waved Brynne's comment off with the wave of his hand. "I'm sure it'll come out in time. I can wait." He wouldn't let his innate curiosity show, not when they'd laid the mystery out there like a challenge.

Brynne caught Leah's eye and shook her head. "Don't you dare tell him until you make him squirm for a while first."

"Hey, you're the lieutenant. I have to follow your lead. Sorry, Dean, you'll have to wait until the boss lady gives the okay."

A rap at the door interrupted their conversation. Dean answered it, surprised to see a police officer when he opened the door. He couldn't remember the guy's name, but he was one O'Malley's colleagues in the police version of Station U.

"Hey, what's up?" Dean asked, stepping back to let the cop into the squad room.

"They sent me over to check on you folks. Everything okay here?"

Brynne nodded, concern creasing her brow. "What's the problem, Seth?"

"We had a prisoner escape from the hospital. You all transported him there after a fire this morning?"

Dean and Leah glanced in each other's direction. Dean took the lead. "I remember. I'd had a run in with him before and he said some things to me on scene that might be construed as threatening. We dealt with it and took him in without a problem."

"Well," Seth said. "He broke out of the prison ward when they took him down for some X-rays. He killed one of the security guards at the hospital and was last seen jumping into a dark SUV that sped away from the scene."

Brynne jumped in, saying, "Have you checked the area outside?"

Seth nodded. "I did. It seems clear, but the sarge told me to make sure you all got home safely since it was shift change time."

Dean hated this. He refused to let Manton and his threats scare him, no matter how easily the werepanther had beaten him before. "I don't think that will be necessary, Seth. I can get home fine on my own."

"What about your partner," Seth asked, glancing at Leah.

She shook her head, too. "He'd be a fool to come after me."

Brynne said, "Maybe we're better safe than sorry here. I think it would be a good idea for the nice officer here to shadow you both on the way home. Leah, your apartment downtown is on the way to Dean's place. He can follow you that far with Seth following in his squad car."

Dean knew better than to argue with Brynne. Her serious tone made it clear that this wasn't a request.

Leah, however, didn't recognize the signs, or she ignored them. "I said I don't need any special treatment. If this cat comes after me, it'll be the last thing he does. I can take care of myself."

Seth snorted a chuckle. "Look who thinks she's all badass. What are you, some sort of hunter-medic with a death wish?"

Leah's eyes narrowed, and her fists clenched. Before Dean knew what was happening, short orange fur had sprouted all up and down her exposed arms. Black and tan splotches appeared, dotting the orange fur until she'd assumed the coloring of a jungle cat of some sort. Dean thought it might be a variety of panther.

Seth held up his hands in surrender. "Hey, I'm sorry I said anything. I didn't know you were a shifter yourself."

Brynne stepped in front of Leah, blocking her from the police officer's view. "You know what? Why don't you tell your sergeant I'll take care of security tonight? If you could have a unit swing by here a couple of times later to check on the station while we're out on calls, that would be great."

"You sure?" Seth asked. "I don't know. The sarge was pretty clear."

Brynne nodded. "I'll call him for you. I'll let him know I'm taking responsibility. I've kicked this guy's butt once already. He won't want a repeat performance."

Seth took a few seconds and then nodded. "I guess with a vampire and a werejaguar in the house, you've got things well in hand. I'll do a last sweep around the building before I leave."

Barry called out from his seat behind one workstation, "Come in after your sweep and I'll have Freddy pack up some dinner for the road since you took the time to check up on us."

"I'll do that, but it'll have to be in an hour or two when I do the second check. I have to report in to the sarge first."

"Suit yourself. He's made lasagna and his homemade pasta is amazing."

"Don't worry, I will be back," Seth said. He waved one last time and headed out the door.

Dean shook his head. "Brynne, I'll be fine. I'm going straight home. Nobody'd be stupid enough to jump me at Errington's HQ."

It was Leah's turn to be surprised. "You live at Errington Security? I didn't know they rented apartments there."

Barry laughed. "The apartments are for family members only."

When Leah's confused expression continued, Barry added, "Dean's wife is Jaz Errington herself."

Leah's gaze took in Dean and seemed to appraise him in a different light.

He shook his head. "I just married into the family. I'm not a hunter. I'm here on this earth to heal and that's it."

She nodded and forced herself to smile. "I, of all people, shouldn't throw shade on others for their family connections. Brynne's right, though. The Errington building isn't all that far from my apartment complex. I could follow you there to make sure nothing happened and then head on home."

Brynne nodded. She answered before Dean could object. "Perfect. You do that. Maybe you can both follow each other in first thing tomorrow morning, too, just to be safe."

Leah nodded. Dean reluctantly followed suit.

"Let's go, then. My wife is expecting me home for dinner."

Leah nodded towards the kitchen. "What about that delicious food Freddy made?"

On cue, Freddy came from the kitchen with two large paper bags. "I overheard the discussion and made an executive decision. Here are double servings for each of you. I didn't know if you had anyone else at home, young lady, so I erred on the side of caution."

Leah smiled. "Nobody else at home on my end, but that means more leftovers for me." She took one bag and Dean took the other.

"Fine," Dean said. "Let's get this little safety caravan on the road. Brynne, you and Barry have a *quiet* night, okay?"

Barry and Brynne groaned in unison.

"Agh," Barry said. "The 'Q' word. I can't believe you'd do that to me. It's Brynne who pissed you off."

"Sorry, pal. Make her do all the dirty work."

As if on cue, the radio squawked with alert tones and Dean laughed as he and Leah left the station for the parking lot.

He got in his white pickup truck and waited until Leah pulled around in a beat-up Nissan. It had mismatched quarter panels making it look like it had been assembled from spare parts in a junkyard. Dean didn't judge, though. He knew what kind of money new paramedics made working for the city.

He waved at Leah and started home with her right behind him. He decided not to tell Jaz about the situation with the missing werepanther and the threats. She might decide to make him take a driver from her security detail, and he did not want that. For now, a mysterious werejaguar trailing him home was good enough.

Chapter 18

DEAN DROVE up in front of the gates and pulled out his keycard to access the lot beneath the Errington Security building. Leah waved from where she'd pulled up on the street behind him. She drove off as he pulled down the ramp to the underground garage.

Gibbie's beat-up white van sat in one of the visitor spaces by the elevator. Dean smiled. He wondered how the vampire had fared over the last twenty-four hours, chauffeuring the Interpol agent around town.

After parking in his assigned slot, Dean walked to the elevator. James, the guard on duty in the windowed office beside the elevator, waved at Dean as he walked up. It had taken some getting used to living in a place that seemed to have more security than the White House sometimes. It was why he chaffed at the need to have an escort outside of these walls.

He rode the elevator car up to the top floor, using his keycard to access the private level. The sound of laughter greeted him as soon as the doors opened on their dedicated floor. Dean dropped his keys in the bowl by the elevator and hung his duty jacket up in the closet.

"That you, Dean?" Jaz called.

"Like anyone else could get up here besides me without an alert coming over your phone?"

Dean walked into the living room.

Jaz smiled. "I know you like me to pretend we live a normal life in a normal house. I'm just playing the dutiful wife welcoming her husband home."

Gibbie, seated in a recliner in the corner, mimed gagging himself with a finger. Dean laughed out loud at the gesture.

Hangbe, seated in a plush straight-backed chair beside Gibbie, shook her head. "Don't let him domesticate you, girl. I spent too much time helping to foster your wild side."

"Don't worry, Hangbe," Dean said. "I don't think anything I do will ever get rid of that part of her. I wouldn't want to, anyway. It's part of what drew us together."

Jaz smiled. "Good answer, hubby. What's in the bag? I could smell it as soon as you came in."

"Freddy's lasagna, garlic bread, and probably a few cannolis, if I know how he thinks."

Hangbe leaned forward. "It smells delicious."

"It is, and lucky for you all, Freddy always packs extra. There should be enough for all three of us." Dean glanced at Gibbie. "Sorry, bud. No blood in the house for you."

"It okay, I ate earlier while milady was sleeping."

Hangbe shot him a mischievous grin. "What did I tell you about calling me that?"

"Well, you shouldn't have told me you're descended from royalty."

Dean hid a chuckle behind one hand at the byplay between the pair. Apparently, Gibbie had gotten over his nervousness around the African Amazon.

He caught the expression on Jaz's face, too. She hadn't missed the exchange, either.

"Hey, hon," Dean said, turning towards the kitchen. "Do you want to come help me get the plates together? Maybe you can crack a bottle of wine, too."

"Good idea. We'll be right back."

Jaz followed Dean into the kitchen. He started unpacking the bag while she got out plates for them and turned on the oven to heat the garlic bread. The two of them had a routine down for reheating their chef-quality meals from the Station U cook.

Dean glanced back around the corner into the living room. Gibbie and Hangbe were chatting about something.

He smiled, saying, "Hey, is it just me, or is there something going on between those two."

Jaz laughed. "Hangbe and Gibbie? Give me a break. He's not her kind, AT ALL."

"I don't know. I sense some kind of chemistry between the two of them."

Jaz gave him a playful whack to the back of his head. "Maybe that knocked some sense into you. There's no way she'd have anything to do with a vampire, especially not Gibbie."

Dean didn't belabor the point. He was usually pretty good at spotting things like this. Maybe she was right, though. She knew Hangbe better than he did. She could just be humoring the strangeness of her tour guide around the city.

He finished plating the food after zapping the larger container in the microwave to rewarm it. Then he and Jaz carried everything in and set their small, round dining room table.

"Food's ready," Dean called. "Gibbie, I poured you some wine. I hope that's okay."

"Perfect, Dean. Like I said, I'm full already."

Hangbe came in and sat beside Gibbie. Dean took his spot beside Jaz. Once they'd sat down, Jaz raised her wineglass. "To friends, old and new."

Everyone raised their glasses and gentle tapped them together before sipping at the nice red Jaz had selected.

Hangbe took a bite and said, "Dean, there was a fire downtown today involving some deaths. Did you happen to know anything about it?"

Dean nodded. "In fact, we got called in today to pick up a patient there. It wasn't a pretty scene. At least thirty dead, and it definitely had something to do with our trafficking ring."

"What makes you say that?" Jaz asked.

Dean filled her in on what the firefighters had found in the basement. He skipped over details about his patient. Despite that fact that Manton had threatened him, Dean wouldn't divulge confidential information. He settled for describing bystanders witnessing cat shifters locking up the building's exits before the fire broke out.

Gibbie's jaw dropped, and he shook his head as Dean finished his description of the scene. "That must have been awful for those poor people. Why would anyone do something like that?"

"Probably because they know someone is tracking them," Hangbe replied. "They have to know I'm on their trail by now. I should have made the connection and come here sooner. Those people died because I didn't get here to America in time."

Jaz shook her head. "Don't you dare. You had no way of knowing where they were taking people until you met with me and we both made the connection together. You taught me a long time ago that the bad guys are the ones responsible for what they do. We can only do so much."

Hangbe shook a finger at Jaz. "I taught you too much. Those rules were for you to learn. They were not for you to recite them back to me years later."

"What's good for the goose," Jaz began.

Dean asked, "What if that's the end of the trail? Do you think they'd pack up and move on to some other city?"

Hangbe shook her head. "No, I think they were tying up some loose ends. They are probably hiding somewhere in the city, hoping we'll believe they've moved on."

Jaz stared at Dean and pursed her lips like she was going to say something but changed her mind.

"What?" Dean asked.

"I was waiting to see if you mentioned the police dispatch to your station this evening about the time you got off work."

Dean resisted the urge to scowl at her. He'd forgotten that she had people monitoring the radio transmissions of the city agencies about Unusual activity.

"What do you want to know? It was a routine check based on an earlier event. It turned out to be nothing. End of story."

"Were you going to tell me a shifter on a call threatened you earlier today?" Jaz had stopped even pretending to hold back. She was full on pissed at this stage.

"Jaz, maybe we can have this conversation later, when we don't have company over."

Hangbe decided it was time to insert herself into the conversation. "If you tell me who this shifter is, I'll take care of it so you and Jaz can pretend it never happened."

Both of them said "NO!" at the same time to that suggestion.

Dean took a deep breath. He was going to have to tell her the whole story anyway at this point. "Look, it is the same jerk who jumped me in the parking lot a few weeks ago. He was injured at the scene of that fire."

Hangbe leaned in. "So, he was the shifter connection to trafficking you mentioned."

Dean sighed. "Yes. I avoided saying anything because he's technically a patient. I shouldn't tell you anything about my encounter with him."

Gibbie countered with, "I don't know, Dean. If someone attacks or threatens you, that probably voids the caregiver arrangement. It would for me."

"The vampire's right," Hangbe said. "So this Cretan was the one who had locked the people in the building?"

Dean nodded. "It looks that way. He was injured. We took him to the hospital until he could regenerate enough for them to take him to the Unusual unit at the jail. He escaped from custody and the police are looking for him."

Jaz asked, "Why do you think this isn't a big deal, then? What happened that makes you think he won't come after you?"

"Because the probie I worked with today scared him off."

Jaz laughed, "What new academy graduate paramedic could scare off a werepanther with a grudge?"

"That's what I wondered," Dean replied. "She said something to him about her father, and he sort of shut up and stopped being so scary."

"Who's her father?" Hangbe asked.

Jaz shook her head and said, "Back up. What's this girl's name? Let's start there. What do you know about her?"

"She's a shifter of some sort herself, maybe a leopard or some other jungle cat with spots."

Hangbe glanced at Jaz and then said, "A jaguar, maybe?"

"Possibly, why?"

Jaz leaned back and shook her head. "What's her name?"

"Leah, Leah Casado. She just came through the new accelerated paramedic program. She's very good for her first day."

Gibbie shook his head. "It can't be the real Leah Casado. There's no way she'd work as a paramedic in our city. I'd heard rumors she was around here somewhere going to college, but I thought it was all just rumor."

Dean glanced around at the others. He leaned back in his chair and folded his arms. "Okay, now it's your turn to fill me in. What am I missing here?"

Jaz said, "Dean, if it's the same girl, and it sounds like it is, your new partner is the daughter of the leader of the underworld cartel called the Jaguars. They're criminal royalty of the highest order. Here in North and South America, jaguar shifters are very rare, and very powerful. They descend from the high Incan priests and gained their power through blood sacrifice and magic. That's how they've held onto their power all these years later."

"So, she's the daughter of a criminal kingpin?"

Gibbie shook his head and leaned in towards Dean. "No, she's the daughter of THE criminal kingpin, at least the biggest one in this hemisphere."

Dean thought they were pulling his leg. He glanced from Jaz, to Hangbe, to Gibbie, and back to Jaz. They all nodded.

"I still don't get why that's important. Based on the way she reacted to my questions about her background, she clearly wants nothing to do with her past, something which I totally get, by the way. Why else would she take a job like being a paramedic unless she had broken all ties?"

Jaz said, "Except she didn't. She still felt perfectly comfortable dropping daddy's name with that werepanther to make him settle down. It worked, too, based on what you said."

Hangbe said, "I must talk with this girl. She might have valuable information for this investigation."

"No," Dean said. "You will not."

"You can't tell me no. I can investigate whatever and whoever I want in order to close my case."

Dean shook his head. "Not this time. She's my probie. That means she's under my protection. If you want to talk with her, you ask me, and I'll see if she wants to talk to you. I don't think she knows anything about what's going on. She's been in the academy for the last six months studying. Believe me. She's had no time for socializing."

Hangbe protested, but Jaz held out a hand. "Hangbe, I have to back Dean on this one. He's on our side and he wants to break this ring as much as you and I do. If he thinks she has nothing to do with it, then that's probably correct."

"But—" Hangbe started.

Jaz shook her head. "Let Dean find out what she knows. If he thinks she can help us, he'll let us know. Right, hon?"

Dean nodded. "Believe me, Hangbe, I want these animals in jail as much as you do. I saw those bodies piled on top of each other, trying to claw their way out of that burning basement. So did Leah. If she can help, I'll let you know and have her tell you herself. She wants to be a paramedic, then she's going to own the full responsibility of what that means in my book."

The words hung in the air for a few seconds. The last few minutes had been tense and everyone in the room seemed lost when it came to what to do next.

Gibbie finally broke the silence saying, "Hey, I've some dice in my coat pocket. How about we play a round of Yahtzee?"

After an exchange of glances, everyone broke out laughing. Despite the laughs, it turned out Gibbie had the perfect solution to diffuse the tensions building between the four of them. They played a few rounds and kept the conversation to lighter subjects. When the topic returned to work at the end of the evening, everyone had relaxed and worked out a plan of action.

Walking Gibbie and Hangbe to the door with Jaz, Dean said, "So, tomorrow, after work, Jaz and I will head down to the Irish Shop and talk to Dougie about closing the portal. There has to be a way to shut it down temporarily. That will cut off the traffickers from their support network and source of victims."

Hangbe nodded. "Good. In the meantime, Gibbie and I will concentrate on tracking down these cat shifters and their contacts here in the city to narrow down who the boss is here in Elk City."

Gibbie gave a thumbs up. "I'm right there with you, Hangbe. This vampire will hook you up."

Hangbe shot Gibbie a strange look, then said, "We'll all check back in tomorrow night and see what the next steps will be."

Everyone agreed and the two guests headed back down to the garage while Dean and Jaz prepared for bed. The weight of the long day at work suddenly hit Dean, and all he wanted was to climb in the sack. He had to be back at work in time for the next shift in the morning with Leah.

Jaz smiled as he yawned while helping her clean up from their dinner. "You go to bed. I've got this. You're back in early tomorrow anyway."

"You sure?"

Jaz nodded. "Go. I won't be up long. I'm tired, too."

Dean smiled and headed back to their room for a much-needed night's sleep.

Chapter 19

GIBBIE PULLED the van onto the street from the Errington building's garage and turned south towards the apartment he'd arranged for Hangbe. She sat in the passenger seat checking email or something on her phone. After a few minutes, she looked up and scanned the darkened sidewalks outside as he drove.

"Where are we going?"

"I thought you'd want to get some rest. You only had that quick two-hour nap when we dropped off your bags at the apartment."

"No time for that. I found some information in the Interpol database that might link to Manton. There's a werepanther by the same name who's associated with a clan out of southern France."

Gibbie didn't know how she kept going like this. He didn't technically need rest, and he was tired after their day tracking leads and locations Gibbie had turned up. He hadn't even gotten out of the van on most of them since it was daylight out. She'd been up for at least two days based on what Dean had told him about their time in Ireland.

"I don't know any French shifters in town, if that's what you're asking."

"No, but there has to be a place, a local pub, or something where we might get a lead on who picked up that guy when he broke out of the hospital. There aren't many who'd hide someone associated with killing a human in a public place like that."

She wasn't wrong about that. He didn't know anyone, even among his shadier contacts, who'd put up with that in the community. Still, if she wanted to find someone who did, that meant going to The Watering Hole. A werewolf family originally from the hills of western Maryland and West Virginia ran the bar. They had contacts that came there from all over the country. They'd been closed earlier in the day, so he hadn't taken Hangbe there.

"I know a place. I'm not sure if you'll be able to find what you're looking for there, though. Most people here in Elk City are decent folks."

"Just get me in the door. I'll take care of rooting out the scum."

The gleam in her eye sent a chill down Gibbie's spine. It was both terrifying and a bit of a turn on at the same time. He kept his focus on the road as he turned off the original path home and took her deep downtown. He stole a few glances in her direction while he drove. There was something about this woman that excited him more than just about any woman he'd ever met.

Maybe it was that she was so far out of his league, or that he knew she'd kill him out of hand if he crossed her. He'd dated dangerous girls before. More than a few had tried to kill him, mostly in a fit of anger at something he'd done to piss them off. Hangbe was different. If she decided to kill him, it wouldn't be because he said the wrong thing or winked at the wrong waitress. There was something refreshing in that.

A few minutes later, Gibbie pulled the van to the side of the street in an empty parking space. He hopped out and fed a few quarters into the meter and waited while Hangbe came over to join him.

He pointed up the street. "The Watering Hole is up there one block. If someone downtown knows where this guy is hiding, they'll be in there. Otherwise, all those involved are probably locked down."

"Do I need a password to get in?" she asked as she slipped a silver Kukri knife under her jacket where it fit into a sheath hidden there. He knew she had a pistol hidden in a shoulder holster on the other side.

"No, I'll go with you. I know the bartender there. Just remember, if you cause trouble there, I can never go back."

"If there's trouble, it's probably a good idea for you to find a new place, anyway. You're a decent enough guy for a vampire, Gibson. It'd be a shame for anything to happen to you."

She dropped a sly grin as she said it and started across the street. He jogged along to catch up with her stride, propelled by her exquisitely long legs. He caught up with her as she turned and angled up to the next block. He pointed at a nondescript gray door in between a locksmith shop and a dry cleaner.

Hangbe pulled open the door and walked down the stairs just inside. Gibbie pulled the door closed and followed her down just in time to stop her from taking out the bouncer.

The big werebear had a hand pressed against her chest, glaring at her and shaking his head. "Lady, I think you're in the wrong place. This is a private club."

Hurrying down the last few steps, Gibbie rushed up to stand beside Hangbe. "It's alright, Anson. She's with me."

"Another one of your human floozies, Gibbie? She's not like your usual type."

"Uh, yeah, well, I'm trying to turn over a new leaf. Can we come in?"

"You know the rules. You're responsible for her behavior while she's here. You okay with that. With that hidden body armor she's got on, it seems like she's looking for trouble."

"Oh, that, we were paint balling earlier. We just want a drink and a chance to relax, right, honey?" He snaked an arm out and around her waist, hoping she didn't lop off his arm for being so forward.

To his surprise, she leaned into his embrace and smiled. "This is all so exciting, Gibbie. I never even knew this place was here. I've walked past it dozens of times."

Choking a little in surprise, Gibbie recovered, saying, "Oh, yeah, sweetie. Just remember, you're my guest and you can't just waltz in here any time you want."

He glanced at Anson. The big shifter nodded and moved to one side to let the two of them through. The noise of the live metal band washed over them both as the door opened. Gibbie steered Hangbe over toward the bar where he saw a pair of open stools.

As they worked their way through the crowded underground club, she leaned in close and whispered in his ear. "If you ever touch me again without telling me first, it might be the last time you touch anything."

Gibbie almost tripped over his own feet at that moment, casting his eyes down to catch the wicked grin on her face. He gulped and said, "Understood. I just thought we needed to work up a cover story."

"It was good work, just don't make a habit of it."

Gibbie nodded and let out a sigh of relief. He let his hand drop from around her waist to show her he'd gotten the message. To his surprise, she reached down and pulled it back into place. He settled his hand over the curve of her hip where the waistband of her tight jeans rode just below the bottom of the thin layer of body armor covering her torso. He tried unsuccessfully to hide the goofy grin on his face at being so close to such a magnificent woman.

Breck, the bartender saw Gibbie and Hangbe sit at the end of the bar and came over to take their orders. Gibbie ordered his usual, a sangria with a wedge of orange. Hangbe ordered a double Scotch, neat.

As she went to make their drinks, Gibbie leaned in closer to Hangbe and whispered, "What's the plan?"

"I've got to identify who in here is related to our trafficking ring. Let's wait for the drinks to come back."

Gibbie had no idea what she was going to do, but she clearly had something in mind. Breck returned with their drinks. He picked up his as soon as it arrived and sipped at the tangy beverage.

Hangbe left her drink sitting on the bar. Her right hand rose instead to touch her fingertips against two of the beads in her ornate necklace. A gentle crooning came from her throat. He only heard it because he was so close to her. He doubted anyone else had any idea she was up to anything.

He opened his mouth to ask what she was up to, but clapped it shut as she raised the forefinger of her left hand. The tune wafting from her never stopped, even after she turned her head in a slow pass so she could scan the whole place. She twisted back and forth twice before settling back to stare across the room at a lone door in the far wall.

"There, that is where I'll get my answers."

"What's back there? What did your magic show you?"

"I don't know. I only know that the ones I seek are behind that door."

Gibbie scanned the area and spotted the hulking form of a guard standing in the shadows not too far away. "You'll never get in there unnoticed. There's a guy watching it, see."

Hangbe batted his arm down. "Don't point, you fool. I see him. Look, I'll get up and head to the women's room. The bathrooms are in the corner nearby. You get up and distract the guard."

"Me? What do you want me to do?"

"Just get his attention on you and not the door. You do that and I'll be able to get inside. Can you get it done or not?"

Gibbie saw her beautiful eyes staring back into his, and he didn't hesitate. "Of course. One distraction coming right up. Just be ready to go."

Hangbe stared at him for a second longer, then got up and wound her way through the crowd towards the restrooms. Gibbie watched her go and looked around the room for the best way to get the guard's attention. A crazy idea formed in his head. Sliding off his barstool, he paused long enough to down the rest of his drink and scribble something on the napkin beneath his glass before heading into the crowd to put his plan into action. It just might work in this bar full of shifter bikers and other rough sorts.

He made his way to the bandstand and leaned close to the spike-haired woman running the sound board. "I'll buy all the band's merch for sale on that table over there if you get them to play this song for me." He handed her the folded napkin.

She opened it and read the words there. Raising one eyebrow, she glanced up at him. "Really?"

Gibbie nodded. "All the merch, but you have to do it up right."

"Okay, it's your funeral. I'll be right back."

He waited while she made her way to the rear of the stage and waited for the band to finish the current song. She handed the napkin to the shirtless and tattooed drummer and pointed at Gibbie. The guy read the napkin and squinted through the lights. Gibbie raised a hand and waggled his fingers at the guy.

The reaction he got was not what he expected. The drummer's face split into a broad grin. He called over the rest of the band, who all clustered around his drum set. Realizing his plan was about to go into action, Gibbie swallowed hard. The song was only part of it. The next part was all him. It would succeed or fail based on what he did next.

The band members spread out back to their instruments. The lead singer on keyboard said, "We have a special request from one of our biggest fans and we couldn't say no. It's one of our favorites and I'm sure yours, too. Join in if you know the words."

Dropping his hands to the keys, the music started with a familiar trumpet fanfare and a driving disco beat. The bass and lead guitar joined in right away with the intro. Gibbie knew it was now or never, and he let out a yell and charged to the center of the now-empty dance floor. He reached the middle just as the singer started in on the 70's anthem, Y.M.C.A.

Gibbie threw his hands in the air as he let himself fall into the music so it carried him away. By the time they got to the chorus, the dance floor had filled to bursting and everyone joined in with voices and arm motions as they all spelled out the letters.

While everyone danced around him, Gibbie craned his neck and spotted Hangbe slipping through the door to the back rooms of the bar. Smiling that his plan had worked, he continued leading the dance party, only partly worrying if he had enough room on his credit cards to pay for the pile of t-shirts and stuff the band had for sale. All that mattered was that his plan had worked.

Chapter 20

HANGBE STOOD by the women's room door as Gibbie approached the bandstand. She wondered what he was up to. She waited and worried the vampire wouldn't be up to the task she had set for him. She was about to break into an improvised Plan B to get into the back room when the music started up again.

Her jaw dropped as her ridiculous guide to Elk City began dancing and gyrating around the dance floor in front of the band. To her amazement, the crowd cheered and began singing along, joining in the dance. When the chorus came around, everyone in the room began spelling the letters with their bodies, shouting at the tops of their lungs.

Two female shifters came running over and tugged the guard away from his position by the door. He'd been dancing in place for the first verse and chorus and didn't resist when they pulled out to the dance floor. Shaking her head, Hangbe slid along the wall, catching Gibbie's eye as she opened the door and slipped inside. He actually winked at her, which she'd have to deal with later. For now, his ridiculous plan had worked. Now, she had a job to do.

Letting the door close behind her, muffling the noise from the bar on the other side, Hangbe let her eyes adjust to the even dimmer light on this side. A hallway with several doors stretched ahead of her. The only light came from the open door at the end. Her sensitive ears picked up at least two male voices and the sound of someone sobbing softly from that direction.

Touching her beads of seeking, as she had done earlier at the bar, she reached out to find the source of the presence she'd felt earlier. It was someone linked to one of the missing persons cases she'd followed to Elk City, though she couldn't be sure which disappearance they related to. It was the first solid lead she'd found in the several months she'd been tracking this case.

Her magical necklace connected to the presence right away, and she got a sense of proximity that meant whoever it had linked to. They were probably in one of these rooms off this hallway. The voices at the end of the hall got louder and a loud smack followed by a cry of pain echoed down the hallway.

The male voices laughed as the sobbing grew louder, following the cry for help. Hangbe moved down the hallway, checking the other two doors on the way to the one that was open. Both were locked. She continued on until she reached the end and peeked into the open room.

A metal desk occupied most of the room. Four hulking forms stood around a woman tied to a metal chair. One man with his back to Hangbe raised his hand to deliver a backhand blow and said, "Are you going to try to escape again, girl?"

The woman in the chair wore a torn dress with a plain blue print fabric that had seen better days. Her brown hair hung down around her face but didn't hide the bruised cheeks and the tears running down them. She lifted her head to answer but stopped as her piercing blue eyes met Hangbe's brown ones. The girl gasped in surprise and Hangbe cursed under her breath. There went her advantage.

Just like that, the four men turned to stare in her direction, their eyes narrowing in anger as they spotted her. The largest of them pointed at her. "What are you doing back here? This area is closed to patrons of the bar."

Thinking fast, Hangbe stood from her crouch and shrugged. "I'm sorry. I was told the bathroom was this way."

She knew right away they didn't buy her act. The werepanthers closest to the door reached for her and dragged her into the room. Damn, they were fast. Still, that worked to her advantage.

Letting her momentum towards them help propel her forward, Hangbe launched off her back foot, snapping a kick with her boot into the midsection of the nearest shifter. As he doubled over, she reached into her jacket for her pistol.

As her hand came free with the gun, a fist like steel cracked down on her wrist. The blow sent a jolt of pain up her arm and loosened her grip on the Glock. Cursing as it clattered to the floor, she ducked under the two pairs of arms reaching to pull her closer.

The closest of them had doubled over from the force of her kick and she rolled sideways, using his back as support to move her away from his partner. That brought her nearer to the boss man, but he hadn't expected the move, so she caught him by surprise.

His eyes widened as she slipped the Kukri free from inside her jacket and hacked the silver alloy blade down into the side of his neck. Blood spurted free, the razor-edge cutting vital vessels that would never regenerate. His hand came up and clapped against the spurting wound, gasping in pain. He fell backward and she turned to face the others. The leader would be dead in under a minute with that wound.

"Who's next?"

The one she'd kicked hugged his midsection as he stumbled towards the door, but the other two came at her, both shifting into their humanoid panther forms. Claws extended, they raked at her from both sides as she twisted to keep away from their grasping reach.

Her body armor took most of the damage and she was able to sneak in a hit on one of them with her Kukri that brought a yowl of pain as he yanked his injured paw back.

Hangbe tried to follow up on that strike but that exposed her back and she realized too late the other shifter had the reach to grab onto her shoulders. His iron grip pulled at her and slammed her to the floor hard enough to knock the wind from her.

Gasping and trying to recover, she realized she'd never get away in time to avoid the next attack. Reaching for her neck, Hangbe's questing fingers found the large glass bead just in time. Accessing the magic with her mind, she let the stored spell loose as the raking claws got too close.

A blinding flash of white energy pulsed out from the Amazon on the floor. Both attackers flailed at their eyes, trying to clear them.

Knowing she only had a second or two, Hangbe slashed at the ropes binding the girl to the chair and leaped over it, yanking the stunned prisoner to her feet.

"Follow me."

The girl nodded, stumbling after Hangbe into the hallway. The one she'd kicked had reached the door to the bar and stood talking to the guard who'd returned to his post.

As Hangbe and the girl entered the hallway and raced towards them, both men squared off to block her path. She reached for her pistol, forgetting for a second she'd left it on the floor in the room behind her. Cursing as her hands met an empty shoulder holster, Hangbe shifted gears.

She shouted at the girl, "Stay behind me and keep up."

Not waiting for an answer, Hangbe leaped forward, feinting left and then attacking to the right, leading with her blade. It worked, and she avoided the incoming attacks enough to slice across the torso of the one she'd belly kicked. He howled in pain and fell to the side, clutching at his slashed abdomen.

Ducking low and punching back to the left, the Amazon delivered a blow to the solar-plexus with a fist.

She didn't wait to follow up with a killing blow. She had to get the girl out of here to safety. Standing, Hangbe reached back for the girl's hand and tugged at her, pulling her into the crowded bar. The action at the doorway had drawn unwanted attention, though, and several werecats headed in her direction.

"Go, run for that door. There's an old white van parked down the street to the left. Meet me there." When the girl hesitated, her eyes wide with fear, Hangbe shoved her in the right direction with a hand between her shoulder blades. "Go!"

The girl stumbled in the right direction at least. Hangbe had hoped to hand her off to Gibbie, but the vampire was nowhere in sight. A pair of muscled, furred bodies blocked her view of the bar a second later just as more clawed hands grabbed for her from behind.

Spinning in place, she struck out with her blade, trying to drive the attackers backward. The silver alloy kept the attackers wary since the wounds wouldn't regenerate the way normal injuries would. There were too many of them, though. She got in a few hits, but then the claws pulled her to the floor.

Hangbe lay on her back, most of the attacks absorbed by her body armor, and reached for her necklace. There weren't any offensive spells there, but she could heal her injuries at least. Then she'd figure a way out of this.

A booted foot stomped down. Pinning her free hand to the floor before she could activate the healing bead. A black panther's face snarled down at her.

"Let's finish her. Hunters like her need to know where they can and can't interfere with us."

Yowls of agreement from the shifters all around her, holding her immobile to the floor. Hangbe gathered her strength, determined to make them pay before they killed her.

A wild scream unlike anything she'd heard before interrupted the incoming attacks. The shifter standing on her free hand flew backward as a shadowy blur pitched him into the wall. The blur continued around the circle, taking down each of the shifters. The final two let go of Hangbe and backed away, trying to defend themselves.

The blurred shadow solidified. It was Gibbie. "Hey, you need a hand up? We should probably leave now."

He reached down and Hangbe nodded, taking the help. Her wounds were more severe than she realized.

Gibbie turned and bared his fangs at the nearest cluster of shifters, stomping his foot in their direction. They all backed away a step.

Now that they had some space and path to the door, Gibbie pulled Hangbe's arm across his shoulder and helped her run for the exit. They burst through and raced up the stairs, reaching the street a few seconds later.

Hangbe paused as her head swung back and forth, searching the sidewalk in both directions. "Where is she?"

"The girl you brought with you is already in the van. I took her out first, then came back for you."

Shouts from the open doorway behind them stopped the conversation. Hangbe nodded down the street. "Let's get out of here."

Gibbie once again assisted her as they half-limped, half-ran to the van. The girl huddled against the far corner of the bench seat behind the driver's seat. Hangbe nodded at her as she eased herself into the passenger seat.

The driver's door popped open and Gibbie hopped in. "Wow, that was exciting. I didn't know what you had planned when you went back there, so I kind of had to improvise. Sorry it took me so long to get back to help you."

"You did everything right. The girl was the one who needed saving." Hangbe paused, realizing how that sounded. "Uh, thank you for returning to check on me, though."

"Think nothing of it. After all, what kind of guide would I be if I abandoned you?"

Hangbe nodded and stole a glance at Gibbie, suddenly seeing the frumpy, unlikely partner in a new light. As the passing streetlights flashed overhead, they lit up his smiling face. A grin spread across hers as well.

She settled back and touched her healing bead, waiting for the healing warmth of the magic to wash over her. She swiped a hand across her forehead and shook her head. For some reason, she was already a little flushed before the spell started.

Chapter 21

DEAN'S ALARM startled him from a nightmare. He'd been trapped in a basement with fire all around him. He woke gasping for breath, surprised at first that he wasn't hacking from inhaling caustic smoke.

"You okay, hon?" Jaz asked, still half asleep beside him.

Dean ran his hand through his hair, scratching at his scalp to wake himself as he checked the clock. "Yeah, just a bad dream. I have to get ready for work. Go back to sleep. Sorry to wake you."

Jaz mumbled something he didn't quite get as she rolled over. He asked her to repeat it, then noticed she'd fallen back to sleep.

He gathered a fresh uniform shirt and pants from the closet and carried it all into the bathroom. He'd shower and get dressed in there so he didn't wake her again. She'd been up late working on some paperwork left over from the day in the office.

A half hour later, Dean rolled out of the parking lot. Leah had pulled up on the curb outside the ramp, waiting for him. He waved as he passed her. He'd forgotten about her driving in with him this morning.

She followed along behind and together they reached the station about twenty minutes later. Dean always enjoyed this time of the day.

There weren't that many cars on the road yet, and it always made the city seem so peaceful.

Leah parked next to him and by the time he'd gathered his backpack with a spare change of clothes, she was waiting by the back bumper of his truck.

"You could've gone in. I'm fine."

Leah shook her head. "Nope, I'm not losing my job because my training officer died on my watch."

"Gee, thanks." They both chuckled at his response as they headed for the station.

Barry and Brynne sat at the table inside, already started on their breakfast. Barry worked on a stack of waffles and Brynne sipped some warmed blood from the stores Freddy kept on hand for her.

Dean smiled as he took in their relaxed state. "See, I didn't jinx you after all. Neither of you look any worse than you did last night when we left."

Barry's smile turned to a scowl. "Oh, the jinx was in full effect until about two hours ago. It finally settled down enough for us both to catch up on our reports. I just sat down to eat."

Brynne raised her mug and gestured to the ambulance bay door. "We left the rest of the shift checks for the two of you. A gift for your impertinence. We ended up dealing with the aftermath of a bar brawl at some shifter club downtown. Some pretty serious injuries, though no one was talking about how it started."

Dean laughed, and Leah joined in after a second. "All's fair where the jinx is concerned. Let us catch some breakfast and we'll take care of it so you two can get out of here."

As the four of them finished their breakfast, Dean asked, "Anything from last night we need to know about?"

Brynne thought for a moment and said, "No, not really. Nothing more on the trafficking thing and everything else was pretty normal, aside from the thing at the bar. Just back-to-back calls that kept us running all night."

Dean nodded and finished his waffles and sausage. He waited for Leah to finish then said, "Ready to get started?"

She nodded.

The two of them went to get the ambulance squared away for the day while the other two packed up their gear.

Brynne stuck her head into the ambulance bay to say goodbye before leaving. Then Dean and Leah were alone while they finished their checks on the equipment. They settled in after that to go over the in-house training on the computer network, since Leah was new to the system.

Their first call came in on the radio an hour into the shift, followed by a succession of routine medical emergencies, all excellent tests of Leah's skills.

Before he realized it, they'd finished their last run of the day and were headed back to the station. His stomach growled loud enough they both started laughing. They hadn't had a real lunch, only able to grab a few snacks from the supplies at the hospital between dropping patients off. He looked forward to whatever Freddy had for them when they got back.

Brynne and Barry had already arrived back for their next shift by the time they rolled back into the station. Dean plugged in the land line electric to the ambulance to keep everything charged and checked to make sure Leah was working on restocking from their last few calls.

"I'll fill in the log for the last two calls. How are you on your reports?"

Leah looked up from where she'd been digging in the med bag. "I'm in good shape. I probably have a half hour left to finish up."

"Okay, Brynne will check them over for you before you submit them. I have a meeting I have to get to."

"You sure?" Leah asked. "I figured I'd be following you home again."

"No need. No one's seen any sign of Manton since yesterday. I'm sure he's long gone."

Leah's doubtful expression lingered for a second, but she shrugged and went back to work.

Dean headed into the squad room and dug into his last few items to complete the shift. He let Brynne know about double checking Leah's reports and then he changed into his civilian clothes to meet Jaz.

Freddy had a sandwich ready made with the roasted chicken he'd made for dinner. He dropped it in the brown paper bag he held. "I made one for Jaz, too. That girl forgets to eat just like you."

"Thanks, she'll appreciate it. And you're right. She skips lunch most days. This'll hit the spot." He waved goodbye to the others and headed out to his truck. Checking his watch, he knew he'd have to make good time to meet Jaz when he told her he would.

She already had the black SUV fired up and ready to go when Dean pulled into the garage and parked his truck. He left his bag and EMS gear in his truck. It was safe enough in the pickup truck here beneath the Errington building.

"You're raring to go," Dean said as he climbed into the SUV.

Jaz leaned over for a kiss hello. "I've been out checking on some local clients today and just got back. I thought you might beat me here."

"Seems like perfect timing, then."

Jaz smiled and backed out of her spot. Dean buckled up and leaned back in his seat. It was time to have a talk with the resident leprechaun of Elk City about shutting the portal to Ireland. He wasn't looking forward to what they might learn when Jaz confronted Dougie about the trafficking ring.

To Dean's surprise, the shop's lights were turned off when they arrived outside. He checked his watch. "That's weird, I know he keeps the store open until at least eight most nights."

"Maybe he closed early tonight. Let's go around back and see if his car is here."

Jaz pulled the SUV into the alley that ran beside store and drove to the rear parking area. Only one of the parking spaces in the back was occupied. A green and white Mini Cooper sat in the spot right next to the shop's rear door.

"Is that his car?" Jaz asked.

Dean shrugged. "I've never seen what he drives. It could be his."

"Let's try the door. Maybe he's still here."

Jaz and Dean got out of the SUV. Jaz wore her usual low-key tactical outfit of black military fatigue pants and a black T-shirt.

Instead of her usual holstered Glock on her hip, she had a smaller semi-automatic tucked into a holster at the small of her back.

Dean got to the back door first. He was about to knock when he noticed it was partially ajar. "That's strange, this door has always been shut and locked when we've come here before."

"Step back, Dean. Let me go first." Jaz had drawn her pistol and approached the door from the side, opening it a few inches and checking the interior from beside the opening before pushing it open the rest of the way.

Dean followed her inside. He could see right away, there'd been a struggle of some sort. One of the free-standing shelves in the storeroom had tipped into the wall. Most of the shelf's contents had spilled to the floor. Several snow globes had broken, and water and green glitter covered a portion of the floor.

Jaz pointed at the puddle. "Careful, don't slip."

Dean stepped around the mess and looked around for any sign of Dougie. His mind turned to worry for his friend. This looked like it had happened within the last few hours based on how wet the floor was.

"Do you see him anywhere, Jaz?"

She'd moved into the next room and as soon as he asked her, she called out. "I found him. Dean, get the medic bag from the truck."

Dean resisted the urge to rush in to see what had happened. Jaz could handle any life-threatening situations as well as he could. If she thought they needed the first aid bag from the back of her SUV, he trusted her judgement.

By the time he got back with the med bag, Jaz had already pressed a wad of paper towels against a gash on the leprechaun's head. The big leprechaun looked up and Dean and gave a weak grin.

Dean set the bag down, happy to see Dougie was conscious. "Hey, what happened to you?"

"Oh, nothing really. I fell down. That's all."

"Bull," Jaz said. "I know a shakedown when I see one. What did they want?"

Dean added, "And who is it who did this to you?"

Dougie pushed Dean's hand away from his head, taking the gauze pads himself and pressing them against his scalp. "Really, my friends, I'm fine. Just patch me up and I'll go home."

Dean leaned in to get a better look and shook his head. "You're not going home. You need stitches for that laceration on your head at the very least, and the doc will want you to get a CT scan as well for the potential head injury."

When Dougie protested again, Jaz cut him off.

"Douglas O'Nolder, you listen to me. I need to know what happened and if this has anything to do with a group of werepanthers running trafficked women and men through your portal."

As Dean took more gauze and pressed them against the gash on Dougie's forehead, the leprechaun glanced at the floor to avoid the Hunter's glare. Jaz kept her gaze locked on him until he threw up his arms and gasped in exasperation.

"Fine, yes, it was the cat shifters. They found out about my portal about six months ago and offered to pay me to use it. In the beginning it was just to bring in some crates of Irish whiskey without paying the duties, but then they branched out into other types of smuggling. I tried to stay out of it, but something must have happened while you all were over in Ireland. They got furious about what you were doing sticking your nose into my business. They worried you'd found out what they were doing."

Jaz nodded. "They thought you told us. You're lucky they didn't just kill you outright. They've murdered others to cover up their trail."

Doug started sobbing and said, "They might as well have killed me. I told them if they killed me, the portal would close forever. Instead, they took me pot-o-gold. Now I've lost all me magic and they control the portal and my riches."

Dean's anger bubbled up. He wanted to yell at Dougie. The big lug had helped those who killed all the people in that basement. And who knew how many others they'd injured or killed over the course of six months. Instead of shouting at him, Dean swallowed his anger. He had to try to salvage something they could use to shut the operation down.

"Dougie, you can help us. How do we shut the portal, even temporarily?"

"You can't," Dougie blubbered as tears streamed down his cheeks.

"Now that they have my gold, they control my magic. I'm just a poor shopkeeper now. I have nothing else to my name."

Jaz growled deep in her throat. "Cut the pity party. You bought yourself this trouble trying to add to your little pot of gold. If you'd wanted to stop them, you could have gone to the police, or even too Dean and me. You had options."

All the leprechaun did was continue wailing.

Hoping to salvage something from the encounter, Dean asked, "At least tell us where they're hiding out in the city. You must know that much. Who's their leader? How do you contact them?"

"I never met the boss. I know he's named Finn something or other. I know nothing else about him other than he's relatively new to Elk City."

Dean glanced at Jaz. She shook her head. The name meant nothing to her. He shrugged and went back to his care of Dougie's injuries. He'd quieted down to simple sobbing now.

Jaz took out her phone and called in to the direct line at Fire Headquarters, calling for an ambulance to take the shopkeeper in for an evaluation. It didn't take them long to get there. Brynne and Barry came in, loaded up the leprechaun, taking Dean's report as they did.

The two of them watched the ambulance leave, then locked up the shop and walked to their SUV. As they drove away, Dean asked, "How do we close the portal if we need the pot of gold to control it? We can't let them bring any more people through it."

"We don't have to close it. We just have to restrict access. Between my people and Rudy's security teams, we should be able to take care of it. We'll mount a large enough guard force on both sides of the portal to discourage them from using it for now."

"We're still not any closer to finding Kaylee's family or Verity. If they're still alive, we have to find out where they are."

Jaz nodded. "We will. There aren't that many places they can hide in the city. We can narrow things down by a process of elimination. Any chance that new girl working with you has a way of tracking them down? She has to have underworld connections with the werecats in the city."

"Why use her?" Dean asked, instantly on the defensive to protect his probie from anything that could affect her chance to become a full paramedic.

"I'm just asking. Her family has to know who's behind this, even if they're not part of it."

Dean stood his ground. "I'll mention what we're doing, but I won't directly ask her for help. It's unfair to get her involved if she doesn't want to get involved. There are other ways we can do this. What about Gibbie and Hangbe? They might be able to use what we've found out from Dougie."

Jaz thought about it for a few seconds and said, "They might at that. We'll leave your girl out of it for now, but it might end up she's our only way in."

Dean knew Jaz was right. He didn't have to worry about it right now, though. "Let's exhaust our other leads first, okay. Call your teams and I'll reach out to James and Rudy about getting his pack and their security squads on the case, too."

When they got home, Jaz pulled out her phone and started making some calls while Dean did the same. Within two hours they had guards on both sides of the portal. It wasn't what they'd wanted at the beginning of the night, but it was a start. He'd do some more work the next day since he switched to night shift with Leah that evening.

Chapter 22

AFTER ANOTHER FITFUL night filled with vivid nightmares of fighting to get out of a smoke-filled room, Dean spent the next day working through a haze of sleeplessness, helping Jaz schedule coverage on the Irish Shop and the pub in Dublin. She was so preoccupied with what she was doing; she didn't notice how tired he was. He didn't tell her about the nightmares, figuring they were just a remnant of post-traumatic stress from what he'd seen in the basement of that building days before.

Jaz tried several times throughout the day to contact Hangbe and Gibbie to pass along their information on the gang, but both had dropped out of sight. Dean had wanted to get some of the other CERT team members and go looking for them, but Jaz told him not to worry. It was typical for Hangbe to do this when on a case. It didn't ease Dean's worry over Gibbie, even though he should be safe with her by his side. The vampire had lived at least four hundred years on his own without anyone's help. Still, between his nightmares and everything else going on, Dean was more than a little on edge.

Luckily, his first night shift with Leah went well, with no particularly traumatic calls or tension. Dean even managed an hour and a half of nap time in the middle of the night when things settled down for a bit. Leah continued to show the knowledge and hard work that had put her at the top of her class. She handled each patient with confidence and poise. She only needed a few checks with Dean to make sure she was on track.

The second night rolled around and Dean got to work even more exhausted. The dream still bothered him, and he only managed a few hours of fitful rest that afternoon. He hoped Leah was up to her usual standards because he was dragging. He needed the evening to go as smoothly as the last had.

He spotted her in the parking lot as he pulled in at Station U. The industrial park's streetlights weren't the best, and he almost didn't see her standing by the back of her car. A jet-black Mercedes sedan had parked beside her. She seemed to be in the middle of an animated conversation with someone through the rear window of her car.

Dean climbed out of his pickup truck and craned his neck to see who she was talking to. The rear window on the Mercedes was down, but the dark interior kept him from making out who it might be. Thinking she might need his help, Dean walked over.

When she turned his way, he stopped. She glared at him, her eyes glowing yellow. "Go inside, Dean. I'm in the middle of something."

Dean held up his hands, palms out, and backed up a step. "Sorry, just checking on you. See you inside."

Whatever had her upset, he had to remember to maintain his distance and remember she was far more able to handle herself in a supernatural world than he was.

He pulled open the station door and entered. Brook and Tammi sat eating dinner at the table and Brynne stood nearby, peering out through the window. She used her hand to lift one of the plastic slats in the blinds to see better.

She glanced his way before turning back to look outside. "Is she still yelling at her father? I can't hear them anymore."

"That's her father? I couldn't see inside the car."

"Brook saw the Mercedes pull up and sit idling in the lot before Leah got here. I ran the tags through O'Malley at the PD. It came back to a company owned by Leah's family. When she drove in and got out to talk to whoever it was, I figured it had to be her dad."

Dean walked over to look out the window with Brynne. "They weren't yelling when I saw them, but she was angry about something. It looked like she was ready to shift."

Brynne nodded. "Her father isn't happy with her career choice. I think he believes in the 'once in the Cartel, always in the Cartel' model of underworld gangs."

"Do you think she's in danger?"

"No, but we should keep an eye on her just in case. Maybe you can get her to talk about it later tonight on shift. I'd like to know what brought her father back to town."

Dean wondered, too. Maybe it had something to do with the werepanthers and the recent fires. Outside in the lot Leah took two quick steps backward, pointed her finger at the car while shouting something he couldn't make out. She spun around and stalked towards the station. Her eyes still glowed bright yellow as she approached the building.

Brynne and Dean scrambled to get away from the window. Brynne sat down behind one of the computers, and Dean hopped into a recliner and pretended to watch the news playing on the flatscreen.

Leah stepped inside and shut the door. She stood there, breathing hard with her eyes closed. Dean half expected her to change into her werejaguar form, but when she opened her eyes, they were their normal human brown color.

Dean tried to act normal and asked, "Hey, Leah. Everything alright?"

"How much did you see?" She asked, turning to Brynne first.

Brynne sat back in her chair. "Enough to know that your father is still trying to get you to quit. I thought you'd worked all this out with him while you were in the academy?"

"Me, too. Apparently, when I had words with one of his minions the other day, it gave him the idea that I wanted back into the Cartel."

Dean didn't know all the backstory like Brynne did, but he understood fathers who had trouble taking no for an answer. "Maybe he was hopeful you'd changed your mind."

"No, he was making sure I understood that I couldn't live in both worlds. I had to either be in or out. He didn't accept my excuse that protecting my colleagues was part of my new job."

Dean shook his head. "Hey, if that run in with Manton is the cause of this, you don't have to worry about me. My wife is more than capable of keeping track of me if there's any sort of trouble."

Leah rolled her eyes. "Your wife came up, too. He must have done some checking on the people I work with. He has informants everywhere. He's worried Ms. Errington will use me to get to him."

Dean looked away, remembering the conversation he'd had with Jaz a few days before.

His expression wasn't lost on Leah. She said, "I figured as much. Look, I'm an open book. I told Brynne and I'll tell you, I'm not in that world anymore. There's nothing I can tell you about anything that involves my family. All I want to be is just another medic."

Knowing it was up to him to mend this since she was his responsibility, Dean said, "You're a very good one. I have no reason to believe you'll have any issues staying in this job for a very long time. If I had any ideas about turning to you for help with anything, you've made your position clear. As far as I'm concerned, the matter is settled."

"Really? That's it?"

Dean nodded. "Discretion is part of our job here at Station U. Usually it has to do with our special patients and who they are, but there's no reason it shouldn't apply to you as well. Share as much or as little of your life as you want. We'll keep our noses out of it."

Leah seemed like she wanted to believe him. "What about your wife?"

"I've had to tell Jaz to back off before and I'll do it again if I need to. It won't stop her from investigating things she's hired to look into, but I won't let her leverage my relationship with you to get information." He held up his right hand and drew a cross on his chest with his other. "Promise."

Brynne stood. "I'm glad that's settled. Now you two need to get to work. The shift's started and you haven't begun any of your regular checks yet. Brook and Tammi finished theirs early. If you hurry, you might get dinner before Freddy cleans up."

Freddy called out from the kitchen. "Don't worry, Dean. I can reheat things if you get tied up."

Good old Freddy, Dean thought. He always looked out for the team and somehow always turned out superb meals, no matter what time it was.

"Come on, Leah. Brynne's right. We should get started."

Leah nodded and followed Dean into the ambulance bay to begin the shift checklist. By the time they returned to the squad room twenty minutes later, Brook and Tammy had left. Brynne still sat at the computer, looking over something. He was sure she heard them enter, but she kept working without looking up.

Dean pointed over at the table. "Leah, grab some food. It's always best to eat while you can. You never know when—"

Before he finished his sentence, the radio alert went off. They grabbed their coats for the first call of the night. They'd have to catch dinner later or grab a snack on the road. Duty called.

Chapter 23

GIBBIE PULLED into the alley and slid the gear lever into park. Hangbe unbuckled her seat belt and swung around to climb into the back of the van where she'd stashed her weapons. He swiped his sweaty palms against his shirt and turned to follow her. She'd found a short sword in the style of a Roman gladius for him. It hid nicely beneath his gray overcoat as he slid it into its sheath.

"Are we sure this is the place?" Hangbe asked, staring out through the back window at the building across the street.

"It's the only thing this size built of that glazed yellow brick Shayna mentioned. I checked with several sources earlier while you were resting. A guy I know at the building permits office talked my ear off about how rare that style was in this area."

When they had gotten back with Shayna, the girl Hangbe rescued from the shifter bar, it had taken them a day to get her to trust them enough to open up about where they'd held her and who'd captured her. She was a from a sea-side village in Cornwall in the U.K. As best she could tell, she'd been here for almost six months, but she couldn't be sure.

Once they gained her trust and got her some food and rest, she told them all about the clan of werepanthers who'd taken her. She mentioned meeting other people from villages like hers, most of them women and young girls. All had similar stories. She remembered three places where they'd kept her together with a group of others. One matched the description of the building across town that had burned down a week before. The other two were harder to nail down until Gibbie seized on the yellow bricks she mentioned.

They were still trying to track the third location, but the building across the street from the alley in which they hid had to be the second building Shayna remembered.

"What's the plan?" Gibbie asked. "You don't have a gun anymore. I still don't know why you didn't ask Jaz for another one."

"Because she'll be angry I lost the first one. The authorities can trace it back to me through my Interpol file. She won't want to loan me one they could trace back to her."

"But you won't lose another one. I mean, what are the odds?"

Hangbe shook her head. "Don't tempt the fates. Besides, I'm more than capable of handling these cats with just my blades." She brandished the yard of sharpened steel she held before sliding it into a sheath at her waist. "Plus, I have you now. You've proven a more than capable companion on this investigation. You've got my back, right?"

Gibbie bobbed his head with so much enthusiasm, he bumped his head on the van's roof. "You don't have to worry as long as I'm around. I'll be your bodyguard as long as you'll let me." He cringed a little as he said the last part. He caught the hint of a grin from her when he said it, and he chastised himself internally for talking like an idiot. This woman didn't need him to guard her back or the rest of her exquisite body.

When he realized he let his eyes linger on her a little too long, he flushed and turned around to fumble with his keys. "I'd better be sure the van's security system is armed before we leave. This neighborhood is pretty sketchy."

Hangbe snorted a laugh. "I don't think anyone will bother this heap, Gibson. Don't get me wrong, it's the perfect van for a stakeout. No one will pay any attention to it at all."

"No offense taken. I know it's a little beat up but me and this thing have been through a lot together." He patted the bench seat.

A flicker of movement caught his eye. He leaned towards the rear window, sliding past Hangbe in the open rear of the van. "Hey, that guy matches that photo of Manton Dean showed me. He's going into that side entrance. This has to be the right place."

"I agree. We'll wait a few minutes, then follow him in. Are you ready?"

Gibbie nodded and reached down and held on with a white-knuckled grip on the hilt of his short sword with one hand. Hangbe grinned and opened the rear of the van, jumping down to the pavement. He followed and shut the doors, toggling lock on the key fob before sliding it into his pocket.

They moved into the shadows near the mouth of the alley and checked the building's windows for any lookouts. The whole place looked vacant, despite the fact they'd seen Manton enter. No lights showed anywhere in the three-story structure.

"Where is he?" Gibbie asked. "We saw him go inside."

Hangbe searched the street in both directions and raised her arm. "There. That's him leaving from that door at the far end of the block."

"Should we go after him or find out why he was here?"

A muffled series of screams reached Gibbie's sensitive vampire hearing. Hangbe's head whipped around back to the building across from them in mid-answer. She'd heard it, too.

"Smell that?" She asked.

Gibbie sniffed the air. "Smoke." He pointed to the door Manton had entered across from them. "See it coming out around the doorjamb?"

Hangbe tapped a bead on her necklace and charged across the street without answering. She moved quickly; he could barely keep up with her. Gibbie reached deep, accessing his vampire speed and strength despite his reluctance to use it.

She reached the door just ahead of him and dashed inside. Thick smoke filled the entry hallway, causing them both to crouch low to see under it. Hangbe coughed and paused to catch her breath. The screams were louder here.

Gibbie turned and found the source. A stairwell leading up and down opened to the right. The smoke came from there, billowing up from the basement. He remembered the fire Dean had responded to last week. They were killing off more of the kidnapped people.

Hangbe had already reached the same conclusion. She bounded past him and down the stairs. Despite the flames from the packing crates stacked in front of the chained double doors below, Hangbe charged forward. Gibbie raced along right behind her.

She leaped over the flaming crates and pulled at the doors. They opened a little but stopped as soon as the chains pulled tight. "Help me!"

Gibbie was already jumping past the flames even as the walls and ceiling burned. The heat blistered his skin, but he pressed on, shouting, "Stand to the side."

Hangbe moved up to the wall, crouching low. She'd produced a scarf to cover her face and mouth. It couldn't be doing much, but it was better than nothing. Gibbie didn't need to breathe except to talk so the smoke had little effect on him. The heat and flames were another thing entirely, but he pushed aside his fear and slammed into the doors with all his vampire strength and speed.

The chains held, but the doors' metal handles pulled free of the steel frames as he burst through to the basement. A huddle of people in the against one wall by a barred window shrieked when he turned towards them. He'd forgotten he was in full vamp mode with his fangs and glowing red eyes.

Settling his face back to normal, Gibbie shouted. "Stay there while I clear the stairs. Get ready to run out to the street." A few nods were all the response he got.

Hangbe had crawled into the room behind him. She appeared weakened as she stood. "Is there another way out?"

"Not sure, but I can clear the stairs of those crates if you can get everyone to run out when I do. The ceiling and walls are on fire, but it's the only chance they have."

She offered a grim smile. "Be careful." She went over to the clustered people.

Gibbie rushed back to the stairs, returning to vamp mode to access his strength and grabbed at the nearest crate. His hands burned from the charred wood, but he ignored it as he threw the crate behind him against the far wall, away from the shrieking people.

Ten seconds later, all the crates now burned in a pile across the basement. The walls and stairway ceiling had caught fire all the way up to the first floor now, but there was a path up in the center of the stairs if they ran. They were shifters and would heal if they got through without dying. It was their only chance.

He waved at Hangbe, and she shouted at the clustered women and girls. They rushed past him as the Amazon led them up the stairs. Gibbie followed the last of them up, picking up the two stragglers under each arm and carrying them up and out of the building. He set them down on the sidewalk and peeled off his tan windbreaker. It smoked and threatened to catch fire until he stamped on it with his booted foot.

He searched for Hangbe and found her leaning up against the side of the building nearby, catching her breath. She stared at him, studying him in a way that made him a little queasy.

"Are you alright?" He asked.

"I am. We should get these people away from the building before it becomes fully aflame."

Sirens sounded in the distance as the two of them herded the people across the street and sat them down on the sidewalk. Gibbie tried providing care, running down his first aid training from his CERT classes.

Hangbe tugged at his arm. "Let the professionals tend to them. We should be gone when the officials arrive."

He didn't understand but followed along after being sure there were no serious injuries among the people. Catching up to her at the back of his van in the alley, Gibbie stopped as she turned on him and yanked the door open.

"Get in." A heat burned in her eyes.

The steady gaze she held on him stirred a host of emotions. He followed her instructions and climbed in the back, sitting on the cushions laid out behind the bench seat. He turned just in time to catch a broad smile on her face as she pulled the door shut.

"That's the second time you've saved me."

"I was just doing my job."

"Shut up." She pressed him back as his eyes widened in surprise. He never heard the air horn of the fire engine pulling up outside. It blocked the alley, hiding the van from the street.

Chapter 24

AS HE DROVE to the address on the screen between him and Leah, Dean waited for additional information to come in from dispatch. He stiffened when the radio announced another building fire downtown with injuries.

From the grim set of Leah's expression, she had the same worry about what they'd find when they arrived. Dean resisted the urge to drive any faster, though. He was already traveling as fast as was safe, and additional speed would only put the two of them in danger from an accident. Then no one at the fire would get their help.

The glow of the fully involved building fire lit the night sky over the city. This time, headquarters dispatched Dean and Leah with the initial response from the fire department units. He hoped that was a good sign and there would be live victims waiting for him.

As they approached, Dean searched for a location to pull over that wouldn't hinder the firefighting operations. Flames thrust high into the black night sky and the first few fire engines on location were still connecting to the hydrants to throw water on the blaze.

He spotted a spot ahead near an alley. A fire truck currently blocked the entrance, but he could get them to pull forward enough to get the ambulance through if he needed to leave in a hurry. A crowd of people sat on the sidewalk nearby, watching the blazing building as the firefighters battled the flames to keep it from setting fire to any of the neighboring buildings. A few fire fighters stood with the people on the sidewalk. They waved to him as he parked. They must have a patient for them over there.

"Get the cot out, Leah. Grab the monitor, oxygen, and airway kits. Anything else we'll leave here. We can bring patients back here for anything beyond that initial care."

She nodded and hopped out to get started.

Dean leaned over and grabbed the mic from the dash. "U-191 to Dispatch. On location and staging for patient care."

"Received U-191. Switch to operations channel two to connect with fireground command."

Dean switched the radio and grabbed his portable unit from the charger beside his seat. He made sure he dialed in the channel and slid the leather strap over his head so it rested diagonally across his chest.

By the time he got to the rear of the ambulance, Leah had everything loaded on the cot and ready to go. He nodded his approval and keyed the mic clipped to his shoulder strap. "Incident command, ambulance U-191 on location in the alley off Piedmont. Are there any patients?"

"U-191," The female voice, that of Deputy Chief Alyssa Rowe, said. "Rescue 11 has two patients with burns and respiratory distress. Take over patient care from them. They should be just down the street from you."

Leah looked over her shoulder and pointed at the ECFD rescue truck halfway down the block where they'd seen the cluster of people and the two firefighters. Dean nodded and grabbed the foot of the cot as Leah pulled the head end towards their patients.

"U-191 received. On the way to Rescue 11 now."

As they got closer, the light from the burning building revealed a pair of firefighters tending to two women seated on a tarp on the sidewalk. Other women and girls stood around, clustered in small groups of three and four, watching the firefighters caring for the patients.

Leah left Dean to manage the cot the rest of the way and moved forward to take over patient care from the two firefighters.

"Hello, gentlemen. What do you have?"

The first firefighter pointed at the pair on the ground beside him. "These two women were here with the others as we drove up. We got to them and started basic care. I'll let them explain the rest of it. We need to get back to our crew."

Leah nodded. "I've got this. Go ahead." She waited for the two firefighters to leave and approached the pair seated on the tarp. They both had oxygen masks over their mouths and noses. Soot covered their faces and tattered clothing. Some of it had burned away, leaving blistered flesh underneath in patches on both, mostly on their arms and hands. They were lucky if the fire was that close.

"Hi, I'm Leah." She let her eyes flash a quick yellow glow to tell them she was an Unusual. Dean showed his UV star of life tattoo, hidden from all but Unusual eyes.

Leah continued after the special identification. "My partner, Dean, and I are here to help you. Can you tell me your names?"

The taller of the two spoke first, the lilt of her Irish accent clear. "I'm Devon. This is Haley."

She gasped a little as she talked, making Dean wonder if Devon had inhaled hot smoke and had some airway burns. He was about to say something to Leah, but she beat him to it, asking the patient about her breathing and airway.

Realizing she had it in hand, Dean took over assisting her with getting vital signs on both patients while she continued getting their history and assessing their injuries. Once again, she impressed him with her cool confidence and poise.

They both had some significant second-degree burns that needed attention. Dean and Leah started applying clean dry dressings to keep them covered for now. The burn center at ECMC would see to further treatment.

As he was applying the bandages to Haley's burns, Dean remarked, "You two were lucky to get out when you did."

Haley shook her head and spit on the pavement beside her. "None of us would have gotten out if those two hadn't come and broken the locks that held all of us in."

"All of us?" Leah asked, startled and twisting her head around to search others standing nearby. "You were all in there?"

Devon coughed when she tried to answer and waved at Haley who said, "The bastards had been holding us to work on various jobs to pay off our toll to come here. Then one of them showed up tonight. But instead of unlocking the doors to take us to work, he set a fire in the stairwell and took off. We would've died in there if not for that crazy vampire and the sorcerer woman he was with. Now that we're free, we aren't sure where to go next or if we're in some kind of trouble."

Dean caught Leah's eye and then said. "You're not in any trouble as far as we're concerned. We don't care how you got here. We just want to treat your injuries. Once that's finished, the docs at the hospital will let you walk out on your own."

"Hospital!" Devon said, bringing on another coughing fit. She tried to stand and pull off the oxygen mask. Leah placed her hand on the woman's shoulder, pushing her back onto the tarp.

She said, "If you don't want to go to the hospital, we can't make you. Merrow like yourselves will heal pretty quickly if you can get to a source of salt water, right?"

The two nodded, eyes shifting from side to side, uneasy with the situation. They sat as if they were ready to jump up and run at any moment. Dean knew Merrow were the source of the legends of mermaids. He'd have to ask Leah later how she identified them. That could wait, though. Dean hung back and watched how Leah handled this. She was, after all, an Unusual just like they were.

"Easy," Leah said, holding a hand out to settle them. She lowered her voice a little and softened the tone she'd been using. "We are here to help you. Dean and I will patch you up enough to get you moving and then you can seek a way to regenerate, okay?"

After a long pause, Devon nodded. "I guess that's fine."

Dean took a chance and asked, "You mentioned the vampire and the woman?"

Haley glanced at Devon, who gave a quick bob of her head. Haley said, "It was strange. A black woman with incredible power and the oddest vampire I've ever seen showed up and broke the chains holding the doors closed. They helped us get free and then the pair took off in that direction, almost too fast to follow."

"Gibbie," Dean muttered. He caught Leah's eye. "I need to make a call. Keep monitoring them. I'll be right over here."

Her brow wrinkled, a little confused, but she nodded.

Dean moved a few steps away while he dialed Jaz.

"Hey, Dean," Jaz said. It sounded like she was hands free in her truck. "You're down at that fire, right?"

He knew she monitored his calls on her police and fire scanner. "Yeah, and you'll never guess who else was here?"

"Hangbe, right?"

"Bingo, along with her vampire shadow. It was a good thing. They freed the people trapped in the building before the fire trapped them."

Jaz cursed and said, "Put her on. She's not returning my calls."

"They're not here anymore. They must have taken off after the ones who set the fire as soon as they got everyone out. I have no idea where they went next."

Jaz was quiet for a second, then said, "I might have a way. Can you get away to help me?"

"I have to stay here and work with Leah."

"Call Brynne. Tell her I have a lead on something. See what she says."

Dean stopped, trying to decide what to do. He hated not sticking with a task. But they needed to reach out to Hangbe and Gibbie. He thought some more and decided Leah was good, solid enough to manage care for a bit on her own. Brynne could take over when she got here.

"I'll call her. How far away are you?"

"I'll be there in five minutes. Be ready to go when I get there."

Dean shook his head. "I think I'd better wait for Brynne. She shouldn't take too long."

Jaz didn't like his answer based on her tone, but she said, "I'll get started without you. See you in a bit."

Dean dialed Brynne's cell phone. She picked up right away.

"Hey, Dean. You two okay?"

"Yeah. Listen, I have a strange request. Jaz needs me to help follow a lead on the guys who set this fire. Leah is here with me handling two Merrow patients with burns and smoke inhalation."

Brynne interrupted him. "And you need me to come take the rest of your shift so you can go play with your wife?"

At first Dean didn't pick up on the fact that she was messing with him. He stammered a bit, searching for an appropriate answer to her question.

Brynne followed up with, "I guess you'll be asking for conjugal honeymoon visits next."

Realizing she was messing with him; he forced a laugh. "Alright, very funny. I'll assume that's a yes. How soon can you get here?"

"I'm already headed down to HQ to pick up supplies. I'll give you the list and you and Jaz can grab them while I take over with your probie."

"We can do that."

"Good, I'll be there shortly."

Dean hung up and returned to Leah. She had taken another round of vital signs. Dean joined in and helped so she could record everything from the monitor for her patient report later.

"Brynne's coming. She's going to finish the shift with you."

"What, so you can go chase the bad guys?" Leah asked, grinning up at him as she crouched by the heart monitor. "I hope you've got some help. It's almost certainly those rogue cats again."

Dean nodded. "I'll be fine. Jaz is coming. She thinks she can track either the ones who set the fire or at least the two who freed these people."

"Hunters hunting in the night. It's the kind of thing my mother used to tell me to scare me into staying in bed." Leah's tone had turned hard. He wondered if she'd had run-ins with other hunters out there."

"My wife only hunts the bad guys. There's no reason for her to go after anyone else. She's on our side in this."

Leah said nothing, turning back to her work monitoring the two women. It occurred to him she might have a different view of who the good guys and bad guys were given her family background. He wanted to tell her that Jaz would never hurt anyone she cared for, but that would be a lie. If her father was mixed up with this somehow, Jaz wouldn't hesitate to take him down.

Dean pushed the disturbing thought from his mind. No need to borrow trouble. As far as he knew, there was no connection to Leah's father. He had to talk to Jaz about this before an accidental encounter caused issues.

A fire department SUV pulled up across the street and Brynne hopped out. She put on her Lieutenant's helmet and crossed over to join them. Before she reached them, Jaz's black SUV parked right behind Brynne's vehicle.

Dean let Leah give a quick report as if she was handing over patient care. It was good practice for her.

Brynne listened until she finished and nodded. "Excellent work. I'll be right with you."

She followed Dean over as he headed for Jaz, who'd climbed out of her truck. She wore her usual tactical gear, though she'd added dual holsters, one on each hip. It looked like she expected trouble. He knew from experience her sword was in the SUV next to her seat, too.

Jaz smiled when she saw them coming her way. "Hey, Brynne. Thanks for letting me steal Dean from you for the rest of the night."

"As long as it's not just an excuse for a midnight booty call, I'm happy to help. I'd like to get rid of the scum setting these fires, too."

Jaz asked, "Has James or Rudy got any idea who's behind this trafficking ring?"

Brynne shrugged. "Until Dean stumbled upon the one girl a week ago, we didn't know they were operating here. I know both James and Rudy are turning over every rock to see how they operated this long with no one telling them."

Dean said, "There haven't been that many werecats around that I've seen since I've worked here. They have to be relatively new in town."

Brynne nodded. "There are a few who live locally, but you're right. I hope you two can track them down and stop them."

Jaz glanced at Dean. "You ready to go? I want to get on the trail so I can go stab someone."

He smiled. "How can I turn down an invitation like that? I hope it's not me."

"If I'm going to stab you, you'll know it, husband of mine."

Brynne laughed. "What you two do in your spare time is up to you, just don't call me to patch you up. I'll get back to helping Leah. Keep me in the loop if you find anything. I'd like to pass it along to James."

Jaz nodded and waited for Brynne to cross to the other side of the street before she said, "Dean, get in. I think I figured a way to track in on Gibbie's cell phone signal. It turns out he's been playing some game app with a few of my guys. When they told me, I followed a hunch and got a friend to hack into his phone using the app as a back door."

"Great," Dean said, climbing into the SUV. "Where is he?"

"According to the last message I got from my friend, less than a block from here."

She fired up the SUV and pulled out onto the street. She did a three-point turn to turn around and avoid going past the fire scene and then headed back up the road.

Jaz was right on the money. They followed the map of the screen in the SUV's dash. It led them around the block and into an alley leading back towards the fire scene. Dean spotted Gibbie's van parked between two brick apartment buildings halfway down. Jaz pulled over and the two of them got out to search around for their friends.

A scream from inside the van sent both of them racing to the rear doors.

Jaz pushed Dean aside, drew one of her pistols, and reached for the door handle. She yanked it open at the same time she switched on the tactical LED mounted beneath her pistol's barrel.

The beam of the light revealed two naked bodies. It took Dean a second to recognize Gibbie on his back with Hangbe right beside him.

Gibbie screamed again, trying to pull some of his scattered clothes closer to cover up.

Hangbe shook her head and cast a glance at them. "Jaz, hon, do you mind? I'm a little busy here."

Chapter 25

AN HOUR LATER, in a diner a few blocks away, a waitress set down the last plate from their orders and refreshed everyone's coffee before leaving them alone again.

Hangbe smiled and continued with her description of the evening's investigative activities. "After we rescued the people from the building, we knew it was too late to follow the trail of our friend Manton. We got a little distracted after all the excitement."

She cast a wicked grin in Gibbie's direction and added, "I guess Gibson and I let the moment get the better of us." She cast a wink at Jaz. "It's an excellent way to relieve stress. You should try it sometime. I certainly don't regret the brief moment of release. What about you, dear?"

Gibbie looked up from his coffee like a deer in the headlights of an oncoming car. "Oh, no, of course not. Always looking to lend a hand for a good cause."

Dean coughed as the coffee he was drinking threatened to come out through his nose.

Jaz covering for her husband's spluttering attempt at a response, said "Um, let's put that part of it aside. We haven't heard from the two of you since we brought you through the portal. You were supposed to coordinate with my teams on this."

"Sorry, Gibson had some excellent leads that took us deep into the criminal underworld of the Unusual community. We didn't really have the time to come up for air and check in. It's a good thing we did. That's how we discovered the location of the building tonight."

Dean had regained control of his voice by this point. "You could have called in a warning to me or Jaz, or even to the fire department. They put firefighters in danger starting this fire. It would have been nice to avoid all that, let alone the risk to the people who'd been trapped inside."

Hangbe leveled her stare at Dean. "I've been after this group for a long time. A lot of people have died and more will die if they're not stopped. Sometimes you have to cut corners to get the job done in a more expedited fashion."

Jaz jumped in before Dean could come back at Hangbe. "What Dean means is you came here to work with our team. We hooked you up with Gibbie to be your connection, not just to the city, but to our broader efforts to stop this ring here in Elk City. Can you at least fill us in on what you've found so far?"

Gibbie had recovered some of his composure and used this opportunity to share what he knew. "It's really fascinating to watch her work, guys. Hangbe used some sort of questioning charm on her necklace to interrogate a few of the people we located. Then we found and rescued one of the kidnapped women. That's how she uncovered as much as she did. Like we found out the gang out of Ireland is financed by a third party who helped them set up shop here."

"Who is it?" Jaz asked. "If they picked this place on purpose, they have to be from here."

Gibbie shook his head. "We're not sure. But, after we got the location from the girl, I figured there had to be a local connection. I tracked down a guy I knew who liked to set fires. It turned out he didn't set the ones in these buildings, but he remembers talking to a cat shifter who asked him a lot of questions about how to burn a building down the right way and the wrong way. That guy matched Manton's description perfectly."

Hangbe smiled as Gibbie got more and more excited by the story. "It really was a stroke of genius by Gibson to track down this fellow. He was quite useful. Now that we know who the arsonist is, we just have to track them back to the source and we can roll this whole thing up with a nice little bow on top."

Jaz glanced at Dean. He could tell she wasn't happy by the firm set of her lips. It was her non-expression that hid her true feelings, though it didn't work as well as she thought it did. Not only did Dean see through it, Hangbe did, too.

"Jaz, I appreciate your expectation for a certain level of cooperation from me, however, I don't have time to file reports with people until I'm finished. I have to follow the case wherever it leads me."

"Even to the back of Gibbie's van, apparently."

"I will not make excuses for my recreational tastes. Besides," Hangbe reached out and gave Gibbie's pale hand a squeeze. "He's so much more than he appears to be at first glance, especially if you've seen as much of him as I have."

Dean almost choked on his coffee again. Gibbie blushed a shade of crimson most would have thought impossible for a vampire. Dean set the coffee down, resigned to not drink anything for the rest of the meal.

Clearing his throat, Dean asked, "Now that we're all here together, what's your next step. Maybe if would be a good idea to work on this as a team from here on out."

"Dean's right," Jaz said. "The time for freelancing is over. We have to catch these guys before they do this again and leave town to set up somewhere else. Manton got away while you worked at rescuing the trapped Merrow."

Hangbe shrugged. "Our lead disappeared tonight, which is a shame. Unless you have a magical way to track them I don't know of, Gibson and I will have to go back into the dark underbelly of this city and rattle some cages until something shakes loose again."

Jaz paused and tapped her chin. "That's actually a great idea. We might have a way to track them magically. I hadn't even thought about it until now."

"What?" Dean asked. "Is there a contact you have that can lead us to the rest of the victims before they're killed?"

Jaz smiled and fixed him with a steady gaze. At first, Dean didn't understand. Then it sunk in. "You mean me? How can I track them?"

"The Geas. The Yakshini woman laid that Geas on you. I had forgotten all about it, but it's how you stumbled upon Kaylee the way you did in Ireland. I think it's still working under the surface. It explains how you've ended up scheduled during the shifts when these fires have been set. You're the connection to all this."

"I thought you said it removed the Geas after we found Kaylee?"

"It appeared to be, but I think there may be some underlying effects still in place."

Dean considered the series of dreams over the last few weeks, all about being trapped and held without a way to escape. Could they be connected to the strange spell the Yakshini seer cast on him?

"I'm not saying you're wrong, Jaz, but if the charm had any power at all, it's not particularly effective. I found a girl wandering a beach. That was definitely magic at play. But the rest? I'm not so sure. So I ended up working extra shifts. I do that all the time. None of it has gotten us any closer to the source of the trafficking in Elk City." Dean shook his head. "Gibbie has gotten more done with Hangbe than I have. The two of them actually rescued some people."

Hangbe leaned forward, excitement twinkling in her eyes. "Yes, and it was your idea to connect Gibbie to me. Jaz might be on to something here. What kind of charm was it? He's absorbed it to the point that I can't sense it."

Jaz said, "I smelled it as soon as he got home from work that day. It had an old school feel to it, not like something a younger caster would come up with. They're always improvising to try to improve upon the classics."

"If that's the case, then there's a component of connection we're missing." Hangbe's hand touched her intricate, beaded necklace, tapping first one bead and then another, lost in thought. "Dean, what were you doing when you first discovered the trafficking ring?"

Dean related the initial encounter with Verity and the later attack by Manton at the station after work. "I think about her a lot, especially since she was scooped up as she left the ER and carried away. I feel like all my hard work was for nothing. I'm pretty sure she died in that first fire. They were almost all Selkies according to the coroner's report."

Gibbie smiled, "It's almost like her ghost is calling you."

"That's it," Hangbe said.

Gibbie laughed. "I was right? Dean's being haunted by a Selkie ghost?"

"No, if she was dead, the Geas linked to her would have dissipated. I think she's still alive. I think she is the connection to the charm."

Jaz nodded. "It makes sense. Dean close your eyes and concentrate on trying to see Verity where she is right now."

Dean doubted this was the right solution, but he played along. He leaned back in the diner booth and closed his eyes, tilting his head back a little as he did. He thought about Verity as he'd seen her in the apartment when he'd first encountered her. It wasn't easy, other thoughts and memories kept drifting in and messing up his concentration. After a minute of trying, he opened his eyes.

Everyone at the table stared at him, waiting for some sign it worked.

"Well?" Gibbie asked, losing patience.

"It's no good. I can't seem to concentrate on her. All I can think about lately are the nightmares I've been having."

"What kind of nightmares?" Jaz asked. "You haven't mentioned them to me."

"It's nothing. Hazards of the job, that's all, honey. I keep seeing people trapped in a dark concrete room. I'm pretty sure it's related to some post-traumatic stress from the encounter at the first fire where all those people died. I probably need to talk to the department's counselor about it."

Hangbe laid a finger on one of the thicker beads in her necklace. The midnight blue painted bead had a streak of white across the center. She closed her eyes and muttered something to herself. With her one hand still touching the bead, she reached across the table and placed her index finger in the middle of Dean's forehead, all with her eyes still closed.

He held still, not sure what she was doing. He waited for her to open her eyes, which took about thirty long, awkward seconds.

When the Amazon's eyes opened, they bored into Dean's as if they pierced all the way to his soul. Her lips curled into a grin. "The nightmares are related to that incident, but only because the Geas heightened your fears they've killed Verity. The dreams are a connection to her in your subconscious. It links you to her and almost ensures she still lives. Describe what you see. Leave nothing out."

Dean closed his eyes again, trying to relax and let the disturbing dream thoughts in, rather than dismiss them. At first they resisted his attempts to focus on them. As he worked at it, though, more details filtered to the top of his mind.

"It's got to be another basement. The cinderblocks look stained in lines at various heights along the walls. People are chained up together, huddled in the cold and damp to stay warm. Their fear permeates everything about what I see."

"The walls aren't stone?" Jaz asked. She'd pulled out her phone and was scrolling through something on it, glancing up at him. "You're sure they're cinder block?"

Dean nodded.

She turned her phone around and showed him a photo from the first fire scene. It showed the scorched walls of the basement where the people had been trapped. The older building had a stone masonry foundation made from blocks of large cut stones held together by a layer of cement. None of the photos she showed him had cinder block walls.

"These are the crime scene photos from the first fire. See, not cinderblock."

"So it's not the fire basement I've been dreaming about."

Jaz shook her head. "Nope. You're dreaming about something that's happening now, not a past vision."

"Then Verity is still alive?"

Hangbe nodded. "Your connection links her to the Geas set upon you. That has to hold the clues needed to find her."

Dean didn't understand how that was going to help. "I can't tell you anything more about what is there but what I can see. It's always the same. The same stained cinder block walls. The same huddled figures, chained in the dark."

Gibbie held up a finger to say something, then changed his mind.

Hangbe glanced at the Vampire. "If you have an idea, my love, share it."

Gibbie blushed again at the Amazon's words. "Uh, yeah, so can you describe the stains on the walls again? You said they form lines. Are they horizontal or vertical?"

"Horizontal, but not straight. They're kind of wavy."

Gibbie smiled. "Of course they are. They'd have to be wavy, wouldn't they?"

Jaz groaned. "Gibbie, you're not making any sense. What do the stains have to do with anything?"

"They're important because they tell me exactly where to look for our missing victims, including Verity."

Chapter 26

DEAN LOOKED out over the waterfront by the Elk River where it led into the Chesapeake Bay. Warehouses and businesses lined the street in front of him. Nothing stood out as a potential place to start.

He shook his head. "Tell me again why you think this is the place to look for our victims?"

Gibbie pointed at the river. "Back in the late 1990s, I was stuck down here during a hurricane. It was during the day and I had to hide down in a basement. That ended up being a bad idea because the storm drove a surge of water up the bay and into the river. This entire area flooded. I was wet and miserable until the water level went down and night fell."

"I don't see your point. What does a flood decades ago have to do with our problem?"

"It hasn't just flooded that one time. This area floods whenever a big enough storm hits. That's every ten to twenty years. I noticed while I watched the water rise in the basement that previous floods had left similar lines as the ones you describe. There can't be another part of the city that has numerous floods in its history."

Jaz smiled. "Excellent work, Gibbie. I think your idea matches up with Dean's description perfectly."

"I guess so," Dean said. "There wasn't any water in my dream."

Gibbie shook his head. "No, Dean, the basements are dry the rest of the time, but you mentioned it was damp. That's what clued me in to how the water left a trace of their passage with each flood."

Hangbe nodded at the buildings down the hill from where they'd parked. "I can accept your explanation. How does that help us figure out which one they're in? We can't go along and break into each one. There are dozens of them."

The vampire frowned. "Now, that I don't know. I was hoping one of you would come up with a way to zero in on it. Can't Dean use the spell cast on him to locate them?"

Dean shrugged. "I guess it can't hurt to try." He closed his eyes and tried to relax, focusing on anything that pulled him one way or another. After a minute of trying to feel the connection, he opened his eyes and tried scanning the buildings, looking for some sign that would trigger the Geas and lead him to the ones he was supposed to help.

After the third time he swept the waterfront with his eye, Dean frowned. "I don't get anything. I have no idea how this works."

"Don't beat yourself up, Dean." Jaz laid her hand on his shoulder. "It was worth a try. Maybe you need to be closer to trigger a reaction."

Hangbe tapped the side of her head twirled one of the long braids hanging down around her finger. "If the building they're in has a cinder block foundation, then we should be able to narrow it down to newer construction. We're also looking for a building without too much foot traffic passing by. They wouldn't want anyone accidentally seeing something and calling police. It's got to be a building that's vacant or looks like it in a section away from well-traveled streets."

Gibbie snapped his fingers and pointed. Dean followed the arm to an area off to the right, away from the restaurants and waterfront shops. There were some businesses scattered around there, but not too many. Most of the buildings looked sort of run down.

"That looks right for what we're looking for, Gibbie," Dean said. "Let's go down there and walk around some. I need to see if I can sense anything."

Jaz shook her head. "We'll drive down. I want my SUV close enough I can get to it for more firepower if we need it."

"Two guns and a sword aren't enough, honey?" Dean asked. Jaz's Katana hung across her back, and she had twin semi-automatic pistols in holsters on each hip.

"Werecats are fast and crafty, Dean. Even with all four of us, it wouldn't take too many to overwhelm us if they caught us by surprise."

"They won't," Hangbe said.

Gibbie cocked his head to one side. "Won't what?"

"Catch us by surprise. I have a spell bead that should protect us from any sneak attacks." She reached up and tapped a red and gold striped oblong stone threaded on her necklace.

"How do you keep all of them straight?" Gibbie asked. "I'd forget which one did what."

"I remember because I earned each one of them in the ceremonies and tests of my birthright as a Dahomey Amazon. They're a part of me now."

Hangbe gave the area one last look and spun around, following Jaz back to where they'd parked their vehicles.

Gibbie tugged at Dean's sleeve as they followed the women. "Isn't she wonderful? I can't believe how lucky I am to have found her. I want you to be my best man, okay?"

"Easy, buddy. You just met her. How do you even know she feels the same way?"

An expression of wide-eyed horror crossed Gibbie's face. "Oh no, what has she told you? I probably came on too strong." He started pounding his clenched fists into his thighs as they walked. "I'm so stupid."

Dean reached out and gripped his friend's nearest wrist. "Calm down. Nobody said anything. She likes you enough to sleep with you, but that doesn't mean she wants to marry you. Take is slow. Enjoy things as they are right now. She's a busy woman and settling down might not be in the cards for her right now."

"Good idea. She's a modern career woman. I've got to respect that. I can wait for her to propose."

Dean shook his head. Gibbie's history with women was questionable at best. This whole thing had a new level of improbability, though.

"You guys coming?" Jaz called. We only have a few hours until the sun rises. "We need to be done searching by then so Gibbie can get under cover."

"Yeah," Dean said. "Be right there. Gibbie has something in his eye."

Gibbie took a deep breath and let it out slowly. "Take it slow. Got it. I can be like molasses slow. From now on, it's all about the Gibbie slow burn. Women can't resist that."

Dean rolled his eyes. "Come on, Casanova. If we don't hurry up, she'll move on without us."

They rejoined the women and loaded into their vehicles. Gibbie led the way in his van until they'd pulled onto a street with a few run-down shops and some vacant commercial buildings. They parked and the four of them met up once again on the sidewalk.

Jaz pointed to the far side of the street. "Dean and I will go up that side. Check the foundations and identify which ones have cinderblock if you can. If we don't find anything definitive in the ones that do, we'll meet back here."

Hangbe and Gibbie nodded and set out up the street. Dean crossed to the other side with Jaz and checked the first building. It was an older one. They made the foundation from quarried stone. He and Jaz moved on to check the next while he kept his mind open to any sensation that might tell him he was close to Verity and the others.

He and Jaz reached the last building on their side of the street. It resembled a big grey barn because of the old, faded wood siding. It appeared to have once been an operation that sold and serviced outboard motors for boats in the marinas nearby. From the padlock on the front door and the empty showroom behind the large plate-glass window, it had been out of business for some time.

Dean knelt down and checked the thin strip of foundation visible between the sidewalk and the lower edge of the siding. Jaz glanced down at him and he shook his head. The foundation was the rough, unbroken grey of poured concrete.

Jaz said, "We'll wait here for Gibbie and Hangbe to finish their side. Maybe they'll find something."

Dean stood, grumbling his frustration. "I feel helpless stumbling around like this. There's got to be a better way to search for them."

He turned and kicked the strip of solid concrete he'd checked moments before. The concrete cracked beneath the steel toe of his duty boot. On a sudden impulse to further vent his anger, he kicked it twice more in rapid succession. The cracks widened, and then the thin layer of concrete veneer fell away to reveal the top of a row of cinder blocks.

As he knelt down to check the patch of missing concrete, Dean reached out and traced the masonry joint now visible between two cinder blocks. A flash of imagery surged into his mine the moment his fingers touched the exposed blocks. This time, the shadowy figures in the dark had more definition, and as he scanned the faces, he recognized one in the group. Verity, her cheeks lined where her tears had left a track through the grime and dirt on her face.

"Jaz, they're here. We found them."

"Are you sure?"

"Look. The cinderblock wall was just covered up for cosmetic purposes, I guess. I got a quick vision of them, just like in my dream. They're here. I know it."

Hangbe and Gibbie jogged over from across the street.

"What's up? Did you find something?"

Jaz slipped the pistol from her left holster. "Dean says they're in this building."

Hangbe reached beneath her jacket and pulled out a short, broad-bladed sword. "Did you see any guards? We need to know how many people from the gang are here."

Dean shook his head. "All I can see is what I saw earlier in my dreams, just with more clarity and definition. The first floor looks deserted."

"If there are people held here, there are guards to watch over them," Hangbe said. "This building takes up the whole block. Let's circle around and see if there's another entrance they have used recently."

She tugged at the sleeve of Gibbie's windbreaker and the two of them started off up to the nearest corner. Dean followed Jaz in the opposite direction. He pulled out his phone and sent a quick message to Brynne to come with the ambulance to this location and stage nearby. There might be a need for medical care once they found the missing people.

The two of them turned the corner and proceeded along the side of the building towards the rear. A chain-link fence blocked off a section of the parking lot behind the building. A pair of newer model sports cars, a black Mercedes sedan, and a large white passenger van were parked inside the locked parking area.

"Someone's here," Jaz said. "They wouldn't leave nice cars like that parked at an abandoned building. Stay behind me. If trouble pops up, take cover."

"Gotcha."

They circled the enclosed parking area and got a closer look at the vehicles. The Mercedes sedan looked familiar. He stared at it, trying to remember where he'd seen it. Then he saw it. The license plate read, "W-CAT1."

"Jaz, I think Leah's father is in there."

"Really? I knew he had to be mixed up in all this."

"I'm not sure, but that Mercedes is the same one parked at the station earlier tonight. It's got to be him."

Jaz glanced around. "Where are Hangbe and Gibbie?"

Dean looked to the far corner of the building. "They should have gotten here by now. Maybe they found a way inside."

"If she did, it would be just like her to barge in without waiting for backup. Let's go check."

Jaz moved up to the corner of the building with Dean close behind. Sure enough, there was a single, windowless steel door in the wall about midway to the front of the building.

Staying a few feet back, Dean followed up to the doorway. Jaz reached out with her right hand and tried the knob. She grinned as it turned in her hand and she pulled the door open enough to peer inside.

Dean wanted to ask what she could see, but he knew better than to make a noise right now. If there were werepanthers inside, they would surely hear him, even if he whispered.

Jaz pulled the door open far enough to slip in sideways and then held it for Dean to follow her. A short hallway extended away from them with a few doors on either side and one at the end.

They checked each door as they moved towards the one at the end. Each was a storeroom that looked like it hadn't been opened in a while. Dust and mold covered the floors inside.

Jaz reached the last door at the end of the corridor. She pressed her ear to the wood for a few seconds and then tried the door. It swung out into a large open warehouse.

In the center of the room, Hangbe and Gibbie knelt with their hands on their heads. A cluster of men and women stood around them. They had pistols trained on the pair. Dean recognized Manton among them, which meant the others were all werepanthers like him.

Jaz had her pistol up and Dean knew she was trying to decide whether to try a rescue or back up.

The decision was made for them when the door behind them leading outside opened. Six armed men entered and stopped leveling their pistols at the two of them.

A familiar voice from inside called out. "Ms. Errington, Mr. Flynn, why don't you come in and join us. I wouldn't want you to miss all the fun."

Jaz paused for only a split second before she relaxed and held up both hands. Dean did the same as the shifters behind them came forward. They grabbed Dean's arms and pulled them down, wrenching his shoulder as they secured them behind his back with plastic zip ties. Another pair disarmed Jaz and secured her arms behind her as well.

Their captors led them into the center of the warehouse and forced to their knees beside Hangbe and Gibbie. Jaz glared at the Interpol agent, who shrugged in reply. Dean scanned the room, trying to see anything that might be a way to escape. He stopped when he reached a tall figure standing in the shadows nearby.

The figure walked forward. At first Dean thought it might be Leah's father, but as the light fell across the face, he gasped.

"Hello, Dean," Artur said. "I told you I'd be back."

Fury filled Dean. This man had caused so much pain and suffering for Dean and his patients, all he wanted to do was start shouting.

Jaz lifted her head and glared at the ancient vampire, dressed in a crisp charcoal business suit. "It's a good thing you have me tied up. I didn't get the chance to finish you the last time we met. Are you up to a rematch?"

"I rarely like to get my hands dirty, girl. I won't give you the satisfaction of dying with a blade in your hand."

Dean looked around behind Artur. "Where's Mr. Casado? I assume you and he were behind the whole thing from the beginning."

Artur grinned. He shook his head. "No, his arrival in town was merely a fortunate accident. I don't like to partner up with others. I prefer to keep the spoils for myself. Besides, my feline friends here were looking for a new leader. I was happy to offer my support for their endeavor."

The response confused Dean. He knew Leah's father had some sort of underworld connection and money. It only made sense that he'd have been involved with this somehow. Why would Artur deny it?

Artur grinned. "I'm sure you have more questions. I will answer all soon enough, including my desire to end your meddling in my affairs once and for all." He nodded at the shifters surrounding them. "Put those two with the others, then finish preparing the building."

Chapter 27

LEAH LEANED FORWARD, searching the street for the address Dean had given them. The GPS in the ambulance had gotten them close, but she and Brynne had to stop and look for numbers on the buildings.

Brynne pointed ahead. "There's Gibbie's van. They're down that way."

Leah searched the sidewalks and buildings as Brynne pulled up behind the van. "I don't see them."

Brynne handed her a handheld radio with a shoulder strap. "Take the ambulance's portable. I'll use my own. Let's get out and have a look around."

Leah took the radio and got out. The pair split up and searched both sides of the street a few hundred feet in each direction. They returned to the ambulance after their search failed to turn up their friends.

Brynne took out her phone. "I'm calling James. We need help. I get the feeling there's some sort of trouble."

Leah cocked her head to one side and sniffed. The faintest whiff of smoke wafted past her. "Do you smell that? Something's burning nearby."

Brynne shook her head. "No, but your senses are better than mine. Which way?"

Leah sniffed again and pointed to the end of the street. She didn't see any flames, but the smell of smoke seemed to get stronger as she and Brynn jogged up the street to the large wooden warehouse at the end.

"It's coming from inside. Look." The inside of the former marine engine repair shop had filled with the haze of smoke. A flash of flame in the back corner broke through the thick smoke for a few seconds.

Brynne raised her mic and pointed to the nearest corner. "I'll call this in. See if you can find a way in at the rear that isn't filled with smoke. Don't enter. Just contact me with what you find."

Leah nodded and took off around to the back of the warehouse. She made it halfway around the fenced in parking area to the rear before she noticed her father's car. It sat alone in the small lot next to a loading dock and door. The gates to the fence were open, so she ran up to the door and started to open it but stopped herself just before she touched the metal knob.

Remembering her fire academy training, she held the back of her hand up near the metal door and knob about a half inch away. When she felt no heat coming off it, she gripped the knob and pulled. When it didn't open, Leah groaned. She had to get inside, and she dreaded what she had to do next.

Releasing a bit of the iron grip she held over her jaguar self, she let the out some of the power instilled in her family by the blood rites of Incan high priests millennia before.

Her eyes shifted first, giving her the ability to see into spectrums no human eyes could see. Tawny fur sprouted on her arms and face, dotted with black and tan spots. Stopping the transformation there, Leah gripped the doorknob again and yanked with all her might while twisting the knob.

A squeal of twisting metal preceded the door popping open as the deadbolt broke off inside the metal door jamb. Smoke poured out through the top of the door.

Leah ducked beneath the smoke so she could both breathe and see, racing inside to begin her search. The open floor of the warehouse area had a few boxes and crates scattered about, but no sign of her father or the others she sought.

The heat and smoke grew as she continued deeper inside. She realized this was like the other fires, and that meant they had to be in the basement.

At this point Leah had to crawl to stay below the smoke. She looked for any sign of a door chained shut from this side.

Her radio squawked. "Leah, where the hell are you."

She kept crawling as she reached up with one hand and keyed the mic clipped to her shoulder strap. "I'm looking for survivors inside. I think I'm close."

"Negative." Brynne's voice cracked with anger. "That's a job for the fire crews. Exit the way you entered. Right now."

Leah knew if she left now, it was as good as condemning anyone trapped inside to death. She reached down and turned down her radio's volume to drown out her lieutenant's voice.

Coughing, Leah continued on and was just about to turn around when she spotted the locked basement door. The chains hung down enough that she spotted them beneath the thick layer of smoke filling the upper part of the hallway.

She banged on the door. <Cough> "Is anyone in there?" <Cough, cough>

Muffled voices from the other side reached her enhance hearing.

Turning around, Leah planted her feet against the frame on either side of the basement door and gripped the padlock and chain with her clawed hand. Sweat poured down her face and her glowing yellow eyes stung from the smoke. She ignored all of it, focusing all her considerable strength on pulling the chains free of the eyebolts, securing them to the wall on either side of the door.

Realizing she had no time for a second try at this, Leah released the last bit of barrier between herself and the wild jaguar inside her. Snarling through the long teeth of a jungle cat, she pulled at the chains. She gave all her strength to it; her rippling feline muscles popping the seams of her uniform shirt at the shoulders.

Letting out a final roar of defiance, she pushed with her powerful legs as she pulled with her arms. The chains finally pulled free and she dove forward to pull open the door.

Her shifted feline visage came face to face with a young woman with long red hair. The woman screamed and recoiled back, almost falling back down the stairs. Leah yelled for her to stop, but all that came out was a long string of ripping snarls.

Cursing in her mind, she wrestled her inner jag back under control enough that she could talk like a person again. "It's okay, I'm not with the others. I'm a paramedic. Hurry up and come out."

"Leah, is that you?" Dean called from inside. "I need help. I can't get them out by myself."

A few timid men and women started up the stairs. Leah pointed back down the hallway. "Go that way and turn right. The door out will be straight ahead. Stay low out of the smoke."

They darted past her and crouched low as they ran back the way she'd come.

Leah bounded down the steps two at a time with her uncanny feline balance keeping her from tumbling to the bottom. Dean waited for her. Bruises covered his face. Whoever had beaten him had ripped his uniform shirt open. Ragged tears in the skin on his chest oozed blood past edges already crusting with scabs.

"What happened? Did my father do this?"

Dean seemed shocked at her question, but then pointed behind him. Two shirtless figures slumped bound to a metal support column with woven silver cable. The restraints left angry red welts against their exposed torsos, sapping their strength so they couldn't escape.

One was her father, beaten into unconsciousness. The other was the portly vampire friend of Dean's. He gazed through listless, pain-filled eyes back at her.

Leah rushed over and reached out to free them, pulling back at the last second. The silver would injure her as easily as it did the two of them.

"I can't free them, Dean. I can't touch the silver, either."

"They stripped me of my gear. Do you have a pair of trauma shears on you?"

Leah's confusion at the request kept her from complying right away.

"Leah, yes or no. Do you have them? We don't have much time. It might already be too late." He glanced up at the floorboards covering the basement rafters overhead. Flickering firelight played through the cracks. It wouldn't be long until the fire burned through to the basement.

Shaking herself from the fog of indecision, she dug in the cargo pocket of her uniform pants and handed Dean her hardened steel trauma shears.

He snatched them and grabbed at the cable, twisted around Gibbie first. Leah winced at first expecting the silver alloy to burn him. She relaxed when nothing happened. She'd forgotten he was human.

Dean gripped the shears and opened them wide as he slid the thin braided cable back as close to the joint where the two blades hinged.

"You'll never cut that," she said.

"An old EMT once bet me he couldn't cut a penny in half with a pair of these shears." Dean grimaced as he used two hands to squeeze the handles together. "I lost that bet."

With a sudden snap, the trauma shears cut through the first cable.

Leah jumped forward. "Give me the shears. I'm stronger than you are. Hold the cable out so I don't have to touch it."

Dean pulled at the bindings and selected the next cable in the line. Leah, in her werejaguar form, powered through all the restraints in less than thirty seconds.

Together she and Dean pulled Gibbie and her father to the foot of the stairs. Flames filled the doorway above.

"We're not getting out that way," Dean said. "Give me your radio. Is Brynne out there?"

Leah nodded and handed Dean her handset and mic.

"Paramedic Dean Flynn to Lieutenant U-1. Need RIT team to basement for rescue of four individuals."

"Dean," Brynne responded. "There's a window on the northwest corner of the basement. Fire crews just arrived. I'll have the rescue teams meet you there."

"Northwest corner. Copy."

Dean oriented himself but had some trouble figuring out which way was correct. Leah pointed to the farthest corner of the cluttered basement. He grimaced. It was a long way, and embers already fell from the floor above. The ceiling could collapse on them at any time.

"My father's lighter than Gibbie. You take him. I'll take the fat vampire."

"Hey," Gibbie's limp protest might have been funny at another time. This time Leah ignored it. If she hurt his feelings, she could apologize later. Her inner jaguar had rougher edges than her human self.

Dean winced as he tugged at Leah's father, pulling him up into a firefighter's carry. He stumbled a little but stayed on his feet as he lurched towards the far side. Leah lifted Gibbie with ease over one shoulder and followed.

They made it to the far side just in time. The ceiling behind them collapsed into the basement as the fire consumed the floor above. Smoke started filling the space around them.

Dean reached out to Leah. "I'll boost you up to the window. Break out the glass so the rapid intervention team knows where we are."

Leah calmed herself enough to shift back to human form, though she held onto some of her shifter strength. She didn't want to alarm the human firefighters outside.

She stepped into the stirrup Dean made with his hands and pulled out the small metal flashlight from her belt. The window was small, only about three feet across and maybe two feet high. Gripping the flashlight in her fist, she hammered the butt against the window until the glass shattered outward.

Gloved hands reached in to pull her to safety. She batted them away. "There are others injured in here. I'll lift them up to you."

The nearest firefighter, wearing a lieutenant's helmet, nodded. He started calling out orders to his team while she climbed down.

"Dean, help me lift Gibbie up first. Then we'll get my father out."

With her partner's help, they lifted their two patients to safety. As soon as the firefighters pulled her father up through the window, Dean crouched down to boost her up.

Leah shook her head. "You're injured. You go first. I can leap up and pull myself out with no trouble."

Dean objected, but only for a second. He nodded and let her boost him up instead. The smoke had become so thick at this point that she had trouble breathing. Coughing, she mustered her remaining strength and leaped up to the waiting hands, letting them pull her to safety.

Chapter 28

DEAN, Gibbie, and Leah's father, Carlos, sat in the back of the Station U ambulance. Dean sat on the bench seat beside Gibbie while the older werejaguar lay propped up on the stretcher. Leah had wrapped the blood pressure cuff around her father's arm and pressed the button on the monitor to start the reading.

"I don't need all this, I'm already healing."

"You're in my world, now, Papa. You'll do as I say. You're not some young cub who got in a scrape."

The elder Casado grumbled a little, but let his daughter continue checking him.

Brynne crouched by Dean, tending to his cuts. He batted her hands away. "Enough. I'll live. I may not regenerate, but I've been through this before. We have to find Jaz and Hangbe."

Waiting until he finished talking, Brynne said, "You done? I've got O'Malley and the rest of the PD combing area businesses for surveillance video. I've called James and Rudy to get them on it as well. Now let me tend to these injuries or I'll strap you down and take you in to ECMC myself."

Gibbie snorted a laugh as he sipped on the bag of blood from the small refrigerator in the ambulance. His injuries had already mostly healed. "She's right, Dean. There's no way you're up to dealing with those werepanther creeps. And Artur is a force to be reckoned with all by himself."

"If we don't hurry, they'll kill them both. That has to be why Artur took them for himself." Dean hissed in pain and pulled away as Brynne dabbed at his cuts, trying to clean them.

"I will deal with this," Carlos announced. "The vampire is problematic, but the werepanthers are in my domain and we must make an example."

Dean glanced outside. "We can't stay here too much longer. It's almost dawn. Gibbie and Brynne need to get inside and under cover."

"I'm as good as new," Gibbie announced, leaning over and dropping the empty blood bag in the wire trash can filled with a red medical waste bag. "I'll get my van. I have a few ideas on where to look around town."

"Gibbie," Dean said. "If this whole situation has proven anything, you're not equipped to handle this alone."

"I won't sit by and do nothing. You've lost your wife. I've lost something, too. She's the one, Dean. Hangbe is the girl I've been waiting for. I won't lose her this way."

Brynne rolled her eyes. Dean understood, though. Gibbie had been through one girlfriend after another in the few short years Dean had known him. Each one treated Gibbie like trash, and the relationship usually ended badly. Despite that, the frumpy vampire never gave up on finding someone. If he thought Hangbe was a chance at that, who was Dean to discount it. He and Jaz hadn't looked like a perfect match in the beginning either.

Dean said, "Okay, Gibbie. Go. But check in with Brynne or I before you do anything. We're going to need extra help on this. Artur will find out soon enough we survived, and he'll know we're coming for him."

Carlos reached over and ripped the velcro free on the blood pressure cuff. "I can help, too. I don't have the resources here I would have at home, but under the right circumstances, I can handle a few werepanthers."

Leah's eyes flashed yellow. "Not alone you won't."

Carlos smiled. "Deciding to join the family enterprise after all, Mija?"

"No, this is a rescue operation, and I'm a paramedic. I can use my Unusual skills to help save the others and keep you from getting yourself killed in the process."

Leah's father didn't hide his disappointment, but he said nothing, only nodded.

Dean stood. "Good, then let's split up. Gibbie, you head out and see what you can uncover. If Artur is back in town and staying somewhere, there has to be a trail. He's not shy about killing or hurting his food source. I'd start there."

Gibbie nodded and jumped out of the ambulance. He gave Dean a thumbs up and left to get his van.

"The rest of us can head back to the station."

Carlos said, "I have a car here. I'll stay."

Brynne shook her head. "If it's that fancy Mercedes parked out back, it caught fire when the building collapsed on it."

Carlos deflated a bit.

Dean said, "Leah can give you a ride once we get back."

Brynne pushed Dean back down to his seat with one hand. "You sit down. I'll drive back. Leah can ride up front with me. You're still injured."

Dean knew better than to argue with her. "Yes, oh wise and ancient one."

"You'll pay for that later once we've rescued the others. Buckle up. I have to get back before daybreak."

Dean did as he was told and settled in with Carlos for a ride back across town to Station U.

James and Rudy waited in the Station U squad room when they got back. Tammy and Brook came into the ambulance bay as soon as Brynne backed the unit into place.

Tammy popped open the ambulance's rear doors. "Damn, Dean, are you alright? I heard you'd been injured, but you look like crap."

"I'll survive. I have no choice until I find Jaz." Dean climbed out, looking around the garage bay while his mind swam with random ideas of what he needed to do. Jaz could already be dead for all he knew.

Brynne walked back from the front of the ambulance. She gripped Dean's arm, spinning him around. "Dean, I see you panicking. Take a deep breath. I called ahead for help. Tammy and Brook came in early to take over."

"What if we're already too late?"

James Lee, vampire lord of Elk City, said from the squad room doorway, "Artur likes to play with his captives. He won't rush this and that gives us time."

Rudy, his werewolf security chief, nodded from behind him. "I've got the entire pack mobilized this time, Dean. I'm also coordinating with the Errington teams. We'll find him and get her back."

Dean struggled to pull himself together, trying to steer his racing thoughts in a coherent direction. Leah stood off to one side, talking with her father in hushed tones. After a few words exchanged back and forth, the elder Casado approached James.

"I wanted to apologize for not notifying you I was back in town. I assure you; I didn't return for business. I came back to deal with a family matter." He glanced back at his daughter before returning his attention to James.

The vampire nodded. "We had an agreement, Carlos. Family or not, you're in this now. What kind of connection do you have with the werecats we're dealing with?"

"As I said, I had no idea this was going on until I was contacted by someone who let me know my daughter had a run-in with the local werepanthers. I came to assure she was staying on the right side of our agreement. That is all. They approached me to parlay with the others, and I tried to make an arrangement with them. In the end, I'm as much a victim here as our paramedic friend and his loved ones are."

Brynne stepped in to break the tension. "His story checks out, James. They trapped him in the fire with Dean and Gibbie. They wanted him as dead as the others they held there."

"This has got to stop. Artur has meddled for the last time in my affairs."

Dean paced as an idea drifted into his mind. James and the others had tried and failed to catch Artur before. He had to have a contingency plan in place to deal with things this time, too. The only solution Dean could come up with was to bring overwhelming force and firepower along when they finally tracked him down.

"I think we need more than the ones we've assembled to track Artur down and catch him. We have to bring in some big guns."

James, Brynne, and Carlos all asked the same question in unison. "Who?"

"There are two women who've been after Artur for a long time. I think they'd be upset if we didn't include them in the search and rescue operation. They'll add some extra firepower and ability to the mix."

Brynne smiled. "I know where Ashley is. Do you have a line on Ingrid?"

Dean nodded. "She's been here the whole time since we closed the gates between the planes, just like Ashley." He checked his watch. It was almost six and then official end of his shift. "In fact, she should be starting an early class right about now."

James and Rudy exchanged a glance before James said, "I don't mind Ashley. She has a sense of self-control. Ingrid is a wildcard I'd rather not cut loose in my city."

Dean shrugged. "She's already here. She never left. I can assure you, if we ask Ashley for help, Ingrid will get wind of it and show up when you least expect it. Wouldn't it be better to include her in the plan from the beginning so you have some level of control?"

Rudy nodded. "He has a point, James. Plus, she brings a certain level of chaotic carnage to the table we might need."

"Fine, see if they're on board, Dean. Rudy, Brynne and I will go back to the Nightwing building and work on finding where Artur is hiding."

Dean glanced at Leah. "What about you two?"

Carlos said, "I have a hotel room downtown. Leah can take me there. I'll reach out to the people I know. Maybe they will have some ideas of where these rogue cats are hiding."

"All right," Dean said. "James, can you have Celeste field calls and coordinate things on that end? I'll fill Gibbie in so he knows, too."

James nodded and pulled out his phone. "I'll send each of you her number. Send anything you get to her and she'll get it out to the rest of the team. If nothing else comes up, we can meet in my apartment in the Nightwing building later and decide on our next moves."

Everyone seemed in agreement and started for the parking lot. The sun was just brightening the horizon to the east as Dean jumped in his pickup truck. He had a lot to do to find Jaz and Hangbe. He bit back the primal scream that kept trying to escape his chest. It held the fear they were already too late to save them. He refused to give it a voice. Hope was all he had left.

Chapter 29

HANGBE ROLLED over on the floor and tried to get some sense of where she was. The pitch blackness of the room in which she found herself didn't help at all.

A gasp from someone nearby in the dark froze her in place as she tried to determine if they were friend or foe. Dammit, she needed to see. They'd disarmed her when the vampire and the shifters took her. They had not removed her most potent weapon. The problem at hand was how to access it with her hands secured behind her back.

The other person in the room gasped again, this time giving voice to their groans. "Who's there? I hear you moving."

Hangbe relaxed. "It's me, Jaz. Looks like they locked us up here together."

"Where's here? I can't see a thing. One of the werepanthers took my Hunter necklace. He said he wanted a souvenir."

"Lucky for us, they didn't take a fancy to mine. I guess antique African beads aren't worth anything to these thugs."

"Wait, does that mean…"

"Maybe. I'm trying to figure that out now."

Hangbe shrugged her shoulders, trying to slide the ropes around her chest up so she could extend her wrists past her butt to bring them around to the front. After working at it for several minutes, she gave up. The ones who'd tied them up had known what they were doing. Time to try something else.

"I don't suppose you have a blade hidden in your boot or something?"

Jaz sighed. "No, they found the small folding knife I keep inside my combat boot. I've got nothing sharp on me."

"Alright, let me think." Hangbe worked through her options. The necklace she wore had belonged to her grandmother. Over the years after her initiation, she'd added to its beads as she'd found additional spells she could store in them. It still held at its core the beads the original Dahomey Amazons had given to each of their number during training. In the past, Hangbe had always had to activate them by touch. But was there another way?

The dark-vision charm was a large black and white bead just to the left of center in the first row of the necklace's ornate pattern. Hangbe tilted her neck, bringing her chin down so it rested on the necklace. She moved her neck and jaw around to figure out which row of beads she was touching. It wouldn't do to release a fireball in this enclosed space by accident.

Sliding her chin to the left and right, she finally thought she had the right bead identified. The dark-vision bead was one of the larger ones in the pattern. The magic it held was long lasting. Spell duration or power seemed to relate to the size of the individual beads making up the collection.

"Cross your fingers, Jaz. I'm going to try something."

"That's about all I can do right now."

Hangbe pressed down with the tip of her chin and summoned the power in the bead beneath it. At first nothing happened. She could feel a distant stirring of power, but it stayed just out of reach.

She redoubled her efforts, focusing her concentration on exactly what she wanted to achieve. After pressing on the bead long and hard enough to bruise the end of her chin, a flash of light almost blinded her.

Hangbe squeezed her eyes shut, fearing the worst. When nothing exploded, she opened them.

She could see.

A blue-green haze tinted everything, but there was enough light to make out where she was.

"We're in some kind of security vault."

"What, like a bank?"

"Yes, exactly that. The metal walls on three sides are covered in small locked doors of various sizes. The fourth wall looks like the interior of the vault door."

"Are there words that tell us which bank it is? Any sort of identification?"

Hangbe craned her neck, scanning the entire room. "No. Just some numbers on each door. You know this city better than I do. Where would there be an empty vault like this that Artur and those werepanthers could hide us?"

"I have no idea. Maybe there's an old abandoned bank somewhere in town. He has a thing for abandoned buildings. Hey, anyway you can help me see better?"

"Not with what I have. I might be able to get us free, though." Hangbe kept looking around. Their captors had secured their wrists and ankles with plastic cable ties. There were also ropes around their chests and knees, further hindering escape. The only thing in the room other than themselves was a small folding card table and an old metal desk chair on wheels.

"I think there's a way to cut the plastic ties. It's going to take a while, though."

Jaz laughed. "For now, time is the only thing we have."

"Agreed. Let me try something." She rolled across the hard metal floor towards the card table. Desperate times called for desperate measures. At least no one would hear her cry out if she cut herself by accident. With a grimace, she gritted her teeth and set to work.

Chapter 30

DEAN STOOD outside the martial arts studio, watching the class inside go through their routines under the watchful eyes of their instructor. They practiced two-handed sword combat with bamboo mockups of the real thing.

As each pairing took their turn, the instructor circled them, watching as they sparred, calling out suggestions, and occasionally stepping in to adjust a student's stance and position. Dean continued to watch for fifteen more minutes until the class ended and the students stopped, bowing at their teacher before heading into the locker rooms.

The instructor, a tall brunette with long braids on either side, glanced out the window at Dean and motioned for him to come inside. Dean nodded and headed in.

"Were you just in the neighborhood, or is the world ending again?" Ingrid asked.

Dean shrugged, worry coloring his expression. "Neither, I guess, though it feels like the world is ending to me."

The valkyrie stopped picking up the few towels on the benches. "It's not like you to mope around. What's happened?"

"It's Jaz. She's been taken and I need help."

"The last time I helped you, I ended up grounded and stuck on earth for who knows how long."

Dean winced at the venom in her tone. He'd been afraid this might be her reaction.

"Artur is back in town. He has her. I thought you'd want to know."

Ingrid resumed picking up towels. "You think dropping that scumbag's name is enough to bring me out of my early retirement? Go see my sister. She enjoys living here. Maybe she'll help you."

"She's my next stop. We need you both."

Picking up the laundry hamper, Ingrid headed for the door behind the counter. "Not my problem anymore. I take my orders from on high and, thanks to you, they aren't talking to me anymore."

Dean hesitated for a second before dodging behind the counter and into the back room. Ingrid finished filling the washing machine and started it.

"You're not allowed back here."

"Ingrid, it's Artur. This is your chance to stop him. You've been after him for centuries."

She stopped folding towels, putting her hands on her hips. "Look at me, Dean. I wasn't meant to teach bored suburbanites how to look cool on their dating profile. I'm a warrior for the light. You did this to me, so explain to me why I should care what happens to your wife?"

Dean stared at her, struggling to find an answer that might motivate her. He'd led with the one thing he was sure would have her drop everything and join the fight.

When he didn't answer her after a few seconds. Ingrid returned to the laundry. "Exactly. Now, if you'll excuse me, I have another class starting in ten minutes and they expect fresh towels or they complain to my boss."

Dean shook his head. "Not so much of a badass now, are you, now that your wings are clipped."

"Watch your tone, medic boy. You know I could kick your ass from here to Sunday if I wanted." When Dean still didn't leave, she cocked her head to one side and said, "I'll tell you what. Ask Gabe. If he's in, I'm in."

"I'm not talking to my father right now. He tried to end the world, remember?"

"I guess your wife's not so important to you after all."

Dean clenched his fists, grinding his teeth together.

Ingrid laughed. "Ooo, that got under your skin. Good, you deserve it. Now get out of here. If my boss shows up and finds you back here, he'll dock my pay and I can barely afford my apartment as it is. Come back if you get Gabe on board."

Dean bit back the insult on the tip of his tongue. He needed her. He couldn't afford to burn any bridges right now.

By the time he got to the parking lot, he'd got his temper under control again. Sliding into his truck, Dean checked his phone. It was almost lunchtime. If he hurried, he might catch Gabe on a break between lessons.

He didn't know what he could say that would make a fallen archangel like Gabriel help him out. It wasn't like their father-son bond was all that tight. Still, he needed Ingrid and her sword. If that meant he had to bring Gabe into this as well, then he'd figure it out.

Dean pulled out of the strip mall parking lot and headed for the highway to take him across town. He checked the clock on the dashboard and pressed on the accelerator, praying he didn't pass any cops. He couldn't afford any delays.

____

Chapter 31

____

THE ROBERT JONAS ELEMENTARY SCHOOL parking lot's visitor spaces were full, so Dean pulled into one of the empty staff slots. He hoped they didn't tow him while he was inside.

At the front door, he rang the buzzer and waited for someone to answer in the office.

"Can I help you?" The bored female voice said over the intercom.

Dean smiled into the camera mounted over the door. "I'm Dean Flynn. I'm a paramedic with the city." He held up his station ID in front of the camera. "I needed to talk with someone who works here about something private."

There was a pause. "Come on back to the office."

Dean waited for the door's lock to click and went inside. Back in the office, a woman with curly red hair sat behind a tall counter.

"I need to see that ID again, please."

Dean handed her his fire department photo ID.

She glanced at it and handed it back to him. "Who did you need to see?"

"I think he teaches trumpet here on Wednesdays?"

"Oh, Gabe. Yes, he's got the third graders right now. He should be done in a few minutes." She leaned forward and whispered. "Can you tell me what this is all about? I won't tell anyone, I swear. Gabe's so mysterious about his background. The others in the office here have all sorts of ideas but nothing we're sure of."

Dean schooled his face to remain calm and dispassionate. "I'm sorry, ma'am. I'm unable to say because of confidentiality rules. You understand." He glanced around. "I don't suppose you have somewhere I can speak with him alone. What I have to ask him is a bit, uh, delicate."

The woman's eyes lit up at Dean's words. "Really? Well, the principal is at meetings at the Board of Education all day. I suppose you could meet in her office. It's right over there. Go on in and I'll send him in as soon as he dismisses the class."

Dean smiled, nodding. She picked up the phone and tapped in a few numbers.

"Mr. Angel? Yes, there's someone here to see you. I've put him in the principal's office to wait for you." A brief pause and she hung up the phone. She smiled at Dean. "He'll be up in a few minutes. They're almost finished."

Dean walked back to the office she'd indicated. He spent some time reading a few of the plaques on the walls while he waited.

A few minutes later, a voice from the doorway said, "Oh, it's you."

Dean tried to hide his surprise as he turned around. Gabe, his biological father, was not the man he'd been a few months before. Since Dean had last seen him, his father had put on at least twenty pounds, hadn't shaved in a few days, and his khakis and light blue oxford shirt looked like the last time they'd seen an iron had been during the previous presidential administration.

Working to cover his shock, Dean said, "Hello, Father."

"Hello? That's all you have to say to me after what you did? What brings you out to the burbs? Did you want to get a look at the carnage your selfish choices made in my life?"

"My choices? I..." Dean choked off the rest of his reply. He wouldn't get anywhere attacking Gabe. As much as he hated being here, Jaz needed his help. Dean could suck down a lot of crap to save his wife.

He waved his hand, trying to cancel what he'd said. "Look, Gabe, I came down here because I have something to ask you."

"Ah, here it comes." He set down the black trumpet case on the small couch against the wall. "What is it you need, Dean? Parental validation? It's a little late for that, don't you think?"

"No, there's a problem and I think it might need your unique skills to deal with it." His eyes fell on the paunch sticking out around the belt of Gabe's Khakis. It was hard to believe this was the fabled Archangel Gabriel, the trumpet-bearer, destined to call upon the armies of the Lord for the last battle. Now he looked every bit the part of an elementary school music teacher.

"I'm sorry, I no longer have to deal with all that stuff. Ever since you cut off the bridge between this world and the other planes, I'm kind of stuck just being another human meat sack."

"Stop feeling sorry for yourself. Billions of people would have died if I hadn't done what I did. And you're far from helpless, despite what you look like."

Gabe shot him a hard glare, and Dean was afraid he'd gone too far. Then his father looked away, reaching down to adjust his belt.

"Look, Gabe. Maybe there's something I can do to help your situation. I need your help with something. What can I help you with in return?" Dean didn't want to owe this man anything, but Jaz needed this.

Gabe's frown turned upward. He tilted his head to one side as he raised a finger to point at his son. "You're really in trouble, aren't you? And it's something you have to have me along to deal with, too. Well, isn't this an interesting conundrum?"

Dean started to speak, but Gabe held up his hand to stop him.

"Don't tell me I'm wrong. Tell me what you need me to do and I'll tell you what I will want in return."

Dean sighed. He began at the beginning, trying to paint his efforts as noble, helping the trafficked people in the city find freedom. He got to the part about Artur and Gabe's grin widened. By the time he finished telling everything, his father exuded the typical Eldara confidence and power he hadn't shown when he first walked into the office.

"So, you need the help of the Eldara, despite what you did to strand us here on Earth all those months ago?"

Dean nodded.

Gabe began pacing, his head tilted back as he walked, staring at the ceiling. After almost a minute he stopped, saying. "I'll help you and convince Ingrid to come along, too."

The wicked grin that followed the statement gave Dean chills. "What is it you want in return?"

"Oh, not so much. I just want you to open up the gates between the planes again, that's all."

"I have no idea how I'm supposed to do that, and I'm not sure it would be a good idea to do it even if I did."

Gabe put an arm around Dean's shoulders. "That's not something we have to worry about right now. I have some ideas we can try after we save your pretty little wife and her friend."

Dean resisted the urge to shrug off his father's arm. It was anything but comforting. He needed his help, though. Jaz needed it. Realizing he could doom the earth to eternal darkness just to save his wife, Dean nodded. "If you'll help, I'll do what you ask."

Gabe grinned, picking up his trumpet case and heading out the door.

"Where are you going?"

"I have the fifth grade trumpet students in a few minutes. Don't worry. Leave a message with Adele out front on where you want to meet up for whatever you have planned. I'll meet you after work and I'll bring Ingrid along, too."

"Have you been in touch with Ashley? She hasn't replied to my message yet."

Gabe chuckled, "I'll bring both the sisters. I know how to reach her wherever she is." He waved over his shoulder, walking away with a spring in his step that hadn't been there before.

Dean shook his head, dreading what might be in store for him once all this was finished. He pulled out his phone and looked up the address for the Nightwing Building downtown. He wrote it down on a slip of paper from the principal's desk and left the message with Adele on his way out.

He hoped they were having success in their efforts to locate Artur. He could bring all the help in the world to this thing, but it wouldn't do any good if they didn't know where Artur held Jaz and Hangbe.

Chapter 32

HANGBE PULLED the ropes from around Jaz's hands and stood. "Can you get the ropes around your feet?"

"Yeah, I think so. I can't see a damned thing in here. When I catch that shifter who stole my Hunter necklace, I'm going to take a little extra time on him."

Jaz's ever-present confidence and adrenaline always brought a smile to Hangbe's lips. She'd enjoyed mentoring the young Hunter when they'd first met a few years back. The girl picked up everything you taught her on the first go around, and she'd turned into just the sort of person you wanted at your back in a situation like this.

"As long as you leave that vampire to me, you can do whatever you want to the werepanther."

Jaz chuckled. "You might have to get in line on that one. He killed my family, has been on the hit list of a pair of particularly dangerous Eldara twins, and I'm sure there are others around who want a piece of him, too."

"I guess we'll see who gets to him first." Hangbe had moved to the inside of the vault door. She traced the mechanism visible behind the glass that covered the interior surface. "I'm not sure we have a way out of here yet, so it may not matter."

"What makes you say that?"

Hangbe twisted her head towards Jaz. She was still working at the knots that bound her ankles. "The inside of the door is covered in what I'm sure is bullet-proof glass. We can't get at the tumblers that would let us open it from the inside."

"Where there's a will, there's a way, Hangbe. You broke apart that card table easily enough to get the metal to cut through your bonds. That glass isn't unbreakable. Hit it enough times with something hard enough and it'll shatter."

The remains of the card table lay in the corner. Hangbe stared at the pieces and considered what her companion had said. It might work. There was one problem with the plan. "They'll likely hear us banging repeatedly on the door if they've got anyone close by."

"Good, then they'll be stupid enough to open the door and check on us."

Hangbe shrugged. That was a possibility. It would give them one last hurrah together before the werepanthers and the vampire over-whelmed them. There were too many for the pair of them to handle all at once. Their only chance lay in sneaking out and dealing with them piecemeal.

Jaz stood; her hands outstretched in the darkness as she stepped towards the broken table. She reached the spot and bent down, retrieving two of the metal tubes that used to be the folding legs. She stood and clacked them together a few times.

"These seem solid enough to do some damage. If they want to come in here after us, I'll be ready to greet them. I've got some payback to deal for killing my husband."

"You don't know he's dead. He's more resourceful than you give him credit for based on what I've seen. Gibson speaks very highly of him."

"Maybe they're both alive then."

Hangbe's eyes narrowed. "They'd better be. I've taken a liking to that particular vampire."

Jaz laughed. "I don't know what you see in him. He's a bit of a goofball. He's had his moments when he's lent a hand, but if you knew what he was like when Dean first met him, you might change your mind."

Hangbe shook her head. "There's something about him. He's…" she paused as she searched for the word. "…comfortable is probably the best word for him. Plus, he's got the stamina to keep up with me. I haven't met too many men who do."

Jaz shook her head. She'd moved over to the sound of Hangbe's voice until she stood next to her friend. "I really don't want that image of Gibbie and you. But hey, you do you, right?"

Hangbe put an arm around her protege. She returned her attention to the interior side of the door. Reaching up, she traced the metal frame holding the sheet of glass in place. Her fingers met the occasional bumps of the screws holding it all in place. Her smile broadened. There might be a quiet way out after all. Now all they needed was for Gibbie to use the special bonding spell she'd laid on him. With luck, the cavalry should arrive about the same time they got out of here.

Chapter 33

DEAN PACED in front of the broad stretch of floor-to-ceiling windows, staring out at the darkened skyline.

"Dean, you're going to wear out that carpet if you keep that up," James said. "Come sit down. I'll get you a stiff drink to settle your nerves."

"I can't drink at a time like this. I need to be at my best for what we have to do."

Brynne smiled. "Dean, he's right. We don't even have a location for them yet."

"Exactly, and every passing minute could be a minute too long."

James and Brynne exchanged glances as Dean returned to his pacing. He didn't care what they thought. Jaz was out there somewhere, and Artur had tried to kill her once already. There was nothing to keep him from doing it for real this time.

The elevator out in the penthouse's entry hall pinged. Dean craned his neck to see who it was. Rudy entered, accompanied by Carlos and Leah Casado. Seeing the pack leader and security expert coming in with the two werejaguars seemed strange. He was pretty certain werewolves and cat shifters didn't get along.

James crossed the room and shook Carlos's hand in greeting. He glanced at Rudy. "Any luck on your end?"

Rudy shook his head. "I've got the pack out looking for any sign of Jaz and her friend. I thought we might catch a break since a lot of them know Jaz and could pick up her scent. There's nothing so far."

Dean threw his head back and stared at the ceiling in a silent scream.

Rudy frowned. "Sorry, Dean. We're trying everything we can think of. Something will turn up. It has to."

Dean lowered his head. "What about you, Carlos? These werepanthers are supposed to be under your control. Surely you have some idea where they hide out here in Elk City?"

Carlos's eyes darkened and flashed yellow.

Leah laid a hand on her father's arm, settling him. "I've impressed upon my father the importance of this to me. He's doubly motivated because these rogue cats sully his reputation. He wants them and their vampire leader as much as the rest of you do."

"More. Much more, Mija." Carlos said. "James and I had an agreement in place, limiting the scope of my operations here. I honor my word and they have broken that promise. In my line of work, honor is everything. Others must know what befalls those who step in my way."

Dean snorted a laugh. "Pardon me if I don't get all shaky at the mention of your criminal empire. It is that criminal empire that started all of this to begin with. Even if it was a group of rogue cats, they were still yours to begin with. If they hadn't been here, my wife would be safe."

Brynne stood, walking to stand in Dean's eye line to Carlos. "This bickering isn't getting us anywhere. Stop it right now. That's an order, Dean. Let's go through what we know now that we're all here."

"Not all of us," Dean said. "What about Gibbie?"

James frowned, but said nothing. Dean knew the vampire lord didn't think much of the frumpy member of his undead community. Brynne jumped in, saying, "Maybe you should call him. He might have fallen asleep or something."

"That's not fair," Dean replied. "He's a lot better than you all give him credit for. He may not look like much, but I've learned I can count on him in tough situations. I only hope he didn't go after them alone."

The elevator pinged. Everyone's head turned to see who it was.

Gibbie charged from the elevator and raced into the room. "I found them. At least I'm pretty sure I did. I was just driving around town, moping mostly. Then I remembered this thing that Hangbe did to me when were together the first time. She's got some awesome magic, among other talents. She used one of her spells to…" He skidded to a stop when he realized how many people were in the room. Everyone had stopped and now stared at him.

Dean broke the awkward silence. "What did she do, Gibbie? How do you know where they are?"

"Oh, yeah, well, I tried to think about what I could do to contribute to finding Hangbe and Jaz. There wasn't much that came to mind. Then I remembered what Hangbe did to me in bed that first night."

"Gibbie," Brynne said. "Focus. Stay on target. Are you sure this is relevant?"

"I am. I wasn't going to mention the sex. I mean, it was A-mazing, of course. Oh, yeah, where was I? Um, okay, so that first time she traced a sigil on my forehead and over my heart. She repeated the move three times and then said something in a language I didn't recognize. I asked her what it was, and she said it marked us for each other."

When no one said anything or showed they understood, Gibbie said, "Yeah, well, I didn't know what she meant either. She told me it was so she'd always know where I was and how to find me if she was nearby. So I wondered if I could do it in reverse. I went down to that old Rakshini you took care of, Dean. I told her about the spell and she took a pinch of powder, blowing it in my face until I sneezed. Some powder fell on my chest and it made the sigil glow so I could see it."

Carlos asked, "I'm sorry, Mr. Gibson, is this going somewhere?"

"Yeah, it is. I left there and started driving around downtown. I used the standard square search grid system you and Brynne taught me in CERT class. Anyway, that's how I found them. I think."

James let out an exasperated gasp. "Where did you find them, Gibbie?"

"Oh, I think they're hiding out in the old Gnome's lair a few blocks from here. Once I knew what to look for and got close enough for our bond to light up, I spotted the werepanthers hiding out, watching the place as if they were guarding whoever was inside. It has to be the right place."

James nodded. "Alfonse left the place vacant when things turned bad during the pending apocalypse. He hasn't returned that I know of. If there's activity there, it's not him."

Rudy pulled out his phone. "If there are lookouts, we'll need more people." He turned away as he started tapping out a message on it.

Dean remembered the gnome's hideout. "That place is an underground fortress. I'm not sure we could get in there with an entire army behind us."

A voice from behind Dean startled everyone.

"You don't need an army if you have us along," Gabe said.

Dean spun around. Gabe, Ashley, and Ingrid stood in the doorway to the balcony. They each had flown in with wings now folded against their backs. Then the wings disappeared into whatever inter-dimensional hiding spot that hid them as the trio walked into the room.

"You came," Dean said.

"I said I would," Gabe said, displeasure tinted his tone. "Don't you forget you owe me for coming."

Ashley stepped forward and pulled Dean close. "You don't owe me anything. I remember how you came to find me when I needed it most."

Ingrid snorted, saying, "Yeah, yeah, everything is always kittens and rainbows where my sister is concerned. Gabe said you could open up the gates to Valhalla again, so I suppose I can help to get things back to normal."

Both Brynne and James shot Dean a startled look at the revelation of what he'd promised Gabe. Neither of them said anything, though. Dean shrugged as he caught their stares. They'd been there when the demons had tried to come through the open portal to Hell. They had the same questions as he did.

Ingrid, wearing her gleaming silver chainmail and winged helmet, crossed to the liquor cabinet against the far wall and poured herself a tumbler full of James's best Scotch. "So, is this a war council or what? You all sounded like you were in the middle of planning this little rescue mission. Carry on."

Dean said, "Gabe, you mentioned the Eldara could help us get inside without having to fight through every fortified inch to get to the central part of the lair."

Gabe smiled. He sauntered over to Ingrid and took the bottle from her, pouring a glass for himself. He wore a golden breastplate and a helmet of Spartan design. He pulled off the helmet and tucked it under one arm as he sipped at the liquor.

"The Eldara cannot be banned from any place on earth. It's part of our charge as messengers of the gods. We wouldn't be very good at it if we couldn't deliver the messages."

Ashley said, "What he means is that we can get at least part of the way inside. That should cause enough of a distraction to allow the rest of you to come in the front entrance." Ashley had a chainmail shirt like her sister's. Instead of a helmet, she had a silver chain woven through her dark hair and across her forehead. A triangular silver rune hung down against the skin between her eyebrows.

James clapped his hands together. "Sounds like we have the beginnings of the plan. Gibbie, you and Dean sound like you've been inside. Come over and draw out a map of what you remember and let's work out the rest. Time is of the essence now that darkness has fallen. Artur is a traditionalist and sleeps during daylight hours. He will have risen by now."

Dean and the others moved over to the large dining table nearby. James's assistant, Celeste, appeared with a large sheet of grid paper and Gibbie and Dean sketched out a rough diagram of the layout. Within a few minutes, they had a plan for how to get inside.

Chapter 34

DEAN GLANCED out the passenger window as Gibbie pulled his van over to the curb. Behind the van, two black SUV's stopped as well. Behind Dean sat Leah Casado and her father. Dean tried to ignore the rumpled covers on the mattress behind the seat. Every time he thought about it, the image of Gibbie and Hangbe tangled in the sheets kept creeping into his mind.

Gibbie twisted and rested his arm on the back of his seat so he could see all of them. "Okay, this is as close as I want to get with the security cars behind me. You three duck down in case anyone is looking this way. I don't think the werecats will recognize the van, so I should be able to get in with my keycard from when Alfonse used to live down there."

Carlos cleared his throat, "I don't like that we're leaving a lot of our muscle outside, even if they are just wolf-kind."

Dean said, "Stick to the plan. You two are here to do whatever mojo you can do on the werepanthers at the entrance. Then we can let the others in without sounding the alarm."

"Don't worry. Leah and I know what we have to do. We have a score to settle as well. I still don't understand why you're along. You have no abilities that I can sense. Surely someone else can alert the

Eldara when we are ready."

"Ashley said it had to be me. Something to do with our history together." Dean let it drop at that. He really didn't want to go into their past as a romantic couple.

Gibbie pointed out the rear window as lights flashed behind them. "That's the signal. They're all set. That means the Errington team is in place to cover the exit after everyone goes in." He settled back behind the wheel and pulled back out into the street. "You all hide. We can't let anyone see I'm not alone in the van."

Dean ducked into the back. He and the two werejaguars pulled a quilt from behind the center seat and ducked under it. It was musty beneath the covering; with just a hint of funkiness he didn't want to identify. He was glad he didn't have the sensitive noses of the two werecats, judging from the wrinkled noses and expressions on their faces.

The van continued on, then stopped. The driver's window hummed as it opened.

A gruff male voice said, "Hey, where do you think you're going?"

"My girlfriend lives here. She gave me this keycard. I'm just here to pick her up and then we're leaving. What's with all the security. I've never seen two guards out here before."

"Just something new the building management is providing. Hurry back out. Don't make us come in there looking for you."

"Yes, sir." Gibbie replied. The van lurched forward and then tilted down as it started into the garage.

After a few seconds, Gibbie put up the window. "There are two up at the entrance and two more just inside. Are you sure both of you can take them out without raising the alarm?"

"You'll see," Carlos said, lifting the blanket away and shoving it behind him. "There's a reason the other jungle cats fear us."

Once again, his eyes lit up with a fierce yellow color. Leah's flashed as well, though she shifted uncomfortably when she caught Dean watching her.

Gibbie pulled the van over once it was down to the second level, out of sight from the entrance. As he stopped and waited, three figures stepped out of thin air into the beams of the headlights.

Dean started to call out a warning until he realized it was Gabe, Ashley, and Ingrid.

Ashley walked over to Gibbie's window. "We are here. We will breach the entrance down on the lower level. If Artur has any vampire or werepanther guards just inside, we will deal with them for you."

Dean nodded. "We should be down with the rest of the team shortly. Once we're in, you three will hold the entrance so no one escapes past us, especially Artur."

"Don't worry. If he tries, we'll take care of him." Ashley returned to the other two Eldara. They all turned and stepped out of the headlight beams, winking out of sight in the blink of an eye."

"Neat trick," Carlos said. "I wonder what it would take to hire one of their kind. They'd make a very effective assassin."

Dean shook his head. "I don't think they'd be all that interested. They're helping us because it furthers their own agenda, otherwise, they'd stay out of such matters."

Carlos snorted as if he didn't accept the answer.

Gibbie said, "Maybe you can ask them about it once we're finished today. Right now it's time for you two to go to work."

Leah nudged her father. Both Casados, dressed in tight-fitting black athletic wear, stepped from the van and closed the sliding door. They were out of sight for only a few seconds, but when they moved around to the front of the van, the headlights showed two heavily muscled werejaguars. One was shorter than the other, but both looked fierce and powerful. They loped on two legs into the darkened garage, heading back up towards the entrance.

"I hope this works," Dean muttered.

"Don't worry, Dean. We'll get Hangbe and Jaz back. Knowing them, they're already halfway out with an escape plan of their own."

Chapter 35

HANGBE SLAMMED the metal table leg twice against the temple of the werepanther coming at her. On the second hit, his eyes rolled up in his head and he slumped to the floor. He'd still raked at her side with his claws, tearing open the body armor at its thinnest point.

Pressing a hand against the wound, she glanced to the side. Jaz had dispatched the final one of the group they'd encountered. The pair had stumbled into the four guards as they'd run from their last encounter outside the vault.

"You okay?" Jaz asked, nodding at the blood seeping through Hangbe's fingers.

"I'll live. We need to get away. The noise from this fight will draw more down here."

Jaz nodded at the two possible exits from the room. "The question is, which is the best option? We don't even know where here is."

"Pick one, we know we can't go back the way we came."

The Hunter shrugged and started down the concrete corridor on the right. Hangbe followed. Unlike the rest of the rooms and hallways they'd seen so far, this one had no decor or fancy carpets covering the drab concrete walls. Maybe that was a good sign. It could mean this led to an exit.

Shouts sounded behind them a few minutes later. She glanced back to check the twisting passage behind. No sign of pursuit, but they'd be coming.

Ahead of her, Jaz picked up speed to a loping jog. Hangbe tried to match it but fell behind almost immediately. Fatigue and shortness of breath had set in, setting off alarm bells in her mind. The bleeding had slowed, but the way she felt almost assuredly indicated an internal injury of some sort.

"Jaz, slow down."

Jaz stopped. When she saw Hangbe lagging, ran back to her. "I knew we should have stopped and treated that injury sooner."

"Whatever's going on," Hangbe gasped, trying to catch her breath, "it's internal. I think I might have a punctured lung."

Jaz pointed in the direction they were heading. "It looks like it opens into a room down this way where the passage turns. I'll help you down there. Then we can see about treating this wound."

Pulling Hangbe's arm over her shoulder, Jaz lifted her friend up and together they staggered to the corridor's end. It opened into a small storage room lined with metal shelves. Judging from the dust and the old civil defense markings on the containers and boxes, this was part of an old nuclear bunker.

Jaz lowered Hangbe to the floor in the corner, propping her up against one of the shelves. "Let me take a look at that."

She pulled Hangbe's bloody hand away, revealing a deep gash in the skin. It looked deep and bubbled a little when she took a breath.

"You're developing a pneumothorax. That's why you can't catch your breath. Here, press your hand back against the wound. Try to press hard enough to seal it and keep air from leaking out."

Jaz started rummaging through the shelves, pulling boxes down and examining the labels.

"What are you looking for?"

"There has to be a first aid kit stored down here with all the survival crackers and expired meal kits. I need to find something to decompress your chest. Air is escaping your lungs and filling the chest cavity. If I can release that pressure so I can control it, it should ease your breathing. If Dean were here, he'd probably improvise something from what he had in his pockets."

Hangbe smiled. "Being married to that medic has rubbed off on you."

"I've picked up a few things. He's taught a few classes to a few Errington assault teams. Nothing too advanced, just basic combat and tactical first aid."

Jaz kept looking and then let out a quiet "yes" as she pulled down a cardboard box with a red cross on the side. She unsealed the tape around the lid and opened it. After digging through the contents, she smiled and held up a syringe. It was an old model, made before disposable plastics with a metal frame around a glass tube leading to a long stainless steel needle.

"This will do nicely. Here, hold this. I need to find some plastic to seal that wound in your side before I do the decompression."

Jaz searched through the room and came back with a roll of aluminum foil.

"What's that for?"

"Not plastic, but this should do the trick. We have to seal the wound off, and this will stay airtight if you hold still."

She tore off a piece of foil and folded it into a twelve-inch square. Pulling a roll of adhesive tape from the first aid kit, she taped the foil patch in place, leaving one side open.

"Exhale as hard as you can."

Hangbe did as she was told. Frothy, bloody bubbles oozed out from the open side of the foil patch. Jaz wiped the blood away, pressing on the seal to hold it in place before Hangbe took another breath. She taped off the last side as best she could and then wrapped several rolls of gauze around Hangbe's waist to hold it all in place and help the tape hold a seal.

Hangbe glanced down and nodded. Pretty good work for a makeshift occlusive dressing. Her breathing was a little easier now.

Jaz asked, "How do you feel?"

"A little better."

"Good, then I'll hold off on using the needle until you need decompressing again."

A shout from the corridor had them both start to get up. Jaz pressed Hangbe back down.

"You stay put. I think it's just a few of them. Are you sure, Gibbie is close by?"

"I am. Hopefully, he brought help. We just have to hold on a little longer."

Jaz nodded. She started pulling boxes from one shelf by the doorway. Once it was empty, she moved it into the doorway and refilled the shelves. Then she started on another. By the time the shouts grew louder, she'd blocked off the doorway with shelving and boxes.

"It won't hold them long, but it's all I can do." Jaz hefted the two metal table legs and moved over to the doorway. "I can at least make it painful to break down the barricade."

Hangbe closed her eyes and reached out with her mind, calling to Gibson. She could feel him, closer now than before. She tried to urge him to hurry, but she wasn't sure if that worked or not. Darkness closed in as unconsciousness took her.

Chapter 36

DEAN HUNG BACK and watched their backs as Carlos, Leah, and Gibbie fought their way through the werepanthers in front of them. As they took the final two down, he raced past them and squeezed through the partially opened vault door.

He skidded to a stop staring at the broken table in the corner and the two piles of ropes and broken plastic cable ties on the floor. His fists clenched as he looked around for some sign of where Jaz and Hangbe were.

Gibbie joined him, drawing in a deep breath, nostrils flared. "She was definitely here."

"Artur must have taken them. He's going to kill them and get away."

Gibbie pointed to the floor. "I don't think so. If he'd taken them, why untie them? And look, some ropes have been cut free. I think they got free on their own."

"Your mojo with Hangbe brought you here. Where are they now?"

Gibbie walked around the room. He returned to the door, tracing the large plate of glass leaning against the wall, then looking at the exposed locking mechanism. He nodded and squeezed out through the doorway to return to the outer room.

Dean followed. Leah stood to one side, wrapping her father's arm with a bandage. Both werejaguars had injuries, but Carlos's were more severe.

Realizing he'd dropped the ball on his duties on this rescue mission, Dean retrieved his trauma bag from beside Leah and dug through it to pull out a ten-pack of four by four-inch gauze pads. He started applying a dressing to a slashing wound on Leah's shoulder.

"Sorry, I thought we'd found them."

Leah smiled. "I understand. It's not that bad. Check on Gibbie. He's pretty beat up, too. He and my father took the brunt of the last fight."

Carlos shook his head. "I do not understand how it is they will not submit to our wills, Leah. Our power over other werecats should exert control over them. They shouldn't be fighting us. They should be surrendering and begging for mercy."

"Something has broken the control passed to our line," Leah said. "I felt the difference with the first contact we had outside. Somehow they've overcome it."

Carlos flexed his cat fingers, exposing his claws and then retracting them. "I first felt it back in that warehouse when they captured me. I had hoped it was isolated to proximity to the ancient vampire."

Dean finished dressing Leah's shoulder. "They're fighting like they've got no choice. None of them has tried to escape."

Carlos smiled, but it was the sort of smile that chilled the blood. "They know the only way they survive the encounter is by defeating us. If they run after being part of this, they know we will hunt them down and make an example of them. My daughter and I cannot let this affront stand."

"Speak for yourself, Papa. I'm here to help my friend recover his wife. I will not be a part of your vendetta against these others."

Dean moved over and dabbed at the wounds on Gibbie's chest with a dampened piece of gauze. He pretended not to overhear the confrontation brewing between father and daughter behind him. The vampire's wounds were superficial and needed only a little cleansing. They would heal on their own the next time he fed. Despite that, Dean stayed where he was, keeping busy until Leah and her father worked out their differences.

Carlos had had enough. He crossed over to the vault and glanced inside. Then he paced around the room, checking the exits.

Unsure what he searched for, Dean joined him. "Maybe we should reconnect with the other two teams and spread out from here?"

James and Rudy each headed up a separate team from the local werewolf pack. They'd taken two other side passages on the way here after werepanthers ambushed the group from inside one of them.

"We don't need the dogs to help us. The vampire can locate the women, can't you?"

Gibbie let Dean finish and then started pacing around the room. He stopped at each of the three exits twice as he circled. After the second pass, he backed up and stopped at the second doorway. It opened to a long, carpeted hallway with several pairs of doors opening from it.

"This way."

The two werejaguars joined him at the corridor entrance. Leah stopped and glanced back. "I smell death."

Dean's heart skipped a beat. Did she mean a dead human?

Gibbie interpreted it in a much more positive light. "Of course you do. Those two women aren't going to just waltz out of here without a fight. They've got payback on the mind."

He shouldered past the two werecats and started jogging down the hallway, checking the doors to either side as he reached them. Gibbie left the doors open as he continued on. Dean glanced inside as he passed. They appeared to be sparsely furnished guest bedrooms, which struck Dean as odd. Alfonse the gnome had seemed like a solitary individual on the one occasion Dean had met him. Maybe the rooms predated him.

Gibbie passed the last of the rooms and picked up speed. The Casados started speeding up as well. Soon Dean was jogging along alone, shouldering the trauma medical bag over one arm as he tried to keep up with them. He hoped the increased speed meant they weren't too late.

Chapter 37

JAZ BATTED AT THE ARM, forcing its way past the stacked barricade of shelves. She swung with every ounce of strength she had left. A satisfying crack resonated up the metal tubing and into her arm. The attacking werepanther howled and pulled back the broken arm, cradling it with its other hand.

This had been the second assault on the barricaded room. The first had been more of a test of the defenses. This last one had been better planned, with multiple werecats attacking the narrow entrance to the storeroom at once.

Jaz had been lucky. Given her only weapon were the two metal tubes that had been card table legs, she should have been pleased with the outcome she'd had. If she'd had even just her grandmother's Katana, she'd have killed several werepanthers by now, and this assault on their position would be over.

As it was, she'd broken a few bones, but caused no lasting damage to anyone. She might hold them off one more time. This last time, they'd partially dismantled the shelving she'd piled in the doorway. It wouldn't take too much more work to pull the rest away, and then they'd be able to rush in on her.

Jaz glanced back at Hangbe. Her breathing was ragged at this point. Each inhalation seemed a struggle. Anger filled Jaz rather than sorrow. She'd rather avenge her friend and fight to the end herself than give in to self-pity. Hangbe had been sure a rescue was imminent, but Jaz had yet to see any evidence anyone was close.

Artur stepped into view in the corridor outside. Two attractive female vampires flanked him. "Jaswinder, my child. I commend you on an admirable defense, however there's no way you're getting out of there alive. The only thing you're doing at this point is injuring my friends. They will recover and break through, eventually. They're not going to be gentle once they do get in."

Jaz dug her hand into her pocket, wrapping her hand around the makeshift stake she'd crafted from five tongue depressors she'd found in the medical kit. Taped together and hastily sharpened against the rough concrete walls, they made a passable shiv. Under the right circumstances, and with a little luck, she was pretty sure she could reach Artur's heart with it.

"I'll tell you what, Artur. You send your minions away, and I'll come out so just you and I can play. Surely, you're not afraid of a woman armed only with a table leg?"

A fourth vampire, this one a male, stepped into view and leaned in to whisper something to Artur. The ancient vampire's eyes glanced at the newcomer for a second before returning to glare at Jaz.

"Bad new, Artur?" A flash of anger across his face rewarded her guess.

"It is nothing." He waved his hand, dismissing the newcomer. Footsteps ran back up the corridor towards the central lair. "I tire of this, perhaps I will deal with you later. I have some pressing matters that I must attend to."

Jaz smiled. She had a good idea now what the whispered message must have been. "They're here, aren't they? My husband and friends wouldn't sit idly by and let you hold me for long."

When Artur didn't respond right away, Jaz continued. "My guess is they have you trapped down here. You're not getting away this time. This time you're going to die along with your minions."

A moment of irritation was replaced by a sly grin. "I've lived for thousands of years. My plans span centuries. I do not care if this one incursion upsets the balance momentarily. I will merely reset the chess pieces and begin again. That is the advantage I have over those of you with puny, human lives."

Artur flicked his head to the side and the two women with him ran off in the opposite direction, continuing past the storeroom. That rough concrete corridor went on for some distance, Jaz knew.

Shouts and the clash of steel on steel echoed down the corridor outside. Whatever was happening was coming closer.

The vampire's canines glistened as the grin broadened. "It seems, Jaswinder Errington, I must leave. Have no fear, though. I shall return. I have unfinished business with your family line, and I will come for you again."

With a curt nod in her direction, Artur's form blurred as he moved with a speed she could never have matched. He was out of sight before she could blink an eye.

For an instant, she considered tearing down the makeshift barricade to go after him. She decided there was no way she could dig her way out in time to catch up with him. Instead, she went over to Hangbe and did what she could to keep her comfortable until help arrived.

Chapter 38

DEAN JUMPED BACKWARD AS the limp body slid across the floor towards him. Gibbie, armed with the broken arm from a chair, had staked the vampire as he tried to race past and get at the paramedic to the rear.

"You good back there, Dean?" Gibbie called out as he engaged the next of Artur's undead minions.

"I'm still here. We have to break through. We must be getting close."

Gibbie didn't answer. The final vampire had pressed him back against the wall and wrestled to pull away the makeshift stake. He pummeled at Gibbie's face and head again and again with his free hand.

Dean looked around for help. The Casados had run farther down the concrete corridor. The two werejaguars battled a cluster of werepanthers gathered in front of several doors on either side.

Realizing if Gibbie was going to get help, it was going to have to come from him, Dean slid the trauma bag off his shoulder and bunched up the long strap in both hands. Letting out a guttural shout, he charged at the vampire's back.

The heavy bag struck the vampire from behind at the same time he'd pried the wooden stake from Gibbie's hand. The blow caused the chair arm to fall clattering the floor, leaving both vampires unarmed. Gibbie took one more blow to the head. His eyes rolled up in his head and he slumped to the floor.

Dean stepped back to swing the bag around for another strike. The vampire spun on him, leaving him no time to bring the heavy trauma kit around in time to stop the charge.

Before he knew what happened, Dean found himself on his back struggling to hold the vampire at bay. He pressed at the weight laying atop him with one hand on the creature's neck. The corded muscles resisted his fingers digging at the cold flesh.

The face and its dripping fangs dipped down towards Dean's neck despite every ounce of strength he poured into his arms to hold off the vampire.

"You smell tasty, human," the raspy voice whispered as the mouth passed his ear. "Do I detect a hint of something Unusual? Let's see what your vintage really is."

Dean wrenched his head to the side and slammed it back into the vampire's temple. He might as well have bashed it against a brick wall. All he did was knock himself into a daze.

He closed his eyes and tried to gather his wits, expecting to feel the piercing fangs at his neck any second.

Instead of pain, there was a splash of wetness against the side of his face and the full weight of the vampire fell upon him.

Opening his eyes, he blinked to clear away whatever had splashed on his face. His cloudy vision cleared as his tears wiped away the blood from his eyes.

Ingrid stood over him, her blazing silver heavenly sword in her hands.

Dean glanced to the side and gasped. The wide-eyed face of the vampire stared back at him from where the severed head lay beside him.

Groaning, he shoved the headless body away and sat up so no more of the foul vampire blood poured out onto him.

"A thank you would be nice," Ingrid said.

"Thank you," Dean replied as he tried to wipe blood from his face with the back of his hand. All he seemed to do was smear it around. He stopped and reached up to Ingrid. "Can you help me up?"

The Valkyrie extended her hand and pulled him to his feet with ease. Ashley knelt by Gibbie, checking his injuries. Gabe stood watching, his sword hanging in its scabbard at his side.

"Maybe you two could help the Casados?" Dean nodded towards the two werejaguars fighting a desperate battle down the corridor.

"They seem to be holding their own," Gabe said with the barest glance down at the battling werecats.

"If you don't, I'll consider your bargain void," Dean said. "The fight isn't over until Jaz and Hangbe are free and Artur dealt with."

With a gasp of exasperation, Gabe drew his gleaming blade, this one golden. "Shall we, cousin?" he asked Ingrid.

"Always up for a fight."

Together the two strode down the hallway towards the fighting.

Dean retrieved his trauma bag and knelt beside Gibbie with Ashley. "How is he?"

"His injuries are severe and he has a concussion, but he'll live. Most of what he's sustained should resolve after a few feedings."

"Do you think it's safe to leave him here?" Dean wanted to keep searching for Jaz.

Ashley smiled and nodded. "Go. I'll stay with him until he wakes up."

"Thank you." Dean ran down the hallway. The addition of the two Eldara had turned the tide against the werepanthers. They now fought a sort of fighting retreat, trying to disengage from the Casados and the two angels.

He caught up with them as the fight reached a bend in the hallway and turned the corner. He passed a room with junk piled in the doorway.

"Dean!"

He skidded to a stop and returned to the opening. Jaz's beautiful face appeared in between one gap in what he realized was a hastily constructed barricade.

"Are you alright?"

She smiled. "I am. It's good to see you. I knew you'd find me."

"Always. Where's Hangbe? Is she…?" He didn't want to finish the question.

"She's in here with me. She's hurt and bleeding internally. Do you have any fluids in that bag?"

Dean nodded. He pulled at the stacked shelves and boxes. "Clear me a way in so I can check on her."

It took several minutes to widen an opening for him to climb into the room. Dean rushed over to Hangbe and began assessing her. The ashen color of her dark skin told him she'd lost a lot of blood. She felt cold to the touch, but she still breathed and had a flicker of a thready pulse.

"Jaz, go back down the hallway. Find Ashley. I need her to help. I can give some fluids, but this is beyond me. She needs a full trauma suite."

Jaz disappeared as Dean set up the fluid drip and got the IV started. He continued his assessment. Her abdomen felt rigid and distended under his palpating fingers. She definitely had an internal bleed. The fluids might help to stabilize her blood pressure for a brief time, but she'd die without special intervention.

It didn't take long for Ashley to arrive.

Dean twisted his head around and asked, "Where's Jaz?"

"I left her with Gibbie. He's still out cold. What's going on with your friend here?"

"She's in shock, thready pulse, probable internal bleed in the abdomen. She needs surgery and I don't think there's any way to get her there in time."

Ashley knelt beside Dean and placed one hand on Hangbe's head. The other rested on her belly. The Eldara Sister closed her eyes and bowed her head. Dean watched as a golden glow formed beneath Ashley's palms. The glow remained for about ten seconds, then it faded away.

The Eldara slumped a little as she pulled her hands back. Dean knew she'd spent some of her corporeal life energy to heal some of Hangbe's injuries.

The Amazon's eyes fluttered open and seemed confused for a few seconds as she looked around. "Where's Jaz? She was just here."

Dean rested his hand on the woman's shoulder. "Rest easy. She's helping Gibbie. He's injured, too."

At mention of Gibbie, Hangbe tried again to rise.

Dean pressed her back to the floor. "You need to lay still until we can get an ambulance here for you. Ashley was able to heal you a bit, but you're going to need a trauma center to fix what's wrong with you."

Hangbe relaxed and lay back. "How bad is he?"

Ashley said, "He took a knock to the head. He's pretty banged up. I wouldn't worry, though. We'll take him to the hospital, too. A few bags of blood and he'll be good as new."

Hangbe relaxed at the news. Dean continued monitoring the woman's condition while he and Ashely waited for the others to return.

Carlos was the first to come back up the corridor, with Leah close behind. They both had shifted back to human form, though their eyes still glowed yellow.

"Did you find your woman?"

"I did. We found both of them. Jaz is down the hall looking after Gibbie. Leah, do you think you can run down there and check on him?"

The other paramedic nodded and jogged out of sight.

Dean checked the corridor behind Carlos. "What about Artur?"

"I think he made his escape into the night. We caught up to a pair of female vampires. After we dealt with them, we found an exit into the basement of a building about a block away from this one. The two Eldara gave chase, but I fear with a head start, they will not catch him. That one is too slippery by far."

"You're not kidding," Ashley said. She stood, shaking her head. "My sister and I have almost caught him several times in the last two centuries. Each time, he has weaseled out of trouble, either by escaping or using some obscure rule of protection to keep us from dispatching him on sight."

"Well, now he has the Casado Cartel to worry about. I care not about rules or how powerful he is. For the right price, everyone can be found and killed."

Ashley and Dean exchanged glances. The discussion of contract killing, even for someone as reprehensible as Artur, made them both uncomfortable.

Dean changed the subject. "What about the werepanthers behind the trafficking ring? Did you regain control over them?"

"They will no longer bother this area, or any other. They're an example for others who think they'd prefer working away from our oversight. I'm especially pleased with the way Leah has shown her leadership potential in the cartel tonight. Don't you agree?"

Dean hesitated to answer. He knew Leah's feelings about this, and he suspected they hadn't changed despite her participation in the fighting tonight. Aware of the elder Casado's eyes on him, Dean said, "She has a bright future in whatever she does."

Carlos frowned, but said nothing else. Dean decided to look busy and get another round of vitals on Hangbe. Her condition had improved since Ashley's supernatural intervention, but she was still borderline unstable. As soon as Leah returned, he'd leave her with Hangbe while he tracked down Brynne and got an ambulance for both Gibbie and the inspector. James and the others could deal with the cleanup down here.

Chapter 39

DEAN REACHED out to grab Jaz's hand where it rested on her knee as she steered the SUV with her left hand.

She gave his searching fingers a gentle squeeze and glanced his way. "You okay?"

"I'm fine now that you're home safe and sound. I'm not sure how I feel about you leaving again to track down the European side of this trafficking ring."

"Dean, it's been two weeks since the rescue. Hangbe's recovered fully, and she's finally prised herself away from Gibbie's side to get back to work."

"I know," Dean said. "I don't know why you have to go with her back to Ireland. You should be able to let your Dublin team handle things. We found Kaylee's family and Verity. Can't we leave the rest to someone else?"

Jaz shook her head. "There's too much riding on this. We have to follow up and track down the other side of this operation. We didn't have to do that here. Carlos Casado's ruthless retaliation against the remaining werepanthers left us no one to arrest. His cartel doesn't reach outside of the Americas, though. That leaves that clean up to Errington and Hangbe's Interpol connections."

Dean recalled all the news of random gang carnage in the area. He knew it was Carlos cleaning house and making sure everyone left alive had no doubts about who was in charge of the werecats in the western hemisphere. "Do you think we're going to have any trouble from the Cartel now that Carlos has taken things into his own hands?"

"Maybe." Jaz shook her head and sighed. "I'll give him credit for one thing. His hit teams were careful and avoided all collateral damage. We wouldn't have known they were here if it weren't for the bodies they left behind. That's why I didn't have to intervene."

She took her Hunter lineage seriously. As long as no one outside the gangs was hurt, she'd stand down.

Jaz pulled into a parking space at the rear of the Irish Shop. They had allowed Dougie to reopen after a long meeting with James about his part in the illegal activity. Dean thought the leprechaun had gotten off easy with the threat of future sanctions from James and the agreement that Rudy and his werewolves would watch to make sure things remained legal. Part of that agreement was to keep the door to Dublin locked except for specific uses arranged with James or Rudy in advance. To make sure he complied, James held on to Dougie's recovered pot-o-gold as collateral.

Dean hopped out. Gibbie's white van was already here, parked right next to the shop's rear door. Dean figured the vampire and Hangbe must be inside already.

When the back door of the van popped open and a shirtless Gibbie hopped out, Dean shouted and jumped backward.

Hangbe climbed out, pulling a black t-shirt over her sports bra. Gibbie pulled her close and planted a long, energetic kiss on her full lips.

When they parted, Gibbie turned and noticed Dean and Jaz for the first time. "Oh, hey guys. Hangbe and I were just, uh, saying goodbye."

Dean held up a hand. He really didn't need the mental image to go along with what he imagined had just been happening in the back of the van.

Hangbe winked at Jaz. "I'm going to miss this one." She wrapped her arm around Gibbie's neck and pulled him in for another kiss, even more passionate than the last.

Jaz cleared her throat. "Maybe we should postpone the trip for a little while?"

Hangbe held out a hand with her forefinger extended as she continued to press her lips against the vampire's. Dean and Jaz waited.

Thirty seconds later, she came up for air and smiled. "I wanted him to remember what he's waiting for until I return."

Dean couldn't hide his surprise. He'd thought this whole affair with the frumpy vampire had been a fling. "You're coming back?"

"Of, course. Gibson and I have a wedding to plan."

Gibbie blushed, reaching out to clutch at her hand. "I cannot wait. It'll be the event of the year, I promise."

"I don't want a fuss, my love. I just want you."

Dean glanced and Jaz and rolled his eyes as Hangbe leaned in to kiss Gibbie again. The Hunter returned the expression.

Finally, they all went inside and headed to the storeroom with the door to Ireland. Dougie sat at a desk nearby, looking over his books. He stood as the four of them entered.

"It's wonderful to see you all back to visit. James gave me a heads up you'd be here to travel through the portal. Do you know when you'll be returning?"

Jaz shook her head. "I'll have Dean arrange a time with you once I know how long it's likely to take on the far side. Hangbe and I have a lot to do in coordination with Irish and UK authorities."

Dougie nodded and produced the key that unlocked the door. He twisted it in the keyhole and pulled the door open.

Dean decided he'd better make a good show of this after all the attention Gibbie had given Hangbe. He reached out for Jaz and pulled her into an embrace. "Hurry back."

"I will. I'll reach out with a message every day so you know what's going on."

Dean smiled. "I'll hold you to that."

They separated and waited while Gibbie and Hangbe exchanged goodbyes three more times. Finally, Hangbe came over to join Jaz with her bag on her shoulder and suitcase rolling behind her. Jaz grabbed her gear, too, and with a wave, the pair disappeared through the door, pulling it closed behind them.

Dougie locked the portal and returned the old key to his pocket. "What are you two going to do while the ladies are gone?"

Gibbie smiled. "I have to find a new apartment. Hangbe made it clear that my place was way too small for us to stay there long term. Maybe I'll get a new bed, too. We kind of wrecked the one I had."

Dean winced. He really didn't want to know.

"What about you, Dean?" Dougie asked.

"The work of a paramedic never ends. I've got a new shift tomorrow and Leah is still on probationary status. She's good, but there's a lot to learn to be as great as I expect her to be."

"She's a good kid, Dean," Gibbie said. "I'm sure she'll do fine."

"I hope so. There are some conflicts with her family that need to get worked out. As long as her father lets her live her life, she should be fine." Dean shrugged. There wasn't much he could do about that. "You up for a quick bite at Hank's place?"

Gibbie smiled. "I could have a little something. Not too much, though. Hangbe has me on a strict diet. She says she wants me in shape for our wedding night."

Dean shook his head as Gibbie described in too much detail all the things he loved about his new girlfriend. He didn't complain, though. It was all part of his life as a Station U paramedic. He wouldn't have it any other way.

Epilogue

GABE TRUDGED up the stairs and opened the door to his apartment above the music store. He snorted in disgust at the pitiful accommodations. An archangel should live in a palace. He was Eldara royalty and yet here he was.

Dropping his keys on the kitchenette counter, he bent down and picked up the mail someone had shoved beneath the door for him. Seeing nothing but bills and junk mail, he threw the stack of envelopes on the counter beside the keys.

"You never got back to me about your mission," a woman said from across the room.

Gabe resisted the urge to startle, instead slowly turning to stare at the person who'd let themselves in to his inner sanctum. "You came to me. It's not my job to track you down."

The woman, who looked to be in her mid-thirties, stood. She wore scarred tactical body armor from her shoulders down. Her close-cropped blonde hair had been shaved close on one side, and a scarlet streak swept across the other. She glared at Gabriel with her one good eye, the other covered with a black leather patch.

"Did you get him to agree to help you reopen the ways to the upper and lower planes?"

"I got him to say he would try. Neither of us know how he might do that, by the way."

The woman shook her head. "That's for me to work out. I have to make all this right. The problem started the moment he closed off earth from heaven and hell. Until I fix it, nothing will ever be normal again."

Gabe pulled a beer from the fridge for himself and held out another one for the woman. She shook her head. Shrugging, he opened his and took a long pull from the bottle. "Given what little you've told me, I'm not sure I want things to change. I can see across the boundaries of time, at least a little. There's much from the future you describe I like."

The woman stormed across at him, raising her hand to grab at the hilt of the Katana across her back. "Your kind is the reason I'm here. The archangels started it all. Maybe if I kill you now, I won't have to fix anything."

A flash of gold lit up the room as Gabe summoned his heavenly blade. He swept it at the woman's exposed neck. She finished drawing her own sword and blocked his strike with surprising ease. He filed that bit of information away for future reference.

"I'm not so easily dispatched, Gabriel. You're not the first of your kind I've tangled with. I'm still here, which should tell you not to cross me."

Gabe stepped back, lowering his blade a little as he took another sip from his beer. "You're fast, faster than a human should be. What have you done to enhance yourself?"

"What was necessary after the Eldara betrayed humanity." She also stepped back, but kept her sword between them, ready for another attack.

"You can lower your weapon, girl. My attack was just a test. You passed it."

"I won't lower my guard until Dean completes the task he agreed to. Until then, dearest Grandfather, you're stuck with me."

The End

The Paramedic's
Sorceress

Prologue

JOANNA HELD UP HER HAND, fist closed just above her head. Movement on the path up ahead kept her cautious. She crouched to one knee along the overgrown trail that had once been a concrete sidewalk in a nice residential neighborhood. It always amazed her how fast nature had moved in to take over once the people were gone. Twenty-plus years gave the trees and undergrowth plenty of time to move in.

Behind her, the rest of her ten-member hunter squad had also stopped, each assuming a position to watch their own chosen approach vectors. Nothing would sneak up on this hand-picked team. Knowing her rear was safe, she scanned the path and underbrush to either side, watching carefully for any sign of the bit of movement she'd seen seconds before. She had to shift her head back and forth to account for the loss of her left eye, covered now by a simple leather eyepatch.

She tensed for a second as a figure stepped out onto the trail about fifteen yards ahead. Joanna relaxed as recognition registered. It was Flynn. The scout had been watching for trouble ahead of the team. The fact she was here before they'd reached their target wasn't a good sign.

"What did you see?" Joanna asked as the fairy approached and crouched beside her.

"They've definitely got the spell circle staked out. I spotted at least fifteen demonlings of various kinds on this side of the location. I'm sure there were others on the opposite side I couldn't see."

Joanna pressed her lips together in a grim line. She'd hoped this circle might have gone forgotten by the Eldara leadership and their underworld minions. That now turned out to be wishful thinking.

She frowned. "With that many demonlings, there has to be an angel around somewhere, too."

Flynn nodded. She knew their enemies as well as Joanna did. She was a just a few years older than her team leader and had fought in this gods-forsaken war as long as everyone else had.

Joanna looked over her shoulder at the rest of the team. If Flynn had spotted fifteen demons and said there were others, they were there. Add in an Eldara warrior to control them, and the team would be hard-pressed to win out in a standup fight.

Behind her, Joanna's second, an older wolf shifter named Marian, moved closer. Joanna didn't bother to repeat what Flynn had told her. The werewolf's enhanced hearing would have picked up the entire conversation.

Marian leaned in. "You're not thinking of turning around and trying somewhere else, are you? This mission is time-sensitive. You said it yourself."

Joanna thought about the question for a moment, then shook her head. Marian was right. "This is too important. Besides, we have no guarantee any other spell circle would be less guarded. "

Flynn glanced down the path and shrugged. Joanna knew that look. The scout was thinking of a plan.

"It's possible we can catch the ones closest to us by surprise. If we can take out enough of them on this side, it'll even out the fight a little bit." She brought around her crossbow and patted the stock.

Joanna smiled. The woman wasn't just an amazing scout and an excellent medic, she was also a deadly shot with that crossbow. The rest of her team was just as adept with their own weapons. She'd picked the group with care when they left on this mission. Flynn's idea had merit. They might be able to cut down the nearest demons fast enough for Joanna to complete her mission.

"Gather everybody around, Marian. Let's come up with a plan of attack. Flynn's right. It might just even up the odds."

The werewolf nodded and moved back down the path, whispering to each of the team. Soon, all of them had clustered around Joanna. A few on each side turned to face outward, covering their position and watching for trouble.

Joanna crouched down, keeping her voice low. "This isn't going to be easy. Flynn thinks there are probably twenty to thirty demonlings and an Eldara up ahead. They're guarding the remnants of the home in which the spell circle is situated. If I'm going to accomplish my mission, I have to get to that circle. Once I reach the center and start the spell, you can break off and do your best to escape. Until then, we have to keep fighting. Does everyone understand?"

She scanned the grim faces around her in the darkness. The silver hunter charm around her neck gave her the ability to see, even in the dark of the moonless night. Each team member gave a quick nod or met her eyes with a slight smile. They were all with her.

"Alright, we move out now. Spread out into a skirmish line. Flynn will take point." Joanna turned to the scout. "Take out the closest sentries. We'll be right behind you if anyone raises the alarm."

The fairy smiled, her lips parting, showing her teeth. She cradled the crossbow in front of her and disappeared down the path without a sound. The rest of the team spread out on either side of Joanna and moved forward through the remnants of homes burned down long ago.

All that remained were the open foundations and the few tattered walls still standing. The thick cover would help them get closer to the target. Hopefully, it would be close enough to kill the demonlings before they knew the hunter team was on them.

A hundred yards down the path, Joanna encountered the first body. The demonling lay across the narrow track, the stubby feathered end of a crossbow bolt jutting out from between its vacant eyes. It wore shreds of clothing that might have been for modesty or were just to display random colorful trophies from its victims. The rags did little to cover the scaly green hide or the clawed hands and feet. It was harmless now, though.

She continued forward.

The thrum of a bowstring ahead stopped her. She crouched and scanned the area, trying to peer through the vegetation that had once been someone's front yard. Joanna mined the recesses of her memory and tried to piece together where she was in the old neighborhood. She hadn't been here for over twenty years. It couldn't be that much farther to the burned-out shell of the Victorian house that had once been the home to her coven. The witches that had started her training so long ago were now long dead, but their sacred and blessed spell circle should still be intact.

Pushing aside memories she hadn't thought about for a long time, Joanna moved forward in a crouch. She'd heard no shouts of alarm. Flynn was good with that bow. By the time any victim heard the thrum of the bowstring, the speeding bolt would've already found them and they'd be dead.

Joanna found the next demonling lying side-by-side with a third. The first one had a crossbow bolt pinned between its shoulder blades. The second had its throat cut open from ear to ear. She smiled. The scout was just as deadly with that long silver fairy knife she carried.

Taking a few more steps, she was getting hopeful they might make it all the way to the circle without raising an alarm when a shout to her right drew a chorus of demon howls from all around. So much for that idea.

A screeching snarl to the left followed the first shout of warning as one of the hunter squad squared off against one of the demons.

Knowing the need for secrecy was all done now, Joanna stood, gathering her magical strength in from the natural growth all around her. She'd been taught well and knew how strong she was as she honed her magic throughout the long war.

She filled herself with power, not caring that it would alert any magical creature for a quarter mile in every direction. With her left hand, she drew her grandmother's Katana from over her shoulder. Her right, she kept open to cast a spell at any incoming attacker.

Ready for anything, she sprinted forward. It was all about speed now as more snarls and shouts sounded ahead. The demonlings knew they were under attack now.

Joanna kept her eyes open. The Eldara would be around some-where, and they'd almost have to choose her as their target once they sensed her power. She was the most dangerous of their team. Joanna had to make sure she spotted the angel before they found her.

She'd almost made it to the site of the old home and the spell circle inside when shouts from ahead slowed her sprint to a stop. She cursed under her breath. It wasn't one of the Eldara. It was two. That meant there were even more demonlings nearby than her team could hope to handle. Joanna launched a bolt of molten plasma drawn directly from the Sun. It flew at the pair of fallen angels without a second thought. She had to keep them busy so they couldn't exert control over their underlings. It was the only way any of her team were going to escape.

She charged forward, slinging spell after spell at the two Eldara. Her power drained fast, but this wasn't the time to be conservative. The pair separated to come at her from two different directions. Maybe they didn't realize she was just trying to get to the spell circle and didn't care about whether or not they attacked her. If they wanted to waste time getting to a new position, she was fine with that. Anything that delayed their attack on her was a win. Once she was at the center of the circle, she could release the prepared time travel spell she'd worked on for months. It would only take an instant to activate it. They'd never catch her once it went off and sent her into the past.

A whirr of wings from above her gave Joanna just enough warning to dodge the swipe from the glowing silver blade. It was a good thing, too. That blow would have decapitated her. Rolling across the ground, she came back to her feet and blocked the next blow with her own blessed blade.

The ring of metal on metal echoed through the night as the two mighty swords met. Sparks flew from the magical blades as they crashed together.

Joanna pointed a finger and blinding darts of lightning launched from her fingertip at the winged woman fighting her. At this range, she couldn't miss.

Electrical energy surged into the Eldara's chest. With a look of shock, the formerly immortal creature collapsed, dropping the glowing silver blade to the ground as she did. The silvery light faded from the metal, along with the life of the one who'd wielded it.

Joanna didn't have time to gloat. This wasn't the first of the foul creatures she'd killed. She hated all those who'd done their best to destroy the world these last twenty-odd years. Instead, she spun around and raced towards her principal objective while she searched for the other Eldara. Shouts and snarls raged all around her in the darkness as her team fought their way through the ever-growing numbers of demonlings waiting for them.

She kept her eyes open as she moved. A flash of light to her left jerked her gaze that way. She winced as she saw the winged enemy cut down one of her team members. They'd never stood a chance against one of the angels fighting from above. The people with her were good, but few of them could stand up to one of the Eldara alone.

Ripping her gaze away from her friend, she focused on getting through the last bit of brush and into the remnants of the living room with the inlaid marble floor and its spell circle.

She made it to the center and reached up to clutch at the silver charm around her neck, releasing the stored spell. The Eldara from outside had spotted her and charged in at her, wings propelling the angel straight over the crumbled wall. The male Eldara laughed as he neared, his glowing sword outstretched towards her chest.

Just before the blade struck her, the spell went off, and she tumbled backward into the temporal vortex. Her visceral scream of success echoed in her ears alone as she tumbled back to a simpler time.

———

Joanna sat up, wiping the sweat from her eyes, gasping for breath. It was just another dream. She'd made it, though the dreams continued even weeks later. She was here, and now she could make it all right again. Swinging her legs over the side of the stained flophouse mattress, she got up and crossed the tiny motel room to the sink with its dripping faucet. Cupping her hands, she splashed cool water on her face.

These people did not know how good they had it. Most people in her time hadn't had actual running water from a tap in decades. It hadn't taken long for the trappings of civilization to fail once the war began.

That was when the dying started.

Shaking her head, Joanna looked up into the mirror, her one good eye staring back at her from a face she hardly recognized. She avoided her reflection back home. The scars and leather eyepatch reminded her of everything she'd lost over the years. But that was why she was here in the past. She had to find out what had happened when her father had stopped the four horsemen and the Eldara from starting their war to end the world. She had traced it all back to that moment in time. If she could make that right, then her future would never happen and maybe everyone she cared about would still be alive.

Chapter 1

PARAMEDIC DEAN FLYNN finished pushing the syringe and disconnected it from the IV tubing. Beside him, a pair of Elk City fire-fighters performed CPR on the man lying on the living room floor. Dean looked up and checked the heart monitor, watching the tracing of the line that showed the heart rhythm. Ventricular fibrillation, again.

"Leah?"

His probationary paramedic, Leah Casado knelt beside the heart monitor. She glanced at the screen. "V-Fib, shock him again." She reached over and laid her finger on the monitor's shock button, ready to deliver the charge she'd dialed in. Leah glanced around the area around the patient saying, "I'm clear, you're clear, we are all clear." She made a last check to make sure no one touched the patient and pressed the button. The man's body jerked and then went still again.

Leah called out. "Resume CPR."

The firefighter kneeling next to the patient leaned over, beginning compressions again. Kneeling beside the man's head, another fire-fighter continued to operate the bag-valve mask, squeezing the bag and breathing for the patient in between compressions.

Dean watched the monitor and looked over at his probie. "What next?"

"We pump him some more and check for a pulse."

A ripping snarl interrupted their conversation before Dean could reply. On the floor, the man's body sprouted fur along his exposed arms, chest, and face. His fingers elongated into talons and the face pressed outward against the oxygen mask, turning into a wolf-like snout, complete with sharp canines. The cardiac arrest patient had not just revived after the shock but also turned into a werewolf.

The two firefighters performing CPR jumped backward from the snarling creature awakening before them.

"Get back in there. We have to hold him down." Dean followed his shout by diving across the body, pinning the arms of the struggling beast to its side. Clearly, this guy's pulse had returned. As he returned to life, his shifter instincts triggered his change to wolf form.

Dean struggled, losing the battle to control the creature beneath him. Leah joined him, gripping the struggling wolf's arms at the wrist, holding the guy down. She lent her own incredible shifter strength to Dean's paltry human efforts. Together with the two firefighters joining in, they were able to hold the werewolf down.

Behind Dean, a woman's voice came from the open front door. "Another save? That's two this month, Dean. You two are going to get the department's resuscitation award this year if you keep that pace going."

Dean craned his neck to see his supervisor and former partner, Lieutenant Brynne Garvey, standing there. "They never give it to paramedics from Station U. With shifters and other Unusuals who regenerate, truly fatal cardiac arrests are few and far between. More often than not, they resuscitate themselves, like this one did. We just show up to monitor his progress."

Brynne shrugged. "I'll still put in the paperwork. You two shocked him to get him back. They've got to recognize the extra difficulties we have in these situations."

The patient had stopped struggling. The werewolf settled down and shifted back into a man as he regained control of his faculties. "M-m-my chest hurts." A groan followed his gasping words as the pain of repeated, vigorous chest compressions and cracked ribs settled in.

Dean and Leah relaxed. The two sat up from where they'd been laying across him. The firefighters backed away as well, gathering their gear and cleaning up the area around the guy.

"Sorry about that," Dean said. "You went into cardiac arrest and we had to perform CPR on you."

The man's eyes widened at the words. "I was dead?"

"Near enough," Leah said. "We pulled you through, though. You still need to go to the hospital, but I think you'll be alright once the cardiologist gets a look at what's going on with your heart."

The man nodded, then called out as he spotted his wife and children standing in the corner. They'd watched everything.

Before he could say a word, the wife said, "No more cheeseburgers for you. We are switching you to fish and salad from now on."

The man groaned again as Dean and Leah shared a smile. Brynne walked over to the family and took down some additional information while Leah and Dean packaged their patient for transport to Elk City Medical Center. Dean guessed this patient was destined for the hospital's cardiac catheter lab. They needed to open up the arteries that sent blood to his heart. It was just another day in the life of a Station U paramedic.

A half-hour later, Dean and Leah rolled back into the parking lot at their station. The average passer-by would never know an ambulance station sat in the run-down industrial park at the edge of the city. Despite the sketchy surroundings, though, Dean felt at home in this nondescript location. He and his partners here treated the supernatural creatures of Elk City and its surroundings. Their work was vitally important to all the Unusuals in the area.

Pulling around back, he drove up in front of the ambulance bay doors, waiting for them to rise so Leah could get out and help him back in. She hopped out and walked around back.

Once parked, Dean shut off the engine. He plugged in the land line power cord and then headed back to help Leah restock their supplies from their last call. It was almost the end of the shift and there were a lot of things to get done if they were going to leave on time.

"That was weird how he came back suddenly like that. Does it happen like that all the time?" Leah asked.

Dean shrugged. "With shifters, it does. We usually see them come back that way before we ever get to check for a pulse. It's the best sign we have of a spontaneous return of circulation."

Leah shook her head, lost in thought as she considered what her partner said. Being a were-jaguar, she knew much about the Unusual community, but she still had a lot to learn about the medical care they needed. Dean hoped she wasn't the last Unusual to join the team. It was good to have someone from the community they served working alongside the human paramedics that staffed these special ambulances.

Dean nodded towards the rear doors of their unit. "I can finish up here. Why don't you go in and get started on your report? It's almost the end of the shift and it would be nice to get out of here on time for a change."

Leah nodded. "It has been a little busy lately, hasn't it? When will it settle down again?"

Dean smiled. "Your guess is as good as mine. Sometimes things get busier than usual for no reason. Brynne will let us know if anything special is going on."

Leah left to get her patient reports in order. Both of them were more than a little overworked right now. In fact, all the paramedics in the city were feeling the strain with an increase in minor accidents and medical calls causing all sorts of trauma and injury. It could be just a random spike in ambulance calls, but Dean worried it was something else. He'd learned to distrust coincidences.

By the time Dean finished restocking the meds and supplies, Leah had added the finishing touches to her report at the computer workstation inside the squad room. She looked over as Dean entered and said, "Do you want to come over here and check on what I'm doing? I think I've got everything filled out correctly. It's only the second time I've filled out the special form for a cardiac arrest."

"Just drop it into the system. It'll show up in my queue for me to sign off on it. That way it'll send the report to the hospital for their records, too. They'll need it to add to the guy's medical reports while he's there." Dean scanned the break room. "Hey, where's our relief? They're usually here by now."

"Not sure. The place was empty when I came in from the ambulance bay."

Dean scanned the room and called out. "Freddy, are you here?"

"In the kitchen, Dean," a gravelly voice called from the far side of the room. "I'm just finishing up dinner. It'll be ready in a few minutes if you have the time to stick around and eat."

"Where is the next shift? Brook and Tammy should be here by now."

Freddy poked his head out from the small kitchen that served the station. The zombie's gray skin stretched thin over his bones. "They came in early and racked out in the bunk rooms. They both looked beat."

Dean smiled. Both of them were parents and sometimes came into the station early to catch a nap before work since they couldn't often get a lot of sleep at home. He guessed having children around tended to make too much noise. He decided to let them wake up on their own while he finished up the last chores of the shift.

It took Dean and Leah twenty minutes to finish up and sit down to eat dinner. Brook was the first to stumble out of the women's bunk room. She gave a wave and headed into the bathroom to freshen up.

Tammy emerged next and headed straight for the station's coffee maker to pour herself a fresh mug of Freddy's excellent coffee. "How was your day?"

Dean finished the food in his mouth before answering. "Crazy. We haven't been back to the station until now. I hope your evening goes better."

"Me, too. Brook and I have been running non-stop on our last few shifts, too."

"Come. Sit and eat something. The ambulance is ready to go for you so you don't need to do the checks right away. This crab cake sandwich is amazing."

Freddy beamed from where he stood nearby, his thin lips separating in a smile, revealing his gap-toothed grin. "I'm glad you liked it, Dean.

I'm using a new spice blend besides the traditional Old Bay seasoning."

Tammy took a bite of hers and sighed. "Freddy, you're a genius. How do you keep getting better at this all the time?"

The zombie chef shrugged. "It's just nice to be appreciated." He headed back into his kitchen, leaving the paramedics to enjoy the food.

Dean had finished his plate and stood to take his dishes to the sink. He picked up Leah's empty plate on his way by. She nodded thanks without looking up from her phone.

Leaving the dishes in the sink for Freddy to take care of, Dean waved at his colleagues. "I'm getting out of here. Don't stay here too long, Leah. We've got an early start tomorrow."

She waved to indicate she'd heard him while continuing reading what was on her phone. Dean smiled and left her to her texts, chats, or whatever occupied her time after work. She'd earned a break.

Outside, Dean pulled his coat close around him to ward off the late-December chill. He'd be glad when it wasn't dark at both ends of his shift anymore. A person needed a little sunlight once in a while. He checked his phone, hoping to get a message from his wife. She'd been down in Baltimore at a security conference all day, and he wanted to hear she was on her way home.

The screen showed no new notifications. Still no word.

Disappointed, Dean climbed into his pickup truck and started on his way home to wait for his wife to return. He would be glad when her schedule settled down as well. They needed to reconnect and start sharing regular meals again. He almost wished something would come up that required their joint attention, even though that type of thing meant a crisis of some sort going on.

Dean shook his head, banishing the thought. It was foolish to wish for something like that.

As he drove from the parking lot, he never noticed the woman in a long, black duster step away from the shadows beside the station. She watched him drive off, then snapped her fingers and disappeared.

Chapter 2

DEAN PULLED into the underground garage below the Errington security building and stopped before reaching his parking space. His wife's black SUV sat parked in her slot next to his. He hadn't known she was back yet. She usually texted him. Pulling into his assigned spot, Dean checked his phone again to see if he'd missed a message about her return. He had not.

Grabbing his gear and backpack, Dean climbed out of his truck and headed inside the building. The guard greeted him from behind the desk just inside.

"Hey, Jed, when did she get back?"

"A few hours ago, sir. Something came up here and she had to leave her meeting early."

"Anything serious?"

"I think she should tell you herself, sir. She's on the second floor in the armory."

Dean nodded, puzzled by the guard's response. He had a pretty good rapport with the Errington security team members. It wasn't just that he was the boss's husband. He and various employees talked about things going on in the world all the time. It was odd for Jed not to tell him what was happening.

Getting on the elevator, Dean rode to the second floor. He'd only been to the building's armory on a few occasions, like when they set out to fight off the pending apocalypse the previous year. Errington security teams carried a variety of weapons in their assignments as members of corporate protective details. This was in addition to their other hidden work fighting demons and rogue Unusuals all over the world. It had impressed Dean with the weaponry inside. He'd seen it all when Jaz gave him a tour after the building first opened. In his work as a paramedic, it wasn't a place he needed to worry about.

Dean spotted Jaz as soon as he exited the elevator. She stood outside the armory's reinforced steel door. She looked up when he approached but didn't return his smile. He decided that couldn't be good.

Dean approached and gave a brief hug to his wife. She returned it but pulled away quickly. He knew she didn't like public displays of affection in front of her subordinates. Dean glanced into the open armory. "What's going on, Hon? You didn't tell me you were back. I was surprised to see your truck downstairs."

"Dean, there's been a situation. Some of the guys were doing a regular inventory of supplies today. It's something they do every month. They found some pistols and ammunition missing from the armory, so they went back and did an audit of everyone who signed in using a passcode to check out weapons and gear."

"So?" Dean asked. "Someone forgot to check their pistols back in. You guys have weapons stored in the lockboxes inside all the vehicles. They're probably in there."

Jonas Storm, Jaz's second in command, shook his head. "We thought about that. We've checked all the vehicle inventories. Nothing is out of place, and there are no extra pistols in any of the lockboxes. We returned here to see who's been in the armory and came up with a bit of an anomaly, sir."

When he finished talking, Jonas turned and glanced at Jaz with his eyebrow raised in question.

Dean looked back-and-forth between Jonas and his wife. What were they getting at? "What's going on? I get the feeling there's something you're not telling me."

"Dean, it's just that when we checked into who signed in to retrieve the weapons, we came across someone who used the private family code that only you and I share."

"Oh," Dean said with a smile. "So, you're the one who lost the pistols."

"Of course not. I don't lose pistols. They're too important and shouldn't be left lying around. However, that leaves you."

"Me?" Dean raised his hands to his chest, palm outward. "Wait a minute. You know how I feel about guns. I haven't even been in this room since our big fight last year. You logged us in then. I honestly don't even remember what the code is."

Jonas sighed. "I figured as much. Sorry to suspect you about this, Dean. But we had to check." He glanced at Jaz. "You know what this means, don't you, ma'am?"

"It means we have a security breach. I want a complete sweep done of the interior of the armory, especially the locked bins where those two pistols sat. Every weapon requires a separate code to release it from the lock box. I want to know how they got past that. See if we can get a DNA swab or something to identify the person involved. And review the interior camera recordings. Let's figure out exactly when they went missing."

"It has to of been sometime within the last two months. That's when the code was entered." Jonas held up a tablet and scrolled through some information before continuing. "It says here that was entered into the system about a week before the vampire and the werepanthers kidnapped you."

Jaz shook her head. "I know that's a long time and many people have been in there since, but let's do the swabs and check for DNA residue anyway. We pay that lab a lot of money to be available at a moment's notice. Let's put them to work for a change."

Jonas nodded, tapping at his tablet as he walked away. Dean waited until Jonas had entered the elevator before turning back to his wife.

"Hon, I swear I have nothing to do with this."

She reached out with her arm and pulled him close, her hand snaking around his waist. "I know that. We'll sort this out. Now give me a kiss. It's been a long day."

Dean leaned down towards her, enjoying the quiet moment with his wife. They'd had very few of those since their brief honeymoon a few months ago. It would be nice if this problem kept her around home for a change.

Following that line of thought, Dean asked, "I don't suppose you're able to stick around for a few days? Is that conference canceled or do you have to go back tomorrow?"

"I'm staying close until we get to the bottom of this. We need to find out where the security breach happened. That code should've been known only to you and me. I entered it into the system myself, and it's not like someone could've hacked in there to get it. That system isn't connected to the outside world. In order to hack it, someone would have had to come into the building."

"Well, that makes it easy," Dean said. "The camera footage will reveal everything."

"But it'll take time. What if the breach happens again? It's just strange. There are so many other kinds of weapons in there someone could've grabbed. Some of them are quite powerful, both magically and conventionally. But all they took were a pair of Glocks just like the ones I use."

Dean smiled. "I don't suppose you have an evil twin you haven't told me about, do you?"

Jazz gave him a playful punch in the shoulder. "In your dreams, husband of mine. Come on. Let's go upstairs and get something to eat."

"I had something at the station, but I'd be happy to sit down with you while you eat your dinner."

"Oh, what did Freddy make tonight?"

"Crab cakes."

"Ugh, my favorite. Why didn't you bring me any?"

"I didn't expect you home in time for dinner. Let me call the station and see if he has any extras. If you want, I can go get one for you."

"No, don't do that. Knowing Freddy, he'll go to all the trouble of making a fresh batch, and I don't want to make him do that. Just remember next time to bring me home one, even if I'm not in town. It can live in the freezer until I get back."

"That's a deal. Come on. Let's go upstairs."

The two of them headed to the elevator to ride up to the top floor. Having Jaz home early was a pleasant surprise that Dean intended to take advantage of. It would be nice to settle in together for the evening. He could put something on the TV for the two of them to watch and just have an ordinary night at home. This whole breach was probably nothing serious. The building was a fortress, and Dean suspected the whole thing was a mistake.

Chapter 3

JOANNA WALKED up the steps to the second floor of the motel and down the outdoor walkway to her door. She took the brass key from her pocket and slid it into the lock. She froze.

The door popped open on its own as soon as she'd inserted the key. She'd been sure to lock that door when she left, and there was supposed to be a do not disturb sign hanging on the knob. That guy at the front desk was going to get a piece of her mind if he let the maids clean the room after she specifically told him to leave it alone.

Leaving the key hanging in the doorknob, Joanna swept back the long, black duster she wore, reaching down with both hands to draw the twin pistols on her hips. Willing her night vision to engage, she stepped inside the darkened room, scanning from left to right, both pistols outstretched in front of her.

She'd only gone two steps before a voice behind the door spun her around to face the small table and chair there. "Goodness gracious, Granddaughter, is this any way to greet me when I go to the trouble of coming all the way down here to visit you?"

Joanna lowered the pistols, but only halfway. "What are you doing here, Gabriel?"

"You left a message you needed to speak to me." He spread his arms and nodded at her. "Here I am."

Joanna shook her head. "I told you I'd come to you. How did you find me?"

"It wasn't that hard. I knew you didn't have a lot of resources here in the past, so I figured you were staying somewhere like this dump." He looked around, his lip curled up a little in disgust. "This is only the second one I checked. You'd be surprised how easy it is for people around here to remember a person like yourself. You're quite striking, you know. The eyepatch in particular stands out."

"I'll have to have a talk with the clerk at the front desk. I paid a little extra to have some anonymity."

"You're a little hard for people to forget that way, Joanna. I made one mention of a woman with an eyepatch at the convenience store across the street and the guy practically fell over himself telling me all about your coming and going back to this motel."

Joanna ground her teeth. So much for trying to fly under the radar. She had to wonder if anyone else had noticed she was in town. No one knew her back in this time and place, but she didn't want to draw any attention to herself. She'd already taken too many risks as it was, and she had to limit contact with people connected with her in this reality.

"Relax," Gabe said. He gestured at the chair across from him at the table. "I'm here, now. Tell me what it is you want."

Declining a seat, Joanna said, "I want to find out why you haven't leaned on Dean to get him to do what you've asked of him."

"It's not that easy. He doesn't like to hear from me on the best of days. Now that he owes me something, he avoids me like I want money from him."

"Then you need to go see him instead of coming here. He made a deal and he'll stick by it. You just have to lean on him a little."

"Why is this so important to you? You're acting like there's some kind of hurry. Judging from your age, you're at least 30 years in the past. Certainly, you have had plenty of time to do whatever it is you need to do."

"Never mind about that. Just make a point to see Dean face to face and make sure he knows what you expect of him."

"I'm not even sure he knows how to do what you want him to do."

"What WE want him to do," Joanna said. "This is in your interest, too, remember?"

"Tell me again why I want my son to do this?"

Joanna hesitated for just a second before continuing. "Are you happy with being stuck here on earth like this? I would think you'd want to be back in the heavenly planes where you belong."

Gabe studied her, his eyes seeming to bore into her soul. Joanna held his gaze. She couldn't let on how she was manipulating him. It was possible he suspected she was up to something. She could never let him know what the world became and how he had a part in that.

"I'll reach out to Dean again as you ask. Maybe he'll make some time to come see me. When he does, I will need to know the plan. Tell me what it is we want him to do. I'm still not sure how you expect him, of all people, to correct the error he made when he closed the portals."

"You let me worry about that. I'll have information on what he's to do, but first we need him to commit to being ready when you send him instructions. He can't avoid you. Understand?"

Gabe nodded. He got up from where he sat, turning to slip between Joanna and the table before stopping at the door. He glanced over his shoulder. "I don't like it when humans try to trick me, girl. I know you're up to something. When I figure out what it is, you'd better hope I don't think you're working against my best interest."

Joanna said nothing.

Gabe nodded and left, pulling the door closed behind him. She hadn't realized she'd been holding her breath. She let it all out with a long sigh. Part of her hated just being around the archangel. She wanted to execute the Eldara every single time she saw him. It wouldn't be a simple thing to do, but she'd killed his kind before. Now that he was grounded, she'd have a better chance than if he discovers how to recover most of his powers here on Earth. Once that happens, Joanna feared she'd never be able to stop what was to come. Right now, he was her only opportunity to fix things.

She moved to the window, looking out over the parking lot, she watched as Gabe climbed into his used sedan and drove off. She still enjoyed hearing the running of a car's engine. Funny how things like cars, or even guns that still had ammunition were such common place objects in this world of the past. It had been so long since she'd seen either that it made her want to stay here, even though she knew that could never happen.

A thought occurred to Joanna. Gabe had been in here for some time before she got back. She got down on the floor to check under the bed. She relaxed when she spotted the package, still wrapped in plastic, sitting under there. Reaching for it, Joanna slid the bulky object out into the open. She stood and pulled the curtains closed before unwrapping the plastic. Taking great care, she lifted the leather-bound tome up to the table and flipped it open. She stared at the ornate calligraphy before turning to the position marked by a slip of paper.

Gabe was right about one thing. She did not know exactly what it was she needed her father to do. All she knew was that Dean had started this process and, given her understanding of magic and how it worked, he was the only one who could set things right. She sat down and leaned forward, studying the ancient tome on the history of magic and interplanar travel. This was the book she'd first used to come up with her spell to return to this time and place. Now it was the book that hopefully held the answer to how she would get her father to save the world from a war that would kill billions.

It was almost dawn when Joanna found what she was looking for. At first, she didn't want to believe what it said had to happen. She considered searching the book again to see if there was any other way to go about this. Shaking her head, she realized that would only delay the inevitable. This was the only way, and there was a sort of circular synergy to it.

A plan formed in her mind as she sorted out how she was going to get this done. Getting up and stretching a little, Joanna moved to the bed, laying out a towel on the patterned bedspread. As she usually did when confronting troublesome problems, Joanna found it relaxed her to clean her weapons. While she was thinking about how to get this all to work, she disassembled both her pistols and began cleaning them.

Joanna reassembled both before beginning again. She went through this process three times before she slid both weapons in their holsters and set them aside. She got up and walked into the bathroom to stare into the mirror once again.

"Am I really going to do this?"

The face on the other side said nothing in reply, and she shook her head. There'd always been a fear of what she'd discover once she got back here. All she could do now was face up to it and try to get a few hours of sleep before she put things into motion. Waiting for a better plan wasn't an option. She was already almost out of time. She pulled the burner phone from her pocket and tapped out a message to Gabe so he could get the ball rolling.

Chapter 4

DEAN SAT in his parked pickup truck and stared at the building in front of him. He couldn't believe he was using his valuable day off to come here and meet with Gabe. His father had been insistent, however, reminding Dean that he owed him a debt. Gabe had helped to get Jaz back when a pack of werepanthers kidnapped her. Dean didn't enjoy owing Gabe anything and would not stay in his father's debt any longer than he had to.

The whole thing made Dean a little nervous, though. He didn't know what it was his father wanted. He hoped it wasn't anything illegal. That was one reason he hesitated to go inside. Dean didn't trust Gabe. The Eldara had already tried to double-cross him once, hoping to trick Dean into starting Armageddon. Dean had figured a way around that trap. Now he had to be wary of any tricks Gabe had in mind this time.

Grumbling under his breath, Dean climbed out of the truck and went inside a nondescript door beside the music shop. He took the stairs up to the third floor and stopped outside Gabe's apartment. He raised his hand to knock, but the door opened before his knuckles made contact. Startled, Dean stepped back, unsure what to expect.

Gabe stared out at him from where he stood midway across the small room. "Don't just stand there gawking. Come inside and sit down. We've got a lot to talk about."

Dean paused for a moment then stepped inside, pushing the door shut behind him. The apartment was a simple one and not up to what Gabe considered a suitable standard for an archangel. Dean didn't care, though. The fact that Gabe was living in this place was his own fault.

"Come, sit." Gabe gestured to a pair of stuffed chairs sitting in front of the television.

Dean remained standing a few feet from the door. "I'm hoping you can just tell me what it is you want and I can leave. Not sure I want to stay and hang out."

"You're my son, Dean. We should be able to sit and talk a little bit. Is that so difficult for you?"

Dean ground his teeth, then nodded and moved to sit in the chair closest to the door.

"See, that wasn't so hard." Gabe took a seat in the chair beside him.

"What is it you want? I know this is about what it is I owe you. I'm good for my debts, but I'd like to get this one paid and be done with it."

Gabe laughed. "Is owing your father a favor really such a horrible thing? I'm not going to ask you to kill your wife or anything like that. It's not that much of a request when you think about it. I just want you to make things right again."

There it was, Dean thought. Gabe wanted him to start the end of the world. The way he said it off the cuff like that made it seem like the most innocent of requests, but Dean saw through it.

"I will not let you start a war. If you try to start the apocalypse again, I'll do everything in my power to stop you."

"I want nothing of the sort. I only want things to go back to the way they were before you and I met. That can't be such a bad thing. Everything was pretty normal then, right?"

"You're still speaking in riddles. Tell me the specific thing you want me to do for you."

Gabe smiled. "I want you to open the gateways to the upper planes again. Make it so I and the other Eldara trapped here on earth can go back home."

"Tired of living like us puny mortals?"

Gabe shook his head. "Stop being sarcastic. That attitude doesn't suit you. Set into motion what needs to happen to open the gateways again. Do that and I'll be out of your way. I'm not going to start a war. You won't let the demons come up from hell, if that's what you're afraid of. Just think of it as a little reset after the dustup we had here last year."

Dean studied his father's face, searching for any sign of trickery. He knew something hidden lurked behind the man's eyes. That reminded him he couldn't trust anything his father said at face value.

"So what if I do this for you? Does that mean you'll leave, and I won't have to see you ever again?"

Gabe shrugged. "If that is what you want, I can oblige you, but that will be up to you. I'd like to think we can still see each other from time to time."

Dean snorted a laugh. "You act like you and I can have any kind of real father-son bond. You weren't there when I grew up. Then, you show up a year ago to get me to destroy the world. Now, you want me to act like none of that happened and take you back as a father? It doesn't work that way."

Anger flashed across Gabe's eyes. "You owe me. I saved your Hunter wife's life when no one else could."

Dean's voice raised as his own anger bubbled up to meet Gabe's. "I'll satisfy my debt to you. No more tricks or word puzzles. Tell me what it is you want me to do. If it doesn't endanger the entire world and the people I love, I'll help you reopen the gateways."

Gabe's anger disappeared as quickly as it appeared. Dean wondered if it had all been an act. "Well, you see, I'm not all that sure how this is going to work. You're going to have to figure some of this out on your own. You're the one that started this and you're the one that has to figure out the solution."

Dean stared at his father for a few seconds, trying to understand what he was saying. "I do not know how to make this right. I don't even know where to begin. If that's the best you can do, then I'm afraid I cannot satisfy your request."

"I didn't say I wouldn't help. But you need to be the catalyst to moving this whole thing forward. You need to visit the Oracle of Elk City."

"What the heck is that? I've never heard of such a thing."

Gabe nodded. "I know that. Oracles, by their very nature, hide themselves from most of the communities in which they live. There is one, though. I'm sure of it. You'll just have to ask around. You have enough contacts in the Unusual community that you should be able to figure out a way to locate them. Once you do, they will start you down the path to opening the gateways again."

"It's not much to go on. I'm not sure how much time I can devote to chasing this Oracle down. I still have to work, and there are other obligations."

"You'll figure it out. After all, you're my son. I know you won't give up on a task once it's set before you. Find the Oracle. Ask them how to satisfy your debt to me. They will pass along the answer you seek."

Dean stood and opened the door. "I'll see what I can do. I'll reach out when I've discovered what the Oracle wants."

Gabe said nothing, just nodded. That lack of a farewell or good luck from his father irked him, though Dean didn't know exactly why at first. It wasn't until he got back into his pickup that he realized a small part of him, deep inside, wanted a normal relationship with the man. That realization bubbled up anger at Gabe all over again. Shaking off a wave of disappointment in himself, Dean started his truck, wondering how he was going to track down this hidden Oracle he'd never heard of before.

Jaz must've been watching where he was via GPS because as soon as he left the parking lot at Gabe's apartment building, she pinged his phone. Dean answered as he drove away.

"Hey Honey," Jaz began. "I saw you were on your way back. Did it go okay?"

"Yeah, I've figured out what he wants. It seems like my father doesn't like it here on earth very much and wants to go home."

Jaz paused for a second before answering. "He thinks you can do that?"

"He does. Gabe says I'm the one to do it, though he doesn't know how. Not a lot of help when you think about it. He says I have to talk to someone called the Oracle of Elk City. Do you know anything about that?"

She answered right away. "That's not good, Dean. The Oracle is nothing but trouble. She's associated with local crime families because of her ability to help them predict the success or failure of their next underworld venture. There's a price to pay for her advice."

"Well, I don't have much choice in the matter. That's who I have to talk to. Who would I see about getting in touch with her? Would James or Rudy be able to help, or is there someone else entirely?"

"Actually, you might be able to get an answer the next time you're at work. You'll be close to an underworld connection there."

It took Dean a few seconds to realize his wife referred to his new probie partner. He needed to cancel that idea right away. "Leah wants nothing to do with her family's criminal background anymore. That was pretty clear when she last saw her father. You were there. I'd rather leave her out of this."

"I know, but she's the only connection I can think of who might be able to get you access to the Oracle. It's up to you, but that's the best way."

Dean didn't like the answer, but he didn't say anymore. He didn't want to take his anger at Gabe out on her. It wasn't Jaz's fault. "I guess I'll just have to think about it for a while. Maybe there's another way. I hate to get Leah all mixed up in my personal business. She's a good paramedic, and that's all she wants to be."

"She's also a grown woman, Dean. Let her decide what she wants to do."

Dean said goodbye and disconnected the call while he thought about what his wife had suggested. She wasn't wrong about giving Leah the choice, but he wanted to make sure she didn't feel any sort of pressure to help. He was technically her supervisor. Dean would have to think about how best to approach this with her. He took some extra time while he drove around the city, trying to clear his thoughts before heading back home. In the end, he decided he'd bring it up the next day, when he and Leah were on shift together. It was better to get out from under his debt to Gabe anyway he could. He'd make it up to Leah later.

Chapter 5

THE FOLLOWING day Dean and Leah ran nonstop calls from the moment the two of them got into the station. It left him little time to approach her with his request to locate the Oracle. By late afternoon, they drove out on their tenth call of the day. This one had them heading downtown for a twenty-four-year-old male with severe abdominal pain. Dean knew the general vicinity, but it was all warehouses and such. He didn't know about any homes in that area. Dean trusted in his dispatch instructions, though, following the directions from the ambulance's GPS system.

They came off the highway ramp and turned to the left. That took them around so they passed back under the highway overpass. While they were under the highway bridge, the GPS said they should be on location. Dean slowed the vehicle and looked around. What he found surprised him. There, nestled under the bridge, between two massive concrete supports, was a tiny two-story home tucked back so the roof almost touched the overpass's steel girders.

"What a strange place for a house."

"I guess it takes all kinds." Leah picked up the microphone from its clip on the dashboard and called in to dispatch. "U-191 on location."

The dispatcher responded, acknowledging her message. Dean

pulled up in front of the ramshackle house, parking by the front steps. He got out and helped Leah gather their gear to take inside. Abdominal pain could be almost anything, so they grabbed both the trauma and medication bags, as well as the heart monitor and portable oxygen kit.

Leah was in charge, taking the lead as she went first up the three steps to the front door. She lifted the old brass knocker and let it fall twice. A few seconds later, an enormous old woman with gray hair answered the door. She was both very round and very tall, topping Dean by at least six inches.

"Oh, good, you're here," she snapped. "Come with me. He's downstairs in the basement."

Leah glanced back at Dean and shrugged. Dean nodded towards the interior and she followed the woman inside. Dean stepped in right behind her. He paused for a second inside the front door as his eyes adjusted to the darkened home. There were few lights on. In addition, what shades and curtains he saw were all closed to keep the light filtering in from outside to a minimum. The woman hadn't slowed, and neither had Leah. Both of them were Unusuals and could see in the dark just fine. He had to move fast to catch up as she led them down a narrow entry hall into the kitchen.

She turned and pointed to a door in the corner. "He's down in the basement. The door and the steps are right there. Maybe you can convince him to come up and do something constructive with his life for a change."

"Uh, yes," Leah said. "Thank you, ma'am. We'll take it from here."

The new paramedic opened the door and started down the steps into the dark in the basement. Dean was right behind her. He reached for the penlight flashlight in his pocket. There was even less light down here. Leah, with her shifter senses, might be able to see in the dark, but he couldn't.

Just before he switched on the light, his eyes picked up a blue-white glow coming from the other side of the low-ceilinged basement. There, in the corner, sat a short, fat man with long greasy hair, wearing a headset. The swiveling desk chair turned as they approached. Behind their patient, a double row of computer monitors were mounted on the concrete wall. Dean looked around for cues as to the man's Unusual type or identity but could find nothing that helped him figure it out.

Leah called out to the guy as she approached. "Excuse me, sir, we are paramedics. The call to 911 said you had abdominal pain?"

"Yeah yeah, I can barely stand up it hurts so bad. What the hell took you so long? I've been waiting here in agony for at least ten minutes."

Dean resisted the urge to snap at the guy. They'd hurried to get here while still driving safely. Ten minutes wasn't that long to wait. The guy was conscious and talking, so things couldn't be that bad.

Leah had things in hand, though. "Sorry for the delay, sir. We are here now, so why don't you tell us what's going on."

"What do you think's going on? My stomach hurts. That's what I told the idiot on the phone. I don't know where you got that guy, but he's got a bucket of crap for brains. You're lucky Yelp doesn't let you leave reviews for 911 services. I had to tell him four different times to stop asking me stupid questions and send me an ambulance."

"He was just doing his job, sir." Leah set her gear down beside the man's chair and began her examination. The guy had swiveled back around and resumed tapping away at his keyboard. "If you'd stop typing, my partner and I can see what we can do for you. That way we can figure out what's wrong."

"Give me a second," The guy snapped. "I have to finish up this review for the pizza place that delivered my lunch." He tapped a few more times, then hit the return bar and swiveled back to face Leah. "Hey, you're a cute one."

Dean started to say something again. This guy was way out of line. He bit his tongue instead and stopped himself. His partner glanced back at him over her shoulder and gave him a reassuring nod. He had to remember Leah's considerable were-jaguar powers could handle this guy if she decided to put him in his place.

Instead, Dean set down the equipment next to her and asked, "What do you want me to do?"

"Why don't you get his vital signs while I ask him some questions about his stomachache."

Dean took out the blood pressure cuff and plugged the tubing into the heart monitor so it would read on the screen. Then he wrapped it around the man's enormous upper arm. While the patient wasn't as tall as his mother, he certainly had inherited her bulk.

Leah continued asking some basic patient history questions and jotting the answers down on a notepad she'd fished from her jacket pocket. Every answer the guy gave included a snide comment or complaint. At this point, Dean was ready to strangle the guy, but Leah still kept her cool.

As she finished with her standard medical history questions, she asked if she could lift up his shirt and look at his stomach.

"Hey, I didn't know I was going to get undressed by a pretty girl when I called 911. I should've called sooner."

That was it for Dean. "Hey, watch it buddy. She's a professional, and she's here to help you. Treat her with some respect."

Leah glared at Dean and he realized he'd overstepped. He nodded his apology and stepped back a bit. This guy pushed all Dean's buttons in a way no patient ever had before.

Turning back to the patient, Leah asked, "Let me just take a look to see if I can spot any bruising. Have you fallen recently?"

"Fallen for you, if that's what you mean. Maybe I can get your phone number and we can catch up in a few days. I'm sure this will go away on its own."

"Maybe, but let me figure out what's going on here first." She reached over and pressed on his abdomen with her fingertips, checking all four quadrants. When she got to the lower right side and pressed down, the guy winced a little. The stronger reaction came when she released her fingers, though. He jumped out of his chair, screaming in pain.

Dean nodded. Rebound tenderness in that location was a classic sign of an inflamed appendix.

Leah caught on right away, too. "I think we should get you packaged up to go to the hospital, sir. You're likely to need surgery."

"What are you talking about? Can't you just give me something for pain and go away?"

"No, sir. I think you need to get your appendix out. Only the hospital will know for sure, but we probably need to take you in."

"I'm not going to that stupid hospital. The last time I was there, they gave me horrible service. I spent a week leaving horrible reviews for every doctor I saw." The patient looked at Dean. "You guys can't take me if I don't want to go, right?"

"We cannot, but she's correct, sir. That appendix needs to come out. Unless you're prepared to stay here and do it yourself, we should get you in to see a surgeon right away."

A voice called out from the stairs. "Chester, listen to the nice people and go with them. Don't make me have to take you in myself. I won't be happy with you, believe you me."

The guy craned his neck around and snarled back at his mother. "Why don't you stay out of this, Ma. I'm a grown man. I can take care of myself."

She laughed. "If you were a grown man, you'd have your own house and would not be living in your mother's basement like some kind of loser. Now, listen to the paramedics and do what they say, or I'll shut off the internet again like last time."

Dean hid a smile behind his hand as he coughed to cover up his reaction. He moved forward again and removed the blood pressure cuff, returning it to its pouch.

"So what will it be," Leah asked. "You can ride with me in the back of the ambulance and we'll get you to the hospital just as quick as can be."

The guy's snarling visage turned almost pleasant. "Well, if you're going to be there, I guess it can't be all that bad. You're going to give me your phone number, right?"

"We'll see, but first let's get you to the hospital." She moved to help him stand.

Dean finished gathering up the gear while Leah assisted the guy to the stairs and up to the kitchen. He hobbled to the front door, clutching at his stomach the whole time. Despite his angry responses, Dean could see he was in a lot of pain.

Fifteen minutes later, they left him in the care of the nurse at the ER. At least he was nice to his new caregiver, asking for her phone number, too. Dean chuckled as he and Leah put fresh sheets on the cot before rolling it back out to the ambulance.

"At least he stopped asking for your phone number once he saw Barbara come in."

"You just have to know how to deal with his type. They're all the same."

"Who's all the same?" Dean asked. "I never figured out what kind of Unusual he was. I sometimes can see the clues, but this time there was nothing."

Leah looked at him wide-eyed for a few seconds, then started laughing. "Dean, think about it. He and his mother live under a bridge. He's obnoxious and spends all his time on the web with his computers." She stopped and stared at him, waiting for what she said to sink in.

It took a few seconds, but then he realized. "Oh, my God. That guy's a real, honest to goodness internet troll?"

Leah nodded, still chuckling at his response. "I guess you still have a few things to learn, too, eh, Boss?"

"My rule is if you're not learning, you're not living, Probie. I'm learning something new every day on this job."

Leah nodded as they continued down the ramp to their waiting ambulance. Together they loaded up the cot and got it back on the street, ready for their next call.

Chapter 6

ON THE WAY back from the hospital, Dean decided it was time for him to ask Leah about where to find the Oracle. He didn't want to just ask outright, though. He thought that would be rude. Instead, he started off asking her about her work.

"How do you think you're fitting into the job so far, Leah?"

"I don't know. You tell me."

"You're a great paramedic and you have a good bedside manner with your patients. I think you will be a great asset to the Station U team. That's not really why I was asking. I wondered if you still have some issues dealing with your father's response to working here. I know he wasn't thrilled with you."

Leah didn't answer right away, causing Dean to glance in her direction as he drove. She stared at him, meeting his eyes with a quizzical look on her face.

As he looked back to the road to drive, she said, "Dean, we've talked about my father before. You know I don't enjoy discussing him. I have to deal with him from time to time, but I've got a handle on that. You know all that. I have to wonder what you're getting at. Have you heard of problems with my family connections from the Chief or someone else in the chain of command?"

Dean shook his head. "No, no, it's not that at all. I apologize. I shouldn't have worried you. Everyone is thrilled with your performance so far. The EMS Chief told Brynne how pleased he was to sponsor an Unusual cadet through the academy. No, I was trying to come up with a way to ask you something, and I didn't know how to approach it exactly. It's related, at least in part, to your family's background and I wasn't sure how you'd react. It's sort of important to me, though."

"Then just ask me. If it's something I don't want to tell you, then I won't."

"Fair enough." Dean realized his entire body had tensed up and he'd gripped the steering wheel hard enough to make his knuckles ache. He took a deep breath and forced himself to relax. "The thing I needed to ask about was if you knew anything about the Oracle of Elk City? I need to locate them for a personal matter."

"Why would you want that? Trust me, the Oracle is nothing to fool around with. My father has had dealings with her frequently and he's never been happy with the results."

That answer surprised Dean. Based on what Gabe had told him, the Oracle and criminal enterprises worked hand-in-hand. "So the Oracle doesn't work for your father?"

"The Oracles are a thing all unto themselves. They don't work for anyone. They're all a loose conglomerate of seers and soothsayers from various cultures around the world who can see things in the mystical world others cannot see. Each has their own agenda and though they work for different organizations like my father's cartel, they consider themselves independent contractors at best." She cocked her head to one side. "You still haven't told me why you need to talk to this one. This isn't something you should take lightly. There are those who believe the Oracles don't just predict and read what they see. Some say they use their clients to make things happen that benefit them."

Dean didn't answer right away. He wasn't sure he wanted to explain Gabe's request to Leah. The more he thought about it, the more he realized that wasn't fair. He had no problem asking her to open up about her family, the least he could do was open up about his own, too.

"It's my father. He wants me to do something for him and I'm not sure how to go about doing it or even if I want to do it. How do I make sure the Oracle is on my side and not his, trying to fool me somehow?"

"That's easy. Don't do it."

Leah's immediate response surprised him. She continued before he could defend his reasons.

"Look, Dean, I know if my father came and asked me to go back into business with him, I would say no instantly."

"It's not that simple. I owe him a debt and I have to pay it back. I don't like owing him anything."

Leah paused for a few seconds as they drove along. "It's because he saved your wife, right?"

Dean nodded.

She let out a long sigh. "Okay, I can tell you what I know about the Oracle. I'll tell you how you can get in to see her, but that doesn't mean you're going to get any kind of answer to whether or not you should help your father. The Eldara have a way of manipulating things to get their way as much as the Oracles do."

"That's an understatement." Dean hesitated before continuing. Then he decided he'd shared this much, he might as well share everything. "I've told you a little about what he tried to get me to do when the four horsemen of the apocalypse showed up. To fulfill my debt to him, he wants me to undo some things I did then to hold off the end of the world. He assures me undoing them won't endanger anyone, but I'm not so sure."

Leah chuckled to herself. When Dean glanced her way to see what she'd laughed at, she said, "Looks like you have daddy issues just like I do."

Dean responded with a laugh of his own. "Aren't we quite the pair? All grown up and still dealing with stuff like that. Still, I have to do this, Leah. I'll be careful, I promise."

"I'll make a few calls and get you a location and instructions on how to get inside. The Oracle doesn't just let people walk up and ask for readings. You have to jump through a few hoops to get there. It's all part of the mystique from what I've heard."

Dean didn't like the sound of that, but he didn't have a lot of choice. He'd already told Gabe he'd figure it out and go see the Oracle. Now that he was committed, he'd have to go through with whatever it took.

The rest of the drive back to the station was silent. Leah worked on her reports on the laptop while Dean thought about what she had said. It sounded like the Oracle was every bit as tricky a character as his father was. That would require him to be extra careful in the encounter. He might need to do a little extra research before he went.

Bill and Barry were waiting for them when they got back to Station U. Barry stood in the ambulance bay as Dean pulled up. He helped Dean back the unit into position, then closed the overhead door for him.

Bill worked on a checklist for the inventory of medication supplies in the dispenser sitting at the back of the parking area. Dean waved and finished locking down the ambulance and plugging everything in. He didn't know why they'd come in early.

"What are you two doing back in the station before the shift's over?"

Bill looked up from his tablet and smiled. "Overtime, my man. The chief approved it so we could get caught up. He noticed how busy we were. Brynne must have explained how we'd fallen behind on some of the regular duties, so he authorized Barry and I to come in a little early and get caught up."

"Does that mean Leah and I don't have to do normal chores to check out today?"

Barry nodded. "Bill and I are just about finished. Once we wrap up, we're going in and getting an early dinner. Freddy got things started sooner than usual when he heard about the extra OT."

Dean smiled, as did Leah at hearing that some of their regular work duties were put aside for the day.

"Leah, why don't you get your reports finished up. I'll come in and double check them as usual. We might actually be able to take a few moments to relax before our shift ends."

"That sounds great. When I'm done, I'll look up that information you wanted."

Dean nodded, watching her head into the squad room.

"How's the new probie working out?" Barry asked. "You miss me as your partner, right?"

"She's doing great," Dean replied. "And no, I don't miss you and your constant bad jokes. She's much better company."

Barry assumed a melodramatic expression, pretending shock. He threw his arms wide and gaped at Dean. "Well, I am seriously offended. I mean, how could anyone not appreciate my superior sense of humor and clever repartee?"

Bill snorted a laugh as he raised a hand. "I thought I had a terrible sense of humor, but Barry, you take it to new levels I could never attain."

Dean laughed as Barry's expression shifted to his new partner. "You two are perfect for each other."

Barry smiled. "We are, aren't we?"

Dean left the two of them in the ambulance bay, swapping bad dad jokes, and headed into the squad room.

Leah had finished up the final bits of paperwork and sent them to Dean's account. She stood up. "I'm going to go out in the parking lot and make a few calls about that thing you wanted."

"Sounds good to me. I'll look over your reports and get them completed. Thanks for looking into that for me."

Leah waved off his thank you and walked out through the station's front door. Dean logged in and looked over her reports. He rarely had to make any adjustments. She'd mastered that part of the job quite well. It might've been that she already had a college degree and knew how to write pretty well. Maybe she was just good at this job. Either way, he was glad she was working out as well as she was.

He finished up in a few minutes and clicked to send them through into the system with his approval. Pulling out his phone, he checked his messages to see if Jaz wanted him to bring anything back for dinner.

She replied back right away, telling him to pass on that and come home. She said she had something special planned. That got him kind of excited, and he went to double check that the regular end-of-shift duties were completed and got ready to leave.

By the time he'd finished the last check, Leah had returned to the squad room. She sat at one of the computer stations tapping away on the laptop. She finished and glanced his way.

"I was able to contact someone about the Oracle, Dean. I've emailed you some instructions based on what they told me. They want both you and your father to make an appearance together. I hope that's not a problem."

Dean winced, but then held up a hand when Leah started to say something. "It's okay. I'll work through it on my own. The fact that they want Gabe there might be a good thing. I'd like to see him squirm a little, too."

Leah got up to grab her things and headed back outside.

Dean called in to the ambulance bay where Barry and Bill still worked on the med inventory. They waved goodbye, and he followed Leah out to their vehicles. His mind wandered back to what Jaz had said. He got excited about the surprise at home and jumped into this truck. He'd put aside everything about the Oracle for now. There'd be time to worry about that later.

Chapter 7

JOANNA STARED down into the glowing water. The dollar store stainless steel bowl sat on the bed in front of her. The polished metal reflected the light upward, illuminating her face as she leaned over. Her hands wove complex patterns in the air above it as she continued to stare into the depths inside. A shiver passed down her spine as she realized what it was she saw. There was no way it could be true, and yet her scrying was rarely wrong.

"No, it can't be happening. Not yet." She'd planned her spell to return to this time and place carefully so she'd have plenty of time. The incursions weren't supposed to begin for at least another year.

Shaking her head, the sorceress drew in more power and delved deeper, looking for a hidden meaning behind what she'd foreseen. After several minutes, she gave up, wiping beads of sweat from her brow. All she could see was that the first of the netherworld incursions would happen that evening.

Judging from the strength of the impression, it wasn't far from where she sat. Lowering her hands, Joanna let the spell dissipate. The glow faded as the magic left and she stood, taking the bowl and dumping it out in the sink in her tiny bathroom.

Returning to the main room, she grabbed the matched pair of

holstered pistols, clipping them to her belt on either hip. She grabbed the sheathed Katana from where she'd propped it by the door. Once her weapons were in place, she slipped on the long coat to hide them and left. If she hurried, she might make it in time to close the rift before anything came through.

Ten minutes later, the taxi dropped Joanna off at a corner beside an open-air flea market in a parking lot. It spanned a full city block. The street lights over the lot provided plenty of illumination for the stalls as the vendors sold their wares to the public milling around after their long work days. Joanna slipped the driver a few bills, muttering for him to keep the change. As she did, a scream split the night, rising above the buzz of the crowd.

Damn, she was too late.

Joanna charged through crowd. As she got closer to the center of the market, the crowd shifted from folks milling around shopping to people running away from something.

She jostled through the fleeing masses. The terror-filled eyes of the people she passed now told her everything she needed to know about what awaited her. The rift had opened and at least one of the demon-spawn had broken through. She had hoped the bystanders would get away without seeing what the world held for them in the near future.

The crowd thinned. Ahead of her, screams and shouts rang out. Another familiar and dreaded sound rose above the din of the crowd, the ripping snarl of a fetchling. Smaller and less deadly than a fully mature Fetch demon, the greater members of demon-kind often used fetchlings as scouts. It made perfect sense to send one of them through a small tear in space to see if the world on the other side was ready for the coming invasion.

Drawing a pistol in her left hand and her Katana in her right, Jo raced up to the side of a small outdoor shed and peeked around the corner. The red and black scaled fetchling stood over a woman, tearing into her dead body with wanton abandon. This class of demonling weren't too bright and were easily distracted from assigned tasks. It was something Joanna had taken advantage of before.

She couldn't use magic against it because the three-foot gap of the rift still lay open just behind it. If she used any of her powers here, those on the other side would sense it. It might spur them to send more through sooner. That meant she had to kill this thing in a more conventional manner.

That wasn't impossible, just difficult with what she had at hand. She glanced around the shed again to check if the thing had moved and spotted a man with broken and bloody legs crawling away from the hell-spawn and the dead woman.

The fetchling spotted the movement at the same time Joanna did. Distracted from its first kill, the thing bunched up its powerful legs to pounce on a new target.

Cursing, Joanna charged out from behind the shed, shouting at the monster. "Over here, demon-spawn. Why don't you try out someone who is a little more prepared to face one of you scum suckers?" Her noisy approach worked. The fetchling's head swiveled in her direction.

Raising her left hand, she emptied the magazine into the thing's face as she charged straight at it. The bullets impacted, jarring the creature backward until it stood several feet behind the woman's body.

The demon's snarling mouth drew back in an approximation of a human grin. Its mouth opened and a loud, booming voice came out from it. Fetchlings couldn't speak on their own, but they could provide a conduit through which their masters could talk.

"You're too late, sorceress. We've started what you cannot stop. We will have this realm for our own. There's nothing you can do to prevent it."

Joanna growled in reply, holstering the pistol and switching the katana to her other hand. She raising her other pistol and fired off another full magazine into the fetchling.

When she raided her mother's armory, she failed to find any blessed silver alloy rounds, so she'd settled for these armor-piercing bullets. She'd taken the time to inscribe a few spell runes on them, though. They wouldn't kill the thing, but they'd cause a lot of pain and slow it down enough that she could use her sword to finish it.

She holstered her pistol just before she reached the fetchling. Gripping the Katana with both hands, she swept it down at the creature.

With surprising swiftness, the fetchling batted it away, somehow catching the flat edge of her blade before the razor edge contacted its head. The incoming weapon pushed aside, it leaped forward at her.

Joanna planted her foot and pushed with all her strength, launching herself into the air. She muttered a spell under her breath, levitating up and over the creature's attack. The demon lords on the other side of the rift had sensed her presence, so there was no need for secrecy anymore.

Executing a somersault in mid-air, Joanna landed and brought her blade around to strike at the fetchling's back.

She managed a glancing blow that sent the thing howling in pain as it spun away from the attack. She flicked droplets of black ichor from her blade onto the pavement. They sizzled, causing tiny streams of smoke to rise up from the ground.

The fetchling bellowed and turned to charge back at her. The wounds caused by the bullet impacts had already started to close on the creature's face. For a moment, Joanna considered a spell, but decided it wasn't worth wasting the power when she knew her sword could do the job.

As the fetchling charged, Joanna surprised it by lunging forward to meet it. Her sword lanced outward, slashing and thrusting at the same time. The attack caught it across the throat, cutting deep.

With a screech and a gurgling snarl, the fetchling stumbled and slid on the pavement past Joanna as she stepped aside like a victorious matador.

Not satisfied with a suspected kill, Joanna swung downward and hacked through the creature's spine right behind its head with her blessed silver sword. The creature twitched a few times before letting out a groaning sigh. It was done.

Joanna checked the area around for any other demons. There were none, and the rift had already closed. All she saw were the bodies of the woman and the man who'd tried to get away. She shook her head. The guy had bled out before she could get back to him. He lay there, his sightless eyes staring back at her, terror locked on his face's dying expression.

A siren sounded in the distance, followed by another in a different direction. Joanna realized she needed to get away before she had to answer awkward questions from local authorities. She considered casting a spell to destroy the demon's body, but there wasn't enough time. Besides, someone might be watching from nearby and see her do it. She was sure there were others hiding amidst the stalls who'd seen the fight. It was better if they had less to say about the woman who'd killed the monster.

Joanna bent down to clean her blade, using the dead woman's shredded blouse. Then she sheathed the sword, pulled her duster close to conceal her weapons, and jogged away from the sounds of the approaching police.

Once she'd crossed the nearby street and left the area of the flea market, she slowed to a walk and tried to blend in with the crowds. Many people were out and about the downtown shopping and dining district. Once she was two blocks away, she hailed another cab and got in, giving the driver an address a block away from her motel. She'd walk the last bit, just in case they questioned him about where he'd left her.

As she settled back for the ride, Joanna rethought her plans. There was no way she could afford to wait for her father or that Eldara to get a move on. She was going to have to kick things into motion for herself. She'd avoided it until now because of the potential temporal paradox it could cause. Up to this point, the less contact she had with her family, the better. Now that was a luxury she no longer had.

Fifteen minutes later, back at her room, Joanna refilled the scrying bowl and added another pinch of the magical reagents from the pouch at her belt. The powder dissipated in the liquid as she leaned over, whispering the words of the spell. This time she searched for something here in the present related to the future from which she came. It was a more difficult spell to work, but it was important based on what the demon had said back at the flea market. Something it said made her wonder if her return to the past had made a change to things she hadn't envisioned.

For a long time the glowing liquid remained cloudy. Then the liquid cleared and Jo leaned forward, staring deep into the deceptive depths. Her eyebrows raised in surprise. "No, that's not right. It's too soon. They won't understand."

She leaned back, letting the power slip from her. The spell faded along with the glow from the bowl. She stared at the wall across from her while the magic dissipated. She wasn't sure how long she sat there staring into space. All she could think of was whether her parents would understand what was happening? She had hoped to avoid seeing them in person, but now she knew that was impossible. They deserved an explanation. She hoped she could give them one they would accept.

Chapter 8

DEAN ARRIVED home to find Jaz in the kitchen, cooking dinner of all things. She rarely cooked, though she was good at it when she did. As the successful CEO of her own company, she felt her culinary talents were wasted when she could hire someone else to do the same job. It was one reason she encouraged Dean to bring home food from the station when Freddy made extra. Dean smiled, walked up behind her at the stove, and leaned over to give her a kiss on the cheek.

"What's the special occasion?"

"I just thought maybe we could spend some extra time together this evening. I was able to wrap up some things early tonight, so it seemed like a good time to be with my husband. Is there anything wrong with that?"

Dean shook his head. "Not at all. I heartily approve of spending more time with your husband. Let me go shower and change. I'll come back and help you with dinner."

"That's alright, I'm almost done. Get your shower and I'll get things on the table by the time you get back."

Dean gave her another kiss and headed back to the master bathroom. He got undressed and turned on the shower. He always looked forward to rinsing off after a long day at work. It wasn't that he was a germaphobe, rather it was more symbolic than that. He saw people during the worst days of their lives. He usually brought order to the chaos, but he always felt like some of it rubbed off on him.

Standing by the shower, Dean reached in to test the water temperature. As he stood there waiting for the water to warm up, he glanced down, spotting the edge of something plastic in the wastebasket. He leaned over to see what it was, pulling out the 4 inch plastic stick. Turning it over, he spotted a blue plus sign in a clear window midway along what he now realized was a pregnancy test.

He stared at it for at least a full minute, trying to make some sense of the mixed emotions of shock and joy coursing through him. He looked back towards the kitchen. Is this what she had in mind for this evening? Did she want to tell him over a nice dinner? He didn't want to ruin the surprise for her. Dean dropped the test back into the wastebasket, covering it with some other trash. He'd have to try to act surprised when she broke the news.

As he got in the shower and tried to focus on cleaning up, dozens of questions raced through his brain. Foremost among them was trying to understand how they could be pregnant right now. He laughed a little at the thought. It wasn't entirely impossible. The real issue was he knew they were destined to have a daughter together, but not right now. By his reckoning, they weren't due to give birth to Joanna for another few years. Surely she would've told them when she came back in time if she had a sibling.

He dried off and got changed into a pair of shorts and a T-shirt and headed out to help his wife finish setting the table for dinner. He needn't have hurried. She had already gotten everything on the table and sat in her spot waiting for him with a big smile on her face.

Dean smiled back at her as he sat down. "So, what's the special occasion?"

Jaz frowned, then shook her head. "Damn, I left it in the bathroom trash bin didn't I?"

"What are you talking about?" Dean asked, trying to act innocent.

"Oh, stop. You're horrible at hiding things from me. I could tell as soon as you walked in that you'd found it. Ugh, pregnancy brain is already setting in. I meant to dump the trash in the chute in the hallway before you got home and I just got distracted by dinner."

Dean hurried around the table as Jaz stood. He pulled her into an embrace, holding her there for a long time. He whispered in her ear. "When, how?"

Jazz shrugged, saying, "I'm not sure. I was assuming we wouldn't get pregnant until we were supposed to have Jo in a few years."

Dean held her at arm's length so he could see her face. "My thoughts exactly. How far along are you?" He glanced down at her flat stomach.

Jaz shook her head "I have to go to the doctor to be sure. My guess is six or seven weeks, maybe? I'll know more after the appointment tomorrow."

Dean took his seat as Jaz returned to hers. He dished up his dinner and found himself stopping and looking up at her, unable to hide the big grin across his face. It was a feeling he couldn't explain, even to himself. He'd wondered about this moment for a while, but the unexpectedness of it, and the way it had caught them both by surprise, made it special in its own way.

As they ate, they talked about random things, but each time, the subject came back around to the baby, leaving them both smiling back at each other.

Finally, Jaz said, "Look at us. We're like a bunch of complete goofballs here. I would think we would've been able to handle this like adults, but I can't help but feel like a teenager getting caught by her parents with a boy in her room."

"I feel the same way. Maybe it's just because we weren't expecting it right now. Do you think it's Joanna? "

Jazz shrugged. "I guess it could be. Maybe her math was off from when she came back in time. If she's like every other teenager I've ever met, it wouldn't be the first time they got a math question wrong."

Dean joined her in shared laughter. He felt light, almost giddy, and wondered how she felt. He was about to ask her when her phone rang. Recognizing the distinctive ringtone from one of her security supervisors, Dean waited while she answered it.

"This is Jaz." She paused, listening for a few seconds. "Are you sure it's a demon?"

Another pause, followed by a stern shake of her head. Whoever it was on the other end of the line relayed quite a bit of info before she said anything else.

"Alright, work with the local police and start the usual cleanup protocols. I'll be there as fast as I can. We need to make sure the bodies aren't tainted in any way from the demon's teeth or claws. They may have to bring in a shaman or a witch from the local coven to double check. We need to make sure they won't later reanimate."

She nodded once and hung up the phone.

Dean stared at her for a second before saying, "A demon? Where?"

"Downtown. At the Route 40 flea market."

"Here? But I thought you had wards and things set up around the city for that kind of stuff."

"I did, which is how we sensed its arrival. Unfortunately, my teams weren't able to get there in time. Two people are dead."

"Well, at least your team killed the thing, right?"

"That's the strange part. Someone else got there first. They killed it before anyone else from the police or my security squad could get there. People reported it as a woman with short hair, blonde on one side and purple on the other. A few bystanders claimed she wore an eyepatch which should make her easy to spot in a crowd. We'll see. It's probably something they thought they saw or added in the heat of the moment in their minds."

"Could it be another hunter from another clan in town?"

"It better hadn't be. The protocol is to check in when you enter someone else's territory. If they're here hunting on my ground without telling me, that means there's trouble afoot. There'll be hell to pay. There's a reason we do things the way we do among the clans. It's to keep innocent bystanders from being killed like what happened tonight. If someone knew there was going to be trouble like this and didn't tell me first, then I want to know why those lives couldn't have been saved."

Dean understood. The various Hunter clans around the world operated independently, but they had a few rules they followed when working in tandem. He found it hard to believe someone from another clan came here without at least paying respects to the clan leader first.

"What are you going to do?"

Jaz started towards the hallway where the lockbox with her sidearms was located. "I have to go down there. Maybe there's some residue or something I can sense to tell me who it was that dispatched the demon. It might lead me in their direction. I don't like freelancers running around on my turf. You shouldn't either. People like that aren't careful and could kill a peaceful Unusual living here. We don't need that kind of bloodbath on our hands."

"No, we don't." Dean stood. "I'm coming with you. I'd like to see this for myself, and maybe I can help smooth things over with the local authorities. "

"Suit yourself. I don't know how long I'll be and I know you have to work in the morning."

"I can handle a late night if need be. If you're there too long, I can always go back to your truck and sack out for a bit until you're ready to come home."

"Fair enough. Let's go."

Dean followed her out the door, their earlier joy forgotten for the moment in the midst of this crisis.

Chapter 9

DOWNTOWN, Dean sat in the passenger seat while Jaz got out and talked to one of the responding officers at the scene near the flea market. The authorities had formed a police perimeter around the area while they gathered evidence. It was also always a good idea to keep bystanders away from the carcass of a dead demon in the middle of town. Jaz showed her ID and got back in the SUV, driving forward slowly while two officers lifted the yellow crime scene tape so they could drive under and proceed the rest of the way in to the market.

"What did he say?" Dean asked.

"He didn't know that much about what was happening. He thinks it's some sort of drive-by shooting or gang violence. It's probably better that way. He saw a few people from one of our Errington teams go by already, so we should be able to get a better report once we get down there."

She drove forward another block and parked along the curb behind a line of police cars. She climbed out and Dean followed her as she walked into the center of the market. They passed through rows of vendor stalls, all deserted now.

Dean tapped his wife on the shoulder and pointed ahead. "There's Jonas."

They walked forward to meet the Errington team leader standing talking to a police detective. Dean recognized the detective as one member of the police's own Station U team. He couldn't recall the guy's name.

Jaz waited till Jonas finished the conversation, then walked over to talk to him. "Anything new to report?"

"No. The bystanders all report the same thing. A woman armed with some kind of pistol and a sword charged the creature soon after it appeared and killed it. The story we're spreading is that it's some kind of escaped zoo animal and she was one of the keepers."

Dean nodded. It was funny how people accepted excuses for what their mind couldn't understand. If they wanted to think it was an escaped reptile from the zoo, he would not disavow them of the impression.

Curious, Dean walked farther in towards the center while Jonas and Jaz talked to each other. He spotted the demon beside a body with a sheet draped over it. It was one of the two deceased people from the attack. A quick look around revealed the blood stains farther along the pavement where another body must have been. The coroner had already retrieved that body.

He walked over and studied the area. He could tell the person had dragged themselves a little distance along the pavement from the way the streaks along the ground led up to the larger stain of pooled blood.

Someone called his name and he looked up to see who it was. He spotted Barry and Bill coming in from the other direction. "Hey guys. You here to pick up the bodies?"

"We responded thinking there might be other people injured. Now we're just helping the coroner clean up. He's got his van here at least, so we don't have to carry any of the bodies for him in the ambulance."

Barry stared down at the sheet where they stopped with their stretcher. "This one's a woman, Dean. The thing savaged her pretty bad. Hopefully, she was dead by the time it started to dig into her. It looks like it might've been eating on her."

Dean frowned. He crouched down and lifted the edge of the sheet, staring for a few long seconds at the carnage beneath. He'd seen some severe attacks in his day, but this had to be one of the worst.

Lowering the sheet again, he stood back as his colleagues loaded up the body.

Bill nodded to where Jaz stood talking to Jonas. "I sure hope they can figure out who let this thing loose."

"What makes you think someone let it loose?" Dean asked.

"Someone said they spotted the person who killed this thing. My guess is she let it get loose and then had to track it down before it got to somebody. Apparently, she was too late to clean up her own mess."

"Have you talked to the police about this theory of yours?" Dean asked.

Bill frowned and Barry said, "Don't listen to him. Bill's just playing through his usual conspiracy theories. From what I heard, the woman who showed up here saved a bunch of other people from getting killed as well. There's nothing to show she had anything to do with it. Probably just lucky to be in the right place at the right time. The people here were lucky she knew how to deal with the problem."

Bill shook his head. "So you say, partner. I want to know why she showed up armed to the teeth and had the right weapons to do the job. Sounds like somebody who knew what was coming, or who knew something had gotten out."

Dean said, "Maybe it's best if we leave the police work to the police. They've got people trained to do this kind of thing and they might be better qualified to look into who's guilty of what."

Barry and Bill lifted the stretcher up to waist height so they could roll it back towards the other side of the flea market. As they left, Jaz came over and stood beside him. "Any interesting news from those two?"

"Bill thinks the person who killed the demon is the person who released the demon."

"Interesting theory. What does Barry think?"

"He sees it the way I tend to look at these things. People around were lucky someone was here who knew how to deal with the problem. I don't automatically think the same person is guilty of something, but I guess it's something worth looking into, especially if you think it was a hunter who did this."

Jazz said nothing. She paced around the demon, staring at it while she stroked the silver charm around her neck. It was infused with powerful magic, though Dean wasn't sure how it worked. Maybe she could see into the past with it.

She made three circuits around the body before she stopped. "The demon came through a rift just over there. You can see how some of the pavement is split apart from the opening in space and time. Whoever fought the demon used powerful magic of their own. That's probably the woman the people spotted. According to Jonas, the detective said some people saw someone matching her description get into a cab a couple blocks from here. They're looking into finding out who it was. When they have a location, I'll have my team go with them. This person is powerful. That makes her more than the local Station U police squad can handle on their own."

Dean's eyebrows shot up. "Do you think there's going to be trouble? She could be one of the good guys."

"She's powerful and has magic besides her obvious weapons skills. That's not a combination you find very often, and it's definitely not something from one of the other Hunter clans. That alone is enough to put me on edge. Plus, if she's one of the good guys, why didn't she check in to let us know she's in town?"

"I don't know. Maybe she's on vacation."

Jaz snorted a chuckle and shook her head. "Always the optimist, Dean. It's one reason I love you."

He smiled, then nudged the demon carcass with his toe. "What about the demon? Do you know what kind it is and how it got here?"

Jaz crouched down beside the carcass. "It looks to be some kind of little Fetch demon. I've not seen this kind before, but that's what it looks like to me. Once we get it back to the Errington building, I'll have one of our exobiologists come in and do a full autopsy on it. We should be able to match tissue samples to other demons we've tagged in the past and come up with a type and at least some of its abilities in case others like it show up. I'll also have a better idea of what it is and where it came from."

"You said it came through a rift over there?" Dean nodded in the direction she indicated earlier. "Maybe it squirmed through a hole by accident?"

"Something this small doesn't have the power to open a rift like that on its own. Plus you shut down all the major gateways to the other planes, remember? It shouldn't have been able to get through at all."

"Oh, yeah. I'd forgotten about that. So, how did this one get here, then?"

"Good question. That's one thing we need to figure out, and sooner rather than later. If one of these can come through, then there's no reason to think others won't follow. A demon incursion like this on a regular basis could cause a lot of problems and we're already spread pretty thin."

Jaz turned and took a few steps back towards where they'd parked. She stopped and looked over her shoulder. "You coming?"

"What, you're done already?"

"I've seen everything I need to see down here. The police are taking control of the bodies, and Jonas and his guys are bringing the carcass back to our HQ. Until they complete the autopsy, we won't know anything. I've got a taste of the magical residue from the scene. If we run into this mysterious woman, I'll know it right away."

"I guess that means we can get back to our romantic evening, then." He pulled her close.

Jaz's eyes narrowed. Dean stepped back and raised his hands. "Kidding. I know you'll have too much on your mind for the rest of the night to relax. Can I help with anything?"

She shook her head. "No. I need to reach out to the other Hunter clans and see if they've seen anything like this in their regions. Maybe they've spotted this rogue out slaying demons in their backyards, too."

Dean nodded and followed her back to their SUV. Jonas came over to see them off. He told them he'd drop off any additional information from the police in a report via email should anything else come in overnight."

Jaz fired up the engine and pulled away from the curb. She slowed just long enough for the police officers to lift the caution tape up so they could drive under it again. Then she picked up speed and they headed home.

Dean knew from prior experience she had a million things going through her mind at a time like this. She was good at what she did, and it was best to let her percolate through her ideas on her own. It didn't mean the complete shift to the evening's plans didn't disappoint him. He wanted to talk about the baby some more, but now wasn't the time. She was in full on Hunter mode now and she wouldn't appreciate him distracting her from that. She didn't need to add a grumpy husband to the mix. Resisting the urge to say anything, Dean looked out his window and watched as the streetlights went by on their way back home.

Chapter 10

FOR TWO DAYS, Dean hardly saw his wife. They came and went from the apartment, both so busy with work they barely talked. He managed to catch a few important snippets of information from her, though. The autopsy hadn't turned up anything new, other than confirming it was a previously unknown type of Fetch demon.

Her contacts with the other Hunter clans around the world discovered nothing helpful, either. No one knew of any rogue hunter roaming around the world. All of that sent Jaz into a foul mood. She didn't like puzzles she couldn't unravel, and this one affected the safety of her own backyard.

Dean's days on the ambulance filled up with hours of extra overtime as the call volume ramped up even more. He asked Brynne about it, but she couldn't shed any light on why more Unusuals were getting sick or injured than normal. It was like everyone was on edge and making stupid mistakes that ended in trips to the hospital.

He had a couple of days off coming up, though. He looked forward to the respite from his time on the ambulance and maybe spend some more time with Jaz, too. It wouldn't be all relaxation, though. This opening in his schedule allowed him to follow up on seeing the Oracle with Gabe. He couldn't put that task off any longer. He'd looked over the instructions Leah had sent him. While they seemed straightforward, there was a lot left unsaid, including the statement that he and Gabe would have to pass some sort of test before they could get in to see the Oracle. That kind of statement concerned him. It could mean almost anything.

Jaz wasn't there when he got up the next morning. He found a text from her on his phone saying she'd headed down to meet with a demonologist in Baltimore who might have information on where the demon had come from. She'd reach out later about whether she'd be home in time for dinner.

Having the day free to get his task with Gabe over with, Dean sat down and got himself some breakfast. His meeting with Gabe and the Oracle later that morning set his mind to cycling through all the possibilities it might bring up. The apprehension of spending the morning with his father, coupled with tension about visiting the Oracle, merely added to the leftover unease from his work week. He wanted Gabe out of his life, especially now that Jaz was pregnant. He saw no reason for their baby to get to know her grandfather. Only trouble could come from it. The best way to do that was to do what the Eldara wanted him to do and find a way to open the gateways to the heavens again.

Dean checked his watch and got up from the table. It was time to go. Gabe had offered to drive by and pick Dean up, but Dean told him no. He preferred the two of them meet at the location. That way, they could go their separate ways once the Oracle finished relaying her instructions. He checked the directions from Leah to note the address and bring up his phone's GPS. The location was over in a manufacturing district of the city. That surprised him. He would've thought an Oracle with this kind of magical juice would have lived in one of the city's upscale residential neighborhoods.

The directions led him to the front of a two-story brick building with a sign that read "Carrie's Meat Products." He chuckled to himself. That wasn't very specific. What did they mean by "meat products?" He guessed he'd find out soon enough, since he had to go inside to locate the Oracle.

Dean parked out front and dropped a few quarters into the parking meter before he walked inside. There he found a bustling retail business with a combination of glass refrigerated cases and wooden counters lining the wall opposite the entrance. The cases were filled with various cuts of meat and sausages. As he read the tags next to the various steaks and roasts, he saw normal things like beef and pork and even a few chicken cuts. The surprising part was the non-standard meats available. Tags in one case labeled alligator, ostrich and emu, and even bison cuts. He wondered where a butcher in Maryland had found a bison.

The place was busy with about twenty customers milling around. They had been taking numbers at the counter and now waited their turn. Pulling out his phone, he glanced at Leah's instructions again. One thing he hadn't understood earlier told him to get in line. Now it made sense.

Walking up to the machine that dispensed the numbered tickets, Dean took one. His number was sixty-four.

He glanced up at the electronic sign on the wall. "Now serving number 47." Figuring he'd have to wait awhile, Dean walked over and waited his turn in a spot where he could see the rest of the shop. He was standing there when Gabe walked in. The Eldara didn't spot him right away, so Dean walked over and cleared his throat.

Gabe smiled. "Oh, there you are. This isn't what I expected at all."

"Me, neither. I'm not sure what it is we are supposed to do."

Gabe stared at him. "You were supposed to get instructions on how to do this, Dean. I'm not the one who needs to see the Oracle. You are."

"Don't get that way with me. I reached out for instructions. One of them was that you had to be here, too. I guess we'll figure the rest out as it goes along."

Gabe crossed his arms, not saying anything for a few seconds. He looked around and shook his head. "What's with all the people, can't we just go up to the counter and get what we need?"

Dean nodded. "My instructions say to wait in line. My guess is that means we wait for our number to be called." He held up the ticket.

Gabe glanced from the ticket to the number on the electronic sign.

It had moved up to fifty-one. He grumbled something and moved over to the corner where he leaned up against the wall to wait. Dean chose a spot a few feet away where Gabe would be close enough to join him once the number came up, but not close enough to engage in any conversation.

It took twenty minutes. A chime sounded announcing another number change. Gabe spotted it first and nudged Dean so the two of them could walk up together. Dean had been scrolling through his phone, checking messages and emails. He flipped back to the email with the instructions from Leah.

Dean still stared at his phone when the woman behind the counter asked them, "What'll it be?"

He gave the phone one last glance to be sure of what to do next and said, "I think I need to see one of your special cuts."

"You think you need to see it, or do you know you need to see it? There's a difference and a lot will be riding on whether or not you understand that."

Dean thought this matronly woman must be the Oracle herself. "Excuse me for my hesitation, Madame Oracle, it is a pleasure to meet you."

The woman laughed. Several of the other people working behind the counter overheard what Dean said and laughed as well.

"Oh, I'm not the Oracle, kid. But you'd better be damned sure you actually want to go back and meet her before I let you behind this counter. "

Dean swallowed hard. He nodded. "I'm sure. I want to see your special cut."

"Fair enough. Don't say I did not warn you." She gestured to Gabe. "Is the old guy with you?"

Behind Dean, Gabe grumbled, "Yes, we are here together. And I'm not old, I am ancient, ancient beyond years. There's a difference."

The woman smiled. "If you say so. Since you're here for advice with your friend, I suggest you get a better attitude. People don't always like what they hear back there. So don't go unless you have no other choice."

Dean glared at Gabe. "Stop making this harder than it needs to be. Come on. Let's get this over with."

Looking back at the woman, Dean nodded again. She moved aside and lifted up a hinged portion of the counter, revealing a small opening for Dean and Gabe to pass through to the back. They followed her through a doorway covered with thick hanging strips of plastic. They kept the chill of the refrigerated area behind the main showroom separated from the customer counters out front. Dean shivered as he passed through the opening.

About a dozen people in white coats worked next to long, stainless steel tables with drains cut in them. Each dripped blood to the floor beneath, where it followed channels in the concrete towards metal grates set in the floor. The workers cut and hacked at the large carcasses on the tables, cutting away slabs of meat.

They followed the woman as she wound her way among the tables. At one point Dean slipped in a pool of blood next to one of the butcher tables. He nearly fell to the floor next to one of the grates. Dean caught himself just in time, and stared at the iron grate for a moment. Snarls and growls came up from below.

Standing and checking his footing, Dean moved away from the drain in the floor, though he glanced back at it several times. He wondered what lived down there, lapping up all the drained blood from the carcasses.

The woman led them back to a table that stood apart from the others. The woman behind it had to be at least six feet tall and had the build and bulk of a professional wrestler. She wore a plain, white tank top, stained red with flecks of blood as she carved away at one of the largest animal carcasses Dean had ever seen. Her muscles rippled as she moved a two-foot-long, curved blade through the meat with the precision of long practice. He wasn't sure what kind of animal it was, but the roasts and steaks she cut away from the bone were enormous. When they stopped by the table, she didn't even look up. She kept slicing away.

The woman from the front said, "They want the special cut." She winked at Dean and left them there, waiting for the butcher woman to stop working and tell them where the Oracle was.

For a while, she said nothing, continuing to carve away at the giant beast. Dean glanced at Gabe. He was no help, he just shrugged.

"Um, excuse me. We are here to see the Oracle of Elk City?"

"I am the one you seek," she said without looking up. Her accent seemed Eastern European or maybe Russian.

"Oh, good. Look, I am here because I have a task to perform and I'm not sure what it is I need to do to accomplish it. I was told you could help me with that."

The woman stopped cutting for the first time since they'd arrived at the table. She looked up at Dean, examining his face. Her pupils flashed with a red light as her eyes met his.

"You not only don't know what to do, you do not know what will be expected of you to do it. That is the real problem."

Dean waited for more, but she said nothing else, instead going back to her work. He waited for many long seconds. After nearly a minute he asked, "Okay, what am I supposed to do and how am I supposed to do it?"

With a sigh, the woman set her knife down and leaned on the table. Fixing Dean with her gaze, she said, "Your father here wants you to do something that you are not prepared to do. In order for you to fulfill your promise to him, you must embrace that which is within you. You need to embrace that which is the ultimate power you hold. Until you accept this power as a part of you, you cannot accomplish what it is you seek to do."

"But what does that mean?"

The woman picked up her knife and set to carving again. "I never repeat myself. Your foretelling is finished. Go. You will find no more answers here and I have an order to fill."

For a few seconds Dean stood there staring at her. She had said nothing that made any sense. Everything she said was, at best, a riddle with hidden meaning. And how did she know Gabe was his father?

Gabe tugged at his arm. "Come on. We've discovered everything we need to know."

Dean stared at Gabe. How did he glean answers from that cryptic reading? Shaking his head, he followed Gabe back out to the front.

One of the shop women lifted the hinged counter again so they could pass through.

Soon, they stood outside on the sidewalk and Dean stopped, grabbing his father by the arm. "What did she mean?"

Gabe offered Dean a broad grin. "It's simple. She wants you to become one of the Eldara, like me."

Chapter 11

DEAN ARRIVED home a half hour later in a daze. A myriad of thoughts swirled through his head. He had no desire to become anything like his father, even if he could. While he'd manifested a few mystical abilities along the way, he'd shown nothing like what he'd seen from the other Eldara he knew. If he had a divine side to himself, it was pretty well hidden amidst his more mundane human attributes. On top of that, what was Jaz going to say? Dean didn't even want to think about her reaction to all of this.

As he pulled into the underground parking area, he saw Jaz's SUV parked in its slot. That surprised him. He'd expected her to be gone all day. She was going to want to know what the Oracle had told him, and he wasn't ready to share it with her. He decided to stall for time while he thought of a way to break it to her. He waved at the guard behind the desk and opted for the stairs rather than take the elevator. If he was lucky, she'd be down in her office working with the rest of the staff.

Dean climbed to the top floor and let himself into their apartment. He stopped as soon as he stepped inside. She was already here. His shoulders drooped as she called out to him.

"Dean, you're back already? Good. Come in here. There's something we have to talk about."

Dean squared his shoulders and took a deep breath, searching for the best way to tell her what the Oracle had revealed to him. Instead, she cut him off as soon as he entered the living room.

She sat at her small writing desk behind her laptop. She swiveled around in the chair as he walked in. "I'm glad you're here. There's been a development that we need to talk about."

"A development about what?" There were so many things going on in his mind at that moment that he couldn't make sense of what she said.

"Really, something about two different situations. Our lab did some DNA analysis on the crime scene at the flea market. Something interesting popped up and Jonas sent it to me right away.

"Okay, what did he find?"

"The DNA trace they found on the demon's body matches a DNA trace found inside the armory here at Errington headquarters. It matches the person we're searching for who broke in and stole the weapons."

"How is that even possible? Could they have contaminated the source somehow? Maybe one of your operatives slipped up and got his own DNA mixed in with the sample."

"Ordinarily, I'd think that too. However, both DNA samples come back matched to both you and I."

"Well, there's your problem. It can't be both of us."

"Dean, you're not listening to what I'm saying. Think about it for a second." Jaz ticked off points on her fingers. "Someone used a personal family code known only to you and me to get into the armory. That same person used weapons from the armory to kill the demon two weeks later. That person is somehow genetically tied to you and me."

It took Dean a few seconds to figure out what it was she was trying to tell him. "Jo? You mean she's somehow come back to us again? How?"

"I'm checking on that now. Somewhere around here we have a DNA sample of hers, I'm sure of it. She left a few things behind when she went back to her time."

"I can't understand why she'd be back here." Dean said. "I mean, why hasn't she contacted us?"

"My thoughts exactly. I'm a little annoyed about it."

"Let's not jump to conclusions." Dean paused as he thought about everything his wife had revealed. "There could be another explanation. Maybe somehow magic contaminated things?"

Jaz shook her head. "I had them run the sample twice. The second time, we used a spell to cleanse the sample first. Everything matches up to the DNA as a child of ours."

Dean thought for a moment, then stared down at Jaz's stomach. "Could it be…?"

"I thought about that. I'm either pregnant with Joanna, or there's another child she never told us about. She could've done that because she didn't want to pollute the timeline any more than she already had, but that's just a guess."

"It could also explain why she hasn't reached out to us. Maybe she knows what's going on but can't tell us because it would alter her past."

Jazz nodded. "We'll see. We're getting closer to locating her. They tracked her down to a motel on the west side of the city, but she'd already checked out by the time the police went to pick her up. If the woman who killed the demon is Jo, she's much older than the teenaged version we met before. Bystanders said the woman was in her mid to late 30s."

"Great," Dean said. "I get to talk to a daughter 10 years older than I am. How do I explain that to my friends?"

Jaz chuckled a little. "Look, we don't know what she's doing here or why. She may not be able to come see us. Part of me wonders if we should avoid looking for her at all."

"What are you talking about? Of course we have to find her. Don't you want to talk to her?"

Jaz laid a hand on her stomach. "More than anything you know. I have so many questions for her, but maybe we can't. We have to be prepared for that to be the case. We'd have to find her without causing something in our time to go wrong. It could cause a paradox we can't fix."

He nodded, even though he didn't fully understand everything she said. She was much more attuned to these kinds of mystical things than he was. The good news was with this revelation to deal with, she'd forgotten all about the Oracle.

Jaz went back to her laptop and tapped out something for a few seconds before sending off an email. She closed the lid and stood. "I wanted to tell you as soon as I knew something. It's a lot to take in, but you needed to know. I have to head back down to operations and talk with Jonas. There's so much to be worried about, especially if more demons are likely to pop out somewhere around the city. I'm working with the team on a way to track if one of those rifts opens again."

"That sounds great. We don't want any more demons running around the city killing folks. Get that done." He smiled to himself. That would give him some more time to figure out how to tell her about the Oracle's foretelling. "Hey, do you think we might go out to dinner this evening? Then we can both catch up with what's been going on the last few days."

"That would be great. I completely forgot to ask you about how your morning went with the Oracle."

"That can wait until tonight. We can talk about it then."

"Sounds like a plan. I'll meet you up here at the apartment around 5:30?"

Dean let out a sigh of relief as Jaz left to get back to ops on the second floor. With the rest of the afternoon ahead of him, he settled in and took care of some random chores around the apartment while he waited for their dinner date. For some reason he was both excited and apprehensive about it. He hoped Jaz had a positive reaction to what the Oracle told him. This was something they had to talk through together. She knew a lot more about how something like this might work out and what it would mean for the two of them. If he somehow was able to switch on the Eldara half of his genetics, it could change everything.

By the time dinner time arrived, Dean was starving. He realized he had eaten no lunch. He'd been so lost in his thoughts all afternoon that he'd completely forgotten. Now he couldn't wait to get something at the restaurant. He was dressed and waiting when Jaz showed up at 5:15, racing through the apartment as soon as she came in the door.

"Everything good, hon?" Dean asked as she zoomed by him in the hallway.

"Yeah, I'm just running a little late. Let me go get changed and I'll be right back out."

"Sure thing. I'll be right here."

He tried to ignore the pit in his stomach accompanied by the occasional hunger gurgle. Jaz came back out twenty minutes later wearing black slacks with a matching black-and-white checkered print top. He looked her over and smiled. It was nice to see her without her usual tactical belt and sidearm. He couldn't see any weapons on her, but there had to be one somewhere. She never went anywhere unarmed.

"You look stunning. I'm going to be the luckiest guy in the restaurant."

"You say that to all the girls. Come on, let's go. I'm famished."

The restaurant of choice that evening was Sabatani's. Kristof, the Djinn who owned the place, met them at the front doors as they walked up.

"Dean, Jaz, what a surprise. I was so delighted to see your names on the reservation list this evening. It's been too long."

"Yes, it has," Jaz said. "How have you been?"

"Very well, thank you. Things are going so well that I am opening a third restaurant in Philadelphia. That means I'll have one here, one in Baltimore, and now one up there, too. I hope perhaps you can make it there for the grand opening celebration next month."

Dean nodded. "We'd be honored to be there. Sounds like a lot of fun."

Kristof led them to a table in the corner where they could see the whole restaurant. He knew Jaz's preference to see all the entrances and exits from where she sat.

Their dinner was both relaxing and filling. Dean had crab cakes while Jaz enjoyed a steak and lobster combo that was the special that evening. To Dean's surprise, when he told her about the Oracle's pronouncement, she had nothing much to say about it. All she said was that she trusted whatever decision he made. He guessed that meant she'd be okay being married to an Eldara, if it came to that.

They were just about to order dessert when her phone buzzed in her purse. She excused herself while the server stood ready to take their orders. Pulling out her phone, she glanced at the screen. "It's Jonas. He wouldn't call if it wasn't urgent. I have to take this."

She stood, putting the phone to her ear. She walked away towards the restrooms for some privacy.

Dean smiled at the woman standing there waiting to get them dessert. "Why don't you come back in a few minutes. I'm sure we'll order something then."

Less than a minute later, Jaz hurried back. "Grab your stuff. We have to go. Jonas thinks he figured out how to track the demonic rifts before they open. He says there's one opening right now across town."

"So much for dessert." Dean followed her towards the restaurant's exit. Kristof came over to see what was going on.

"Is everything alright? You looked upset about something."

Jaz nodded as she put on her coat. "There's a little something we have to deal with, Kristof. The food was delicious. Can you charge the bill to my corporate account? And please give the server a twenty-five percent tip on top of it. She did a fabulous job."

"Of course. I hope everything is all right. Please stay safe."

"Safety is my middle name," Dean said as he followed his wife out the door. He hoped she had some backup coming from her security teams. She didn't need to be facing down a demon all by herself. He jogged after her as she raced across the street to their SUV.

Chapter 12

DEAN PRESSED his fingers into the armrest, gripping tightly as Jaz raced through traffic to get across town. She wove the SUV in and out of the busy downtown flow of cars with surprising ease.

"What did Jonas tell you?"

Jaz kept her eyes focused on the road ahead as she answered. "He picked up a magical surge that he thinks is related to another rift opening. He said it was a pretty strong one, but he couldn't be sure if it was what we were looking for or not."

"So he's on his way with the security team to back you up?"

Jazz cursed and swerved around another car ahead of her, then slammed on her brakes, narrowly avoiding a minivan moving across the intersection as they zoomed through. She passed within inches of it before zooming onward.

"He's not coming. There's some kind of situation going on with a pair of shifter gangs on the other side of town. The two go teams are already committed there. He put a call in to local police, but you know better than I do how quickly they'll respond in support."

Dean shook his head. "You can't handle this all by yourself, hon. If it's a bigger incursion than before, there could be multiple demons running around out there."

Jaz kept driving, though she glanced his way. "Failure is not an option, Dean. I'm a Hunter and this is what I do. It's what I was born to do."

Dean started to object, but stopped himself before he said anything. He used similar arguments when talking about his work as a paramedic. She was just as devoted to what she did as he was to his career. Pressing his lips together in a frown, he kept his thoughts to himself. He knew she could handle herself in most situations. He had to trust her to do the same here.

"How much farther?"

"It should be a couple of blocks ahead."

Dean stared out the windshield, getting his bearings. They'd entered an older residential neighborhood of closely packed row homes. Jaz slowed a little as she craned her neck as she looked out the windshield.

"What's the address?" Dean asked. "I know this area."

"Jonas said it would be in the vicinity of Fourth Street and Wilson."

Dean pointed down the road. "That's straight ahead. It's about two blocks to where Wilson crosses Fourth."

Jazz nodded, accelerating again. Dean grimaced, hoping no one was out tonight walking their dogs or kids right now. They'd never be able to stop in time if someone were to…

"Stop!"

A shadow darted out between two parked cars on the right. Instead of slowing, though, Jaz sped up. She hit the shadowed figure at full speed, bouncing up and over it before coming to a screeching stop about fifteen yards away.

"Good God, Jaz. I think you hit somebody."

Her eyes stared into the rear-view mirror. "Dammit, it's still alive."

Slipping the gear into reverse, she watched the rear view camera screen on the dashboard while she accelerated backwards. Another few bumps under the tires and she stopped.

Dean tried to control his breathing, ready to run out and help some poor pedestrian. Then he saw it in the headlights ahead. A red and black scaled demon like the one from the flea market twitched in the street, its body twisted and wrecked by the impact with the SUV.

"Stay in the truck, Dean."

Dean wrenched his eyes away from the twitching carcass in front of the SUV to stare at his wife. "What?"

"Listen to me. Stay in the vehicle. I'll be right back. There might be more around."

He nodded and returned his gaze to the thing in the road ahead of them. She reached behind her seat and pulled out her sword. Then she opened her door and stepped out, drawing the katana, leaving the enameled scabbard propped on the driver's seat.

Standing beside their vehicle for a few seconds in silence, she lifted her head a little as if sniffing the air. A grim smile formed as she walked up to the demon twitching in the road in front of them. She hacked down once at the back of its neck with her blessed silver alloy blade.

The twitching stopped.

Another quick sniff in the air and she took off, heading back in the direction from which the creature had come, disappearing into the darkness between two sections of row homes.

Dean sat watching the spot where she'd disappeared for many long seconds, waiting for her to come back. A chill raced down his spine as he sat there alone. The soft sound of eighty's pop played in the background on the radio.

He checked his watch, deciding to wait two minutes for her to return. The time passed. He put the window down a little to see if he could hear anything. A scream right next to the SUV startled him and he shouted in alarm.

Someone pounded on the back of the vehicle. He looked up into the rearview mirror to try to see what it was. There was no one there.

"Oh my God, oh my God, let me in!" The woman screamed from right beside his window. "Open the door, please."

Dean unlocked the door and opened it, jumping out to stand in the street to check on her. "What is it? What do you need?"

In the light coming from the vehicle's interior, he made out blood dripping down the side of her face. He couldn't tell if it was hers or perhaps someone else's. "Are you bleeding? Tell me, are you alright?"

"Get out of the way. That thing's gotta be right behind me."

Before he could react, she shoved him away from the SUV and climbed into the front passenger seat. He reached out to stop her, but she yanked the door closed.

Dean tried the door, but she'd locked it. He gave up as a ripping snarl came from the darkness nearby.

Spinning around, he stared into the night, wishing once again for some way to see in the dark at times like this. He backed around the vehicle, keeping his face towards where he thought the sound had come from. Whatever it was snarled again. It seemed to get louder and he tried to keep the vehicle between him and whatever was out there.

Another of the red and black demons leaped atop the car parked beside the SUV. It scrambled across onto the SUV's hood and bounded at Dean, now standing beside the driver's side door.

Dean screamed and raised his arms to block it aside. Before he could bring up his arms, a series of shots rang out, exploding into the night. The creature lurched to the side in mid-leap, glancing off Dean's shoulder before rolling across the pavement and coming to a stop ten feet behind him.

He took a step towards the twitching body. An arm shoved him in the chest, pushing him up against the hood of Jaz's vehicle.

"Look out, it's not dead yet."

A tall woman wearing a knee-length black coat stalked past him. The demon had rolled over and climbed to its feet. It bunched up its leg muscles to spring forward.

The woman swept a sword from a scabbard at her waist, a Katana very similar to Jaz's. She met the demon's charge with a single stroke, then spun and kicked it aside to slam into the driver's door. It struggled to rise, but she brought the sword blade down two more times, finishing it.

Dean stared at his rescuer. The woman had short, close-cropped blonde hair. Her scalp was shaved on one side, just above her ear. On the opposite side, where the hair hung down to her shoulder, it was colored deep magenta, lit up now in the light from an overhead street light.

Looking back over her shoulder, she studied Dean. Her one good eye stared back at him. A black leather eyepatch covered the other. "Are you alright? Did it bite you or scrape you with its claws?"

Dean shook his head. "Um, no, I'm fine. It bumped up against my shoulder when you shot it. That's it." He studied her face. She didn't look like the Joanna he knew. He couldn't tell if it was her or not.

The woman turned to search the area all around the truck, scanning the darkness. "Where did she go? Tell me."

Dean thought she meant the woman who'd climbed into the SUV. He turned to point at her. The passenger door was ajar.

"I think she left."

"Not the housewife, I mean your wife. There's a fully grown Fetch demon out there. It came through with the others. She'll never take it out on her own."

Dean pointed off to the right where Jaz had disappeared into the dark minutes before. The woman didn't wait. She raced off in that direction.

Dean called out. "Wait, I'm coming with you."

She stopped and started to say something to him, then shook her head. "I can't stop you, and I don't have time to argue. Stay close and try not to get in the way."

Dean struggled to work out who this person was. She looked nothing like his daughter. Maybe Jaz had been mistaken about everything.

He stayed close as requested, just a few feet behind the woman as she ran between two sections of row homes and turned right down an alleyway running parallel to Fourth Street. A shout of alarm ahead caused her to pick up speed.

Dean recognized the voice. It was Jaz. She sounded hurt.

Running behind the newcomer, Dean searched the pools of light down the alley coming from a few street lamps. He saw the demon well before he spotted his wife on the ground a few feet away. The thing had to be at least twelve-feet-tall, with great, curving red horns growing out of either side of its head. Like the smaller demons it bore a partial resemblance to, its scaled hide was green and red, with patches of coarse fur sprouting from its shoulders and back.

From where she lay on the ground, Jaz waved her sword in the demon's direction in a feeble attempt to fend it off.

"Hey," Dean shouted. "Leave her alone. Come fight me if you want to."

Strangely enough, the demon turned to look at the pair racing his way, its toothy maw opening and filling the night with a bizarre cackling laughter. "Puny human, what do you think you can do to me?"

Before Dean could answer, the Hunter woman responded, charging forward with her sword held high. "He can't do anything, but I sure can. Prepare to die, demon spawn."

The ridiculousness of it caused a crazed, maniacal laugh to slip from Dean. The woman looked so small charging at that gigantic creature. It bellowed in defiance and reached out with a clawed hand to grab at her. Somehow, she dodged the attack, swinging her sword, and hacking off a bit of one talon as she ran past.

Screaming with rage and maybe pain, the demon tried to catch her with its other arm. She spun and bounded straight upward, executing a double flip, sailing through the air impossibly long before landing on her toes, ten feet away. Her free hand came up holding a swirling ball of white-hot plasma above her hand. With a twist of her arm, she hurled it straight at the demon.

Bellowing in surprise, the creature fell over in its efforts to back away from the speeding bolt of fire streaking in its direction.

The ball of fire impacted against the demon's shoulder, exploding and covering it with dripping burning goop that clung to the scales and melted them away. It threw its head back and screamed in pain into the night sky.

Two giant bat-like wings emerged from its back. They beat at the surrounding air twice, and the demon rose into the air. The wings beat faster and it soared upward to disappear into the night.

"Damn, damn, damn." The woman turned in a circle, staring upward.

"What's wrong?" Dean asked. "We survived. There's no way we could've killed that thing by ourselves."

"Don't you see," The woman said. "We had to stop it. Now that it's loose and it can go about its mission. It'll ruin everything."

Dean shook his head. He didn't understand what she was talking about. He was about to ask more questions when a groan from nearby reminded him of Jaz.

"Oh, my God." Dean raced down the alley to where she lay, propped up on one elbow on the broken pavement. She clutched at her belly with the other hand.

"Where are you hurt? Let me see."

She started to say something, then groaned again as she pressed harder against her stomach. Dean stared as blood welled up around her fingers.

"Let me have a look. Lay back." He pressed against her shoulder to lower her to the ground then pulled her hand aside to look at the injury. One of the demon's talons had pierced her just to the right of her navel. It looked to be pretty deep. Dark red blood filled the hole, flowing out of the puncture wound. Dean slapped his hand down over the opening, applying pressure.

Reaching into his pocket with his other hand, he pulled out his phone, dialing 911.

"911. State the nature of your emergency."

"This is Paramedic Dean Flynn, Station U. I'm located just off of Fourth Street near the corner of Wilson. We're in an alley behind the homes on the southern side of the street. I've got a woman, 25 years old. She's got a traumatic injury and is bleeding from a puncture wound to the abdomen. I need an ambulance right now. Also, alert the trauma center at ECMC."

He listened as the 911 operator went through the standard questions. He felt slightly annoyed, even though he knew she had to ask them. An ambulance was already being dispatched by another member of her team sitting nearby.

He half listened to the questions and studied Jaz. She tried to talk but gasped in pain instead.

The other woman came running over. "Oh my God, Mom."

Dean stared into the woman's face. "Joanna? It is you. How?"

She shook her head. "No time for that. Move your hand."

"No, I have to keep pressure."

"Don't argue with me. Move your hand." She reached down, grabbing his wrist with surprising strength and yanking it away. She held her other hand a few inches over the injury as her palm glowed with a faint pink light. The glow seemed to infuse into the wound. The flow of blood slowed, then stopped.

Jaz gasped once, then fell silent as she lost consciousness.

Dean checked for a pulse. He lifted her wrist, catching a rapid, thready beat beneath his searching fingertips.

Joanna lowered her hand, her shoulders sagging. "I've done what I can to stabilize her. The baby's fine, too, thank God. She'll still need a surgeon and maybe a witch-healer, too. Is the ambulance on the way?"

Dean nodded, at a loss for words as he stared at the grown woman who was his daughter. He had so many questions, but they could wait. The two of them shifted all their focus to Jaz, waiting for the ambulance to arrive.

Chapter 13

DEAN THANKED Brook and Tammy one more time as they rolled their stretcher back out through the doors to the ambulance outside. They'd done excellent work stabilizing Jaz during their trip to ECMC. Now she was in the able hands of the trauma surgeons upstairs. His hands formed fists as he fought back the urge to scream out his frustration that he couldn't do anything to help her. Thank goodness Joanna had been there and had possessed the healing ability to stop her mother from bleeding out in the street like some common mugging victim.

Staring down at his clenched fists, Dean forced his fingers to relax and tugged at the bottom of the scrub shirt Ashley had gotten for him to wear after he'd arrived. His clothing had been smeared with Jaz's blood. Self-conscious in the medical attire, Dean tried to shift gears and focus on something else. Jo was probably out in the waiting area. She'd driven the Errington SUV to the hospital while he rode in the back of the ambulance with Jaz. He should check in with her and tell her what was going on.

He didn't see her as he entered the waiting room and walked outside to the ER's visitor parking lot to look for her. She stood behind the SUV, closing the rear liftgate as he approached.

She spotted him coming and hooked her thumb over her shoulder towards the truck. "I figured I should lock up my weapons in the box in the truck's rear. The people in the waiting room were giving me odd looks after one of them noticed one of the pistols underneath my coat."

"That's probably a good idea." He smiled. "You got the pistols from the armory back home, didn't you?"

"Oh, you noticed that."

"Not right away. I suspect your mother's going to have a few words with you about taking weapons from her without at least saying hello. Besides, it's not normal to walk around these days armed to the teeth unless you're a cop or in the military."

Joanna shrugged. "Things are a bit different in the future."

Dean waited for her to say more, but she didn't elaborate. He struggled with how to strike up a conversation with her. He longed to understand how the fresh, teenaged witch he'd met a few years before had become this hardened and battle-worn woman. She was his daughter, and he cared about her, even though she was now easily ten or fifteen years his elder. It was strange, but he tried to get her talking anyway.

"Jo, you mentioned your mother's pregnancy when you healed her. Is the baby—?"

"Me?" Joanna finished for him. "Yes, she is. That's something else that altered in this timeline from what I thought the last time I came back. That's why I tried to keep my trip here a secret from you."

"Your mother knew you were back before we came out after the demon. You left enough DNA both in the armory and at the scene of the last demon incursion for her to piece together who you were."

"I forgot about DNA sequencing. I should have masked that and been more careful." Her statement seemed more to herself than a response to Dean.

"You could have just asked for the pistols, and anything else you needed, you know."

She shook her head, her eyes meeting his again. "I couldn't come see you, at least not right away. I had to limit contact as much as I could. If you'd stayed away tonight, we wouldn't be talking right now."

"You know her better than that." Dean smiled, trying to soften his words. This Jo was so different, he didn't feel like he was getting to know her at all. "Once we figured out another incursion was happening, you know your mother was going to come and do what she could to stop it."

"She should have left that to me. Look what happened to her."

"You act like this is her fault," Dean said, his smile disappearing. "Don't blame your mother for getting hurt. If you'd communicated with us, we could've coordinated. We would know what the hell is going on."

"You don't need to know everything that's going on. It could spell disaster. Things are already bad enough because of what's happened back here."

Her reaction startled Dean. He'd seen that type of pained expression in her eyes before. It was like some of his paramedic colleagues who were dealing with traumatic stress injury. Some in the military called it a thousand-yard stare. What had caused her to have that kind of reaction?

He studied her face in the glow of the parking lot's overhead lights. For the first time, he made out the white, jagged scar that traced down her forehead, disappearing beneath the eyepatch and emerging out the other side to continue down her cheek. There were other scars he could make out on what little skin he could see.

Part of him wanted to ask about each past injury, to try to piece together her past. Instead, he focused on the present. "Jo, I think the time has come to tell us what's happening. You didn't come back here for a random visit with the family. Tell me what's going on." He cocked his head to one side, watching her and hoping she'd open up and share with him.

After a few seconds, Joanna let out a long slow breath and said, "I came back the first time to help fix what we all thought was a problem with you and mom getting together the way you were supposed to. I made that right, but something else happened because of it." She paused before continuing. "Or maybe after it."

Dean nodded to encourage her to keep talking.

"Dad, things are awful in my future. They'd changed so much from when I left. After you sent me back, I woke up in the burned-out shell of the coven's home. The coven members were all dead or scattered. I ended up wandering alone in a wasteland of what had once been this vibrant city. Something happened to change the future, making it even worse than the coven had feared when they first sent me back."

"You survived, though. It looks like you lived a long time after you returned."

"It was pure dumb luck at first." She let out a sad smile. "Demons and other netherworld creatures had overrun most of the world by that point. I had to fight for my life every day for weeks until I found a place of refuge amidst a group of survivors. Some of them recognized me and took me in. A lot of them were Unusual friends of yours and they gave me shelter because of my relationship with you and mom. Since then, we've all fought a losing war, trying to dislodge the invaders and carve out a safe home for humanity again."

"That's awful, Jo." Dean noticed she didn't mention what had happened to either him or Jaz when she talked about the future. He decided to let that question lie for now. "Jo, if we'd known you were going back to that, we would never of sent you. You know that, right?"

"Of course." She wiped at an errant tear dripping down her cheek. "Look, I don't believe what happened in the future, or at least that version of the future is your fault. But I knew something had happened sometime in the two years after I left to go back. We were able to piece together what I remembered of how it was supposed to be and what happened in the new timeline. It took us a while, but I think I've tracked down what it was. It all tracks back to when you stopped the Four Horsemen from trying to end the world."

Dean shook his head. "Why does everything always comes back to that? That's like what the Oracle told me, too."

"You've spoken to the Oracle, then? Good. I thought Gabe would try to pull a fast one. I was the one who convinced him to ask you for that favor."

Initially shocked at that last revelation, he bit back an angry response at her involving Gabe in something she could've handled more directly. He thought about it and decided this powerful, competent fighter and witch likely had good reason for doing what she did.

Now that she was in contact with him, though, maybe she could help him understand what he had to do.

"I will not disagree with you about trusting Gabe. I don't trust his motives, either. But, if you didn't trust him, why involve him in what you needed me to do at all?"

Joanna fixed him with a dark, steely gaze, holding his attention with her one eye. "Because it's all his fault, and I wanted to make sure he went back to heaven where he came from."

"I'm sorry, I don't understand."

"Do you know what we call the battle to save humanity in the future, Dad? We call them the Eldara Wars. They started because Gabe and a demon lord made a pact to rule the earth on their own, knowing the upper planes couldn't intervene and stop them anymore. You made sure of that when you closed the pathways upward."

Dean didn't understand why she shifted everything to an attack on him. "I didn't know. I just wanted to stop the end of the world."

Joanna sighed. "I know that. Now, we just have to fix it. What specifically did the Oracle say you have to do?"

"She said I could harness the Eldara side of my nature to open the upper planes again."

A puzzled expression crossed Jo's face. "That's it?"

"Yep. She didn't say much at all, really. I have to find a way to activate the dormant Eldara in me. Given everything you've told me tonight, it makes me even more reluctant to do so. Why did the other trapped Eldara side with Gabe to take over things? The Eldara are a force for good in the world."

A snarl erupted from Joanna. "There's nothing good about the Eldara. There have been a few who've taken our side over the years but never for long and always to serve their own ends. They're not good or evil, they just look out for themselves, and they don't care who they step on to do it. Believe me, they're not all that special except in how hard they are to kill.

The vitriol in Joanna's voice took Dean aback. He had always thought of the Eldara as creatures of the light, they were, after all, the inspiration for the legends and myths about angels. The way she described them as self-serving and power-hungry didn't entirely fit with an Eldara like Ashley. The more he thought about it, though, he could see it with Ingrid, and definitely in Gabe. Perhaps the healing sister was an aberration and not the standard for the Eldara.

Squaring his shoulders, Dean asked, "So what do I have to do to stop all this from happening? I do not know how to empower my immortal half. As far as I know, it's nonexistent."

Joanna laughed. "Dad, why do you think it is I'm so powerful? I've become one of the strongest sorceresses to have ever lived. That's partly because of the Eldara blood in me. It's that power that's enabled me to survive against odds that were always stacked against me. That blood comes from you, and so does the power it carries."

"How did you turn that part of you on?"

"For me, it was finding a powerful artifact and using it as a catalyst. It awakened something in me and brought that power to the forefront. For you it will have to be something similar, I assume."

"Oh, okay, if that's all." Dean let out his sarcasm with a laugh. "All I have to do is find some left over relic lying around and everything will be fine. So where do I locate this hidden power source?"

Joanna shook her head. "Dad, that's the simple part. One thing you taught me, long ago, was to trust in my friends. That advice has stood me in good stead through many battles and tough times. You have a lot of wonderful people here who will help you, if you ask."

Dean stopped and thought about it. She wasn't wrong. When he thought about it, there were a lot of folks here in the city who would drop everything if he asked them to. "Look, let's go back inside and up to the surgical waiting area. We should be able to get some word of how things are going with your mother. While we're there, we can come up with a plan to figure out what we're looking for and who can help us locate it."

Jo nodded and even smiled a little as she followed him inside. They had something to occupy their time while waiting for the doctors to put Jaz back together again.

Chapter 14

BACK HOME THE NEXT NIGHT, a knock at the apartment door
interrupted Dean while he chatted with James and Rudy. He left the
others while he went to get the door. He opened it to find Gibbie
standing there with a big grin on his face, and he wasn't alone.

"Hey, Dean. I hope you don't mind, but Hangbe was in town and I
didn't think she'd want to be left out."

The West African Interpol agent pushed past the vampire and
pulled Dean into an embrace. "I heard about Jaz. How is she?"

"She's doing well and recovering, though she hasn't regained
consciousness yet. The docs are hopeful, though. She might just need
the time to heal."

"Gibson wouldn't tell me what it was you wanted us to do, but I
hope it's to hunt down that demon." A wicked gleam shined in her
eyes. "I'd love to say I took out one of those things, or at least helped."

"If we run into the demon, we'll have to try to kill it, but that's not
our primary target." Dean gestured for them to proceed down the
hallway towards the living room. "Everyone else is here, so we can go
ahead and get started. I'll fill you in with everyone else."

The new arrivals walked into the living room to join the rest of the
team. He followed them in and studied the odd collection of friends

he'd assembled. The group included Jonas, the head of the security team at Errington, James Lee and Brynne, as well as Rudy and his daughter Marian. Rounding out the group were Kristof and the two dryad twins, Wim and Dora from the CERT team Dean had trained. With Gibbie and Hangbe here, the group was ready.

He opened his mouth to ask everyone to sit when another knock at the door interrupted him. He went to see who it was, surprised when he found Leah Casado at the door.

"What are you doing here?"

"I got the word from Brynne that you might need some help. She told me to be here tonight. Sorry if I'm a few minutes late."

"Uh, yeah, come in. We were just about to get started." Dean felt awkward having this probie here helping out, but Brynne wouldn't have asked her if she didn't think she could lend a hand. At the very least, she was a powerful shifter in her own right.

Dean returned and opened his mouth to get started when Gibbie asked, "Hey, where's Ashley? I'm surprised she's not here, too."

Joanna answered from the other side of the room before Dean could. "No Eldara. They can't be involved with this."

Dean had initially objected when Joanna had stipulated that Ashley was not invited. He tried to explain to her that the healer could be trusted, but Joanna was adamant. Knowing how she felt about Gabe and others like him, he'd let it drop. If they needed her later, he could always reach out on his own.

Using Jo's outburst as a cue, Dean announced, "Everyone, this is our daughter Joanna. A few of you have met her before during her previous visit. "

Gibbie laughed. "Gee, kid, you sure grew up fast."

Everyone chuckled, even Joanna to his surprise. It reminded him of why he'd included him when he pulled the group together. He had a way of lightening the mood at times like this.

Once everyone settled down after the bit of levity, he and Joanna went over everything they'd discussed together the night before. He explained what the Oracle had told him and also what Joanna foretold would happen in the near future.

"Well, I for one have never trusted the Eldara any farther than I can throw one," James said. "I know that sounds amusing coming from a vampire, but honestly, they've always had their own agenda."

Kristof Elgar shook his head. "Surely, some of them are to be trusted."

Joanna shook her head. "None of them can know what we're doing. I can't stress this enough. In what is coming, they are key players against humanity, including Unusuals who don't come to their side. I will not say who's good and who's bad in my future, but no one trusts the Eldara, and most we try to kill on sight."

That last bit quieted the room down. Based on the grim expressions on everyone's face, Dean figured it had set the mood for what they needed to do pretty well.

Wim, one of the twin dryads from the CERT team, raised her hand. "You asked us to come here because you needed us to do something. Tell us what we need to do and we'll do it. None of us want anything to do with the future your daughter just described to us."

"In order to set things right," Dean said, "I have to do something to enable my half Eldara side. Jo thinks once the Eldara can return and serve their true masters, there won't be any need for them to remain here on earth and try to take over. The heavenly powers won't allow it."

James smiled, "You've pretty much denounced that side of yourself, Dean. How do you plan to awaken something you've buried so deep?"

"That's for me to deal with. Right now we need to figure out where some key relics are located. We think one of them will be the catalyst that will allow me to access the power we need."

Jo took it from there. "The two of us think we've come up with what we're looking for. When you all fought against the Four Horseman, they were vanquished and fled. But I believe each of them left a piece of themselves here on earth, an artifact of power of some sort. One of those relics, from Malificar the horseman of the plague, is what the Eldara and their demonic allies used to bring through hordes of netherworlders to Earth in the early days of the war. That kind of power might also be used to open a gateway in the other direction. In order to do that, though, we need to find the artifacts from one of the other three."

"Oh good," Gibbie said. He rubbed his hands together with glee. "I love a scavenger hunt. Where do we start looking? "

Dean shrugged "That's the problem. We don't know where any of these things might be. We have to assume they're somewhere close by, though. The Fetch demon that broke through a few days ago came here for a reason. We have to assume he didn't come just to talk to Gabe. He had to come to recover the Malificar relic for himself since we know he'll use it to invade this world soon."

Rudy raised his hand with a concern. "With a demon on the loose potentially looking for the same things we are, it puts all of us in a lot of danger. We will not be able to break up into smaller teams and spread out the search. We'd never be able to fight something like that."

"I agree." Dean could see the concern in the eyes of everyone in the room. "Look, I know this is going to be dangerous. I'll understand if any of you want to bow out. No one will think anything about it if any of you don't want to help."

Brynne stood. "No one's bowing out, Dean. This is too important for that. We do have to plan carefully while we search, though. Rudy's right. None of us want to run into a Fetch demon unprepared."

Joanna nodded. "My father and I have come up with a plan for two teams to include strength and other abilities that might be useful in both a search and a fight. There's enough muscle in this room to deal with either one if it comes to that."

Gibbie pumped his fist. "Yeah, this demon had better watch out. He doesn't know what's coming for him."

Hangbe laughed. "Easy does it, Gibson. The best outcome would be to avoid meeting the thing altogether."

"Absolutely," Dean agreed. "I'm hoping we can come up with a plan to locate and grab the artifacts without alerting the demon to what we're doing. Jo assures me that once we have the relics, she can use their own power against any demons after I do what is needed to open the gates."

James stood and Brynne came to her feet beside him. The vampire lord glanced around the room. "Then it's settled. When do we start?"

"Tonight," Dean said. "I looked up and went through Jaz's notes from when we faced the Four Horsemen and came up with some likely locations where they'd have left the artifacts. I'll text you all the instructions, then give out the team assignments. Once that's finished, we can split up and start looking."

He pulled out his phone and sent out the prepared message. He hadn't included Hangbe or Leah, but he'd work that out. The Interpol agent could accompany the team with Gibbie, Marian, Kristof, and the twin dryads. He kept the CERT team together and added Joanna for some extra muscle. Hangbe would lend even more power to the group. Leah could join his team with James, Brynne, and Rudy. Everyone seemed ready to get on the move. It was time to go hunting.

Chapter 15

AS GIBBIE'S beat up white van rattled through the nighttime streets of Elk City, Joanna sat in the seat behind him, studying the other members of her team. She'd asked her father to assign her to ride with the CERT team members. She'd known many of them since she was little. However, the real reason she'd chosen to go with them was that she'd also fought alongside many of them in the future. She knew their grit and determination under pressure.

Of course, she couldn't tell them any of that. She had to be so careful about how much she told anyone about what their own future held. She'd already skirted the boundaries of what she considered allowable by telling them about the war that was coming. It was necessary to fulfill the mission and prevent the war.

Their chosen target this evening was the location where her father had first encountered Bellum, the horseman of war. He and her mother had found the demon in an underground tunnel beneath the city. Gibbie drove them to a location that would give them access to those old steam tunnels. She'd hoped that by searching the locations where the horsemen each first appeared, there might be some trail or hint of an artifact linked to them.

Around her, the team chattered about random topics. Everyone shared what they'd been up to since the last time they'd gathered. Wim and Dora had opened a landscaping design business together. Marian had started community college, skipping past her senior year in high school. Kristof and Gibbie also shared their recent projects. Even Gibbie's partner, Hangbe, shared details about a recent Interpol case she'd closed in Turkey.

The easy-going way they all interacted despite their unique backgrounds brought a smile to Joanna's face. This was the kind of camaraderie she was used to with her companions in the future. Many of the world's Unusuals sided with their human neighbors to fight off the demons and their Eldara overlords. People and supernaturals had worked together and put aside centuries and even millennia of old grudges and feuds to fight against a common enemy. It was good to see how much of that had been fostered already here in Elk City. She knew her father and the other medics from Station U had done a lot to bring people like these together in unexpected ways.

The conversations stopped when Gibbie pulled the van to a stop in a deserted parking lot beside an old factory. A tall brick smokestack stood next to the structure, stretching up into the dark, cloud-covered sky.

"Well, here we are. I'm pretty sure there are access points to the old steam tunnels from the old days beneath this factory. That smokestack leads to one of the boilers that heated many of the homes in this area. We should be able to get into the basement and find an entrance. We'll have to search, though. I'm sure the one I remember has been closed off for years."

"Don't worry about it, Gibbie," Joanna said. "We've got what we need to break through if we have to, right?"

Kristof answered from the third row seat behind her. "I brought along the tools we might need, including several crowbars and even a pickax if we need to do some heavy demolition."

The team unloaded. Hangbe and Gibbie opened up the rear of the van and everyone grabbed one of the tools to carry inside. Joanna picked up a small sledgehammer. She slid the wooden handle into her belt. It would do as a weapon in a pinch.

Gibbie led them to a side entrance to the factory, right beside the smokestack. "This should let us in near the basement stairs if I remember correctly."

"You act like you've been here before," Dora said.

"Yeah, this factory's been here for a long time, just like me. There was a time when I hid out in the tunnels beneath the city. People weren't always so forgiving about having a vampire living next-door."

Marian snorted. "Like they're okay with it now. Half the people in the city would crap themselves if they knew a werewolf like me or a vampire like you were their neighbors."

"Those that know respect us and do their best to get along," Gibbie replied. "That's a lot different than it used to be."

Hangbe reached out and tried the knob. "It's locked. How do we plan to get inside, Gibson?"

Gibbie took a step back and looked around. "Well, we can break in with the tools we have, I guess. That'll make a lot of noise, though."

Wim pointed to the second floor of the factory. "That window is open. I can probably squeeze through the opening if someone can get me up there."

Hangbe nodded. "Human pyramid time. Marian, you and I take the base with Gibbie. Then Joanna and Dora climb up on our shoulders, with Kristof spotting and boosting people up. Wim should be able to climb up on top of them and reach the window."

Everyone nodded and moved over until they stood beneath the open window. Hangbe braced her arms against the building. Beside her, Gibbie and Marian did the same, except they interlocked their arms across the others to form the base of the pyramid. Kristof boosted Joanna and Dora up onto their shoulders. As she climbed and settled into place, she hoped her booted foot wasn't digging into anyone's shoulder too badly.

Wim clambered up, steadying herself against the wall as she stretched up. She gripped the windowsill with two hands and scrambled with her feet against the brick as she pulled herself up and into the narrow gap between the open window and the sill. She wriggled in and disappeared.

Joanna jumped down. "Now we wait."

They all returned to the locked double steel doors, watching and listening for some sign Wim was unlocking them. It took Wim five minutes to find her way down to the first floor and make it to the entrance. The door wasn't chained on the inside and all she had to do was press on a panic bar to open it. She smiled broadly as she let them into the even darker interior.

None of them needed flashlights. Each had a way to see in the dark. Most of them had that ability inherently. Hangbe and Joanna had a little magical manipulation each enabled as they entered. The interior lit up as bright as day for Joanna as soon as she enabled her Hunter charm's spell to enhance her vision.

"All right, Gibbie," Joanna said. "You've been here before. Lead the way."

"I think the stairwell down to the basement is this way. It's been a long time since I've been here." He took off down the hallway with the rest of them following in single file.

He led them to a musty stairwell and down into the basement. They wove through the cluttered stacks of stored furniture and rusty equipment until they reached a concrete wall and stopped.

"I am pretty sure the entrance to the tunnels used to be right here. We should be below the smokestack now."

Joanna pointed in both directions. "Let's search along this wall and see if we can find anything. This area seems to form a footing for the smokestack, so let's check it and see if we can find anything that might lead us inside."

It only took a few minutes before Kristof called out in the far corner and the others joined him. The concrete had been chipped away already, revealing a hole in the brick wall beneath. Now, loose bricks were scattered all over the floor, exposing a jagged opening in the smokestack's base.

"Looks fresh," Marian observed. "That's the bad news, I guess. The good news is, we don't need all these tools now."

"Yeah," Joanna said. "But who created this hole and why?"

Hangbe shook her head. "We'd better be careful. Do you know of any reason why someone else would be looking for the same thing we are?"

"I hadn't thought about that. If the Fetch demon is looking for the same thing we are, then we have to hurry. We can't let them recover the artifacts first."

Joanna darted into the circular opening and scrambled through. She realized as she got to the far side there was no way a twelve-foot major demon could've made it through that opening. That meant if any demons were down here, they were probably just underlings and would be more easily dealt with. Jonas had provided her with armor-piercing silver alloy pistol ammunition that should take out a lesser demon, if enough shots struck a vital region. She also had her sword. The only other person armed with something that could take down a demon was Hangbe with her Amazon sword and a pistol with a magazine of the same ammo Jo had.

As Joanna stood and waited for the others, she studied the old tunnel stretched out before her. It proceeded left and right for some distance. It was arched with a gap in the floor through which ran old, rusted pipes. She assumed they were the steam pipes that once carried heat to the surrounding buildings.

Once everyone stood around her, she looked at Gibbie. "You've been here before. Which way to the location where you all found Bellum?"

Gibbie looked both ways, then pointed to the right. "I wasn't with him until the end of that fight. I can get us in the general vicinity, I know about where they were searching when they found him. Other than that, we'll have to just look around."

Joanna nodded and let Gibbie lead the way.

Chapter 16

GIBBIE LED them through several intersections until they came to a larger junction. He pointed down a large circular tunnel to the right. "This is where they came out the last time. Me and the rest of the CERT team met them there and Kristof used his wild magic to close off the entrance." He pointed at a smaller, round tunnel straight ahead. "My guess is that is where they went to find Bellum."

Joanna smiled. "Now we start searching."

Unfortunately, they never got the chance to go any farther. The group hadn't even made it to the smaller opening when snarling growls echoed from inside.

Joanna barely got her hand down to draw her sword before two fetchlings launched from the opening, charging straight at the group. She spun to the side and avoided the one coming at her. She couldn't afford to use her pistols for fear of warning others nearby of their presence.

The other fetchling charged towards Wim and Dora.

Jo shouted in alarm, fearing the worst. The two were the most vulnerable of the team.

The dryads turned to face each other and gripped wrists. Clutching close together, they transformed into a thick trunk of oak stretching from floor to ceiling in the tunnel.

The fetchling ran into it and bounced off, stunned by the sudden and unexpected impact.

Hangbe was there in an instant. She swept her Amazonian sword downward, hacking into the demonling as it struggled to rise.

Joanna took a stance to gut the fetchling circling back towards her. Just before it reached her, a snarling, furred form hurtled into it from one side. The teen werewolf pinned the demonling to the side of the tunnel, teeth and fangs ripping at the scaly hide.

Joanna ran up and waited for an opportunity where she could be sure of her blow. Seeing an opening, she thrust deep with her sword, finishing it.

Marian backed away from the now inert carcass as she shifted partially back to human form. She smiled at Joanna with black blood dripping from her mouth, then with a groan, she bent over and heaved, losing the contents of her dinner all over the tunnel floor. She stood up and wiped her mouth with the back of her furred hand. "That thing tasted horrible."

"Maybe just use your claws next time, eh?" Joanna suggested.

Marian spit several times on the floor in reply, trying to remove the taste from her mouth.

Joanna pulled a cloth from inside her coat and wiped at the black demon blood smeared on her blade. She had to clean it before it could etch the silver alloy and damage the metal.

Kristof moved to the tunnel from which the two demons had come. "If there are two down here, what are the chances there are more?"

"Pretty good," Joanna replied. "Let's be on our guard. Fetchlings are pretty stupid and don't act on their own. Something else is down here with them."

Joanna and Gibbie led the way into the opening. Hangbe and Marian followed, then Wim and Dora. Kristof brought up the rear. They didn't have to go far before Joanna held up her hand, stopping them. A chittering screeching sound echoed down the tunnel in their direction.

She turned, whispering back to the others. "That's demon speech. There must be a group of them ahead."

"Can you understand what they're saying?" Gibbie asked.

Joanna shook her head. "Never bothered to try to learn it. But there's enough of them down there to be talking to each other. That tells me they're up to something. They're usually not much for communicating."

Hangbe stepped forward. "Let me scout ahead. I can mask myself so they can't see or hear me. We don't want to stumble into a group larger than we can handle on our own."

Joanna nodded. She and the others waited while Hangbe stroked the beads on her necklace of spells. A few seconds later, the Amazon faded from sight.

Gibbie smiled over at Joanna. "She's just wonderful, isn't she?"

"She is at that. I'm sure she's handy to have along."

In truth, Hangbe had been a valuable asset for the freedom fighters in the future. It wasn't just the magic she held, or her abilities in a fight. She was one of Joanna's most trusted advisors. It had been partly her idea for Joanna to come back and try to make things right in the past.

They didn't have to wait too long for her to return. A few minutes later, Hangbe reappeared right in front of Joanna.

The Amazon wore a frown. "There's seven of them, just like the ones we fought. There's also another who walks around on two feet like us wearing a hooded cloak. I couldn't make out their face in the shadows. They might be human, or they might be another demon. I couldn't be sure and didn't want to get too close."

Joanna didn't like the sound of that. If another major demon had come through, then things were progressing far faster than she'd expected. "Alright, if we catch them by surprise, we should be able to handle this. But let's be careful. We don't know the capabilities of this other creature."

Something about the way Hangbe had described the creature in charge bothered Joanna, but she couldn't figure out exactly what it was. Most demons didn't bother with clothing, though a few of the humanoid varieties did.

"We'll charge in and take them on as we meet them," Joanna said.

"Hangbe and I will lead, followed by Gibbie and Marian. Kristof, you, Wim, and Dora come behind and finish off anything that we leave wounded or disabled behind us. We don't want the leader getting away, so we're going to move fast and cut our way through to them. We'll hold back on using our pistols. I'm worried about ricochets in these tunnels."

Everyone readied themselves and lined up as she'd arranged. She glanced at Hangbe, who nodded in return. The two women took off at a dead run down the tunnel.

Ahead, it opened up into a broader space. Someone had lit up the area with a magical glowing green orb floating above the chamber's center.

The first of the fetchling demons spun around as the pair entered. It barely got off a screech of alarm before Hangbe's Amazon blade skewered it through the neck.

To the left, Joanna sliced downward, almost severing another of the demonling's head. It still twitched and tried to rise. She left it behind, trusting in the others to finish it. She had her focus on getting to the cloaked leader ahead. They still had their back to her.

The five remaining fetchlings came at the group now, alerted to their presence. Joanna and Hangbe spun and dodged their way through, dealing blow after blow. Most of them were not fatal, but all five of the smaller demons had injuries of one sort or another by the time the pair made it past them. Gibbie and Marian would have to deal with the least injured remaining. Hangbe and Joanna focused on the leader.

The hooded figure turned to meet them, dealing both women with a surprise. The demon leader swept their hood back to reveal a stunning blond woman in silver armor.

"It's an Eldara warrior," Joanna called out. Her heart sank. Things had progressed much farther than she'd hoped if the Eldara were already consorting with the demons. That meant the Fetch demon had already forged some alliances to start the war.

Hangbe didn't even pause, charging in with her sword leading the way.

The Eldara laughed. In a flash, a silver heavenly blade appeared in her hand. She swept it around, parrying the West African's magic blade. As she moved to the side, she held up a glowing red disc in her free hand.

"Looking for this? Once we find the other three talismans, your hopes of stopping what is to come will be over, Sorceress. Even with all your power, you cannot beat all of us."

Joanna cursed and flung out her free hand, fingers splayed wide. Ropy tendrils launched from her fingers towards the Eldara and the artifact. Two of the five tendrils connected with the disc while the other three wrapped their sticky ends around the woman's wrist.

Tugging with all her might, Joanna tried to pull the Eldara off balance while also hoping to dislodge the magical remnant of Bellum.

Hangbe darted in, taking advantage of the momentary standoff to land a strike against the arm held by Joanna's spell.

The magic attack took the Eldara by surprise, but she recovered faster than Joanna anticipated. With a twisting move that would have dislocated most people's shoulders, the other woman managed to both parry Hangbe's attack, and slice through all five of the strands holding her arm and the disc.

Bellowing with rage, Joanna charged, hoping to distract the Eldara so Hangbe could come in from the opposite side. It didn't work.

The Eldara launched herself straight up, inverting so she stood upside-down on the domed ceiling above. The move caught Hangbe by surprise, and the Eldara managed a slicing blow that caught the Amazon across the shoulders.

Hangbe went down with a yelp of pain as the silver-clad Eldara Warrior flicked the blood from her blessed blade. She beckoned to Joanna. "Come on. I've never killed a human before. It's always been forbidden until now."

"Well, I have killed Eldara. I've found it's nothing special at all."

The blast of spell energy Joanna launched wasn't at the laughing woman on the ceiling. It was at the worked, rectangular stones of the dome. A section of the ceiling cracked and fell away, dislodging the woman so she fell back to the ground.

Stunned, the Eldara struggled to rise as Joanna rushed in.

Just before the sorceress reached her, the woman grabbed Hangbe and pressed her sword up against her throat. "Stop, or I'll end her right now."

Joanna skidded to a stop. The chamber fell silent. All the fetchlings had been killed and the rest of their team came up to form a semicircle around the Eldara and Hangbe.

"You can't escape, Eldara. Give up the disc and I'll give you your life."

"You're in no position to bargain, girl. I can take this one's fragile life and still fight my way free. However, rather than expend the energy, I'll trade her for safe passage."

"Don't do it," Hangbe shouted. "Kill her."

The Eldara jerked her blade a little and some blood trickled down from the Amazon's neck.

Beside Joanna, Gibbie growled deep in his throat. "Don't you dare."

"Or what, Vampire?"

His bluff called, Gibbie shook his head. "I swear if you kill her, I'll hunt you down and end you."

Marian added, "We all will."

Joanna needed to get control of this situation or things were going to go downhill too quickly to turn back. "Stop! Everyone freeze."

Once she was sure everyone had listened, she turned back to the Eldara. "What guarantee do I have you'll keep your word?"

"I swear upon my heavenly blade. I'll let this one go as soon as I exit the chamber and am sure none of you pursue me."

"Fine, let her through."

The others stared at her for a few seconds, then stepped back to make room. The Eldara lifted Hangbe with ease and walked through the open space until she reached the room's exit. She laughed and kicked Hangbe in the small of her back, sending her flying into the room. By the time the others turned from Hangbe to look for her, the Eldara was gone.

"You shouldn't have done that," Hangbe groaned as she rolled onto her side. Blood streamed down her back where the blessed blade had sliced open her body armor and the skin and muscle beneath.

"I had no choice. Wim and Dora, help Gibbie tend to Hangbe's injury. Marian, see if you can catch a scent of the Eldara's trail. Maybe we can follow her."

As the others set to work, Joanna walked over to Kristof. "You're older than the rest of us here. Have you seen anything like that disc before?"

The Djinn shook his head. "No, but I could feel it's power. It contains both dark and wild magic, though I can't understand how. If that is the type of relic we're looking for, it would definitely possess the power needed to do what you want Dean to do, in theory at least."

Joanna frowned. That wasn't good news at all. She hoped the others were having better luck.

Chapter 17

DEAN TURNED the SUV into the entrance to the university, just outside the city limits. He glanced over at Brynne beside him. "Are you sure this is where Famis first landed in the city?"

Brynn, sitting next to him in the passenger seat, nodded. "James and Rudy tracked down reports of the four horsemen dating back to when we think they arrived. Several witnesses at the time reported seeing a robed figure walking from the weather observatory atop the science building on campus. He apparently assaulted and killed several security guards who tried to stop him.

James added from the back seat, "It was dumb luck we discovered it. Rudy's son goes to school here and happened to read an article in the campus newspaper mentioning the attacks. Otherwise, we never would've known anything about it. When we followed up at the time, there was definite magical demonic residue."

"Not to mention the smell," Rudy said.

Dean drove through campus, trying to remember exactly where the science building was located. He'd known there was a planetarium and observatory on the roof, but hadn't known about the weather station set up as well. Given how Famis came in on the heels of a blizzard that fateful night, Dean was sure it was the right place to start looking.

He slowed and looked around. He'd pulled over in back of what he thought was the right building. "I think I can park over there, but we still will have to figure out a way to get inside."

Rudy held up his phone. "I called ahead to campus police. They're going to have an officer open the building for us. He should be meeting us soon, if he's not already here."

Dean pulled the SUV into the lot on the side and parked facing the three-story building. A sign on the side of the building confirmed it was the right place.

"There's a campus police vehicle parked right there. Your guy must already be here, Rudy."

The five of them all got out and walked around to the front of the building opposite where the police car had parked. Both James and Brynne stopped suddenly. Dean, Leah, and Rudy stopped as well.

"What is it?" Dean asked, searching the darkness outside the circle of light cast by the street lamps by the entrance.

Brynne bared her fangs. "I smell fresh blood."

"Me, too." James added. He pointed towards the front doors.

Dean spotted a crumpled figure halfway inside an open door. Rudy bounded ahead, followed closely by Leah. Both the shifters had started their transformation as they ran. James and Brynne kept up right behind them.

Given the super powers of the other four, it did not surprise Dean to be the slowest of the group by far. The others had already taken in what had happened and spread out around the body, searching for clues by the time he got there.

"Is it the police officer?" Dean asked as he ran up, gasping for air.

Brynne knelt by the body. "Something with a lot of strength and claws gutted him. They cut right through his Kevlar vest like it was butter."

Leah pointed inside. "I smell something odd. It seems like a cross between a burning campfire and an entire book of matches lighting up at once."

Rudy growled. "I smell it too. That's brimstone, and that means there are definitely demons around."

Dean didn't like the sound of that. He couldn't let them beat him to the artifact if that's what they were here for. "We have to stop them."

James pointed inside. "Rudy, find the nearest stairwell. We shouldn't take the elevator. Leah, you watch our backs. You'll smell the demons before you see them. Don't let anyone sneak up behind us."

Rudy disappeared inside and Leah hung back as the others entered the building before coming in herself.

Ahead of them, Rudy had already raced up the steps to scout by the time Dean made it into the stairwell. He'd just caught his breath from racing to the front door and he stared at the steps, shaking his head. "Man, I've really got to get into better shape."

Brynne smiled at him "What's the problem, probie? Do I need to carry you?"

"Don't you dare. I'll be fine.

Leah came into the stairwell. "Go, Brynne, I've got him."

Brynne nodded and raced up the stairs to follow James and Rudy to the roof. Dean smiled and thanked Leah with a nod. He started up the steps, trying to go as quickly as he could and still maintain some semblance of reserve in case of trouble. Leah stayed at the bottom until he reached the first landing, then came up after him.

By the time Dean got to the top of the stairwell, the other three stood at the foot of a ladder bolted to the wall. It led up to a hatch in the ceiling. Dean could make out stars above. The hatchway was already open.

James said, "It's not good. Rudy went up and peeked over the edge."

"Yeah, there are definitely demons up there. I can't tell how many, but it's more than just one or two. I also smell something else, but I'm not sure exactly what, or who, it is. It's almost familiar. The demon smell is messing with my nose and I can't be sure."

"Could it be another demon?" Brynne asked.

"Maybe, but it doesn't smell like that. It smells almost like…" Rudy trailed off as he thought about his answer. As Leah reached the last landing and stood beside Dean, Rudy finished his sentence. "It smells almost like one of the angels."

"You mean the Eldara?" Dean couldn't believe that. "Why would one of them be working with the demons?"

The others all shook their heads.

"Maybe…" Brynne began, thinking out loud. "Maybe the Eldara is here tracking the demons just like we are."

"Well, if that's the case, then I'll be happy to have the help." Dean looked at the others. Something about this didn't add up, but he found it hard to believe someone like Ashley or even Gabe would side with the demons. Even after everything Joanna had told them about the future, he couldn't get his mind around some of heaven's messengers doing anything so dark.

"So how do we want to do this?" Rudy asked.

James looked at the ladder. "Brynne and I will go up first. We can get up there the quickest. Rudy, you follow, and then Leah. Dean, you come up last and be careful. There don't appear to be any demons down here, but watch your back."

Dean nodded and stepped aside as the others readied themselves. James and Brynne stood on either side of the ladder, giving each other a brief glance. They took off up the ladder side-by-side. The pair moved so quickly, they disappeared in a blur of motion. Rudy raced up right behind them.

Leah spared a glance to Dean as she flexed her shifter muscles beneath her tawny fur. Snarls and growls echoed down to them from above. "Watch your back. It already sounds like a serious fight up there."

Dean barely got off a nod before he followed the others up onto the roof. He stood alone in the stairwell, listening to the sounds of snarls, growls, and occasional shouts from above. He looked up at the night sky visible through the square hatchway at the top of the ladder. Fighting down the dread rising inside him, Dean climbed to join the others.

Whatever it sounded like from down below, Dean wasn't prepared for the fierceness of the battle happening on the rooftop above. Leah and Rudy stood back to back, fighting off four of the smaller demonlings. Each was the size of a large dog, like a German Shepherd. The two shifters held their own, but were mostly on the defensive.

Dean sidled along the roof's edge, staying well away from that fight. He stopped and ducked as Brynne ripped the throat out of the small Fetch demon, the blow sending it cart-wheeling past Dean.

On the opposite side, James tumbled across the flat black tar of the roof. He fought a desperate hand-to-hand fight with a tall, thin man wearing a gray overcoat. As they rolled across the roof, a silver sword blade scattered away from the pair to come to rest at the parapet beside Dean's feet.

Dean took all this in over the space of a few seconds then without a thought, bent to pick up the sword. He studied the blade, realizing the man whom James fought was one of the Eldara.

That fight puzzled him. Why was he fighting with James and helping the demons?

A pulse of energy ran down the blade, alerting Dean to trouble just in time to swing it around to meet a charging demon. The thing leaped for Dean's throat and he brought up the blessed sword just in time to skewer it through the chest. The snapping jaws closed to within inches of his face before the fetchling fell limp against him, nearly knocking him over the edge.

Steadying himself, Dean drew the blade free. It left a smoking black hole in the dead demon at his feet. He hefted the sword, which felt somehow right in his hand, and shouted, "Yeah, that's right. I'm not just a puny human right now, am I?"

Brynne called out. "Don't get cocky. Hey, behind you!"

He spun around in time to fend off another of the demonlings. It skittered backward, avoiding the glowing silver sword he wielded.

In the background, Dean made out that Leah and Rudy had finished off two of the four demons they fought, though Rudy favored his left side and clutched at his leg. Brynne couldn't help him. She had to jump over to take on another demon, and James still tumbled along with the swordless Eldara.

Knowing he was on his own, Dean did his best to keep the pointy end of the sword facing towards the fetchling. The demon circled, trying to get around behind him. Dean turned in place with the glowing silver blade between him and the snarling beast. The thing jerked to the left then back to the right, trying to fake Dean out.

The snarling beast gave up trying to flank him and charged in. Dean hacked down at it, using an awkward two-handed chopping attack that didn't land as effectively as he'd hoped.

The demon screamed as the blade scored a blackened line across its back. It skittered away before reaching Dean.

He'd hoped to kill it with his mighty blow. This was one of the few times he fretted that he wasn't as savvy in a fight as his friends.

He screamed as the demon charged in at him again. Hacking down with the sword again and again, Dean lopped off bits of flesh and scaly hide as he dug with the sword at the top of the demon's head. The whole time, he kept kicking at it to keep its teeth from connecting with his legs. He must've finally caused enough damage. The creature slumped to the ground with a groan and lay still.

Dean stumbled backward, catching himself before he fell over the side of the building, slumping instead to the crushed stone and tar of the rooftop.

Leah saw him fall as she finished the last demon facing her and Rudy. She raced over, took one look at his shredded pants leg and dug into a fanny pack she had buckled around her waist.

Dean recognized the field emergency triage kit issued to all paramedics to carry in their private vehicles.

"Hey, easy."

"Quiet. You're bleeding."

Surprised, Dean looked down and realized she was right. The pain followed the realization, and he gritted his teeth against the searing agony coming from his thigh.

"How bad is it?"

Leah smiled. "It's not as bad as I first thought. Mostly superficial, though I think you're going to be sore for a while. You might need a few stitches."

She finished bandaging his leg and helped him stand. The fight was over. Well, over except for the standoff between James and the Eldara.

The two stood facing each other near the university weather station.

James leveled an accusatory finger at the angel. "What are you doing here? Your kind is supposed to fight demons, not order them around."

The Eldara sneered at James, "I could say the same for you. Why are you siding with humans over your own kind? You could rule alongside us, you know. Those of us who have joined together with the netherworlders realize we could rule this whole planet. The humans are so easily controlled."

"I like things the way they are." James pointed at the Eldara. "Give us what you retrieved from the weather station."

"What, you mean this?" He reached into his overcoat and pulled out a shining green disc. It was about a half inch thick and about the same diameter as a DVD. "If you're looking for this, that means you've discovered the others exist as well. Know this. We're going to find them before you do. We will not let you stop us."

"You're not getting off this roof," James gestured to the others. "You're outnumbered. Give me the disc and you can go."

"I think you forget who you're talking to, bloodsucker. I'm not trapped anywhere."

Before James could move, the Eldara raised his arms straight up as wings sprouted from his back. With a mighty thrust of the feathered pinions, the angel soared into the sky. Even with all that, James almost managed to grab him with a giant leap. He landed on the other side of the roof, tucking and rolling back to his feet. He stared up into the dark nighttime sky. The Eldara and the disc were nowhere in sight.

"What was that disc he carried?" Dean asked.

"I expect it was the relic we were looking for," Brynne replied. "The good news is, now we know what the others will look like. Hopefully, we can find them before the Eldara and their demonic allies do."

James came over, staring down at Dean's injured leg. "How bad is it?"

Leah shrugged. "He's lucky. It's not too bad, though he'll need help getting down the ladder.

"Hey, I'm not an invalid. Prop me up on somebody's shoulder. I've still got one good leg."

Dean pushed himself to his feet, swayed a little, and sat right back down again. Staring up at Brynne and James, he smiled. "Okay, I guess I need a little help."

"You think?" Brynne said. She glanced at Leah. "I brought a med radio. It's in the SUV. Call in and tell them we have someone who needs a few stitches."

Leah dashed for the open hatchway, leaping out of sight down into the stairwell.

Brynne gestured to Rudy. "How are you?"

"I'll heal up shortly. I can help you get him down the ladder. I'll go down first and you and James can hand him down to me."

Embarrassed, Dean tried to keep them from fussing over him. They got him down the ladder to the stairwell. They took the elevator down to the ground floor, though. Leah already had the SUV running and they drove to the hospital to get him and Rudy checked out.

Chapter 18

DEAN WAITED as the elevator doors parted before limping out into the hallway that led to his apartment. The ER had been busy and he'd had to wait several hours to get stitched up. It was mid-morning by the time they released him. He was still a little sore from the stitches as the numbing injection wore off. He reached for the knob to the apartment door, but before he could turn it Joanna opened it from the inside.

She stared down at his leg and the white gauze dressing where his pants had been cut away, then back up at his face. "When I heard what happened, I feared it injured you much worse than it appears. They seem to have patched you up for the most part."

"I guess so." Dean shrugged. "I'll be happy if I never have to worry about getting attacked by one of those things again. Given what the demon could've done to me, I guess I shouldn't complain about a little pain and a few stitches."

"You should've been more careful. Didn't you always tell me you were a healer, not a fighter? You're best off leaving the fighting to those who know what to do."

"I was. I swear. One of them got around the others and came after me. In the end we defeated them, but not before one of the Eldara spirited away the artifact we were searching for. I heard what happened with your team as well. With two of those things taken from us, we need to find the others before it's too late."

Joanna moved aside to let him enter the apartment and closed the door behind him. "How bad is the pain?"

"It's not so bad. Rudy drove me home just to keep me from pulling at the stitches so soon. I should be fine in a few days."

Joanna's face took on a look of disdain that matched one he'd seen from Jaz countless times. "Let's try to avoid getting between demons and what they want anytime soon, okay, Dad? It's bad enough Mom is out of commission in the hospital without having to worry about you, too."

Dean sat on the sofa and raised his leg over the coffee table while Joanna slid a throw pillow under his ankle. He let out a sigh of relief. "On the bright side, I did get to see your mother while I was at the hospital. She's all right from what I can tell, though she's still unconscious. I'm worried about that. The doctors can't explain, though they say all her vitals are in normal range."

Joanna smiled. "She'll be alright. It's a normal reaction to the magical healing I used. I drew a lot of that energy to heal her from her own internal reserves. She has to restore those reserves before she'll wake up again. It should only be another day or so before she's back with us. "

Dean glanced down at his leg and then back at his daughter. He raised an eyebrow in question.

Joanna shook her head. "No, I can't heal you the same way. Well, I should say I won't heal you the same way. Your life isn't threatened and that spell it takes a lot out of me, too. I need to conserve my strength. There are at least two Eldara working with the demons, and we need to be very careful about how much energy I use. I might need it to fight them later. Also, we can't afford to have you unconscious right now. I feel like you're going to be pivotal to how this whole thing resolves."

That brought to mind something Dean didn't understand. "Why have these Eldara teamed up with the demons? It doesn't make any sense. They're natural enemies. I know you explained it before, but I still don't get it."

"In an ordinary world without barriers between the planes, you're right. They're enemies because their masters are enemies. However, now that these Eldara are trapped here on earth, and more or less living as mortals do, they've lost some of their heavenly connections." An expression crossed Joanna's face, and she looked like she was about to spit in disgust. "Where I come from, Dad, the Eldara are our enemies, or at least most of them are. They are the ones who sided with the demons and began the takeover that would eventually destroy most of the world and almost all the people in it. In the world I come from, we're fighting a losing battle. That is why I'm here. We have to open the gateways to heaven and allow the Eldara to resume their roles as messengers for the gods of light. Until then, we can't let up. If some of the Eldara have realized they can work alongside the demons, then others will too."

Dean picked up on something in the way she said that last sentence. "Others like Gabe, you mean?"

Joanna nodded. "Gabe's an Archangel. His power and notoriety is what will solidify the union between demon and Eldara. Then the war begins."

Dean shook his head. That was new information. He found it hard to believe. "Look, Gabe is not the best person in the world. I, of all people, know that. I can't see him doing this, however. It would destroy everything he's existed for."

"But that's not how he looks at it, Dad. Gabe sees this as the natural evolution of things. He and others like him think he and the demons can rule this earth with no interference from those who used to be their masters. To him, this makes perfect sense."

When she explained it that way, Dean realized Gabe might just be that mercenary about things. He'd shown no caring about all the billions of people who might have died if Dean had allowed Armageddon to happen. That had been to serve the light, but what was all that different about starting a war with demons as allies? It all made him worry even more about finding the other relics from the horsemen. There were only two left, and he had an idea about where at least one of them was.

Dean nodded to himself, saying, "I think I have to pay a visit to the morgue. If I'm right, that is where Mortis, the horseman of death, will have left his artifact. It's probably hidden somewhere inside the room where we fought them at the end."

"If that's the case," Joanna said. "Then maybe I should go with some of the others and leave you here to heal."

"No," Dean said. "I need to be there. I'm the one who faced off against Mortis. I think without me, you'll never find the artifact on your own."

Joanna shrugged "Suit yourself. I will not argue with you, but we're going to take some more firepower with us this time. The Eldara have teamed up with enough of the demons to stop us if we don't show up in force. Contact the others and let them know what we're doing next."

Dean nodded. He slipped his phone from his pocket and began tapping away, sending messages. The sun was up and that meant James, Brynne, and Gibbie were all sacked out while the sun was up. Rudy would be awake, though. He could pass along the messages. They could all meet downtown outside the morgue after nightfall and see what they could figure out.

Dean put the phone down after sending his messages and yawned. Realizing that he was going to be heading out later that night, he needed to get some rest. Rather than get up and move to the bedroom, he lay back against the cushions and soon fell asleep. His dreams turned fitful as he encountered Gabe. They argued over his father starting a war. Each time, Dean lost the fight despite knowing he was in the right. He kept reliving the argument, losing again each time. When he awakened later, he worried if his nightmares were a sign of things to come. He hoped not.

Chapter 19

JOANNA WATCHED as her father dozed off on the sofa. She waited a few minutes to make sure he was in a deep sleep, then gathered her coat and weapons and set out. He'd be safe enough here inside the Errington building while she went and took a look around Gabe's apartment. He should be at work, and she needed to see if he'd already contacted the Fetch demon. The two Eldara they'd encountered hadn't mentioned the archangel, but their involvement worried her. She'd hoped to keep Gabe insulated from what was to come as much as possible. Once he became involved with starting the war, she feared there would be no way to turn back the timeline.

She checked out one of the SUVs from in the garage downstairs, retrieving the keys from the guard at the desk. Dean had given her access to that much, as well as the armory, so she could restock her ammunition as needed now without having to break in. As she pulled out of the lot and started across town, Joanna planned what she'd have to do if it turned out Gabe was already working with the demons.

The archangel was a formidable opponent. He'd proven that time and again in the world she knew. She'd made numerous attempts to get to him with her Hunter teams. Each time she'd hoped to end the war. They'd all ended in failure. She'd lost a lot of good people on those missions. That was what had set the decision for her to come back to the past and try to stop it all. She didn't want to risk anyone else to get the job done. Now it all seemed to be falling apart back here, too.

Her thoughts returned to her parents and her brow furrowed with worry. She'd sensed the life stirring within her mother when she'd healed her. It confirmed what she'd foreseen in the scrying bowl. The timeline had changed back here, too. Being in this time and place reminded her of the previous trip back and how her teenaged self had returned to a changed future.

Her finger scratched at the edge of her eyepatch as she remembered that first day back, landing by surprise in a world destroyed by demons. She'd lost the eye soon after she got back, attacked and almost killed by a pack of ravenous demons before she knew what was happening. It had been a rude awakening in the worst way.

Joanna shook her head. She shouldn't entertain such thoughts. She'd learned long ago not to dwell on what had already been written. Few things could be changed for her memories. All she could do was continue on with her plan and make sure the future she knew never happened to these good people here.

She pulled up in front of Gabe's building and walked upstairs to his door. He usually taught his trumpet lessons this time of day, so she could search his apartment uninterrupted for a little while. If he'd been in contact with the Fetch demon, there had to be some residual clue to sniff out.

Pressing her palm against the door knob and crossing her middle and ring finger together, Joanna muttered a few words in the fairy tongue, unlocking the mechanism. As the door popped open, she pushed it open the rest of the way and stepped inside, pushing it closed behind her with her foot.

The apartment had a musty feel to it, both in odor and appearance. It didn't appear much different than it had the last time she was here, but something had changed. She looked around, trying to decide what it was about the place that felt off to her senses. A loaf of moldy bread wrapped in plastic sat on the counter. She stared at it for a few seconds before it hit her. Gabe hadn't been here for days. She pulled open the refrigerator. The food inside had also all soured or spoiled.

Dammit, she thought. He'd had one of the demons here in the room. Nothing could foul food like that all at once except a visit from one of the unclean ones. That meant Gabe had already had a conversation with the Fetch, or one of its senior Hellspawn. Her grandfather had abandoned this place, knowing she'd come looking for him here.

She began her search in earnest, trying to find some clue that might tell her where he'd gone. She found nothing after fifteen minutes and turned her thoughts inward as she conjured a spell to sense the residue of magic in and around this place. It was a powerful spell, though extremely localized. It would suit her purposes here. Gabe's apartment consisted of just a bathroom, a bedroom, and the living room kitchen area. She didn't need to cover much ground.

Closing her eyes and concentrating, Joanna summoned the power that would allow her to sense magical auras and artifacts, too. If she got lucky, maybe she'd find where Gabe might have hidden something, expecting to come back and get it later.

She immediately caught a hint of arcane residue. Joanna kept her eyes closed, opening her mouth and running her tongue across her lips to taste the aura, then sniffed the air to gather in more of the flavor of that which she sought.

Her hand raised, pointed to her left. That way.

Opening her eyes, she headed back to Gabe's bedroom. She realized as soon as she stepped inside that Gabe had already taken whatever it was she'd sensed. While the residue was strong, it wasn't strong enough to still be close by.

Getting down on her hands and knees, she searched under the bed, following the scent. She reached out with her spell until she found the loose floorboards hidden there. Sliding the bed to the side, she removed the wooden panels, revealing a small cavity inside. The residue was strongest here.

It tasted of rot and disease, making her nose wrinkle as she peered down into the gap. Gabe had already found one of the artifacts and had hidden it here in his apartment. Judging from the aura around the opening in the floor, it had been hidden here for some time. He must have discovered it soon after Dean defeated the horsemen. The Eldara possessed powerful magic of their own, so he might have thought to use it for his own purposes somehow, even before the Fetch demon returned.

Standing up, Joanna looked around the apartment one last time then headed for the door. She was sure now. Gabe wasn't coming back here. He'd decided to leave this place behind and that worried her. It probably meant he'd decided to work with the demons already.

Maybe Dean or the others would have some clue where Gabe would hide out. There was still a chance to keep him from cementing the deal that would forever doom the planet to a literal hell on Earth.

Shutting the apartment door, she returned to the street, letting the spell she carried fade away as she did. As the power drained from her, she felt that familiar remorse at letting it go. It was one thing she'd learned about herself long ago. That power was seductive and sought to control her as much as she sought to control it. Using it too much or too often could lead her down a path she didn't want to contemplate. She'd already opened herself too much when healing her mother.

Just thinking about it caused her to crave the rush of the arcane force again. Thrusting away the thought of opening herself up to draw in the energy once more, she climbed back into the SUV and drove across town back to the Errington building. She'd wait there until her father awakened. She'd join the others at the morgue downtown that evening. If they recovered the last artifact, they'd be able to do what was needed without confronting the archangel. If not, then she'd fill in the assembled team about what needed to be done. Maybe it wouldn't be too late.

Chapter 20

STANDING at the top of the ramp leading down to the county morgue's underground loading dock, Dean got an instant flash of his past from the last time he was here. Facing down the four Horsemen of the Apocalypse had left an indelible impression on him. Shaking off the memory of that night, he looked to either side at the people assembled with him. Some of them have been there that night, too. They had fought to get him inside to confront the demons intent on ending the world. It was strange to be back here for a mission that seemed oddly related.

"Let's get down there," Dean said to the assembled teams. "If what Joanna said is right about Gabe, he could already be here."

Gibbie stared down at the well-lit loading dock area and shook his head. "Everything looks fine from here, Dean? What makes you think he's already here?"

Dean shrugged. "He and the demons have been one step ahead of us the entire time. I think it's best to be on our guard and assume they're here." He strode forward towards the bottom of the ramp. The others fell in behind him, with Joanna and James in the lead.

When he reached the bottom of the ramp, everything looked

normal, just as Gibbie had said. The coroner's vans sat parked in a row on one side in the underground space, opposite the loading dock. At this time of night, they would lock the entrance unless someone was out making a run for a fresh body in the middle of the night.

James pointed to either side. "I smell fresh blood. Spread out and look around before we try to go inside. This might be a trap."

The others did as he asked. It was Marian who discovered the first sign of trouble. She'd started up the narrow stairs leading up to the loading dock's concrete deck. "Ewww, there's sticky blood all over this railing." She pulled her hand back and held it up to show the others.

James shook his head. "Maybe they dropped a dead body while carrying it up and into the building?"

Brynne studied the railing for a few seconds. "No, that doesn't make any sense. When the bodies get here, they're zipped up tight in sealed body bags. There's no blood to worry about." She brought her bloody fingertips up to her nose, sniffing at them. "Plus, this is fresh."

She pointed to the top of the steps where a smear of blood across the floor led toward the double doors leading inside. "I think they killed someone and dragged them inside."

No sooner had she said it, than the doors burst open and at least a dozen of the small fetchling demons charged out at them. The group had spread out to search for clues, so all most of them could do was to prepare to defend themselves wherever they stood.

"There seems to be an endless supply of these little buggers," Dean shouted as he backed up to get behind James and Brynne. "Where are they getting all of them?"

Jo came to stand beside him, her pistol in one hand and her sword in the other. "Once the fetchlings are here, they can lay eggs and reproduce dozens in little more than a week. They grow very fast."

She fired off a series of rounds into a cluster of the ones charging their way. The magical rounds she'd liberated from the Errington special weapons armory succeeded in slowing down the initial surge. The ones she hit dropping and rolling onto their backs, their clawed arms and legs twitching a little as the life leeched out of them.

Jo's attack proved enough of a break for James and Brynne to charge forward and meet the remaining stragglers on their side. Joanna holstered her empty pistol and raced after them. Dean struggled to keep up, if only to stay close to the support of the others.

James ripped the head from one demon, hacking at the neck with a sort of Roman short sword. The gladius gleamed now, slick with black demon blood in the overhead lights as he spun around to take on another one.

Brynne kicked one demon in the side of the head, sending it bowling head over heels into a pair of others running right behind it. The tumbling demon tripped up one of them, but the other leaped over and bolted to the left, right at Dean.

He backpedaled to get away. Before he'd taken two steps, Joanna slid into place between him and the demon. She hacked down twice with her shining blade in a motion so fast, he found it hard to follow. When she finished, the demon lay bloody and twitching at her feet.

The attack began quickly and ended just as fast. The expanded double team had taken down all the demons. Hangbe and Gibbie had accounted for a surprising number on their own, judging from the pile of bodies piled in front of them.

Dean searched to see if anyone needed help. "Everyone okay? Sound off if you or someone nearby needs medical attention." Wim and Dora came over to join Dean with their field triage kits, ready to treat any wounds.

Hangbe shook her head, rattling the beaded braids in her hair. "It'll take more than a few minor demons to damage this group. They'll know we're here now, though. We must press forward."

"Agreed," Dean said. He started for the steps up to the double doors, but Joanna pulled him back.

"Not so fast, Father. Let's let someone with some firepower go in their first." She started towards the stairs, loading a fresh magazine in her pistol.

Hangbe beat her to the entrance. The Amazon bounded up the steps with Gibbie right behind her and disappeared inside. Dean and the others raced in a tight group to follow them.

Hangbe had paused a little farther down the hallway until Gibbie pointed her in the direction of the main autopsy theater where the showdown had happened the last time they were here.

As Dean entered at a run behind Gibbie and Hangbe, he skidded to a stop. Gabe was already there.

The archangel stood across the room with its steel autopsy tables in a row. Beside him stood two others. Dean recognized one as the man who'd flown away with the artifact from the university's rooftop. He assumed the other one, a woman, was the one the others had encountered underground.

Gabe smiled as the group entered and held up a hand, stopping their advance. "That's far enough. I didn't think you'd have any trouble with the pitiful few demons set to guard the entrance."

His offhand manner angered Dean. "What the hell, Gabe? Why are you consorting with Demons? I thought you wanted me to reopen the pathways to the upper realms."

The Eldara shrugged. "Someone pointed out to me that if I was going to be stuck here on earth, trapped with a bunch of mortals, it might just be my opportunity to become a god among men."

Joanna snarled. "You are no god, angel scum. You're nothing but a lowly servant. The messenger boy of beings who've forsaken you, nothing more."

Gabe frowned. "I will not be baited into attacking you, Granddaughter. Though we three are powerful, I have no doubt you would eventually defeat us. You sought to deceive me when you first arrived, trying to keep me from discovering what was to be my true destiny in the future."

Joanna took a step forward, leading with her blade.

"Hold up, Jo. We will not change his mind." Dean shook his head and turned back to his father. "Now what? Do we just stand here and stare at each other?"

Gabe smiled. "You all could just leave. There's nothing to find here. We've already searched. Someone else must've found Mortis' artifact already. At first I thought it was you. Seeing you here and now, though, I realize that is not the case."

Joanna said, "If we kill him now, maybe the war will never happen."

"There doesn't have to be a war," Gabe replied. "If the right people side with us, then the others will learn to become our servants. Those who do so will survive. Those who don't will die. It's that simple."

"How many other Eldara have sided with you?" Dean asked. "Have you talked to Ashley or Ingrid, or others like them? I can't believe they'd stand with you in this insane attempt to take over the world."

It was the woman beside Gabe who answered Dean. "I don't know what the healing Eldara will do, however, the other Valkyries will come around as I have. They will realize that our job to collect souls for the battle at the end of the world is no longer needed."

Gabe added, "She's right, Dean. The rest of the Eldara stuck here with us will eventually join up as well."

Dean didn't know what to say. It seemed like they had all the answers. He also didn't like the idea of a fight with them down here. It was a good bet he and his friends could take them, but at what cost?

He looked left and right at all his assembled friends. "Let them go. Fighting them here now will only end up with a lot of us dead or injured. We'll deal with them later."

Joanna looked like she was going to resist and attack the angels. Dean held her gaze, pleading with his eyes until her grim expression softened and she gave him a brief nod.

Gabe laughed. "It's good to see she has respect for at least one of her elders, son. You know, you could rule alongside me. You are half-Eldara yourself. I'm sure we could find a way to awaken that part of your being, as the Oracle said was possible. It would set you apart, above the others."

"No, thank you. I think I'll stay human for now. It seems like being an Eldara is not all it's cracked up to be."

"Suit yourself." Gabe turned and waved to the other two. They moved along the far wall and down the side of the room towards the door. The group moved to the side to let them pass, though everyone kept their eyes on the trio, as if expecting an attack at any moment.

As the door closed and they moved down the corridor away from the autopsy theater, Dean nodded towards the door. "Leah, Marian, go after them and make sure they're really leaving. It could be a trick to lull us into a false sense of security."

The two women did as they were told. Both had already shifted partially into their were-animal forms. Marian had the look of the wolf about her, while Leah's forearms sprouted tawny fur dotted with the tan and black spots of the jaguar.

James shook his head. "This isn't good, Dean. If the artifact is already taken, who else would come to retrieve it if it wasn't us or them?"

Dean started to answer that he didn't know, but stopped as Joanna moved to the center of the room. She turned and stared around her, though her gaze seemed blank and unfocused, as if she were looking into the distance. Raising her hands straight out from her shoulders, palms facing outward, she closed her eyes and began to hum a droning tune. She murmured something in words Dean couldn't quite make out. A subtle, bluish glow outlined her hands and forearms as she slowly turned in place.

After about thirty seconds, Joanna stopped her rotation and lowered her arms. The glow faded from her arms and hands as she opened her eyes. She smiled at Dean. "The Eldara can be such fools sometimes. They always think they know everything. Once they decide something is a certain way, they never take a moment to look backward and reassess their decision."

"What are you saying?" Brynne asked.

"The artifact is still here. It's hidden somehow, though. It wouldn't have been readily available to even an archangel's enhanced vision. Something has locked it away behind some sort of concealment. It's puzzling."

"Does that mean we can find it?" Gibbie asked. "I love puzzles. It'll be like one of those escape rooms."

Hangbe laughed. "Darling Gibson, you are always such a breath of fresh air. I'm sure if the sorceress is right, then we will possess the necessary skills to unravel the clues to its location." The Amazon glanced at Joanna. "What do we need to do to reveal the artifact?"

Joanna smiled. "It's going to take me some time, but I think I can at least discover where it is in the room. How we remove the wards that are guarding it is another question."

She set to work right away, getting the others to help her clear the room by pushing the autopsy tables and carts to the sides so the center of the room was empty. Then she sat down on the concrete floor and began another spell. Dean and the others stood by and watched, giving her the quiet she needed to locate that which they sought.

Chapter 21

IF DEAN EXPECTED Joanna to complete her spell searching for the location of the artifact quickly, he was mistaken. In fact, it took her almost 3 hours before she uncovered a result. In the meantime, Dean and the others did what they could to keep the city morgue building secure in case Gabe returned with reinforcements.

Marian and Leah returned soon after they followed the Eldara out to inform them the trio had flown away as soon as they reached the exterior of the building. The pair were sent back out to keep watch over the loading dock area. Dean gave them strict instructions not to fight but to retreat to the autopsy room if the Eldara reappeared.

While the two shifters took up their sentry positions, James and Brynn contacted Elk City officials to apprise them of a situation requiring a perimeter and lock down of the building until further notice. A few police units would be dispatched to watch outside, and any coroner cases would be diverted to the auxiliary morgue at the hospital. That should give them some privacy.

All that remained for them now was to settle in and wait until Joanna found the artifact, if it was still there as she thought. When she finally opened her eyes and let out a long exhausted sigh, she had sweat streaming down the sides of her face, plastering her hair in place. Dean had never seen a magical spell cause that kind of exertion before, though his experience with such things was admittedly limited.

"Did you find it?" Dean asked as he moved forward to help her stand.

"I did." She flexed backward with her hands against the small of her back as she tried to stretch out the kinks from being seated so long. Then she walked to the far side of the room and pointed to a spot on the cinderblock wall.

"It's here. It's been placed behind a complex set of wards creating a sort of magical pocket dimension. Someone has to unlock it before we can remove it."

"How?" James asked. "Does it require more magical help? I could send for the local coven and see if they can offer their resources."

Joanna shook her head. "No, what we require is for me to reveal the entrance. Then someone will have to go in and decipher the puzzle inside to unlock the artifact from its hiding place."

Brynne shook her head. "There's a real puzzle to solve, like a riddle or something?"

Joanne nodded. "Whoever locked this artifact in place had a sick sense of humor. If the puzzle is not unraveled correctly, it will likely kill whoever attempts to remove the talisman."

Dean stared at the spot on the wall his daughter had pointed towards. "Send me in. No matter what the risk, we aren't leaving here until we recover the artifact."

"I don't think you understand," Joanna said. "We all can't work on it together. Someone has to enter the dimension to solve it. Once you're inside, you are committed to finding the solution or die trying.
"

"I understand. How do I get in?"

"From what I can tell, you walk up and placed your hand on the correct spot. My spell revealed it. I think it also activated the transport mechanism for the puzzle. It will draw you into the pocket as soon as you touch the wall."

Hangbe smiled. "All is not lost. All we need to do is to stack the odds in our favor."

Gibbie nodded and smiled along with her. "I like the sound of that. What do we need to do?

"Magic often operates outside an understanding of technology. Those who cast such spells often disregard ways technology could be used to circumvent their traps. Some technologies can penetrate the magical veil hiding the pocket dimension."

"What did you have in mind?" Dean asked.

"I'm sure you have the standard Errington security load out in the back of the SUV?"

"I suppose I do. I didn't check. There's nothing back there I've ever needed other than the medic bag. What are you looking for?"

"You'll see. Give me the keys. I'll be right back."

Everyone waited while Hangbe and Gibbie disappeared. They returned about ten minutes later, each rolling a large black case in front of them. Setting the cases on the floor, the Amazon opened first one, and then the other. An array of electronic surveillance devices were stashed inside foam compartments in each case.

"What's all this stuff?" James asked. "It looks like it's standard radio gear."

Hangbe nodded. "Exactly. In my experience, standard radio waves can pierce most basic magical glamours, which is almost certainly what this is. Whoever enters will go in with a surveillance link. We'll set up the base station out here so we can transmit and receive information from them. The Errington teams have gear with both audio and video capability, so anything the individual inside sees, we will see, too."

Joanna smiled. "It's ingenious. I hadn't thought about it until now, but you're right. This should work, in theory at least."

Brynne looked around at the gathered team members. "Why does it have to be Dean who goes in? I think someone else should go in."

Several of the others raised their hands.

Dean shook his head. "It has to be me. I'm the one who fought Mortis at the end. My guess is there's something about this test that will require me to be there."

"You don't know that, Father. It's entirely possible that some sort of magic will be required inside. That limits it to me going in."

"Or me," Hangbe added. She reached up, stroking her fingers

across the ornate necklace she wore. "I have quite a few spells stored here that might come in handy. I should go."

Dean shook his head. "No. It's going to be me. Let's get the system set up and arranged so that I can go in. The longer we wait and argue about it, the more likely it is Gabe will come back to see what we're up to."

He stared around the room, meeting each individual's gaze for a second before moving on until he got a nod from everyone. Hangbe and Gibbie started pulling the gear out of the boxes and setting up the radio base station. They pulled one of the steel autopsy tables over and put a flat screen monitor on it, along with a keyboard and a small antenna array.

They handed Dean a belt pack from the other case. He clipped it onto his waistband. With Hangbe's help, he attached a cord that went to a headset with a single earpiece and microphone. He settled it into position and angled the microphone down so it rested in front of his chin. The ear cup of the headset also had a small tubular camera about the diameter of a standard number two pencil. It would pick up anything in the direction in which Dean faced.

He pressed the power button on the belt pack. A crackle of static squawked in his ear and he quickly dialed down the volume. He glanced towards the base station and video monitor, smiling as he saw the image on the screen showing exactly what he was looking at.

"This is great," Dean said. "With this, we can all help out. Together we should be able to solve the puzzle inside without a problem."

Dean moved over to face the cinderblock wall and Joanna came to join him.

She leaned in close, whispering, "You need to be careful in there, Dad. This is risky and you are the most mundane and human of all of us."

He shrugged. "Who knows? Maybe that's my biggest advantage. Come on, let's get this over with. The sooner I get that artifact, the sooner we can go back to the apartment and figure out our next steps."

Joanna nodded and pointed to a place on the wall. She'd marked it with a black felt-tip pen. "All you should have to do is place the flat of your palm over the X. Think about Mortis and what it felt like facing him. That should draw you into the puzzle."

Dean nodded and stared at the wall for a second before lifting his hand and pressing it against the mark. As soon as he did, something jerked him forward, pulling straight at the center of his chest as if someone had attached a rope around him. It startled him and he yelped in surprise. The tugging sensation stopped as soon as it began, and he opened his eyes. He stood in a stone passageway. Torches lit the corridor every twenty feet or so, stretching straight ahead into the distance. He couldn't make out the end of the hallway.

"At least it's not a maze. Are you guys getting this?"

A bit of static crackled in his ear, followed by Brynne's voice. "We hear you loud and clear. We can see the hallway, too."

"Okay, I'm going to move forward. If you see something, don't assume I do, too. Tell me to stop. This is a team effort."

Dean walked forward, taking his time and searching the walls for anything that might be a clue to whatever puzzle he was to solve. Although initially it appeared to go straight for a long way, the corridor ended about a hundred yards ahead.

Seeing something on the flat stone wall ahead of him, Dean stopped short. Four square ceramic tiles hung in a square pattern on the corridor's end. Each was white and painted in black with a different symbol. A leather thong connected each to a wooden peg inserted in a circular hole.

"Are you all seeing this?"

"Yes," Joanna said. "Move a little closer, but don't touch anything."

Dean did as he was told, stopping about five feet from the wall. He kept his hands down at his sides as he studied the four tiles. The runes or symbols made no sense to him, but hopefully the others would understand what they meant and what he was supposed to do.

"Dean," James said. "Lean forward to look at each tile in turn so we can get a good shot of each one. I'm capturing screen images so that we can compare them to what we can find from an internet search. Rudy and Brynne are using their phones to try to find comparable symbols that might help us determine what the tiles are supposed to do."

Turning his head, Dean held his gaze on each tile for a few seconds and then moving to the next one until he'd captured a good shot of each one. As he did, he noticed that while the tiles were arranged in the corners of a four-foot square, there were other peg holes at the midpoints of each of the square's sides. It looked like the pegs holding the tiles could be removed and re-inserted into another location if he wanted. He relayed his thoughts on to the rest of the team on the other end of the radio line.

There was a lot of discussion as the team tried to brainstorm what the puzzle meant. It took about five minutes before someone had an answer for him.

Joanna shushed the others and said, "Dad, Rudy and Brynne have found historical representations of what they think match the symbols you're looking at. They represent the four horsemen. Each one corresponds to a different one."

"Okay, so what am I supposed to do?"

"I think you're right that you're supposed to rearrange the tiles in a certain order, but we're not sure what that's supposed to be."

Dean thought about it for a few seconds. "It has to be the order in which they appeared here in Elk City. They each showed up with their own signs and effects on the people around them."

"I guess that makes sense," Joanna replied. "We only get one shot at this, though, so it's not as much as I'd like to go on. It's up to you, Dad."

Dean nodded. This made sense to him and felt right somehow. "The first horseman to manifest here was Malificar, the horseman of pestilence. Then came Bellum, the horseman of war, Famis, horseman of famine, and finally Mortis himself. If I can figure out how to arrange these, we should be good to go."

Gibbie's voice came over the link. "That works, we just need to figure which symbol is which."

"Exactly," Dean replied. "Which one is Malificar's?"

Brynne responded. "According to the search we did, the one in the lower right corner is his."

Dean stared straight ahead and took a deep breath and then reached out for the corresponding tile for the horseman of pestilence.

The wooden peg with the tile suspended from it slid out of the hole with ease. The leather cord that ran from the tile up to wrap around the peg was smooth and worn. Moving with care, he slid the peg into place in the top center between the two top tiles. He pressed the peg into place until it stopped and pulled his hand away.

"Nothing happened, so I guess that's a good sign. Next is war and then famine."

Brynne relayed the next two identities for the symbols. Dean moved to the upper left corner first, pulling the tile for Bellum from its hole in the wall and moving it downward to the middle left hole. Once again it's slid into place easily with no outward signs of any change.

He reached down and pulled out the peg for famine in the bottom left corner. He moved it over and placed it in the middle right hole. That left the final tile with the symbol for death. It was in the upper right corner. He pulled it from its spot and replaced it in the bottom middle hole below the first tile he moved. This time as he pressed the peg in place, an audible click sounded in the hallway. Dean froze.

"What was that?" Joanna asked.

"I don't know. Something happened when I pressed in the final one."

Dean took a step backward and looked around. That was when he saw it. In the ceiling just above his head, an opening had appeared. Inside was a dark circle glowing with a sickly purple light. Standing on his tiptoes, Dean reached up and closed his hand around the disc. It came away easily in his hand.

He pulled it down and stared at it for a second. Instantly, he felt the jerking pull at his midsection again, this time dragging him backward. He let out another yelp of surprise. He gasped for breath for a moment until he realized he was standing in the autopsy room again, staring at the X marked on the wall. He glanced down at his right hand. He held the ceramic disc they'd come for.

Everyone came over to cluster around him.

"You did it," Joanna said. "We have the final artifact."

"But will it be enough?" Dean asked. "They have the other three."

"True, but I think they needed all four. As long as we have one, they can't complete what they need to do. This should give you some leverage now, and maybe it'll be enough to do what needs to be done."

"And what exactly is that?"

Joanna shook her head. "I'm still not sure. Now that we have one of the artifacts, we'll find out, though. Then we will make sure the Eldara wars never start."

Chapter 22

BACK AT THE APARTMENT, Dean headed into his bedroom and shut the door. Joanna sat out in the living room watching a movie streaming on the TV. She seemed to get lost in the shows she watched there. He figured she missed the shows from her past. Based on what little she'd let slip about her future, things were pretty dire there and she hadn't watched any TV for years.

Dean lay back on his bed and stared at the ceiling. It was almost one in the morning. Despite his exhaustion, so much had happened in the last few days that he was a jumble of thoughts, all fighting for his conscious attention. He reached into his pocket and pulled out the disc he'd retrieved from the hiding place in the morgue. It seemed rather unremarkable given who it had belonged to.

He studied the artifact in the light of his bedside lamp. The black ceramic gleamed a little as he turned it in his hand, but it no longer glowed with the purple light he first saw as he grabbed it. The enameled finish had a glossy look to it. Runes had been etched all the way around the center in a spiral pattern. There was something else there besides the black background. The more he stared at it, the more it gave him a queasy feeling in the pit of his stomach.

He'd wondered if they needed to decipher the runes, but Joanna had told him it was merely common script of the demon tongue. It identified the owner of the disc. In this case, it belonged to Mortis, the horseman of death.

Rolling to his side and holding the disc closer to the bedside light, Dean studied it, trying to understand what he was supposed to do with it. Joanna seemed convinced he could use it to re-open the gateways to the upper planes, but he did not know how he was to do that. She had offered no guidance. All she'd said was that somehow he was to awaken a hidden part of himself. It was much the same as what Gabe had told him.

Ordinarily, he'd have wanted nothing to do with anything belonging to one of the horsemen. He'd just as soon put that part of his life behind him. Given the alternative, though, perhaps his unwillingness to make the sacrifice seemed petty. Joanna's vague references to what could be coming sent a chill down his spine. He would do what had to be done to avoid her predictions.

She had faith that he would figure it out. He had little understanding of things magical, though, and doubted her confidence in him. He thought back to the situation when he'd confronted Gabe in the morgue. Even though his father had tried to trick him in the past, it seemed a bit much even for someone like Gabriel to plot to take over the world while siding with demons risen from the netherworld.

If only he could talk to someone else about his thoughts. Unfortunately, Jaz was still unconscious in the hospital. She would have been the person in whom he'd have confided. Ashley might have been a good resource, but Joanna had been adamant not to include any of the Eldara. She'd warned him against involving any of them. He found it hard to believe that he couldn't trust the Eldara sister with his confidence, but his daughter's vehement response when he'd brought it up had changed his mind. Until he understood more, he'd abide by Joanna's wishes.

Setting the disc down on the nightstand, he switched off the light and climbed under the covers. He fell asleep as soon as he closed his eyes, exhaustion overriding his busy thoughts.

The buzzing of his phone awakened him, and he pawed at the top of the nightstand to find his phone. It took him a few tries before he grabbed it and pulled it closer. Glancing at the screen, he saw Brynne's number. It was almost three in the morning and he wondered what she was calling about at this time of night. She knew Dean wasn't working right now and would be on a more normal schedule, so it must be important.

Dean tapped the screen to pick up and held it to his ear "Yeah, Brynne, what do you need?"

"Dean, I know you're off for a few days, but we've got a situation. There's a major mass casualty incident across town. All the on-duty Station U teams are tied up there, and I got a strange text from James about a situation that needs checking on. Are you able to help?"

"Sure, I'll do what I can. What's the emergency?"

"I don't have a lot of information. James just texted an address and said someone there was injured. He hoped you could deal with it. They're only a few blocks from your apartment. I wondered if you might grab the med kit out of an Errington SUV and go take a look at them. It would be a huge favor."

Dean didn't balk at the strange request. Helping people was what he did. "I can do it. Text me the address and I'll head right over. What kind of person are we talking about here?"

"I'll see if I can get some more information out of James. He hasn't responded to my replies yet. I'm heading over to the other incident to help out, but I'll keep trying and get back to you."

"Well, be careful. I'll go and check this out and let you know when I'm done."

"Perfect. If it's more than a simple injury, call me and I'll send an ambulance." She hung up the phone on her end as she finished talking.

Dean sat up in bed and reached for his pants folded on the chair nearby. He tried to keep quiet. He didn't want to involve Joanna if she was asleep. She had a perpetual look of sleeplessness about her, like she never really got a good night's sleep. If he woke her, she'd just want to come with him and he didn't think he needed the help. Slipping on his shoes, he stood and grabbed his phone. On a whim, he reached out and picked up the artifact from the nightstand. He shouldn't leave it lying around unattended.

Out in the living room, Joanna snored softly on the sofa. A movie played on the flatscreen across the room. Smiling, Dean grabbed his keys and headed down to the parking garage. He'd sign out one of the SUVs and go to check on this injured patient.

Ten minutes later, Dean pulled up in front of a four-story row-home matching the address on his phone. It looked like they had converted the building into apartments. Checking his phone once again for the unit number, Dean got out and retrieved the medical bag from the back, then started up the front steps. An intercom panel marked with the apartment numbers was set in the wall beside the front door. Pressing the button marked 4-B, Dean waited for a response.

A raspy voice replied through the intercom speaker. "Who is it?"

"Hi. I'm Dean Flynn. James Lee said someone here was injured and might need some help. I'm a paramedic and I came by to help out at his request."

The door buzzed as the person upstairs released the electronic lock to let him inside. Dean pulled the door open and entered the foyer. Stairs led up on the right, while a long hallway stretched to the rear of the building. Shouldering the medic bag, he started up the steps for the fourth floor. Someone needed his help, and it was there that he tried to focus his attention as he climbed, both sleepy from being awakened in the middle of the night and still a little sore from his injured leg. He reached the top landing and caught his breath. He looked around and spotted the door marked with a B on the left.

Dean rapped a few times on the door, then waited. It took a minute before the door opened. An old, gray-haired man peered at him in the dim light of the single bulb lighting the upper hallway. He studied Dean, staring up and down at him for a few seconds before opening the door and gesturing for him to come inside.

"Hi, I'm Dean Flynn. I talked to you over the intercom. I wanted to come by and see if you needed some help. What seems to be the problem?"

"It's my son. He was out with friends at a bar tonight and when he came home, he'd been beaten rather badly. I did the best I could for him, but I'm worried he might need more attention."

"Sure, I can help with that. Show me where he is and I'll see what I can do. If it's not too bad, I can probably treat him with what I have in my bag. If it's serious enough, though, I might have to recommend he goes to the hospital."

"No, no hospitals. I'm sure you can take care of it yourself."

Dean followed the man into a back bedroom. A groaning form huddled on the bed with the covers pulled up so they hid the person's face. Crossing the room, Dean introduced himself again and set down in his bag before opening it and pulling out his trauma supplies.

He reached out to pull the covers back, then jumped backward as the fully dressed person in the bed sat up and reached out to grab him. Dean shouted in alarm and turned to retreat. He froze as he came face to face with a seven-foot-tall serpent with a spread hood like a giant cobra. It stood where the old man had been standing seconds before.

Shouting in alarm, Dean tried to swerve around the giant snake coiled in his way. He didn't make it very far. A spray of wet mist enveloped him, coming from the fanged mouth of the giant serpent. His limbs went rigid, and he toppled to the floor. His body no longer responded to his mind's commands, including his attempts to call out for help. All that emerged from his mouth were a few strangled gurgles.

As he lay on the floor staring up at his attackers, the enormous snake wavered and changed back into the old man.

The other one, much younger, but with a distinct family resemblance, climbed out of the bed. He knelt down beside Dean, staring down at him. "Is he alive?"

The old man chuckled. "I only paralyzed him. He's unable to move, though I'll bet he can see and hear everything we are doing." He bent over and waved his hands in front of Dean's face.

Dean let out a gasping croak in response but could not say anything else.

"See, he's fine. Search him for the artifact, but be gentle. The Eldara was adamant about keeping him alive and safe."

The man from the bed started patting at Dean's clothes, pulling out his phone, car keys, wallet, and Mortis' disc.

With a snap of his fingers, the old man held out his hand. "Give me the artifact. Leave the phone, keys, and wallet on the floor, then help me pick him up. We'll put him in the trunk of your car and take him to the rendezvous."

The two lifted Dean by his arms and legs and carried him out and down to the street. It was becoming harder to stay awake as the paralyzing poison continued to work on his system. Despite that, he tried to force his mind to focus as they lowered him into the trunk of the car parked in front of Dean's SUV. As the trunk lid closed, shutting off the available light, he lost his fight to remain conscious and everything slid into darkness.

Chapter 23

JOANNA OPENED her eyes as she lay on the sofa, blinking to clear the sleep away. She'd fallen asleep in the living room watching TV. Judging from the amount of light coming in the windows, it was early morning, perhaps just after dawn. She stood and looked around. Something nagged at the corner of her mind. She studied the room, trying to understand the sense of unease filling her. Starting as a young witch, she'd learned to trust her well-honed senses, built from years living during a war. She wasn't sure what was wrong, but something was definitely off.

Moving through the apartment, Joanna checked each room. No one was home. She knew her mother was still in the hospital, but Dean should've been there. He was off today and had mentioned looking forward to working with her on how to use the disk to reopen the gateways to the upper planes. She supposed he could have gone out to get breakfast, but why not leave a note?

Unable to shake the sense that something was wrong, Joanna left the apartment and took the elevator down to the parking garage. One of the Errington security team members sat behind the desk just inside the entrance.

"Hi, Jed, isn't it?" The guard nodded, and she continued. "Have you seen Dean this morning?"

"Uh, no ma'am, but let me check the logs. I saw his pickup truck parked in its usual spot, though I remember seeing one of the SUV's missing from the garage when I came in this morning. He might have taken it out for some reason."

Joanna waited while the guard logged into a laptop on the counter. He scrolled through a few items and then pointed at one entry. He turned the computer around so she could see.

"Right here. He signed out the SUV last night a little after three a.m. It doesn't look like he checked back in after he left. If he had, they would have checked off the box here on the entry. Also, someone on the night crew would have made sure they fueled it for its next user. There's no sign of that either."

A sense of foreboding filled her. Something had happened to him. She knew it. "Is there any way to figure out where that vehicle is right now?"

The guard seemed uneasy for a second before saying, "I'm not sure I should be checking in on the boss or her husband."

"You know who I am, right?"

The guard answered with a slight nod.

"Then believe me when I say that something is wrong. I'm not sure what, but Dean should've been back by now wherever he went. That means he's in trouble."

The guard paused in thought for just a second, then nodded and swiveled the computer back around. He tapped a few things on the keyboard, staring at the screen as he continued to search for Dean's location. "Here it is. I pinged the unit's GPS transponder. It looks like he's just a few blocks away. According to this, it's been sitting parked on the street for several hours."

"Give me the address, and is there a spare key to that vehicle somewhere?"

"There is, but I need to kick this up the chain of command. Let me call Jonas. He just arrived and should be up in his office on the second floor."

"Just give me the key. You said it's four blocks from here?"

"Yes ma'am."

"Then drive me there and drop me off. I'll bring it back if I can't find Dean."

"I can't leave my post here, but Jonas will know what to do. He can drive you if that's what is needed." The guard made a phone call while Joanna paced back and forth between his desk and the garage entrance. She was just about to leave and walk there on her own when the Errington Security Team's second in command, Jonas Storm, stepped from the elevator.

"Hello, Joanna, what can I do for you?"

She repeated what she'd told Jed about Dean's location and her sense that something was wrong. He listened and replied as soon as she finished with her request for a ride over to the SUV's location.

"Let me call him first. It might be a misunderstanding."

Joanna fumed, but said nothing. Nobody trusted her sense of danger here. She was used to being in charge.

Jonas listened to his phone until Dean's voicemail picked up. He cut the connection. "He's not answering. I'll drive you. Jed, pull up Dean's phone logs. See if you can locate him that way. If you find him, call me on the radio." He gestured towards the door to the garage. "Follow me, Ms. Errington. Let's see why he hasn't checked in."

Joanna forced a polite smile and nodded. Her mother had always trained her people to think proactively and take initiative when needed. She wished they could have acted a little faster, but the result was the same and they were on the move. Her instincts were still telling her there was a problem. She had a sinking feeling about what they might find.

In the garage, she circled the vehicle Jonas led her to and climbed in the passenger side. Soon they were on their way to find the missing SUV. Traffic was already picking up with the morning rush-hour, so it took a little longer than she'd have liked. They found Dean's SUV parked on the street. It was in front of a set of row homes on a residential street.

Joanna climbed out and walked to the parked vehicle to look inside. No sign of her father, nor were there signs of foul play. Jonas put on his emergency security flashers and got out with her.

"If he's not in the SUV, he must've gone inside one of these buildings. Most are apartments so there's no telling how many units there are to check on."

Joanna shook her head. "That might not be necessary. I might be able to locate where he went after he arrived. Do you have the keys?"

Jonas handed over the spare set for the parked vehicle. She unlocked it and climbed inside the driver's side. She placed her hands on the wheel and closed her eyes, trying to focus on her father while murmuring the words of a clairvoyance charm.

After a few seconds, a picture formed in her mind of an overhead view of where she sat. A shadowy image matching the vehicle pulled up and parked in her location. A translucent figure got out, though she couldn't see who it was. They just had a sort of anonymous form about them. They retrieved something from the rear compartment and walked inside the building to her left.

Opening her eyes, Joanna looked at the building the figure had entered. It had to have been Dean. Wondering what he'd gotten from the back of the SUV, she got out and opened the rear lift gate.

Jonas came to stand beside her at the back of the vehicle. "What are you doing?"

"I'm not sure. Is anything missing?"

Jonas opened the armored weapons locker, looked inside, then closed it. "Everything is fine there." He moved a few cases around in the back before he nodded. "The medical triage bag is missing. He must have taken it with him when he got out."

"That makes sense. He would have come out to help someone in need of medical attention in the middle of the night." Joanna pointed at the building the figure in her vision had entered. "He went in there."

She and Jonas walked over to entrance. They stared at the keypad with the intercom. "Give me a second," She said. "It is possible I can figure out which apartment he wanted."

Concentrating on her father again, she closed her eyes while focusing her attention at the door and the buttons corresponding to the apartments inside. No matter what she did, though, she couldn't figure out which button the shadowy form pushed.

After a few minutes trying, along with an increasing headache behind her eyes, she sighed. "I know he went into this building, but not which unit number. There are eight apartments in here. It could be any of them. I don't want to knock on every door and alert someone we're coming."

Jonas said, "Let me try something. I'll be right back."

He returned to his vehicle, retrieving a small black brief case from the back. He opened it on the steps by the building's front door and removed an electronic device with an elaborate keypad on it below a rectangular screen. It looked kind of like a large calculator.

Jonas held the device up to the buttons corresponding to the apartments inside. A red scanning laser lit up as he passed the unit along the row of buttons several times.

"What's that doing?"

Jonas smiled. "It's a fingerprint scanner. It can pick up latent prints on some hard surfaces. Dean should be in our system and I've told it to limit its search to prints in our employee database."

He stopped scanning when there was a soft beep from the device. An image of the array of buttons appeared on the small screen. Beside it was a fingerprint labeled "Flynn, Dean."

On the video image, one button now had the fingerprint superimposed over it. Joanna leaned forward and peered back and forth between the screen and the actual panel of buttons on the wall. She pointed at one of them. "It's 4-B."

"I'm glad it worked," Jonas said. "That's the first time I've used it. We've had it in the back for about a year, but never had the need until now."

"Magic can't do everything, so I'm glad you had it with you." Joanna pressed the button and waited for a response over the intercom. When nothing happened, she pressed it and held it down for a few seconds. Still no response.

Jonas tried the door, but it was still locked. He shrugged. "I could get a crowbar and break it open, but that's all I've got."

Joanna shook her head. "This, I've got." Despite the nagging headache, she pressed her hand on the door, holding her palm flat against the lock where you'd insert a key to enter. A second later, a click sounded followed by the door popping open a few inches. Pulling it open all the way, the two of them bounded up the stairs to the fourth floor.

The door to apartment 4B was ajar. Joanna drew one of the two pistols hidden under her coat. Jonas drew his from a shoulder holster as the pair stood on either side of the entrance.

Peering through the partially opened doorway, Joanna didn't see anyone inside. She nodded at the Errington security captain. He returned her nod with a grim expression and pushed open the door, stepping inside while he swept the room for any danger with his outstretched weapon. Joanna entered right behind him.

Together, the pair tactically cleared the small apartment. There was no one there. They did find the missing medical bag. It sat on the floor beside the bed along with Dean's wallet, phone, and the SUV's keys. There were no other immediate clues about his whereabouts.

They split up, searching for anything that might point them in the right direction before giving up.

Jonas asked, "Any magical way you can see where he went from here?"

She shook her head. "No, I saw him enter the building, but that's where my clairvoyance spell stopped. It didn't show him leaving. That likely means they carried him out, because if he'd walked, my spell would have spotted him again."

"If someone has taken Dean, I need to get a full alert going to locate him," Jonas replied. "We've got to alert the Elk City authorities, too."

Joanna shook her head. She had a good idea who had her father. Gabe must've known they had the fourth disk. She didn't know why they didn't just take it and leave Dean behind, though. That seemed to show the archangel had some reason for needing both Dean and the artifact. She didn't like the way that sounded in her mind.

"I think I know who has him, Jonas. That means you won't find him through conventional means. I need to reach out to some of the others in the Unusual community. Maybe one of them knows where he's been taken."

"I still need to start an investigation, at least until Jaz gets out of the hospital. You understand."

"Do what you have to do. I'll hang onto the keys to the SUV, if you don't mind. Don't worry. I'll be sure to check in with you if I find anything."

Jonas nodded and picked up the med bag from the floor. Together, the two of them headed down to the street. Joanna drove off in one direction, while Jonas returned in the opposite way towards the Errington HQ.

Dean needed help. Joanna hoped she and the others could find him in time to provide it.

Chapter 24

DEAN GROANED, his eyes fluttering open as he tried to get his bearings. The last thing he remembered was the trunk lid closing, sealing him in darkness inside the vehicle. He twisted his head to look around, realizing in that moment he had regained the ability to move after that snake shifter had paralyzed him. He tried to sit up and realized he still couldn't move his arms and legs.

Lifting his head, he stared down at his body. He lay on a cot of some sort with a metal frame. His arms had been bound at the wrists and then secured to a rope around his waist that wrapped around the mattress, disappearing underneath. His legs were similarly bound at the ankles and secured to the bed. Unable to move his arms and legs, Dean could still roll from side to side a little. He used that bit of mobility to survey the room in which he found himself.

Besides the cot, there were several cardboard boxes stacked in the corner, though he couldn't see any labels or markings to tell him what was inside. The rest of the room was empty. It wasn't that large, maybe only ten feet across with a bare light bulb in a fixture overhead. A single door set in the wall opposite the cot was the only exit he saw.

Turning his attention back to himself, Dean pulled at the ropes securing his wrists together, trying to loosen them. They were too tight and, if anything, his struggles only made them tighter. He'd already lost some of the feeling from his fingers. Dean didn't think he'd be able to get free from them without some assistance. When he tried to move his feet, he found his ankles bound just as tightly.

Dean looked around for some way to cut or loosen the ropes nearby. There was nothing. The cot was situated, so it wasn't near any of the boxes and it wasn't as if he could reach out and open any of them to examine the contents anyway. He heard voices from the other side of the door and stopped, craning his neck to look around. He recognized one of them right away.

The door opened revealing a corridor with cinderblock walls just like the room he was in. The first person to enter was the old man who'd changed into the giant serpent the night before. Entering right behind the old man was Gabe.

"We tied him up to make sure he didn't get away, sir. We made sure he was unharmed, though, just like you ordered."

"That was a smart move." Gabe's eyes met Dean's as he kept talking. "My son is very resourceful and might have found a way to escape otherwise. You can untie him now, though. I am here and he won't go anywhere while we're watching over him, isn't that right, son?"

Dean frowned. "You have me kidnapped and you want me to be nice and agree not to try to escape?"

"I needed to speak with you alone, and I didn't think you'd come if I asked. I knew you and the others could probably find Mortis' artifact after I was unable to. I didn't think you'd just give it to me. Now that I've got it, I wanted to have a discussion with you about what happens next. Because Joanna's poisoned you against me, I really had no choice."

"You're right about that I still don't understand how you could side with the demons."

Gabe smiled. "I didn't think you'd understand what's going on here. You've gotten it all wrong. I'm not siding with the demons. They are siding with me. The Eldara will rule this world. We will finally see the power that should've rightfully been ours when this planet was first created. The demons will serve us and help us rule over mankind as it always should have been."

"And you expect us to all just roll over and let you take over?"

Gabe laughed and shook his head. "No, of course not. Humans are far too stubborn for that. No, we will have to make some examples of those nations that choose not to listen to reason. Eventually, though, others will come around. No one want's to die and in the end, I'll offer life and peace to those that come around, after a fashion."

"You're insane. I see now that your drive to end this world has not changed, even after I stopped you the last time."

"Why should I stop what I've already started? You only delayed the inevitable, son."

"Don't call me that. You may have donated genetic material to me, but you've never been a father."

The archangel shrugged. "Suit yourself. I have you now, along with the final artifact. I will convince you to serve alongside me, or I'll use you to complete what must be done. Either way, I'll get what I want."

Dean started to answer, refusing to help Gabe, but he stopped himself. The Eldara was feeling chatty. Maybe this was Dean's opportunity to figure out what he intended to do. Eventually, his friends would come for him. All he had to do was bide his time. That meant he had to humor his father.

"Tell me why I should join you? What's in it for me?"

Gabe smiled, beginning an explanation of what he needed Dean to do and how he expected his son to stand by his side. Dean listened, occasionally nodding, filing away the information as he waited for the rescue he hoped was on its way.

Chapter 25

JOANNA WINCED as Brynne let out another string of expletives. James and Brynne had invited her over that evening after she spent the entire day failing in her efforts to track down any trace of her father.

The vampire paramedic paced across the penthouse apartment atop the Nightwing building. "I swear, when I get my hands on that guy, he's going to be busted back to probie status. He knows better than to walk into a situation where he can't watch his back."

"In all fairness, my dear," James said. "It was you who sent him there without checking on whether the text from me was legitimate."

"How was I supposed to know someone had hacked into the phone system and made it look like you sent me a text message?"

James shrugged, unable to answer the question.

Rudy had an answer, though. He stood on the opposite side of the broad living room. "Whoever is behind this has the resources to do a lot of things. None of my usual contacts have any leads to offer me." He glanced at Joanna. "Are you sure there's no magical way to track him down? I've turned over every stone I can think of. No one seems to know where Gabe might be hiding. I mean, it can't be that easy to hide three rogue Eldara, a twelve-foot Fetch demon, and a growing horde of ravenous demonlings."

Joanna shook her head. "I tried everything I can think of. The Eldara are protected by powerful enchantments and even disconnected from the higher planes, those protections still remain in place. If they don't want to be seen, they are practically invisible. Even Dean with his half Eldara blood might be blocking my attempts to locate him."

"But how?" Brynne asked. "Dean doesn't know how to access that part of himself. I know for a fact he chooses not to even try. I find it hard to believe Gabe could convince him to do it."

Joanna shrugged. "I'm just answering the question, Brynne. He may not be aware of doing it. It might be inherent. Believe me, I wish I could find him as much as you do. We have to figure out another way to track them down."

James walked over and laid his hand on Brynne's shoulder stopping her from pacing. "Let's try to come at this a different way. We can't find the Eldara directly, but we still have some evidence of a few isolated demon attacks all over the city this evening."

"I see what you're getting at," Rudy said, snapping his fingers. "If we can figure out where the demons are coming from, we might have a way to track them back to Gabe, or at least the Fetch demon who is summoning them."

James nodded. "Exactly. If we can get to one of the attacks soon enough, we might be able to let one of them get away and track it back to its original location."

Brynne threw her hands in the air. "You can't just let one of those demons run free. They're out there killing people."

"I don't see another way to do this, my dear. If you have one, make sure and tell me. Otherwise, I think we might have to go with this plan."

Joanna didn't like James's proposal any more than Brynne did. She'd seen what could happen in a populated area if even one demonling escaped their tracking. Still, it might be the only way they had of narrowing down Dean's location. It was a longshot, but at this point it was all they had.

She crossed to the broad floor-to-ceiling windows lining one wall. She stared out into the night sky, studying the city lights below. Common people, going about their common business without any clue what waited for them in a few short months if she failed in her mission. She'd only been up here one other time, and that was back when the world had already fallen apart. Most of the world's governments had collapsed and yet somehow, James had managed to hold Elk City together by the thinnest of threads. He held out longer than almost anyone else had. It was his influence that helped Joanna first expand her magical knowledge into the sorcerous arts, far beyond the simple witch charms from the beginnings of her magical training.

"I agree with James. I don't think we have a choice. I'm concerned about what Gabe is planning. If all he needed was the disk, then why did he take Dean, too? They could've killed him just as easily and taken the disk, leaving his body behind. Gabe must've requested that Dean be captured along with the artifact. I just don't know why."

"Maybe I can lend a few thoughts about that," a new voice said from the hallway leading to the elevator. Hangbe and Gibbie stood in the entryway.

Joanna raised her eyebrows in a hopeful expression. "Were you able to find him?"

Hangbe frowned, her beaded braids rattling softly as she shook her head.

Gibbie answered with, "We tracked down every lead we could think. Hangbe even tried to use an old tribal tracking charm. No luck."

Hangbe said, "I also wondered why Gabe needed to take Dean. Then it came to me. He's the one who originally closed the gateways, so it makes sense he'd be the one who needs to reopen the gateways, or at least just the ones to Hell."

Joanna frowned and nodded. "Of course, why didn't I see it before? For the same reason I wanted Dean to re-open the gateways to the higher planes, Gabe also needs Dean to gain broader access to the creatures of the netherworld. I never made the connection in the other direction. Somehow he gets Dean to allow the demons to gain free travel back-and-forth between the lower planes and Earth. That's why there's an unrelenting horde of demons invading this world just a few months from now."

Everyone went silent. This was the first time Joanna had outlined so clearly what awaited them in the future. She'd hinted at it a few times but hadn't laid out the stark reality it was so close to happening.

After a long silence as her words sunk in, James said, "Well, we're not going to let that happen. If it takes us having to let a demon go so we can track it back to their lair, so be it. It's not the best plan, but it looks like the only option we have." He gestured to Joanna and the Amazon, standing on opposite sides of the room. "You two are our strongest spell casters. You two put your heads together and see if you can come up with a way to prevent Dean from opening the netherworld gates. If you can block whatever magic they get him to use, maybe that'll buy us enough time to break him free and get him to safety."

Joanna didn't think they'd have much luck but what else could they do? Her eyes met Hangbe's. Judging from the other woman's expression, she wasn't too hopeful about it either. Still, the Amazon held powerful, old-world magic in that necklace around her neck. Joanna wasn't without her own resources, either. While the others prepared to track some demon spawn, the two of them would come up with something, anything, that could stop whatever Dean was supposed to do.

Failure wasn't an option.

JOANNA JOLTED in her seat hard enough to make her gasp. The beat-up white van careened around a corner, then sped forward down a new street.

"Watch it, Gibbie. I'm trying to form a delicate spell here."

"Sorry. Rudy told me to hurry up. They think they've found one of the lairs the demonlings are using. This could be where they're holding Dean."

"Gibson, dearest," Hangbe said. "Jo is right. We're in the middle of something requiring intense concentration. It wouldn't do to have it go off here in the back of your vehicle."

"Understood, I'll try to be more careful."

As he said it, he hit a monster pothole, jolting the back seat passengers once again.

Joanna's eyebrows lowered as she struggled to regain her focus. She'd never tried to load a spell this complex into a locus like one of Hangbe's magical beads before. It wasn't just tricky, it was near impossible under the best of circumstances.

"You've got this," the Amazon said as she held the necklace still beneath Joanna's fingertips. "We're almost finished."

The sorceress nodded and redoubled her effort, trying to finish before Gibbie bounced them off a parked car or a telephone pole. He drove like a madman. The magical energy flows writhed in an intricate knot of power floating between the two women. She wasn't sure if Hangbe could see the spell or not. It pulsed with so much energy, Joanna squinted at the brightness streaming from it.

One more piece to tie down on the back side and they should be finished. Then she could release it into the gem-encrusted bead in the center of Hangbe's necklace. Al—most—got—it.

"Done!" Joanna's exultant shout rang out as the glowing mass of energy compressed into a marble-sized ball before disappearing into the bead between Hangbe's fingers.

Hangbe let out a gasp, dropping the necklace as she rubbed her fingers against her thumb. "That stung a little. I think it worked, though. Now we have to find Dean and hope the plan works."

Gibbie glanced back over his shoulder, smiling at the two women. "We're almost to the corner where Rudy told us to meet him. This has to be the right place."

Joanna wanted to believe the vampire was correct, but this was the third such race across town tonight. The other two had turned out to be small demon nests. They'd cleaned them out and killed the occupants, but they weren't the primary location they'd all hoped to find.

Taking a deep breath, she tried to slow her pounding heart. That spell had taken a lot of power from her already dwindling reserves. She'd spent so much since she'd returned to this time and place without taking the necessary time to rest and rejuvenate her personal qi. It was a calculated decision based in no small part on her desperation to succeed. The risk she'd burn out her magical core and never be able to summon even a simple incantation to light a birthday candle was real.

Shifting her attention to the problem at hand, Joanna thrust away her concerns. She knew the risks of what her former instructors would call reckless spell usage. If she and Hangbe were successful tonight, she could take all the time she'd needed for so long to rest up. A part of her looked forward to the near comatose state such a rejuvenation required. No dreams, no worldly worries at all, just rest.

The van squealed to a stop at the corner where the residential street they'd driven down met a broad, partially wooded avenue beside a park. Gibbie leaned forward to peer out through the windshield. "Anyone see Rudy?"

Joanna brought her attention back to the present and searched the outside through the tinted side windows of the van. Hangbe popped open the sliding side door and stepped out to get a better view.

In a flash of movement almost too quick to follow, Hangbe drew her sword from beneath her long, leather coat and pointed with it towards the park. "I hear fighting that way."

Before either Joanna or Gibbie could exit the van, the Amazon stroked one of the necklace beads and took off in a blur of magically enhanced speed. She disappeared into the darkness amidst the clustered trees at the park's edge.

"She's amazing and all," Gibbie said as he met Joanna in front of the van, "but I hate the way she charges into trouble without waiting for me."

Joanna smiled. "Let's go catch up with her, then. You go first, I'll be right behind you."

Gibbie nodded and raced into the woods, using his vampire strength and speed. He hefted an impressive double-headed silver battle axe. Joanna would have been able to keep up with just a little magical boost, but after casting that spell, her body resisted pushing past the exhaustion she felt. Drawing her Katana in one hand and a pistol in the other, she jogged after the other two towards the distant snarling and shouting of the fight taking place somewhere deeper inside the park.

By the time she caught up to Gibbie and Hangbe, the fight was over. A few of Rudy's werewolves finished off the few fetchling demons that were wounded but not dead. A single naked human body, a man Joanna didn't recognize, lay on the grass near the center of the clearing. His body bore numerous bloody injuries. A ring of demon bodies surrounded it. It must be a member of Rudy's pack and security team. He'd died while shifted into his full werewolf form, which explained the transformation back to his naked human self. The young werewolf named Marian knelt next to the body, two fingers pressed against the man's neck, searching for a pulse.

"Anything?" Rudy asked her as he jacked a fresh magazine into his pistol.

Marian shook her head and stood. Her eyes glowed a brilliant amber as a low growl rose from her throat.

"What happened?" Joanna asked as she walked over to the pack leader.

Rudy shook his head. "I had Willam tracking one of the demons from an attack we responded to. He radioed that it had come here to the park and disappeared somewhere. I told him to wait for back up before investigating. He either didn't listen or they caught him by surprise. He took a bunch with him before we got here. We finished off the rest."

"So it's another localized nest and not the nexus we'd hoped for?"

"I'm not sure." He pointed to the far side of the clearing. "I have a few scouts checking that hill over there. Some old caves were sealed up there years ago to keep the neighborhood kids who played here safe. It's possible that's where the demons came from. There's no other sign of a nest anywhere around here."

Joanna pressed her lips together as she looked around, using the magic in her hunter charm to scan the darkness for anything that might give her hope they'd located where Gabe held her father. If the caves were sealed, then it was unlikely the demons had taken up residence there.

A crackle of static sounded over the radio clipped to Rudy's belt. He lifted it to his face and keyed the mic, "Say again?"

"The concrete over one of the cave entrances has signs someone has tampered with it."

"Wait for me and others. Don't try to move it yourself."

"Roger. I'll take cover until you get here. I'm on the far side of the rise."

Rudy brought two fingers to his lips and whistled two quick chirps. As the others in his pack glanced his way, he pointed towards the rocky hillside rising amidst the trees. Three of Rudy's pack mates moved in that direction. Before following, he gestured for Marian and one other pack member to stay with Willam's body.

Joanna fell in alongside Hangbe, Rudy, and Gibbie, saying, "If this is where they're holding Dean and they're trying to bridge the gap to the netherworld, hidden caverns would be a perfect place to open a more permanent gateway. No one would know it was there until it was too late to stop them."

"I've never been down there," Rudy said. "They've been sealed for at least fifty years. I only know about them from the former pack leader. He mentioned getting lost down there when he was a kid. It took two days for the search parties to find him and get him out. The way he'd talked, the tunnels and caverns are extensive."

"Should we call James and Brynne to bring the other team here?" Hangbe asked.

Rudy paused in thought before answering. "Let's see what we find first. If it looks like this is the place for sure, we can call them."

The group fell into silence as they moved quickly through the trees surrounding the base of the hill. As they reached the far side, the scout from the radio conversation stepped from behind a cluster of bushes.

Pointing to the rocky slope to their right, he said, "The concrete plug is right over there next to that larger boulder." He led them over to where he'd pointed. "You can see the places around the edges with the fresh scrapes and chipped cement?"

Everyone moved closer to look. As soon as he pointed out what he'd discovered, it was clear the concrete had been altered. If a person wasn't searching, they would likely ignore it, but the signs were there if you studied it for a few seconds.

Joanna moved to the side with the most signs of work. "There's a definite gap here. I think this can be moved without too much trouble. Someone help me."

Rudy tapped her shoulder. "Step back and let Gibbie and I take a try at it. We're the strongest ones here."

She nodded and moved to stand beside Hangbe while the two men positioned themselves on either side of the slab set into the hillside. As soon as they managed to find a grip and tug, the concrete tipped away from the opening, revealing it was no longer a thick plug of poured cement. It was now just a thin concrete panel about six inches thick. Behind it lay a dark oval cave entrance disappearing into the side of the hill.

The unmistakable stench of a demon nest wafted out at them. Unfortunately, the smell was followed by a rush of six more of the small fetchling demons from inside. They charged at Gibbie and Rudy first, since they were the closest.

Both Hangbe and Joanna tried to get a clear shot at them, but the dog-sized demons moved too fast. Neither wanted to risk shooting either the vampire or the pack leader by mistake. Their special pistol rounds would just as easily wound or injure any supernatural creature.

Joanna holstered her pistol and charged in with her sword, held before her in a two-handed grip. She sliced open the side of a demonling who'd leaped up and landed on Rudy's back. It had shredded a portion of his leather bomber jacket as it tried to get through to the skin beneath.

The thing let out a piercing shriek and dropped away. Joanna kicked at it, rolling it onto its back. She stabbed down and finished it with a single twisting lunge.

As she turned back to take on another one, she realized the others had taken care of the threat. Rudy shrugged off the remains of his jacket and dropped the tattered, torn leather to the ground.

"Damn, I just bought that."

"Be glad you did," Joanna said. "It was enough to keep that one from tearing you apart."

Rudy nodded and turned his attention to the cave entrance. "If I were a gambling man, I'd say this has got to be the right place. I'll text James that we're checking it out, just in case our phones don't work once we're inside. There's a lot of iron in the ground around here."

Joanna took a few steps inside the cave, trying to listen for any movement or voices from deeper inside. Rudy made his call to James and left his three-person security team to cover the entrance. It wouldn't do to have another returning horde of demons come in behind them.

Once that was finished, he joined Joanna, Hangbe, and Gibbie inside the cave. "Shall we delve a little deeper and see what we can find?"

Joanna started to take the lead, then thought better of it. She wasn't at a hundred percent, and Rudy's sense of smell and hearing was likely the best of the four of them. She gestured for him to go first.

Gibbie followed the pack leader, with Hangbe and then Joanna right behind. After the initial ten feet or so, the tunnel sloped down. Someone had taken the trouble to work the rock into rudimentary steps, which helped with the steep descent. It would be easy for a four-legged fetchling to navigate, but it was a little more difficult for a person balancing on two feet.

It wasn't long before they heard voices ahead. One sounded more like a deep-throated growl. The other was more human and recognizable. Joanna was sure it was Gabe. This was the right place.

Rudy slowed their pace as they drew nearer the source of the voices. Odd snarls and barks formed a strange sort of background chorus to Gabe and the other voice arguing about something. She could only pick up a few words amidst the noise. It wasn't enough to understand what they were talking about.

The pack leader stopped and stooped low. He gestured for the others to wait there while he approached a bend in the tunnel a few yards ahead. A flickering yellow light played shadowy forms on the wall at the turn.

Rudy moved around the corner and out of sight for almost a minute. When he returned, Joanna realized she'd been holding her breath. She let out a long, slow sigh as he came back up the tunnel to where the trio waited.

Keeping his voice low, Rudy filled them in on what he'd found. "Gabe's down there with Dean in a broad cavern that opens up just around the bend. He's arguing with the biggest damned demon I've ever seen."

"That would be the Fetch demon," Joanna said.

"Well, if that's what put Jaz in the hospital, she's lucky to be alive. There are also a few dozen of the smaller demons."

"What about Dean?" Gibbie asked. "Is he okay?"

Rudy nodded. "He's standing a few feet away from Gabe. His hands are tied behind his back, but otherwise he seems alright."

Some of the tension in Joanna's back melted away at word her father was here and unharmed. Now they just had to see if the plan she and Hangbe had come up with worked. She leaned forward, drawing the others in as they did the same. Then she started to describe what the four of them needed to do next. The plan wasn't a sure thing, but it seemed like they might be out of time to come up with anything better. Time to see if it worked.

Chapter 27

DEAN TESTED the bonds securing his wrists behind his back. Focusing on that while standing this close to the enormous Fetch demon kept him from feeling all the terror that threatened to overwhelm him. The thing emanated evil like terrible body odor. Just getting within ten feet of it made his skin crawl.

He tried twisting his wrists a little to give his fingers access to the loose ends of the rope. He managed to grasp them a few times with his fingertips, but tugging on them didn't do anything to loosen the knots. Dean refused to give up, though, just like he'd refused to give in to Gabe's demands that he embrace his Eldara blood. Eventually the archangel had stopped trying to convince him.

That had led to Gabe bringing him here. He wasn't sure where here was. They'd put a hood over his head before leaving the room where they'd held him before. He'd been placed in a vehicle of some sort and driven in the vehicle for a while. Then they'd walked him here into this cavern. He wracked his brain to try to remember where an underground cave system like this might be near Elk City. He didn't remember ever hearing of anything like this.

Gabe stopped talking to the Fetch demon. They'd conversed in a guttural language Dean didn't recognize. For all he knew, it was Demonese or something.

"The time has come, Dean," Gabe said as he tugged at Dean's arm, pulling him along towards a section of the rock wall on the other side of the cavern. The area had been polished smooth to a glossy finish. He could almost make out his face in the reflection of the torches lighting the area.

"I told you I won't help you. I have no desire to reveal my inner Eldara side."

"The time has passed for that, unfortunately for you. My nether-worlder friend here informs me we don't really need your consent for this. He is convinced that nephilim like yourself can be forced to embrace your hidden assets, IF you're given enough incentive."

Dean didn't like the sound of that. If they could force him to comply in some way, then he'd never be able to stop them. He still had a small hope that help would arrive. He knew his friends had to be searching for him. Maybe he could stall them or somehow interrupt their plans.

"You keep calling me that. Isn't nephilim some sort of bastard child of the gods?"

"Actually, son, it's the word for the product of any immortal being and a human, be it an angel, a god, or even a demon. According to Baelzap here, his ability to invade the mind of mortals should give him the power needed to bring forward your Eldara half. Once that is completed, we will use you and the four artifacts to open all the lower gates to the netherworld. We'll start with this one here beneath the city, then you and I will travel around the world opening more until the nations bow down before us."

"I feel like I'm in a poorly written horror movie."

"What's that?" Gabe asked. He clearly hadn't been paying atten-tion to Dean in that moment.

"Nothing," Dean replied. He'd hoped to glean some knowledge of what they planned in hopes of finding a way to stop them or mess up their plot. The more Gabe talked, though, the more he sounded like a megalomaniac in a low-budget film.

Gabe held Dean in position about six feet away from the flat stone wall. Baelzap moved to stand on Dean's other side. The demon reached out with one of its massive, clawed hands and gripped the top of Dean's head. The strength of its squeeze gave him an instant migraine. Then it spoke to him but not aloud. This time it talked directly into his mind.

"Eldara spawn, you will serve your purpose on this world whether you desire it or not. I have you in my power now."

As if to prove its point, Dean's left foot lifted from the ground and stomped down again, followed by the right foot. This motion repeated against Dean's will, as he sort of ran in place, unable to control his own body. It was as if the Fetch demon controlled him with strings like a marionette puppet. After about thirty seconds, his legs stopped.

"Now you know I can control you in every way. I control not just your mortal muscles, but also your emotions and senses."

Now Dean's vision swirled around as if he were spinning on an impossibly fast merry-go-round. The motion stopped as suddenly as it started, and he found himself standing on a cliff high up on a snowy mountain peak. The freezing winds bit at his exposed skin, chilling him to the bone. Soon his teeth chattered and uncontrollable shivering took over his body.

The spinning swirl began again after a few minutes. When it stopped, he found himself back in the cavern, standing between Gabe and Baelzap. Dean tried to talk but was unable to control his voice. Changing tactics, he focused on the demon's presence in his mind.

"That's a neat trick. Was I really there or did you just trick me into thinking I had left this place?"

"As far as your puny human brain is concerned, there is no difference between the two. I control you in every way you can think possible. I tell you this so you can know true despair as I compel you to do what we wish."

Something tugged at Dean's wrists behind his back. Gabe used the edge of his heavenly blade to cut his bonds. His arms now hung straight at his sides. Of course, it didn't matter. Baelzap held his head in its massive, clawed hand and thus controlled Dean's every move.

There was a flash of pain in both hands, followed by a wet, sticky sensation dripping down his fingers. His hands lifted up in front of him. Long gashes in his palms dripped blood down his forearms to his elbows. Holding his hands before him, palms out, he marched forward until they pressed the bloody cuts against the smooth stone wall. The stone wasn't cool, as expected. Rather, it was warm, almost hot to the touch.

Baelzap spoke aloud now, in guttural English. "He is ready, angel. You may begin the ceremony."

Gabe came forward and pressed his hands against the backs of his son's while he chanted in a rhythmic lyrical language Dean didn't understand. It was the polar opposite of the guttural tongue used with the demon earlier.

Golden sparks erupted from around the edges of his bloody hands. The dripping crimson liquid sparked as it splashed to the stone floor. The sparks increased in intensity, and something happened in the back of Dean's mind. He felt as if a presence long hidden in the depths of his memories fought to come to the surface. Something horrible rose up within him.

Gabe pulled his hands away and dug the four disks from his jacket pockets. He pressed them into the stone around where Dean's hands pressed into the stone. When they touched the wall, they adhered in place as if magnetized.

As the fourth artifact was applied in a crescent above Dean's outstretched fingers, all four began to glow with a sickly, purplish light. The golden sparks changed color, too. The shower of sparks now echoed the color of the glow from the four disks.

In his mind, Dean fought to push back the thing that rose up from his subconscious, fighting back the only way he knew how. It seemed to be working for the time being, even though he sensed the increasing pressure from Baelzap to draw the thing forth.

A shout echoed through the cavern from behind them. Dean couldn't turn to see who it was, but he didn't need to. He'd recognize Gibbie's crazed battle cry anywhere.

"Cha-a-a-a-arge!"

The cavalry had arrived.

Chapter 28

JOANNA CURSED UNDER HER BREATH. She and Hangbe weren't in position yet.

Rudy had led them up and around the corner. They all stayed low, keeping behind the natural rocky protrusions and formations to stay hidden from the several dozen fetchling demons milling around the cavern. The goal was to get as close as they could to where Dean was held captive before setting their plan into motion.

The demons were grouped in clusters around the cavern and didn't seem to be paying a lot of attention to whatever Gabe and the Fetch demon were doing with Dean. That could work in their favor if they could stay out of view. The pulsing energy emanating from the other side of the underground chamber sent shivering chills up and down her spine every time a wave hit her. They'd begun a ritual of some sort, judging from the chanting of the Fetch demon. It didn't bode well for any of them if it meant what she thought it did.

Joanna had almost made it to the hiding place she'd chosen, when the others noticed what the Eldara and the demon were up to. Before anyone could stop him, Gibbie whispered, "They're doing something to Dean. We have to stop them."

He let out a bellow of rage and leaped from his hiding place. "Cha-a-a-arge."

The vampire hefted the battle ax he carried and raced forward into the room, using his vampire strength and speed to its utmost advantage. Rudy didn't wait. Seeing the plan was blown, he raced after Gibbie.

The cry of alarm alerted the demons all around the cavern. Most raced towards the bellowing vampire and the snarling werewolf running a few steps behind him.

Realizing the fetchlings would overwhelm the pair with the weight of their numbers alone, Joanna stood from behind her hiding place and drew her pistols. A dozen yards away, Hangbe did the same.

The pair emptied their magazines into the demons racing towards Gibbie and Rudy. They'd loaded specially charmed cartridges from the Errington armory. Each bullet contained a mixture of silver, elemental iron, and lead. They had inscribed a rune warding against evil across the head of each projectile. It should allow the otherwise conventional weapons to strike down the demons. Joanna would have traded a lot to have even a few cases of these to use in the future. Any kind of firearm ammunition was almost unheard of in her time.

The leading demons tumbled to the ground, rolling and skidding across the cavern floor, struck by the hail of bullets. They lay twitching and dying just a few feet from the charging vampire and werewolf.

The rapid-fire attack had another effect on the remaining fetchlings. Half of those left noticed the secondary attack and peeled off from the primary group. Seeing Hangbe first, they let out a chorus of howls and charged in her direction.

Dropping her empty magazines free, Joanna slapped another two into place as she raced to join the Amazon. As she ran, she fired again, this time taking more careful aim and picking off the demons scrambling towards the other woman.

Across the cave, Rudy had shifted completely into his werewolf form, shredding his clothing as it fell free in tatters. He and Gibbie squared off, ready to take on the remaining fetchlings closing on them.

Joanna reached Hangbe's position as she fired her final rounds. She dropped the empty pistols in their holsters at her waist and drew her sword just in time to catch the first of the charging demonlings. Though they had cut down a lot of them, the fetchlings still outnumbered the four rescuers.

Hangbe and Joanna moved closer together and took a position to fight side by side. Within a few seconds, the pair's attacks turned into almost a choreographed dance of martial arts as they slipped into a combined rhythm of strike and counterstrike.

The Hangbe Joanna knew in the future was a wise old sage who offered advice and counsel to the warrior sorceress of their Hunter clan. It amazed Joanna to see her old mentor fighting like this. The two melded their styles together instinctively, avoiding incoming attacks, all the while helping to fend off attacks coming at their partner.

The charging demons raced into a spinning machine of death. They never had a chance.

A ripping snarl from nearby drew Joanna's attention for a split second. She spared a quick glance in that direction. Two demons had leaped on top of Rudy, driving him to the ground. One of them had clamped down on his shoulder, biting down hard while the other tried to get at the werewolf's throat.

Just as Joanna thought about trying to break away from her fight to go and help, Gibbie appeared beside Rudy. He gripped each of the demonlings by the backs of their necks, ripping them free and flinging them across the cavern. They smashed into a nearby outcropping, sliding to the cavern floor. One lay still. The other tried to rise, only to fall back down again with two of its four legs broken from the impact.

Her attention returned to the fight with the surrounding demons. The number had thinned down to just four, but she and Hangbe gasped for breath at this point. They had to finish these last ones quickly if they were going to get in position to put their desperate plan into motion.

More yelps and howls came from somewhere nearby. That meant more of the fetchlings were on their way. They'd never be able to keep fighting and rescue Dean at the same time if they didn't hurry.

Joanna hacked down one of the demonlings closest to her. "We have to finish these off. We're running out of time."

Hangbe nodded, lunging forward and skewering another through its open mouth. Her blade emerged from the back of its head. Its teeth snapped down around the blade several times before finally realizing it was already dead. Wrenching the blade free, she said, "I'll work my way around to the left. You go to the right. We need to have Dean's position squarely between us when we enact the spell."

Joanna nodded as she swept her blade down, slicing through the last demonling's spine.

With the nearest fetchlings taken care of, the two split up. Hangbe moved to the left and Joanna shifted over to the right until they each reached the far cavern wall. They each stood about ten feet to either side of where Gabe, Dean, and the Fetch demon stood. The power emanating from whatever spell they were using on Dean had gained in strength, and a spectacular light show of cascading purple sparks came from where Dean's hands pressed against the cavern wall. Joanna could tell the spell they were using was almost complete. She and Hangbe were running out of time.

Joanna moved towards Dean and his captors. Maybe she could interrupt the spell before she and Hangbe resorted to their desperate plan. Before she took her second step, Gabe turned his head her way. His eyes glowed with an incandescent white light. Streaks of the same dark purple lightning flashed across them in time with magical pulses of power emanating from whatever they were doing to Dean.

"Stop right there, girl. He lives only because it suits me to have my son live up to his ultimate potential. Come any closer, and I'll release my protection. He'll still open the gateway, but the dark magic will consume him at the same time."

She froze. Appearing to comply with Gabe's command. She had to be careful not to alert him to what they planned. As long as he thought she would do as he said, Dean was safe.

On the far side of the trio, Hangbe caught Joanna's eye and nodded. Her hand rose to her necklace, tapping the special bead they'd prepared earlier. The rhythmic motion of her tapping tied to the pulsing purple emanations playing across the flattened stretch of wall.

Joanna smiled a little and focused her concentration on the spell she'd prepared. It was a version of both a clairvoyance and clairaudience spell she'd used dozens of times before to spy on her enemies during the Eldara wars of her future. Now she'd adapted it to combine with the astral projection magic stored in the bead in the center of Hangbe's necklace.

Gabe turned his head towards Hangbe for a few seconds, then looked back at Joanna. "What are you two doing? I can sense other magics in play here. I warned you not to intervene."

Joanna smiled. It was too late. With a triumphant shout, she released her spell, sending the power flowing towards Dean.

On the opposite side, Hangbe's magical necklace flared with a brilliant blue-white light as the specially prepared bead released its magic.

The spells met in the center, enveloping Dean in an incandescent white nimbus almost too bright to stare at. Both Gabe and the Fetch demon stepped back from the trapped paramedic. Once the demon released his head, Dean's hands fell away from the wall, dropping to dangle at his sides. The rest of his body remained rigid as the magic coursed through him.

Joanna had done everything she could. Now it was up to him. It was up to Dean to make the spell really work.

She hoped he would understand what to do, because she hadn't had any way to coach him. She couldn't even try to shout instructions. Gabe charged at her, his golden heavenly blade appearing in his hands. She brought out her Katana, parrying the incoming attack just in time.

On the other side, Hangbe fought the Fetch demon. Gibbie had left the injured werewolf and joined her. The two of them were holding off the monstrous netherworlder's attacks so far.

Gabe swung at Joanna's head and she ducked under the slicing attack just in time to avoid decapitation. She had to keep Gabe occupied long enough for everything to work. Hopefully, her father did his part soon. She had little energy left to hold off the archangel for much longer.

Everything now revolved around Dean.

Chapter 29

DEAN HEARD all the fighting around him, though he couldn't see much, staring at his bloody hands pressed against the wall. The gunshots and sounds of demon snarls reached his ears as the magical power from Gabe and the Fetch demon coursed through him.

Then he heard Gabe's warning to someone to Dean's right. He called her "girl," so he knew it must be Jo.

A few seconds later, his entire body jolted as a new, ice-cold sensation coursed through him. It started at his feet. The burning fire of the demonic spell from the Fetch demon cooled and faded. The sensation reached his chest and the sparks around where his hands pressed against the cavern wall stopped. His arms dropped limp to dangle at his sides. He still couldn't move anything, but at least something had interrupted the opening of the portal to Hell.

As the cold surge swept up his body and enveloped his head, everything went white. It was as if he'd teleported to the inside of a cloud. Cold, white mist floated all around him, obscuring his vision beyond a foot in any direction.

It occurred to Dean that he could move of his own volition for the first time since the Fetch demon had begun its spell. Choosing a direction, he moved through the mist. He wasn't walking. It was more like floating with his feet just an inch off the floor, or whatever it was he'd stood on when he'd arrived here.

He hadn't drifted very far when a bright light flared in front of him. He raised his hands to ward off the painfully bright beams flashing in his eyes.

A voice echoed in his head. It could have been male or female, or maybe somehow both. "Why are you here?"

"I don't know. Something brought me to this place. Where am I?"

"You stand in the place between the upper and middle planes. That gateway has been closed for some time, though. Strange that you would come through it now. The last human to pass through this place was a witch of the Dahomey people."

Surprise spread across his face. That was Hangbe's tribe. Was this connected to magic she wielded? He had little gauge of her skills and powers. He supposed she could have made this happen. Then something the voice had said registered with him.

"You said I'm in a gateway between earth and heaven?"

"Yes. I am the keeper of the gate. Not long ago, the ways were closed. A result of a brave choice made at great sacrifice. Because of it, we lost touch with the people of the middle realms, and those of the upper realms trapped there."

Dean nodded. He'd closed those portals, trapping any Eldara currently on earth. He thought he'd closed off the netherworld, too, but they had somehow found a way around what he'd done, at least in part.

"If this portal is open," Dean asked, "does that mean the netherworld gates have opened, too?"

The presence in his mind chuckled. "Perhaps, and then again, perhaps not. It's hard to tell with our netherworld kin. They have their own interpretation of the rules of the game."

"Game?" The characterization angered Dean. "People are dying down there. Do you mean to tell me all of humanity are just playing pieces in a gigantic chessboard to you?"

A gentle chuckle drifted across his consciousness. It didn't anger him, rather it calmed him some. "I am sorry for the characterization. The word I used doesn't translate well to your human concepts. Suffice it to say that your world, indeed all the middle planes, are a testing ground for a contest that has consumed countless millennia. The light and the dark have warred so since the dawn of this universe."

"I know, that is why I closed the gates in the first place. I wanted to stop you all from using us as playthings."

Curiosity tinted the consciousness in his mind. "Come closer, so that I may see you more clearly. There is something about you that intrigues me. I wish to know how you have come to harness such power."

Dean took a few tentative steps into the fog. The blinding light grew even brighter somehow, though it didn't burn him. He squinted, trying to peer through it, but couldn't see anyone. The voice seemed closer somehow, though, when it next spoke.

"Ah, you are one of the nephilim. I sensed a power in you when you first arrived here. Something has awakened your Eldara self. It has now taken precedence over your human side. That is why you have been able to make this journey. The combination gives you a foothold in both planes."

Dean realized Gabe's spell forced out his inner divine self, since he'd refused to let it out on his own. "I may be a nephilim to you, but I'm a man to those I love and care about. I only want to set things right so that the world may return to a path that doesn't lead to destruction and ruin."

"What do you mean, son? I see only the usual human warring and ruin when I scry your world."

"It's what Gabriel was trying to get me to start. He wanted to begin some sort of demonic takeover of the Earth using his loyal Eldara as overlords."

"Gabriel, you say? The archangel always had an ambitious streak about him. I suppose if he were trapped and saw no way out, he'd seek to use his Eldara powers against humanity."

"That's exactly what I was trying to stop when he captured me and tried to turn my Eldara side against me."

The voice in his head chuckled in amusement. "But that is not how it works. Gabriel has always fought against the tenets that founded the great contest. He didn't see the reason for the creation of humanity in all its various forms across the universe. He only sought a way to conclude the game, not understanding that the true contest was in the playing, not the winning."

That made little sense to Dean. What kind of contest didn't have a winner? Then he thought about the world in which he lived and all the joy alongside all the suffering. Each tempered the other. It was what made up life as a person. It made them all human.

Thinking about what the voice said, Dean replied, "It was never about ruling the world and humanity, was it? It was about the daily lives of the humans who lived there."

"And the choices they make. Yes, you see it now. You, who are only half Eldara, understand so much more than a lord among angels. You should embrace your Eldara side and join the heavenly hosts. A voice such as yours would be a welcome addition to our servants."

Dean shook his head. "No. I want nothing to do with that. I serve, but on my terms and on Earth. I'm one who serves my fellows, healing and taking care of those who can't care for themselves."

"As an Eldara, you'd have the power for healing beyond anything you could do as a mere human."

His thoughts drifted back to what he'd seen Ashely do with her powers. For a second it tempted him. Think of the things he could do.

"Why can't I do both?"

"To have the powers of an Eldara, you must give up the power possessed by humankind. That is the greatest power of all."

"Humans have no power."

"No?" Amusement tickled the corners of his mind as the voice continued. "Who was it who closed the gates to the upper planes? It wasn't your Eldara half. It was a decision made by your human side that did it."

Dean took a moment, as he puzzled over the beings response. Then he understood what they were asking him to give up. "Free will. Humanity has free will, and that gives us all power the others don't have."

"That is correct. The Eldara are our servants. They do what we wish when we wish it. Sometimes they stray from the path we set, but ultimately, we pull the strings to set them back on course."

"And if I choose to keep my humanity and relinquish my Eldara side, what would happen? Could I go back and stop what Gabe is trying to do?"

The voice pondered what he asked for a few seconds before it responded. "If by stopping the archangel, you mean to end the war that was to begin, the answer is both yes and no."

"Which is it?" Dean asked. Their answer made no sense.

"Free will is the root of the contest. Most choices a person from the middle planes makes are small and inconsequential. However, there are those pivotal moments when a choice has more meaning and power over the direction of the universe. You made such a choice when you stopped Armageddon. That choice set a certain path into motion."

"Yes, and now I want to stop it and put things back on the right path."

Sadness swept through the voice as it said. "You may right the flow, but the alternate path created will continue on in the direction you set it."

Confused again, Dean parsed the words from the voice several times before he thought he understood. "You said 'alternate.' Does that mean there is now an alternative version of things somewhere else, no matter what I do?"

"Such is the power of free will. Choices always have consequences, good and bad. The greatest of choices, more so. You may try to right a wrong, but some of the original choice remains. Those that are on that path must carry it out to its natural conclusion, though that ending has yet to be fully written. It's all part of the same contest."

Dean understood, but the realization saddened him. Sometimes a paramedic had to make hard choices and try to save those who could be saved, while letting others go. It wasn't easy, but he understood that he couldn't do both things he wanted. He had to choose the greatest good, even if there would be alternative consequences he didn't like.

"I choose to reopen the gateways. Return the Eldara on earth to those to whom they must answer."

Though he still couldn't see the people behind the combined voice in his head, he envisioned them nodding with approval. "The nephilim has spoken. He renounces his Eldara nature and chooses life as a human. So it shall be. Farewell Dean Flynn. You have chosen well."

The mist thickened around him as the blinding light dimmed and faded away. When the mist thinned out again, Dean once again stood between Gabe and the Fetch demon. He wondered if it had all been a dream, his mind drifting away for a split second.

Then his father shouted at him. "What have you done? You fool. You could have had it all, the whole world at your feet."

Dean smiled, realizing he'd regained the ability to move again. He stepped back from between Gabe and the Fetch demon. "No, I couldn't. The only way I can have all I want is to be the man I was born to be. I choose to help those who need it, to save those who can't save themselves, and to stand up for those who cannot do it alone. The gateways to heaven are opened again. That means you have no power over me anymore."

The Fetch demon snarled and took a step towards Dean. Dual flashes of blinding silvery light slashed down. Ashley and Ingrid stood between Dean and the advancing demon. The two sisters, arrayed in shining silver armor, glowed with power, a silvery nimbus coursing around them.

Gabe shouted again as the demon backed away from the sisters. "No, how did you do this? It cannot be real."

Another flash of light left two more Eldara, these clad in golden armor, standing on either side of Gabe.

One of them said, "Brother, they have summoned you. Why are you still here?"

"Michael, Raphael, you don't understand. You have not been trapped here as I was. Join me, and we may still prevail."

The archangel Michael shook his head, peering with stern eyes out from beneath his golden helmet. "Nay, Gabriel. You have strayed from the path set for you, and now you must answer to the powers above. Come with Raphael and me. We must set right that which you started here."

Gabe shook his head and backed away. Before he'd taken two steps, two more of the golden clad angels appeared behind him. They snatched him up, one taking each arm. Another golden flash and, in the blink of an eye, all five disappeared.

A yowl of pain from the Fetch demon drew him to look to his right. Ashley and Ingrid forced the enormous hell-spawn backward. A circular black opening appeared in the cavern wall. As they advanced on the demon, he retreated towards the opening. Scaled hands reached through and grabbed at the demon, pulling it backward until it disappeared from sight.

Ingrid raised her hand, fingers spread wide and closed them into a fist. As her fingers tightened, the blackened hole to Hell narrowed and winked out. Ashley nodded and glanced at Dean, giving him a little wink. Then the two sisters disappeared in a flash of gleaming silver.

Dean stood still, trying to take in all that just happened. Joanna and Hangbe stood along the wall to either side. Both looked spent and exhausted. Nearby, Rudy stood up, his shoulder and arm bandaged, hanging in a makeshift sling.

Gibbie approached from where he stood by Rudy and clapped a hand down on Dean's shoulder. "Wow, I guess we saved the world once again. All in a day's work for us, right?" He paused, a big grin on his face. "Anybody else here hungry?"

Dean's smile soon broke into laughter. Joanna, Hangbe, and Rudy joined in, leaving Gibbie standing there with a big, albeit perplexed grin on his face.

Chapter 30

DEAN CURSED as the pen slipped out of his hand. The bandages covering the cuts on his palms made it difficult to hold on to anything that small.

"Sorry about that," he muttered as he retrieved the pen from the check-out counter and scrawled his signature on the old-fashioned paper receipt.

The diner's manager smiled and slid the signed receipt into the register's cash drawer. "Do you need your receipt, sir?"

"No, thanks. Just toss it."

Joanna met him outside by the entrance to Hank's Place, the diner where he'd first met her teenaged self just a year and a half before. He stood on the steps out front, staring at the stretch of Route 40 where she'd dashed out in front of Jaz's SUV.

"Seems like only yesterday teen witch Jo was trying to keep her parents from killing each other."

Joanna smiled. "That was a long, long time ago." Her hand came up and she absently scratched next to her leather eyepatch.

"You never told me how that happened to you."

"It's a long story for another time. It's been so long, I almost forget it's there. I lost the eye on that first night back from this timeline."

Dean waited, hoping she'd elaborate, but she said nothing else. They'd come here for dinner after visiting Jaz in the hospital. She was due to be released the following day. The doctors said she had made a full recovery, though they gave no answers as to why she'd been in the coma for the last week. Joanna's explanation about the magic she'd used to heal her mother was looking like the only answer any of them would have.

They returned to Dean's white pickup truck and started back across town towards home. He still had something to tell her, but he'd balked at saying anything every time he mustered the nerve during dinner. He needed to tell her what he'd learned from the guardian of the gateways about her timeline. She deserved to know, but he was at a loss about how to break the news to her.

As he turned onto the interstate to take them across town, he noticed her staring at him. "What? Is there something on my face?"

"No, I'm waiting for you to tell me what you've been hiding since we rescued you at the cavern."

Dean shook his head. She saw through him just like her mother did. "How did you know?"

"You're a horrible liar, Dad. Don't get me wrong, I think it's an outstanding trait. It bothers you not to be honest with people. I can tell there's something you're hiding from me. I'm leaving to go back as soon as we bring mother home, so I'd like to know now rather than later."

Dean let out a long, slow sigh. "You're right. It has to do with why you came back here in the first place. I learned something when I was opening the upper portals, something the powers of light told me before I came back. I just didn't know how to tell you."

"My plan to fix everything didn't work, at least not completely."

He glanced her way. She had a matter-of-fact expression on her face, as if it didn't surprise her.

"How did you know?"

"It was always a possibility. I knew it was a long shot when I came back the way I did. It was the only choice I had, desperate as it was. Now I know that there's no hope for my dying world after all."

"That's not exactly it." Dean tried to organize his thoughts and wrap them around the paradox of what he'd learned. "When I stopped Armageddon, I broke something. That is what created your timeline and started the Eldara Wars in the future."

Joanna nodded, waiting for him to say more.

"There was something else I was told. We could reset the original timeline to fix the future of this world, however, it wouldn't erase the alternative future. When you go back, I don't think anything will have changed. The Eldara and Demons will still be trying to take the world, your world. I'm sorry, Joanna. I know that's not what you wanted to hear."

"At least a version of my teenaged self will be able to live out her life in relative peace and happiness. I can take comfort in that, I guess. We saved one version of the world I love."

Dean tried to think of something else to tell her that would cheer her up. He remembered something the guardian had said to him.

"... *though that ending has yet to be fully written.*"

"I'm not certain your future is as dire as you think it is. You and your companions there still have the power of free will. That is what defeated Gabe and the Fetch demon. It was my humanity and its greatest power. I could choose the light. Don't give up when you return, Joanna. There still may be a way to win in the end."

She seemed unsure of what he said, but she didn't argue with him. She nodded and the two of them fell silent. He hoped his interpretation of the guardian's words was correct. He thought it was. When he gave Joanna the advice just now, it felt right.

A calm assurance passed over him, and he believed in the core of his being that she'd survive and somehow save her world. That gave him hope. Sometimes, hope in the future and belief in their skills were all a good paramedic needed to save the day.

He thought it might be the same for his daughter, the sorceress.

The End

Check out the spin-off series - The Eldara Sisters - starting with *The Nightingale's Angel.*

Help the With A Review

I Need Your Help ...

Without reviews indie books like this one are almost impossible to market.

Leaving a review will only take a minute — it doesn't have to be long or involved, just a sentence or two that tells people what you liked about the book, to help other readers know why they might like it, too. It also helps me write more of what you love.

The truth is, VERY few readers leave reviews. Please help me out by being the exception.

Thank you in advance!

Jamie Davis

Also by Jamie Davis

Get a free book and updates for new books.
visit JamieDavisBooks.com/send-free-book/

—

Eldara Sisters Series

The Nightingale's Angel

Blue and Gray Angel

—

The Huntress Clan Saga

(A 6-book Urban Fantasy series starting with)

Huntress Initiate

—

The Broken Throne Series

(A 5-Book Dystopian Urban Fantasy

starting with)

The Charm Runner

—

The Accidental Traveler LitRPG Series

(with C.J. Davis)

(A 6-book Epic Fantasy Series starting with)

The Accidental Thief

—

Lone Wolf Squadron Scifi Series

(A multi-book space opera series starting with)

Marshal the Stars

—

Follow on Facebook for updates, news, and upcoming book excerpts

Jamie's Fun Fantasy Readers Facebook Group

About the Author

Jamie Davis is a nurse, retired paramedic, author, and nationally recognized medical educator who began teaching new emergency responders as a training officer for his local EMS program. He loves everything fantasy and sci-fi and especially the places where stories intersect with his love of medicine or gaming.

Jamie lives in a home in the woods in Maryland with his wife, three children, and dog. He is an avid gamer, preferring historical and fantasy miniature gaming, as well as tabletop games. He writes LitRPG, GameLit, urban, and contemporary paranormal fantasy stories, among other things. His Future Race Game rules were written to satisfy a desire to play a version of the pod races from Star Wars episode 1.

www.jamiedavisbooks.com